WHEN BIRDS FLY

Cindy Harris

Battle Press
SATELLITE BEACH, FLORIDA

WHEN BIRDS FLY

Battle Press books may be ordered through booksellers or by contacting:

Battle Press
1-919-218-4039
steve@battlepress.media
www.battlepress.media

ISBN: 979-8-9887-6514-1 (softcover)
ISBN: 979-8-9887-6515-8 (eBook)

First Edition.

Disclaimer:

This is a work of fiction. All the names, characters, businesses, places, events, and incidents in this book are either the product of the author's imagination or used in a fictitious manner. Any resemblance to actual persons, living or dead, or actual events is purely coincidental. This book is intended for mature audiences.

Other Books by Cindy Harris:

How Did I Miss That????

If you enjoy *When Birds Fly*, I would really appreciate a short review, your help in spreading the word is highly valued and reviews make it much easier for readers to find the book.

Amazon Link:

https://www.amazon.com/dp/B0CXLVYDGY

Dedication:

This book could not have been written without the spiritual input from my daughter Victoria, who I believe guided my thoughts and fingers to let me write this story. She loved this type of thriller and I lovingly dedicate it to her.

Chapter 1

The heat had scorched every living thing. The dust laid low in the air from a horse drawn cart that had passed a few minutes before. The air was still and stifling. In the pond just across from the farmhouse there wasn't much water left. Many of the birds had flown off to find more water. The seaport was close by. The red farmhouse stood out sharply in the fields of long brown grass and a pathway that was well worn gave a clear view of the front door. The pretty stained-glass piece above the top of the door was unique. A gift from her father to her mother on a birthday long ago. The beautiful small glass pane depicted the smallest Edelweiss flowers in brilliant yellows, whites, greens, and blues. When the sun came through it strongly in the morning hours, the colors entered the room like the prisms of Rose's precious crystal vase that was always filled with the most exquisite flowers and kept in the center of the kitchen table.

This day was a special day. Special because it was a Friday and there would be no school the following day. It was also special because it was the day Elinore would turn 7 years old. As soon as her teacher rang the school bell signaling the end of the day, Elinore ran quickly home. Running was hard in her wooden shoes, and the slipper socks inside kept sliding towards her toes, but she was determined to make it home as quickly as she could. Elinore was becoming impatient as her younger sister, Margaret, struggled to keep up. Margaret was less than a year younger and much shorter. Margaret was not a healthy child, born earlier than the doctors had predicted. Her legs were thin and weak, but she wanted her sister to have a splendid day, so she did her best to keep up. Feeling like a leaf blowing in the wind, tethered to her sister's hand, she giggled with delight as she ran as fast as she could. Elinore envisioned all the things that awaited her at home for her big celebration day. Almost out of breath, with her heart pounding and the heat of the day making her cheeks a bright red, she fought to get her shoes off. She knew she would not be greeted well by her mother if she dared to wear her wooden shoes inside the house. Margaret got her shoes off easily. They were already a little too big for her.

Elinore burst through the door; the sweet smell of her favorite cake entered her nostrils. Rose called it Eierschecke. All Elinore knew was that it was her favorite. Made of vanilla pudding and things that made her tummy and mouth very happy. She loved the delicious toppings that her mother would adorn the cake with. Apples were her favorite but sometimes it would be only poppy seeds or quark. As she bolted toward the kitchen, her mother Rose quickly kneeled down to pick her up and spin her around. With her feet lifted high in the air under her mother's grip, her eye caught a large package on the kitchen table wrapped in brown paper with a big yellow ribbon. This heightened Elinore's delight even more. Elinore dreamed of what could be in that package! She was so excited she could barely hold it in. As she reached to shake the package, she caught a quick sideward glance from Rose who had strict rules about washing up before dinner and changing into play clothes after school. Elinore immediately knew to withdraw her hand. With her bottom lip protruding, she went to her room to change.

She knew supper would not be for a few hours and decided to go to the pond to pass the time. She sat down on her favorite rock, caught a butterfly, threw a few rocks in the pond, even tried to catch a frog, but her mind still held the image of that package with the beautiful yellow ribbon and the secret it held inside. The time stretched on to what seemed like an eternity. Finally, she heard mother ring the big bell that was tied to the outside post. Rose shouted for her to come inside. Running like the wind, she made her way inside and sat down quietly. Her mother ladled out some pork and cabbage for the family. Elinore ate quickly that night, barely taking time to taste it. Still, she kept her manners in telling her mother the food was delicious. When dessert came, that was a different matter. She took time to savor the sweetness of the apples and cream. Rose was a very good cook, which made Porter happy. His round belly and hardy laugh were evidence of this.

Eventually came the time for Elinore's long-awaited moment. What gift did her parents have for her? She wanted to just scream! Finally, Porter placed the gift in her hand as they all shouted HAPPY BIRTHDAY!! The brown paper was tough and seemed to want to hold the secret back for as long as possible, but Elinore tugged at the paper wildly until it finally loosened. Inside was a zoetrope reel! A sort of magic lantern. The lantern created the illusion of movement by spinning drawings inside a drum. As Porter placed the reel inside the drum pictures began to emerge. By turning the wheel, she could make them come alive. Elinore became addicted to the amination of this toy. She was quite an imaginative child in her own right. Then her father said he had something else for her. Elinore's eyes widened with curiosity. This was her lucky day! She could hardly contain herself! Almost about to burst, she waited for her father to come back into the room.

He began to explain he had not had time to wrap it, but Elinore didn't care. Porter was a busy man and ran his own business in the textile industry. Supplying the uniforms for the Prussian Army, he worked hard into the evenings. Every day he came home exhausted, though he always took time to laugh with his girls. Porter Downing was on his way to becoming a wealthy man. His dreams were running wild, and endless. He had hoped that his family would someday never need to want for anything. He dreamed of a beautiful home, the newest modern invention of the automobile, double breasted suits with top hats and as much Goldmark as he could spend.

Finally, Elinore caught a glimpse of what Porter had tucked in the crook of his arm. He was carrying a beautiful doll. The doll had sparkly blue eyes with eyelids that opened and closed. She had long blonde hair that Elinore could brush if she wanted. She loved the traditional German dress the doll wore but quickly thought of a ribbon she had tucked away that would be perfect for her hair. She began to think of a name she would call her new dolly. That night as Rose tucked her and Margaret into their beds the moonlight came through the window brightly. Elinore thought to herself, this had been the best day of her life! She pushed her new doll under her arm and slowly fell off to sleep with the corners of her mouth turned upwards.

Weeks passed quickly in the small town of Cuxhaven and days were filled with lots of mundane things to do for Elinore. Homework from school, feeding the horses, watching after Margaret, and helping mother with the washing. One day Elinore came home from school and heard arguing in the side room off the kitchen. It was her mother and father having a very loud conversation. It wasn't often she heard her parents speaking in such a manner and it made her tense. The door was slightly ajar, and Elinore tried hard to listen for clues without making it obvious. She knew eavesdropping wasn't a nice thing to do, but her curiosity got the better of her. Then she heard her father slam his hand down on his desk and proclaim, "Then it is settled Rose! If you won't move, I'll build our castle here!" Porter stormed out of the room. He was very upset and now Elinore was upset. Elinore froze as her father stormed past her and she tried desperately to fade into her surroundings.

Porter's paperwork lay strewn from one side to the other inside the small room. Elinore shuddered and knew her father was angry about losing his way with mother. She could hear the crack of the horse whip and her father bellow loudly, "YA!" as the wooden wheels of the buckboard wagon headed down the road toward the market. She knew it would be late before her father came back and she'd probably be fast asleep by that time. Elinore peeked into the room and saw her mother sitting and crying with a handkerchief, dabbing her eyes. Elinore asked, "Why are you crying mother? Don't cry," she said. Rose tried to hide her face, but Elinore was persistent. She wanted to know what her father meant when he spoke about a castle. Rose began to explain to Elinore that her father wished to be closer to his work so he could spend more time at home with her and her sister. Elinore liked that idea; she loved it when her father would play games with her like flying a kite and when they dressed up for tea parties. So, Elinore innocently asked, "Then why are you crying mother? That isn't so bad."

Rose felt Elinore was old enough to understand so she began to tell her, "Your father is earning much more money now and wants to have a house with nicer things. He would like to move closer to the city. And we wouldn't have to draw water from the well anymore. There would be water in the house. The markets would be closer, and we may have a person come to help with the chores. Your father said the rooms would be bigger and you and Margaret could have your own rooms, would you like that?"

Elinore needed to think about that before she answered her mother. She had questions. What else would change, she wondered. She did not want to make her mother cry again. Sheepishly she asked, "Would Miss Ilse still be my schoolteacher?" Elinore really liked Miss Ilse. She was kind. The worst thing she ever saw Miss Ilse do was make a boy stand in the corner of the room holding the heaviest book in the classroom. And she was really cross that time. Elinore thought Miss Ilse was very pretty, and she always wore a well-kept bun in her hair with curled locks that framed her face. She was a small woman and soft spoken. Elinore was one of her most favorite students. She took an extra kindness to Elinore, and always helped her for a few minutes after school with her spelling. Elinore sometimes had trouble with this subject.

Rose was always honest with her children and told Elinore that she would have to go to a different school if they moved. Immediately, Elinore was no longer happy about what her father's wishes were. Now she had a tear coming from the corner of her eye too. She stomped her foot in protest. "NO MOTHER! I DO NOT WISH TO MOVE FROM THIS HOUSE! WE'VE LIVED HERE ALL MY LIFE!" Rose had to hold in her laugh. All 7 years of her life, she thought. Rose scooped Elinore up and whispered in her ear. "Don't worry child, everything will be ok." Rose was not so sure about that but would never let on to Elinore.

Elinore broke from her mother's embrace and went outside. Dragging her feet as if she had boulders attached to her legs, she fretted about her father's thoughts. She sat down by the pond again. This seemed to be a place she was visiting more and more lately. There was so much to think about. She didn't want to change schools at all. Mostly because of Miss Ilse, but Elinore had a secret she shared with no one. She had begun to have a fancy for a boy seated two seats away from her at school. Carl seemed to notice Elinore too. He would carry her books halfway home for her every day and sometimes he brought her an apple. Elinore loved apples. Carl was a year older than Elinore and she thought he was so charming. Carl was much taller than she and she liked the way his nose perked up at the tip. It was the cutest nose she had ever seen. He had blonde hair, the same as hers, and small ears much like her own too. The only thing she didn't like about him was that he had a habit of punching her in the arm. Not hard, but she couldn't understand why he did that.

One day while she and Margaret walked home from school Elinore found that her sister had caught on to their side glances and smiles at one another. Margaret had run ahead of Elinore and only after she had gotten some feet away, broke out in song. "Elinore and Carl sitting in a tree, K.I.S.S.I.N.G!" Elinore felt her face turn red with embarrassment. She didn't want her secret out. She ran after Margaret, furious. Her embarrassment and anger fueled her body. Margaret's eyes widened and she ran for her life! Elinore had no problem catching up to her. Her stride was much longer, and she could run much faster. When she got close enough, she leaped through the air with her shoes flying off her feet and her books spilling out over the ground. They both landed in a pile tumbling over each other screaming. Elinore clutched at the ground looking for something to help her but Margaret, being smaller but much scrappier, picked up a rock. Elinore pried the rock from Margaret's hand and started to swing it straight for her head. But in a clear moment of thought, Elinore dropped the rock to the ground. Realizing in a flash the harm she could do to her; she instead grabbed her face tightly between her thumb and forefinger. She glared into Margaret's eyes and said, "If you ever tell anyone about me and Carl, I will make your life miserable!"

With that, she got up, gathered her books and shoes and started to walk home, leaving Margaret where she was. She had to dust herself off as all the tumbling made her dress gather the dirt and dried plants around them. She had to admit to herself, she kind of enjoyed the power that rock gave her, but she loved her baby sister. It only took a few minutes to reach the front door of their home when she felt a small tug on her apron. To her surprise, it was Margaret behind her. She wondered how she was able to catch up so fast. Gasping for air, she motioned to Elinore to bend down to her so she could tell her something in her ear. Margaret was out of breath. She whispered, "I will never tell a soul your secret. I'm sorry El." Margaret never spoke about Carl again in that manner.

Elinore woke early the next day. She heard what sounded like a large crowd just outside her window. She jumped out of bed and rushed to the window. Her eyes saw a crowd of men working and digging just behind their farmhouse in the open field where her mother used to plant her vegetable garden. She ran to the kitchen while Margaret was still fast asleep. Elinore could smell coffee brewing. Rose entered the kitchen at the same time. Elinore asked her mother what the men were digging for.

Rose explained to Elinore with a smile, "You better get used to it dear, those men will be here for a while." Porter had hired a bunch of men to build many new additions onto their farmhouse. Porter wanted a large room to entertain in. He expected he could have as many as 50 people at times. He also wanted to add another bathroom so he wouldn't have to share the small one they had with the children. Porter wanted a separate smaller house too. One that resembled their own farmhouse but smaller, so the housekeepers and horseman could have their own quarters. Porter also planned to have a new barn built. The one they had was very small. They only owned two horses, a covered wagon and a buckboard wagon, but Porter wanted another horse and he had heard of a new gasoline internal combustion powered automobile that was recently made available to the public. Porter wanted one so desperately that he'd even dreamed of it in his sleep. It was well made and produced by a big corporation called the Daimler Group right there in Germany. It was called the Motorwagen, and the cost was 1000 Goldmark. A hefty price, but with all the money that was coming in from the endless orders for the Prussian Army, he could well afford one. Finally, he wanted two more bedrooms so the girls could have one each and a spare for visitors. He had the horse keeper pull the wagons to the other side of the house by the pond and tether the horses to the hitching post where Rose's cowbell hung. She needed that bell to call the girls in for the evening meal.

Rose and Porter had met in 1886. Rose was introduced to Porter by her sister Agnes Seals. They had gone to a small church together in Cuxhaven. It was a small northwestern city in Germany with one of the largest fishing ports that bordered the North Sea. They spoke in Plattdeutsche to one another. Rose Seals and Porter Downing quickly fell in love and were married in August of 1887. Rose became pregnant, and Elinore Rae was born August 16, 1888. Just less than 9 months later Margaret Ann was born on May 28, 1889. Rose had difficulty in carrying Margaret and she was born early. Margaret was only 2 pounds when she entered the world. Doctors feared she would not survive. Rose had terrible depression after her birth and remained despondent for many months after. That was until she found solace in planting a vegetable garden; watching things grow and making delicious meals from her harvest. Her depression left after the first harvest, and she continued to plant the following year, but keeping up with her two little ones and running a household wasn't easy so Rose decided it would be best to just visit the market. Though she always remembered the difference in taste from the store-bought produce to her own homegrown.

Rose's sister, Agnes, was much more stoic. Agnes wasn't like her mother or her father at all. "She marched to a different drummer," Rose remembered her mother saying. Rose, however, was much like her mother. Agnes was taller and bigger boned as some would say. She had a harshness in her voice and spectacles that she looked over the top of as she spoke down to people. Rose did not seem to notice this as she had grown up with her, but as a result, Agnes did not have many real friends. Agnes, however, was someone who could take charge and run a tight ship. Rose could and would step toe to toe with Agnes, but Porter would never dream of it as many others would not. Agnes had long hair like Rose, but she would braid it tight and wrap it around the top of her head. The two sisters were born 2 years apart, but both women were completely opposite.

Porter enjoyed Rose's sense of humor and the fact she was such a petite wallflower. He was still very attracted to her in the years that followed and couldn't imagine coming this far in life without her. The things she did often made him laugh. One day, word had come from her mother that Agnes had informed the family that she didn't feel she could continue on with things in Germany and was going to relocate to America. It broke their parents' hearts. They begged her not to leave, but she left anyway.

Occasionally Rose would receive a letter from Agnes with tales of her adventures in the states, and all the money to be made for women in the domestic service areas, factory work, and midwifery. She would tout about how you could make an honest living at dressmaking which she already knew how to do from back home. Agnes boasted of the endless opportunities in her letters and Rose often wondered if these were just tall tales. She bragged about friends of hers working as laundress workers, and saleswomen in large department stores. Rose couldn't really picture Agnes with a gaggle of friends. She just wasn't that type of person. When Rose shared this with Porter, all he would say was that she was sure tough enough. Rose often wondered if Agnes would ever find a suitor to make a life with and start a family. Rose knew her sister was tough on the outside but could have a kinder side at times. She was a survivor with great instincts. But to find a suitor she would need to clean herself up a bit. Agnes snorted on the rare occasion that she laughed. Her fingernails were unkept and she was very tense most of the time. Agnes loved eating but had horrible table manners. Rose always hated the way she slurped her soup and ate with her hands. Most of all Rose thought

Agnes would look far more beautiful if she loosened her locks once and a while. She wondered if the tightness of her braids made her as stern as she was. Porter had often joked about that with Rose. Agnes had worn that same hairstyle since they were young children.

It was November of 1897 and almost the end of autumn. There was a crispness in the air. The trees had nearly lost all their leaves by then. Elinore felt badly for the men who were still working around the house outside. The weather was growing colder with each passing day. The men were already finished working on the new barn but still had other work to finish. The horses and wagons were all stored in the new barn now. Porter had purchased two more horses, one of which Elinore fell in love with immediately. He was a tall black beauty standing almost 18 hands high, with a silky black mane and tail. Elinore loved to look him straight in the eye. His soft eyes brought her such a warm compassion, she felt it was as if she had known him all her life. When her school day was over, she would always visit him before going inside. With her books in hand, and the apple Carl would always give her, she would call out to him. Elinore had given him the name Lucky, but for now, she was the only one who called him by that name. Lucky seemed to know she was there before she even called out to him. It was as if he knew the sound of her footsteps. Elinore would put her books down in front of his stall and wait for him to lower his face to her. She loved the small white patch on his nose. His hair was soft and beautiful. She made a habit of taking the apple out once she had his full attention, then taking one bite for herself and then another for Carl. After the first crunches, she would give the rest to Lucky. Elinore confided a lot of things to Lucky. Lately most of the conversations had been about Carl. She asked Lucky if he thought it was proper for her to give Carl something small at Christmas.

Elinore was already thinking about Christmas. She had been shopping with her mother the day before and the market was already preparing for the holidays. Bright red ribbons and bits of garland were beginning to pop up everywhere. She thought it would be nice to write Carl a poem for Christmas. Elinore had no money, but a poem could allow her to express herself to him. It was either that or maybe tuck a few of mother's lovely biscuits under her apron for him. Elinore's thoughts fleeted for a moment to the wind she could hear howling outside the barn. It was a chilly and gray day. Branches were breaking off the limbs of the trees above and landing on the barn. Elinore loved the snow and knew it would be coming soon. There was lots of fun to be had in the snow for her and Margaret. She made her way inside after saying goodbye to Lucky; making sure to give him a gentle pat on his muzzle before she left. As soon as she entered the kitchen, Rose wanted to know what took her so long to come home. At once, Elinore thought to herself there must be some trouble. Her mother had never asked about her delays before. Elinore quickly answered, "I just wanted to check in on Lucky." Rose knew she had a fondness for the horse. Rose and Porter had a plan. "Your father wishes to speak with all of us in the front room now. Run and fetch your sister," she said.

Elinore ran quickly, almost sliding as she rounded the corner to their room where she knew she would find Margaret. As she entered their room, she saw Margaret sitting on the floor brushing her new dolly's hair. Her eyes grew large and darker. Elinore was furious. Snatching her doll from Margaret's grasp, she said "What do you think you're doing? That's my doll!" Margaret stood and put her hands on her hips. Defending herself, she shouted, "I was bored, and I wasn't hurting her!" Elinore's teeth clenched down as she looked at Margaret. She howled, "Don't ever touch my doll again!" Angrily she tucked the doll under her pillow. She pushed Margaret hard toward the door and said, "Father needs to speak to us, NOW GIT!" She pushed her again forcefully toward the door. She was cross but had what her father needed to say on her mind. What could he be wanting to tell them? She was hoping that the anticipation of the next few moments would have a good outcome.

Elinore and Margaret entered the front room. Porter was sitting in his favorite chair tapping his fingers on the round table positioned between his chair and Rose's. His legs were firmly planted on the floor. His voice became very serious. He said, "Come and sit girls," as he pointed to the circular rug on the floor in front of him. Rose entered the room and looked weighty, as well. Porter slowly began to speak. "Girl's, we have a serious situation, your mother and I need both of your help with." He placed his one finger on his bottom lip looking most pensive. He looked down at his girls sitting anxiously awaiting his secret and he just couldn't hold back any longer. Rose knew what he had planned to say but kept up with his charade. Porter felt he would burst into laughter if he waited just one more second. A sly grin came across his face and he blurted out, "I think tomorrow we will be going to the forest and bringing home the nicest balsam we can find! This house needs a Christmas tree for Christmas!" With just a month left, they would need to start to make decorations. The girls were so excited.

Margaret ran and leaped into her father's arms, almost knocking him over. She then grabbed her mother's hands and pulled her up to dance circles around the room. They were bursting with excitement. Elinore started to dance too, and her father picked her up swinging her over his shoulders as he ran into the kitchen and back. Elinore screeched with excitement. Tomorrow will be a fun day! She knew they would soon be gathering tinsel, apples, roses, and wafers to decorate the tree with. Mother would always make popcorn and they would all sit around the large kitchen table together to string the popcorn, alternating it with cranberries every year. Elinore always thought the red cranberries were a nice contrast against the deep green pine. She had a keen eye for details for someone as young as she was.

As Porter had promised, they were off to the forest the next morning. They rode in the buckboard wagon this time expecting the tree would hang off the end. They seemed to walk a long way, Elinore thought, as it was hard to plod through the deep marsh. She thought to herself she may need to carry Margaret back to the wagon on her back. Her tiny legs were having a hard time managing. Finally, Elinore and Margaret's eyes together spotted a tree 20 paces from where they stood. They both shouted out and pointed at the very same time, "I like that one!" Rose and Porter stood back and looked at the tree for a moment. Both wondered if it would fit through the door. This pine was surely a tall one, but both had to admit, the girls had picked a beauty. Margaret ran up to the tree to touch it. She pulled at the limbs and twisted the needles. She turned to her mother and said, "I love that smell." Taking a big breath of air from her sticky pine oiled hand for herself, she held her tiny hand out to her mother and said, "Smell."

Rose smiled as she watched her children enjoy the smallest pleasures of life. Margaret turned to reach for the same branch again, when a small bird suddenly flew straight out at her, almost knocking her over. The bird was stuck in her hair! Margaret began screaming, running in circles, as she pulled at her hair. Elinore was laughing so hard she was absolutely of no help to Margaret at all. Suddenly the bird broke free leaving Margaret's hair looking as if she had just gotten out of her bed. Elinore continued to laugh at the unsightly mess Margaret now was in. Margaret's face turned red, and she shouted at her sister. "It's not funny!" Rose and Porter tried to contain themselves too, covering their mouths with their hands. Porter chopped the tree down fast and Rose helped him load it into the wagon. The tree was heavier at the base, so Porter took that end and Rose tugged at the other. There was barely enough room for the four of them to sit on the bench, but they made it home safely. Porter called loudly to the men who were still at work to come help him bring the tree inside the barn. It was colder now, and it would stay fresh inside the barn until Christmas.

The girls were tired from the day and flopped to the floor like rag dolls. Rose quickly put some potatoes on the fire, with some cured pork she had bought the day before at the market. Soon it was bedtime as the sky became darker more quickly in the month of November. They kissed their parents and went off to bed. The next day they would need to be up early because it was Sunday, and they would be expected to attend church. It was also the day they could wear their pretty dresses and leather shoes, with ribbons in their hair. It was the only day they were allowed to dress in their fancy clothes. Both girls loved their leather shoes, even though they pinched their feet. They were so pretty; neither were bold enough to complain. The button up, black leather booties with tassels at the top made each of them feel so special.

Church went the way it always did that Sunday. The girls fought off their sleepy eyes as the preacher spoke. After the sermon was over all the boys and girls could enjoy some biscuits and milk that the preacher's wife always offered. They were surely worth the wait. Elinore loved the biscuits with the cherries on top, most. Afterwards, she went outside where there were a few of the older boys and girls standing and talking. Elinore saw someone coming over the hill behind the church. As he got closer, she realized it was Carl. She ran toward him calling out, "Carl, Carl, it's so nice to see you! What brings you here?" Elinore knew it was a long way for him to have come and he attended a church closer to his home. "I came looking for you," he told her. Her eyes squinted, wondering if something was wrong. "It's not that I'm not happy to see you, please don't think that Carl, but is everything okay?" she asked.

Carl began to explain. "My father has fallen ill, and I will need to start working to help my mother with the farming and the cost of food for my family." He then began to tell Elinore that Mr. Schmidt was willing to have him help him at his shop. Mr. Schmidt owned the local blacksmith. He needed help and had plenty of work. Carl said he may be missing some school because of this, and Elinore became sad. She thought, surely, he would work for Mr. Schmidt after school. Even though Carl had promised to come to see her, Elinore began to doubt that would really happen. She told Carl that she hoped his father would feel better soon, and that she knew her father would need to bring their horses to Mr. Schmidt to be tended to. She told him that she would ask to come along with her father when he went. Elinore really felt like crying at this news. He was the first boy she had ever taken interest in. She remembered the first time she saw him, what he was wearing, his beautiful eyes and smile. She remembered all their talks as they walked home from school, every word he said to her, every punch in the arm he gave her. Everything. She leaned in to whisper in his ear and felt the warmth of his face against her lips. Her heart was racing, but at the same time sadness overcame her, and all at once, she decided a kiss on his cheek wouldn't hurt. She quickly looked around to see if anyone was watching and pecked him one.

He looked sort of bashful to her as she heard her father's voice calling her. She told him she would see him again soon and took off running. She was hoping that her father had not seen her kiss Carl. Elinore knew her father would be angry with her for it. She and Margaret climbed into the wagon, as Porter helped Rose up. With a quick snap of the reigns. Porter and his family were on their way home. Elinore and Margaret sat quietly all the way. During the long bumpy ride, Elinore did her best not to cry. She felt as if she had just lost everything. She had already begun to picture herself married to Carl.

Elinore was very mature for her age, and it wasn't uncommon for girls just a little older than her to start thinking about their wedding day. She even thought of the house they would have of their own. But that wasn't going to be now, and it was all she could do to keep herself from crying. Soon they arrived home, and Porter guided the horses into the barn. The barn still had the smell of fresh cut wood, and the dampness made it stronger. The wind was picking up and the smallest drops of rain began to fall. The children and Rose ran for the house. Rose threw some more wood on the fire in the kitchen. She had set a pot of soup on the fire before they had left for church and now it was almost ready. She had planted some peas in the spring and had picked and dried them. She was using them in the soup, and she couldn't wait to taste it. She had also purchased some smoked hocks to add to the soup and with the fresh bread she had made earlier, it would warm everyone.

Porter came in and shook the rain off his coat and hat. The water splashed everywhere which sent a hairy eye from Rose in his direction. It was raining harder with each passing minute. Rose and Porter knew it was going to be a bad storm that night. They had both noticed how fast the sky was turning ominously on the ride back. The black sky made the moon and stars disappear. Rose had lanterns and candles burning in the kitchen. She took Porter's coat and hat and hung it closer to the fire to dry. Porter felt the chill of the November rain right through his bones. He took off his leather boots and placed them near the fire also. He sat down on the wooden chair they kept next to the fire and held his hands out to catch a bit of warmth from the flames. The evening meal was ready, and he called to the children to come and have a bowl of soup. They sat at the table quickly. Rose poured the soup and sliced off a piece of fresh bread for each of them.

Rose loved the smell of fresh bread, and it made her happy. The rain outside was beating on the window in the kitchen much harder now. The leaves passed by the window like birds, when suddenly there was a huge crack. A flash of light lit the entire room. A bolt of lightning struck the tree just outside the kitchen and a heavy branch hit the ground hard with a thud. Elinore covered her head and Margaret screamed. She dove under the table shaking. "Come here you poor thing," Rose said to Margaret as she lifted her into her lap. Rose wrapped herself around Margaret until she felt she could sit in her chair again to finish her soup. They were all hoping the blue skies and sunshine would return by morning.

And indeed, it did. Porter got dressed and went outside before even having a cup of coffee. He wanted to see if the storm had caused any other damage other than taking that branch off the tree. The hole the men had dug for the newest building that was to be the smaller version of their own house, was now completely filled with water. Porter just stood there gazing into the pool of water, discouraged and disappointed. Shaking his head, he saw some birds flopping around at the water's edge. He muttered, "At least someone is enjoying this." He went back inside for a cup of Rose's coffee. As he began to tell her about the water, he couldn't help but show his disappointment in the way things were going. But just as he began to speak, the men began to show up outside to start working again. They seemed to have a plan already, as Porter watched from the window. They started digging a trench that would allow the water to drain into the pond. The landscape helped because the pond was a bit lower than where they had planned to build the house. Porter went outside again to speak briefly with the men. When he came in, he had a grin on his face. Rose didn't ask why; she just took that as a good sign. The men stayed late that day to make up for lost time. It was hard work, but they were making great progress. Rose noticed one of the men. Every time she would go outside, she would catch him eyeing her. She felt uncomfortable with him watching her so intently.

That evening Porter was late coming home. Rose was busy in the kitchen, while the girls played in their rooms. The man came to the backdoor and knocked softly. Rose went to the door and opened it just slightly. She asked the man what he wanted. He asked if she wouldn't mind if he used their bathroom. She hesitantly let him in and as he passed her, he brushed against her apron. She felt the hardness of his hips pressing against her. He didn't try to hide his liking for her. She had noticed the smile on his face. Her thoughts turned to the children. Rose began to regret letting the man in. It was only her and the girls in the house. It was just a minute, and he was back in the kitchen again. As he headed for the door, he said thank you Mam, and reached for her hand bending as if he were going to kiss it. She pulled her hand back quickly. Rose sternly said to him, "That is not proper sir and I want you to leave now!" The man continued toward the backdoor with no apology, and Rose could see by his risen cheekbone that he was again smiling. Disgusted, she slammed and locked the door behind him.

She decided at that moment she would not tell Porter just yet. She knew it would make him angry enough to let the entire crew go. With Christmas so close it would be horrible for that many men to lose their jobs because of one of them. She would be more careful of him in the future. If there was another incident, she would have to tell Porter and she dreaded what the outcome of that would be. Soon Porter was home, but he was too tired for much conversation that night, as another very large order for more uniforms had come over the telegraph. Rose didn't mind. She filled the bathtub with warm water and put fresh towels in the bathroom for him. He thanked her, told her how much he loved her, and made a straight shot for the bathroom to soak his aching bones. She put the girls to bed and waited for Porter in their bedroom. By the end of that day, she too was tired.

It felt to Rose as if she'd only been asleep for a few minutes when she was awakened by the birds chirping outside. That was her signal to put on a pot of coffee to brew in time for Porter to have a cup before heading off to work.

The days were flying by, and it was much colder now. Porter's visions for their home were all but complete. The small house behind their farmhouse was almost finished and the men had framed out the additions for the extra two rooms plus the larger bathroom next to where Porter and Rose slept. The men left breaking through the walls for last so as not to interrupt the lives of the family inside. Rose was tired of all the constant hammering and shouting. She couldn't wait to have her peace and quiet back again. Even though the temperatures outside had grown colder the ground was still warm. It would be another month before it was all frozen. She began her days early; there was a lot to do, and she started to think about how nice it would be to have someone to help with some of those things. She thought about the tree in the barn and the Christmas things they needed to purchase. She had noticed a wooden rocking horse in a store window when she and Porter were in town last. She thought about how happy the girls would be to receive the rocking horse as a present. Rose also noticed how much Margaret loved the doll that Porter had given Elinore. Rose thought maybe Margaret could have one also.

There was still a little time before the holiday. Rose planned to start early so she wouldn't need to rush. She had already begun to think about the feast she would prepare and what friends of Porter's would be coming. Of course, Rose's parents would be there to share in the festivities. She began to daydream, getting lost in a moment of the day while staring out the window of the kitchen. Her mind drifted off like it was above her looking down at all that was happening around her. The girls were growing fast. She was alone quite often during the days, while Porter worked longer days at his shop. She thought of all the new buildings that were going up around her. There were so many changes. The man who had touched her inappropriately bothered her. Suddenly, Rose had a feeling of uneasiness. Things were happening all too fast. Her gaze was broken by a sound that was unfamiliar. It was a steady puttering sound. It was strange enough that Rose opened the front door to see what was making the noise. As she opened the door, she could see Porter. She prayed to herself, please dear God, what has he brought home now? Rose stepped outside and watched Porter slowly pull up to the front of the house with a huge smile that showed all of his teeth. He was seated high on a bench on top of what looked like a metal horse to her. It had 3 wheels and a pole in the middle which he used to steer it with. There was a smaller bench opposite from where he sat, and a folded-up leather cover was harnessed behind him. The wheels were very big, and it had a landing board on the side to help a person step up into the vehicle. Porter shouted to Rose, "Come on up!" He waved to her with excitement. She thought to herself, the children aren't home from school yet, why not give it a whirl? Porter extended his hand to help her and soon they were riding along.

Once again, the two felt like they did when they had first met. They laughed loudly as the sun brilliantly blazed down on them. Careful not to burn up too much gasoline, Porter steered back to the new barn behind the house after a few minutes. Rose got down, looking over the vehicle and then at Porter. Her eyes showed concern when she asked Porter if he thought they were not taking things too quickly. She knew this machine must have cost a massive amount of money. Porter and Rose spoke quietly in the barn among the horses as he explained all the reasons why he thought this was the best purchase he had made yet for his family. Rose still had her doubts but what could she do now? Porter also didn't think it was the right time to tell Rose he had done a bit of shopping before he had come home with the automobile. He could see Rose was overwhelmed by his latest purchase. He had bought new leather shoes, fancy dresses of silk, with hats to match, for all three of them. He knew they would be happy to have these new garments. He decided it would be better to wait to give her the gifts he had purchased for her and the children at a more appropriate time, so he gave them to the horse keeper to hold for him, in his house till the perfect moment came. They would be safe with him. Rose would never go to the house that Hans lived in. His house looked much like Porter's on the outside, but inside it didn't have much furniture or decorations. Hans had been around horses all his life and had a great way with them, but he was a simple man. Porter and Hans had known each other a long time and Porter relied on him to oversee things around his house as well as the horses. Porter knew Hans worked long hours. In turn, Hans remained loyal to Porter, and they always seemed to see eye to eye on things.

Rose felt things were moving faster than she liked. The skies were mostly filled with gray days lately, and winter was there in all its glory. The trees were barren sticks against the sky and the birds were only dark specks floating between them. The ground had frozen solid, and it had snowed a few times already. It made it hard for Porter to use his new automobile, but when he did manage to use it, he would always complain about his sore backside. It was a rather bumpy ride on the local dirt pathways, so he was using the wagons for the time being. The children had collected all the decorations to adorn the tree with. They had strung the popcorn and cranberries and had found the most beautiful red roses. They tied little red ribbons on almost everything that was in sight. There was a miniature violin in the corner by the fire in the kitchen. Rose even placed a red ribbon on that. Rose had already bought food for the Christmas feast. She purchased potatoes, green beans and carrots. Porter would be bringing home a huge pheasant Christmas morning. He planned to give her the gifts he had bought at that time so she could wrap them. Porter even made a quick decision to buy a set of the finest silverware from Hanau. Porter had invited a few people from his shop for Christmas dinner and Rose's parents would be visiting for a few days.

Finally, Christmas morning came. It had snowed the night before and everything was covered in white. The snow sparkled in the sunshine. Porter stepped outside and took a deep breath into his lungs. He loved the smell of freshly fallen snow. He planned to go into town, very early, to pick up their bird. As he entered town there was a small woman sitting on the corner with baskets at her feet. Porter stopped to see what she was peddling. Inside the baskets, were beautiful lace tablecloths. He thought to himself, Perfect! He gave the woman more Goldmark than she had asked for, said "Merry Christmas," and was on his way to the butcher. He had to pass the silverware shop on the way. Like women loving pretty dresses, Porter had a thing for silver. He couldn't pass that store without stopping for a minute. As he studied every item in the window, he a strong desire to buy all that was displayed. He started to narrow down his list as he stepped off the wagon onto the frozen ground. When he entered the shop, he immediately thought, yes, I must have that tea and coffee set on the first table! Then he saw a solid silver set of falcons on another stand. He just had to have those! And oh yes, he added an enormous serving tray to his bundle. Then he thought, oh, I mustn't forget that silver vanity set for Rose! He thought, Perfect! A Perfect gift for a perfect wife! He had the owner wrap it all up but as he headed out the door, the most magnificent centerpiece he had ever seen was there in front of him. It was an enormous cast figure modeled like Triton holding a trident. It was massive, and remarkable! He paused only a moment before adding it to his bundle of things. With that, he swore he was finished. He made his way quickly to the butcher and then home. He needed to set up the spicket for Rose. The pheasant was so big that it would take hours to cook. He arrived home with many bags.

The excitement had begun. The tree was up, Rose's feast was cooking, and the house was filled with glorious smells. There were gifts wrapped in brown paper under the tree as they awaited their guests. Elinore and Margaret could hardly keep away from the gifts until after they ate. They fidgeted and twitched with excitement that just seemed too much for little Margaret. She ran in circles, dancing and singing loudly. Porter couldn't wait to give them their dresses as a gift, so he gave them to each, earlier than he had planned so they could wear them for the holiday. All the things Porter had purchased for his family fit beautifully. Elinore and Margaret tip-toed around the tree looking and feeling very regal. Rose set the table like never before. She had to admit, Porter had lovely taste. Her table had never looked better. She finally began to think that maybe she could get used to this way of life, but still had some reservations. Rose was looking forward to dancing that night. Her father could play their mini violin well. Porter could also play it, but not as well. Porter had begun teaching Elinore how to play and she was catching on fast. Her thin fingers made it very easy for her. Rose settled into a chair at the table. Taking it all in, the exquisite silverware, the crisp white lacy tablecloth guarded by the falcons on each end and Porters new centerpiece temporarily taking the place of her crystal vase. What a magnificent sight! On the sideboard sat the new tea set and the most fragrant roses in Rose's vase. In fact, there were so many of them that it was impossible to fit another stem into the vase. Rose did not mind moving her precious vase off the table. She had thought even before the holiday it might be safer there, especially since the girls were getting older and were starting to do their homework from school in the kitchen where it was lighter. Rose had had that vase for a long time and would be very upset if it were to be broken. Rose took in all the smells and glitter of all the decorations; thinking to herself, this would be the best Christmas ever!

Chapter 2

The winter hadn't brought a lot of snow and spring came early. The pretty snowdrops were followed by blooming brilliant purple and white crocuses. The renewal of life was in the air. The birds came back, and other green bits were popping up everywhere. The bees were buzzing, and the warmer temperatures were finally returning. All the holiday decorations were put away and Rose was back in her daily routine. It was a sunny, warmer day when Rose decided to hang some laundry outside to dry. Porter had hung a clothesline for her the day before. She wanted to wash all the curtains in the kitchen to freshen things up. With the fire smoking, and the smells from cooking, things could get awfully smelly. Now that it was warmer at least she could open the windows. Rose wanted to hang them out early, so she squeezed the curtains tightly, releasing most of the water and placed them in the basket. She hastily made her way out the back door, carefully looking around to see if any animals were there. Immediately she saw Hans and felt safe. She closed the door with her foot and started to pull on the line.

She was all but finished hanging the curtains one by one and pinning them with the clothespins she had tucked into her apron when the line got stuck. She tugged at the line, but it wouldn't budge. Rose grumbled and was becoming impatient. Hans was watching from the front door of his house and couldn't help but find it funny as he saw her starting to argue with the clothesline. Rose was really struggling, so Hans figured he better see if he could help. Hans had only taken a step toward her, when Rose gave the line another hard tug with all her might. Suddenly the line let loose, and she fell to the ground hard. A few seconds later Rose began shrieking in pain.

Hans began running toward her quickly. His amusement had now turned to panic. He could see Rose was swatting at herself and stumbling to get up. Rose had fallen straight on top of a hornet's nest. Hans always wore leather boots and chaps which provided some protection against the stinging bees that now were swarming around Rose. He picked her up and ran for the pond. The bees chased him right to the water's edge when he jumped in still holding Rose. He and Rose landed with a splash. He kept her under the water for as long as he could hold his breath. But when he came up the bees were still there. He pushed her down again as she gasped for air. They went under one more time before the bees gave up and left. When they were finally able to come to the surface Rose was crying. Covered with bee stings, swollen and in quite a lot of pain.

Standing in the water, Hans told her to take off her clothes. Rose looked at him strangely. Hans continued explaining that she needed to cover herself with mud to make the bee stings less painful. He turned around until she was covered with mud from head to toe. He gave her his jacket and took her inside the house. Hans sat her down and reached for an onion in the storage bin that was next to the sink. He took a large knife and cut several slices from it. Rose couldn't imagine what he was going to do to her now, but she trusted him. He placed the raw onion on her face. Now Rose's eyes began to tear. She started to push his hand away, but Hans kept his hand firmly against her face holding it in place. Rose sat there, in only his jacket, covered in mud, stinking like raw onion, and completely embarrassed. She thanked Hans for his tender care. In turn, he tried to make her feel as comfortable as he could. She had to admit, the onion made the stings less painful. It surely hurt though. After a while, Hans could see an improvement; the swelling was starting to go down. He felt it was safe to leave her, he knew Porter would want to be made aware of what had happened.

Hans quickly went to the barn and chose the newest horse since he was the fastest and he wanted to waste no time. Hans set out in the direction of Porter's business to deliver the unfortunate news. Within the hour, Porter came through the door of the house, his face showing fear and concern. When Rose was a child, she had almost died from a bee sting. Her tongue had swelled up and the doctors had to keep her breathing. She was not having this type of reaction now, which pleased Porter considerably.

The sun was beginning to set on what had been a very long day, and Porter was determined to take care of those bees once and for all, for good. He left through the back door, went to the barn and returned in a moment. Porter was on a mission. Rose could see Porter had set a can down with a spout on it just outside the door. He also had brought a large stick inside the kitchen in his other hand. He wrapped an old rag around the end of the stick and stuck it into the fire. Rose could see the determination on his face and did not want to get in his way. He quickly went back out with the torch and picked up the can that he had left by the door.

When he lifted the can, Rose could see the word "gasoline" printed on the other side. In her loose-fitting sleeping gown, she moved painfully and slowly to watch what he was about to do. She saw Hans and Porter standing together near where she had fallen. Porter poured gas into the ground and lit it. Suddenly, a blast of fire exploded from the ground and even caught some of the surrounding grass up with it. After a short time, Porter was back inside and said, "NO MORE BEES!" He came closer to Rose, and looking at her arms and face he asked again how she was feeling. His concern was most evident.

Elinore and Margaret could see the pain their mother was in and were worried too. Elinore made some tea for Rose and Porter. Porter and Rose went to bed early that night. As Porter laid beside her, he was careful not to bump into her. When he had looked at her in the kitchen, he could see that she had been stung at least thirty times. If Hans had not been near, Porter could not imagine what would have become of his beloved wife. Porter kept it to himself; he felt somewhat guilty for not spotting the hive when he hung the line the day before. That night, Porter decided that he would stay home the next day to look after Rose and the children. He wanted to give her a little time to heal.

That morning Rose awoke sore from head to toe. The bee stings on her fingers and face hurt the most. Elinore made oatmeal and tea for her mother and father. As they sat at the table and ate, both parents noticed how Elinore was starting to become more independent. She had not been asked to do anything for them. She just did it. After they were done, Elinore and Margaret began to clear the dishes from the table and wash them. Elinore washed the bowls and laid them to dry next to the sink; Margaret brought her the teacup Rose had enjoyed drinking from. Elinore put the tea bag on a spoon and carefully handed it to Margaret to place in the trash bin. When the bin was full, Porter would always bring it to the pit to be burned.

Just as Margaret was about to drop the teabag in the bin, her father called out to her, "Fraulein, you have forgotten to take my cup too." Poking fun, Porter was light-heartedly jesting with her, but Margaret's youth made it hard for her to understand. She turned around quickly and looked straight at her father. Her jaw was jutting out; her upper lip raised on the left side of her face and her one eye partially closed. Her contorted face made Rose let out a belly laugh all the way from her toes. Now armed with the spoon and tea bag, she aimed it straight at her father. She put on the most threatening face she could. With her finger placed at the tip of the spoon, she was ready to use the teabag catapult! Margaret hollered, "Stop laughing at me!" All of a sudden, her finger slipped off the spoon and the teabag hurled through the air hitting Porter square in the eye with a splat! Margaret's face now had a look of sheer terror. Her mouth hung open in disbelief of what she had done. She stood there frozen and terrified, waiting in shock and fear of her father's reaction. She hadn't really meant to let the teabag go. She only wanted to make them stop laughing at her.

Elinore too, stood frozen, waiting…not believing, what her sister had done, when a roar broke out between Rose and Porter. Porter was laughing hard enough to make his eyes tear.

With their parents laughing, Elinore and Margaret began to laugh too. Margaret ran to her father and said, "I didn't mean to do that! It was an accident!" Porter was laughing so hard but managed to slip out the words, "I know dear, it's Okay." He held his belly and slapped his knee. His belly was beginning to hurt from laughing so hard. Margaret felt relief at her father's laughter. She thought, surely, she would be punished, but in the end, she found it very funny herself. Margaret knew that would not be something to try again in the future.

That night, Elinore went to bed with thoughts of Carl again. She had heard his father was coming along well and beginning to feel better. She really wasn't sure what his illness was specifically, and Carl never did elaborate on it, but she was excited to hear he would be returning to school. She hadn't seen him in months and to her, it seemed even longer. She wondered if he had changed much and if he'd kept his job with Mr. Schmidt. She was disappointed they never got to see each other over Christmas. She had written him a poem but never had the opportunity to give it to him. She hoped they could pick up their relationship where they left off. They both were a little older now but would still attend the same school with Miss Ilse as their teacher. The seasons were coming and going like the waterwheel at the grain mill. The mornings always seemed to come most quickly. Elinore felt as if she'd only just gone to bed when it was time to get ready for school again. She and Margaret had their own rooms now so getting ready in the morning was a little less complicated. It saved so much time since they now had two bathrooms to use as well.

Elinore started to look over her wardrobe; not finding much to her liking. She flicked through her dresses in her closet not liking one after the other. Elinore wished she could change her wardrobe as often as she liked; that would be magical. She knew Carl would be at school today and she wanted to dress for the occasion. As she brushed her long hair, she couldn't help but stare at her reflection in the mirror. Her body was starting to develop curves. Her brassieres were feeling so much smaller, and she noticed her lady lumps were starting to escape from under her arms from them being too tight. Her hips were struggling to fit under her apron; there just wasn't enough fabric to cover. And her apron seemed shorter now too.

It was very cold in the early morning and the smallest of snowflakes were falling from the sky, but not hard enough to cancel school. She and Margaret had a quick bite to eat and were off to school. They walked at a quick pace, and the entire time all Elinore could think about was seeing Carl again. The cold air made their cheeks red, and they wrapped their scarves tight around their necks and shoulders. Margaret walked close to Elinore. Her coat provided a little shelter from the ice-biting wind. They passed the apple tree that Carl had picked an apple from one summer for Elinore. The memory of that warm day and the butterflies in her stomach made her smile. The apple tree looked gnarly now against the gray sky with no leaves or beautiful red apples on it. She missed Carl very much. In just a few minutes she would be seeing him again. Her legs began to feel wobbly as she approached the schoolhouse. Her heart was racing and even with the cold air in her face, it felt warm to her, and indeed she was. Margaret even asked her why she seemed to be blushing. Not much got past Margaret. She picked up on the slightest detail of things. Elinore brushed her comment off, telling Margaret she was being silly, and her face was just red from the cold. Of course, she knew better, but didn't want to admit it.

They both climbed the small staircase and entered the schoolhouse. The younger children sat on the left, and the older, on the right. Elinore looked around and began to feel disappointed. Carl wasn't there. School would begin in just a few minutes. She took off her long coat, hung it up, and took her seat. The desk where Carl was supposed to sit remained empty. Miss Ilse was outside ringing the bell when she heard Carl's voice. A voice she would recognize anywhere. Elinore started to grin from ear to ear. Happily, her eyes met his. He took his seat and all at once the butterflies returned to her stomach. Her heart was pounding, and she couldn't concentrate on what Miss Ilse was saying. She wished their lesson would go quickly so she could finally get to speak with Carl.

As soon as class was dismissed, she ran out and down the steps of the school ahead of Margaret. Carl seemed to know what she had planned because he was right behind her. School provided some social communication and Margaret, knowing Elinore would want to speak with Carl, took her time to meet with her sister outside. Carl and Elinore stood facing each other. She noticed how much taller he was now. Carl's eyes dropped to Elinore's bosom. He admired how her body had filled out since the year before. He put his hands around her waist and pulled her towards him for a kiss. Elinore wilted in his arms, becoming intoxicated by his masculinity. She could feel his arms through his coat. They were much thicker than she remembered, and his shoulders were broader. They stood frozen in the moment, not wanting to break the spell that they both seemed to be under. Elinore found herself focused on Carl's eyes again. They had not changed. Still pools of blue she could find herself lost in. They both began to speak at the same time but broke out in laughter. Always being aware of who was around them, he leaned in again toward Elinore. He could smell the sweetness of her hair. Mesmerized by her beauty, he kissed her lips again, but harder this time. With her eyes partially closed, she could feel a warmth inside her that was slightly below her navel. It was almost too much for her to take.

Elinore backed up slowly. She didn't want Carl to read her coyness the wrong way, but she feared Margaret would be around shortly. Each told the other about how often they had entered their thoughts. Elinore asked Carl how his father was doing. He responded that the doctors said his father had a mild stroke, and would need to walk with a cane, but was recovering nicely. He would have to leave school again in the spring but as for winter, he was going to cut back his hours with Mr. Schmidt to get more learning in. This made Elinore happy. She would be seeing him on a regular basis again. Soon they would be considered adults, but for now they both decided to keep their relationship a secret.

Carl told Elinore he needed to go see Mr. Schmidt and would not be walking her halfway home that day when school let out but would tomorrow. Elinore called out to Margaret who was still inside the school. As soon as she heard Elinore's voice, Margaret came running out. Each step on the staircase was half the size of her leg. She could only take one step at a time but scurried down the stairs as fast as she could. She waved to Carl and grabbed Elinore's hand when they started home. All the way home, Elinore couldn't stop thinking about the kisses Carl had given her. The softness of his lips and his embrace. Everything that was going on around her at that moment seemed so unimportant as thoughts of him began to consume her.

Chapter 3

Nearly six years had passed since Porter made the decision to build onto his farmhouse and construction had finally come to an end. The year was 1901. Porter and Rose's lives were everything they could have wanted. Porter had hired a woman to help Rose. The children were healthy but for a few special needs for Margaret. Hans was still Porter's loyal hand. Porter enjoyed throwing lavish parties and celebrating every chance he could, however with the hours he worked he had to admit it wasn't that often.

Porter also was aware that Elinore fancied the black stallion he had purchased. Almost immediately from the time he had brought him to the stable Elinore had a fondness for the horse she named Lucky, so he gave Lucky to her as a birthday gift. She had proven to be quite a good equestrian and she and Lucky had developed a special bond.

Porter had accomplished obtaining most of the things that were on his wish list. He now had his ballroom and his own bath, which he still had to share with the girls from time to time. It annoyed him slightly, but he chalked it up with the price to be paid for living with three females. The girls had their own separate rooms. Hans was always busy putting final touches to his own house. The new barn was the perfect size for storing their horses, wagons, and Porter's fancy automobile. Porter was making more Goldmark than he had ever dreamed of and now was the well-respected businessman around town that he'd always hoped to be.

Porter was also a generous man. He gave to the church and the school. He took great care of his family and hired the help that was necessary. Rose adored this part of the man she had married. Rose loved Porter with all of her heart. He was her first and only true love. It always showed in the way she fussed about him. Her life had come a long way since they had first met. She never imagined her heart could be so filled with love between her children and her husband.

As children would be, Elinore and Margaret were looking for something different to do on this boring Saturday morning. It was still very cold outside, but it didn't seem to bother either of them. They both went down to the pond. Sliding around on the ice was always great fun. Porter had bought both girls ice skates. Today, they decided would be a fine day to try them out. They both sat on their favorite rock and laced up their skates. They began to glide across the pond. Elinore seemed to skate effortlessly. She liked speeding across the pond as fast as she could. The wind caught her lovely blonde hair, and it flew back behind her the faster she skated. She tried skating backwards and that came easily too. It gave her such a thrill. Margaret's legs struggled to keep her standing but she was still having a grand time. She sat down on the big rock for a break. She was envious watching Elinore glide along effortlessly and having the best time. She spun in circles and moved with the greatest of ease.

Margaret was feeling cold, and she wished she had a hot cup of something. She began to take her skates off and put her shoes back on, deciding she'd had enough. She got up and turned to go but as she headed up the hill, she heard a huge crack. It sounded like thunder, but it couldn't possibly be, the skies were bright. She turned to look and saw the ice on the pond had separated in half for almost the entire length of it! There was now a line right in the center that continued to the edge and Elinore was still on the ice. Panic set into Margaret's soul. Her sister was in great peril! Out of her mouth came a voice no one had ever heard before. She screamed to her mother for help. She continued to scream, calling Elinore to try to make it back to the edge. The alarm sounded through the crisp, cold air. Rose was inside and couldn't hear a thing coming from outside. Margaret stood watching as Elinore tried to make her way slowly to the edge. Elinore was as afraid as she could be. She began to feel the ice beneath her feet becoming unstable. Margaret's face was now stained by the tears running down her face. She stood frozen as the horror unfolded before her eyes. She couldn't believe what she was seeing.

Margaret was still sounding out a cry for help when Hans came running down the hill. He didn't see Elinore at first. Thinking the problem lay with Margaret, he rushed to her. But she quickly pointed to Elinore who was lying flat on the ice now. Her one foot had broken through the ice, and she was partially submerged in the frigid water. Elinore was turning blue. She was shaking visibly from where Margaret stood. Hans quickly ran to the stable, grabbing a rope and Lucky and made his way back to the pond. Margaret's panic transferred to Hans. He knew this was a bad situation. He told Margaret to run inside to tell her mother to get blankets and inform her of what had happened. She ran as fast as she could, ripping the door open, not even bothering to close it behind her. Her screams conveyed the message of panic to Rose's ears. She tore the blankets from her bed and ran with them to the pond. Hans had tossed a rope to Elinore and tied the other end to Lucky. Elinore managed to get the rope around her shoulders and the horse slowly backed up. Elinore slid across the ice and with every inch Lucky pulled her, she could feel the sharp edges of the ice cutting into her flesh. It hurt her legs badly. She was now so cold; she couldn't feel anything but the ice shredding her skin. Elinore was crying, bloody, scared, and frozen. As she reached the edge of the water Hans and Rose quickly scooped her up. Rose rubbed her daughter to warm her. Her skin was bluish on her toes that were submerged in the water for the longest of time. Rose had seen frostbitten digits before and hoped her foot would turn pinkish again soon. Elinore had never felt so cold in all her life. She felt very overwhelmed about all that had just happened.

Rose was also not feeling well. She had been nauseous the past month. This stressful moment made it that much worse. Rose moved her daughter to her bedroom and gave her a hot cup of tea. She covered her with blankets and tended to her wounds.

Rose needed to use the bathroom. As she stood staring at herself in the small mirror above the sink, she noticed how tired she looked. There was now a little bump in her belly again. Could she be pregnant? She thought she was just gaining weight because of eating too much over the holidays. She had still been having her strawberry week regularly, but on second thought it had been less than normal. She wondered how Porter would react when she told him about her suspicions. The thought of another baby made her happy. Elinore was 13 now, and Margaret was 12 years old, and very independent for the most part. Rose laughed for a moment as she thought, "Poor Porter, he'll never be able to get into the bathroom again!" With their two girls and herself in the house and a new baby on the way, his chances were slim. She would need to ride into town soon to see the doctor. Even though she was happy, it had been a while since Margaret was born and she had to admit, she was a little frightened. The birthing process frightened her most. She began to vividly remember the hard time she had to bring Margaret into the world. But now she was much older.

She washed her face with cold water; the smell of the violet scented soap she always loved began to bother her nostrils. It seemed to smell so strong to her now. She took another sniff and her nose scrunched up with dislike. Setting it down on the pretty petite soap dish, she promised herself to buy another piece of soap next time she went to town. Rose had started some stew earlier that day; she knew it was one of Porter's favorites. She needed to tell him when he arrived home about what had happened with Elinore. Rose decided that before they went to bed that night, she would tell Porter about her suspicions about being pregnant too. She was pretty sure she would be expecting a baby soon.

When Porter came through the door, he could smell Rose's stew which brought a smile to his face. His happiness though became concern when Rose told him what had happened with Elinore. He went to check on her. Elinore's toes were pretty and pink again. Rose had already fed the children and with sleepy eyes, they wished their father a good night.

Finally, Rose had time to speak alone with Porter. She made some tea and called Porter to the kitchen. As she sat in her wooden chair, she couldn't remember her back ever hurting as much as it did at that moment. Porter was quick to taste the stew Rose had made and he was hungry! The fire made it warm and inviting. He sat down and raised the teacup to his lips. It warmed his belly with each sip. He was tired from the long day at work. Rubbing his sore eyes, he noticed his wife's beauty. Her eyes sparkled as the flame from the hearth cast a glow about the room. Rose sat close to Porter and said, "I need to tell you something." Her voice was hushed. Porter leaned in toward her and asked, "Is something wrong?" Rose didn't know quite how to respond. She decided to just blurt it out. "I think I'm pregnant again." Porter's eyes opened wide. He asked her if, she was sure. Rose told him about all her suspicions. Porter rose to his feet, offering his hand to her. As she stood Porter placed both his thick hands on her belly. With a huge smile, grinning from ear to ear, he pulled her close and kissed her. He was so overjoyed. Rocking gently back and forth; staring into her eyes, she could see the happiness from her news in him. Rose told him she would need to see the doctor soon. They would need to know when their little bundle of joy would be arriving. The two headed off to their bedroom. As they climbed into bed Porter pulled Rose close to him. He wrapped himself around her and whispered in her ear. "I love you so much Rose," then kissed her cheek as the sleepiness set into both of them. Morning would come quickly, and the children would be off to school.

Rose slept so well that night. When the sunlight began to stream through the room, she opened her eyes slowly. She turned to look at Porter but there were only rumpled blankets where he had slept. She had not heard him get up. As she rose to her feet the cold air hit her. She reached for her house coat and tied it close to her body. She called out to the girls but there was no response. A set of 11 lines appeared on her forehead between her eyebrows. Had they overslept too? She hurried into the girls' rooms thinking how late they would be for school, but when she peered through the doorway, she found they were gone too. Porter had left enough hot water for her to make a cup of tea. He had placed a teacup, spoon and the cannister of tea on the table for her. Thinking to herself how nice this was to have the morning to herself, she poured the steaming water into the dainty cup that had been left for her. Suddenly, her stomach felt queasy again. She barely made it to the toilet as she hurled whatever was left inside her from the night before. Looking in the mirror she couldn't help but notice her tangled hair and pale face. She moistened a washcloth and washed her face, then taking a deep sigh, she went back to her bed.

Hours went by and Rose's housekeeper Elsie decided to poke her head in to see if Rose needed anything. Elsie had never seen Rose in bed so late. She hadn't been working for the Downing's long, but was already quite comfortable around the house, and Rose much preferred Elsie to the other workers who had passed through. Elsie was a young girl only in her twenties but very well groomed and knowledgeable in domestic matters. She had attended a finishing school which made her complete in Rose's eyes. Rose liked her proper attitude and was pleased with her cooking as well. It was almost as good as hers. Elsie came from a large family having 14 brothers and sisters. She had even helped give birth to a few of them herself.

Rose was very comfortable with her feet up and buried beneath her blankets, but she could feel the presence of someone, so she peeked out with one eye from under her cocoon. She saw a slender neck and the eyes of Elsie at the very edge of the doorway. Rose said to Elsie, "Please don't look at me, I'm a dreadful mess!" Elsie laughed as she entered the room. "Come now, I've made you some oatmeal and tea. Maybe it will make you feel better." Rose put her feet on the floor, but her head was a little dizzy. She grabbed Elsie's arm and together they walked to the kitchen. For extra measure, Elsie put her hand around Rose's hip to brace her. If she was dizzy, she didn't want her to fall. Rose sat down, covering her face with her hands. A look of concern came over Elsie. "I don't mean to pry Mam, but are we expecting?" Elsie had a large family and surely knew the signs of an expectant mother from early on. Rose looked quickly at Elsie with piercing eyes and Elsie was now worried. Had she overstepped her boundaries? Rose asked, "Does it really show? Do I look that bad already?" They both began to laugh.

Elsie assured her as she placed her hand on her shoulder, that everything would be fine. Elsie left the room and in the blink of an eye, she returned. In her hand she was carrying the vanity set Porter had given Rose. She set the powder-puff music box down and wound it up. A Tchaikovsky melody began to play. Elsie gently handed Rose the mirror and began to stroke her hair. Rose was enjoying the attention and Elsie was enjoying the personal time with her as well. It made her miss the times when she was younger and with her own mother. She hadn't seen her parents in some time. Rose decided she'd better get out of her bedclothes soon. The children would be home in a few hours, and she ought to be dressed. Elsie put the vanity set away and cleared the table. She had much work still to do. Quickly she helped Rose dress and went to her work.

Chapter 4

Miss Ilse had just dismissed class for a bit of free time. All the children rushed outside to play. Elinore took Margaret's hand to help her down the staircase. As they reached the doorway Elinore could see Carl standing by the tall Oak tree, but this time he wasn't particularly looking for her as she had expected. Instead, she saw him speaking with Anna. Elinore wasn't happy about this at all. Her one eye began to close, and her bottom lip began to push up and out. She called out to Carl, but he did not hear her. Then she noticed how Anna was giggling and smiling wildly as Carl spoke. Carl seemed to be enjoying himself to make matters worse.

Elinore broke into a sprint directly toward them. Imaginary green horns were protruding from the top of her head. Elinore had never had a jealous bone in her body before, but she did now. As she barreled toward them, Anna's eyes widened, and she trembled with fear. Elinore came to a quick stop just inches from Anna's nose. Anna was terrified just as Elinore had intended. Elinore quickly turned to Carl and asked if she could have a word with him privately. Her face told him that she was more than angry with him. He willingly obliged. Elinore made sure to give Anna a glare of disgust before leaving. She was much bigger and taller than Anna and wanted her to get the message; Carl was hers.

Carl was very much aware he had made Elinore upset. He quickly apologized, but Elinore was not so quick to accept. She told him if he wanted Anna that he could have her and all he had to do was say so. Carl felt badly about what he had done to make Elinore angry, and he could see she needed time to cool off. He even offered her the apple he had brought for her, but she threw it at him narrowly missing his head. He now saw a side of Elinore he had never seen before. She was a force to be reckoned with. He knew he would have to wait until tomorrow to see if she would still have him. He also knew to be careful in the future with his actions. As kind and lovely as she was, Elinore had a jealous side and a hot temper.

Angry and wounded, Elinore went to look for Margaret, but she didn't see her. She began to call out to her. Over and over, she called out loudly to Margaret. Wondering where she could be, Elinore went back to the schoolhouse. Inside she saw a bit of commotion. One of the other children was screaming, catching Miss Ilse's attention. The child told her how two of the other children had used the empty rain barrel to roll down the hill in. At the bottom of the hill was the stream. The ground was frozen hard but because the stream ran constantly, it was not solid. There was still water flowing and the girls were laying among the broken pieces of the barrel. Somehow Elinore knew one of those girls had to be Margaret. Running down the hill as quickly as she could, not understanding why Margaret would do such a thing, she reached the stream. There lay Margaret and her good friend Gertrude. Both were bumped and bruised. They were having trouble trying to grip the slippery wet and icy rocks. Elinore grunted as she reached out to Margaret. Hanging off a tree limb, she called to Margaret to grab her hand, but their fingertips wouldn't meet. Elinore was stretched as far as she possibly could reach, yet she could still not touch her.

She started to look around for a stick long enough to make it down the embankment when suddenly Carl reached past her and lifted Margaret to safety. Then again, he reached down to pull Gertrude up. Elinore began to dry the two after pulling her apron off beneath her coat. She kept asking Margaret why she would do such a silly thing. The only excuse Margaret could come up with was that she thought it would be fun. Elinore decided to stop being mad at Carl and thanked him for his help. She kissed him and thanked him twice. She was glad he came to their rescue. Carl told her he would be walking with them home to make sure they arrived safely. And so, he did.

The walk home was long and windy. The cold air blew against them hard enough that each had to keep pulling their coats closed. Margaret didn't seem to mind so much. The cold felt good on her bruised face and body. Carl put his arms around both of them, pulling them closer to himself. The three walked quickly against the bitter wind. Above, the clouds were becoming dense, and the air smelled like snow. Carl knew a bad storm was on its way. He hoped he would have enough time to get home before the snow began to fall. He knew he could run quickly without the girls. Finally, they arrived at Elinore and Margaret's house.

They exchanged farewells and gratitude promptly but before he left, he handed the apple to Elinore; the one she had thrown at him earlier. She smiled and with a small laugh, she reached out for the apple. "Lucky has been looking forward to this." Elinore kissed him again, but this time she kissed him on the lips. He instantly had become her hero. Slightly dazed, she took him by surprise. He smiled back at her. He felt a warm rush inside and for a split second felt love entering his heart. Carl knew now he was back in her graces again and he needed to be more careful with himself around other ladies. The snow began to gently fall as Carl arrived home. All the way, he couldn't help but think about Elinore, and as he lay down to sleep that night thoughts of her filled his head. The next time he would see her couldn't come soon enough.

When Margaret and Elinore entered their home, they were greeted by Elsie. Elsie immediately noticed the bruises on Margaret's face. She kneeled to Margaret's height and began to examine her more closely. Her head tilted to one side as she began to look poor little Margaret over. "What in God's name happened to you Margaret?" asked Elsie. She started to explain, when Rose came around to the door. Rose's back was hurting badly this day, so she relied on Elsie to see how badly Margaret had injured herself. Rose turned to Elinore and demanded an explanation as to how this happened and why she was not able to protect her sister. Elinore hesitated for a moment as Rose's foot began to tap against the floor in frustration. Suddenly Margaret spoke out and said, "It was my fault, Mama. I ran off with Gertrude while Elinore wasn't looking." Elsie had a look of concern on her face. Margaret had a large bump on her head and cuts to her face. Elsie went to the kitchen and grabbed a dish towel, gathered some snow from just outside the back door and gently placed it on Margaret's head. She winced and Elsie apologized for causing her more pain. Elsie was still worried, so she held up a few fingers and asked "Margaret, how many fingers do you see?" "Three!" Margaret shouted, insisting she was fine.

Elsie decided she would sit up and watch her that night and told Rose of her intentions. Rose knew she was right about Elsie being a blessing and thanked her. It was snowing hard when Hans came through the back door a while later. When he opened the door a rush of cold air entered the kitchen. Hans had come to see if Porter had safely made it home. Rose had not realized how late it was. Now not only was she concerned about Margaret, but she was worried about Porter too. She invited Elsie and Hans to have something to eat and stay with her at least till Porter came home. Rose did not like being home alone at night, especially now. Her belly was becoming heavy, and she was always tired. Some days she felt as if she could sleep the entire day away.

Rose made some carrots and onions with Bratwurst. The smell made everyone gather in the kitchen around the table. As the darkness of the night crept in, Porter still had not arrived home. The snow outside was starting to pile up. Hans was reading Roses mind. She was more than worried. Hans asked her if she wanted him to go after Porter, but she felt safer with him being there and insisted on him not going anywhere. Elsie was quick to remind Rose all the worrying she was doing was not good for the baby and that Porter probably stayed at work. He was smart enough not to try to travel in the dark during a snowstorm. Rose had to agree with her.

When morning came there were still a few small flakes falling from the sky. The sun was really bright, and the snow started to melt and fall to the ground from the tree branches. Across the field, the snow was flat and smooth with not even an animal's paw prints on it. It sparkled like a pool of precious diamonds as the rays of the sun illuminated each crystal. Rose put on a pot of coffee and found Hans and Elsie with their heads lying on the kitchen table. She tried to make her way around the kitchen without making any noise, but the wooden floor creaked with every step. Elsie was the first to hear her. She quickly rubbed her eyes and told Rose she would put the coffee on, but Rose insisted that she just go check on Margaret. Rose shook her head and whispered under her breath, "I'm pregnant, not lame." Elsie heard her though and could only smile to herself. Rose always had a quick wit and it made Elsie laugh at times.

Elsie left the room and Rose saw that Hans was still asleep. She didn't want to startle him, so she gently touched his shoulder. He still didn't flinch. Rose leaned over him placing her hand on his neck. She whispered softly into his ear and noticed how rugged he'd become. He smelled like the horses that he spent so much time with. He had a thick beard and wore mostly leather clothing. Rose leaned closer and Hans woke. He hastily turned his head and for a brief second, Rose and Hans' lips touched. Realizing what had just happened, both their faces expressed extreme surprise. Hans jumped up from his wooden chair and nervously smoothed his ruffled clothing. Rose started to laugh. She quickly put a cup of coffee in his hand. They began to talk about Porter.

Elsie smelled the coffee too and came looking for some. Taking a cup off the hook, she told Rose that Margaret still had a bump on her head, but it was smaller, and she thought she'd be fine. As Elsie savored her first sip of coffee, the front door could be heard opening. Porter was finally home! Rose rushed to help him off with his coat and asked what had happened to him during the night. He told her he had slept on his desk at the factory and that it was the hardest bed he had ever slept on. Hans looked outside and only saw his horse tied to the railing. "What happened to the wagon?" he asked. Porter had left the wagon under cover at the factory. Seeing how high the snow was, he thought it would be better to leave it there. Hans put his cup in the sink, thanked Rose, and left to tend to the horse.

Elsie made some oatmeal. She thought Porter and his family could use something warm and hearty in their stomachs after the long night. As she began to pour the milk for the girls, she noticed how low the jug had become. "Rose," Elsie said, "We are going to need milk soon." Porter was a provider, so his mind was already turning at Elsie's statement. The snow was halfway up the front door and the sun's rays had not done much to melt it. Porter had dug out a small pathway so they could at least open and close the door. He did the same at the back door. When Elsie spoke about the milk, he remembered seeing something peculiar while he had cleared the snow. He had noticed way across the field, someone had abandoned a wagon. The Adler's lived on the land next to his, but he knew that wagon did not belong to them.

Porter always kept a pair of binoculars on the hook by the back door. The more he thought about that wagon, the more he felt he needed to have another look. Porter took his binoculars and tried to see inside the wagon that was still there. He could see clearly large cans in the back that had small handles on each side. They surely looked like milk cans! With the cold temperatures, if there was something inside them, it would definitely be frozen. Porter knew it would be a while before they would be able to get into town to the farm where they usually bought their milk. He came inside with a childish look on his face. Hans took one look at him and knew he was up to something. Porter had an impish grin and a twinkle in his eye. Hans was smiling too. It was as if they were reading each other's minds!

Porter then told Hans to saddle up two of their horses. Hans asked, "Should I bring a rifle?" He laughed as he said it. Porter had a way of getting what he wanted by almost any means necessary. Hans never really minded that about Porter. As a matter of fact, he mostly enjoyed where their every adventure took them. As Hans quickly went through the door to the barn Rose asked, "What are you up to Porter? Haven't you been out in the cold long enough? You are going to catch a cold!" Porter kissed Rose on the cheek and gently rubbed her round belly. He told her not to worry, that he'd only be a minute. As he said that he could hear the horses right outside the door. Porter wasted no time putting his boots back on. He could feel they were still damp inside. He put his hat and coat on and secured it tight around his neck. His gloves were dry and warm because he had laid them on the floor close to the fire when he came in earlier. The warmth felt good to him as he held them to his face for a moment.

Elsie watched from the window as the two men made their way across the field. She could see the horses were having difficulty stepping through the deep snow. The cold air forced her to close the window tight. With her neck shrunk into her shoulders and eyes closed; she shuddered from the cold. When she turned and opened her eyes, she found Rose staring at her. She seemed to be looking at her as if she would be able to provide an explanation as to what the men were doing. Elsie shrugged her shoulders and sat down at the table. She was confused about what to do next. After about a minute, Elsie stood up again. Without speaking, she grabbed for the meat cleaver, put her coat on, and went out the back door too. Rose looked at Elinore and simply said, "Goodnight Irene!" She rolled her eyes and left the room. Elinore could never understand why her mother said that, but she often did when she was frustrated. It made her laugh. Who was Irene? she thought.

Soon Elsie returned. Her apron was bloody, and she was holding a headless chicken by its neck. Rose had a few chickens in the back by the barn, but they had not been producing eggs lately. Elsie told Rose she was going to make some chicken soup. She began to cut up the vegetables and clean the chicken. Rose put a few more pieces of wood on the fire under the kettle. The house was starting to smell good. Rose was wondering again about Porter and Hans. She looked out the back door again impatiently and finally saw the two men heading back. They seemed to be dragging something behind the horses with ropes. Sucking her teeth and letting out a lot of hot air, she began to think, "For heaven's sake, what are they bringing home now?" When those two men were together it would surely be the death of her to follow, she thought. They were always up to something!

Rose ran her house very orderly, but lately it seemed like sheer chaos to her. Porter and Hans came through the door laughing loudly as if they had just been to the pub. They rolled a heavy milk can through the door with them. Just outside, under a canvas, sat three more cans. Rose knew they were milk cans. She asked Porter, "Where on earth did you find them? Are they full?" Porter proclaimed, "TO THE TOP! It just needs to melt down a little." He had the happiest face as he spoke to her. He was always happiest when he was solving problems. They now had enough milk to last a month or more.

Rose went straight away to making some biscuits to put in the hearth, to be served with Elsie's soup. Hans and Elsie would be joining Porter, Rose and the girls for a celebration dinner. To Rose it didn't seem to matter much anymore where her husband had gotten the milk from. She was just glad he was home, and she knew they had only taken enough for their family. If they found out who owned the milk cans, they would gladly pay for them. But with two daughters and a baby on the way, milk was very necessary to have in the house to drink. That night was a good one for everyone at Rose's table. Fresh biscuits, fresh milk and lovely chicken soup. A light and lively mood filled the room. The hot soup was tasty and warmed the coldness from each of their bodies. As they enjoyed the meal, they also enjoyed the laughter and conversation. Even the girls added a sense of humor to the evening.

The hours passed and Elsie began to yawn. Hans humorously said, "Now stop that, Elsie!" And in the very next moment, he found himself yawning too. Elsie pursed her lips and stared a hole into him. They laughed at the silliness of it all. Hans knew it was time to go home; he was tired. It had been a long day, so he stood up and said thank you for the wonderful evening, nodded his head at Porter, and made his way home. Rose felt tired too. She had already put the girls to bed by that time. Porter and Rose left the room ready to turn in, but Elsie still had work to do. She would be the last to have the sandman throw sand in her eyes that night. She quickly washed the bowls and things and prepared for the next morning's coffee.

Finally finished and exhausted, Elsie headed off to her quarters which was on the opposite side of the house that she shared with Hans. She started to make her way across the frozen snow. With each step the crunching snow seemed to make it colder. Elsie began to pick up her pace. The cold air was biting at the back of her neck. As she took her next step, the apron she was wearing caught under her shoe. Landing face first in the snow she began to laugh. Having trouble getting onto her feet, only made it funnier to her. She began to roll around like a child. Her face turned upward, and she couldn't help but gaze at the beauty of the night. The moon was brighter than she could ever remember. She took a deep cleansing breath and thought about how lucky she was to be in her own quarters and working for the Downing's. She really liked her job, and the pay was not bad either. Rose and Porter paid her handsomely, but most of all, they appreciated her.

Before she got up, she took another deep breath and began to move her arms up and down, next her legs, out and back again. She rose to her feet more easily now that she had cleared the snow with her own body; she smiled upon noticing the snow angel on the ground before her. She felt the coldness of the winter and decided to just leave it there thinking no one would see it anyway and made her way home. Nearly there, Elsie could see a small light on inside the front of her quarters through the darkness. She knew she had turned down all the lamps before she left earlier.

She tapped on Hans' door lightly, hoping he was not asleep yet. Hans came to the door looking a little confused. He asked Elsie what was wrong. She replied, "I'm not sure Hans. The lamp is on." She was pointing to her side of the house. Whispering now, "I know I turned the lights down before I left." He started to laugh. Hans was smiling like the cat who ate the bird. His eyebrows raised and he began to bite on his lower lip. Feeling a little uncomfortable that he was the one who would be breaking the news to Elsie, he said, "Well Elsie, I think you're about to meet your new helper. I guess Rose and Porter forgot to mention it to you."

Elsie couldn't understand why they needed another helper. All the other hired help that came through had not measured up. She began to wonder if she'd done something wrong. She approached her porch slowly, trying to size up this new girl before entering. She peered through the small window and sure enough, there was a girl sitting with a book. The girl appeared to not look more than maybe 18 years of age. Elsie thought she was no match for her immediately. She thought to herself, "If she intends on taking my place, she has surely met her match." Elsie entered the house; there was an awkward moment that followed. Elsie shook the snow off her coat and sat down to take off her shoes. The girl suddenly came to her feet excitedly. Maybe it was her nervousness, but she seemed to want to make a good impression apparently. She held out her hand and blurted out, "I'm Emma, nice to meet you." Elsie smiled and reached for her hand. Then quietly she said, "I'll show you your room."

Elsie made up her mind at that moment to reserve her judgement on what she thought of this new girl for the time being. Emma had not struck her as anything special. The only real thought she did have of her was that at least her hair was neatly tucked up into a bun. Her hands were soft, which told Elsie she had not done any hard work. Emma was also very thin. Elsie guessed maybe 110 pounds at the most. Emma followed Elsie to her room. Her room had a small desk, chair, and a bed with a beautiful blanket. Emma paused a moment and then said, "Mrs. Downing told me that you would be telling me what to do and if I had any questions, I needed to ask you."

Elsie felt she should have been made aware of all this coming and was in no mood for this stranger's questions about anything. Being a little short, she introduced herself, "I'm Elsie," and went right into the itinerary for the next day. "We start work early here. Putting on coffee for Mr. Downing is the first thing in the main house to be done at sunrise sharp. Then Oatmeal for the girls and getting them off to school, then Mrs. Downing, then getting the evening meal started, afternoon dishes, laundry, sweeping, more cleaning up, and let's just say, we finish last." Emma shrugged her shoulders and said, "Okay…I'm here to help you." Elsie liked her positive attitude but also knew the proof was in the pudding from experience.

Elsie then said, "You better get some rest, morning will be here soon," and closed the door behind herself. As she walked to her room the wooden boards beneath her feet made noises. She put a few more pieces of wood in the pot belly stove in the corner to keep it going throughout the night and went to bed. Elsie didn't sleep well that night. Having someone new in the house put her on edge. She planned to ask Rose in the morning what this was all about. It worried her. She knew Rose liked her but wondered if there was something she did not know.

That morning Elsie purposely did not wake Emma. She made her way to the house to start the coffee. She passed the chickens and saw they had laid a few eggs. She stopped to pick them up knowing what a delight it would be to have some eggs for the morning instead of oatmeal. Gently she tucked them into the pockets of her apron and opened the back door of the house. As she opened the door, Rose was on the other side. Rose was surprised to see Elsie standing there at the very same time. Rose became unbalanced because of the size of her belly, making her fall backwards landing with a thud to the ground. Elsie rushed to help her up. Both their eyes widened by what had just happened. Elsie was afraid Rose might have hurt herself or the baby. "Are you okay?" Elsie asked nervously, several times. Rose stood up slowly. She felt ok. No pain. She went to the bathroom to check herself with Elsie waiting just outside the door. Elsie asked again if everything was okay. Rose opened the door; "Yes, yes Elsie. Stop worrying so much," Rose told her. "I'm so sorry," Elsie said, "I didn't mean to scare you." Rose assured her everything was fine.

They headed back to the kitchen where Elsie began to take the eggs from her apron. Elsie wanted to ask Rose about Emma badly but before she could, Rose asked her if she had met Emma yet. Elsie said, "Yes I have." Rose told her that she was enjoying their dinner so much the night before she had simply forgotten to mention it to her. Then she explained the reason she hired the girl was because with the new baby coming, she wanted Elsie all to herself but realized they needed another person to help with the housework. That would be too much to put on her alone. A huge relief came over Elsie's mind with her words.

While the coffee was brewing, and the eggs were finished cooking in the pan on the rack above the fire both women sat down at the table. Suddenly Emma burst through the door. Realizing she was late on her first day and a bit embarrassed, she apologized profusely. She made herself busy around the kitchen, picking up the broom and sweeping. Rose and Elsie were looking at each other with puffed out cheeks and bulging eyes. They held back the laughter that begged to come exploding out. Emma bounced around the kitchen like a butterfly trying to find things to do. Rose called out to Emma to come sit down.

Emma was about ready to jump out of her skin at that point. She was thinking she was in real trouble now. Being late to rise on her first day was not a good sign. As she placed the broom in the corner it slid down the wall, hitting the floor with a crack. Elsie and Rose couldn't contain themselves any longer and exploded with laughter. Emma wasn't sure if they were laughing at her, or they expected her to laugh with them. She was a bundle of nerves as the corners of her mouth turned upward with embarrassment. Rose put her arm around her shoulder and pulled her in for a hug. Emma finally felt it would be okay to laugh outwardly. It really was kind of funny. Rose motioned to her to sit down once again. Emma was less nervous now, and Rose began to tell her in detail what was to be expected of her and the role she was to play in their household. It was now apparent to Emma; Rose was very orderly. She ran her house with strict rules but could cope with the problems that everyday life threw at her. Rose had a great sense of humor. Emma began to understand the pecking order too. She knew to go to Elsie before bothering Rose about anything. Also, it was quite noticeable that there was a baby on the way. Rose called the girls in to meet Emma. Elinore and Margaret had been busy doing homework from school. They were both hungry and thought their mother was calling them for an early lunch. They came barreling for the kitchen but stopped dead in their tracks upon seeing a new face in their house. Margaret piped up, "Who is this person mother?" Rose quickly scolded her to mind her manners. Rose continued, "Girls, this is Emma. Emma is here to help with the chores." After meeting the children Emma was beginning to feel a bit more comfortable.

Margaret only had one thing on her mind and didn't really care about who did the chores. She was smelling something cooking. Margaret spouted out, "Mother, are those eggs I smell?" She rubbed her tummy and licked her lips. She had forgotten all about the introduction of Emma and her stomach had her full attention. Elsie nodded to Emma, pointing to the eggs with her lips. Emma understood she was about to serve her first meal of many. There were enough eggs for all of them, so they all enjoyed the deliciousness of their late morning feast. The biscuits left from the night before were a nice compliment.

Rose was enjoying her cup of tea when she felt a pain in her belly. Elsie with her watchful eye noticed the change in her face immediately. Elsie insisted that Rose go back to bed for a while. She wasn't sure if the pain was from her fall or something else, but she had experienced women who were this close to delivery sometimes having false labor pains. Either way, she felt better with Rose in bed with her feet up. She already knew about the early delivery of Margaret. It would not be good for her to have another premature baby. Elsie planted a chair right outside Rose's bedroom. She wanted to be within earshot if Rose called out for her. For now, Rose was without pain and comfortable.

Elsie slept in the chair that night. It wasn't easy and Elsie's backside was hurting from it. She had a huge blanket wrapped around her and at times all you could see were her eyes popping out from the top. The next morning, Elinore and Margaret were getting ready for school, and they couldn't help but poke a little fun at Elsie. She had cocooned herself in the blanket and Margaret began calling her Miss Pickle, partly because somehow in Margaret's mind, she looked like a pickle sitting in a chair with the green blanket she was wrapped in. As both girls headed off to school they hollered out, "See you later Miss Pickle!" Both enjoyed the fun they were having with poor Elsie. Elsie grumbled under her breath. "I'll give you Miss Pickle!" The girls closed the door hard enjoying themselves, which woke Porter. Emma had the coffee started in the kitchen and the smell of the fresh brew was starting to reach the rest of the rooms. Porter looked out from his bedroom and saw Elsie all bundled up in the chair. He thanked her for her caring nature and told her how much he appreciated her help. Elsie tried to stand acknowledging Porter but felt more like a pretzel from the wooden chair she had rested on. Porter helped her to her feet and told Elsie to go home for a bit, have a hot bath, and a cat nap. He would be staying home that day and she could rest easy.

Feeling grateful to be going home and having Emma to fill in, she went straight away to the back door. She walked up the hill and across the field; the sun warming her face. It felt good to her. She stood still for a moment noticing how the sun had melted down the snow quite a bit. There was a slight breeze in the air that blew her messy hair back. No one would see her raw beauty or her unkept hair, so she stayed frozen in the moment enjoying the warmth, when she heard Hans's voice call out to her. Damn! Quickly smoothing her hair and tying it into a knot on the back of her head. "What?" she hollered back at him. She was grouchy from her rough night. Pulling her coat closed and fixing the collar tightly around her neck, she turned toward the house again.

There Hans stood on the porch with a cup in his hands. Slowly she began to walk toward him. She noticed a snide look upon his face as he couldn't help but notice her disheveled appearance. She was in no mood. Hans seemed to be having fun with her as he cast his eye over her from top to bottom. In a pejorative manner, he intended on giving her the business for being out all night. Completely unaware that there had been trouble the night before, he began by saying, "Look what the cat dragged in!" Elsie pressed her lips hard together. Her eyes became cold and dark. He called out again, "Aww Fraulein, did I hit a nerve?" Elsie was about to let him have it for all his mocking. "Where's a snowball when you need one," she thought as she looked at the mostly melted snow around her. Elinore and Margaret had already given her grief. She picked up some bits of snow she could gather and threw it at him. Missing him, he laughed loudly ducking out of the way. She shouted at him, "Are you always this brainless? The horses have apparently made you into a soft-headed numbskull. You can really be a blockhead at times Hans!"

Elsie was usually soft-spoken and an easy target for poking fun at, so Hans was speechless at Elsie's harsh return. He stepped down off the porch and walked in her direction. He wanted to make sure she knew he was just toying with her. She walked quickly toward her quarters, and he really had to pick up his pace to catch up to her. "Elsie," he said, "I was only joking with you, is something wrong?" "Yes," she said and began to tell him how Rose had some pain the night before and how she slept in the chair all night keeping an eye on her in case there was any blood or problems. He was bewildered at her news. He hadn't even seen Porter the day before and thought he had just worked late. Elsie told him Porter was at the house and was staying home for the day as she stepped up onto her porch. "Pardon me now, I've got a hot bath waiting for me." Hans tipped his hat to her and realized why she had been so upset. He thought he'd wait a few hours and then go talk to Porter to get the details.

Chapter 5

There had been heavy rain the night before making the ground saturated along the path to school. Elinore and Margaret began stomping the mud off their shoes before entering the schoolhouse. Margaret was happy when she spotted Gertrude sitting in the corner. She quickly took off in her direction to chat a while before Miss Ilse started her lessons for the day.

Elinore scanned the room for Carl. He was wearing a new coat which she did not recognize immediately. But soon enough upon hearing his voice; walked right up behind him. Elinore was a tall girl who stood almost shoulder to shoulder with him now. She leaned over and whispered in his ear, "Nice coat handsome." Carl turned quickly to pull her toward himself for a kiss. Surprised he would do that in front of everyone there, her expression was that of shock. The classroom of children caught the action and all of them began a harmonious "Ewwwww." Elinore covered her face with her hand. Miss Ilse shouted, "Children, children, take your seats please!" Carl took his seat; embarrassed by the chaos he had caused. Elinore and Carl were among the oldest students in the classroom. She had one more year to go after finishing the current year they were in. Because Carl had lost so much time working to help pay the bills, he now had one more year as well. They sat across from each other in the last aisle seats. There were only 4 other children as old as them. Elinore had begun to think about where her life would take her regarding Carl. As she gazed at him, she noticed he'd begun to grow hair on his face. He was looking stockier to her with each year that passed. The chair he sat on seemed even too small for him now. Thoughts of marriage and children of her own with him began to enter her mind. She had known him since they were young. It was forever to her. Elinore felt they both had strong feelings for one another, and she really couldn't picture herself with anyone else at this point.

Miss Ilse's lesson seemed to last forever that day. When the bell rang signaling the end of the school day Elinore was so grateful. She asked Carl if he would walk with them home and he happily agreed. They walked the same familiar path and Carl reached for her hand. Elinore felt the warmth of his hand in hers. Margaret understood her sister's relationship with Carl better now that she was a little older. Walking along side of them left her feeling like a third wheel, so she began to walk ahead of them most times. With her house in sight now, Carl gave Elinore the apple he had in his coat as usual. She smiled at him and suggested they go give it to Lucky together right away. Margaret had already gone inside the house when Elinore and Carl made their way to the barn.

Elinore reached out and unlatched the barn door. The smell of fresh hay for the horses filled the air. Elinore had always liked that smell even as a small child. The two entered the barn and Carl closed the door behind them. Elinore walked quickly toward Lucky putting her hand gently on his muzzle. She loved her horse more than almost anything. Lucky's eyes were dark and beautiful. She knew he could hear her when she entered the barn. Looking into his eyes, she raised the apple to her mouth and took a bite. The crunch of the crisp apple perked up Lucky's ears. Elinore put the apple in the palm of her hand and extended it over the rail of Lucky's stall. The horse bit the apple and chewed it to pieces within seconds.

Carl seized the moment, turning Elinore around to face him. He could no longer hold his growing passions for her. Without speaking he gently reached for the strands of her hair that softly hung around her face. He began to run his fingers through them as he inhaled her sweet smell. Afraid to move, she partly closed her eyes, and at that moment he tasted her sweet lips. Carl began to spread his moist kisses over her throat as he tried to unfasten her coat. Finally breaking it free, his hands rushed in to pull her closer to him. Now he could feel the softness of her skin and it drove him mad. He pressed his lips over her bosom. Elinore wrapped her arms around his shoulders feeling the heat building between them. Wanting him, enjoying his masculinity, the warmth inside her grew fast. Carl pressed himself against her and Elinore backed up against the rail behind her. She was held in his grip that left her breathless. He eagerly picked her up, hiking her legs up, around his waist. Elinore began to lean back offering herself to him, revealing only what she wanted him to see. Her motion teased him and in a heated frenzy he carried her to the long wooden bench at the back of the barn. They kissed passionately and she could feel his hardness against her thighs that were still wrapped around him. Carl couldn't contain himself any longer and reached to unbutton his trousers. Raising her long dress up around her hips Elinore half gasped with her desire for him that had become overwhelming too. His hardness began searching, probing between her thighs, finding and entering that first small bit, when both heard a noise that came from outside the barn.

Panicked, they rose to their feet and straightened their clothes. They rushed out of the barn to see where the noise was coming from. At the back side of the barn a broken tree limb lay on the ground and partially against the barn. It was the force of the wind that rubbed the branch against it. Upon seeing this they both laughed. Elinore smiled and shook her head. They thought they'd been caught! It had spoiled the moment but they both found it funny. She looked at Carl and said, "You're losing daylight, better be on your way." Both didn't want the moment to end but it had despite their desires. Carl nodded his head in agreement and started off but then stopped. He turned to Elinore who was still watching him. He walked back to her and whispered to her, "You know, I love you, Elinore." She placed her index finger over her smiling lips and quickly pressed it against his. She answered, "I love you too, Carl." Lingering for just a moment, they parted ways and Elinore returned to the house.

She saw Margaret in the window and thought, "Oh Boy, here we go again." The minute she opened the door, Elinore could smell Elsie had something wonderful cooking. She passed Emma who was folding some laundry in the front room. When she passed her parents' room, she saw her mother lying on the bed. Elinore asked, "Mother, are you feeling alright?" Rose patted the mattress and asked her daughter to come sit next to her so they could speak. Elinore was concerned; not knowing what to expect. Rose told Elinore that the doctor had been to the house to see her. He rarely came to the house; Mother usually went into town to see him. Elinore wanted to know what he said. Rose told her he said he wanted her to keep her feet up as much as possible and that the baby would be coming soon. A surprised look came across her face. "Mother, I thought that wouldn't happen for a while." Rose then said, "Well you never know Dear, it could be, but it's not guaranteed." She went on to say that because she has had some pain, the doctor thought it was best to take some pressure off. Elinore then asked, "But you're okay, right?" Rose assured her she would be fine. Elinore kissed her mother's forehead and went off to her room.

Margaret could hear her sister coming down the long hallway, she had been lying in wait for Elinore. This was the moment! She listened for Elinore's footsteps. She began kissing her own arm up and down and then turned wrapping her arms around herself, moving her hands up and down her back. "Oh Carl," she exclaimed. Before anyone could see, Elinore gave Margaret a hard shove, sending her into her room and slamming the door behind her. Elinore sat on her bed thinking about her moments with Carl. She wondered how far they would have gone if that branch had not interrupted them. She was excited but frustrated at the same time at what had just taken place. She took her coat off. She could still smell Carl on herself. She would see him tomorrow at school but that couldn't come soon enough for her. For now, she would have to wait. She sat down on her bed and tried to do her homework but couldn't concentrate. It was no use. Again, she thought about what could've happened if it had not been for that stupid branch against the barn. She threw her books to the floor and leaned back, placing her hands on her forehead. The sun was getting lower in the sky and Elinore's room was filled with an orange glow. She looked out her window and thought, what a beautiful sunset! A few clouds were highlighted by the sun as it dropped behind them. For a moment she wished she were a painter, because it was one of the most beautiful sunsets she had ever seen, but her thoughts were broken when she heard Emma call out to her and Margaret that supper was ready.

Elinore, Margaret, Porter and Rose sat in their places as Emma and Elsie scurried around the kitchen. Emma had made Bratwurst with onions, peppers, and carrots. She had also made some potato salad which Rose couldn't wait to taste. Her mouth watered with the delight of tasting something she hadn't had in a long time and her expectations were met. "Ummmm…this is very good!" She savored the forkful. "Very good Emma!" Elsie and Emma smiled at one another happily. If Rose was happy, they were happy. Taking a bowl for Hans, Emma and Elsie walked home to have their meals. They would return after a while for the clean-up and preparation for the following morning. On their way up the hill Emma asked, "Elsie, do you think Rose is happy with me now?" Elsie's brows raised. "Why do you doubt yourself? If she didn't like you, you would've been gone already." Emma smiled. "Supper did come out good, didn't it?" The two were laughing as they tapped on Hans's door. Hans was delighted when he opened the door to find food in Elsie's hands. He took the bowl and inhaled the steam that came from it deeply. "Wow, this smells great!" Elsie piped up, "Courtesy of Emma." Feeling a little embarrassed, Emma just stood there. Hans put his hand on her shoulder and said, "Thank you." He couldn't wait to eat, he was hungry.

Elsie and Emma enjoyed their dinners on the opposite side of the house with some conversation too. Elsie finally began to think Rose had made a good decision about choosing Emma. The hour passed quickly, and it was soon time to return to the main house. Putting their coats on again and opening the door, they could hear howling off in the distance. Elsie picked up her walking stick from the corner by the doorway. She didn't like the howling of the wolves. They walked past Hans' porch to pick up his empty bowl he had left out for them. It was completely clean. Then they entered the main house to clean up and set up for the morning. Emma looked at Elsie and started to laugh. Elsie's eyes squinted, "What's so funny?" Emma returned, "You weren't kidding when you said we finish last." Elsie could only smile back. Everyone had gone to bed so they worked as quietly as they could, soon returning home to their own beds. Elsie put a couple more pieces of wood in the stove before turning down the lantern. She could still hear the wolves howling outside which made her skin crawl. "Rotten animals," she muttered and pulled the covers up over her head. Emma sleepily said "Goodnight". Her voice sounded like she was already more than halfway asleep already.

On the other side of the house Hans was still very much awake. He had also heard the wolves. He also knew Rose's chickens were a big draw for the wolves. He knew he would have to do something if they did not move on to a different hunting ground. After the long cold night, the sun began to rise. Elsie's eyes slowly opened. "Ughhh, I feel like I just went to bed," she said out loud. Emma had heard her. She let a small laugh loose and began to beg for just another 5 minutes. Elsie was amused as she began to gather her clothes for the day. She then said, "Emma, you can have 5 minutes more if you like, but I wonder how Mr. Downing would like to head off to work without even a drop of coffee when he has the two of us working for him." "Alright, alright!" Emma said. "I'm up!"

By this time Elsie was mostly dressed and told Emma she would meet her down at the main house, and that she was going to speak with Hans for a moment. Elsie grabbed her coat off the hook and put it around her shoulders. Her coat was still warm from hanging next to the stove. It felt good to her. When she opened the door, the cold air hit her face and her eyes closed. It was bitterly cold this day. It made her shudder, and she buried her neck beneath her shoulders. Walking quickly to Hans's door, he opened it. He had been looking outside and saw her stepping onto his porch. He rushed her in quickly, closing the door fast. Elsie told Hans that she thought Rose's baby might come early like Margaret did. She asked, "Can you take me to town soon so I can purchase a few things for Rose to have for when the baby does arrive, please?" Hans asked her if she wanted to go in a few hours as he only needed to care for the horses that day. He paused, considering that would leave Emma by herself. He asked, "Do you think Emma can handle everything by herself?" Elsie was quite certain she could by now, so she was delighted to know she'd be going soon. She assured Hans that things would be fine.

In the meantime, Emma had made her way to the kitchen and had started the coffee. Porter loved his coffee and gulped down his first cup. Rubbing his hands together, he held out his empty cup for another fill up. He took a few sips and realized he needed to be on his way. With one last gulp he handed his cup back to Emma. "Thank you," he said. Porter was late, and swinging his coat over his shoulders, he headed for the door. As soon as Elsie came in, she explained to Emma that she was going to town with Hans to visit a shop she knew of that sold things for expectant mothers and newborns. "Do you think you can handle everything till I get back?" she asked. Emma only asked what she should prepare for evening meal and Elsie replied, "We're making Bluefish tonight and I'll be back soon enough to help you."

She rushed back outside to meet Hans who was already waiting. Hans had pulled the wagon up to the door and helped Elsie up onto the wagon. The ground was frozen solid still, which made it easier for the horse to pull the wagon as it glided over the hardened earth. Elsie knew exactly what she wanted from past experiences. She knew Rose would need some receiving blankets, a bed jacket, a sleep sock, and some nappies. Rose still had the basinet she used for Elinore and Margaret. Elsie also wanted to ask about some sheets and burp cloths.

Hans steered the horse down the street as Elsie pointed out where she wanted him to stop. She saw a familiar face as the wagon slowly came to a stop. Marie was outside washing the store's front window. Elsie leaped to the ground and ran to Marie. Hans stayed on the wagon, not wanting to do more than be the driver. Marie was happy to see her old friend. "It's so nice to see you again!" she cried out, "Come in, come in!" opening the door for her. The two women talked light heartedly and laughed out loud. Marie was one of the nicest people Elsie had ever met in her life. She could surely purchase all the perfect needs for a newborn baby from her. When Elsie's mother was pregnant, Marie supplied everything necessary to fit her mother's needs perfectly. Marie's husband had died many years prior, but she still had a positive outlook on life and kept the store open. Elsie imagined it must be difficult running the store by herself when she saw a young boy working in the back of the store. She looked at Marie puzzled. "Did you finally get yourself some help?" Marie replied, "Yes, he's very good and unloads all the deliveries for me. He's a fine lad, I must say too!" Marie couldn't help but wonder where Elsie had been since the last time she saw her. And better yet, who was this handsome fellow in the wagon waiting on her? She finally had to ask, "Is that your husband dear?" She was pointing to Hans. "Good Lord, Nooo!" Elsie laughed loudly. "He's the horseman of the family I work for now," she explained. "Actually, he's a very nice man and so is the family I work for." "And who are they?" Marie inquired. Elsie proudly responded, "The Downing's." Marie knew of Porter's reputation, so she led Elsie to the most beautiful and best baby things she had to offer. Soon, Elsie had two full bags of things to bring home.

Marie helped her carry the bags to the wagon and the two women hugged each other and promised to see each other again soon. Pleased with what she had purchased, Elsie knew Rose would be too. When they finally arrived home Hans put the bags in Elsie's room for her. He knew she needed to see how Emma was doing. Elsie rushed into the kitchen. When she opened the door, the fish was already in the blue and white speckled pan. The cover laid beside it on the table. Emma had just finished pureeing the tomatoes and slicing the lemons. Elsie only needed to put it all together and on the rack over the fire. Emma had also made some red cabbage which smelled heavenly to Elsie. What an excellent choice of a side dish, she thought, and she hadn't even asked her to do so. She wondered where and how someone so young learned to cook so well. She complimented Emma with a "Well done!" Elsie just couldn't wait for dinner or resist having a forkful of the lovely red cabbage sitting in front of her. Licking her lips with a huge grin on her face, she tasted it. "Perfect!"

That made Emma happy. She was becoming more confident with each day and was glad Elsie was pleased. Elsie quickly put the fish together with a few spoons of butter and set it over the fire. It would be a couple hours before they would all be ready to eat. Elsie decided this would be a good time to check in on Rose. Slowly she peeped into Rose's bedroom and could see she was sound asleep. With the extra time she had now she decided to tidy up before the girls came home from school, and with that thought the girls erupted through the front door. Elsie was confused. They were home much earlier than usual. Before she could ask why Margaret blurted out "We got to leave early today, Miss Ilse wasn't feeling well."

Margaret was ecstatic. No homework, out of school early, and it was still daylight. She dropped her books on the kitchen table and ran outside toward the pond. She was delighted to go outside and enjoy the fresh air. She began to pick up rocks to skip across the water when she saw something pop up out of the water. It was late March, and all but a few sections of ice had melted. It was still bitter cold during the night, but daytime was becoming warmer with each passing day. Watching the water closely, she waited for something to happen. But nothing did. She figured it must have been her shadow or something that she saw. She picked up a few more rocks and raised her arm to launch one when she saw it again! She was sure this time. She looked closer and she saw a turtle's head. Quickly, she reached down to snatch it, but it was too fast for her, and it escaped her grasp. She scanned the water sharply, intent on capturing the little creature when she saw his small head pop up again. Margaret had already experienced how slippery rocks at the water's edge could be, but that was not on her mind now. She was determined to capture it as she stepped closer to the edge. Waiting and watching, the turtle seemed to taunt her. Finally, she could see him just under the water. With lightning speed, she scooped down and tightened her hands around its shell and lifted it out of the water. She examined him closely, noticing the pretty green hues on his shell. Completely unaware of where she was placing her feet, Margaret was once again a victim of the slippery wet rocks. She hit the water with a splash. Her dress now was covered with the muddy silt, and she was soaked. The turtle had escaped too. She knew her mother would be upset with her. Disappointed about losing her prize, she threw the rest of the rocks down that she still had in her pocket.

She made her way back to the house but saw no one. What luck, she thought and ran to the bathroom to quickly change her clothing. She thought she had gotten away with going unseen, but Elsie's watchful eye indeed saw the entire accident. Elsie had a good laugh about it. Poor little Margaret, she thought. After Margaret left the bathroom, Elsie quickly went behind her to rinse her clothing so the dark mud from the pond wouldn't stain her pretty dress. Elsie hung the dress to dry and neither Margaret nor Elsie mentioned it to each other or anyone else.

Elinore had been sitting in her room the entire time. Carl and Elinore's relationship had reached a boiling point. Elinore was lovestruck and Carl was mostly all she could think about. Emma was closest to her age in the household. She couldn't talk things over with Margaret. Margaret was much too immature to understand. Emma already had noticed a change in Elinore over the past couple of months. Emma decided it might be a good time to approach Elinore to see if she could convince her to talk to her. Emma knocked softly on Elinore's door. Elinore quietly called out, "The doors open." Slowly, Emma entered to find Elinore sitting on the edge of her bed, deep in thought. Emma closed the door silently behind her. Emma had soft eyes. She said, "Elinore, I think something is troubling you and I wondered if you'd like to get some things off your mind." Elinore began to explain the feelings she had about Carl, and once she started, it spilled out uncontrollably. "Please don't tell anyone," she pleaded with Emma. "I don't know what to do. I want my mother and father's approval, but I think they'll be upset." Emma asked why. Holding her hands up in the air, Elinore exploded saying "I don't know!" She sat down on her bed again, placing her fingers on her forehead and closing her eyes. Elinore paused only a moment and said, "Emma, I really love him so much." Emma thought for a minute trying to think of the right thing to say. "Elinore, you really haven't known him that long." Emma was unaware that they had known each other since they were small children. Elinore's neck stuck out with her chin pushed forward, and she made a strong stand. "No!" she said. "You are wrong! I have known him since I was 7 years old." "Elinore, I didn't know that," Emma said, and sat down on the bed next to her. Putting her arm around her, Emma began to tell her that when two people are just friends and then become more, things can get complicated unexpectedly. "Maybe take a deep breath Elinore and slow down a bit," she said. "There's no hurry, right? Enjoy your time getting to know this different side of Carl."

Elinore looked intensely at her as she thought about what Emma had just said. Elinore nodded her head slightly and blinked her eyes, understanding what Emma was trying to convey to her. Elinore didn't like admitting it, but Emma made a valid point. She took a deep breath and exhaled hard. Elinore decided to take Emma's advice and felt better about it. Happiness returned to her eyes, and she said, "Thanks Emma, but please don't tell anybody." Emma assured her again, "Of course." Emma hoped she had said the right thing as she left Elinore's room gently closing the door. She felt good about their chat and hoped she had made a difference.

Emma knew food would need to be served up soon and hurried back to the kitchen. Passing by Rose's bedroom she looked in as she breezed by. She stopped dead in her tracks when she saw Rose in the bed looking as if she was doubled over. She raised her voice and rushed in. "Mrs. Downing, are you feeling, okay?" Frightened by her position, she hoovered over her. "What can I do to help?" Rose shouted back at her, "Sohn einer Hundin! Just help me out of this damn bed! Nothing is wrong Emma; I just feel like I swallowed an elephant!" Rose began to weep at her frustration. "Oh Emma, I'm sorry. It's just so hard. I need to use the toilet badly enough, I could wet myself, but I can't roll out of this damn bed!" Rose continued, "My belly is so big, and I feel so ugly!" Her face was turning red from her tears and Emma tried to comfort her.

"Come now, getting upset isn't going to help." Emma started to swing Rose's legs off the side of the bed. Holding onto both her hands, she began to pull Rose to her feet. Rose wiped the tears from her eyes and thanked Emma for her help; rushing to use the bathroom. Emma took the opportunity to straighten out the bed linens when suddenly she heard Elsie calling her from the kitchen. Elsie needed her to get some of the frozen milk from the cans outside for the girls to have with supper.

Elsie and Emma worked quickly now putting the food together. There was not much time for talking because they were running late. Elsie served up the meal quickly as the time passed fast. Elsie had a surprise for Emma. She was looking forward to showing her all she had bought from Marie. It was a few hours later when the women finally were on their way back to their quarters. That was when Elsie could tell her about the surprise she had. Taking only a minute to put more wood in the stove, Elsie began to show Emma all she had purchased. Emma saw the quality of the items and began to feel bad about not purchasing something too for Rose. But then Elsie pulled out a sparkling silver spoon from the bag. Elsie handed to Emma and said, "Here, this is for you." Emma gazed at the spoon. "Was it expensive?" Elsie pushed it into her hand and told her not to worry about that. Then, Elsie handed her some tissue paper with a piece of gold ribbon and said, "You just need to wrap it up." Emma was grateful for Elsie's thoughtfulness.

Exhausted, she reached to turn the lantern down and whispered, goodnight. As Emma pulled the blanket over herself, she called out to Elsie, but Elsie was simply too tired to talk. Painfully, she answered with an impatient "Yessss?" Emma knew she had to say what was on her mind quickly. "Thank you for everything you do for me, Elsie." Elsie responded, "You're welcome, NOW GO TO SLEEP!"

Chapter 6

Before the sun crept into the sky, Hans was already up and awake. He had heard the wolves again the night before and they sounded closer now. He worried that they were coming dangerously close. Wolves were vicious creatures and would stop at nothing to feed. They had even been known to eat small children. There was a fog that morning rolling into the large field that Porter owned. The sky was still a deep Prussian blue and the mountains, in the far distance, were just an outline against the barely illuminated sky. Hans put his leather riding gear on and clutched his heavy jacket with his thick rugged hands. Fastening it around himself, he walked across the field to the barn. His mind was set on checking the vast posted wire fence that outlined Porter's land. He put the saddle on the horse and gently placed the bit in its mouth. Putting his boot in the stirrup, he hoisted himself up. With a small kick to the horse's belly, he headed off into the darkness.

He had brought his rifle with him just in case and made sure it was fastened in its holster tightly. Hans always carried extra bullets in his jacket and ran his hand over the pocket assuring himself he was ready to get to work. As he rode, his sight focused on inspecting closely every post and every inch of wire. He was halfway out into the field when he began to notice signs of digging under the fence. Hans assumed the wolves were responsible. Hans became keenly aware of his surroundings. He watched for signs. He continued to ride along the outskirts of their land when he saw a tree that had fallen, knocking over one of the large posts, taking some wire with it. Hans had not brought tools with him. Only his trusty rifle. Not getting off the horse, he made a mental note of it. He continued but saw no other breaks in the fence. He knew Porter would be relieved the damage was only minor.

Hans's horse had only gone fifty meters when he began to act strangely. Spooked by something, Hans nervously began to look around. The darkness still covered the fields and he continued to ride cautiously. The last part of his ride took him through the densest thicket of the land. Hans was ready to head back to the barn after one last look. He was riding closer to the fence when a reddish reflection of what looked like two animals' eyes appeared. Through the darkness there was no telling what it was, but the horse's reaction told him all he needed to know. The hair on the back of his neck began to rise. Hans reached down to unfasten his rifle. The horse let out a loud whinny and bolted off running. Hans leaned down close to the horse's mane, as its hooves thundered across the ground. The mane whipped at his face and his hands held the reigns tight. For a split second he couldn't resist looking behind them to see what they were running from. He couldn't exactly count how many but there was an entire pack of wolves not far behind them and the horse was putting distance between them.

It appeared the wolves were giving up, when Hans was thrown forward hard. He was launched up over the horse, landing on the ground with the horse landing partly on top of him, then rolling off to the side. Startled in the moment, Hans now felt the burning shear pain in his hip and thigh. In the distance he could see the wolves had watched them go down and were beginning to surround them. There were at least ten wolves in an organized pack! Having only seconds, Hans looked for his rifle. Stumbling to his feet, and breathing heavily, he saw his rifle just inches from the horse, which was now down and neighing loudly in pain. Hans quickly picked up his rifle, targeting the wolf that was leading the pack. He took aim and fired, hitting him directly. It went down with a yelp and the other wolves slowed their pace. Hans fired off three more shots, striking another three wolves. Hans was a great marksman and rarely missed his target.

Han's pain was becoming extreme as he walked over to the horse. Looking around again, he could see the remaining wolves had given up and disappeared into the woodland. He looked down at his horse and could see its leg was badly broken. Close to where it fell, he could see many small holes dug by Maulwurfs. It was clear the horse had stepped into one of their holes. Saddened by what he knew he had to do next, he began to speak to the horse, "I'm sorry I have to do this, you've been a good horse." He put his hand on the horse's muzzle and closed the animal's eyes. Lowering his rifle once again, he pulled the trigger and began his long walk home. Limping and in a lot of pain, he could finally see the house after what seemed to be a long time. The walk was grueling, and it felt as if he might not make it at times, but he was within sight now.

Porter was just finishing tying the laces on his boots and getting ready to head off to work. Making his usual rounds about the house, he checked in on Rose and the girls first, then raised his binoculars to his eyes. Looking across the field, he could see someone walking toward his home. He focused in a little clearer, to have a second look; he could see it was Hans, and he appeared to be injured. Porter put his binoculars back on the hook and bolted for the barn. Quickly throwing a saddle on Lucky, he headed out to meet Hans. Hans was glad to see Porter coming. The pain in his leg was almost unbearable. "What happened Hans?" "Well Sir, I went to check on the fencing because the wolves have become a problem. I had to shoot the horse because it broke its leg. We were being chased by the wolves, maybe ten of them and there's some downed fence on the far-right side of the field from a fallen tree." Porter didn't care about the tree or the fence. He was more concerned about Hans. Porter only asked if he was okay; he could see his face was twisted from the pain. Hans could only tell him that it hurt a bit. Porter got off the horse and told Hans to get on, he would walk Lucky home and let Hans take a break.

Porter needed to get to work but he had to make sure all was well at home first. Now he would have to stop to see about purchasing another horse for the family too. He knew it was going to be a long day when he headed off to the barn to harness Lucky to the wagon. He had to pass his automobile once he was inside the barn and thought to himself that spring could not get here soon enough! Then he could use the automobile and it would save time for sure. It would be nice to use his treasured auto again, but he had more important things to think about now. He missed the days when he wasn't so busy. He missed the long talks he and Rose had over a nice cup of coffee. He also missed having fun with his two girls. They were growing so fast, and he knew it wouldn't be long before they were all grown and married with children of their own. He thought about the baby that was on the way. He was grateful to have such good help with Hans, Elsie and Emma. Porter sighed heavily and began his journey toward town. He knew he would be at work for another long day to hopefully fill as many of the orders he had now that were piling up. He also had a little surprise for Elsie and Emma. With the large orders he had received over that last week, he planned to buy a washing machine. He thought it would be of good use with all the soiled nappies that would be coming their way.

It was an early Saturday morning and Margaret had finished her breakfast already. She wasn't very hungry, but Emma had managed to get her to eat a piece of toast, tempting her with a bit of raspberry jam on it. Emma knew that was her favorite. Rose had just picked it up while in town, especially for her. Margaret sat for a minute staring at the floor. With her elbows on the table and her hands pushing her cheeks up, Emma asked, "Is something wrong, Liebchen?" Margaret pouted and replied, "I'm bored!" Emma laughed. She asked, "Would you like to help me with the laundry?" "NOOOO!" Margaret howled. She was sucking her teeth with an evil eye aimed directly at Emma. She reached for her jacket that she had left on the back of the chair. She pushed her arms into the sleeves with a big huff for each arm. Then she stood up and marched to the back door. Opening the door, showing great irritation, she closed the door loudly. Emma couldn't help but laugh at her display of attitude and remembered how hard it was to be that age.

Looking for something to do, Margaret walked toward the barn. Margaret tugged on the heavy barn doors, determined. Finally, getting them open, she expected to see at least one of the horses. But the only thing she saw was her father's automobile. Wondering where the horses were, she searched the barn. Maybe Hans had brought them out for a brush, or maybe a walk. She looked over the big bales of hay that were behind the barn, but still did not see the horses. She wanted to find Hans now and started up the hill to his house. But as soon as she turned, she saw some movement from the corner of her eye. Curious as usual, Margaret needed to find out what the cause of the motion was. She began to push the hay around and a small animal looking like a squirrel came out. Margaret picked it up. "Awwwe, aren't you a cutie!" She stroked the little creature. Smiling at it, she asked, "Now where has your mother gone?" Before she finished her question, another one appeared. To her delight, she picked them both up cradling them in her arms. She intended on bringing them inside to show her mother, but just then another two popped out. "Oh my!" she exclaimed. Margaret bent over to try to gather all four and met eye to eye with the mother! Looking into the small dark beady eyes, both her and the animal were frightened by each other. Then she noticed the mother was quite dark. Almost black really. And then she saw that white stripe down the small animals' back! Margaret screamed. She now knew what she was looking at.

She turned to run, dropping the little ones, but it was too late. The skunk had already raised its tail and sprayed her. The odor was so strong; she began to spew vomit but kept running so as not to be sprayed again. Margaret was screaming like a siren, heading straight for the house. Emma heard her. She opened the door to see what was wrong but was greeted by the strong odor from the skunk. Stopping Margaret from coming in, she ordered her to take off all her clothing and threw a towel to her to wrap herself in. Leaving her clothes in a pile near the door as she had been told, Margaret was whisked into the bathroom by Emma who reached for the washing soap and tomato juice on the way. She had become a victim once again!

Margaret was crying and Rose crossed the front room to see why. She immediately could smell the skunk which made her nauseous too. She had to go back into her room, closing the door. She was glad Emma was taking care of Margaret because she simply could not. Margaret sat crying in the tub and Emma poured the tomato juice over her head. Emma tried to comfort her, but Margaret was inconsolable. Then, through her tears, she told Emma she had left the barn door open. Emma told her not to worry, that she would take care of it as she dried her off with the towels. She still smelled like a skunk but not as bad. Elsie brought in some fresh night clothes and Emma helped her to put them on. Margaret went to her room with tears still in her eyes. The skunk oil still smelled very strong.

Emma now had the ugly task of bringing the clothes down to the pond to rinse them. After throwing them in at the water's edge, she hiked over to Hans's house. Hans answered his door, still clearly in pain. His nose scrunched with one whiff of her. "Whew Emma, isn't it time for a bath?" He had a grin which angered Emma. "Ha, you're funny Hans! Margaret left the barn door open and got sprayed by a skunk. Can you please go close the barn up?" she asked. Shaking his head, he returned, "Sure." Emma finished rinsing the clothes and put them in a basket by the back door to air out. Then, she sought out Elsie to tell her she was going to have a bath herself, when she heard Rose call out to her, "Emma?" Frozen, standing still but wanting to leave, she waited. Rose thanked her and apologized for not being able to be of more help. Emma replied, "It's ok and you are welcome." She just couldn't wait to get into a hot soapy bath. On her way home, she couldn't help but think to herself what a horrible day it had been.

Hans had heard Emma close the door on the other side of the house. He felt bad for her. Having to deal with the oil of a skunk was never a fun job. Hans's leg was all black and bruised deeply. He was glad the horse's weight had not broken his leg. He also felt sad about having to shoot the horse. He really liked that horse. Hans took a swig of whiskey from the bottle he had on the table next to his bed. He shook his head as the whiskey began to burn his nostrils and sat down. Looking around, he began to feel useless. Hans was one to always be busy. There was always something to be done, but Porter had insisted he take a few days to rest. His mind was busy thinking of all the things that he needed to do, but especially thinking about that fence he needed to repair. Every day that wire was down, the wolves would feel welcomed to roam the area freely. Porter had given Hans an old pair of binoculars. Reaching for his saddle bag, Hans let out a low groan. He pulled it closer; his leg and hip pained him some more. Placing his forehead in the palm of his hand, he closed his eyes. He ran his fingers across the top of his head through his thick hair. Exhaling hard, as if he was trying to breathe out the pain, he clutched the bottle of whiskey for one more sip. Raising his saddle bag, he dropped it hard onto the bed with a thump. He pushed the flap over and started to dig for his binoculars. Limping to the door with them in his hands, he figured he'd sit outside for a while. Placing his jacket over his shoulders, he opened the door.

The cold air felt good to him, and he breathed it deeply into his lungs. He liked the way it cleared his head. On the porch were two wooden chairs. Sitting down in the one closest to the door he let out another grunt; he looked up to the sky and could see large groups of thrush birds beginning to migrate. With that he knew spring would be on its way shortly. He raised his binoculars to have a closer look. He now could see some redwings flying too. He rarely had time to watch the birds but loved doing so. He often thought of Porter's two girls as little birds because he knew one day they would fly off leaving the nest of their parents to have families of their own. He had hoped he would be a part of that in the future. Deciding he'd had enough, he returned to his bed for a bit of an afternoon nap. Hans laid on his bed, staring at the wooden beams above him and wondered where his life would take him. He thought about the mountains and how beautiful they were. He thought about his love of horses and how he had hoped to have cattle of his own someday. There was a lot of money to be made with a dairy cattle herd and he was quite comfortable in a saddle. He thought about Elinore, Margaret and Rose. They were the only family he had. His mother and father had died many years ago from influenza. Hans had no brothers or sisters. He had one uncle, his father's older brother, but he had never met him, and he had no idea how to locate him. Hans had dated a few women, but never found any that he wanted to spend more than an evening with.

Hans was OK with being on his own, but he did consider Porter to be somewhat more than just his boss. He thought fondly of the family he had adopted. Just then he heard a tapping on his door. He struggled to push his legs off the bed and grunted as he stood up. Slowly making his way to the door, he thought, "Who on earth could it be now?" He opened the door to see Porter standing there. "Porter?" Hans asked. "Is everything okay?" It was an odd time for Porter to be home. Hans stood there waiting for Porter to respond. The two men stood in the doorway for a minute. Hans's eyebrows began to lift. "Porter, come in please, you're letting all my warmth out the door." Startled, Porter seemed deep in thought, then he said "Yes, yes, sorry Hans." Porter had brought Hans a wooden cane he had owned for some time. He held it out to him. Hans let out a laugh. "What is that for Porter?"

"It's for you, I thought you could use it." Hans's lips widened and he couldn't help but laugh again. "Porter, I'm not that old that I need a cane!" The two laughed like old friends do. "Yes, yes Hans, I was only trying to help." Porter held out his other hand which firmly gripped a full bottle of unopened bourbon. He said, "Well maybe this will help a bit more." Hans's eyes smiled with delight. "Now you're talking, Porter!" Porter and Hanns sat down at his little round table by the stove. Hans reached over to put another piece of wood on the fire. Opening the stove door, and placing the wood on top, he asked Porter why he was home so early. Porter began to tell him he was beginning to worry about being at work so much, with Rose being so close to having the baby. Porter also worried about his girls and what effect it would have on them, with him being gone so much. Hans assured him he would be there to stand in his place, for whatever was needed. But Porter still had a troubled look on his face. Hans opened the bourbon bottle and handed it to Porter. "There isn't much this won't fix." Watching Porter take a few glugs from the bottle, he told him, "Give it a minute, you'll feel better." "Um, that's good stuff," Porter breathed out hard through his nose. "Just like drinking turpentine!" Laughing loudly, Hans stuck his finger out toward Porter and told him it would give him more hair on his chest too. Hans paused and asked Porter if he'd like to play a game of cards. "No," Porter said, "I just came by to see how your leg was doing."

"It hurts still," Hans bent forward slightly. Hans waited a minute, thinking maybe this was a good time to approach Porter about purchasing a few Holstein Friesian cattle. He knew they produced a good quantity of milk. "Porter," Hans said. "If you have a minute more, I'd like to talk to you about something." "What's on your mind Hans?" Porter's curiosity was apparent by the expression on his face. "Well Porter, I was thinking." Hans was rubbing his chin between her thumb and fore finger. As he twisted his thick beard around his fingers, Hans began to tell Porter about his thoughts on getting some Holstein Cattle. He even added, with some dairy cattle he wouldn't need to be taking anyone's milk again. "Just think about it for me Porter, okay?" Both men laughed together again, and Porter agreed it was something to think about.

Hans walked Porter to the door, placing his hand on his back. He told him, "Don't wait so long to come back again," and that he'd have some more whiskey waiting for him when he did. They stepped towards the door, opening it. Slowly, Porter asked Hans if he knew how much Holstein Friesian was going for these days, as he considered the idea. "I'm not sure, Sir," Han's replied. Porter seemed stuck in the doorway. A few seconds passed and Porter turned around, still inside, he closed the door again. "Hans, do you know Elinore has a serious interest in that young man Carl that she attends school with?" Hans had not noticed. He said, "No," shaking his head. His forehead wrinkled as he waited for more information. Hans asked, "Porter, does that worry you?" Porter began, "Well it's just that the only thing I know about him, is that he works at Schmidt's place as a blacksmith hand. I guess I am a little worried." His face looked strained, as he stood there for a moment. He opened the door, tipped his hat to Hans and left. Hans knew why he was worried. He was watching his first born become a young lady. As Hans lay back down on his bed, he thought to himself maybe he ought to keep a watchful eye out for this young man.

Chapter 7

The smell of coffee brewing opened Porter's eyes. He rubbed them and slowly rose to his feet. He followed the alluring smell to the kitchen. Elsie and Emma had flour all over their faces and on their aprons when he entered the room. "What have you two been up to?" Porter asked. The women were a dreadful sight. Elsie held out two plates heaped with biscuits filled with raspberry and apricot preserves. Porter took one in both hands. Licking his lips, he inhaled them deeply. Porter loved biscuits and these would be a real treat. Pausing momentarily, he said, "These biscuits smell heavenly!" Porter took one bite of the first one and then one bite of the second. It only took another second before Porter had both biscuits rolling across his tongue. His cheeks puffed out with all that he had stuffed into his mouth. He tried to speak; something sounding like words came from him but neither Elsie nor Emma could understand exactly what he was trying to say. The cookie bits made it hard for him to speak but his grin spoke a million words. Elsie and Emma felt good about having pleased Porter. After all, Porter had always treated them well. They had a good laugh about the way Porter looked like a big kid devouring his luscious treats.

Rose and the children soon came to see what the excitement was all about. Margaret was the first to enter the kitchen. The vision of the heaping mound of biscuits excited her. "Wow!" Margaret shouted, taking a biscuit in a hurry. "These are delicious!" The girls were elated over the abundance of tasty treats. Margaret asked for some milk, while Rose and Elinore made themselves a nice cup of tea. They all sat down at the table and enjoyed the Jamy goodies the women had made.

Porter hated to leave but he knew there was a lot of work for Greta to handle by herself at the factory today. He needed to be on his way to work. But before he left, he took his usual round about the house and kissed Rose and the girls goodbye.

Hans was just getting himself together as the sky began to change from its darkest hours to splashes of yellow. It was still early and only an outline of himself was visible inside his room. Hans felt he was strong enough to tackle the fence that had been on his mind. He went to the barn to gather the tools he needed. Taking Lucky out to the field with the wagon, things went much easier this time. Hans loaded much of the wood from the fallen tree into the wagon and with the necessary tools, fixing the fence went smoothly. Hans's leg was still giving him grief, but he pushed himself through the work until the sun started to go down. When he was finished, he took a minute to look at the now fully repaired fence and felt happy about what he had accomplished. The wagon was heavy and loaded down with wood. Lucky was a strong beast and seemed to have no problem pulling it. They traveled back to the house to stack the wood off; it would help heat the house during the cold winter nights.

Hans was looking forward to a hot meal and finally reaching his bed for a good night's rest. Elinore and Margaret were busy thinking forward to what their next day had in store. They anxiously picked out what they wanted to wear with matching ribbons for their hair, and of course, wondering what kind of cookies they would be having after church. Margaret had her bet on the cookies with the chocolate dots in the middle while Elinore was convinced it would be the Linzer cookies. Both girls laid their clothes over the rocker chair in the corner and placed their leather shoes next to it. Sunday mornings were always a rush, so Elinore and Margaret always picked their clothes out the night before. Margaret was excited because she knew Gertrude would be there. With all the snow that had fallen over the winter, they hadn't been to church for some time. Elinore had her own reason for her jitters. She knew Carl would likely be there.

They had been on a break from school over the winter months and she hadn't seen Carl much since the day in the barn either. Just the thought of that day made her warm inside. She hoped he would be there and maybe they'd have some time to themselves to speak privately. She gazed out the window to watch the twilight take the day away. Her daydream carried her off to another place for a moment, when she heard Margaret calling her name. "Elinore? Are you going to wear your hat too?" With her trance broken, she responded with a stutter, "N-No." Elinore was still not focused but gradually looked at Margaret, noticing the doll that her father had given her long ago on her pillow. Gently, she picked it up. Stroking its hair, she asked Margaret, "Do you still like this doll?" Margaret clamored, "Oh yes Elinore! She's the most beautiful doll I've ever seen!" Elinore took Margaret's hand and placed the doll in it. "I want you to have her now." "Really?" asked Margaret. "But I thought you loved her." Elinore explained that she thought she was now too old for dolls, and she couldn't think of anyone else who would love her doll more. Gladly, Margaret took the doll, placing it on her pillow, then she almost knocked Elinore over with a forceful hug that she had taken a running start for. Elinore smiled because she knew she had just made Margaret's day.

Porter and Rose were still in the kitchen. Now that the girls were in their rooms for the night, Porter poured Rose a cup of tea and handed it to her. After pouring himself a cup, he sat down at the table with her. The fire was still glowing from their evening meal and Rose complained that it was quite warm in the room.

Porter looked at her lovingly and told her that she'd never looked better to him. Being almost eight and a half months pregnant she still had a glow about herself. She looked at Porter with a bewildered expression. "You should have your glasses checked! Are you serious? Have you looked at my elephant ankles?" Porter could only smile as he pulled her chair closer to him. He reached for her with both hands, holding each side of her face. With a long-fixed look, he kissed his wife ever so gently on her lips. "Are you ready for bed Rose?" She nodded as he took her hand to help her up. Putting his arm around her, they walked to their bedroom. With nothing but the glow of the fire illuminating the hallway, the Downing family fell fast asleep.

Rose was the first to rise when morning came. With her protruding middle she hadn't been sleeping well anyway. They needed to hurry with a quick bite to eat. Rose did not like being late for church. They hurried in and seated themselves in the pews, waiting for the sermon to start. The hard benches bothered Rose's back and she became restless. Trying hard not to be noticed, she squirmed back and forth. Margaret couldn't wait for refreshment time and a chance to socialize while Elinore couldn't keep her eyes off Carl. Carl had come to church with his mother and father. His father looked well to her, and she was glad he hadn't suffered any setbacks from his illness.

Soon the sermon was over, and socializing began. Rose was surrounded by all the ladies there, asking many, many, questions. Porter was off with his gentlemen friends discussing business and sipping coffee. Margaret and Gertrude were busy stuffing their faces with as many biscuits as their hands could hold. No one, including Porter, noticed Elinore and Carl were nowhere in sight. Carl had slipped out of the back of the church. Elinore went unnoticed, leaving from the front and walking around the side of the building. Both thought they were so clever about their secret meeting. Carl was waiting for her by the shed where the church kept their tools and supplies. Running as quickly as her feet could carry her, she leapt into his arms. They spun around in the excitement of seeing each other again. They kissed, laughed, and kissed some more. Elinore cried out, "I've missed you so!" Carl brushed her long hair back with his hand, pulling her ribbon out with his fingers. "I've missed you too." Out of his pocket, Carl handed her some expensive chocolates. He then told her that Mr. Schmidt was considering making him a partner. Elinore exclaimed, "Oh, that's wonderful!" Her mind quickly filled with thoughts of the two of them being already married, with her in the kitchen making the evening meal, waiting for him to return home from work. Snapping her attention back to her handsome man standing in front of her, she took a piece of chocolate and placed it just halfway in her mouth. Extending her neck, she invited him to bite the other side of the chocolate from her lips. He smiled and gladly helped himself. They both knew they didn't have much time before people would notice they were missing.

Keeping that in mind, Carl had something he wanted to ask Elinore. He began, "Elinore?" She tilted her head slightly and began to listen intently. "I brought you something else too but..." She interrupted. "What, tell me!" Out of his trousers' pocket he pulled a small, polished steel ring. Holding it tightly in his hand, he said, "Elinore, I want us to be more serious about our relationship." Elinore looked confused. "Carl, I have never even had an interest in anyone but you." Carl immediately took the thin band and placed it on her right-hand ring finger. "I just needed to say that before I gave you this," he said. He lingered, holding her hand before releasing it. She thought for a moment, "You know this means you'll have to come meet my parents, right?" Carl barely got the word yes out and Margaret came around the shed. "Elinore, mother is looking for you!" Margaret blurted out. She quickly kissed Carl goodbye and promised to see him again soon. Both sisters headed into the back of the church and came out of the front.

Rose wasn't interested in anything but going home. Her back hurt and her feet were so swollen that her shoes were feeling uncomfortably tight. The baby had not been kicking much but the weight pressed heavily on her bladder. With every bump on their way home, she tossed Porter an awful look. She knew it wasn't his fault, but she had to blame someone. As soon as they returned, she went straight to her bedroom.

Elinore took the ring off her finger and placed it in the small wooden box under her bed where she kept all her treasures. She knew it would anger her father if she didn't discuss it with him first, which she now planned to do as soon as the right time presented itself. They all sat down for an early Sunday dinner that evening with Elsie and Emma included. Rose was noticeably missing. Elsie asked Porter how Rose did while they were out. Porter took a minute to answer. He was busy pushing the last bit of his delicious meal onto his fork with his thumb. Pressing it against his lips and licking the last morsel off his thumb, he said, "I think she's okay. Maybe a bit tired."

Elsie decided to bring Rose a small plate of food and a cup of tea. She knocked on the door and poked her head in slowly. Rose was awake and saw her. "Come in Elsie," she said. Seeing the food in her hand, Rose told her she wasn't hungry, but welcomed the tea. Elsie asked Rose to lay back in her bed. She wanted to see how far down the baby was now. Placing her hands on her lower abdomen, Elsie pressed down on her. "Does that hurt at all?" Rose replied, "No, but if you keep doing that you are going to make me wee in my bed." Elsie laughed. She could feel the baby was low now. She said to Rose, "Maybe two more weeks at the most and the baby will be here." Elsie had everything ready for when the baby came, or so she thought. Now it was just the waiting that would be the hardest part.

The following morning went its usual way. Porter made his rounds, kissed his girls, and left for work. Margaret and Elinore busied themselves and Elsie and Emma did their housework. That afternoon Elsie went to the barn to give the chickens some of the bread that had gone stale. While she was outside, she saw Hans by the pond, filling a few buckets of water. She waved to him, and he motioned her to come over. Begrudgingly, she made her way to the pond. She knew he would ask her to help him carry the buckets of water and they were very heavy, but she also knew he would help her if she needed him to. Sure enough, the two carried three full buckets towards the barn. "Hans, why do you need this much water inside the barn?" "Not inside Else, over here," he said. Turning the corner of the building she saw a beautiful white horse. "Where did he come from?" With her eyes wide and her mouth dropped open, she waited for him to answer. "Porter brought him home Friday, I guess he hasn't mentioned it to anyone yet." He told Elsie that he thought Porter had been worried about Rose. As she listened to Hans, she noticed how high this beautiful creature stood in front of her. She had a leftover carrot in her apron from dinner, so she offered it to the new horse. Hans patted the horse and asked, "Making friends already, huh?"

Hans was going to get the horse cleaned up. He began to brush some soap into the brush he held and started to clean the horse's hair. Brushing and rinsing, he began to get as wet as the horse. Elsie headed back to the house and told Hans she would see him later with his supper, before he asked her for any more help. Elsie never gave horses much thought, but this one was a real beauty. Hans was soon finished with his work for the day and Elsie still had not come by. He picked up the broom that leaned against the building at the corner of the porch. The wind had blown a lot of dirt around so he decided while he waited, that he would give it a good sweep. The sun was getting lower in the sky, and he wondered what was keeping Elsie. His stomach was growling and for that matter, he also wondered what was keeping Porter. Lucky was still not in his stall, so he knew Porter was not home from work yet. Hans sat down on the steps, resting his chin on his closed fist. He noticed the gorgeous sunset taking place above him. Suddenly, he heard the back door close from the main house. Emma was carrying a bowl and heading in his direction. Hans's mouth began to water. He was indeed hungry. Emma placed the bowl in his hand with the fork laid on top. "Thank you!" Hans said, wasting no time in devouring the luscious meal he had been presented with. Emma proceeded to tell Hans that Porter had not returned home yet and because it was getting late, they decided to serve up the evening meal and get everything cleaned up. Hans just nodded, barely taking time to breathe between bites. Emma went back to the house shaking her head. She only muttered a single word, "Men!"

A few more hours passed as everyone was still waiting for Porter to arrive home. Elsie would not leave until he was home. Emma would not leave until Elsie did. She busied herself getting the coffee ready for making in the morning. Rose called out to Elsie. Elsie popped her head in the doorway to see what Rose needed. "I think I had an accident, Elsie," Rose whispered. "Something's not right." Alarms went off inside Elsie's head. "Come now, let me see." Elsie was a little nervous and pulled the blankets from her. "Rose, that's not wee, your water has broken." Her next question was if Rose was feeling any pain. Rose said she felt fine. Elsie told Emma to go get Hans. Elsie quickly went to Elinore's room and explained to her what was happening and that she may need her help. Elinore left her bedroom door open, and now had a watchful eye out for her father's return to break the news to him. Elsie heard the creak of the back door and was glad to be greeted by Hans in the kitchen. She told him, "I think we have some time, but I just wanted to let you know Rose's water broke and I may need your help," she explained. Hans was a little frightened by her news. After all, he had never played a part in a human baby being born before. Only cows and horses. But he remained within earshot none the less.

He was a "fix it" type of guy, so already Hans's mind was preparing on what to do should Porter not come home in time. Elsie decided it was time to get Rose cleaned up. She helped Rose to the bathroom and put fresh linens on the bed. She knew Rose needed to put loose clothing on for what was about to happen next. It had only been about an hour since her water broke and Rose thought she was beginning to feel a few waves of pressure. She felt a sudden urge to use the toilet again. That happened three more times over the next hour and the waves became more intense. Rose was worried because Porter still was not home yet. Elsie insisted Rose stay in the bed, but Rose didn't want to. She felt the need to walk. She paced back and forth, and it seemed harder for her to breathe. Rose was starting to panic. So was Elsie, but she would never let anyone see it.

Elsie knew she was on her own with this. There were no hospitals nearby. The nearest ones were in Berlin and Munich. In the north, most German women used midwives. Elsie had some experience but was never formally trained. Rose let out a hellish howl that came from the depths of her soul. That alone sent Elsie running toward the bedroom again. Even Elinore and Margaret were worried now. Both wanted to know if their mother was going to be okay and waited for Elsie nervously. Emma tried to assure the girls that everything would be okay, but she honestly didn't know if it was the truth. Elsie opened the bathroom door just enough to speak softly to Rose. She wanted to know if she was alright. Rose was drenched in sweat and was holding onto the edge of the sink white knuckled. "NO!" Rose shouted. Elsie called out to Emma loudly, "Go get Hans NOW!" In a flash, Emma and Hans stood waiting for Elsie to tell them what to do next.

Wide-eyed, neither had a clue what they should be doing. Elsie began to sort things out in her mind. She needed blankets and pillows. She told Emma to boil some water and let it cool. She told Hans to be ready to lift Rose's legs. Just then, Hans had a quick thought. In the pub that he frequented in town he knew there were Nun's that lived on the floor above. He had seen them once or twice coming and going. Hans had never really given it much thought before, but he was sure they could be of some help with the delivery of the baby. Not wanting to insult Elsie, he began to tell her about the Nun's. Elsie's eyes opened wider as she listened to Hans closely. "Yes, yes, that's a wonderful idea, Hans! Go get the covered wagon!" Elsie shouted to Elinore and Emma to run and gather as many blankets as they could carry. Margaret just stood at the end of the small hallway alone. She had tears streaming down her face. Confused and silently watching everyone running around, she feared for her mother as she listened to her moan from the bathroom. Elsie had no time to explain, but she patted her on the shoulder and told her not to worry, that it would all be alright, and that she was about to have a little brother or sister. Only half believing Elsie, that did little to help Margaret feel better as she watched Elsie, Emma and Hans struggle with her mother from the bathroom. She could see her mother was in a lot of pain.

Rose could barely walk now. Her face strained with the increasing intensity of pain and holding her lower abdomen tightly. As each wave came, Rose's voice grew more guttural. Hans couldn't take it any longer. He scooped Rose up and carried her out the back of the house to the wagon. Elsie and Emma jumped onto the footboards as Elinore and Margaret watched their mother being whisked away. Hans drove the wagon like he never had before. Running through the darkness of the night, the full moon was the only light he had to go by. The newest horse was light and sure footed, but with every bump, Rose's screams grew louder. Hans felt badly for her, and his fears were getting the best of him now, he hated feeling so helpless.

Back at the house Elinore and Margaret wondered where their father was and what would happen to their mother. Elinore took the water off the fire that Emma had placed there hours ago. She sat at the kitchen table, opposite Margaret, whose cheeks were still stained from her tears. They both stared into each other's faces. Neither knew what to say, so they said nothing for some time.

Hans finally reached the pub and jumped down before the horse came to a stop. He rushed in to speak with the innkeeper, Walter. Quickly, he explained the situation and Walter ushered them inside. Hans flew up the stairs carrying Rose. Emma and Elsie followed close behind. The patrons in the pub hardly noticed them breeze by. Hans reached the top of the stairwell, breathing hard and his chest heaving from the adrenaline that coursed through his veins. A crowd of Nun's swarmed Hans and took Rose quickly from him. Rose was panting and almost hyperventilating. She felt nauseous and asked a nun for a bucket. The Nun's knew exactly what to do. Hans, Elsie and Emma sat down on the bench at the top of the stairs. The smoke from the cigarettes inside the pub was visible from where they sat, and the smell made Emma feel sick. The Nun's carried Rose to a room in the back of the house. They began to strip down Rose as they laid her down on a bed. Propping her legs up with pillows, they tried to make her comfortable. An older Nun checked Rose to see if she had dilated enough to begin pushing, but as she placed her fingers inside her, she noticed something terribly wrong. The baby's head was not in the right position. It felt to her like the baby's face was up. She knew that would make the delivery for Rose more painful and could possibly make her hemorrhage.

Sister Frances went to speak with Hans. She asked Hans if he was the father. "Oh no, Sister." Hans began to explain that Rose was his friend's wife. Then she asked Hans if he thought he could get the father because she feared Rose would be having a long hard labor with this birth and would need some emotional support. With that news, Hans told Elsie and Emma to stay with Rose while he would run back to the house to see if Porter had arrived home yet. His heart was racing as he hurried down the stairs to the wagon that was still sitting in front of the pub. Grabbing the reigns tight, with a crack of his whip he raced off into the chilly darkness again.

In the room above the pub, Rose's pain was getting worse. She faded in and out as she tried to remember times from long ago. But with each wave of pain, only two minutes apart, she was finding it impossible to distract herself. Now, all she could think about was Porter. The baby was making its way slowly down the birth canal. The oldest Nun, Frances told Rose it was time to push. As two other Nun's held her trembling legs, she began to push. Inside herself, she could feel her flower being torn apart. This was more painful than Margaret or Elinore had ever been. Throwing her head back, the veins in her neck and forehead were clearly visible; a blood curdling howl could be heard by Elsie and Emma outside the closed door. Rose, with her head back, noticed how foggy the room had become as the white and green drapes looked so far away. At that moment Rose fell unconscious. Frances feared they were losing her. She reached inside Rose to try to turn the baby. She could also see the umbilical cord was wrapped around the child's neck. With the cord still pulsing, she gently slid it over the baby's head.

With it now free, she slowly tried to redirect the baby's position. Suddenly the baby's head began to show. Frances asked one of the Nun's to wipe Rose's forehead with a cold wet towel. As soon as the cold water hit Rose's face, her eyes opened. The sweat was dripping off her profusely. She cried, wanting to know the baby's condition. Another Nun wiped her head again, and another offered her a sip of cool water. Rose smiled as she laid back on the bed again. Frances told Rose to push again. Preparing for the coming pain, she clenched her teeth and pushed hard. Frances now could see the baby's shoulders because the baby's neck was stretched way too far. Knowing this could cause the baby to be born with paralysis, she urgently told Rose to stop pushing. Confused, Rose asked, "Why, what's wrong?" Frightened, tears began to well up in her eyes. "Please tell me the baby is okay."

Hans arrived back at the house to find Elinore and Margaret anxiously waiting. He started to tell them that their mother was in good hands when he heard Porter pulling his wagon into the barn. Hans quickly went outside to talk with Porter. "Porter, are you okay?" he asked. "Yes," Porter growled. "I had a huge problem at the shop because I gave my horse to a worker to fetch some supplies and he got lost; let's just say it has been an irritating day! But I'm finally home!" Hans barely let him finish and blurted out, "Rose is having the baby!" "What?" Porter's eyes were bulging, "Where is she?" he demanded. Hans told him he would take him to her. Porter dropped his things down on the barn floor and ran to the wagon that Hans had waiting for them. The two men raced off back to the pub. Hans explained what had happened and how Rose wound up there on the way. In the back of Porter's mind, he began to feel angry with the worker for his delay in getting home. He should've been there to help Rose. He even considered firing him when he saw him next. In the close distance, they could see the pub's lights glowing like a beacon. Walter was waiting outside to bring them in and up the stairs. Porter took his hat off and sat down next to Emma. Taking a deep breath, he placed his hand over his eyebrows and rubbed his forehead. He asked her, "Have you heard anything? How is Rose? Is the baby here yet?" "No," Emma answered. Elsie looked at Porter and just shook her head, closing her eyes. Hans stood in the corner by himself. Placing his boot on the wall behind him, and standing on one foot, he could see Porter was a nervous wreck. He started to walk in Porter's direction when Rose's screams filled the air. It was all Porter could do to stop himself from bursting through the door. Elsie stood up, placing her delicate hand on Porter's shoulder.

"Have patience Porter, I'm sure the Nun's will be out to tell us something shortly." At that same moment the doorknob began to turn. Porter rushed to the door; barely able to breathe. "Are you the father?" the tall older woman asked. Frances was looking at a very anxious Porter. "Yes," he said. "How is she?" Frances placed her hand on Porter's and said, "I think she'll be fine, but there were problems with the baby being in the wrong position. She's had quite a painful process and I'm worried as she's had some blood loss. We're doing our best. Please let me return to her and I will come back in a little while to talk with you again." Frances turned to go back inside, but Porter stopped her. With his hand on her arm this time, she turned back around. She understood how much Porter wanted to see his wife. She tried to comfort him and told him to stay calm, but Porter pushed on. He asked, "When will I be able to see her?" Frances patted the back of his hand and said, "Not right now, but don't leave. She'll need you after the baby comes." Frances's faithful expression transferred her calmness to Porter.

He began to remember the many different occasions that made him fall in love with Rose. He had loved her since he first laid eyes on her. He had Agnes to thank for that. Another few hours had gone by and most of the patrons had left the pub already. It was getting very late as the four waited patiently. Now there was a different sound coming from the other room. It sounded like a bunch of women having a party. Then Porter's ears heard the sound of a baby's cry. Smiling from ear to ear, Hans said, "Congratulations Papa!" Porter was speechless and began dabbing his eyes with his handkerchief. Elsie and Emma were crying and hugging each other when Sister Frances brought out the beautiful bundle of joy. She placed the baby in Porter's arms and said, "Congratulations, it's a girl." Then she told Porter he could see Rose now. He wasted no time and entered the room carrying the baby. Rose could see he was ecstatically charmed by the new life she and he had created. He sat on the bed beside her, but she could barely speak. He kissed her forehead and told her how beautiful she was. Porter was overjoyed. Rose was exhausted but wanted to see the baby. Porter laid the baby on her chest. She gazed into her newborn's eyes feeling so much love in her heart for her new spark of life. Rose then looked at Porter and quietly asked, "What should we name her?" Porter just shrugged his shoulders. His bottom lip pressed hard against his top lip, pushing it out to almost a frown. He really hadn't even given it a thought. With all the work he had been doing, getting all his orders filled at work, having to purchase a new horse, finding out about Elinore and her interest in Carl and worrying about Rose, he hadn't had time for much else. He turned her question around and said, "Oh lovey, I think you would pick a much more appropriate name than I ever could." Rose admitted, "Well, I did have one name in mind. "Delilah." Porter thought that was a wonderful name. He could only say, "enchanting!" But then Rose continued. "Porter, I would like her middle name to be Frances to honor Sister Frances. After all, she brought her into this world. "Don't you agree Porter?" Rose waited for Porter to respond. He looked happily at her for a moment and said, "I think that's perfect." Rose felt as if her body had melted into the bed she laid upon. Having no energy left and being exhausted, all she wanted to do was sleep.

Just then, Sister Frances entered the room. She had a kind way of taking charge. She told Porter to kiss his wife and baby goodnight, and to come back tomorrow to collect them, but for tonight Rose needed rest. Sister Frances began to gather Rose's family and move them toward the exit. She kept one hand on the door and with the other pushed them toward the stairwell. She smiled the entire time. Before he had realized what had just happened, Porter found himself looking at the closed door again. Using his knuckle, he gently tapped against the door, but no one answered. He tried to gently turn the doorknob, but it was locked! "Well, I'll be damned," he said as he looked at Hans, sucking his front tooth. Hans threw his arm around Porter, and they all walked outside to the wagon. Hans shouted thank you to Walter as they left. He knew Walter was busy closing the pub, washing out all those beer steins. He shouted out again, "We will see you tomorrow," not wanting to keep him from his work.

When they arrived home, Elinore and Margaret were still up and waiting. Elsie, Emma and Hans were glad to be home and walked up the hill to their house. Porter went inside and didn't have to look far for his girls. He knew they were worried. The girls hadn't seen their father this happy in quite a while. Porter sat down to give them the news. "Well girls, you now have a baby sister!" Margaret was happy. Now she would no longer be the youngest. Elinore really wanted to know how her mother was doing. She asked, "But father, how is mama?" "Ya Elinore, she is good," replied Porter. Relieved, Elinore felt a huge weight come off her mind. "Did you and mother name the baby?" she asked. Porter told her that her mother had thought of a wonderful name. "Delilah Frances, what do you think?" "Oh yes father, it is a beautiful name!" she exclaimed. Then she asked, "When will mother be home?" Porter was so tired but didn't want to be unfair to Elinore since she had waited so long to hear any news, so he simply said, "Tomorrow." Elinore then asked her father if he was hungry, but Porter just simply wanted to go to bed. Elinore told her father that she thought he had had enough excitement for one night and it would be good for him to get some rest. He began to laugh. His little girl was really growing up fast. He crawled into his bed, pulling the covers up to his chin. He felt so strange. He hadn't slept alone in that bed since Margaret was born. He clutched Rose's pillow and could smell the scent of her hair. Holding the pillow tight against his barrel chest, he hoped slumber would come quickly.

Rose was home the following day. She was still very tired, very pale and quite sore. Elsie stayed close to Rose doing as much as she could to make her comfortable. Rose was thankful that Elsie had come along when she had, she was a big help through her pregnancy. She had slept the entire night, while with the nuns but was still exhausted. Rose hadn't breastfed in quite some time and was having difficulty helping the baby to latch on. Elsie knew it would come naturally, in time. As Elsie held the baby, she was enamored with her beauty. So small, she ran her hand softly over the top of the baby's head. She loved the feel of the small spot on an infant's head that would not be fully solid for some time. She also loved the shape of baby lips. In fact, she really loved babies in general. Their tenderness and innocence. Elsie wrapped the baby tightly in one of the blankets she had bought from Marie. As Porter and Rose sat at the table having a little oatmeal, Elsie and Emma presented them both with their gifts. Rose was splendidly surprised. She looked forward to using all the items Elsie and Emma had gifted her with; they were all so beautiful. Elsie handed the baby to Rose and took all the gifts to her room putting them neatly away.

Staring at the baby, Rose noticed Porter's features in her face. She even had his fingernails. Her eyebrows were the same as her own, and so was the shape of her nose. Then Rose realized the blanket Delilah was wrapped in was new too. She assumed Elsie was responsible for that. Now, feeling completely exhausted again and ready to crawl into her own bed, Rose called out to Elsie to come take the baby. All she wanted to do at that moment was sleep.

In the weeks that passed, Rose noticed her brain seemed a bit foggy. She also felt sad with tears not far behind her eyes. She just couldn't understand why she felt this way. After all, her family had just been blessed with a beautiful, healthy baby. All was wonderful in the Downing family, yet she still felt like crying. She was frustrated at not being able to concentrate. Rose had not been to the market in a few days. She simply couldn't drag herself there. Elinore had become quite a mature young lady, so, Rose made a list and asked Elinore if she could take Lucky with a few saddle bags and go to the seaport for some fish and other bits. Elinore was excited at the chance to take Lucky out. The past winter had been awful. The weather was becoming beautiful this May. Crocuses and Edelweiss were visible nearly everywhere one could see. It was still very cold at night, but the days brought warm sunshine.

Elinore headed off to the barn carrying Rose's list and some Goldmark. As she opened the door to the barn, Hans was already there feeding the horses. "I'll be taking Lucky today," Elinore told Hans. "Oh? Where to?" Hans asked. He was unsure about her request. He knew she was a diligent horse rider, and almost considered an adult, but a woman traveling alone concerned him. "Where are you heading off to?" he asked again. Throwing her shoulders back and thrusting her neck out she proudly stated, "I am going to the seaport to pick up some things for mother. Now would you be so kind as to saddle up my horse and I will need at least two saddlebags for the things on mother's list." Hans had a smirk on his face, but did not let his eyes meet hers, he said, "Okay then!" Whilst he saddled up Lucky, he still was irked by something. He turned to Eleanor and asked her if she'd like him to come along. "No," Elinore told him, "I'll be fine, and thank you for your help." In her silent mind, the thought occurred to her that Hans must still think that she was a baby! A small "humph" came from her lips. With that, she stuck her shoe in the stirrup and hoisted herself up, looking down at Hans who seemed so small now, she said, "I'll see you later." With a quick snap of the reigns, she headed off.

It was the first trip she would be taking with Lucky off of her mother and father's land; it was almost hard for her to really believe that her mother had asked her to go. Elinore knew it would take her mother hours to just come home with a few apples and a jar of jam. Rose inspected every morsel of every piece of food she ever bought. Elinore attributed that to the tastiest of meals her mother would serve. As she rode the well-worn path that many other travelers had passed over, she noticed how beautiful the many wildflowers were painting the fields with color. The soft breeze swayed the long brown grass, that was now tinted with shades of green. Life was coming back to the meadows and fields. The sound of Lucky's hooves sounded over the solid dirt. The soil was still moist from all the winter snow.

The breeze blew her hair back as her beautiful black stallion trotted on toward the seaport. Elinore had never felt so free. The sun was so bright, that it made the highlights in her long blonde hair sparkle. She took a deep breath into her lungs. She noticed too, that the closer she got to the seaport, the more birds were appearing. She was hoping she could surprise her mother with a nice piece of bluefish. That would surely make mother happy, she thought. As she got closer to the port, she could now smell the sea air. Her mother had told her to leave Lucky with a man named Gus at the first barn when she entered the town. He was a longtime friend of Porter, and he always took care of his horses when visiting the port. Gus loved horses and always had plenty of fresh hay and water for them. There were many travelers entering and leaving the port, so Gus was always busy at his work. Riding up to the barn she dismounted and began to look for this man her mother had told her about. A tall skinny older gentleman came out from behind the barn. He had a long grey beard and wire glasses, that he looked over the top of. Elinore asked, "Are you Gus?" Gus smiled, and as he did, Elinore could see that he was missing a few of his teeth. With this unkept appearance and with holes in his pants at the knees, Elinore was slightly nervous about his ghoulish outward form. "Ya, I am Gus. And who might you be, Fräulein?" "I am Elinore Downing, Sir," she told him. "Ah, you must be Porter's oldest. Come in, come in," Gus said as he took Lucky's reigns and led him into the barn. He took a large carrot from the bushel he had lying in the corner of his barn and offered it up to Lucky. "Tying them up with a nice treat makes them happy," he said to Elinore with his toothless grin. He patted the horse on his chest and told Elinore she could leave him there for as long as she'd like. Elinore told Gus she'd only be a few hours and then she'd be back to collect him. She waved goodbye and shouted thank you to Gus as she headed off with her small satchel and a few cloth bags.

She walked quickly to her first stop which was only a few buildings away. Picking up her first bunch of potatoes, she could see a few rotten ones on the bottom of the large wooden box they were displayed in. The smell was earthy, and she didn't like it much. There was a woman inside the building who came out to help her. As she looked through the wooden boxes of vegetables, the woman called out to Elinore, "Let me help you dear." Elinore smiled big and said, "I'm trying to get everything on this list for my mother," as she held the list up to her. "Ah, such a good girl. Here, let me see it," she said, taking the list from Elinore. "I see you brought your bags too. Good, good!" Patting Elinore's arm, she took two of her cloth bags and began to fill them with the things on her list. The woman started to hum a tune that she seemed to pace herself by as she placed each piece of vegetable in Elinore's bag; much like her mother did. Elinore was carefully watching. Her mother would be angry if she brought home any rotten food with her father's hard-earned money. When she was done, Elinore offered up some currency, and the woman placed an extra potato in her bag for good luck. She waved goodbye to the woman and headed onward.

The weight of her bags didn't seem to bother her much, and she thought briefly of bringing them back to the barn where Lucky was. Deciding against it, Elinore kept going and hoisted the bags up over her shoulder. The next stop was quite a bit further down the road. As she walked, she noticed more insects flying around. There seemed to be a lot of flies, and bees. After a few more minutes, she realized why. Now, she could smell fish. But before she would go down to where the ships were, she needed to stop at the cheese store and maybe she would be able to find the dried meats her mother wanted.

Elinore was starting to feel her legs straining and decided to sit for a minute or two. She found the perfect rock to rest on. Placing the bags at her feet, she stretched her arms upward toward the sky. Feeling a little thirsty, she took a few sips of water from the small canteen Hans had given her for the trip. Elinore began to look around. There were many people coming and going. There was a lot of chatter and noise from the horses and wagon wheels as they crunched the earthy stones beneath them. Finally, she spotted the cheese store. Picking her bags up, she flung one over each shoulder. The cheese store was only a few stores down from where she stood. Peering through the door, she could see some of the meat hanging on hooks and a big round wheel of cheese. There was a shopkeeper behind a large wooden counter. He wore a white apron tied tightly around his middle. It had bits of meat and things all over it. There were a few people in the small shop already, so Elinore decided to look around for a few minutes before going in. She could see the tips of the masts on the fishing boats. There was a pub just two buildings away with a lot of men inside talking very loudly. She also noticed a group of boys playing on the side of the cheese store. They looked like they were playing marbles against the brick building. They were neatly dressed. Two even had hats on. They all looked very serious, and Elinore thought the till must be a high wager. The one boy kneeling on the ground had very chubby legs and a coat too small for him. His boots were little and stubby. The expression on his face lead Elinore to believe he wasn't liking the outcome of the game much. Some of the people began to leave the store and Elinore took that opportunity to go in and have a look. Immediately, the smell of cheese filled the air. It smelled delicious to her. She filled her sacks with all she came for. Now it was time to head for the boats.

She could tell she was getting very close to the water; she could smell the sea in the air. The smell was pleasing to her. There were many fishing boats docked and many fishermen walking about. She really wasn't keen on the fish smell though. The dead fish smell wafted past her as each fisherman passed her by. And then she saw him. He was a younger fisherman tying down a rope from the large mast on the biggest boat in the port. She could see he was very strong and muscular. He whipped the ropes into place with ease. He had no shirt, only his fishing trousers and boots. From where she stood, she could see he was sweating, and the sun made his skin glisten. His arms were bulging, and his very masculine appearance made her want to fan herself. She thought he was the most handsome man she had ever seen. Carl had not entered her mind for a second. She stood on the gravel pathway gazing at him, when he noticed her. He waved and winked at her from the deck of the boat as his long hair blew wildly in the wind. Sheepishly, she waved back only using her index and middle finger.

There were many things going on in the busy port that day. Just then a small woman caught her eye. She was climbing up a ladder picking some apples off a tree, across from the harbor. There were many apple trees planted there and the woman was selling them by the crate. That explained all the bees to Elinore. She asked if it was possible to buy some loose ones and the woman gladly agreed.

Elinore had not noticed the boys that were playing by the cheese store were watching and following her. Elinore continued walking toward the boats where they had fish for sale. She took her list out and began to look it over. She needed to get tomatoes, fish and preserves, yet. She tucked her list back into her pocket when suddenly she found herself lying on the ground amongst her fruits and vegetables. The boys had rushed her from behind, knocking her to the ground. Their intent was clear as they quickly carried away her satchel with the rest of her Goldmark inside it. In a flash, Elinore left her things scattered all over the ground giving chase to them. Elinore was a fast runner and she gained on them quickly. Her heart was racing. Her anger was about to explode on the boy carrying her money away. Breathing hard and running as fast as she ever had, she was nearly close enough to grab him. Her eyes were fixed on the back of his neck like a fighter pilot ready to take down its target. Just as she reached for the scruff of his neck, that same fisherman that had winked at her picked up that boy with his feet still running and slammed him to the ground. He rolled him over and stepped on the center of his spine, retrieving Elinore's satchel. Elinore was so grateful and couldn't thank the man enough.

Now, she just had to pick up all her things off the ground. As she walked back, the man offered to help pick it all up and she accepted the help gladly. They began to talk as they picked up the apples and potatoes. Elinore was enticed by his steel blue eyes and his rugged appearance. Her apron was dirty from having been knocked over and it made her uncomfortable. She told him she still needed to purchase some jam, fish and tomatoes. He told her he knew just where she could find everything she needed, and again offered his help. As they walked along, she was slightly ahead of him. He noticed the way she walked. He watched closely as her hips swayed back and forth with each step. He began to wonder what her skin tasted like. His desire was heightened by her youth. He had a complete view of her luscious bosom as she picked up her spilled items. It had been some time since he had been with a woman and his lust for her was becoming hard for him to control. They began to walk towards the water's edge. The water sparkled as the rays of sunshine bounced off the gentle waves.

Elinore was experiencing what she thought was the most magical, romantic, moment with a man she didn't even know.

She vibrated inside as she stood next to him and that even seemed to contribute to the mysterious attraction of it all. He was reading her like a book though. He knew this young woman was captivated by him. He continued to entice her with his offers of helpfulness. And it was working for him. He led her to a boat that had just come in which he also knew had bluefish. He helped her pick a nice piece and had it wrapped in white parchment paper for her to take. Elinore found the rest of the things she needed easily and now her bags were very heavy, almost cutting into her shoulders.

She began to head back to the barn to begin her journey home when he asked her if she'd like to stop and have a splash to quench her thirst before she started her ride home. She thought that would be okay and was looking for a reason to put her heavy bags down for just a few minutes anyway. He told her he had an out of the way place to sit when he visited this port so he would be out of his captain's view and invited her to come sit with him. Along the side of the pub, down a small alley, there were several bales of hay and a makeshift table. He had a few bottles of water and a bottle of spirits hidden behind them. The alley was dark and didn't seem to have a purpose, and it smelled funny to her. Not too unpleasant, but for just a few minutes it would do.

Elinore followed him into the small space where the two sat down on the bales of hay. He offered her some spirits, but Elinore said, "No thank you, I have a long way to go before I reach home." "Where is that?" he asked. She replied, "Cuxhaven." He listened intently to her, and she was enjoying his attention. Then he said, "You know, you are one of the most beautiful women I have ever had the pleasure of talking with." Elinore felt her face getting warm. She was blushing. She turned her eyes to the ground almost embarrassed by his compliment. In an instant, she found his hand on top of hers and he was leaning into her neck area. Stunned, she pulled back to look at him sternly, but he already had a firm grip on her. His hand had now moved to her waist and with the other he had a tight grip on the back of her neck. He wanted her. He could not control his desire for another second. She asked angrily, "What do you think you are doing?" He replied, "I'm giving you what you want."

Elinore quickly tried to break free of his grasp, but it was of no use. He overpowered her easily. "You are such a tempting lass; I can resist you no longer." Elinore's back was pressed against the brick wall behind her. "Don't try to fight me," he said smugly and began kissing her neck. "I do like a bit of force if I need it but if you are willing, I won't need to hurt you." He sneered at her. "No! Get away from me!" She shouted at him as she began to fight him off. He only laughed in a terrifying way. He had fire running through his veins. He instantly picked her up and pressed her over the table backwards under his heavy weight. His lips were sticky and wet, and he kissed her throat. She began to feel sick. Her head was dizzy, and she felt as if she would faint. She continued to struggle against him, but her strength was no match.

His lips traveled downward, and she tried to kick out from underneath him, but his weight seemed to increase, pinning her legs against the table. He had an iron grip on her, and she wondered if her ribs would crack from the pressure. In her panic she remembered the bottles behind the haystacks behind him. "Wait!" she said, with a smile. Suddenly, she felt a renewed strength in her struggle with him. He liked where she seemed to be going. Elinore was using her brain to defend herself now, but she wasn't sure if it would work. She began to loosen the strings on her bodice. He rushed in drooling with desire and began kissing her bosom, liking her willfulness. Frantic, inside herself, she began to think of ways to escape, withdrawing her mind from what was happening to her body. Feeling numb; she was in survival mode. She could hardly breathe from his heaviness, when he lifted her legs up onto his shoulders. In a flash, his trousers were wide open and hanging from his hips. Elinore's back became stiff and resisted his pressure; he reached under her dress ripping her underclothing away. He held her almost completely folded over tightly, probing his heated loins against her bottom.

Just as he began to enter her, she whispered in his ear. "I think I would be much more comfortable on the hay." He looked hard into her eyes and said, "Whatever pleases you, lass." Not having a clue, she was feigning. He quickly picked her up, pinning her legs still wrapped around his waist so she could not escape. He moved her to the bales against the wall. She knew her cries for help would not be heard over the loud crowd inside the pub. He dropped her hard and began to penetrate her. Elinore laid back closing her eyes as tears began to well up under her closed lids.

All while putting on an act, she dropped her arms to the side. With each thrust, she was getting closer to his bottles. Her hand was brushing the loop on the neck of his bottle of spirits. Her fingertips could feel the bottle and she clutched her fingers around it in quiet desperation so as not to alert him. One more push and at last, she had slid her slender finger through the loop and was ready. Staring at his shoulder that lay against her chin, she tapped him on the other shoulder with her other hand. He raised his head to look at her. Like a windmill, her right hand came hurling up and over, cracking him square in the forehead with the large glass bottle. Shattered glass and spirits covered his face. Bloodied, she had knocked him out cold.

She looked at him with disgust. She spat at him with her darkened eyes. She wasn't sure if he was dead or just unconscious, but she didn't care. Quickly, she got up, clutched her bags, and ran as fast as she could. She ran all the way to Gus's barn. When she reached his fence, she set her bags down, brushing herself off. She wanted to fix herself so no one would notice she'd been torn apart. She called out to Gus. Gus brought Lucky out and helped her load her bags onto the horse. He told her he was glad to have met her and to tell her father he sent his best regards. As soon as she was out of sight, she began to cry. With no one to see, she was free to let all her emotions spill out. The entire day played over in her mind. She began to feel angry at what had happened. She wondered if she had somehow brought on the circumstance herself. She would remember those rotten little boys and especially that disgusting man for the rest of her life. She rode slowly along the same path, heading back toward her home.

She tried to think of what she would say if anyone asked about her disheveled appearance. The sun was just starting to set, and the sky was a pinkish purple. It somehow made her sadder. Finally, she could see her house. Finally, she could get off Lucky who seemed tired too. Hans had already been looking for her to return. He could see her off in the distance. It only took her a few minutes more before she was there. Hans was waiting as she rode straight for the barn. He helped her down, removing the bags from Lucky. Hans took the reins and led the horse into the barn for some water and fresh hay. He completed his job by taking the bags to Rose, who was anxiously awaiting them.

As evening fell, Elinore just wanted a hot bath. She prepared it herself and was grateful no one asked any questions about her day. Closing the bathroom door, she placed her head against it. Tears fell from her eyes hitting the floor. Standing still for a moment, she looked down at her own body. Never again, she thought to herself! Never again would she allow someone to put her in that position! Her anger was swelling up inside her and she punched her one hand into the palm of the other. She slowly stepped into the hot water. Soaping herself with the fragrant soap her mother had bought. The smell made no difference to Elinore. She scrubbed her skin furiously. Nothing would take away the unseen marks that were burned into her mind. She cried silently. She analyzed the fact that the only two men she could really trust in her life now were her father and Hans. She wasn't even sure about Carl anymore, and certainly didn't want to see him the following day at church. She thought about it and came up with a plan. When her mother woke her and Margaret up in the morning to get ready, she would ask to be excused, feigning tiredness from the long ride to the port. Surely, she knew her mother would understand. Elinore soaked in the hot soapy water till it was cold. Still traumatized, Elinore dried herself fast, putting her night clothing on. Everyone in the house was already getting ready for bed and Delilah was crying for attention. Rose sat on the edge of her bed, nursing Delilah before turning in herself. When Elinore walked past the open bedroom door she quietly said, "goodnight" to her mother. She only wanted to get to her room now. Burying herself beneath her blankets, she lay in the darkness and could still smell his sweat on her skin. She was feeling sore from what he had done to her. She continued to cry in the silent darkness, wiping her tears with her blanket. She wondered if she should tell someone, but who? And what good would it do?

That fisherman was probably long gone off to sea by now. If she told Hans, he would hunt that man down and kill him. Her father would do the same. She decided to never, ever tell a soul. Her trust in men was now broken forever.

Next morning came and mother was hustling through the house getting ready for church. She cried out to Margaret, who was already dressed and almost ready to go. Rose peeked into Elinore's room only to find her with the blankets still pulled up over her head. "Elinore!" Rose shouted. "It's almost time to leave and you haven't even gotten out of bed yet!" A low moan came from beneath the blanket. "I'm so tired mother. Please don't make me go," Elinore whined. Rose continued to swaddle Delilah as she stepped closer to Elinore's bed. Rose reached to pull the blanket from Elinore's face, but Elinore pulled it back and up further from her mother's grip. "Mama please! Let me sleep!" Elinore moaned and pleaded. Rose couldn't help but laugh. One trip to the port and all tuckered out, she thought. Rose was completely unaware of what had happened to her daughter. "Okay, okay," Rose said. "Just this once." Rose kissed the blanket where her head lay below, and gently closed her door. Elinore thought to herself, "Thank you Lord!" She began to think of how disappointed Carl would be because she didn't come. But she knew Margaret would explain it to him.

Elinore waited and listened for the wagon to head off. Only then did she dare peel the blankets off herself. She walked toward the kitchen; she was looking for some time alone. Emma and Elsie's eyes were focused on her as she entered the room. Rubbing her eyes, Elinore began to make herself a cup of tea. She sat down at the table quietly. She felt their stare would burn a hole in her. Elsie wasn't really paying her much mind. Elinore had sat on the chair she had pulled out intending to put the laundry basket on. After wringing the laundry, Elsie took it out back to hang on the line. Emma sat down next to Elinore. Emma waited for her to say something, but it never came. Elinore sat silent. Emma's eyes were drawn to the small tear running down Elinore's cheek. "Why are you crying?" Emma asked. Elinore just shook her head. She couldn't talk. If she did, she would surely burst out weeping. Emma asked her, "It was bad, wasn't it?" Emma had noticed Elinore's strange behavior since she had come home. "What happened Elinore?" she asked. With tears now welling up in her eyes again she said, "Not here. Meet me by the barn in a few minutes, okay?"

Elsie came back in, and Emma asked her where the chicken feed was. "I already looked under the sink," she said. Elsie declared, "There is none, because we ran out!" Elsie quickly realized she was being a bit short and apologized. She handed her a bag of stale bits of bread and started to sweep the floor. Elsie had not slept well the night before and was irritable. Emma took the bread and went to the barn, being careful not to let on that Elinore was out there too. The two women stood close while Emma began to feed the chickens. Elinore found herself wanting to tell Emma what happened. She had already told herself she wouldn't tell a soul, but if anyone would understand, it would be Emma. And so, her words began to spill out like a waterfall. Once she started, she just couldn't stop herself. Emma listened, putting her arm around Elinore's shoulder as she told her story.

Then Elinore thought for a minute and said, "Emma, do you think I did something to deserve it?" Emma couldn't believe what she was hearing. "Certainly not, Elinore! No one deserves that!" "Please Emma, swear you won't tell anyone! Swear, please!" Elinore begged. Emma couldn't believe what Elinore had just confided to her. She had no words except to tell her she was sure she should not feel guilty. Emma handed Elinore her handkerchief and told her that if she ever had to go to the port again to not go alone. She promised Elinore her secret was safe with her and headed back to the kitchen before Elsie started to ask questions. Still, as Elinore was left standing alone, she felt that somehow, she had caused what had happened. She certainly shouldn't have sat down with him. She promised herself never to let herself be that vulnerable again. This was a painful lesson. One she would never forget.

It was almost midafternoon when Porter and Rose returned home with Delilah and Margaret. Elinore was now sitting down by the pond watching the turtles' heads bob up and under the water when she saw Margaret heading her way. Excited, she reached into her pocket as she told Elinore, "I brought you something," and with a smile, she pulled out a handful of cookie crumbs. Then she said, "Well, they were cookies when I put them in there." Margaret shrugged her shoulders. "It's okay, thanks Margaret." Elinore asked, "Did you see Carl?" Margaret said, "Yes, he wanted to know why you didn't come. I told him you were tired from your long journey to the seaport. I think he was very upset." "I'll see him next week," Elinore said, seeming not to care much. Margaret was confused but decided not to ask questions.

The two sisters sat by the water's edge as they watched the sun sink low in the sky in all its splendor. Nature was painting a glorious portrait which was reflected in the stillness of the water. Elinore picked up a rock, throwing it into the pond. A ripple soon raced across the pond. Ironic, Elinore thought, my life is something like that now, a broken picture. She and Margaret stood looking at the beautiful sunset when the dinner bell rang, cracking through the air. They both knew not to procrastinate when food was waiting on the table. So, off they ran to devour their supper. Nightfall came quickly and moonlight filled the rooms in the house.

The familiar sound of crying could be heard. Delilah often cried at night, and Elinore's nerves were becoming frayed. Rose had explained to her that poor Delilah was cutting teeth in, and nights were more painful for her, but Elinore could still hear her cries through her closed bedroom door. Laying in her bed, looking hard at the ceiling, she tried to take her mind to another place, but the images of the seaport still played on in her mind. Elinore could still feel tears, just behind her eyes. And now, with the constant cries from Delilah, Elinore buried her head under her two pillows. Even under the pillows she couldn't muffle the sound. Her head was spinning. Elinore herself wanted to now cry. She was feeling depressed too. She didn't know what to do to make herself feel better. It was too late to go to the pond. Elinore went deeper, pulling her blankets up over the pillows with an annoyed huff. But now the blankets left her feet exposed! Violently, she began to kick her feet and the pillows and blankets became an erupting volcano from the anger that was building from deep within her. Tossing back and forth, fists and feet flying, Elinore started to cry. She fell from the bed and sat there stunned for a minute. She had scraped her back on the way down against the wooden bed rail. Elinore shook her head as she reached double fisted for her hair. Entangled around her fingers she pulled hard.

She could hear herself screaming from within, when Margaret burst into her room. "Elinore, what happened?" Margaret asked. Elinore wasn't in the mood to talk. Instead, she just shook her head. Margaret was carrying a small pouch. She held it out and said, "Want to play?" Elinore had long forgotten what it was like to play on the floor. A smile started to become visible at the corners of her mouth. Margaret sat down and pushed the blankets, exposing a small portion of floor between them. She opened the pouch and turned it over as a small wooden ball and sheep knucklebones spilled out. She bounced the ball on the floor and picked up one of the knucklebones with the same hand. As they took turns, Elinore's spirit became lighter. Soon neither could hear Delilah's cries. The game passed a few hours of time for the girls and finally they began to rub the sleep from their eyes. It was clearly no use, and the two found themselves sleepily slumped over on the floor. The house had grown quiet now, so both decided it was time to climb into their beds for the night.

Chapter 8

As the night sky turned lighter, his eyes started to open. Elinore was still on his mind that morning. It had been three days since church services and there was a break from school now. Carl didn't know when the next time would be that he would see his lovely Elinore. He was missing her desperately. Smoothing his rumpled hair with some water, he yawned from his long night's sleep. He began to dress himself, deciding he would see Elinore today! He washed his face and drank a cup of coffee before going to the small barn behind his house to saddle up his horse. He was on a mission, and nothing would stop him. The sun's rays were bright and warm. Squeezing his horse tight with his knees they trotted off.

The ride to Elinore's went quickly as he thought about what he would say to her when his eyes finally met with hers. He couldn't understand how Elinore could be too tired to see him, as Margaret had explained to him. Soon, Elinore's home was in sight. His heart was racing. Visions of her beauty raced through his mind. Impatiently, he pushed his horse to go faster. Finally arriving, he already had one foot over the horse's back to dismount. Scrambling to the Downing's front door, he grabbed the doorknocker. Tapping it four times, he stood waiting. His insides anxiously vibrated. His hands were sweating.

Rose answered the door with her fore finger pressed against her lips. She shushed him. Rose had been up most of the night with Delilah and she was finally asleep. She signaled to him to come in. Closing the door ever so gently behind him, she whispered, "I'll go get her." She disappeared down the long narrow hallway. Carl was excited. He was only moments from seeing the girl he was falling in love with.

Rose opened Elinore's door to find her brushing her hair. Rose whispered, "Elinore, you have a visitor. Carl is here to see you." Elinore was startled and surprised. Rose could see she was not expecting him. As soon as Rose closed the door, she rushed to reach under the bed for her wooden box. Clutching it tightly, she opened the lid to slip the ring he had given her onto her finger. Elinore really didn't want to see Carl today, but he was already there. She had no choice. Her body was moving without thought. Slowly she walked to where he waited. Her eyes were focused on the floor. Carl was so thrilled to see Elinore that he didn't notice she was not quite herself. Not wanting to wake Delilah, Elinore took Carl's hand and led him outside.

Without speaking, the pair walked toward a small pear orchard that had long been abandoned, many years ago. Small white blooms were appearing on the branches which added to the romanticism of the moment. While they walked, all Elinore could think about was that miserable fisherman. She wondered if Carl would be able to tell that her innocence had been desecrated. Torn from her forcefully by a man she didn't know. She began to think about what he would think if she were to tell him. What would his reaction be? Would he be disenchanted with her immediately? Would he see her differently? She wasn't sure it even mattered anymore. The brutal force she had experienced somehow had demoralized her. Her free spirit was broken. She felt more guarded.

Carl could see she was distracted but he was determined to make her smile. He decided to climb up a pear tree and hang from one of its branches. Swinging around on the branches, he climbed higher and carried on like a monkey. Scratching himself and hooting, when suddenly, a great crack pierced the air. The branch he had chosen to hang from snapped, sending Carl to the ground with a thud. The branch laid across his chest and he moaned in pain. Elinore rushed to him, crouching by his side. "Are you alright?" Quickly, she removed the branch and began to check to see how badly he was injured. Carl took that opportunity to wrap his arms around her. He laughed loudly and rolled her over into the long yellow grass that surrounded them.

They laughed together and finally Carl had his old Elinore back, or so he thought. Carl commented, "I've missed you so much," he said, as they laid beside one another. Elinore responded with just a hint of a smile. Unsure where this was going to take them, she sat up quickly and began to brush herself off. Carl asked her, "Are you Okay?" He was puzzled by her reaction. Elinore responded without hesitation, "Yes, it's just I haven't been sleeping well. Delilah has been crying constantly lately." Elinore hoped that would be enough to satisfy his curiosity.

She turned to face him but found him looking straight up into the brilliant blue sky. There was an awkward silence, when SPLAT, a bird perched higher up in the tree he had just fallen from, relieved itself, landing directly in the center of his forehead. Elinore's eyes widened. Her jaw dropped, and a hearty laugh came out from deep within her. Carl began to laugh too. "Oh Carl, you are really not having any luck today, are you?" Elinore could barely get the words out over her laughter. She had forgotten about everything that had been bothering her for that moment. Unwittingly, Carl had broken through the ice, and unknowingly, Elinore was beginning to heal from her awful experience.

It was a lesson she would carry with her for a lifetime but didn't want it to define her. Her parents had taught her how to be a strong girl and that was something she would rely on for the rest of her life too. Carl knew from the sun in the sky that he needed to be on his way home shortly. He needed to be there before darkness descended. He did not want to cause his parents any grief, but he didn't want to go either. Carl placed his hands on Elinore's cheeks. Her skin was soft and supple. Her long hair spilled over her shoulders. He could smell the sweetest scent exuding from her, and he did not want to leave her. Carl pulled her face closer to kiss her but felt her hesitation. She pulled back; not letting him. Carl dismissed her hesitation, placing the blame on her lack of sleep. He walked her to her door and began his ride home. Elinore took a few minutes to watch him as he left before reentering her house. She thought seeing Carl would have been worse, but realized she felt better after having seen him. He truly was her hero.

Elinore made her way toward the back of the house when she heard a familiar voice. It was her grandmother! Elinore was delighted to see her and her grandfather. They had come to visit and to meet their new granddaughter. Margaret was already seated next to their Opa. Elinore kissed her Oma's cheek. Rose was happy to have her parents come to visit as she shuffled around the kitchen. Margaret and Elinore both knew their grandpa was full of fun and they both had good reason to be excited. Their grandfather was a true prankster and always a lot of fun to be around. There were no rules or limits on the games they would play on each other.

Rose made a nice brew of fresh coffee which her father Eddie was anxious to get his hands on. He always said there was nothing like a good cup of coffee, and Rose could remember him saying that for most of her life. That was one thing everyone knew about grandpa; he loved his coffee and when he didn't have it, Rose swore you could literally see him dragging his bottom lip around, especially in the morning. Porter was much the same way and so Rose thought it was probably a man thing.

As her grandfather sat at the table Elinore could see something else was brewing too. Trouble, and she knew the fun would begin soon. Her suspicions were confirmed with a quick wink from him. Oma was devoting her attention to Delilah and was paying little attention to much else. Rose poured some of the fresh coffee into her father's cup. He stirred in two lumps of sugar and a small amount of milk. Elinore knew what was coming next! Margaret did not, for if she had, she would not have sat so close to Opa. Elinore watched as he slowly stirred his coffee with his spoon when in a flash, he took the spoon out and placed it against Margaret's exposed calf. Margaret let out a cry loud enough to wake the dead. Rose knew what he had done and scolded her father. "Papa, why do you do that?" "It is so mean!" Rose placed a cold wet washcloth on poor Margaret's leg. Elinore was trying her best not to laugh. Opa had done that to her many times before she learned never to sit that close while grandpa had coffee with a spoon in it.

Margaret decided it was time to let the games begin. She snarled at her grandfather. Eddie laughed and the corner of his lip curled upward. He was delighted to be the one to be first out in their games, he secretly looked forward to them, and had the heart of a child. But Margaret had a few things up her sleeve too. This would be an interesting weekend for sure. Rose and Porter were just glad to have the extra help. Adjusting to having a newborn in the house was exhausting at times. Having Rose's parents come to visit also provided a wonderful break for them. Katherine and Eddie loved doting on their grandchildren. Katherine always adored little babies and it had been a while since the birth of Margaret. That evening Margaret waited till everyone had gone to bed. Quietly, Margaret snuck into the kitchen taking the jar of mustard with her. She knew her grandfather would be the first to use the bathroom. She slowly crept to the bathroom being careful not to cause the floorboards to make noise.

She poured out a bit of mustard onto the toilet seat and spread it around. She began to sputter from holding in her giggles as they pushed out through her nose. Silently, she returned the mustard to its original place and laid in the darkness of her room waiting for her booby trap to work. It wasn't long before all that coffee sent Opa to the bathroom. Suddenly she heard it! Grandpa groaned loudly and Margaret had to cover her mouth with her blanket. She couldn't contain her laughter any longer. She knew Opa had mustard all over his butt! It was several minutes before her grandfather popped his head into Margaret's room. He quietly whispered, "That was a good one, little one. I have a good one for you coming." He laughed sinisterly as he left her room. Margaret heeded his warning and thought maybe she might need to sleep with one eye open, but she still couldn't stop laughing from her vision of her Opa with a mustard butt!

Elinore and Margaret were up early the next day. Both were ready to hatch their next plan. Before everyone else was up they had decided to take their grandfather to their favorite place for a bit of fishing. Elinore opened the icebox where she knew her father had left a small piece of Limburger cheese. It had been there a long time, and she was sure her father would not want it. Margaret went to the hooks by the front door to retrieve their grandfather's hat. Gripping it tightly in her hand, she scurried silently back to the kitchen like a mouse. Elinore was waiting. She wanted to make sure no one had heard Margaret. Margaret was impatient. "Come on already!" she said as she pushed the hat hard into Elinore's hand. Elinore hushed her. She neatly and slowly folded the stinky cheese inside the sweatband of her grandfather's hat. Margaret watched her, smiling from ear to ear. When Elinore finished the dirty deed, Margaret returned the hat to its hook with a quick grin. It wasn't long before everyone was in the kitchen eating what Emma and Elsie had made. Rose's chickens were starting to produce many eggs now and it all tasted wonderful to Eddie. Not a speck of food remained on his plate after he was through. He washed everything down with the last sip of his coffee and rubbed his stomach in a circular motion. He was well content. Katherine asked Rose if they were going to attend church the following day. Rose knew her mother always went to church on Sunday. She dared not answer no.

Now that the fuss of the morning meal was over the girls began to set their plan in motion. Margaret entered the kitchen carrying two fishing poles. She set them against the wall; put her cutest face on and pulled up close to her grandfather. Tapping him on his thigh, she said, "Let's go fishing!" He couldn't resist her charms. He patted the top of her head and stood up, reaching for the fishing poles. "Let's go." Eddie loved to fish and thought he could give the girls a few pointers while they had some fun. He told her to go get his hat as he looked for something to put the fish in. All three of them bounced around as they walked toward the pond. Elinore caught the first one, but it was so tiny she threw it back into the water. Margaret caught the next. It was a good size. "Well done, little one!" her grandfather told her. "That one must weigh at least three pounds!" He took it off the hook for her and tossed the line back into the water. Sitting on their favorite rocks in the warm sunshine, their grandfather began to stare at Elinore and Margaret. It made Elinore uneasy, and she asked, "What's wrong Opa?" He said, "I think one of you girls made a stinky." Elinore's eyes got big, and she put her hand on her chest. "Me? Not me?" shaking her head. Margaret chimed in, "Nope, not me either! You smelled it first, so it must be you grandpa!" "No." he said, tossing another line into the water. He handed the pole to Elinore, telling her that nature was calling, and that he'd be right back.

As their grandfather walked back to the house, Margaret and Elinore wondered if they had been caught. Both of their eyebrows rose as they stared at each other thinking about what to do next. Eddie was onto them and had a trick up his sleeve for them too. Above the door in the kitchen there was a small piece of loose wood. It had been there for many years. Taking some thread from Rose's sewing box, he carefully tied several strands, cutting them to the perfect length to brush against their faces when they came through the door later. The girl's eyes would not adjust that quickly from the bright sun outside. He knew how much the girls' hated spiders, and the threads brushing their faces would feel like a spider web and quite literally send them into spasms. As he passed his wife and Rose, both got a whiff of something bad. "Papa," Katherine said. "Go use the bathroom!" He thought to himself. They smell it too. Hummmm. He took his hat off to inspect it. There it was! That little stinky piece of cheese!

Rose knew that all three of them were in the middle of a prank war. Katherine and Rose shook their heads and couldn't help but find it funny at the sheer enjoyment they all got from the silliness of it all with every visit. Eddie enjoyed himself as much as his granddaughters. They had his sense of humor but when it came to pranks Katherine would have none of it. He tossed the cheese into the bin next to the sink, carefully covering it under the other waste. He had to laugh at how clever they were becoming as they were getting older. Heading back to the pond he pictured their faces in reaction to the trap he had set for them. He also knew there was a good chance Katherine would rat him out. He hoped that his plan would go unhitched.

Katherine was just enjoying the smells of what Emma was making for dinner. Emma was making Bratwurst and potatoes with onions. It was one of her favorite meals and Emma knew everyone would enjoy it including Hans. It had been a long time since Rose's parents had visited and she wanted it to be special.

Porter was busy with his paperwork but the smells from the kitchen were distracting him. His mouth began to water, breathing the delicious aroma. He hurried along to finish in time for the feast. He was looking forward to making a food baby in his already large belly.

Eddie had made his way back to the pond and found Margaret squealing with delight. She held up two more fish that she and Elinore had caught. "Good job! Now we have evening meal for tomorrow! Your mother will be proud!" he said. The girls had mistakenly let their guard down. Certainly, a dangerous thing to do around their cunning grandfather. And especially now that he knew he had to step up his game with them. They all continued to fish for a while longer, but after only catching one more they gathered up their things and brought the fish back to the house. Eddie was careful to go in the door first. He was anticipating the girl's reaction to the threads. Now, Eddie was the one who couldn't stop grinning from ear to ear as he turned to watch his prank unfold.

Margaret entered first and Elinore followed close behind her. They were excited and proud to show their mother what a catch they had made, the fish were large enough to feed the entire family. But as they entered the doorway fishing poles and fish went flying into the air, everywhere. Margaret and Elinore were screaming, clutching at their faces, trying to wipe away whatever bug they assumed was crawling on them. Margaret looked at her grandfather. He was busting apart at the sight, covering his mouth at the success of his prank. She ran to him swatting him on the leg. "That wasn't funny!" she yelled as she began to pick the fish up off the floor and put them in the sink. Elinore just rolled her eyes. She thought for a moment that she may be getting too old for this kind of stuff. She had to admit though, it was funny and Margaret's stink eye was even funnier.

The next day started early. The entire family dressed in their Sunday best. Katherine enjoyed showing off her new granddaughter to all her old friends after the service. Porter and Eddie were talking with all the men about the latest business things and Margaret was busy with Gertrude chasing butterflies, while Elinore got to see Carl again. Things were a little easier between the two of them and she was enjoying his company again. Rose was enjoying her free time speaking with the other ladies while Katherine kept Delilah busy. She was enjoying her coffee and gossip thoroughly. This special time was enjoyed by all who attended, and it created a place to air out any problems a family might have. A sort of community tapestry.

As the sun began to get lower in the sky and late afternoon came, Rose approached Elinore and Carl. Elinore had already had her eye on her parents and quickly spotted her mother walking toward them. She whispered to Carl, "My mother is coming." Feeling slightly uncomfortable, the two became quiet. Rose's right eyebrow raised, remembering a time when her mother had interrupted a moment between herself and Porter. She smiled and said, "Don't stop talking on my account now." She smiled and touched Carl's arm. Breaking his uneasiness, she asked if he would like to come for dinner sometime. Carl replied, "OH YES! I would love to!" Rose continued with her thoughts. "I think it is time we get to know each other." Rose faced her daughter and said, "We'll be leaving soon darling, so say your goodbyes."

Elinore hated to say goodbye. She wasn't sure when the next time would come when she would see Carl again. She looked sad, but she did as she was told. As Rose walked back to find Porter, she laughed to herself. She was thinking of how much fun she would have when she was able to tell Carl some of the things Elinore did when she was a baby. Rose had not intended to embarrass them but knew she probably did.

Carl hugged Elinore tightly and she whispered in his ear, "Kiss you next Sunday, I promise." She needed to hurry now because she knew her mother did not like to be kept waiting. Carl found a little humor in the entire situation but was also a little embarrassed. He knew the day would eventually come that he would need to meet Elinore's parents. And so, he looked forward to that meal, after all, Elinore had always bragged about her mother's cooking.

Porter had gathered everyone into the wagon, and all was secure. The family started home looking forward to Emma's delicious meal. Rose knew her parents would be leaving the following day, which saddened her. Rose really enjoyed having a lot of people coming through the house. She would miss her parents terribly until their next visit.

Hans was sitting on his porch early that next morning watching the sun rise. He sipped his coffee, enjoying the quiet moment to himself. It tasted especially good to him this morning while he gazed at the beauty of the big sky. He found it truly inspiring. The corners of the sky remained dark, but the sun, as it peeked out between the distant mountains lit a small portion with an orange and yellow hue that was growing quickly. He was enjoying his most favorite time of the day with only the sounds of nature. The sun's rays were quickly reaching the ground around him as he watched the dew create a mist that burned off every blade of grass that grew. He was very content, and his mind began to wander. He thought about the last time he used his rifle and decided it would be a good time to clean it. He took it apart, laying the pieces on the porch in front of him meticulously. He was entirely protective of his rifle as he knew someday it may save his own life. He never went far without it. It was just a few short minutes when he saw Porter headed toward him.

Porter greeted Hans with a cheerful good morning and a wave of his hand. He told him that Rose's parents would be heading home shortly and asked him to get their wagon ready. Hans told Porter that he would have it pulled up to the house in two minutes' time and they continued with some small talk about the visit. Hans kept his word, and it was only a few minutes before the wagon was ready to go.

Katherine was already waiting with bags in her hands. Hans and Eddie placed the bags inside the wagon and Katherine tried hard to hide her tears. She hated saying goodbye. She hugged each of her grandchildren tightly, and then hugged Rose. Eddie and Porter shook hands, and quickly, he jumped onto the sideboard winking at Margaret and Elinore. He knew Katherine would be anxious to get home. As they rolled down the dirt path, both girls were already missing them. Rose was saddened by the sight of the wagon leaving carrying her parents away.

Elinore wanted to visit the pond again to be alone. She was heading off in that direction when she spotted Hans, who was already back on his porch finishing what he had started with his rifle. Slowly she walked toward him. Placing her chin on the handrail of his porch, she looked up at him with her big blue eyes and asked, "What are you doing?" Elinore was always curious about how things worked. Taking things apart and putting them back together was absolute entertainment for her. Hans began to explain to her how all the rifle's pieces fit together. She asked him if she could fire it. Hans wasn't sure what to say and his face mirrored his uncertainty. He bit his lower lip hard and thought for a minute. It occurred to him that maybe it could be useful to her at some point to have some small knowledge about how to fire a gun correctly. He began to tell her to always treat a gun as if it were loaded, even if it wasn't. She took the rifle and began to look it over. Staring down the long barrel, unknowingly, she was pointing it right at him. He began to jump up and down, waving his hands and yelling at her to put it down. Hans angrily snatched the rifle from her, looking sternly. "What did I just tell you?" The dark hardness of his eyes told her everything! He repeated himself, "Don't ever aim a firearm at anyone unless you mean to take their life! Do you understand me?" He paused, taking a deep breath. "Now listen to me. Never put your finger on the trigger until you are ready to shoot and always keep your eye on your target including what is behind it." He asked her again if she understood him. "This is not a toy!" he said in a raised voice, handing the rifle back to her.

They walked together toward the pond. Hans took the gun from her again and placed one bullet in the chamber. Then he placed the rifle against her shoulder, placing one of her hands under it to support the barrel and the other behind the trigger. Hans then said, "Okay Elinore, when you are ready, pull the trigger." Elinore did not hesitate. She squeezed the trigger, releasing the firing pin that moved with great force, causing it to explode. As the bullet whirled toward the pond, the gun landed beside her. The enormous force threw her to the ground. Stunned, she looked at Hans with widened eyes. They looked like two bright white saucers and her mouth hung open. "Holy Moly!" she said. Hans had to laugh. "Had enough?" he asked. Surprisingly, Elinore had not and wanted to give it another try. Hans agreed and picked up the rifle from the ground. Still laughing, he asked if she remembered everything, he had just told her. She nodded and replied, "Yes, I do." Once again, he loaded the cartridge and placed it on her shoulder.

Just at that moment Porter's voice rang out loudly enough to be heard by the people in the next field. "What the hell are you doing?" Elinore stopped dead in her tracks. She could tell by her father's tone of voice he was not pleased. Handing the rifle back to Hans as if it were hot, she was afraid of her father's fury. Porter was coming quickly toward them. He told Elinore to go back to the house and wait for him there. Elinore felt badly that she had made her father mad and worse yet for causing trouble between him and Hans. Porter had never been this angry with Hans before. "Why, in heavens name, would you teach my daughter how to fire a rifle?" he snarled.

Hans could see by Porter's hardened stare and flaring nostrils that he was beyond angry. Hans quickly offered an apology and the smallest explanation. "She's quite a sturdy girl Sir, and I thought it could be useful to her if she ever needed to defend herself. I'm sorry if I have upset you." Porter's eyes turned to the ground, and he moved his hand in a motion as if he were wiping something away. He growled under his breath, "Okay," and walked off in the direction of his home. Hans was left with feelings of guilt. He had not figured that he might be overstepping his boundaries. He always thought of Porter's family as his own and for the first time it was clear he shouldn't. He was feeling stung and thought about going to the pub to smooth his ruffled feathers. Wounded, he went to the barn to get Lucky to visit Walter for a drink or two.

Porter hesitated a moment before going inside his house. He knew Elinore would be seated at the kitchen table waiting. Porter wanted to make sure she was aware of how dangerous a firearm could be. He really knew and trusted Hans with his daughters but thought that he would be the one to teach her something like that. It occurred to him that maybe he was just a bit jealous for lacking the time to teach her about important things in life, while Hans had nothing but time. He sat down next to Elinore, calmer now than a few minutes earlier. Elinore was nervous, awaiting her scolding. Instead, she was surprised as Porter began to explain how things can go terribly wrong in the blink of an eye when handling guns. She assured her father that Hans had gone over everything thoroughly with her. Porter was starting to feel bad about the way he reacted and hugged Elinore. He knew he needed to make things right again with Hans and went back up the hill to talk to him, but when he knocked on his door there was no answer.

Hans was already seated on a stool at Walters pub and downing his second drink. He sat thinking about Margaret, Elinore, Delilah and Rose. Hans always thought of Porter's family as his own. He knew Porter was aware of this, but now he wasn't sure about if what he had thought he had known for a very long time was true. The beer was going down easily, and his wounds seemed to feel a little better. The alcohol was doing what it was intended to do. A younger female patron inside the pub had had her eye on Hans and she approached him. Putting her foot up on his footrest and placing her elbow on the bar, she looked flirtatiously at him. She said, "Hello handsome!" She had a twinkle in her eye, and he knew what she likely wanted. She was a pretty lass, but Hans was in no mood. He turned his back to her to push her off. He didn't want to be rude, but he could only think about his friendship with Porter and why things went wrong the way they did. He had always displayed his loyalty to the entire Downing family. He felt Porter had treated him unfairly. It was very late, and Hans had watched most of the patrons come and go. He decided to have one more drink before he left and made small talk with Walter about how things had been since the birth of Delilah. Placing his empty stein on the bar, he headed out the door, giving Walter a nod of his head.

In the darkness he walked to Lucky. It was very still and quiet that night, the sound of his boots echoed off the trees with each step, when he saw a man sitting against the post beside Lucky. He called out to him, but he did not move. Pushing into him with his knee intending to wake him from his stupor, the man fell over. Hans knelt to shake him. His arm felt stiff, and Hans was stunned. He tried again to shake him, but he knew it was no use. The man was already showing signs of rigor mortis. Just to be sure, Hans placed his fingers against the man's neck but wasn't surprised to feel no pulse. Hans was shocked and ran back inside the pub to get Walter who was already cleaning up the nights business. "Walter, come quick!" Hans shouted.

"I thought you left," Walter replied. "Please Walter, come with me!" Hans's voice had an urgent tone. He and Walter went to where the man was laying. Walter said, "Oh boy, Helmut had one too many I suppose. Help me get him up, Hans." Hans knew the man was already dead. He said, "Walter, that man isn't going anywhere." "What do you mean?" Walter asked. Wrinkles appeared on his forehead not understanding what Hans was trying to tell him. "I mean he's dead," Hans said bluntly. Walter replied as he looked wide-eyed at Hans, "You better get out of here, I'll take care of this."

Without another word, Hans got on his horse and rode quickly away. He couldn't help thinking about what an awful night and day this had been. Now he was just looking forward to resting in the comfort of his own home with no interruptions or chaos. Finally arriving at the barn, he tended to the horses as fast as he could and headed for his bed, only to find Porter sitting with his lantern on the chair beside his door. Exhaling deep enough to blow a small strand of hair upward from his face, Hans was not looking forward to this conversation. He felt awkward and tense. Porter would not be out this late waiting on him if he had nothing to say. He walked up the hill toward his home warily.

"I owe you an apology," Porter blurted out to Hans. Porter began to explain that he thought his work was taking over his family life. He said, "I wish I could spend as much time with my girls as you do. I should never have taken that out on you. I am grateful I have you to help my family when I can't be here."

Hans looked sternly at Porter and said, "Sir, I am not trying to replace you. You are like a brother to me; your children are my children too." Porter smiled and gave Hans a manly bear hug. "Now that we have that straight," Porter shook Hans's hand. Hans smiled, and with one hand on his door, he winked at Porter. "You have a good night, Sir." Hans opened his door, took his boots off and buried himself under his blankets. The image of the dead man's face was still in his mind. He was glad he was home and now the day seemed to end on a good note.

Days passed quickly now, more than ever. Porter was sitting at his desk once again. At his work he had plenty of money but didn't have the thing he missed most and that was time. Time with Rose. Time with Margaret, Delilah, and Elinore. He felt he missed a lot of special moments of his children's lives. It made him angry. "These damn uniforms!" he said, as another order came in over the telegraph. He slammed his thick, gnarly fist down on his oak desk. The force of his frustration sent papers flying everywhere! Now he wasn't just frustrated, he was angry again because he had to pick up all those papers off the floor. He was having a temper tantrum and could feel his insides vibrating from disgust. Clenching his teeth and bending to the floor over his round belly, he clutched at the papers, not caring about wrinkling them around his very tight grip. He placed the thick stack down hard on his desk when he noticed The Montag. Greta had bought the newspaper during her lunch break and placed it on Porter's desk when she had finished reading it. Now she was back at her desk getting Porter's paperwork prepared for the next day's orders.

Porter picked up the newspaper and licked his thumb, leafing through the first few pages. The newspaper had a lot of articles that Porter was very interested in. Porter had a fondness for shopping for new things and he hadn't had time for any of that lately. Porter bellowed to Greta to come into his office.

She picked up on his tension but wasn't quite sure what it was about. Looking cautiously around the corner of the doorframe, she poked her head in before she entered. Hastily he demanded, "Come in, Greta! Did you leave this newspaper on my desk?" he asked, waving it at her. She reached out to take it, but he pulled his hand back before she could. "It's mine now," he said with the faintest smile. Greta knew the stress of the job was beginning to weigh on Porter. He needed something to take his mind off things for a while and that was precisely why she had left the newspaper where she did.

Porter then began to ask Greta her thoughts about some things that were advertised inside the paper. There were these tablets they called aspirin. They were also being sold in a powder form. He wondered if the claim it cured headaches and other pains was true. He also wondered if Greta, or Rose for that matter, would actually try them. Another item that he found of great interest was called a coffee filter. Apparently, a housewife named Melitta Benz was tired of the bitter taste of her coffee, so she used blotting paper from her son's school notebooks as a spacer, placing it between the boiling water and a brass pan with holes, thus protecting the coffee cup from the grounds. The coffee filter was attracting attention. It was just an idea at this point; however, Porter found the information brilliant. He didn't like the bitter taste his coffee had sometimes either. Greta agreed, she didn't like it either. The last page of the paper mentioned a new bacteriological soap called Kavon that sounded wonderful, and he wanted to try that as well.

Porter's weakness was getting the better of him. Subconsciously, he was already on his way to do some shopping. He told Greta he was going to leave early and asked her to make sure all the paperwork was finished before she left. Greta was well liked by Porter. She was efficient and competent. Greta's feelings about Porter were mutual.

Porter was also still thinking about Hans. He felt bad about how much he had hurt him and wasn't sure how he could make good on that. He did remember Hans expressing his desire to have some Holstein-Friesian cattle to milk. Porter thought about the large room he had built for entertainment. He had never had much time to use it so he thought it could easily be turned into stalls by the same men who built it. He also wanted to stop by

Frieda and Gus's delicatessen. He knew Frieda's potato salad was the best he had ever tasted. Mayonnaise was mostly available in France, but somehow Frieda had a connection with a friend of a friend who could get her supplies of the best kind. She used that mayonnaise in her salads. Porter tried to get the recipe from her, but she remained tight lipped about it. Frieda would not share her recipes under any circumstances.

The farm was just next door to the delicatessen so Porter decided he would visit there at the same time. Maybe he would buy six Holstein and borrow a few cow herders to bring them home. They could stay in the field till he had the reconstruction completed. Porter hadn't been shopping in a very long time and looked forward to it. According to 'The Montag,' there were many new things coming. He especially liked the things developed right where he lived in Germany as they were easily available to him. Porter soon was on his way home, singing a song as his horses pulled the wagon. He had at least ten paper bags filled and six Holstein-Friesian cows following close behind. He was quite a sight heading homeward.

Rose knew Porter would be arriving home shortly. She took a moment to look out the window and her mouth dropped. "Oh my, he's at it again! Elsie, come look at this!" she shouted. Elsie could hear a bit of humor in Rose's tone of voice. She looked out the window beside her and began to laugh out loud. She wanted to fall onto the floor. "I guess we'll never have to worry about milk again!"

Hans had heard the cowherder's noises and whistles and rushed out onto his porch. He couldn't believe his eyes. He had no idea what Porter's intent was, but he did remember their short conversation. As Porter pulled up to the house everyone stood bewildered. Rose asked, "What have you bought now Porter? Good grief!" He handed some bags down to her and the girls. Hans took the last two bags. They were heavy and he had a most confused expression when he asked about the cows.

"You wanted them, didn't you?" Porter boldly asked. Hans looked over the cattle and asked, "You mean they are mine?" "Of course!" Porter said. Before Porter got down, he asked the men who had already started working on the barn, to put them in the field. Once he made up his mind, Porter worked quickly. He had seen the workers outside the delicatessen, and they had started working before he even got home. Porter told Hans that he would explain everything later.

Hans carried the last two bags inside with a restored sense of belonging. He couldn't believe Porter bought him cattle. Incredible! Inside, Rose began unloading the bags and found all sorts of things she had never even seen before. There were little white pills and metal tubes marked "Sample Toothpaste." There were two jars of what looked like mayonnaise. She was so confused. "Why would you buy mayonnaise?" she asked.

Porter told her that Frieda gave it to him, and it wasn't from France but made by a fellow right here in Germany! Porter was so excited, and his shopping spree had done him a world of good. His spirit was restored. He also brought home some scotch tape, which Margaret was now sticking to everything in the kitchen. He bought a thermos and aspirin too.

Elsie wanted to know what the aspirin was for. She held the small glass bottle up between her thumb and forefinger, examining the bottle. Looking at Porter she asked, "What do these do?"

Porter answered her, "Next time you have a headache, take two." Elsie was skeptical. She put them back in the bag, looked at Rose, and shrugged her shoulders. Delilah was curious too. She seemed to like the crinkle sound that came from the brown paper bags and was having a great time playing with them. Porter was happy to bring these treasures home to his family. Many other things filled the bags. Porter bought potatoes, onions, meats, fish, canned tomatoes and plenty of fresh vegetables. He couldn't control himself, but he also knew Rose would be pleased that she didn't have to go shopping at the market.

When all the bags had been unpacked, Elinore started for her room. She had a good book to read that Miss Ilse had lent to her. But before she could get away, Porter called out to her. Turning her head to the side, she displayed a small amount of impatience, before her father said, "It's okay if you don't want these." He was holding up two Milka chocolate bars. Not giving her father a chance to pull them back as he often did, she quickly grabbed hold of them. With a grand smile that allowed all her teeth to show she said, "Thank you!"

Margaret saw the chocolate and asked, "Hey, what about me? Did you bring me something?" Porter asked, "You are not happy with the scotch tape?" Margaret began to pout. Her shoulders dropped with disappointment. Porter was having a good time razzing her. Then from the last bag where he had hidden her treats, he reached in and handed her two packages of vanilla sugar wafers. Margaret squealed with delight. She absolutely loved sugar wafers and ripped wildly at the outer wrapper.

Porter slept well that night knowing he had made everyone happy. Hans was not as lucky though. He tossed and turned that night. He couldn't believe he was now the owner of six registered Holsteins. He dozed off here and there but at the crack of dawn while the morning dew still hung low in the air, he headed off into the field to inspect his cows. Standing in awe for a moment, taking in the massive beasts that stood before him, he decided to approach them cautiously. He knew they too needed to adjust to him and their new surroundings. The sun was starting to peek over the mountains, and Hans knew this would be an interesting day. The sun's rays began to burn the dew off the grass, creating a light fog over the field. He saddled up the white horse this time, thinking she might blend in better with the cows. Hans rode slowly around the field. He knew he would need to begin milking them shortly or their udders would likely clog. As he looked the cows over, it was clear to him he had five cows and one bull! He was glad to learn this because he knew each cow took an hour twice a day to milk. It dawned on him that it might be better to keep his little herd in the smaller penned up area instead of the larger field. He coaxed them with some of the horse's fresh hay which they seemed to be very happy with. Only one cow didn't seem so willing. She showed her dislike for him by stomping her cloven hooves. Each cow was huge and bulky. Hans estimated each weighed upwards of 2,400 pounds. The bull was massive. He guessed that he weighed no less than 3000 pounds. Hans already knew that bulls could be more aggressive, so he decided to leave him in the larger field for the time being. He also knew his cows would be in heat every twenty-one days, so he needed to regulate the bull's visits until Porter had some type of shelter built for them.

Hans did not have to wait long for this to happen. Porter had a well thought out plan for this too. That same day at 1 p.m. sharp, the men who Porter had hired previously were back. Like an army they filed in and commenced working on what Porter called his ballroom. A great change was underway. Saws were blazing, hammers were pounding, and lots of shouting between the men had already started.

The uproar outside woke Elinore and Margaret early that next morning. Off from school this glorious day, with bright blue skies and wispy white cotton-candy clouds, both seemed unconcerned about the noise. The sound was familiar to all who were still trying to sleep inside. Both girls bounded to the kitchen to see if Emma had anything to offer. They both were excited to be able to go outdoors to find something interesting to do. Plopping down hard on their chairs, Emma pushed two bowls of Oatmeal and two glasses of milk in front of them. Emma added a splash of cinnamon to each of their bowls to sweeten their little faces. They inhaled their food and were soon outside enjoying the day finally.

Porter had already left for work, and Rose was getting herself and Delilah washed up. Elsie had finished the laundry and asked Emma to hang it outside for her. She needed to tend to Delilah. She had plans to take her outside to let out some of the energy she had pulsing through her small body. Elsie always said Delilah had more energy in her pinky toe than she had in her entire body! Elsie had a special fondness for Delilah. As noon approached, all the banging and noise came to a stop. The men were taking a break for lunch.

Margaret paid no mind to it all and continued playing. She was busy picking wildflowers, as many as her tiny hand could hold. Elinore had Carl on her mind again. It had been a few weeks since they really had any time together outside of school. He had not been invited for dinner yet so now she was growing impatient to see him again. Whilst her daydreams took her to another place, a feather floating in the breeze caught her eye. She watched it as it gently floated over the pond's surface, touching down in the water creating a small ripple effect. She watched the waves race across the pond until they all but disappeared. Her concentration was broken, however, when just out of the corner of her eye she saw someone walking toward her house. Elinore looked up again but only caught a glimpse of the person's back. It was not Hans. It was a man's shape but unfamiliar to her. Her thoughts quickly returned to Carl and their upcoming graduation. She was also beginning to worry about what she would do after she finished her schooling. Maybe she could get a job in town. She thought about becoming a teacher briefly but dismissed that quickly as she knew she really didn't have the patience for small children on a regular basis. Sitting on her favorite rock, with her thumb on her chin, her mind wandered.

Inside the house, Rose was alone. She was in her room getting dressed to meet Delilah and Elsie outside when she heard the back door close. She called out, "Elinore is that you?" There was no answer. Rose was not particularly alarmed and continued dressing. Opening her dresser drawer, she reached for her precious brush set and began pulling at her hair. She saw a reflection in the small handheld mirror Porter had bought for her. She could see someone standing behind her. Rose gasped, turning to face her intruder. His face was familiar to her. It was the man who had made a pass at her the first time Porter had hired these same workers. Frozen, she stood in terror. "What do you want?" she shouted at the worker trying to cover her partially exposed body. With an evil look he replied, "You know what I want," pleasing himself with his own hand at the same time.

He moved closer to her after he closed and locked the bedroom door behind him. His salacity was untamable. He reached for her, but she pulled away. Catching her by her neck with his powerful grip, he picked her up and slammed her down onto the bed. Rose began to kick and scream. Kicking as violently as she could she landed one right to his manhood. He groaned and winced in pain. Rose saw a small opportunity to escape and ran for the door. His hand landed on top of hers as she reached for the doorknob. Picking her up again as if she was a rag doll, he slammed her down hard onto the wooden floor knocking the wind from her lungs. He was angry now. His face was red, and Rose could smell the stench coming from his mouth. He pushed himself over her, biting her neck and shoulders. Rose continued to fight. Kicking and punching him, Rose was determined to free herself. He bit her harder as she landed many more kicks to his body. She screamed, "Let me go you bastard!" He began to tear away what little clothing she had already put on. He glared at her. He was breathing hard and with a closed fist he punched the right side of her face. Her right eye hemorrhaged from the impact. He hit her two more times in the face and Rose began to bleed heavily from her nose and mouth. The blood drained down, covering her neck and chest. Shrieking, she gathered up the strength to run for the door one more time. But as she turned the knob his thick bulky hand slammed the door shut again. He pressed against her back, and she felt his hardened member through his trousers. His musky scent made her want to vomit. Rose turned around fast intending to club him in the face, but his weight was too much for her. He overpowered her once again and slammed her to the floor again. The back of her head was swollen from the brutal force with which he threw her down. With his pants open wide, he began to spread her legs apart. But as soon as he came to lay on top of her, she bit him hard again taking a chunk out of his shoulder. He wrapped his hand around her hair and jerked her head back and forth. Her neck twisted in pain as he dragged her across the wooden planks. Rose screamed with everything she had left as he clubbed her once again. He was determined to have his way with her by any means necessary.

Outside, Elinore thought she had heard a scream. It was strong enough to break her thoughts of Carl. She thought about it. She had not seen that man come out of her house. She called out to Hans but couldn't see him. Elinore ran to his house to see if he was inside. She flung open his door, but he was not inside. Elinore was starting to panic. She shouted his name out again, but he didn't respond. As she went to close the door, there in the corner was Hans's rifle. She checked to see if it was loaded. It was. Holding the rifle carefully, she ran toward her house. Her heart was pounding. Busting through the door with her foot, she had the rifle aimed ahead of her. To her surprise, there was no one in the kitchen where she expected her mother to be. She entered the house further and saw that her mother and father's bedroom door was closed. Trying to open it without alerting who was inside the room, she found it locked. She reached above the door frame for the extra key her father had placed there in case Delilah locked herself inside the room. Turning the key, she could hear her mother whimper. Her low broken cries and the sounds of a struggle made Elinore tense. Suddenly, she was aware of a faint awful smell entering her nose. Rose had taken out the fish earlier and set it out in the kitchen for Emma to finish later. Elinore was immediately taken back to the seaport where she herself had been violated. She knew what she must do. She broke through the door. Her mother was screaming and still fighting off the man who hardly seemed to notice Elinore standing in the doorway. With the rifle against her shoulder, she pointed it right at him. Elinore growled, "Get off her now!" The man turned his wicked bloodied face to her and with a menacing threat, he lunged at her. Elinore's fear did not freeze her this time. She pulled the trigger hitting the man square in the chest. He fell to the floor. Blood gushed from the bullet wound, and she could hear his gasping last breaths as his life ebbed away.

Hans heard the gunshot and came running to the house. The group of workers were unaware and unable to hear anything, above all the banging and shouting. They had resumed work and were oblivious to the fact that one of their workers was missing. Hans entered the bedroom to a bloody scene. Hans's rifle was on the floor next to the bed where he found Elinore cradling her mother who was bloody and badly beaten. Her face was almost black around her eyes from the violent blows she had taken. He felt the man's neck. Elinore had shot him dead.

Elinore held her sobbing mother, stunned at what she had just done. Hans had been busy with the cows and had not heard Rose's cries. Holding Delilah by the hand, Elsie came in to find out what was keeping Rose and walked straight into the grisly scene. Aghast at what she saw, she covered Delilah's eyes and looked at Hans. He placed his hands on each side of her face and looked straight into her eyes, "Elsie, GO GET PORTER! Take Lucky and go now!" Dazed, she took off running for the barn as fast as she could.

Hans handed Delilah off to Emma and asked her to go find Margaret to make sure she did not come into the house till he called for them. Hans started to clean up Rose. He looked at her bruised face. He picked her up and brought her broken body to the bathroom, gently pouring warm water over her, washing the blood away. He found Elinore shell-shocked but physically unharmed. Rose held onto Hans tightly and wept uncontrollably. In her mind she knew she should have told Porter the first time the man had made a pass at her. Now he lay dead on her bedroom floor. Hans continued to clean off Rose, covering her body with blankets.

Elinore moved to stand over the dead man. She focused on him, overwhelmed and filled with the emotional impact of what had just happened. Everything went into slow motion. Clips began to flood her memory of her own struggle in the seaport alleyway. Suddenly she kicked the man hard with her wooden shoe. It wasn't enough. She stomped on his head and kicked him some more. She kicked him again and again ferociously. She beat his face with her fists, punching wildly at him. Hans heard her and looked out of the bathroom to partially see her. He had to leave Rose for the time being to gently pull Elinore away. He guided her into the bathroom where Rose was. With his large arms, he held both women as they both sobbed damping each of his broad shoulders.

Porter had just gotten home, and Elsie had already told him what she had seen. He entered the bathroom passing the dead man on the floor. With one look at Rose's face, he went back to the man, flipped him, and began punching him brutally till his thick hands were coated with his blood. Hans stood next to Porter, placing his hand on his shoulder and said, "He's dead Porter. You can't hurt him anymore." Porter in a hushed tone asked Hans, "Who killed him?" "Elinore did, Sir," Porter's eyebrows raised, "Elinore?" he asked. "Yes, she did." "Good," Porter replied. It was all he could say. Then Porter took a minute and asked Hans to dig a hole to bury the garbage, pointing to the dead man. He took the bloody clothing from Rose and told Elinore to change and bring him her clothing too. He gathered the sheets and everything else that was soaked with the man's blood and took them to the pit outside. He threw gasoline on the clothes and burnt them to a charcoal.

The workers had left for the day and the hole was ready. Hans and Porter dragged the burly man out to the field where Hans had dug the hole and threw him in it face down. They buried him with everything he had come there with. Erasing him from the surface of the earth. Porter went back inside to put clean sheets on the bed. He mopped the bloodstained floor clean. By the end of the day, Porter had decided to hire another foreman at his own business so he could be home more. He blamed himself for what happened and vowed no more harm would ever reach his family again. If he was present, he knew they were safe. He also took the time to thank Hans again for teaching Elinore how to shoot that rifle. He was now worried about Rose's health and Elinore's state of mind. The workers returned the next day to finish the job. It was a quick fix, not requiring much work at all. Putting large strong stalls in for the cows and opening the building on one end to install a huge barn door was all that was really needed.

Rose was in a lot of pain the next day and barely able to eat. Her bottom lip was split badly, and both her eyes were blackened. Hans was disappointed in himself for not being there to stop the intruder. He sat across the table watching Rose's every move. He apologized a hundred times. Rose told him to stop and that he could not have possibly known what was happening. It still did not stop his guilt pangs. Hans also was watching Elinore. She was so young. He wondered how the kill would affect her. He waited to speak with her; to give Porter a chance to talk to her first.

His next thought was about all the work that was piling up in this time of tragedy. He knew he needed to begin the milking process with the new cows. Porter had bought everything he would need including milk cans and buckets. He was glad the barn was finished completely now. He could begin taking care of the milking rain or shine comfortably. They had built enough stalls for each individual cow and even made extra for any additional ones that may be born thereafter. Hans was happy with the way everything was turning out. He thought they had done an especially good job with the large barn door. Deciding there was no time like the present, he went to the barn. What a perfect opportunity to take his mind off things.

It was only late afternoon, but the sky was dark already. The air was damp and heavy. Hans knew a heavy soaking rain was on its way. He herded the cows to the barn and secured them. There was one last thing to do. He went to the barn for the horses. He needed to check on them and give them their feed. He opened the door, and he heard the funniest sound. He didn't have the slightest idea what it could be. Apparently Lucky had become a jester. His head was bobbing up and down and he swung his long tongue back and forth. It made a slapping sound that he found entertaining. Lucky lifted his head as Hans moved closer to him. Lucky's large teeth produced a smile that made Hans laugh out loud. "Come on Lucky," he said, "We have work to do." Hans shook his head, still laughing because he had never seen a horse do that before.

They rode off to the penned area where the females had been left but was surprised to find they weren't there. They were all in the larger field with the bull. He was confused, he had put them in the smaller field purposely. He wondered if Porter had moved them. But why would he do that? It wasn't like they were small or easy to move. He began to herd them back into the smaller penned area. It was closer to the barn, and he thought if he got them closer it would be more manageable. He planned to bring the bull in last. The cows didn't seem to be giving him a hard time today so he thought they must be getting used to him. Hans was about to find out he had a lot to learn about cattle. He managed to get two of the cows locked into the smaller area and went back to get the other three. Heading back, he couldn't believe what he was seeing. Cows are a lot smarter than he realized. To his amazement, the cows had watched him when he locked the gate and now one had her long pink tongue stretched through and over the rail to unlock the gate again. "Damn! This is not going to be easy!" he said to himself, approaching the cow. He was going to have to be a lot smarter. He needed to have a chat with a few of the local farmers shortly to get some advice.

He finally got all the cattle in the pen and locked the gate as the rain began to fall. Water was dripping off the brim of his hat, and from his jacket when he finally got back to his house, The rain from his coat splashed all over the floor. He was glad to see the fire was still going and pulled up a chair in front of it to dry off. He was tired but satisfied he had at least gotten some milk from the cows releasing their build-up. His mind drifted as he watched the fire. He thought about Rose and Elinore again. He knew Rose would likely be okay, but he was really worried about Elinore. She was so young to have to defend someone to the death.

Chapter 9

Elinore sat in her room staring out the window. She was remembering when her life was much simpler. Her first special memories were filled with sweetness.

Other moments began to filter in as time changed and she became older. Indelible dark images started to flash over and over, of the man's face whom she had shot. She squeezed her eyes, closing them tightly, trying her hardest to push them away. Without realizing it, she was rocking back and forth, and had developed a nervous tick from the horror. She wiped her nose constantly even though there was nothing there. Her shoulder began to occasionally lift at times toward her chin now too.

Porter pushed his head through the cracked door. He wanted to ask her how she was feeling. She had her back to him but turned her face slightly when she heard her door open. Somehow, she knew what he was going to ask and saved him the trouble. "Yes, I'm fine," she said. Stepping into her room, he wanted to know more. He wanted to see for himself. He started by saying he knew how much courage it took for her to rescue her mother. He told her he was proud of her for protecting her family. He asked her if the man had said anything to her before she shot him, but she honestly could not remember. There were a few blanks in her memory it seemed. All she could remember was her mother's screams and his bloody face when he lunged at her. Porter put his arm around her shoulder and sat down next to her. "I think you need some rest Elinore," he said, kissing her forehead before leaving her room.

Taking his advice, she laid back down on her bed. Her legs curled up into a fetal position clutching her pillow. Her mind would not let her rest. She thought over again about everything that had happened. She couldn't understand why some men acted the way they did. Why would they think they had the right to take what they wanted from a woman? She was angry. They have no right, she thought. Then suddenly she felt worse than the minutes before. If she hadn't been so deep in thought about Carl, she might have noticed that bastard entering her house. Then, she thought, "It was no matter now, he got what he had coming!" Her mind was everywhere and nowhere. She decided in that moment that she was never going to let another man take advantage of her or her family again. She decided she needed to sharpen her skills. She needed to be more observant and aware of her surroundings at all times for starters. Her inattentiveness only brought her trouble.

She decided she would never let her guard down from that moment forward. Elinore stood up with a renewed feeling about herself. She had done nothing wrong and was not going to feel bad about it. Elinore left the house to see Lucky. She always felt a calmness come over her when being around him. She picked up the horse brush and ran it over his back. She looked into his eyes, holding his face in her hands. As she stroked his muzzle, she began to speak to him. She told him all that had happened and how she was feeling about it. She told him she thought she would really like to see Carl and asked Lucky if he thought that was a good idea. Lucky's eyes remained fixed on her. She took that as a yes. She went back to the house for a brief minute to tell her father where she was going. She returned quickly and mounted Lucky to ride off to see Carl.

Carl had not expected to see Elinore that day. Out in the field tending to his crops, he could hear hooves pounding the earth. He looked up to see Elinore riding toward him. There was a gladness followed by a sinking feeling in the pit of his stomach. He knew she must be coming to tell him something important. He started to walk toward her to help her down. Lucky was a tall horse and Elinore landed right on top of Carl's foot with hers. With a nervous laugh, she quickly apologized.

Carl was only interested in finding out if everything was okay with her. She launched into her story, rapidly explaining every detail of the grizzly scene, hardly taking time to breathe between each sentence.

Carl's eyes widened as he listened. He couldn't believe what he was hearing. Elinore had taken a life! He felt fear in her words. He could see she was not physically injured, but asked if she was alright anyway. He asked her if she wanted him to come home with her. She told him that he could if he wanted to, but Hans and her father were there taking care of everything. Carl didn't know what to do or say to make things better for her. He kissed her forehead and took Lucky's reigns from her. Together they walked to his home and sat down on the bench just outside the door. Carl was observing Elinore closely. He had never killed a person himself. But he noticed she wasn't crying. As a matter of fact, she almost seemed angry. And then he noticed that her shoulder lifted nervously as she spoke to him, but she didn't seem to be aware of it. He decided the best thing to do was to just listen and pay close attention to what she had to say. He wanted her to know that she could count on him for whatever she needed. He reached for her hand and held it tight. He wanted to assure her and asked her if she knew how much he loved her.

"Of course, I do Carl, I love you too," she said as she kissed the back of his hand still firmly attached to hers. Carl's mother could hear talking from inside the kitchen of their small home. She came outside to find her son and Elinore. Happy to see Elinore, they exchanged pleasantries and then she offered her usual cup of coffee to both. Heidi had no idea what they had been discussing and gave them their privacy.

The coffee tasted good to Elinore, and she thanked her for it. Elinore's mind had been shattered and her thoughts were becoming scattered. She changed the subject from the horror she had just experienced to talking about their future. She was intentionally putting distance between what had happened and her future life, trying hard to forget that it had happened at all. Carl just listened to her, but he had noticed the slight change in Elinore. Nothing specific, but it worried him. He attributed her change to the shock she still seemed to be in but her callous comments about the murder made him shiver. She seemed hardened to it. But then again, he thought, most anyone would surely feel that way after something of that kind. Elinore finished her coffee, kissed Carl goodbye and headed home. Carl decided not to go with her. Simply watched her go. She stopped briefly, turning to blow him a kiss and then continued on her way. Carl smiled and hoped all would be fine in a few days.

Elinore secretly was glad Carl did not come home with her. She honestly was exhausted and didn't want any company. When she got back to the house, Porter was waiting and asked how Carl was doing. She answered, "He's fine." Porter was not used to her being so short with him. He was sure now that Elinore was not quite right. She was never like that with him before and she didn't even have the faintest smile when she spoke of Carl like she normally did. Porter suggested to her again that maybe she should give herself a little more time to heal by getting some more rest.

Maybe her father was right, she thought. She was kind of sleepy now. She didn't even feel hungry either. Elinore went straight to her room through the kitchen and spotted some lovely biscuits and cheese on the table that Emma had put out. She stopped for a minute and couldn't resist. She helped herself to a biscuit and a slice of cheese, gobbling it down before laying down to rest. Elinore changed her clothes, throwing them right to the floor in a pile. She climbed into her bed and pulled the blankets up over her head. It felt so good, she thought. This was her favorite place to be. She shifted back and forth until all her body parts were in their most comfortable position. Elinore's eyes became heavy within minutes as the warmth of the blankets overtook her.

It seemed like she had only been asleep a few minutes when she heard a few taps on her window. The room was completely dark now with not even the moonlight to make out any shapes. Terrified about the thought of what could be lurking just outside her bedroom window, Elinore hid in her closet behind her clothes. A few minutes passed, which seemed like much longer to her when she heard the sound of shattering glass. Remaining there, behind her clothes, she sat still like a mouse. She could feel her skin becoming moist and her breathing was labored. Horrified, she listened to the footsteps wandering about her room. She could hear the footsteps coming closer and closer. Suddenly, what she dreaded most; the closet door opened! Elinore sat breathless. She closed her eyes tightly and her muscles trembled. Then, two bloody hands split the clothes apart! A man's hands reached deep into the closet clutching and swiping at anything he could latch onto. One of his hands found her! Elinore screamed as he dragged her out. She felt the wooden floorboards beneath her scraping into her back. She clutched around for something she could use to defend herself with. Kicking and screaming, she saw the face of her intruder! She realized it was the man she had just shot! He was still bloody but alive! She could see into the open wound in his chest, the rhythmic contraction and expansion of the arteries with each beat of his heart. She even could hear it beating! Thump-thump. Thump-thump. Elinore screamed again!

All at once her eyes opened wide. Her blankets were on the floor and her nightclothes were stuck to her skin, drenched with sweat. Her chest was heaving while she gasped for air. Elinore sat straight up in her bed, fearfully looking around her room. The window was not broken. Her closet door was closed, and she was unharmed. Elinore went to the bathroom looking for a washcloth. Wetting it with a bit of water, she wiped the sweat from her forehead. Trying to calm herself from her nightmare she took a sip of cool water and returned to her room. Sitting in the darkness she started to think. It was useless to try to go back to sleep. She decided when tomorrow came she would go see Carl again and ask him to help her purchase a small pistol. She had a small billhook in the barn, which she used to trim the thatch around the house for her mother. She was fierce with it, and it would more likely be her weapon of choice if needed but it was too big to carry concealed. She would need the smallest of ones for her own personal protection. Carl's boss, Mr. Schmidt, could make one for her. She would tell him it was a gift for someone. The pistol though, her and Carl would probably need to go to Berlin for. Elinore leaned back resting her head on her pillow again. She knew she would feel safer once she had something to protect herself with. Her mind felt clear now, making it possible for her to sleep again. She had a plan and vowed always to keep some sort of weapon within arm's reach. Sleep fell upon her quickly after that.

Within hours, Elinore was on her way again to see Carl. Following through with her plan, she would be asking Carl to visit Mr. Schmidt that day to get her first choice of personal defense in motion. Carl had already seen Elinore coming. He had been up very early that morning, and he was eager to see her. This would be her second time in one week. But this time there couldn't have been much that happened since she only left him hours before.

Elinore was feeling better with the new day. "What brings you back to me so soon? Did you miss me?" Carl teased her. It was the first time in a long time that Elinore laughed so lightheartedly. She looked down at him from the top of Lucky's back. The sun blinded Carl's eyes as he tried to look back at her. Shielding his eyes with his hand he asked her to come sit with him and enjoy some coffee.

"What a perfect way to begin her new day and latest request," she thought. Willingly, she accepted his invitation. The two sat close together as they sipped the hot beverage. Carl looked at Elinore, hesitating for a moment, then blurted out, "Do you want to get married?" He loved to make her laugh. Elinore was stunned. "Carl, you haven't even spoken with my father yet! Where would we live, and what about your parents?" she asked. Carl began to giggle and playfully poked her in her waist. "I didn't mean tomorrow El, I wanted to know for the future if you would." Elinore thought that was a crazy question. How could one know what would happen in the future? Many things over the last year had happened to her that she had never dreamed would ever have taken place. She looked at Carl with her neck pulled back and squinted eyes. "Marry you? No way!" His face dropped, not expecting that response. Elinore couldn't hold it in anymore. She had caught him in his own game. She burst out laughing. "Of course, I want to marry you! For God's sake, what's wrong with you?" Now they both were laughing while they continued to finish their coffee. She had thought about them being married since she was a child.

"Now that that's out of the way," Elinore said, "I have something I need to talk with you about." Carl asked her what was on her mind. She explained to him that she wanted a small billhook. One small enough to keep in her apron. After what had just happened to her and her mother, he completely understood but didn't know where she could buy one. Elinore asked him if he could speak with Mr. Schmidt to make one for her as an intended gift for a special person. She knew Mr. Schmidt would automatically assume it was for Hans and probably ask no further questions. She told him to make sure Mr. Schmidt made it small because it would be used to cut the wild raspberry bushes back without sending them into shock. Her explanation made sense to him and so he told Elinore he would ask the very next day.

In her own thoughts she had already decided to wait till she got the billhook before she asked Carl to help her get a pistol. Elinore and Carl spent that entire day together. It was a breath of fresh air for her. She had been uptight for a few months now, and Delilah's constant crying made it worse. She was enjoying herself and didn't want to go home as evening inevitably came. She kissed Carl tenderly before riding off without enthusiasm. She knew her mother would need extra help until her wounds healed completely. All the way home, her thoughts were filled with Carl and how long it would take for Mr. Schmidt to make her billhook. Her first stop was the barn. She put Lucky in his stall and made her way inside. Right away she smelled something wonderful, Eierschecke cake! Her favorite! She could smell the apple topping as it baked in the hearth next to the fire. What a perfect ending to a nearly perfect day. She inhaled the sweet aroma deeply and sighed with a smile. Her mouth was already watering.

She just needed to see how her mother was doing before she did anything else. Surprisingly, Elinore did not hear Delilah. Looking in her mother's room, she saw Rose seated on the chair watching over Delilah as she slept. Rose quickly held one finger up near her mouth, being careful not to touch her badly broken lip. She smiled faintly at Elinore as she met her in the doorway. Closing it slowly, she leaned into Elinore's ear to speak softly. She asked how Carl was. Elinore smiled and motioned to her that he was fine. Rose remembered when she had first met Porter and how she felt. In a hushed voice, Rose said, "As soon as my face clears up, we'll have him over for our evening meal, Okay?" Elinore nodded happily. Rose needed to check on her cake and hurried off to the kitchen. Emma was busy taking care of the rest of their meal.

On the way to her bedroom, Elinore passed by Margaret's room and caught her blowing a ball of dried long grass across her bed, that she had brought in from outside. With a huge gust from her lungs, she blew it off her bed and swatted it against the wall hard enough for it to break apart. Elinore stood watching her do this a few times until Margaret finally noticed she was there. Elinore thought her sister had lost her mind and started to laugh. Margaret covered her face and was embarrassed. Elinore shook her head and continued to her room, she just wanted to get her feet out of her riding boots and sit down. Then she heard Delilah's cries again. She thought to herself, "God I never want children!" She covered her ears and closed her bedroom door. Gazing out her window across the open field she opened it to the smell of burning wood. She hated to put her shoes back on but reluctantly she found herself doing just that. She wandered around the front of the house but found nothing unusual. Then she made her way past the barns, and all was fine there too. Then she made her way toward the pond where she saw Hans burning wood in the fire pit. Sitting on a wooden chair, he held a long stick over the fire. At the very end she could see he was toasting a marshmallow! She instinctively picked up her pace. Quickly walking over to him, she asked if she could have one.

He said, "Yes, for one Goldmark." Hans enjoyed having a bit of fun with Elinore. She was quick-witted, and he was always up for the challenge. She stared at him making a pouty face. "You know I have no money." "Awe El, I was just kidding," Hans said handing her a marshmallow from the end of his stick. She placed it in her mouth and smiled. She tried to say thank you, but it came out garbled. Her mouth was completely filled with the hot marshmallow fluff, and it made it hard for her to talk. Hans held his hand up, laughing, and he answered, "You're welcome." He could see she was enjoying herself and handed her another.

Sitting down on the ground next to him, her sight became fixed on the flames. She watched them rise to lick the air above them. Elinore didn't realize it, but Hans was paying close attention to her. Elinore sat motionless, transfixed by the flames which seemed to have her spellbound. Hans had been waiting for the right moment to have a talk with her. Hans called her name out loud, piercing through and breaking the trance she was under from the flickering flames. Hans asked, "How have you been feeling lately, Elinore?" She wasn't quite sure exactly what he was trying to get at, but she had a pretty good idea. She asked, "You mean about that worker?" "Yes, that is exactly what I mean," Hans shot back, deciding to cut to the chase. She licked the sweet stickiness from her fingers. She was thoroughly enjoying his treats. She smiled at Hans with her eyes and hoped he saw her gratitude as they both sat at the fire, watching the sun fade from view. She purposely did not answer his question, instead Elinore decided there would be no time like the present and quickly decided this was the perfect moment to ask Hans for help with purchasing her pistol. She knew she only had two options. Carl or Hans. Those were the only two men she could ask on this matter. Each had her trust, and both had enough money to help her. She had already asked Carl to get the billhook from Mr. Schmidt. But on second thought, it seemed Hans was the much better choice for purchasing a pistol. He was much more knowledgeable than Carl about guns.

She looked at Hans and just spit it out. "I'm fine but I need your help with something." "Sure, little one, what is it?" He thought this would be an easy fix. What he heard next blew his mind. Elinore put it bluntly, as she always did. "Hans, I want a pistol." He didn't know what to say. "Please don't tell my father or anyone else." Hans explained to her that if her father ever found out that he had bought her a pistol it would more than likely end their friendship. "That's a lot to ask Elinore," he replied. "He would never forgive me," he added. Elinore sat there just staring at the ground in front of her. She didn't know what to do now. Then she said, "I know it's a lot to ask, but I promise I would never let on that you had anything to do with helping me, I swear." She went on to tell him she felt she needed one in case she ever had to defend herself or someone in their family again. Just one small enough she could conceal within her clothing.

Hans was baffled as to what to do next. He decided to give her limited help. Information wouldn't hurt, but he would not buy one for her. He told her the only place he knew of that might have something like what she wanted was in Berlin or Munich. He knew she would not be able to go there. He also mentioned he could never be gone that long from the house without a proper explanation to her father. Elinore was disappointed but she knew he was right. Then Hans snapped his fingers, catching Elinore's attention. "I do know of one man at the end of the seaport that might have what you want but he is a shifty character," he told her. She knew that would mean she would need to pass all the ships there. She tried to mentally justify her fear by saying to herself that the likelihood of ever running into that son of a bitch who raped her again was slim. It still disturbed her. She decided if she went, it would be after she got her billhook. Elinore rose to her feet and hugged him tightly around his neck.

Hans was glad he could help and understood completely why she felt the need to protect herself, but he also had Porter in the back of his mind. He could put himself in Porter's position and understood this would be upsetting to him. Hans hoped that Elinore would never really follow through with going there for that reason. At just that moment, Rose rang the bell outside signaling that their evening meal was ready. Elinore turned to thank Hans again and boldly kissed him on his cheek. She pressed her finger to her lips and made a 'shhhhh' sound. Hans just told her to get going. He really wasn't sure he had done the right thing. He knew he would have to deny having anything to do with her scheme if someone should find out about it. He prayed she wouldn't follow through with her plan but knew he didn't want anything further to do with it.

Hans's stomach was grumbling. He was hungry and the marshmallows were of no help. He wanted a good meal now and was looking forward to Elsie's visit within the hour. Lifting himself off the chair, he picked it up and carried it towards his house. He placed it back down in its original place by the door. While he waited his thoughts drifted off to his empty coffee cup on his small table. It would surely be nice to have a cup with his dinner, so he began the process. He sat on the porch and waited to see Elsie's hands holding his meal. The smells that drifted across the field told him something good would be along shortly. His belly was making loud noises, and his anticipation grew with each minute that passed. Finally, Elsie and Emma appeared. They were carrying a heavy basket in his direction. Hans told Elsie that he had made some fresh coffee and invited both women to eat with him. They happily accepted and all three were soon enjoying themselves. Hans really liked the sauerbraten Emma had made. He hadn't had it in a long time. Rose had also given each of them a generous portion of the Eierscheke cake. That was a real treat! All three ate, drank, and laughed late into the evening.

Hans felt his eyes beginning to become very heavy when the ladies left to get ready for the next day's affairs. It felt like he'd only been asleep for a few moments, when he was awoken by loud bangs and mooing coming from the barn that held the cattle. Quickly he put his boots and jacket on to rush to the barn. Not knowing what to expect, he opened the door slowly. Everything seemed fine and he wondered what all the noise was about. He walked around the barn and noticed one of the piles of hay was untouched. He spoke to the cows, "What's the matter, you don't like this hay?" He couldn't understand why they did not like this particular bale when they ate all of the others. He lifted it to inspect it and saw a snake coiled up, ready to strike. He dropped the bale and ran to the tools hanging on the barn door. Unhooking the shovel, he ran back to the bale again, but the snake was gone. He looked around frantically for where it had slithered off to. All he needed was to have one of the cows he was just gifted, die from a snake bite. He knew it couldn't have gone far without the cows reacting to it. He waited silently. Soon the cow that seemed to least like Hans the most was stomping her feet again. That was a clear sign to him. He moved slowly toward the cow, gripping the shovel tightly. Sure enough, he saw the gray V-shaped head poking out from some of the uneaten hay. He struck hard and fast with the blade of the shovel, cutting the snake in half. He picked the snake up and walked it over to the pit. It would be burned with the next batch of garbage.

Satisfied, he wiped his hands over the pit. Now he could finally have his morning coffee before he needed to return to do the milking for the day. He was enjoying the way his life was now. All things seemed perfect, and he felt he could continue in this lifestyle for a lifetime. Sitting in his own quietness, he looked across Porter's land. He sipped his hot steaming coffee on his porch as the morning dew began to disappear off the blades of grass. Hans was feeling very content when he saw Porter leaving for work. The two men raised their hands to one another from a distance in greeting. Porter wasted no time getting on his way.

Inside the house, Rose had things on her mind. She had discussed with Porter details of Elinore's upcoming graduation. She wanted to buy her a new dress and have a small celebration for her. Their conversation the night before was lengthy, and Porter was thinking on a much grander scale. Rose had become accustomed to accepting the help around the house, but still thought in a frugal way, especially when it came to running the household. She was a firm believer in waste not, want not. There would only be a few more months till Elinore's graduation would be here. Rose never liked waiting until the last minute to do anything. She went to her small desk in the front room to retrieve some writing paper and a pencil to begin marking down what she would like to purchase for Elinore's special day. A dress was at the top of the list. Rose scratched the paper with the dull pencil. Then she wrote cake and the point on her pencil broke off. She opened the drawer to find all her pencils with no points! She knew Margaret had been in her desk! Delilah was not smart enough to be able to open the drawer yet. Rose was annoyed. Margaret knew how to use the pencil sharpener. She picked herself up from her chair and went to Porter's room to sharpen a few in a huff when she heard Porter's voice. Surprised, she opened the back door, still holding her pencils to see Porter tying the horses up. She asked him if something was wrong and if he felt alright. Porter was never home this early.

He smiled at Rose and reached for her. Drawing her to him, he kissed her and asked, "I can't come home to see my beautiful wife?" Porter was happy to be home early for a change. He told Rose that only two orders had come in over the telegraph that day, so he asked Greta to take care of things. Rose took the gifted opportunity to tell Porter about her list for Elinore's graduation and what she needed to buy before the end of the next month. Soon after they entered the house, Porter felt Rose nudging him to her desk. She pulled up a chair for him and together they sat down closely. Porter squirmed from the tightness. He blurted out, "Rose, you need a bigger desk!"

Rose looked at Porter, cracking a smile but tried hard not to show it. She began to scold him, "Could you just concentrate on this for a minute please." She was doing her best to remain stern but felt his hand reaching for her leg as he pulled her closer. The two started to giggle and Rose slapped his hand. She hollered at him, "Now cut that out! We need to do this!"

Porter had a childlike grin and said, "Yes, mother," as he made another attempt at her leg. After swatting at him again and trying to maintain the seriousness of the matter, she managed to slide her list in front of his eyes. He looked over his spectacles and saw the two words she had written. He looked sideways at her, and a confused expression came over his face. "That's it?" "No silly," she said. "That was all I could write down before I discovered that Margaret had been in my pencils. I was just about to sharpen them all when you came home." Porter pulled a fountain pen from his shirt pocket. Rose was used to writing with a quill and ink well, but it had run dry. Rose took the pen and thought for a minute. "I'd like to buy Elinore a bible, maybe some new shoes and of course, we need a fancy cake, a pretty dress for her and maybe a gold locket. Yes, that would be nice!" Before Porter knew it, Rose had a dozen things on her list, and he could almost see the steam coming from her ears as her thoughts began to run rampant.

Porter decided to get a cup of coffee as Rose continued to ramble on with her random thoughts. She hadn't even noticed he'd left his chair when she asked, "Do you think we could buy Elinore some nice writing paper and…?" Rose stopped midsentence. She sat stunned looking at the empty chair. She raised her voice, "Porter, where are you?" It was humorous to him that he had made his cup of coffee, added a splash of milk, and swirled it with a spoon and Rose hadn't even noticed he was missing. "Coming my darling," he said as a small laugh exited his nose. It was not that he didn't care, but Porter knew when Rose was brainstorming something as important as this, it was best to just stay out of the way until the dust settled.

Just then Elsie came through the door holding Delilah. She was excited. "Look Rose!" Elsie squealed. She held Delilah's tiny hands in hers placing her feet on the ground. Rose encouraged Delilah to step forward.

Rose held both her hands out to receive her youngest daughter as she leaned toward her. Rose was excited too to see her baby's first steps, but Elsie gave her fair warning. "This child is going to be running before you know it Rose, her legs are so strong! We will have our hands full; you mark my words." She covered her mouth as she said it. Elsie did not know Porter was home. Hearing the women talking, he came out of his study and nearly knocked Elsie into the wall. "Porter why are you home so early?" She was never expecting to see him at home when he bumped into her. "OH, here we go again!" he said, "I guess I'm not allowed to come home before nightfall!" He was becoming irritated with the comments about him being home. Rose saw this and said, "Porter it's not often we get to enjoy your company this early," doing her best to smooth his ruffled feathers. He wasn't really mad, but he wanted to lead them to think he was so they would stop. The children got most of the attention in the house but this time he wanted to try his hand at receiving a little from the ladies for himself. It bothered him that business was slow that day and hoped it would pick up. He soon forgot his irritations though when he could smell what Emma was cooking for the evening meal. Porter loved to eat, and Emma had become quite a cook.

Chapter 10

The Downing's were slow to rise when daylight entered the house. That is everyone except Margaret. Margaret had already gotten dressed and was outside looking for adventure and found some. She raced back into the house straight for Elinore's room. Elinore was still fast asleep, buried deep beneath her pile of blankets and pillows. Margaret was anxious to show Elinore what she had found. Margaret shook her hard and whispered her name. "Elinore, you need to see what I found!" She hissed in a hushed voice. "Come on, Elinore!" She remained determined. She continued to poke and pull at her until she got her way. Elinore had had enough. "What?" Elinore barked. Margaret's voice was but a whisper, and Elinore could barely make out her words. Margaret began to tell her secret to Elinore. She told her that she had wandered off near the Adler's field and found this strange thing made of metal hidden under some thick brush. Elinore got dressed and put her shoes on. She was curious and she knew Margaret would never give up till she went with her to view her big discovery anyway. Margaret couldn't wait for her to even get out of her bed. Excited and impatient, she pushed Elinore to move faster. As soon as Elinore was dressed and put her last shoe on Margaret grabbed her hand and pulled hard, launching her off the bed like a rocket. Together they ran from the house; Margaret barely gave Elinore enough time to close the door behind them.

They ran across the field and Elinore started to swat at the bugs they seemed to be disturbing. Both were now sweaty and red in the face as they finally reached the place Margaret was so desperate to show her. She pushed through the branches, parting them slowly to reveal what was hidden. Neither had ever seen anything like it before. There were two large copper barrels, each having long pipes leading into and down a tall column which stood beside each barrel. There was a huge stack of corn wrapped in a hessian bag between the barrels. The two sisters stood wide-eyed looking over the massive heap of metal and wondered what it could be used for. And what did corn have to do with it? They approached the barrels carefully so as not to disturb anything inside them. In the air, Elinore could detect a distinct smell. It wasn't terribly unpleasant, but she had thought she had smelled it before. Elinore bent down to look at the underbelly of this metal skeleton when something zipped past her ear. She looked at Margaret puzzled. "Did you hear something?" Margaret just shrugged her shoulders when it happened again. This time it ricocheted off a small rock just in front of where Margaret stood. That was all she had enough time to say, for in the next second, a loud sound echoed through the trees. It was the sound of dogs angrily barking.

A look of terror came over Elinore's face. Someone had been shooting at them! Her eyes captured the bullet that lay next to Margaret's shoe. Elinore knew someone was watching and had released the dogs on them that were headed their way. Elinore grasped Margaret's hand tightly and screamed at her, "Run Margaret!" The two ran like lightning toward the open field. Elinore turned briefly to see if they were being followed. Behind them were two angry Rottweilers in fast pursuit. Elinore continued running as fast as she could. She felt her heart pounding and it was becoming hard to catch her breath. Poor Margaret couldn't keep up and if it wasn't for Elinore dragging her along, she may have become a bloody treat for the vicious dogs. Elinore didn't know what to do except to keep running. It was only when all she could hear were her own footsteps, did she turn around. The dogs had stopped chasing them! Grateful, Elinore stopped running. Leaning over, she heaved onto the ground. Her heart was pounding in her chest, and it left her with a sick feeling in the pit of her stomach. She wiped her mouth with the back of her hand. She felt as if she would pass out and needed water badly. The sisters walked the rest of the way home without speaking. Both were exhausted, sweaty and very thirsty. Neither wasted any time once they arrived home. Elinore filled the sink in the bathroom near her mother's room and submerged her head into it. The cool water was exactly what she needed. She kept her head under the water until her lungs needed to breathe. Lifting her head, the water dripped off the loose strands of hair that hung around her face. She cupped her hands and drank all the water she could hold. She looked in the small mirror at herself and said, "That's it! I need a pistol soon!" Tired, she went to her room to sit when Margaret joined her seconds later. The two stared at each other. Still, they said nothing until Elinore shook her head in a side-to-side motion. Looking at Margaret, she said, "Promise me you won't go on anymore adventures off our land, promise me!" Margaret agreed and promised. Both laid back on Elinore's bed. Staring at the ceiling, Margaret admitted that she was really scared to think about what could have happened. She said, "I'm glad you were there with me! Thank you for saving me." Elinore smiled and could only let two words escape. "You're welcome."

Nightfall came quickly and after their evening meal both girls just wanted to forget what had happened earlier in the day. Each was yawning uncontrollably; they could almost hear their beds calling them. They finished their last morsels and went to their separate rooms. Elinore had already decided earlier that day to see if Carl would go with her to find the man at the seaport that Hans had told her about. That night Elinore gave a lot of thought to the seaport. Going back there still scared her. She still thought about what had happened to her there, but she wanted a pistol more than ever now. Bad enough for her to take the chance of running into that monster again.

Rose and Porter were the last ones left in the kitchen that evening. Finally, they could talk about Elinore's graduation again. Porter told Rose he had seen a beautiful dress at a shop in town. It was a lovely white cotton dress with eyelet trim and a blue satin sash. Rose told him that she thought that would be wonderful and Elinore would surely love to have it. He had also seen a beautiful gold bracelet at his favorite store and wondered if he should buy that too. Rose was delighted. She was enjoying the time with her husband alone. Just the two of them sitting by the fire in the kitchen. Rose imagined the only thing that would make the evening better was a nice cup of tea. She offered Porter a cup of his favorite Earl Grey tea. He was happy to accept. Carrying the two cups, she sat down. Porter reached out across the table for Rose's hand. He gently kissed the back of her hand and thanked her for the tea that sat steaming on the table in front of him. Porter looked at Rose, admiring her beauty. He felt grateful for the life he and Rose had created. He also wondered if he could have ever gotten this far without her. They had been married for a little over fifteen years and were blessed with three beautiful daughters. Porter was as successful as he wanted to be in his business and had even obtained most of the assets he'd always dreamed of. He was grateful that Rose had always been there to support him. Soon the two cups sat alone on the table in the darkness.

With the first rays of the morning light, Elinore's feet hit the ground. It was already warm out. Her skin was slightly damp as she began to get dressed. Hans had already been outside and was busy with the horse's grooming when he saw Elinore walking toward the horse barn. Hans entered the barn behind her to find she was already saddling up Lucky. "Where are you going today, Elinore?" he asked. "I'm going to see Carl today," answering shortly. "Alright," he said. Her tone of voice bothered him. He fired back, "Did you mention this to your mother or father?" Hans looked keenly at Elinore for details as to why she would be leaving so early. He wondered if this was the day she'd be going to look for the man he had told her about. "No, I haven't, but if they ask would you please tell them I'll be home by late afternoon." Elinore could sense Hans didn't like the way she had answered him. She tossed Hans a sheepish look with a wink. She knew she could wrap Hans around her little finger by doing that. And she was right, Hans had trouble saying no to Elinore. He had watched her grow from the little girl she once was, to the beautiful young woman she was becoming.

Elinore was always silently aware of this. She could wrap him and her father around her finger to get just about anything if she played her cards right. The fact was she thought of Hans as her second father; how lucky she was to have two. Each of them meant the world to her, but each were also very different. Her father was a bit more stoic, whereas Hans she felt was a little easier to confide in at times. Both men though, seemed to be able to fix whatever she was having a problem with. Elinore wasted no time heading out. She had a lot to do, but as she left, Hans bellowed a foreboding warning. "Be careful with yourself little one!" He hoped that Carl would not let her travel far alone. She rode quickly to see Carl, passing the market. Just then she had a thought. It might be nice to stop at the bakery and pick up some nice biscuits for Carl's mother and father. After tying Lucky to the hitching post outside the bakery she began to smell the aroma of all the breads and pastries that were just inside the doors in front of her. The air lifted a heavenly scent as she took a deep breath and sighed. She just had to have some of those tasty treats she enjoyed so much. She opened the door and gazed at all the lovely biscuits and breads that were displayed so elegantly on white paper doilies on the wall behind the register. Also displayed were a great variety of the daintiest cookies in the front case, behind glass, closest to her. Her eyes smiled. A tall woman came out of the small opening behind the counter. She had a white apron on and was covered with flour. She even had flour on her face.

She smiled at Elinore as she stood looking at all the deliciousness in front of her. The woman asked her if she would like to try one. "Oh, yes please!" Elinore accepted her offer gladly. Pointing to the Linzer cookies, she said, "These look yummy!" The woman handed her one and told her that the Linzer's were her favorite too. Elinore raised the cookie to her lips and before she knew it, she had the entire cookie in her mouth. Her cheeks puffed out at the sides. The muffled words "thank you" tried to escape through the cookie bits but were mostly unintelligible. She was feeling a little embarrassed and quickly covered her mouth with her hand. She knew her mother would have pulled her ear for being such a glutton. The woman put a dozen in a bag for her. She couldn't help but laugh and gave Elinore an extra one for the ride home. She folded it over and sharply creased it closed. Now that Elinore's mouth was empty, she could properly thank the nice lady. She paid for the cookies and left. The thought crossed her mind that the cookies may not make it to Carl's so she tucked them into her saddle bag where she couldn't get to them on the way.

Outside the bakery, there were many people, but three men caught her eye. She could hear them talking. She untied Lucky trying to listen to what they were speaking about. Because they kept glancing in her direction, she had the distinct feeling their conversation was about her and she was terribly uncomfortable. She had promised herself to always be aware of her surroundings ever since those young boys tried to rob her. Just then she overheard one of the men comment on how ugly she was. All the men seemed to find humor in the conversation of her outward appearance. Hoisting herself quickly atop Lucky, she rode off fast. Their comments had hurt her. They didn't even know her! Why would they say such mean things about her? Elinore felt tears very close to her eyes, but she'd be damned to let them make her cry. Instead, she became angry. Vowing if she were a man, she would shove her boot up their rear ends.

She began to re-focus her thoughts about getting to Carl's and traveling to the port as soon as possible. His small house was in her sight shortly. Carl saw her and raised his hand to wave to her. He was happy to see her. He had a surprise for her too. Mr. Schmidt had finished her billhook. He motioned to her to ride to the shed behind his house. He disappeared inside the shed for a moment as Lucky leaned into the bushes beside it to eat the tender green leaves. When he came out, he purposely held the billhook behind his back. Carl knew it was the perfect size and exactly what she wanted. Mr. Schmidt had even placed a beautiful garnet on the back of the wooden handle. The blade was only 15 cm. long which could easily be concealed within her apron. Elinore was not expecting to receive anything from him, so she was quick to get right down to business in what she had on her mind. The minute he came out, she began by asking, "Carl, I need you to come to the seaport with me today. Will you?" she asked. "Of course, I will," he said, "But first I have something for you." Elinore was excited now. "Really, what is it?" she asked looking curiously at him. He handed the billhook to her. "Wow! Carl, this is exactly what I had pictured, it's perfect!" She held it up to look at it more closely and thanked him. She leaned down to kiss him and partially lost her balance. They both began to laugh, and Carl pushed her back up onto the horse again to steady her.

She took the small bag of cookies from her saddle bag and handed it to him. "What's this?" he asked while slowly opening the bag. Elinore replied, "I brought your mother and father some biscuits." Reaching in to treat himself to one, he held up his index finger and ran inside his home. Quickly returning, Elinore and Carl were soon on their way to the seaport and pushed the horses to get there fast. They made it to Gus's, and she was happy to see his familiar face. He came out from behind his barn carrying a few apples. Gus was also happy to see her. It had been some time since the last time he had seen her, and he let out the biggest toothless smile she had ever seen. Elinore introduced Carl to Gus, as he took the reins of both horses offering an apple to each of them. She and Carl walked hand in hand toward the boats. They passed the cheese shop, and she began to remember vividly what had happened to her there, not quite a year ago. Little snippets played in her mind as she started to recall that awful fisherman who literally changed her personality forever. Next, she found herself walking past the pub where the worst of that day from the past had occurred. She held Carl's hand tightly. She closed her eyes and looked away, trying to push it out of her mind. They continued to walk on.

Elinore began to explain her reason for coming to the port and what Hans had secretly told her. Carl knew how important this was to her and understood why. They continued their search for the man when Elinore saw a woman selling cosmetics from a small cart. She remembered what those miserable men outside the bakery had said and soon found herself handing money to the woman for some things that promised to make her prettier. She tucked the small bits into her apron, and they moved on in a hurry. This was only her second time to the port, and it seemed even busier than the first time, and it was a lot warmer too. The nice woman whom she had bought apples from the first time was still there. Elinore waved to her, but she did not return her gesture. Elinore wondered if she even remembered her.

It was then that she noticed a man walking in their direction. His gait was odd, and he seemed to have to flex his hip to get his one leg to move forward. He also appeared to have trouble navigating the uneven dirt surface. As the man came closer, Elinore noticed he was only able to maintain stability from a wooden leg that supported him. It was only in a few more steps did she notice the man's face. Her hand clutched Carl's hand even tighter and her blood ran cold. She wanted to run but couldn't. Frozen in fear, it was the same fisherman, but he looked half of the man he did the first time she saw him! She wondered if he recognized her. His eyes were fixed on her as he passed them. She desperately wanted to turn to see if he was still looking at her but didn't dare. As he passed them, she now was focused on the thumping sound of his wooden leg. The corners of her mouth began to turn upward. Her final thoughts were that of righteous indignation. He had gotten what he deserved for what he had done to her. Elinore felt that maybe now it might be possible for her to let go of that miserable memory that haunted her. She had been still angry that someone could get away with doing something like that to her without consequence, but now that she saw him struggling with the wooden peg leg, she somehow felt vindicated and free from the guilt that gripped her. She immediately thought of her father's words, "What comes around, goes around." She secretly wished that she could have seen the day that his fate came to even the score with him.

Carl did not know what distracted Elinore, but he quickly reminded her of the position of the sun, and that they needed to move faster. Finally, they reached the edge of the port. There sat a man on a small wooden chair leaning against a large tree near the last building in the port, just as Hans had told her. Elinore still wasn't sure this was the man she was looking for, so she approached him slowly. Placing Carl between herself and the man, she began a conversation with Carl loud enough so that the man could overhear her. She began to confide in him her made up tale about being the victim of a robbery and even managed to shed a few crocodile tears. Carl leaned in to hug her. Playing along, he said, "Don't worry, it'll be okay." She broke away from his embrace, now posing anger. "If I had a pistol, I would've put some holes in them!" Elinore was deliberately speaking loud enough to see if the man would take the bait.

The man stood, but kept his shoulders hunched over, concealing his face. Soon the man called out to Carl. "Come here young man," beckoning him. Carl was nervous and he told Elinore to wait there for him. He went to speak to the man. His palms were sweaty, and he hoped he wouldn't be shot himself. Elinore desperately wanted to go with him but did as she was told. The man asked him what type of pistol he was looking for. From just behind the tree, he pulled out a small black bag. Reaching inside, he pulled out a browning handgun, a colt and a luger. He explained briefly how much power each had, and he showed him the ample supply of ammunition he had to go with the purchase. Carl shook his head. "No, no." "I think those are too big for my lady. Do you have something small enough for her to hide within her clothing?" The man's right eyebrow was raised, and Carl could see he was thinking hard. The man told him that he might just have what he wanted and went to the other saddle bag that was harnessed to the opposite side of his horse's back. Reaching deep into his bag he pulled out a very small ladies' pistol. It was handmade and probably wouldn't kill someone from a distance but surely could from point blank range, he explained. The man then offered, for just a few marks more, he could purchase a beautiful silver tin that contained 24 extra bullets to go with it. It had pearls along the handle for an extra firm grip and he thought Elinore would be extremely pleased to have it. Carl bought the pistol and bullets, hurrying back to where Elinore stood waiting. Careful not to let anyone see them, he quickly showed it to Elinore. She was very happy when she saw it! Carl was just happy to be finished with the deal. He then turned to nod a farewell to the man but to his surprise, he had already disappeared. Gone without a trace. Carl took Elinore's hand and led her quickly back to where they had left their horses. He did not want to answer any questions as to where they went from Hans or Porter if they raised suspicions by getting back late. Elinore knew her mother and father would be looking for her and didn't want any trouble either. The ride home seemed shorter to them than the one going there. The horses ran fast and pushed clouds of dust up into the air. They rode side by side and enjoyed the company of one another.

Porter was home early again from work and he and Rose had wrapped her gold bracelet with her graduation dress into a pretty package while she was gone. He could see them coming home through his binoculars from the back door. Alerting Rose so she could be ready, together they waited. He watched the two bring their horses into the barn. Once inside the barn Carl showed Elinore the pistol and how it worked. They gave the horses feed and water. They stole a few kisses from each other and headed off to the house. Porter opened the door when they were within a few steps of the doorway. "And where have you two been?" he bellowed with piercing eyes looking just above his glasses. Dumbfounded, Elinore's mind raced to come up with something. Elinore began to explain she had been with Carl all day, when Porter interrupted. Looking at Carl, he said, "I hope you plan to stay for dinner, Emma made us a tasty meal." Carl really wanted to get home but was afraid to refuse, so quickly he agreed to stay.

Entering the kitchen, Carl and Elinore found everyone inside. Emma and Elsie were setting the table and preparing the delicious meal to be served. The mouthwatering delectable smells made Carl's stomach rumble and he was glad he had decided to stay. Elinore was a little confused by the large gathering in the kitchen. She glanced at Hans, and he returned with a wink. Soon they were all sharing conversation and devouring the savory meal in front of them. Rose was thumping in anticipation throughout the entire meal. Finally, she had fulfilled her promise to have Carl for dinner but more importantly she was anxious to see what Elinore thought of her new graduation dress. Impatient for the cleaning up process to begin, Rose began to take pieces off the table that weren't being used anymore. Porter called her out on her behavior, and asked what the rush was. Rose looked crossly at him, but then changed her expression to a smile. He knew what she was being impatient about, but he couldn't resist poking fun at her.

Elinore had barely finished eating when Rose suddenly left the room. Elinore now knew for sure something was going on. Her mother and father were acting so peculiarly, and they were always horrible about keeping secrets. Carl was still busy burying his head in a second helping of food which delighted Porter. He had never had a son of his own and was enjoying watching how much he could eat. Rose placed the package she was holding on the table in front of Elinore. Elinore's eyes widened, looking at the beautifully wrapped package her mother had bestowed upon her. "What is this for?" Elinore asked. "You will be graduating in a few weeks; it is a gift from me and papa for all your hard work darling," Rose answered. Elinore opened the gift to reveal the most beautiful dress she had ever seen. Quickly she stood to give her mother a peck on the cheek. She squeezed her father and rubbed his head. Her father swatted at her hand and laughed. Then he told her that she had missed one. Wrinkles appeared on her forehead between her eyebrows. "Huh?" Porter pointed to the small package still on the table. She picked it up and started to shake it. "What is it?" she asked her father. He just grinned and motioned for her to open it. The brilliant gold bracelet sparkled as she placed it on her wrist. "It fits perfect!" she exclaimed.

Margaret admired the bracelet and commented on how beautiful it was. Elinore was grateful for her gifts and felt blessed to have such a wonderful loving family. She held the dress up in front of her and twirled around the table with it. She looked at Hans and asked him if he liked the dress too. Hans told her she surely would be the prettiest girl at graduation. That made Elinore happy. Elinore ran to her room with her new dress to hang it in her closet. She wanted it to stay as pristine as it was. A wrinkled dress would not be as nice, she thought. She also thought about the cosmetics she purchased while she was at the port. She needed to learn how to apply makeup. She had never had any before and her mother never wore much. She wondered what Carl would think when he saw her with makeup on. She was deep in thought when Rose entered her room.

Elinore didn't notice Rose watching her as she put her dress away. Rose was remembering the days when Elinore was a small child. She felt proud of her oldest daughter. It was a great accomplishment, graduating school. Most children only made it to the eighth grade because most families needed help on their farms. Rose and her girls were very fortunate that Porter was in the textile business, and it was quite lucrative. Her family was very lucky they did not have to work hard. As Elinore turned to return to the kitchen, she saw her mother watching her. Rose was happy. She asked Elinore if she liked her new dress. "Oh yes mother!" Elinore declared. Rose told her that her father had picked it out for her. Rose agreed with her that it was indeed a very pretty dress. Rose put her arm around Elinore and pulled her in tightly for a hug. They walked together back to the kitchen to join everyone still there.

Elsie, Emma, and Hans were getting ready to leave and Carl, Porter and Margaret were still seated, chatting about what he would do after graduation. He told Porter that he planned to stay with Mr. Schmidt and become a partner in his business. Mr. Schmidt had no children of his own, so he had offered him the partnership. Porter was glad to hear he had a plan. If the relationship between him and his daughter continued, at least he wouldn't have to worry where Carl would be working. He would be able to support the two of them.

Carl rubbed his belly. He told Porter he was stuffed like a chicken. Carl knew it would be difficult to climb onto his horse and get home with his huge stomach, but he really wanted to be home before the complete darkness of the evening set in. He thanked the Downing's for the lovely meal and began to put his jacket on. Elinore was not about to let him leave without getting one last kiss from him. She followed him to the barn. She watched him closely. Elinore was becoming aware that her feelings for Carl were not those of a child anymore. Carl knew she was behind him and when he turned around, he found her looking very sultry. Carl had always felt Elinore had hidden passion. It was what had attracted him to her. Elinore twirled her hair around her fingers and began to bite the edge of her lip in a sensual way. Carl put the reins of his horse down and reached for her. Pulling her closer fast, he began to kiss her neck. He could feel her heat against his lips, and he could smell her familiar powdery scent. Elinore lifted her chin to invite more of his kisses. They were creating a sexual tension that was hard to ignore. Carl was feeling a warmth inside himself growing. Their passion was becoming intense between them, and Carl could clearly feel that in his soul. He entered a state of trance as he watched her movements. He was hungry for her and was enamored by her in just the few seconds that they had stepped into the barn. He clutched her tightly and they both knew their passion was what sparked the birth of their budding love story.

Elinore exhaled deeply, knowing it was not the time or place for them to continue, yet she couldn't help herself. She was feasting on his masculine essence. They both did not want to part and felt it difficult to pull away from one another. His eye caught a loose string at the top of her bodice which he couldn't resist. Quickly he plucked the string between his finger and thumb exposing her bosom. Carl mounted his horse when he felt Elinore's return fire. She gave him a hard swat on his bottom. With an impish grin, he leaned down to kiss her one more time. They both laughed with the release of some of their tension. Elinore closed the barn door behind them and waved farewell. The wind whipped at her hair. She stood there noticing the change in the weather as Carl trotted off, fading from her view. She worried about her handsome man and hoped he would make it home safely.

Nightfall came and so did a hard, heavy rain. The storm had come quickly without warning. Margaret hated storms, and as Elinore passed her room, she could see Margaret had dived under her pile of blankets, burying her head. Elinore liked storms. She loved the beauty of the rain bouncing off her windowpane and catching an occasional lightning bolt as it streaked across the sky. She could hear the rain against the roof above her head. Elinore crawled into her bed and the sound of the rain made her sleepy. It had been a fantastic day and Elinore slowly began to drift off to sleep when she was awoken by a loud banging noise. With sleep still in her eyes, she dragged herself from her bed to see what the noise was. Suddenly a bolt of lightning lit the sky brightly. Elinore could see that the barn door had blown open and was flapping wildly in the wind against the barn. She raced to put her riding boots on and ran outside. The cold rain hit her face furiously as she ran. Her nightclothes were now stuck to her body as she ran toward the barn. She reached to close the heavy wooden door and noticed Lucky was not in his stall. Terrified, she entered the barn to look for him but could immediately see he was missing. Panicked, Elinore ran from the barn screaming Lucky's name. She ran crying at the thought of losing Lucky. The rain and wind whipped against her body as she ran frantically. She called out his name over and over, but the howling of the wind muffled her voice. The thought of losing her beloved horse crippled her as her tears mixed with the driving rain. She ran as fast as she could to the pond hoping he would be there. Lightning and thunder crashed around her. Then she scanned the field beside the pond, but Lucky was nowhere to be found.

Hans heard her voice howling Lucky's name and came to her calls. Carrying his lantern, he pulled her closer to him to shelter her from the driving rain. Elinore's sharp shrieking calls told him unmistakably that Lucky was missing. They both continued wandering about trying to find the horse. A crack of lightning once again lit the sky up. Hans thought he saw a shadow move with that last brilliant flash of light. Elinore huddled under Hans's large frame and together they ran through the darkness with only the light from his lantern. Hans bellowed Lucky's name and they both ran to the largest field where he only kept the bull. Finally, they found him! Lucky stood motionless, staring at them. Hans always carried a rope and placed it gently over the horse's neck to lead him back to the barn. Elinore was soundless as she stared at Hans. Again, Hans had come to her rescue. Feeling relieved her horse was home and safe, she expressed her appreciation to Hans with a big hug around his neck. Hans patted her on the shoulder and said, "Come on, let's get you inside to dry off." Hans delivered her to her door and headed back to his home.

Inside Porter was waiting. He watched her as she entered the kitchen, soaked to the bone. He wrapped a blanket around her and began to rub her, wiping the wetness from her skin. Standing by the fire, the heat felt good to Elinore. Porter smiled at his daughter. "Well done, Elinore," he said. "Thank you, father, but it was really Hans who was the hero." Elinore just wanted to get out of the clothes that were still stuck to her. She pecked a kiss to her father and went straight to her room. "What a night," she said under her breath on her way. Now that she was warmer and dry, Elinore climbed back into her bed and began to think about her graduation which would be in only a few days, and it made her nervous.

Chapter 11

Elinore's big day had arrived. Today she would be graduating. It would be a good day and a bad day. Elinore had many things going through her mind. She had given a lot of thought as to what she would do after graduation with her life. Now she would have to enter the work field. She would be considered a full-grown adult. She also wondered what would become of all the friendships she had made in school. She had many friends in school, but now wondered how often she would still see them once she started working. For that matter, she knew her time with Carl would be shortened as well. Elinore was, however, looking forward to making her own money and being free to buy what she wanted instead of asking her father or Carl for money. That was important to her.

All the students came to the schoolhouse early on graduation day. Everyone wore their finest clothing. Miss Ilse had decorated the schoolhouse beautifully. She even had made a banner that hung over the doorway that had the words "Congratulations" on it. She had written on parchment paper each student's name, grade and year. Each was tied with a thin white ribbon. All the parents of each child came a little later and were seated in rows near the doorway of the schoolroom. Miss Ilse had to borrow some chairs to make sure everyone would have a seat. She prepared a lovely speech and called each student by name to the front of the room to give them their own graduation certificate. She shook the boy's hands firmly and hugged the stuffing out of each of the girls. She was so proud of her students. A huge community gathering had been planned to follow. Each of the families had brought a dish of food and the celebration was brilliant. Rose and Porter couldn't have been prouder of their daughter. Elinore passed with very good academic skills. Each student exited the schoolroom, passing the parents through the open doors and down the stairs. One by one each followed the other until all of them stood facing the schoolhouse outside. Then in a flurry, all the parents hurried out and many hugs and kisses started.

Elinore had her eyes on Carl the entire time. She worked her way through the crowd to him. Excited and happy, she stood in front of him to congratulate him. She wondered if he would notice the makeup she had applied to her face for their important day. Carl complimented Elinore on how pretty her dress was. Then he asked her if she was thirsty. "Thirsty?" she asked. "Why would you ask such a strange question at this moment?" Carl looked at Elinore and said, "Well your cheeks look a little red, I thought maybe the heat might be getting to you." Elinore's beautiful smile disappeared, and a dark glare from her eyes pierced him. He had seen this look before and knew nothing good would come from it, yet he was still confused. Elinore blurted out, "You can be dumb as a rock sometimes Carl!" Carl honestly had no idea why she had said that to him, but he did know she was angry. She promptly informed him, "I wore this stupid makeup for you today, the bits I bought at the port," pointing to her cheeks. Elinore took another chance and began to bat her eyes at Carl, making a second attempt to receive a compliment from him. Carl looked strangely at her again. He was about to unknowingly, make the same mistake twice. Innocently he asked if she had something in her eye. Furious, Elinore stomped hard on his foot with a huff and stormed off to her mother and father who were seated on blankets, among the scattered other parents.

Carl's foot was throbbing, and he limped his way over to his waiting mother and father. They too, were proud of their son and his accomplishments. His mother hugged him tightly and told him how happy he had made her. His father asked him to introduce them to Elinore's parents. They had become accustomed to having Elinore around but had never met her parents. Carl did not like to deny his parents, even though he knew it probably was not the best time. He granted his father's wish anyway. Cautiously, he wove his way through the crowd to where Elinore sat with her parents. They were all enjoying some pie and lemonade. Carl did not want to wear Elinore's lemonade, so he purposely approached the corner of the blanket where Rose sat. Carl's parents were delighted to finally meet Rose and Porter. Soon they were all chatting and laughing, enjoying the warm summer breeze the day had brought.

Carl decided to exit while the getting was good, but Elinore was on to him. She followed right behind him. Carl could hear her footsteps close behind him and when she tapped him on the shoulder, he closed his eyes preparing for an incoming sock to the jaw. He realized inevitably; he would have to face her. Slowly, he turned partially shielding himself from the incoming fist attack but was surprised to see Elinore just standing there. The words "I'm sorry," escaped from his mouth before he could even think about a plan. Elinore continued to stand in front of him with a blank expression on her face. Then she said, "I wore that dumb makeup for you, stupid, but you didn't even notice!" Carl hadn't meant to hurt her feelings. He didn't know what to say. But saying nothing wasn't going to go over well either so he simply told her, "Elinore, you are beautiful to me even if you were wearing nothing at all." Elinore was a little embarrassed. Carl had already looked around to make sure no one was close enough to overhear him speak to her in such a manner. He leaned in to kiss her cheek and quickly made his way back to his parents. Now, he was the one grinning big at his triumphant win in the match with Elinore. Carl had played his cards right and escaped Elinore's wrath with no injuries except his bruised foot which his boosted ego was making up for.

The day ended well with a fantastic evening meal of pork and sauerkraut with applesauce and mashed potatoes presented by Emma. Rose and Porter lay in their bed that night snuggled tightly together. They spoke in hushed whispers, careful not to wake Delilah. They spoke about where they thought Elinore would go from this day forward and hoped their oldest daughter would be successful. Both yawned at each other trying to stay awake but soon complete silence was the only sound that could be heard in the Downing household.

With each new day that passed, Elinore knew she needed to do something with her life. She soon found herself sitting at her favorite thinking spot. The pond offered some quiet time so that Elinore could sort things out without being bothered. She watched the dragonflies buzz around her, and a few turtles pop up out of the water. She tossed a few stones into the pond, but it didn't make her feel as good as it did when she was younger. It was just then she noticed Hans had sat down beside her. He said, "I haven't seen you down here in a while, little one. Is everything okay?" Elinore thought she would take a chance and talk with him about her concerns. She began by asking Hans what he thought she would be good at when she went looking for work. He really didn't know what to say to her. He knew she loved cookies and suggested maybe she could see if the bakery needed help. Elinore's right eyebrow raised. She started to laugh. She looked at him with a stink eye and said, "I wouldn't last there a minute! I'd probably eat more than I sold!" He looked down at the water's edge and laughed too. "You're probably right." He had to agree with her. He went on to say, "If there's one thing I've learned Elinore, you need to be able to support yourself alone. You shouldn't depend on anyone." He paused and looked very serious for a moment as he continued. "Like Carl." That wouldn't be good, he told her.

Elinore thought about his words carefully. She thanked him and told him she understood. Elinore sat with her open palm under her chin while her forefinger tapped against her lips as if it would somehow give her the answer she was looking for as to what to do. She decided it might be a good idea to go into town to each shop along the way to ask if anyone needed help to see what would turn up. And so, with the next opportunity she would plan to be on the hunt for work. That night, however, Elinore did not sleep well. Her mind was bouncing around. Elinore lay in her bed staring at the ceiling. She was frightened about the uncertainty of what her eminent future would hold. She knew she did not want to be a teacher. Something many unmarried women did. She had little patience for younger children, except for her sister Margaret. She knew Hans's suggestion of the bakery was not really something she could do either. Surely, if she did that, she would be at least two people's weight within a week. The local general store might suit her better. It was something to consider but it didn't excite her much. She was able to cook and clean but wasn't sure how she could use that to earn herself a weekly wage. She knew she could ride a horse well, but that too was not really a way for a woman to earn money. Her options were few unless she went to Berlin or Munich. There, she could make a lot of money but that was a long ride. In fact, she would probably spend more time traveling back and forth than working. And that would leave no time for anything else. Elinore's eyes were finally becoming very heavy. She pulled her blankets up to her chin. The warmth of the blanket began to make her sleepy and soon she was sound asleep.

Margaret had a good night's rest, and she was also happy because it was the beginning of summer break from school. Her room slowly became illuminated as the sky outside turned a little lighter. She felt full of energy. Margaret sat up and put her feet on the floor. The house was still quiet, but Margaret was feeling devilish. She slithered to her sister's room, hugging the wall tightly until she came to her doorway. She pressed her ear against the door and could hear only a small snorting noise which told her that her sister was still fast asleep. A plan was hatching inside her mind and a crooked smile came across her face. Margaret covered her mouth as a laugh started to erupt from within her. She began to run her fingers through her hair and tried to feel for one of the longest hairs on her head that she could find. She carefully followed it to the root and plucked it from her scalp. Her laugh escaped her mouth in a hissing sound. She placed her hand against the door and slowly pushed it open. Being extra careful not to make the door squeak, she tiptoed slowly toward Elinore's bed.

Holding the long strand of hair over Elinore's exposed face, she dragged the hair across it. Elinore, still asleep, swatted at the hair as if it were a bug. Margaret waited a few seconds and ran the hair across her face again. This time though, she ran it across her nose. Because Elinore was deep asleep, she didn't know Margaret was the cause of her irritation. Suddenly,

Elinore swung at something that was crawling across her. Elinore landed a good, solid punch to her own eye. The violent punch brought her fully awake and the side of her nose and eye throbbed with pain. As she opened her eyes in the dimly lit room, she could see a shadow standing in the corner. It was her sister, who was barely able to contain herself. Elinore jumped out of her bed and bolted toward Margaret. She plowed her down at the waist and they both landed on the floor. Margaret was still giggling, which angered Elinore even more. Elinore began to pull at Margaret's hair, hitting her body, and the two rolled over each other on the floor. Margaret shouted at Elinore to stop. In all the commotion, they had woken Porter and his heavy steps were coming toward Elinore's room. Both girls knew they were in big trouble now. Porter burst through the door shouting, "What is going on in here?" Elinore and Margaret quickly separated without speaking a word. Porter told Margaret to go back to her room on the double. His tone of voice was harsh, and he meant business.

Porter closed Elinore's door and as he made his way back to his bed down the darkened hallway, he uttered the words, "It's just too early for this crap!" He slipped back into his warm bed and snuggled up to Rose's back.

Margaret was still laughing. Elinore and her grandfather were Margaret's two favorite victims for playing her pranks on. She had had herself some brilliant fun to start the new day with. Elinore wiped her nose with the back of her hand and a few spots of blood appeared there. Her eye throbbed terribly. She entered the bathroom to see how serious the pain she had was. When she looked in the small mirror, it was apparent she had given herself a black eye. "Oh, that's great!" she said out loud. "This will really help me find some work!" Now, she was furious with Margaret. She knew it would take at least another week before she could look for work. She would have to wait for the black eye to fade.

Porter was already mad because he had been woken up before the sun even rose. Not able to go back to sleep, Porter decided to have his first cup of coffee for the morning alone. He could hear Margaret and Elinore shuffling about, and he knew it was only a matter of time before they would be in the kitchen too, looking for something to eat. Porter's face became contorted with the idea of the girls coming and how their chatter would likely raise Delilah and Rose from their peaceful sleep. Then he would be surrounded by six women, including Elsie and Emma. Within a few minutes, that was exactly what happened. Delilah had learned how to run and now was running everywhere she went. As a matter of fact, he couldn't remember her ever walking. Rose sat at the table across from Porter, still sleepy.

Elinore poured herself and her mother a cup of coffee. As Elinore took her first sip, Porter noticed her eye. He stood up to have a closer look. In response, Elinore quickly pretended to see something on the floor and started to bend to avoid her father's gaze. But there was no escape. Porter grabbed her face with his thick strong hand and raised her chin, inspecting her face. He saw the discoloration. He looked at Margaret with dark eyes. She could see he was not to be played with. "Look what you have done!" Porter shouted. "I was just playing a joke," Margaret answered, defending herself. "Some joke!" Porter fired back. "You need to be more careful Margaret!" Porter scolded her. "Next time you will not be allowed to go outside for an entire week! Do you understand me?" he said, raising his voice. Margaret sat with her head down. The day had started out being very funny, but now she wished she could fade into the walls.

Porter usually enjoyed being around his family, but today he was feeling stressed. He picked up his cup and opened the back door. Rose could feel the hot air come through the doorway as he left the house. It crossed her mind that it would be a good day to do some of the laundry that was piling up. The clothing would dry quickly on the line. Porter found himself standing in front of Hans's home. He hesitated for a moment before he knocked. He wasn't sure exactly how to explain his worries to him and he had kept them inside his head until now. It was early enough, so he was pretty sure Hans had not left to tend to his daily scheduled routine.

Hans had many things to do in a day's work. Three calves had been born since Porter had first bought the cows for Hans. In addition, he cared for the three horses Porter owned, and that kept Hans busy most of the day, every day. Porter stepped up onto the porch, staring at the door in front of him. Just as he started to turn to go back down the stairs, Hans opened the door. "Morning Porter," Hans said cheerfully. "Yes, it's morning alright Hans. I'd like to talk with you if you have a minute?" Porter said, looking troubled. Hans was concerned and wondered what was bothering Porter. Everything seemed to be going very well for him. Hans asked Porter what was on his mind. He began to tell Hans that he had heard rumors that the Prussian Army's newest General Staff needed to pass budgets, but they had no power over the conduct of the government. It made no sense to Porter, he explained to Hans, but what he did know was that their need for uniforms was becoming fewer and fewer. He went on to say his orders over the last month were less than half of the prior month. Hans asked Porter if he wanted to sell off some of the cattle. Porter adamantly replied he did not. He told Hans that it may be their only means of survival at some point. He was deadly serious, and Hans was rocked by Porter's statement. Hans had to ask if it was really that dire. Porter said, "I think it is Hans, and I am worried. It doesn't look good, but please don't mention it to Rose, I haven't told her yet." Hans told him that his secret was safe with him and assured Porter that whatever he needed, he would be there to help. Porter was strained as he walked back to his house; he was genuinely worried that things could get worse.

Inside the kitchen, everything had settled down. Porter went straight for the coffee. He filled his empty cup with more brew and without hesitation, he moved to his study, closing the door behind him without a word. Rose was still cross with the girls for irritating Porter. With her lips pursed she sat quietly, across from the girls at the table. Margaret could feel her mother's angry stare making a hole right through her, but Elinore was feeling much like the victim. Her parents were angry with her too and she didn't think that was fair. Her nose and eye were sore and now she would have to wait to look for work because of Margaret. How could any of that be her fault, she reasoned with herself. Elinore was angry and felt as if she could explode.

She decided to excuse herself and went to the barn. She unlatched the heavy wooden door, and it squeaked as she struggled to push it open. The doors had become swollen from all the recent rain. Elinore entered the barn. She could smell the horse's damp feed. She walked toward Lucky. Briefly she glanced at the long wooden bench that she and Carl had their first kisses on. Her mind filled with the memories of that day which now seemed like a long time ago. For a moment, everything faded away into a vignette of only herself and Carl surrounded by a fog that shaded off gradually into the surrounding ground. That moment, however, was broken within a few precious seconds by Lucky who was demanding her attention. Elinore laughed as she reached to stroke Lucky's muzzle. "I'm sorry I have no apple for you, but I can give you some nice hay," she said to the horse. The horse kicked its head up as if he were answering her and he stomped his hooves. Elinore decided it might be nice to go for a ride, just her and Lucky. Elinore saddled him up and hoisted herself atop him. They bolted out of the barn fast. The wind whipped through Elinore's hair and Lucky's mane whipped at her face. Staying close to Lucky's thick neck, they thundered across the large field. She could hear the horse's heavy breathing. He was a massive horse with a huge chest. Lucky could run faster than any horse Elinore knew. The speed invigorated her. She felt free from any inhibitions. Elinore pushed Lucky to go faster. Finally, they reached the small stream that ran between her father's field and the Adler's land. Lucky was drenched with sweat and thirsty. Seeing the water, he stretched his long thick neck downward to sip the cool water that encircled his nostrils. Elinore lowered herself on to the ground and took a sip of water too. She took a deep breath into her lungs and stretched her back, raising her arms as if to reach for the sun. She stood there in deep thought. Elinore looked at the blades of long grass that surrounded her. They seemed to dance in the gentle breeze, and she lost herself in the moment. No thoughts entered her mind at all. Only her and her horse standing freely in the open air. She felt a welcome peace which made her smile. She looked at Lucky again and kissed his face. Going back home was the last thing she wanted to do, but knew it wasn't an option, so she started home.

This time though, she and Lucky took their time going back. Elinore was feeling a little better by the time she reached home. When she opened the door and entered the kitchen, Delilah ran right for her knees. Elinore picked her up and swung her up over her head. Delilah giggled with joy and begged for her to do it again. Elinore was happy to do that. She loved Delilah's laugh. It was infectious and made her laugh as well. Placing her on the floor again, Delilah took off running down the hallway toward the bedrooms, looking back to see if Elinore was chasing her. Elinore caught her eye and a frantic chase ensued. Delilah was running as fast as her little legs would carry her. Squealing loudly, she continued to run, all the while, still looking behind to see if Elinore was still giving chase. At the end of the hall when there was no place else to run, Elinore said in a raised voice, "Aha, I got you now!" Elinore tussled her to the floor and began tickling Delilah. She was laughing hard and curled up into a ball on the floor, but the minute Elinore stopped, she begged for more.

Finally, Delilah gave up, releasing Elinore's attention, to find her mother for something to drink. Elinore sat down at her desk in her room. She pulled the top drawer open where she had placed her newly purchased cosmetics. Soon she found herself staring into her small handheld mirror inspecting her eye. It didn't seem to look so bad to her now. She tried to cover it with a lighter shade of makeup. She began to blot the deep bruise until it looked a normal color again. "Amazing!" she said to herself as she smiled in the mirror. Maybe she wouldn't need to wait so long to look for work. Elinore was determined. Only three more days passed, and Elinore found herself sitting at her desk again with her mirror in hand. An unusual thought crossed her mind. She could hear the words, "Let's try this again." Looking closely at her eye, her bruise now was turning a lovely shade of greenish yellow. She patted the cosmetics onto her face trying to cover the dark discoloration again.

"That looks better." Her thoughts seemed to be coming out of nowhere. As if someone were speaking to her from another place. Confused, she put her mirror down and went to search for her mother. Of course, she knew where that would most likely be. She went straight to the kitchen to find her mother and as she suspected, Rose was there sipping a cup of coffee with Delilah on her lap. Elinore apprehensively sat across from Rose. Elsie was washing dishes and asked Elinore if she wanted anything to drink. Elinore made sure to lock eyes with Rose and Elsie, but neither seemed to notice her concealed bruised eye. She asked her mother if she thought she would be able to find work in their small town.

Rose replied, "All you can do is try, darling." Rose didn't know if anyone in town needed help, but she didn't want to discourage her daughter. It was a rite of passage for her leading to adulthood. Rose encouraged her to try their town first and then asked Elinore what she thought about something being available in Carl's town. That gave Elinore a little more hope. She had felt so boxed in by her own town. There weren't many options there. Where Carl lived, there were a lot more shopkeepers which came with many more opportunities. Elinore could feel it in her bones that she would be successful in her search there.

A few more days had passed when Elinore couldn't wait another minute. She carefully picked out her nicest dress and went searching for work. She stopped at every shop in town including Walter's pub. Walter had just hired a boy and so did Marie at the edge of town where her children's store was located. Even the general store didn't need any help. She was determined not to let that discourage her. Before she started home, Elinore stopped at the bakery to buy a few biscuits. She felt she deserved a reward for being so diligent in her search. Her nose filled with the luscious smells again. It was surely her favorite shop. Elinore made sure to get a few of Margaret's favorites and enough to share with everyone. It had been a long day and Elinore was worn out.

As the sun set, the sky was a brilliant combination of a beautiful orange and fiery red color. Elinore enjoyed the view, but it left her feeling somewhat melancholy. She was disappointed, but not crushed by not finding employment. At a slow pace, she and Lucky headed down the same path they had taken earlier that day. Elinore was accustomed to talking over what was on her mind with Lucky and this day was no different. When Elinore finally arrived home, Hans was in the barn. He lent her his hand as she got off Lucky's back. He took the reins from her as he always did and asked, "How did you do today?" Elinore tipped her head to the side and rolled her eyes. "Not so good," she replied.

With her shoulders hunched over, she dragged herself to the house. No one was in the kitchen, which slightly surprised her. There was always someone in the kitchen. She placed the bag of biscuits in the middle of the table, knowing if Margaret found them first, there would be none for anyone else. It made her smile. Elinore was sore from the long day and just wanted to soak in the tub to relax and get some of the dirt off her face. Then the thought occurred to her she might need to take a break the next day. It was a lot harder than she ever imagined it would be, looking for work. It surely wasn't for sissies! Suddenly she could hear Margaret shrieking with joy from the bathroom and knew her biscuits had been discovered, which brought another smile to her face. The simplest things made Margaret so happy. Elinore loved that about her sister. Elinore could also hear the hot sudsy water calling her as she added the last bit of hot water to the tub. The tub was finally filled, and she dipped her toe in to check the temperature. "Ah perfect," she said to herself. Sitting down, the water encircled her. She could feel all her muscles relaxing. She closed her eyes, resting her head against the tub. Her mother's scented soap floated across the water, touching her chin that was now just barely above the surface. Elinore closed her eyes again and enjoyed the moment.

And it was just one moment when Margaret came bursting through the bathroom door. Elinore shouted, "I'm taking a bath Margaret! Get out!" But Margaret didn't care. She had something on her mind. She sat on the toilet seat with her elbow on her knee and her hand resting under her chin. Elinore was becoming irritated and tried to hide her nakedness beneath the suds. "What do you want?" Elinore shouted. Margaret tapped her finger against her lip. A mischievous child-like look came over her. "Mother said I could have Gertrude over tomorrow." Elinore was about to explode. The warmth of her water was fading fast, and she was losing her patience even faster. She replied, "So?" With a drawn out "wellll...," Margaret continued, "Could I give your biscuits to Gertrude?" Elinore just wanted some peace and quiet, so she snapped back at her with a quick response. "Sure, now get out!"

Margaret jumped off the toilet seat shouting, "Okay, thank you Elinore!" She slammed the door behind her and now Elinore was happy to be left alone. She could hear her sister scramble off toward the kitchen to retrieve her goodies before anyone else could help themselves to them. Elinore let out a sigh of relief and sunk her head below the surface of the water. The water was already feeling cooler. It surely seemed she had only been in there a few minutes but in fact it had already been half an hour. And when she looked at her fingers, they were all pruned, so she knew she would have to get out of the water shortly. The time had gone so fast and with Margaret's interruption, it went even quicker. She gave herself a final rinse and dried herself with the fresh towel Elsie had put in the bathroom. She made her way to her room and collapsed onto her bed. Looking up at the ceiling, she thought that maybe right after they had their evening meal, she might just fall asleep before her head hit the pillow. Maybe tomorrow she would have time to see Carl.

It was only seconds from that thought when she heard her mother calling everyone to the table. The food was ready to be served. Elinore was hungry, but her legs were still sore. She dragged herself to the table and the rest of the evening was a blur to her until she was awoken again. Margaret had not learned her lesson. In the darkness, Margaret was up to no good. Slowly, she approached Elinore's bedroom holding a small candle just under her chin to give herself a ghostly effect. As she neared Elinore's bed, Margaret's giggles began to explode from her mouth once again. Try as she did, she couldn't avoid the temptation of playing another prank on an unprepared victim. Creeping closer, Margaret began making ghostly noises. Elinore was resting solidly. Her deep sleep, however, was interrupted by sounds as Margaret moved closer to her. Moving her blankets to see what had broken her sleep, her eyes began to focus on the small glow. Elinore was in a state of confusion. She called out, "Who's there?" Still groggy from her slumber, she tried to clear her vision by rubbing her eyes another time.

Margaret was barely able to control herself. She continued with her ghoulish noises, but they were mixed with small giggles. The giggles gave her away. Elinore could take no more of Margaret's nonsense and began swiping out into the darkness. Her first five swipes hit nothing, but at the sixth swipe she struck hard into Margaret's stomach. With a guttural sound, Margaret was bent over. Holding her stomach, she growled in pain. Elinore struck out again, landing a second blow to Margaret's arm. In a spontaneous reaction, her hand released the candle she was holding, and it dropped to the floor. The flame was close to Elinore's bed and began to lick the corner of the blanket. Elinore was quick to jump out of bed but was unaware of the danger that was within seconds of becoming a very real problem. She shouted at Margaret, "What's wrong with you? Are you crazy?" Suddenly she could smell something burning. Looking at the floor, there was an orange glow. She could see the flames making their way up her blanket toward the bed. Her jaw dropped in fear and her eyes widened as she grabbed hold of the blanket. Pulling it to the center of the room, she slid her hand down and over the burning edge, successfully extinguishing the flame. But her hand was hurt now. It was burnt badly, and Elinore was angry again. She told her sister to go to her room. She was incensed by her sister's pranks. It infuriated her even more because Margaret didn't seem to even recognize the danger; she had put the entire family at risk this time! Elinore knew she would need to have a scathing talk with Margaret soon. She also knew if she told her father, his wrath would be awful for Margaret.

Elinore now stood in front of the icebox, looking for some butter to put on her wound. She smoothed a pat of butter over her wrist, but it didn't seem to make it feel any better. When Elinore finally got back to her bed, she found it hard to fall back asleep. Soon she could see the sun making its first appearance over the tops of the distant mountain peaks. She figured she might as well go and wash up. She wanted to see Carl anyway. She stopped in the kitchen for a quick bite to eat and a gulp of coffee before leaving for the barn. The morning dew created its usual foggy effect as it began to burn off with the warmth of the sun. She was used to the foggy mornings in her father's field. It happened quite often. Even with the dim murkiness of the dawn, she could make out the silhouette of Hans. Pausing for a moment, she made her way to him.

Hans viewed the object of a person coming from the house too. As she came closer, the outline with a featureless interior became recognizable to him. He called out to Elinore. "Good morning, Hans!" she replied. "I'm going to take Lucky today to go see Carl." Hans looked at her with a grin. "Things are beginning to turn serious between you two, aren't they?" Elinore laughed and punched Hans in the arm. Her cheeks were giving away her embarrassment and she tucked her chin in with bashfulness. Hesitantly, she replied, "I guess." She took a minute and looked up at Hans. She admitted to him that she did care for Carl. She swayed back and forth nervously, feeling a little uncomfortable talking about her relationship with Carl to Hans.

Wanting to lighten the mood, he asked Elinore if she needed to wee. Hans was joking with her, and she smiled sideways at him. Elinore was used to Hans's sense of humor. She tossed him another smile and asked what he had to do during his day. He began to tell her his long boring list of cow milking and letting the bull out. Brushing and feeding the horses, taking the white horse for new shoes and buying some more feed for the cattle in town, were also on his list. Elinore was fighting a strong urge to yawn. He continued to tell Elinore that the herd was getting bigger and that two new calves had been born last week. Elinore enjoyed talking with Hans most of the time, but this time it seemed like all she could hear was blah, blah, blah.

Just when she thought she couldn't take another second of it she had a thought to just change the subject. She asked Hans what he thought about her working in Carl's town. She explained she had tried all the other shops in town, but no one seemed to need help. Hans asked her if she had tried the general store. She shot back that she had and that they did not need help either. Hans raised his eyebrow and said, "Well, I guess you have no other choice, little one." He asked her why she hadn't asked Carl what he thought, and she shrugged her shoulders. She thought for another minute and pointed her finger at him. "I think I will do that!" She raised her hand to wave goodbye and took the signal to escape.

The heat of the day was evident to her now because the sweat on her forehead was building. She could see Lucky was feeling the heat too and gave him a good drink before riding off. She reached Carl's quickly but didn't see him outside as usual. Gently tapping on the door, his mother answered. "Hello Elinore, it's so nice to see you, come in." She ushered her in, closing out the heat of the day behind them. "Would you like some lemonade?" she asked. Elinore gladly accepted and then asked where Carl was. She said, "Oh dear, I'm afraid he's gotten himself a bad case of poison ivy. He's in the bath right now with some baking soda and soap." Elinore took a long sip of the refreshing lemonade and told Carl's mother she'd check on him for her. Carl's mother thought Elinore's artful playfulness was quite humorous. She laughed at Elinore's bold coyness, and under her breath the words, "Young love," escaped.

Elinore was just out of Heidi's sight when she entered the bathroom. Opening the door slowly, she called out to Carl. He was not expecting to see Elinore. Recognizing her voice immediately, he placed his washcloth over his manhood. Elinore sat down on the stool beside the tub and noticed all the redness the poison ivy had made on his body. Carl was slightly embarrassed and felt a bit vulnerable. He asked Elinore why she had come. Elinore didn't answer. She couldn't take her eyes off him. She was stunned as she took in the sight of her handsome man soaking in the hot soapy water and didn't hear his question. Carl asked again, breaking her trance. She laughed and said, "I came to ask you…" There was an awkward silence as she could not complete her sentence. The sight of Carl completely without clothing left her speechless.

Carl took a handful of water and splashed her with it. They laughed together and became comfortable in each other's company. She told Carl she was going to look for work in his town because she couldn't find any in hers. Carl told her that he thought that was a good idea. Elinore could see the rash on Carl's skin and asked, "How did you get all that poison ivy on you?" He told her he had pulled some of the weeds that were beginning to cover their shed and didn't know they were poisonous. Elinore was finding it hard to take her sight off Carl's body. The water made his skin glisten. She could see the cuts of his muscles in his shoulders and back that he had developed. Fully exposed, were the ripples in his arms and abdomen above the water. Elinore was mesmerized. She had never seen Carl completely naked. She was hypnotized by him and in order to break the spell she was under, she offered to wash his back for him. Elinore couldn't help taking advantage of his helplessness. With an open mouth smile, she reached for the washcloth. She made sure to give his member a good tug when she took it. Her fingers tingled and she would have given anything for this occasion to be under better circumstances.

Amused, but with a seriousness about him, he told her if she kept playing like that, he would pull her into the tub with him. Elinore wasn't one to be intimidated, however, she did not need a case of poison ivy and it was his parent's home she was in. It was becoming hard for her to behave herself. With the washcloth in hand, she began to rub the sudsy water over his shoulders. Although she knew this was not the right time or place, her passion was igniting a fire in her heart. She felt she might explode in her desire for him. Elinore couldn't resist getting a little closer to Carl. Quickly, she leaned in and playfully stuck her tongue right inside his ear with a slight giggle. Again, he splashed her good with more of his bath water.

Then, all at once, Carl stood up as if he were about to leap out of the water to possibly drag her in with him. Standing there, the water ran off him. Elinore's breathing became shallow. His physique absolutely took her breath away. She was in full frontal view of him. His skin was wet, and his stomach muscles tightly rippled into small squares down to where his hip bones protruded. His biceps bulged and his forearms were thicker than both her thighs put together. Suddenly, Carl lifted one of his tree trunk sized thighs up and over the side of the tub. Elinore gasped. "Carl, what are you doing?" "Get back in the tub!" she ordered him in a hushed tone being careful not to let his mother hear her. Taking a deep breath, she told him she'd fetch him some fresh towels.

Escaping the bathroom fast, she wiped her brow and slowly the corners of her mouth turned upward from the lingering thoughts of Carl standing naked in front of her. She quickly checked her dress and found that the water Carl had splashed her with was almost dry from the heat of the day already. She asked Carl's mother for some towels to bring to him and returned to the bathroom. She placed the towels on the stool and Carl reached out to pull her down to him with her arm. He kissed her mouth, and her eyes closed when his lips touched hers. For a moment, Elinore felt intoxicated. Nearly falling over, she was satisfied for the time being, and told Carl she'd wait for him in the other room with his mother. She left the bathroom with a fantasy playing in her mind. Suddenly, she was in her own home with Carl, and they would be eating their evening meal shortly, followed by a blissful night's sleep in their own bed. Of course, she wasn't sure how much sleep she'd be able to get with Carl that close, lying next to her. She was brought back from her daydream when Carl sat down next to his mother, and she began to apply the paste of clay and baking soda over him that she had made while he bathed. Elinore helped by scooping a bit up with her finger and placing it on Carl's nose. Carl made a low growling noise to show his displeasure with being painted but the itch was the worst of the poison. Elinore had spent much of the day at Carl's, and it was time for her to go home. She told Carl that if she wasn't too tired after looking for work the next day, she would stop by again to see him. He kissed her goodbye, and she began her journey home. The dust of the earth kicked up into a small cloud under Lucky's hooves behind them. Elinore thought about how dry things had become and noticed how the grass had turned brown.

That night Elinore's thoughts drifted far from the image of Carl in the tub, in all his splendor. She wasn't familiar with any other town except her own. She had put her clothing out for the next day and laid them over the chair by her desk. She planned to wear her riding boots which she knew would be uncomfortable but necessary. Emma had been kind enough to make sure her white cotton dress was without wrinkles. She picked the simplest of her dresses to make a good impression. She worried the scoop neck on it might reveal too much of her bosom, but the short sleeves provided a full view of her strong arms. It was tied at the waist which gave a hint of femininity, and it was accented with a strategically placed small flower pinned on her right shoulder. That night went by quickly and soon she found herself riding through the center of Carl's town. There were many shops along the way. There was a fruit and vegetable shop. The man inside had shown some interest in hiring Elinore. He drove a black, horse-drawn wagon with a large block of ice that was stored beneath it, that kept the vegetables cold. He explained he had a daily route to service the people of the community. When Elinore told him of her riding experience, he was pleasantly surprised. He told her he would be making his decision by the week's end and to come back next week. He would let her know then.

There was also a cosmetic shop, a general store, a shop that turned sheep wool into clothing, and a leather shop that sold saddles and bags. In addition, there was a candy shop, a dairy farm, a lady's dress shop which also sold hats and so many more. She would surely find some type of work, she thought. And at the very end of town, there was a huge building that Carl had mentioned the day before.

It was a laundry service business that did regular laundry as well as diapers. Elinore didn't really want to work there and was sure that would be the last place she would visit. The building looked horribly depressing and even a little scary to her. But it did seem that many people worked there. She passed by it at just about quitting time and saw a massive number of people leaving through its gates. There were still quite a few places Elinore wanted to investigate before ever going there. Working with smelly diapers and dirty laundry disgusted her but she was excited about her many new options. As she had promised, she stopped to tell Carl what she had found and all about her days search. Carl was happy she would be working so close to where he lived. He told her that he was sure she would find something shortly. He offered to ride home with her, but Elinore said she would be fine, and it was just a short ride. She started off in the direction of her home, anxious to tell her family what she had found, when she heard Carl call out to her. She turned to face him, and she could hear the three words he had only said once before. He shouted to her, "I love you!" A grand smile came across her face and she raised her hand to her mouth to blow a kiss to him.

The sun was setting like molasses in the sky and there was no time to waste. Elinore felt good about what the day had brought and couldn't wait to tell her father and mother. She knew Hans would probably be the first person she would see, and she was looking forward to giving him the news too. She hoped by the end of the week she would be working. Elinore finally reached home and raced to the door to tell everyone. The kitchen door slammed behind her as she raced through the house to find her father first. Porter was in his study running through his piles of papers. He was worried about his own business, but he was keeping it to himself, for the time being. Porter was unaware that the worry showed on his face. Elinore began to spout off about what the man had told her about the vegetable route and how much he seemed to like her. Porter was preoccupied with his own worries about adjusting his slimming budget and trying to find a solution to it all when Elinore noticed she did not have her father's full attention. Elinore exclaimed, "Father, I thought you would be proud of me!" Feeling disappointed, her eyes dropped to the floor.

Porter quickly apologized and put his arm around his little girl. "What makes you think I am not proud of you? I know you will always find your way Elinore; I know that if I know nothing else." Porter continued by asking what else she had found. He did not want her to know there was something wrong, but Elinore did notice. She made a mental note of it but could not stop her own exhilaration at her newfound options to come out. After all, her father had much more experience in the work field than she did. Elinore was looking for guidance. Porter told her not to close any options and to remain vigilant in her search. Satisfied, she left her father, thanking him. Rose was busy bathing Delilah, so Elinore decided to go tap on Hans's door to see what his thoughts were about how her day ended.

As soon as Elinore had closed the door, Porter buried his head back in his paperwork once again. His money was being spent quicker than he was making it. He felt it hard to concentrate on anything else in the house. He also felt guilty for not sharing this information with Rose. It bothered him to keep secrets from her. He was determined to find a solution.

Through the kitchen window, Elinore stood looking across the field at Hans's home. There was a small light in the window that glowed from inside. It was quiet that night and the earth crunched beneath her shoes as she walked toward the light. She could hear the crickets chirping and noticed the lightning bugs just starting to glow. Everything was so dry and parched. As evening approached, the temperature remained uncomfortable, and it had been a long time since the last heavy rain. Elinore gently knocked on Hans's door. He opened the door and was surprised to see Elinore standing there. "Is everything alright?" he asked. She responded, "Yes, I just wanted to tell you about my day." Hans was honored that Elinore considered him important enough to share her story with him. They chatted for a long time, sharing some laughter together before she returned to her bed for some rest. When Elinore entered her room, she glanced at the chair beside her desk. Even though she was tired, her thoughts were clear, and she was in no mood for any of Margaret's shenanigans. Placing the chair against the door assured her some uninterrupted solid sleep. Pleased with herself, she laid across her bed. A movie, like the kind she watched on the zoetrope reel her father had given her on Christmas day long ago, played through her mind of the day's events. And then again, Carl's face appeared. She found it hard to get him off her mind for any length of time. Her eyes began to feel heavy, and she whispered, "I love you too, Carl," before she fell off to sleep.

Only a few blissful hours had passed in the Downing household before they were all awakened by a loud, heavy pounding on the front door which shook the entire house. Porter sat straight up in his bed, startled. He wasn't sure if what he had heard was a dream or real when he heard it again. Yanking his night robe from the hook on the back of the bedroom door, and pushing his feet into his slippers, he raced to the door. A feeling of dread came over him as he placed his hand on the doorknob. He knew this could not be good news at this hour. Not knowing what to expect, Porter opened the door slowly as Rose, Elinore and Margaret gathered close behind him. Holding his small lantern out into the darkness, a familiar face appeared. It was Carl! Porter asked, "Carl, what's wrong? Are you okay?" He pulled him inside when he noticed Carl's parents, both sitting on the horse behind him. Porter was confused and concerned. Carl's head dropped and he could barely get the words out. Porter started to notice that he could smell the distinct odor of burning wood. The smell seemed to be emanating from Carl's clothing.

Carl, in a barely intelligible voice said, "Our house burnt down." Porter noticed some soot on Carl's face as he continued, "My father is singed, and my mother has burns on her hands, I had to pull them both from the fire." Carl was beginning to lean heavily on Porter's arm. He was clearly exhausted. Rose helped Heidi in and sat her down in the kitchen to examine her burns. Porter brought Otto in and sat him beside his wife. Elinore was frightened. She didn't know how badly Carl was hurt. She threw his arm over her shoulder and led him to the kitchen where his parents were. Carl began to insist he was fine and only asked for some water. Porter asked Carl what had happened. Heidi began to cry, and Otto pulled her closer to him to kiss her. She began to say, "It's all my fault," as her tears turned to sobs. Heidi explained she accidentally knocked over the lantern and the next thing she knew, the entire room was on fire. Trying to put it out with a wet dish towel only seemed to make it worse. Since Otto had his stroke, he had lost much of his strength and wasn't much help in putting out the fire. Heidi then started to say that if it weren't for Carl, she didn't know what would've become of them.

Rose was feeling badly for Heidi and offered her a handkerchief to dry the tears from her face. She applied some butter to the wounds on her hands. Otto looked at Porter and his eyes started to well up. He closed them and covered his face with his hands, moving his head slightly from side to side. He looked at Porter again, "I don't know what we will do now, our house is burnt to the ground. We have our lives and our horse. We have no money and lost everything we owned." Otto put his face down again, covering it with his hands in despair.

Porter was witnessing a completely broken man. His heart broke for him. Porter looked at Rose and realized how rich he was, even though he knew his finances were dwindling. Porter blurted out, "Don't worry Otto, I will help you," as he put his hand on Otto's weak shoulder. Otto looked up at Porter with a grateful expression and thanked him. Otto was also doing his best to comfort Heidi, but she was simply inconsolable. Elinore and Margaret weren't sure what to say. They had never experienced such tragedy before. Both were in shock from the news. Elinore stepped closer to Carl and dropped herself around his shoulders from behind him. She gently whispered into his ear, "I'll get a job and I will help you too." This really didn't make Carl feel any better, but he knew better than to try and stop her. Thinking it was best, he just said thank you and gripped her arms that were wrapped around his neck.

Rose began to prepare her house for her guests. She knew they would need to stay with them for a while and started to process the necessary preparations. Immediately, she told Margaret to move her things into Elinore's room. She'd have to stay there until they sorted things out. Rose put a pillow and a heavy blanket on the settee in the front room for Carl to rest on. She tapped him on the back and placed her hand on the pillow. She told him to make himself comfortable and to just ask if he needed anything else. Rose guided Heidi and Otto to Margaret's room, pointing out the location of the bathroom on the way. She also told them to help themselves to anything else they wanted or needed. She knew Elsie and Emma would be down in the morning to make breakfast, so she jotted a quick note and left it on the kitchen table. The note simply read: We have company. Make extra for three, please.

Snuggled together back in their bed, Porter and Rose held each other tightly. All Rose could think about was how badly she felt about it all. Porter knew he needed to help them, but more importantly, he needed to tell Rose about what was happening in his business. He couldn't and shouldn't keep it from her any longer. The long night seemed to last forever for the two families, but when morning came, they both woke to the wonderful aroma of coffee wafting through the air from the kitchen. Rose had gotten up early. She had trouble sleeping that night and decided to give Emma and Elsie a hand and begin the coffee and biscuits for them. Elsie entered first and immediately noticed a slight odor that was different from the usual morning smell of food. It smelled like something had been burnt. She asked Rose what had happened the night before and Rose began to explain everything to her. She told her that the workload would be getting a little heavier for the next few weeks because of what had happened to Carl's family.

Emma soon came through the door noticing the same thing and listened to catch the tail end of Rose's story. Emma had an apron full of eggs. She had stopped by the chicken coop to gather some of their eggs for breakfast. Elsie explained the entire situation to Emma as she still was processing the details herself. She couldn't imagine how horrible it must have been to experience such a tragedy. Losing everything they owned! She shook her head in disbelief. The three women worked quickly and soon the smells from the kitchen were becoming more pleasant. It soon brought everyone in the house to the table. Each plate had a full portion of eggs, leberwurst, and biscuits with jam and cheese.

Porter finished half his plate before he began to discuss with Otto what the plan would be to restart their lives. Porter had planned to take his vehicle to Otto's house to see the damage and what needed to be done first. After he cleaned his plate, he hurried to his room to look for clothes to fit Otto. Otto was much thinner than Porter. He had many clothes that could not accommodate his growing torso anymore. He piled a few things in a stack and handed them over to Otto. He asked him to wash up so they could leave to see what was left of his home. Porter hadn't started the vehicle up in a while, but it gave him no problem. Otto met Porter in front of the house and was amazed. He hadn't ever seen an automobile. Porter helped Otto up and they were on their way. It only took a few minutes compared to what it would have taken if they were forced to go by horse.

As they approached the house, both men could still see a pillar of smoke rising into the sky with a small glow at the base of it. The main beam had fallen to one side and most of the roof had caved inward. The smell of burning wood was strong and filled the air. Otto's eyes began to well up again. His distraught mind wouldn't allow him to think clearly. He didn't know how he could fix this for his family, and he prayed for a solution. Porter already had in his mind, in consecutive order, what he would do to begin setting them back on their feet and tried to assure Otto that all would be fine.

It was a hot, dry day and Otto thought to himself that heavy rain would surely help put the fire out completely. Porter placed his hand on Otto's arm to comfort him briefly. They could see tall beams still standing but most of the house had caved in and was still smoldering in an orange ashy glow. Porter could see it was not a total loss though. The shed was still standing unscathed, and Otto's crops were untouched. It was not so bad in Porter's mind because he knew his men could have this house rebuilt in just a few days. Otto could only think about how much he had lost and didn't know how he would replace it all. It would certainly be a big burden to place on his son. Otto couldn't work himself anymore, which made him feel that much worse.

Back at Porter's house, Rose was doing much of the same. Wanting to replace some of their items, she was busy gathering things that her family didn't need or use anymore. She had quite a pile growing in the front room. To distract Heidi, she drew her a bath, gave her a washcloth and clean clothing. Rose asked her to go relax in the tub while she finished up with her mission. She knew it would not stop Heidi from worrying but maybe it would take her mind off things for a while. Rose called out to Elinore for help. Carl and Elinore helped Rose, and all three of them began to carry other things throughout the house to add to the pile. Soon Rose had a grand supply of almost an entire household of supplies, including clothing. Wiping her hands against each other back and forth, she said out loud, "I should have done this sooner!" Elinore smiled as she watched her mother coming to the rescue of her boyfriend's family.

In a matter of a few days Porter had the crew of men that he always did business with, working on Otto and Heidi's new home. It would be a modest home but slightly bigger than the one they had before. Porter had given some thought into what Otto's needs would be in the future, so he had the men enlarge the doorways to accommodate a pushchair to make it easier for Heidi to care for him.

Porter always seemed to be in deep thought lately and Rose was noticing. She wasn't sure why. They had had a few complications in recent months, but she thought none of them were enough to make him as grouchy as he had become. She hoped it would pass as soon as Carl and his family were in their new home and their lives returned to normalcy. Still, Rose couldn't help but enjoy the company of a full house of people. She always felt the more people in the house the better it was. She did wish it was under better circumstances though.

Elinore was also at her happiest moments. Having Carl near all the time was a splendid situation. Their interest in each other did not go unnoticed by Elsie and Emma who secretly enjoyed poking fun at the two love birds. Just as Elinore was getting comfortable, word arrived that the house had been completed and it was time for Carl and his family to leave. Rose asked

Emma and Elsie to prepare a celebration meal and they all enjoyed one last meal together before they left. Porter drove Otto and Heidi back to their new home the following day and Carl followed on horseback. The day was bright with blue skies and Otto hoped it was a good sign of better things to come. Otto and Heidi didn't know how to show their gratitude but said thank you many times to Porter.

Elinore was feeling sad about Carl leaving and he could see it in the expression on her face. He gently kissed her lips at the doorway and Elinore felt as if she would cry. She hated to see him go. Carl pulled her closer, and whispered to her that he would see her the following day. She smiled at him and closed her eyes. She didn't want him to see her cry. But finally, she did open them to see him far off in the distance. Elinore closed the door gently and placed her hand on her heart. As she slid down the back of the door, she wiped the one small tear that escaped slowly down her cheek with her other hand.

When night came, Elinore tried to take her mind off Carl and started to think about looking for work again. She was in a hurry to see the man with the vegetable cart, which she knew would be ideal for her. If nothing turned out from that, she would be forced to find quick work at the laundry factory. She wanted a job quickly now more than ever. She wanted to help Carl and his family get back on their feet again.

Elinore was comfortable in her bed and in deep thought when Porter pushed her door open to say goodnight. He knew she would be thinking of finding work again. She was stubborn like that. He knew his daughter's thought process well. A no-nonsense type of girl, and he liked that about her. He was proud because in many ways, she reminded him of himself. Elinore was tough and certainly a survivor. Of all the people Porter worried about, she was the one who concerned him least. She always landed on her feet no matter what problem she was faced with.

Before Porter could close the door, Elinore called out to him from the darkness. "Father, I plan to go to two places day after tomorrow to find work." "Where my darling?" he asked. Elinore spoke thoughtfully. "I would really like to do the deliveries for the man who sells produce, I hope he hires me." She continued, pausing briefly, "But there is a laundry factory I found that I'm sure would hire me on the spot." She asked her father what he thought. In the silence of the darkness, she waited.

Porter did not like the idea of any of the women in his family working, but he knew not to argue with Elinore on the subject. It would be of no use. The more he said he didn't like it, the more she would push to do it. He tried to remain indifferent. Porter just responded, "I know you'll make the right choice. Keep an open mind," he told her. Porter closed the door quietly and began to think about the conversation he would need to have with his wife very soon. Even with everything that had been happening, he still had trouble thinking of anything else.

Chapter 12

It had been more than a few days since he had decided to tell Rose about what had been happening at his shop and how it was beginning to affect their money. Still, he never could seem to find the right time to talk with her about it. He went to bed that night trying to piece together what that conversation would sound like. He was a bit restless in their bed that night and Rose found herself pushing Porter over more than once, just to get a corner of the blanket they shared. She was thankful Elsie would be taking Delilah in the morning so she could get some rest. With Porter off to work, and Delilah with Elsie, she would be left alone. Rose was looking forward to that. The girls were outside and that was one less thing she had to worry about. It was comforting to know that Hans was always nearby. Rose had just finally started to fall off to sleep when she was awoken by Delilah's cries. Delilah was tugging at her ears and crying. Rose suspected she may have developed an ear infection. She tapped Porter on the shoulder, pulling him from his deep slumber, to warn him that they may need to take Delilah to the doctor.

Elinore was just falling into a solid sleep herself when the sounds of screaming pierced the warm air coming down the hall to where she laid comfortably. It felt as if the screams wormed their way into her brain through her ears. Elinore rubbed the sand from her eyes. A bit disgusted she grumbled, "I can never get a good night's sleep in this house anymore!" Delilah's cries were getting on her last nerve. She plodded her way down the hall and was met by Rose, who was holding her wailing sister. "What's wrong with her now, mother?" Elinore asked impatiently. Rose was exhausted and was short with Elinore.

"I'm not sure, go back to bed!" Elinore's eyebrows raised, not expecting that type of response. She dragged herself back to her room as her mother had demanded. She thought about her mother's reaction to her question and found it difficult to go back to sleep. A while had passed, and the birds were beginning to chirp outside her window. All at once, the blankets on her bed started to rumble and Elinore kicked them off in a fury. Throwing herself out of the bed with a huff, she went to the closet to pick out some clothing. She was so agitated it seemed like a good idea to go looking for work, if not for any reason but to simply get out of the house! She thought about her Oma's favorite quote. *Silence is golden.* Boy was she right, Elinore thought to herself. She brushed her hair, pulling it hard and fast. Her hair made a whipping sound as she quickly stroked it. Next, Elinore quickly hurried through getting ready to leave. She reached for a biscuit on her way out. Elinore was saddling Lucky and giving him water, unaware Hans was standing in the doorway of the barn behind her. He sipped his coffee as he quietly watched her. She caught him from the corner of her eye and was startled.

Hans thought it was funny to watch her jump, but Elinore didn't find humor in it at all. "Where are you going this time, little one?" he asked. Elinore was already annoyed and shouted at him, "Why do you call me that? I'm not really so little, you know!" she protested. Hans let out a hardy laugh, and returned with, "You'll always be my little one, little one." With that being said, he left the barn. He knew she would completely understand once she got older. He shook his head, still laughing as he began his long day of work. Tending to the horses and cattle took up most of his day, but he enjoyed his work.

Elinore wasted no time. Her mind was dead set on finding work. She rode straight to the place she most wanted to work at. She was only a short distance away and could see a tall skinny young man, standing next to the produce wagon that was in front of the shop. As she came closer, the shopkeeper came out and handed the man a long list. She couldn't hear what they were saying but it sure looked like that man had swiped the job she desperately wanted, right out from under her. She reached the shop just as he drove off. She was hot under her collar. Elinore tried not to let it show, but she was rattled. She looked at the shopkeeper and asked if the job was still available.

The man had not really expected to see her again. She could see her question made him uneasy. He stood motionless and did not respond. Elinore repeated herself, "Sir! Is the job still available, or not?" Her voice was more direct the second time, and even a bit tense. She could tell what the answer was by the expression on his face. It made her angrier. She knew she should have come back the following day. Her mind filled with the image of that scrawny, poor excuse of a man that left with her delivery list. She wanted to beat the stuffing out of him. She rode off trying to clear her mind and took some deep breaths. There were a few more places she wanted to stop before she went to her least favorite choice. After trying most of the day, and being turned down at every stop, she knew it was inevitable that she would be working at that smelly laundry place. She and Lucky trotted off in the direction of the factory. It looked like a prison of some sort to her. It had iron bars on the windows and a solid heavy iron gate, fenced with pointed tips all the way around the entire building. The building was mostly brick and there were spots around the windows painted with an ugly dark green color.

Just outside the gates, Elinore noticed a young woman sitting on a bench. She was eating something but didn't seem to be enjoying it much. She looked friendly enough to speak with, so Elinore tied Lucky to the hitching post where many other horses were already and walked over to her. The earth crunched under her boots, which made the woman raise her head to look at her. Elinore extended her hand and greeted her with a happy hello. She introduced herself and told her it was a pleasure to meet her. The woman seemed pleased to meet another person so friendly. She told Elinore that her name was Anna. Elinore sat down next to the young lady and asked if she liked working at her job inside the factory. Anna replied, "Not really, but it's a living and the pay is fine." Elinore grinned and then asked if she knew if they were looking for help. Anna laughed, "They're always looking for help." Elinore began to laugh too. Elinore didn't have a full understanding of the meaning behind her wisecrack.

Anna asked her if she was looking for work for herself. Elinore shook her head yes and answered that she was. Anna continued, "You'll need to be careful in there." Elinore noticed a change of expression on her face. It was much more serious. Anna asked, "Is this your first job?" "It is, how did you know?" Elinore asked. "I could tell by your questions," Anna stated. "That's kind of why I'm warning you. You look so innocent, and you could lose that in there if you're not careful." Anna added, "It's dangerous and difficult work." Elinore smiled at her warning as she thought about the things, she had already experienced. She knew she was not as innocent as Anna thought, but she kept that to herself and appreciated her words.

Soon a very loud whistle blew. Elinore was just about to ask her another question, but with the sound of that whistle, Anna's break was over. She stood up, gathering her things, and told Elinore that she enjoyed their chat and that maybe she would see her inside sometime. As a bunch of people hurried through the gates, Elinore decided to slip in too, to see if she could speak with someone about getting hired. She entered the building and the first thing she noticed was the foul smell. It smelled like the lye that Elsie used to make the washing soap with, and the air was humid and heavy. A small woman with a clip board spotted Elinore and rushed toward her. She wore very thick glasses with hefty black frames which from behind she could see with her beady dark eyes. The woman screeched at her, demanding to know where she belonged. Elinore didn't know how to answer her. She stood wide-eyed staring at this woman when she repeated herself in such a harsh tone. "Where do you belong?"

Elinore could smell her rancid breath as she barked out her question. It was a sharp wretched stink that made Elinore recoil. She could see that the woman had many broken teeth. Two ugly yellow snags in her sunken mouth were clearly visible. In a soft voice, Elinore stated that she had come looking for work. As soon as Elinore said the last word of her reply, she held her breath for as long as she could. She doubted she would ever forget this woman's voice or the decomposing smell of a corpse coming from her mouth. She was willing to withstand her blow though in order to find work.

With a malevolent and wicked grin, the woman scribbled something onto her clipboard and told Elinore to follow her. She took her down a long stone hallway to a small room on the right. She gave two quick knocks with her knuckle before entering. "Come on, come on!" she impatiently shouted at Elinore as she pulled her through the door with her. The room was not well lit and rather dusty. Near a window in the corner of the room sat an older man. He was skinny with a long gray beard. He looked kind of scary to Elinore. "Mr. Kraus?" said the woman. The man was annoyed by the interruption. His head popped up from the high stacks of books and papers that surrounded him. "What is it? What do you want, I'm very busy!" The woman explained, "I found this girl wandering in front of the building, and she said she's looking for work." The man shouted back at her, barely looking at them, "Well then, put her to work! Please leave now!"

Elinore was delighted but kept her poker face. She did not want to let on how desperate she was. The woman led her back down the hallway, and Elinore followed at her quick pace. She took her to the iron gate in the front of the building and opened it with a hard push. The woman shouted off a short list of things to Elinore as she listened carefully. "You start tomorrow. Show up at 6am, quitting time is at 4pm. You will receive a half hour for mealtimes, signaled by a whistle. Don't be late, we don't tolerate tardiness. You will start in room number 2. We work 6 days a week, 10 hours a day!" And with her last sentence, she pushed Elinore forward and slammed the gate closed.

Elinore was stunned. The woman was so rude, but at least she had a job now. All she could think about after that was telling Carl she finally was able to earn some of her own money to do what she liked with. Elinore turned toward the horses where she had tied Lucky up and her happiness was cut short. A man in a long black coat had Lucky by his reigns and had one foot up in the stirrup. Elinore ran to Lucky, screaming at the man who was stealing her horse. She ran as fast as she could, and it was hard for her to catch her breath between her screams. Then gaining enough wind, she shouted out to Lucky to stop. With the shrill of her commanding voice, Lucky stood up on his hind legs squealing with aggression. Elinore did not stop her pace. Her boots pounded the dirt as she ran digging in her apron for her billhook. Lucky was still squealing as the man fell to the ground. Elinore was on top of him in a flash. Gaining control quickly, she grabbed the man from behind and with his neck in the crook of her arm, she pressed the billhook against his throat. She shouted at the man, "Move and I will cut you from ear to ear!" The man froze in his position and Elinore could feel his muscles tighten. Elinore wasn't sure what she wanted to do next, but she knew she wanted to make this man pay for trying to steal her beloved horse. She wanted to hurt this scoundrel without a doubt. She let her grip on him loosen only slightly and kicked him hard enough with her boot to curl him over moaning. She looked at him seething with anger. "Next time I will kill you without hesitation!" she shouted at him.

She took Lucky's reigns and placed her hand on his muzzle. Elinore turned to make her way home and found herself staring at an audience of workers from the factory. Her face turned red from embarrassment. Elinore had no idea how many people were watching her. Anna made her way through the crowd toward her as all the people started to break apart. The commotion had ended and there was nothing else to watch. Anna smiled at Elinore. "I guess I was wrong about you being so innocent." The two friends laughed together, and Anna placed her arm over Elinore's shoulder. Elinore looked at Anna and said, "I wouldn't have really killed him, you know," brushing the dirt from her dress. "Sure," Anna said continuing to find humor in it all. As Elinore thought about it, she couldn't believe what she had just done. Her strength came on so suddenly and her anger for that man was explosive. Her reaction to the man's actions took over so fast. Since Anna was still there, Elinore told her what the woman inside had said to her before her scuffle happened. She told her that she was going to start working in room 2 the following day. Anna was happy because she worked in room 2 as well, and now would have a friend to work with. As they parted ways, Anna promised to show her all the things she would need to know at work. The last thing she did was to remind her not to forget to bring her lunch.

Elinore rushed off to give Carl the news. She wasn't sure Carl would be happy about her working the 10-hour days, 6 days a week, but she planned to only work long enough to get his family restored. It would only be temporary, and she planned to assure him of that. Elinore also knew her father would be the harder one to convince. There was one small thing in the sideview of her sight and she couldn't help but notice. A young man, maybe a little older than herself, stood watching her the entire time she spoke with Anna. His gaze seemed riveted on her which Elinore found peculiar. She didn't know anyone in Carl's town and so she wondered what his reason was for looking so fixedly at her.

Elinore had so many other things on her mind, she pushed that thought aside, giving Lucky a soft kick to gallop off. Elinore arrived at Carl's within minutes and started rambling about the details of her day before she could get both feet on the ground. She was vibrating and excited about her success. She told him about Anna and about the man who tried to steal her horse. Elinore told him about the woman with the clipboard too. Carl couldn't say much about Elinore working in the factory. He honestly would have preferred her to work at the general store, apothecary, or even a lady's garment shop. He looked on with aversion as Elinore continued, barely stopping to take a breath. Elinore finally stopped briefly and noticed Carl was not as excited as she had hoped. She was slightly disappointed but was quick to remind him that it was just temporary. She also decided it was not the right time to tell him about the young man who stood gawking at her.

Soon after meeting Carl, Elinore arrived home. Still excited and barely able to contain her good news, she barreled into the kitchen, hoping her thunder would alert her mother and father that she was home. But when they didn't greet her, she went searching for them. They were in her father's study. She pressed her ear to the door and could hear them talking in hushed whispers. Elinore tried the door but found it to be locked. Elinore found it peculiar that her parents would lock any door. She wondered what they were talking about and assumed it must be important. Maybe they just didn't want to be disturbed by anyone, she thought.

Elinore went back to the kitchen to get a bite to eat. She was hungry after her long day and her stomach grumbled. A beautiful red apple sat in a bowl in front of her and she whispered, "Perfect!" She rinsed the apple in the sink, but before she could take a bite, she heard the bolt on the door of the study turn. She only caught a glimpse of her mother, but she could see that she was upset because she was wiping her eyes with her handkerchief. Both her parents seemed to be avoiding eye contact with her and she couldn't understand why but decided not to ask questions. Maybe her news would cheer them up, she thought.

Eventually, Rose and Porter made their way to the kitchen. Rose was not feeling much like conversing and sat quietly. Porter had just finished telling her about the dire situation he now found himself in financially. The news had taken Rose by surprise. She never saw it coming. Worse yet, it was bad enough that Porter was going to sell off his prized possession, his automobile, to recoup some of his money. Porter had even suggested that maybe Elinore could go to the United States to stay with Agnes, if things got much worse. That left Rose in tears. While she loved her sister, she knew Elinore would be devastated by the decision. After all, she and Carl were very serious now, and she had plans to start working. Rose wondered how she would be able to even bring the subject up. Rose thought to herself, she would need to be doing some serious praying this Sunday at church.

With Rose and Porter sitting at the table; coffee cups in hand, they could see Elinore was bubbling with news of her own that she couldn't wait to spill. Rose considered it grand that Elinore was so inspired, but neither of her parents were happy about the long hours she began to tell them about. Again, Elinore stuck to her plan, and finished by telling them that she only planned to keep this work temporarily. She was annoyed that she needed to keep explaining herself but stuck to her plan regardless. They were her parents, and she wouldn't dare dishonor them by showing her impatience. When their conversation concluded, she couldn't help but roll her eyes as she walked away toward her room. Elinore felt that her parents would be delighted if she never grew up at all.

Even though no one was happy about her working, it did not discourage her. In fact, it made her more head strong about earning her own money and taking care of herself. She was proud of what she had accomplished. Rose had taken in so much she was bewildered. Stunned, she sat at the edge of the bed and began to disrobe. She reached for her night clothing that she had laid out on the bed earlier. She had so much on her mind that her head felt like it would explode. The pain inside her head ran from her forehead all the way to her shoulders.

Everything Porter had just told her spun around her thoughts inside her head. She hadn't even noticed the disappointment in Elinore's eyes. Rose suddenly picked up the pillows on their bed and fluffed them with aggression. She set them down hard and began to beat them. Then in an automatonlike manner, she placed Delilah in her crib and hoped she would sleep through the night. Rose pulled the blankets down and climbed into her bed. She tried getting comfortable, but her heavy heart kept her from sleeping well. She thought about all the things she had just given to Carl's family. She thought about the money she had just spent trying to make Elinore's graduation as splendid as it was. That would all need to stop now. She needed to tighten the budget! Rose was going to go back to being thrifty again. Rose knew she had become spoiled by her excessive spending and was somewhat angry with herself because she had not grown up that way. She hoped these small changes would make a difference, but she knew there was little she could control outside of her own family's way of life.

She was cross with Porter. From the time he started the business, he had spent quite an excessive amount on gratuitous items. The automobile was one of the biggest thorns in her side. She never liked that metal horse from the day Porter brought it home. He hadn't even used it much and it was an extra expense that was simply unnecessary. Rose was most upset about Porter's suggestion about Elinore going to live with Agnes in America for a while. She knew Elinore could take care of herself, but she was still a young woman and that wasn't the point anyway. She did not want any of her children to have to leave home in that manner. Rose swore, come hell or high water, she would never allow that to happen as long as she had anything to say about it. Tears started to well up in her eyes and small sniffling noises could be heard as she tried to draw air through her nose. Rose listened to Porter snore in his peaceful slumber. It bothered her how he could sleep so peacefully, knowing all he had just told her. She turned to face him, purposely shaking the bed as hard as she could, but her movement didn't seem to bother him one bit. She wondered as she stared at him, just how long he had known about all of this but didn't think to tell her. For the first time since they were married, Rose found herself truly angry with Porter. She resisted the urge to take the pillow from beneath her head and press it to his face. She knew she could never do such a thing but for the first time in her life she truly considered it. Rose tried again to clear her mind, resolving herself to do what she could regarding the spending they had become comfortable with. Still, she was not able to sleep.

With the sounds of the birds singing their morning songs, Elinore rose quickly. This would be her first day at work. She sprang from her bed and rushed to the bathroom to wash up. Looking in the mirror at herself, she winked and smiled. She encouraged herself by saying, "Today is going to be a good day!" She packed herself a small lunch; the way her friend Anna had suggested, in a paper sack, sealing the top tightly. She fed Lucky well, before heading off for her long day. She didn't want to be late, so she didn't take time to speak with anyone. It was so early, and the sky was barely light enough for her to see where she was going but she and Lucky had ridden this path so many times before that they could have done it with closed eyes. She knew they would make it in plenty of time and maybe she would even have enough time to speak with Anna before entering the facility. Elinore rode steadfastly in anticipation of what her first day at work would bring. She surely wanted to make a good impression with whomever she met. As she approached the gates, they somehow looked more ominous, and the building looked darker than it had the day before. Elinore tied Lucky to the hitching post with all the other horses. An image of the man who tried to steal Lucky from her ran through her mind. She vowed to never let that happen again, so she tied a much stronger knot to untie to be on the safe side.

Elinore had intentionally arrived a little earlier in part, to see if she could talk to Anna before the shift started. During the night her mind had wandered and she thought about what Anna had said to her about being so innocent and exactly what she meant by the other things she had told her. And for that matter, she wanted to know what else she needed to be watchful for. Elinore sat down on the same bench where she had first met Anna. Within minutes, an enormous crowd of people started to gather. There was a lot of loud chatter amongst the workers as they waited for the start of the workday. Soon, Elinore spotted Anna. Quickly, she raised her hand above all the people and with a happy expression, she called out to her. Her waving hand made it easy for Anna to notice her friend. The two had enough time to say hello before the loud whistle blasted. All at once, the large crowd filtered through the gates, while the same small woman with the clipboard stood watching intently. Like a fine-tuned machine, the workers hurried to take their places. Elinore watched as the people seemed to rush in a crisscross pattern in front of her. It seemed like sheer lunacy to her, when suddenly she felt a nudge from behind. It was Anna. She whispered in her ear and pointed to the door that had a large number two, painted red on it. Elinore grinned and with a nod of her head she crossed the hall to the door.

Inside the room, there were countless baskets filled with already cleaned laundry, ready for starch, pressing and folding. The baskets were large and very heavy. Made of wicker, like the one her mother used to pick apples with, but much larger. There were lines that hung across the room and rows of ironing boards from one end to the other except for a small area where a desk sat. There was a person at each ironing board and all the women looked hot and tired to Elinore already. She wondered if she would be doing what they were. Elinore wasn't sure what to do. She stood taking it all in, when two older women carrying one heavy basket between them, came towards her at a fast pace. Elinore was paralyzed for a moment. She didn't know which way to go. Both women on each side of the basket hollered at the same time for her to move, as they struggled with the weight of the basket filled with wet linen. Elinore was startled at the way they spoke to her. She jumped out of their way and brushed against one of the larger baskets at the bottom of the tall stack next to her. The women had hardly made it to the door, when the stack she had bumped into began to teeter. One of the younger women who was watching shouted, "Watch out!" The next thing Elinore felt was pain. Her arm and shoulder were in enormous pain, but her entire body felt the weight of all the baskets and heaps of laundry that had tumbled, covering her. She was completely buried beneath it! She struggled with her other arm to dig herself out. She couldn't even see daylight. Elinore began to scream. "Help, someone help me!" The stabbing pain in her arm nearly made her cry.

It seemed like an eternity, when she felt hands touching her. Elinore had nearly ten full-sized baskets laying on top of her and the men from other rooms had come to help dig her out. Suddenly, she felt a hand on her leg. The hand was reaching around, and then another grabbed at her shoulder, which made her cry out in pain again. Then a third hand began reaching for her bloomers when she heard a man's voice. All the memories of that day at the seaport long ago came back to her. Elinore started kicking wildly. She began to scream. She didn't feel the pain in her shoulder anymore. Sheer panic fueled her now. Escaping was the only thing on her mind. She was in survival mode. Elinore began to tear away at the piles of laundry on top of her when she finally broke through. A set of eyes stared back at her. The man asked her if she was okay. Elinore wasn't sure if she was or not. She lay partially still buried beneath the baskets of toppled laundry, looking out of the small hole she had cleared. The man staring back at her had bright blue eyes and a missing front tooth. He smiled caringly at Elinore and continued to peel the laundry from her. "There you are," he said as he started to pull her to her feet. She could see that there were four other men helping to uncover her. Her panic subsided but she kept it in her mind that one of those men had their hands where they did not belong. She began to laugh as she rose to her feet in embarrassment. She had made such a mess before she had even finished her first day at work. Elinore hoped she would not be fired for it.

A large woman suddenly grabbed Elinore's wrist and started pulling hard, demanding that she come with her. Elinore followed the woman to the end of the very large room to an ironing board that had a wash barrel and ringer next to it. The woman barked out to her, "This is where you will work!" She pointed to two baskets that sat on the floor next to her. Only one of them was filled with laundry. The woman's voice rose and sternly she explained, "You get paid by the basket. Press, starch, and fold all that into that basket," pointing to each. She then said, "Place the finished laundry in the other basket and bring it to me over there!" She pointed to a desk on the far side of the room.

Elinore couldn't understand why everyone seemed so grumpy and uptight. Even almost angry. Elinore picked up a piece of laundry and began to press it. She knew from watching Elsie and Emma, not everything needed starch, so she did those items first. Most of the other women were already on their third and fourth baskets by then. Elinore looked at the barrel next to her with the ringer. It was filled with starch. The starch was much thinner than the way Emma made hers. Elinore was glad because she knew it would be easier to work with. Without knowing it, Elinore had learned a lot from Elsie and Emma. She already knew many clothes needed to be starched before being ironed. She could see she had many aprons, shirtwaists, and undergarments in her pile. She took the things that needed to be the stiffest out first and began to put starch on them. The thickest materials would take the most starch and time to dry. For the other pieces, she would only need to add more water. The humidity began to rise in the room, and someone opened a window which provided little comfort. Elinore had tied her hair into a bun, but strands were already starting to fall out hanging in front of her face. She wiped the sweat from her brow with the back of her hand, looking around the room. She noticed she was looking much like the other women there. She didn't like that. She hated looking so dreadful. But it would only be a short time before she found something better, and she wanted to keep her mind on the goal. She was looking forward to the end of the work week when she would be paid. Elinore had plans. Big plans! The first time she received her wages, she planned to split it in thirds. One for her parents, one for her, and one for Carl's parents. Elinore wanted to buy some things for herself with her portion.

She had seen some very nice riding boots in the shoe shop that she really wanted. They were handmade and a bit higher than her old boots. They were made of black leather and Elinore was excited about being able to buy them herself. She had also noticed some lovely hair pins in the ladies' hat shop that she desperately wanted. They were long enough to handle her long hair and had beautiful garnet gems in a floral pattern on the rounded end that sparkled like the sea waves in the sunshine. Finally, the afternoon meal whistle blew. Elinore thought it would never come! She really needed to sit down. Her first day at work had had a few unexpected setbacks. She left the workroom and could feel the difference in the air on her face as soon as she left. Outside the gates, Anna was sitting on the bench waiting for her. Elinore sat down next to her new friend and opened her paper sack. She had brought two apples. One for her and one for Lucky. She also had some cheese and a biscuit. She brought an orange with her to share and that was the first thing she had a fancy for. As she began to peel it, the zest from the peel squirted into the air which smelled simply wonderful to her. She couldn't wait to taste it when she noticed Anna watching her. Elinore offered half to Anna which she happily accepted. Anna wanted to know if she was feeling okay after having all that laundry on top of her. Elinore admitted she was a little sore from it all, pausing for a moment. Then she began to secretly share what had happened when the men were digging her out. Anna didn't know what to say. She apologized and felt bad about not warning her about the way they stacked their baskets inside the workroom.

Elinore knew their lunch break would be short, and she needed to check on Lucky. She made sure he had water and then gave him the apple she had brought for him. Elinore could see a brightness in Lucky's face when she held the apple out for him and that made her happy too. She ran her hand over his back and beautiful mane. She whispered to him that it wouldn't be long until she was back for him. The loud whistle blew again, and all the workers filtered through the gates once again. Elinore found her way easily this time back to her ironing board and began to work. She worked quickly and soon she was a few baskets ahead of most of the ladies. The break had given her a renewed feeling and she had now developed a rhythm. She began to sing a song in her mind that was one of her mother's favorite songs, Edelweiss. It seemed to make her day go by faster and she pressed the clothing to the rhythm of the song. Elinore had asked Anna how much most people earned weekly while they had shared her orange. She didn't want to offend Anna, but Anna was happy to give her a guess. Elinore at first felt funny about asking such personal questions, after all, she didn't know Anna all that well, but Anna was happy to have someone her own age to talk with and seemed more than happy to answer her questions. Anna told her that she wasn't sure about the other women but that she made almost ten Goldmark per week. Elinore started to add up things in her mind. She knew she could make more if she pushed herself. If she could make fifteen a week, she could give five to herself, and so she set out with her song and stopped at nothing. Starch, press, fold. Starch, press, fold. Over and over as she hummed her tune. Her hard work did not go unnoticed by the woman who counted the baskets. She was impressed at how someone her age could be so disciplined. As Elinore brought basket after basket to the woman, she could tell she was becoming one of her favorites. The woman even told her to call her by her name. Elinore's first thought was how much the name Helga suited her. She was so stoic. She didn't dare make fun of it though. She just wanted to make as much money a week as she could.

At 4pm the final whistle blew. Elinore rushed out and went straight to her horse. She planned to make a quick stop at Carl's and go home. Elinore was pleased with herself. She had done well for her first day. Elinore sat atop Lucky and started down the long dusty road leading to Carl's. Again, she noticed that same young man watching her hard. She was sure she didn't know him and had never seen him before. She decided to smile at him and let him know she noticed his glare but was soon uncomfortable by his lack of a response. Not giving it another thought, she rushed to see Carl. When she arrived, she was pleasantly surprised by the smell of something delicious cooking. She gently knocked on the door. Carl opened the door and greeted her with a kiss. Carl's mother had made a wonderful oxtail soup that made her mouth water. Heidi insisted that Elinore have some after her long day working. They all sat down, and Elinore began to tell them all about her day. Heidi ladled out the soup into four bowls and after a short prayer of thanks, the table fell silent while the bowls slowly emptied spoonful by spoonful. With a full stomach and a few minutes to sit Elinore began to feel sleepy. A huge yawn came from her mouth, and she covered it with her hand. Elinore was embarrassed and let out a small giggle. She knew she had better be on her way and was glad to have her meal over with. Elinore gathered her strength to lift herself from the chair. She placed her bowl in the sink and said goodbye. Carl walked Elinore outside to help her with Lucky, tenderly kissing her before she made her getaway.

It didn't take long for her to make her way home. She put Lucky in the barn and could see Hans was busy building a frame on the ground leading from the larger barn to the horse barn. Elinore was curious now. Hans was hammering away as she walked over to see what he was up to. Hans was on all fours and looked up from his crouched position to see Elinore coming his way. Hans asked, "How did your first day go, little one?" Elinore really didn't like it when he called her that, but let it go. She shrugged her shoulders and asked Hans what he was doing. He began to tell her how he was going to make a concrete footpath between the barns so he wouldn't have to step through all the mud when it rained. The cattle traveled that way so often, grass never grew there. Elinore agreed it was a good idea. She told Hans she was tired, and he laughed. "Welcome to the grown-up world, Elinore!" She could hardly believe he called her by her name. She bent down to kiss him on his cheek.

Elsie saw that Elinore had made it home and greeted her at the door. A bowl of soup sat on the table with steam rising from it. A warm biscuit with butter sat next to it on a separate plate. Elsie told her to sit and nudged her toward the chair. Elinore looked at the soup. She really wasn't hungry but didn't want to make Elsie feel bad. She tasted the soup and couldn't believe it. Elsie had made oxtail soup! Elinore slurped it down quickly and went to her room. She felt she could just collapse in her bed, still wearing her clothes. Elsie followed her to her room with a wash bowl and a face cloth. Elinore had decided to just rise a little earlier in the morning to wash her hair but thanked Elsie anyway. She was asleep before her head hit the pillow.

It seemed that just a few minutes had passed before it was time to saddle up again. She washed her long hair as fast as she could and took the same steps to create a daily routine for herself. Sticking to her routine at work, was also working well. She finished fifteen baskets of laundry instead of ten that day. She took the time to eat with Anna again and she could tell that they would become good friends in time. She left work on the second day feeling much better, but as she headed down the long path to Carl's, that same man again, was standing in front of the general store seemingly waiting for her. It was like he didn't want to take his eyes off her for a second, and as she passed him, Elinore thought his neck would break from staring so hard. She thought about asking Carl to meet her there at quitting time, but the man thus far, had not really done anything to her but stare a hole in her. She changed her mind and decided to go straight home. Elinore was feeling less tired and much more empowered now. She sat on Lucky with her back straight as an arrow. She was happy with her accomplishments and was glad to now have more control over her life. She was looking forward to where this would take her.

She made her way home and entered the barn. Elinore could see Hans still working from a distance. Except this time, he was clearly upset about something. Not raising his voice but he was throwing rocks and kicking up dirt. Behind him, which was now visible to Elinore, was Delilah. She had made a path down Hans's freshly laid concrete to where he was working. Elinore burst into laughter at Hans who was now holding Delilah up by her arms. The concrete dripped from her shoes. Hans would have to fill in the footsteps Delilah had made and smooth the surface all over again. Elinore took Delilah from him to the pond to wash her off. She found it all quite funny and had a hard time swallowing her laughter. Elinore knew Hans was cross and she didn't want to make it worse for him. Hans was talking to himself and still working when Elinore brought Delilah inside. Elinore was glad to be home in time for an evening meal with her family and felt more relaxed than she had all week. The meal seemed like a time from the past. They all sat happily talking and sharing conversation. Margaret made a few jokes, and Elinore was enjoying the moment. Elinore made sure to finish the last bits of her sausage and potatoes. Elsie and Emma would be back shortly to clean up the kitchen.

Elinore decided to offer to bring Hans his meal and Elsie was happy to let her. That would be one less thing she needed to do. Hans saw Elinore heading his way holding up a large portion of food. It made his stomach rumble. He knew there was something delicious in the bowl she carried. Elinore handed it to him, and he immediately took a bite of it. "Ah that's good," he mumbled with his mouth full of food. "Thank you," he said pausing to swallow. "How did things go today?" he asked. Elinore told him things went well and that she had got more done today than she had yesterday. Hans nodded, "Good," shoveling another bite into his mouth. "Hans," Elinore said, "I'd like to tell you about something but I'm not sure what the meaning of it is." "Ok," Hans said and tried to listen closely. He was finding it hard to concentrate on anything but the delicious meal that was in his hands. Elinore began to tell him about the young man who had been staring at her every day outside of work so far. She told him that he hadn't said anything, but he made her uncomfortable. Hans wasn't surprised. Elinore was a beautiful young woman and he told her that that was probably the reason. Elinore smiled. She somehow knew that wasn't the reason but didn't know what was. "Yeah maybe," Elinore said and winked at Hans. Elinore thought a nice hot bath would be great to finish out the day with, and so she did and felt much better for it. She made her way down the hallway to her room where she found Margaret playing on the floor with her sheep knucklebones and wooden ball. The pouch she kept them in was tossed to the side. Elinore asked Margaret, "Why must you always play in my room?" Margaret grinned from ear to ear. She asked Elinore to play a game with her. Elinore really didn't want to, but she did. One game turned into four and it was then that she told Margaret that she needed to go to bed.

Grateful she had got her sister to play for awhile, Margaret didn't argue. She just missed spending time with Elinore. Elinore was finally able to get to her bed and enjoyed the warmth of the blankets that covered her. It was her happy place.

The week went by fast, and Elinore was excited. As she rose that morning, she knew it was payday. The sun brought warmth to the air, and it was particularly warm inside her job with the steam from the pressers. The day went the same as usual, starch, press, fold. She was exhausted by the time the day was over. The whistle blew at 4 o'clock sharp and within seconds, most of the women were lined up at Helga's desk. Luckily, there were only ten women in front of her. Anna was one of those women. She passed through the line and waited for Elinore outside.

Elinore eventually made her way to the desk. Helga handed her 14 Goldmark with a few coins. Elinore knew that was wrong. She knew she had done 10 baskets every day for the past six days. Her pay should have been 15 Goldmark. Elinore stood eyeing Helga. Helga motioned to Elinore to move along, but she wouldn't budge. Elinore knew how to add, and she had kept track of every basket. Her father had taught her well about adding and the cost of things. She stood firmly in place and held her hand out. "Miss Helga, I believe you owe me a few more pfennige." Helga drew her chin toward her neck and her bottom lip pushed out. With one eye almost closed, her eyebrow reflected doubt. She looked down again at her paper and re-counted with a grunt. Helga looked up and said, "I'm sorry dear, I did make a mistake, it seems. Here you go." Helga placed the rest of her money in Elinore's still outstretched small hand. "Thank you, Miss Helga." Elinore rushed out hoping Anna would be waiting for her. Anna was exactly where she had expected to find her, and they spoke for a good while. Elinore wanted to give Carl's parents some of her money before going home. She knew it would make their lives a little better and it made her happy to help. But when she turned to say goodbye to Anna, that same young man was there, and he was walking toward her! Elinore quickly turned around again, clutching Anna's arm and thrusted her forward. Alarmed, Anna sensed something was wrong, and they both moved very fast in the opposite direction. "What's wrong?" Anna whispered frantically. Elinore peeked over her shoulder, carefully covering her face to see that the man was now lighting a cigarette. Elinore asked Anna if she knew the man with the cigarette, but Anna did not. They spoke in whispers. She had seen him around but had no idea who he was. Elinore asked Anna to walk back with her to get Lucky and she agreed. By then, the man had disappeared. Elinore was glad and thanked Anna as they said goodbye again.

Elinore was still rattled when she arrived at Carl's, but gingerly jumped down from Lucky's back attempting to hide her nervousness. She took the money from the deep pocket in her apron, being careful not to nick her hand on her billhook and put it in Carl's mother's hand. Heidi was reluctant to take the money from Elinore, but she really did need it. Heidi didn't know how she would ever repay her. She took the money and hugged her tightly. Carl and Elinore then stole a few minutes alone together. She told him she loved him, and he told her the same. He was grateful for her help. Carl was having trouble getting ahead since the fire happened and the extra money would be a great help. Elinore wanted to make her visit short, so with a kiss she was on her way again.

As soon as she got home, she gave some of her money to her mother with a grand smile. She was proud of herself indeed. Her mother didn't like to take the money from her daughter, but she had a plan. She would hold that money for her and eventually give it back to her. Elinore ran off to her room to put the remaining money in the small wooden box under her bed with the ring Carl had given her along with her other small treasures. There would be only one more day until she could rest. Elinore wanted to spend a good part of that day with Carl, but she also wanted to give some of her time to Margaret. She knew Margaret felt abandoned and bored since she started working. Elinore hated to see her sister unhappy. She thought it might be fun to go to the pond and catch turtles or do some fishing like the way they used to. Elinore hoped the weather would be nice for them.

Elinore woke the next morning after a great night's sleep. She peeped into Margarets room before she left for work. Margaret was sitting on the edge of her bed, brushing her doll's hair and having an active conversation with her. Elinore couldn't help but smile at her little sister. She asked, "Are you up for some turtle hunting tomorrow?" "Oh yes Elinore, I would love that!" Margaret jumped off the bed in delight. She ran across the room and hugged Elinore around her waist.

She could see that spark in her sister that she always loved. While Elinore had grown nearly as tall as her father, Margaret only seemed to have grown slightly more since she was ten years of age. Elinore didn't really feel like going to work that day but off she went anyway. She pushed through the day, slopping her garments with starch, pressing and folding. She was already beginning to hate her mother's favorite song which she kept great pace with. The whistle blew as she completed her last basket of laundry and brought it to Helga. She ran out of the factory with her apron whipping her legs. She only paused briefly to wave to Anna. Quickly, she untied Lucky and bolted home. Lucky ran fast enough with a two-beat stride that allowed all four of his legs to leave the ground at once. A thick cloud of dust formed as they shot down the familiar path.

Near home, Elinore could see a wagon parked just outside the door. She harnessed Lucky in his stall with fresh food and water. Even giving him an extra apple for good measure. She hastily made her way to the door and when she opened it, she was pleasantly surprised to see her grandparents had come for a visit. Elinore was overjoyed. She kissed her grandmother and blew air on her grandfather's cheek with her lips pressed tightly against his face making a raspberry sound. This sound always produced huge peals of laughter between the two to signify the beginning of games and pranks to come. The following morning came with brilliant sunshine. "What a glorious day!" Katherine exclaimed, as she poured herself and Eddie their first cup of coffee for the day. Delilah had wrapped herself around her grandmother's knees. Katherine hoisted her up and sat her on her hip. Speaking baby talk to her, she placed her finger on her bottom lip. Katherine pushed down on her lip and Delilah made a humming sound which came out like a musical instrument. Katherine set Delilah down to hand Eddie his coffee, but Delilah wanted no part of that. She began to cry with her hands held up over her head in protest. Delilah wanted her grandmother to pick her up again.

Elinore knocked on Margaret's door to ask if she was ready. Margaret was already dressed and had her shoes on. Her fishing pole leaned against the wall. "I thought you wanted to catch turtles?" Elinore asked. Margaret thought for a moment and placed her finger on the corner of her smile. "Well, since Grandpa is here." Reaching for her pole she implied that she had changed her mind. Her eagerness made Elinore laugh. Soon the three of them sat by the pond's edge with their pole's lines casted out into the water. Eddie asked Elinore how she liked her new job. She answered with no excitement in her voice which made him think it might be better to leave that subject alone for now.

Eddie was already beginning to think about what pranks he would play on his girls while he was visiting. There were times he thought it might be that he enjoyed playing games more than they did. But he had met his match with Margaret. Since she was a baby, she had always enjoyed being the practical joker. A grin came over his face and his eyes shifted slightly. Slowly he turned to Margaret and asked how school was going. Excitedly, she told him all about what she and Gertrude had been doing. They had painted a large mural inside the classroom, on one of the walls of a field of flowers. It had added so much color to the room. Eddie then said to Margaret, "So I heard they are teaching a new kind of math." Margaret looked puzzled. "What do you mean?" she asked. Eddie replied, "Yes, I heard it is called Gazinta." Now, Margaret was really confused. "I don't know what you are talking about Grandad." Margaret's eyes squinted. She suspected he was up to no good. Eddie smiled and said, "You know, two gazinta four, twice." Eddie couldn't help but laugh. He was laughing at his own joke, but Margaret didn't find it funny at all. Eddie couldn't stop laughing at Margaret's frustration with him.

At that moment, a fish bit at her line and she began to squeal. "Opa, Opa, I caught one!" She reeled in her line quickly, only to find she had caught a turtle. Elinore was the one who busted out laughing now. She told Margaret, "See, I told you we should have gone turtle hunting!" Now, Margaret was really mad! Her face turned red, and she stomped off shouting at her sister and grandfather, "I'm telling Mama!" Margaret ran, and she could be heard yelling to Rose, "Maaaaa…they're doing it again! Grandpa and Elinore are picking on me!" Eddie and Elinore rubbed elbows and laughed. They had won the first match. They both knew though; this was just the first drawing of blood and Margaret would surely be planning her revenge.

As soon as Margaret entered the kitchen to tell her mother, she knew something wasn't right. Her mother and grandmother were seated at the table, and they were speaking in hushed voices. Her grandmother looked worried, and she could have sworn she saw her mother wipe a tear from her eye. Margaret knew she had interrupted something because both women sat up straight and the room fell silent as soon as she entered. Margaret took a sip of water and left in a hurry. She rejoined her grandfather and Elinore but spoke little. Eddie was determined to put little Margaret in a better mood. He hadn't expected she would be that upset. After a few minutes of silence, he looked over at her gazing across the pond with her elbows on her knees and her fists wedged under her chin.

Eddie stood up and moved closer to Margaret. She looked up at her grandfather. Her face was all twisted. He said, "Come on now, I have a trick that is sure to catch something. Here, give me your hook." Margaret slowly handed him her hook. She was half expecting another prank or joke to come her way. Eddie began to put a worm on her line and pierced it so it wouldn't fall off. He told her to cast her line as hard as she could. Margaret cranked her shoulder up as if she would reach the other side of the pond. With all her might and a grunt that sounded like it came from her toes, she flung her line forward. But Margaret had left too much line loose and as she thrust it forward the hook flew high up from behind her. The line snapped forward, and her hook caught the tail of Eddie's shirt. The hook from her forceful cast managed to pull Eddie's shirt off, over his head, landing right into the water in front of him. Eddie bellowed with a hearty laugh. He couldn't remember laughing that hard in years. He had never seen that happen before! His contagious laugh had all three of them exploding. It surely was a sight.

Eddie patted Margaret on the shoulder and said, "Let's try that again." Margaret cast her line again. Then Eddie said to her, "Now for the trick." From his pocket he pulled a piece of paper with something wrapped inside it. Curious, Margaret wanted to know what it was. Eddie told her it was his top secret for catching fish. Inside the paper, he had a small piece of cervelat, which he threw into the water near where her line had landed. Within seconds, she felt a tug in her line. Margaret pulled fast and hard. She reeled her line with excitement. Eddie and Elinore watched wide-eyed to see Margaret pull out a sunfish maybe 5 inches long. She was very proud of herself even though it wasn't a very big fish. Eddie asked her if she wanted to throw it back, but Margaret insisted on bringing it home to her mother, so in the bucket it went.

It was getting late, and the sun was starting to turn the sky into a beautiful pinkish purple, that continued to turn to shades of red mixed with darker grays and blue colors. Eddie decided it was time to get the girls back home. The wind brushed against their faces gently as they approached the house. Eddie spotted a small sized pile of cow manure in their path. As they got closer to it, Eddie began to act as if he were uncomfortable. Eddie was hatching another plan. He began to dig at his pant leg, all the while keeping his thoughts to himself. Closer and closer they came, until he stood beside the small pile. He lifted his leg slightly and began to shake his pant leg from the inseam. Eddie started to make a sound, much like a chimpanzee. "Ooh, ooh, ooh," he sounded, still tugging on his pants. Elinore and Margaret didn't know what to think. Should they do something? Was granddad in pain, they wondered? Eddie ended his antics with a sigh, and marked his relief with an exaggerated expression, "Ahhh!" Eddie was slightly ahead of the girls, so it did not allow him to see their faces. He waited in anticipation to hear their reaction. Margaret spotted the pile of pooh that their grandad had just pretended to deposit there. "Awwwe, granddad!" Elinore's nose scrunched up with disgust and Margaret pinched hers with two fingers. "Geeze granddad!" Elinore and Margaret moaned in harmony.

Margaret flung the door open to the kitchen, stunning Rose and Katherine, who were setting the table. Margaret screeched out loudly, "Maaaa…granddad stinky just poohed in his pants!" Rose shook her head in disbelief. Her father's pranks had gone to an all-time low. Eddie caught a foul look from Katherine, which told him there would be trouble later for him. Katherine didn't like disgusting jokes like the one he had just played, and he would wind up paying for that. Elinore secretly knew all along that it wasn't from granddad's pants, but she played the game and didn't let on, however, she was disgusted at the thought. She knew she was getting older now because she could understand why her mother and grandmother reacted the way they did. It was funny though watching Margaret be fooled by it all and she wasn't going to spill the beans.

Margaret watched her mother move through the kitchen with her grandmother when suddenly in a flash, she remembered the conversation between them that she had interrupted earlier. Everything seemed fine to her now, but it still bothered her. The seriousness on their faces had left but she still wondered what they had been talking about. She was still too angry with Elinore for laughing at her to talk to her about it. Delilah was busy trying to get one of the four women in the kitchen to pay attention to her. She cried to Elsie and Emma first to pick her up. Rose was too busy and so Katherine carried the child on her hip as they continued readying the kitchen for the evening meal. Elsie and Emma had prepared a nice ham with potatoes, and it smelled good.

It wasn't long before all that was left was a bone on a plate with some dirty dishes. Sleepiness entered the bodies of all those who remained around the table. Katherine covered her mouth in her usual lady-like fashion, with Delilah slumped over her shoulder, but Porter didn't try to hide the fact that he had had enough. He yawned big so that all could see clearly into his mouth exposing his back teeth. The sun outside had set, and the moon was bright. Elinore and Margaret made their rounds with kisses and left for bed. Elinore needed to be up early to leave in the morning for work. She felt that her one day off was not enough. She resented the fact that she had no time to herself but moved along anyway. Knowing the night would go by fast, she closed the door tightly so she would not hear any of the noises inside the house. She was also upset that her one day off didn't include one moment with Carl.

Eddie stepped outside for a bit of air and to have a look at the brilliant moon that was shining. He stood gazing at the stars. In the distance he could hear an owl. It was eerie and he was glad that nightfall had come already, for if it were still daytime, as folklore would have it, something soon would be on fire. Katherine opened the door to step outside for a minute herself when she was surprised to see Eddie there already. Katherine closed the door quietly behind herself. "Eddie, I need to tell you something." Eddie's eyes squinted curiously. "What is it?" he asked. Katherine didn't know how to tell him what Rose had told her. "Eddie," she said, "Porter is not doing so well in his business. The rumor going around is that the Prussian Army is going to disband and they've all but stopped ordering uniforms. Rose told me that they may have to send Elinore to live with Agnes for a little while." Eddie's shoulders shrunk and he was now looking at the earth beneath his feet. He shook his head in disbelief. "Maybe we could take her for a little while, what do you think, Katherine?" Eddie hoped it wouldn't come to that. Thoughts circled in his head, because he really didn't think Agnes would be a good influence on his young granddaughter. His daughter, Agnes, was much too ridged. Katherine told him that it wasn't definite yet but that it was a very real possibility. Eddie was sad at this news. He knew he and his wife were too old to be of any help, and their house was only big enough for two people. Eddie found it difficult to sleep that night and worried about his daughter, granddaughters and son-in-law.

Elinore was up early that morning. She was shocked to see her grandfather was already in the kitchen looking for his first cup of brew. He had already made the coffee instead of waiting for Elsie and offered her a cup. Elinore held up her hand as she whizzed by. "No thanks, I have to go now." She pecked him on his cheek and was gone in a flash. Eddie looked around not really knowing what he was looking for. He still was disturbed by what he'd been told. He made his way around the kitchen lifting things up and putting things down, when he came across the core of an eaten apple lying beside the drainboard. The ants had come in from under the door, up the side of the sink and were swarming over the remains. He took a cup and filled it with the lye Rose had stored in the closet. He started to sprinkle it over the ants, and he followed them down their trail which led him out the door.

Margaret had heard Elinore leave, but she could still hear someone talking. She wanted to know who that someone was, so in her nightclothes she wandered through the house in the direction of the voice. She found her granddad in the doorway of the kitchen. "What are you doing Opa?" she asked. He looked at her with one eye closed and his upper lip curled up on one side. In a serious pirate voice, he told her that he was telling the ants to leave. Margaret was convinced her granddad had lost his marbles. She asked, "Why are you talking like a pirate?" With the most serious expression he could muster up and voice to go with it, Eddie explained, "These are pirate ants, Liebchen. One must speak in pirate to them so that they understand." She couldn't believe he told her that! She ran to Rose's room as fast as she could. Her siren going off, "MAAAAAA. Granddad is at it again!" Her voice could be heard throughout the house.

Rose came out of her bedroom wrapping her house coat around her tightly. She had one finger pressed against her lips, shushing Margaret. "Do you want to wake everyone? Quiet down!" she hissed. Rose hurried to the kitchen quickly and whacked her father on the top of his head with two fingers. "Why do you have to make that child crazy?" Eddie ducked trying to cover his laugh, but he couldn't hide his sputtering. Rose went in for another whack, but Eddie had enough experience avoiding blows from Katherine to know how to avoid a direct hit. Eddie squeezed his daughter's side. He knew she was ticklish there and made his getaway to the door as fast as his feet could take him. Rose could laugh now that her father was outside. He had been a prankster for as long as she could remember and now, he had Margaret in training. She took a deep sigh and went to check on Delilah. Thankfully, the child had not been awoken by the chaos and Rose could sit for a minute to collect her thoughts.

Elinore had arrived at work with a few minutes to spare. She sat on the bench and waited for Anna. She hoped they would be able to chat a little before the workday began. Elinore's thoughts soon turned to Carl. It would be another week before she could spend any time with him. She was already missing him. Again, she thought about the fact she was only allowed one day off from work and that simply was not enough. She considered that maybe in another month she would ask to cut her schedule by one day. She wasn't sure they would let her, but it was worth it to ask. Her next thought was that if she wasn't too tired at the end of the day, she might be able to go see him. Elinore knew he would understand why she hadn't come by as soon as she told him about her grandparents' surprise visit. The day went by fast, and Elinore's pace picked up nicely. She had worked out a routine that worked like a clock, in such a short time. She left the building as soon as the whistle blew. Elinore had told Anna all about her grandparents and so she didn't wait for her. She hurried out past large gates and lifted herself onto her horse.

Elinore clutched the reigns tightly, but before she could move, the man that had been stalking her, placed his hands over hers. He had come out of nowhere. Elinore was frightened. "What do you want!" she shouted at him. "Why are you following me?" The man tried to pull her down off Lucky, but she sat firm and pushed him away. She could see his rage building. In a fury, he reached for her again. Elinore had her eyes fixed on his movements. She was not ready to pull her weapon just yet, but she was becoming irate herself, and up for the challenge. This man was no match for her. He was thin and she felt she could easily land him on his bottom. The man wrathfully shouted out, "I know who you are!" Elinore was stunned. Again, she demanded to know who he was and what he wanted. And again, he shouted out to her that he knew who she was and what she had done. Elinore had no idea what this man was talking about. He fell silent, but a look of hostility remained on his face. Then he spoke spewing his venom. "My father disappeared while he was working at your father's house! I want to know what you've done with him!" he demanded.

Now, Elinore knew what this was all about! The man that stood before her was the son of the man she had shot! Her memory flashed back to that awful moment but all she could remember was the man's eyes and bloody face as she shot him. Her blood ran cold, but Elinore kept her cool. "I have no idea what you are talking about, Sir, and I am asking you politely to leave me alone!" she shouted off to him. He faced her. He was only a few feet away but charged at her, closing the gap within seconds. She landed on the ground as he pulled her down off her horse with her dress. Instantly, he was now on top of her reaching for her throat. Elinore's instincts kicked in as they rolled over each other through the dirt. Again, he screamed, demanding to know what had happened to his father. He had managed to distract her for just enough time to gain the upper hand. Elinore was flat on her back, and he straddled her with a leg on each side of her waist. Elinore was not about to give up yet though. He looked straight into her eyes. Froth dripped from his lower lip and his face was darker than before. "If you don't tell me what your family has done with my father, I am going to the Prussian Secret Police!"

That word sent shivers down Elinore's spine. She had only been coming to Carl's town for 3 weeks for work and trouble was already brewing. She knew they would know who her father was because he was a big distributor for their uniforms. The man would still have to prove that she and her family were responsible for any wrongdoing, and she also knew that they had buried his father with everything he had come with in the field. His words still sent shockwaves of fear through her veins. She needed time to think and there wouldn't be a lot of that coming in the near future. Still, she insisted that she knew nothing about his disappearance. It was clear the young man did not believe her, from the expression on his face. She quickly lifted herself onto her horse and charged at him. He began to flail, his arms swinging wildly attempting to stop her from escaping. Lucky sensed the danger and kicked the man with his rear leg hard enough to flatten him, allowing her to ride off in a quick getaway. She arrived at Carl's looking a little disheveled. Straight away, Carl wanted to know what happened to her. Nonchalantly, she answered his questions, and changed the subject to her grandfather and Margaret. She apologized for not having enough time to come by the day before but promised to make it up to him. The entire time she spoke to Carl, she couldn't stop thinking about what she should do about the man outside her work and what he had said.

She had been at Carl's way too long and needed to get going. Elinore leaned in and kissed him affectionately. She squeezed him tight, whispering that she must go now. Carl was disappointed and wanted her to stay longer. Her schedule was weighing on her and she knew she would find it hard to keep up with, even in the short time it had already been. It bothered him that it seemed like Elinore had no time to spend with him, but she promised him it would be just a few more weeks and she would cut back on her days. That made Carl happy. She kissed him again and Carl watched as she rode off.

Elinore wasted no time searching for Hans. She needed to talk to him and then probably her father immediately. As she suspected, Hans was outside working, and she could see him from quite a distance before she completed her journey. She hurried over to him, not knowing what could be done about it all. Elinore was scared about the man's threat of sending the Prussian Secret Police after her and her family. She picked up her pace, running toward Hans, and he saw her coming. "Hans, I need to talk with you now, it's very important!"

Hans could see that she was not joking around. She had a bewildered look in her eyes, and he could see the fear in her. He knew it was something urgent. Hans led her into the cattle barn and closed the sliding doors shut. Hans placed his hands on each of her forearms. He could see she was upset, and he tried to calm her. "Tell me what this is all about. What's wrong?" he asked. Hans was concerned; knowing Elinore was not one to worry or overreact. "Hans, remember the man?" She stopped for a second. Elinore lowered her voice to a whisper. "Remember the man I shot?" Hans looked down at the ground. "Yes, Elinore, what about him?" His face took on a grim appearance. Hans knew from her question, trouble was coming. Elinore continued. "Well, remember the young man I told you about at work that has been glaring at me? I fought with him today." Hans was still listening intently waiting for more details. Hans was the type of man that liked to get to the bottom of things fast and be done with it. "He told me he knows either I or someone in my family killed his father. He told me he hadn't seen his father since he worked here. He's threatening to go to the police. Hans, what are we going to do?" Elinore was frantic. Hans put his arm over her shoulder to comfort her. He ran his fingers down the long strands of her hair. Hans carefully thought for a minute and said, "I'll take care of everything. Don't worry, but I will need a little help from you tomorrow, okay? Do you understand me, Elinore?" Hans spoke to her with a very serious tone. "After evening meal, I want you to meet me back here," he continued. Elinore looked at him with tears in her eyes. She asked, "Hans, do you think we should tell my father?" Hans, without hesitation, said no. He knew Porter already had his hands full and this would make it worse. Hans was already thinking up a plan to take care of this problem before it got any bigger. He knew what he needed to do. There were a few people who owed him a favor or two and now he would need to collect on them. Elinore rushed through her meal that evening and finished before anyone else. She asked Elsie if she wanted her to deliver Hans's meal to him. Elsie was glad to accept her offer. Elinore scampered through the field and tapped her knuckles against the barn door. Hans opened the door just enough to pull her through and quickly closed it behind her. He set the bowl she carried down and said, "Okay, tomorrow you will speak to that man," he began. That was the last thing Elinore wanted to hear. She had no idea where Hans was going with this and started to scratch her head. "Why?" she asked. "Just do what I tell you Elinore!" Hans said sternly. "I want you to tell him that you will tell him everything you know the following day and then get on your horse and leave! Do not turn to look back!" Again, he asked her if she understood him. Elinore could tell Hans was very serious and she quickly told him that she did. "Now go, and do everything I told you to do tomorrow, exactly as I told you!"

When the morning came, Elinore rose to go to work. Except this morning, she was nervous. She went through her usual course of steps and waited for Anna on the bench. She worked without thinking, in an automated way. She really couldn't think of anything else except her conversation with Hans and looking for that man after work. When the whistle blew, Elinore brought her last basket to Helga and left quickly. Elinore did not see the man outside right away, but as she neared Lucky, there he was standing in between her horse and the horse next to hers. Elinore was frightened and her hands shook from the nervous tension building within. "You don't give up, do you?" Elinore asked putting on a front. She wished he would just leave her alone and go away. "What do you want?" she asked. Elinore's teeth were beginning to clench, and her jaw jutted out slightly. The man replied, "You know what I want." He had an evil sort of look about him this time and at that moment she could see his resemblance to the man that she had killed. Elinore got on her horse and said to the man, "I have no time to speak with you now. Come back here tomorrow and I will tell you everything I know." And with that, she gave a gentle kick to Lucky and left, exactly as she had been told to do. She did not look back.

Elinore made her way to Carl's and was happy to see him. She needed to release her anxiety and he was the perfect person to help with that. She was glad to be able to spend some time with him but didn't share the thing that bothered her most. She pushed it out of her mind as Carl told her about his day at Mr. Schmidt's. Someone had brought a horse in for new shoes, but the horse had a very bad infection in its hoof. It was messy. All Elinore heard was his voice but nothing he actually said. She tried her best to look like she was interested in what he was saying. She did her best not to yawn. Just when she thought she couldn't take another moment of his blabbing, she pressed her finger against his lips and kissed him hard. Finally, she found a way to shut him up! Carl couldn't recall where he had left off in his story after that. They walked together to the side of his house where he had planted a garden. Everything was growing nicely, and Carl's mother would have a lot to do soon, preparing for the winter. Elinore stole a few more quiet moments with her love before she thought about leaving for home. Oh, how she wanted to stay, but she had something she needed to take care of that needed her attention.

When she completed her journey, she began to look for Hans, but he was not in either the barn or his house. She wondered where he could be. She really wanted to see him. She had done everything according to plan. Elinore wondered why he was not home. What could be more important than the problem they had, she thought. Elinore felt herself a bit upset with Hans. After she ate, she went again to look for him, but still he was nowhere to be found. Unknown to Elinore, Hans had been outside the factory when she left. He watched carefully, obscured from view. He waited from a short distance and watched the young man that Elinore had left standing there.

Hans's eyes focused on him. A tall gangly man who moved with a loose-jointed awkwardness about him. He had no horse, which told Hans his home could not be far. He watched him walk down the center pathway through the village. Hans followed him slowly, making sure not to draw attention to himself. He knew he had to make this problem go away. This man would become a big problem if he didn't. And Porter had enough problems. He followed, closing in on the young man, when he watched him enter an improvised building, seemingly made from bits and pieces discarded by the villagers. It was sort of a shanty home with a large wooden barrel just outside the opening in the front. It had another opening to go in and out. The house was mostly made of wood and mud, and poorly constructed for a German made building. Hans watched him enter the building while he waited patiently.

When nightfall came, Hans was still in a position to observe his every move closely. He noticed a small light glowing in one section of the house that was visible between the wooden planks. He watched the man smoke a cigarette. He would need to wait just a little longer to be sure no one would see him from under the cover of the night's darkness. He waited until only the light of the moon lit the sky. Hans crept closer to the house. He began to imitate the howls of the wolves he had grown to despise in Porter's field. His call was perfect, and he was the embodiment of a wolf himself. Still, he waited patiently for that exact moment. Hans's howls brought exactly what he wanted from them. They drew the man out of his home. Hans rushed at him with no sound at all. With his branding iron he cracked the man's skull wide open, knocking him unconscious. Hans swiftly pushed him inside the large Hessian feed bag he had brought with him. Hans closed the bag tight and threw it over the back of his horse. He charged through the darkness toward the seaport. The horse was breathing hard, but Hans pushed him to go faster.

As soon as he reached the port, he started to search for a friend of his that he had made long ago. This friend had a small fishing boat, and he knew he could depend on his help. Hans searched the water's edge looking into every boat at the dock.

He had not seen his friend in nearly six months, but he continued to look fiercely for him. Hans scrambled along, making sure not to let a soul see him. It wasn't long before Hans saw the boat he was looking for. He called out to his friend. "Ben? Is that you?" He could see a figure inside the boat. Ben stuck his head out from inside the cabin to see who was calling him. Ben was happy to see Hans. He asked, "What are you doing down here so late?" The waters softly splashed against the sides of the boats that were docked there. Hans spoke quietly, "Ben, I need a favor." Ben could see the seriousness in Hans's expression. "Sure," he answered. "What do you need?" "I need you to take care of that bag on the back of my horse," pointing in the direction to where his horse stood waiting. "What do you mean take care of, Hans?" Hans looked into Ben's face and said, "I need it gone so that it never comes back." Ben was stunned. He asked, "Are you sure?" Hans, without hesitation said, "Yes, I'm sure." The two men lifted the bag off the horse and threw it into the coal bunker on Ben's boat. The man inside the bag moved slightly and groaned in pain. It was clear he was badly injured from the blow to the back of his head and blood had started to stain the outside of the bag. Ben slammed the wooden lid shut with a thud and shook Han's hand. "Nice to see you again Hans, but I must be going now." Ben quickly began to untie the rope his boat was tied to the pier with. Hans stood and watched in the darkness as the small fishing boat chugged off, vanishing from sight.

Ben turned the engine up. He wanted to finish this as fast as possible. Once Ben could no longer see land, he started to think about what he was about to do. The North Sea was cold, and Ben pulled his coat close around his chest. With a grunt he tossed the bag overboard. Ben heard the splash but did not look back. He wanted nothing further to do with it all.

The man in the bag was still alive and could feel the frigid ocean water. He knew he would not survive at that moment. He held his breath until he felt he would pass out. As he was forced to take his last breath, the frigid water filled his lungs and the bag took on the weight, slowly beginning its circling descent to the bottom of the German Ocean floor.

Ben decided he would not return to that seaport for a very long time. He knew whoever was in that bag must have done something horrible. Ben had known Hans a long time and had never known him to be violent unless provoked. He tossed another shovel of coal into the engine and steam coming from the small smokestack became illuminated under the moonlight. The waves gently rippled in the disturbed flow of water from the boat as it moved through it. The moon kissed each ripple highlighting the small waves. Ben recognized it was this romance of the sea that he made his lifetime commitment to. He didn't really mind if he ever visited that harbor again. There were many more he could do business with.

It was still dark when Hans was finally able to lie down on his bed. He wanted to sleep for a few hours before he needed to get up and tend to the horses and cattle. It was only about an hour later though, when he heard a wagon being pulled across the field. Hans sat up and rubbed his bloodshot eyes with his first knuckle. Sand had already started to accumulate in the corners of them and it stung like small cuts when he rubbed them. He splashed his face with the water he still had in his washbowl and quickly combed his hair. He pulled his suspenders onto his shoulders and opened the door to find Katherine and Eddie loading their things into their wagon. He rushed to help and made sure the harness was secure before they left. Soon, he was able to return to his bed for another hour before he would begin his workday.

Elinore went looking for Hans again. She wanted to ask Hans where he had been. Elinore found him sitting on a stool milking one of the cows. Elinore tapped her foot against the ground impatiently, demanding to know Hans's whereabouts. Hans was exhausted and in a bit of a hump. He looked at her standing with her hands on her hips. "Before you say another word," pointing his finger at her, he said, "First off, watch your tone with me little one, and second off, I'm telling you now, don't ever and I mean ever, speak about this again." Hans grumbled under his breath. Aggravated by her boldness, he growled. "The problem is gone and there's nothing to talk about!"

Elinore had a lot of questions, but Hans had ended their conversation. Hans had never spoken to her in that manner before. She left him without another word. Elinore never saw that young man again. He and his dreadful father were just a memory Elinore chose not to revisit from that day forward.

Chapter 13

Porter had left for work early that morning. He had many things on his mind and needed time to himself. He sat staring at his desk for hours while the telegraph fell silent. Porter was depressed. He hadn't ever felt so pathetic in all his life. He had no answers or solutions to his current problem. He wondered how he would explain himself. He hadn't even made enough to pay Elsie and Emma their weekly wages. Porter thought to himself, if only that telegraph would spit out a few orders. He slammed his clenched fist down on his desk and backhanded an old newspaper off the desk to watch it flurry to the floor. Holding his head in his two hands, Porter knew the subject of what to do with his loyal employees would need to be addressed. He would need to slim his payroll completely. Affecting all his workers until business picked up or he could figure something out, was something he hated to do. The only one he planned to keep was Greta for the time being. She could handle anything that may come in the absence of the rest of the staff. Porter still had his local clients too to supply. He wasn't ready to give up just yet. Those small number of clients that bought material from him for other small businesses around town would be necessary to keep him going. It wasn't much but it was at least something. Greta was worth her weight in gold. The thought had crossed his mind more than once about selling his most prized possession, his automobile. He had set up an appointment with a man who he knew had admired his auto for the very next day. Porter's thought turned to Elsie and Emma. They were necessary to keep for now and he would use the money he made from the sale of his auto partially to give them their earned pay. Porter wasn't particularly worried about Hans.

He was very independent, and he and the family could survive on the proceeds of their small herd of cattle. Porter thought about going back to the days of farming like his parents had done long ago, but he didn't like that idea much. Porter never liked getting his hands dirty. Porter could plant a field large enough to support his family, but the thought made him cringe. They were long hours of exhausting physical work.

As night fell, Elinore pulled the blankets over herself and settled in. She couldn't help but be excited. It was her fifth straight week of work and pay day was here again. Elinore slept well that night but was still tired when she rose. Dragging her feet to the bathroom, she got ready for work. As she filled the washbowl, she stared into the tiny mirror. She stood there thinking about how much she'd rather just stay home. She looked as tired as she felt. She splashed the cold water onto her face, but it didn't make her look any better. Her thoughts flooded with all the time she was missing out on, especially with Carl and her sisters. She missed picking wildflowers and catching butterflies with Margaret. But the thing she missed most of all was sleeping until the sun came up. She dragged herself to the kitchen to throw a few things in a paper sack. Elinore didn't have the same enthusiasm as she had in those first two weeks. But today would be her fifth payday and that sweetened the pot just a little. The skies were darker than usual that morning and as Elinore walked toward the barn, she could taste the moisture in the air when she took it in. She pushed Lucky to move faster, trying to reach the factory before the rain came. She could feel the first drops of water hit her face as she came to the huge gates. She fastened Lucky to his post and ran to the small overhang along the side of the factory. Many people had taken shelter there as they all waited for the gates to open. Elinore quickly scanned the crowd looking for Anna from side to side, as the rain began to come down heavier.

Puddles were beginning to form, and Elinore's boots became mostly covered with mud. Elinore rounded the corner of the overhang when without warning, she found herself on her hands and knees. Stunned, she picked herself up and looked at her mud-covered hands. Her eyes lowered downward to her mud-covered apron. It was then that she noticed a young girl leaning against the building pointing and laughing at her. Even some of the men were laughing. Her jaw tightened with anger. Elinore needed a moment to take stock of what had just happened. Before she reacted, she wanted to carefully think about what to do next. She didn't like the way the girl had laughed at her mishap. She really wanted to beat the girl to a pulp, but she controlled herself. She waited and watched the girl closely. She wasn't entirely sure if she had just stumbled, or the girl had tripped her on purpose. Elinore couldn't understand why the girl would be so hateful toward her.

Inside the factory, Helga told Elinore to take a minute to clean herself off so she wouldn't get her basket full of freshly laundered clothing dirty. Elinore returned quickly and began working as fast as she could. She was almost caught up when the lunch whistle blew. Anna and Elinore walked out together and headed for the gates, when the girl from outside spotted Elinore. She didn't like Elinore. She was used to being Helga's favorite and it seemed to her Elinore was trying to take her place. She rushed between the two friends, knocking Elinore to the ground again. Her paper sack went flying into the air and crashed to the ground, spilling her lunch out over the floor. Anna kneeled to pick up Elinore's lunch, and the two met each other face to face. Anna asked, "Are you okay?" Elinore was very angry now. She looked up and saw the girl twitching her way toward the front gates. "No! I am not okay!" Elinore shouted at Anna with fire in her voice.

Anna knew this wasn't going to end well. "Take it easy, Elinore," Anna said, attempting to calm her friend down. But Elinore wanted no part of it. She couldn't let this go again. She sprinted after the girl, jumping on her back. The girl was already way ahead of Elinore and didn't expect the weight of Elinore's body to hit her with such force. They tumbled to the ground, and it was obvious Elinore would overtake her. Elinore began pounding on the girl's head with her fists. Blow by blow, the girl endured the brutal beating of Elinore's wrath. Finally, Elinore stopped when the girl laid still. Soon Elinore found herself surrounded by all who worked in the factory. Some were gawking, some helped the bloodied girl who had started it all, and some of the supervisors were trying to break into the center of the large crowd to break things up. The next person Elinore saw was the lady with the clipboard.

She looked wildly at her. "Explain yourself! What is going on here?" But just as Elinore began to speak, Helga picked her up by her arm. She told the woman that she would take care of the problem and the woman scratched something on her clipboard with a humph. Elinore came to her feet and Helga walked with her to the front of the building. Helga knew what she must do and wasn't happy about it. She told Elinore, "You know, I was really beginning to like you. You're a hard worker and I wish you well." Helga handed Elinore her wages for the week and said, "I'm sorry darling, but you can't work here anymore. They don't tolerate fighting." Elinore began to stutter. "But I didn't start it!" she shouted out to Helga. Helga only turned to go back into the building.

There was nothing to talk about. Elinore hadn't even got to say goodbye to her friend Anna. Greatly disappointed in herself, Elinore mounted Lucky and headed in the direction of Carl's house. Carl was outside his home and was happy to see Elinore coming. He lifted her off the horse, and gently set her down. Her greeting was less than warm. He could see there was something wrong. They went inside the house and Elinore handed Carl's mother some of her money. Elinore then had to give her the bad news. She had to explain that she wouldn't be able to give her anymore until she found more work. Heidi was confused. Things seemed to be going so well for Elinore. Carl followed behind her. He put his hand on the small of her back and gently guided her to his room. There, everything spilled out. Tears streamed down Elinore's face. Carl sat listening intently. He tried to comfort Elinore and told her all would be fine. He put his arm around her shoulder and pulled her close to him. Carl lifted her face with his forefinger under her chin. He kissed her lips softly. "You'll find work again soon, it'll be okay, El." His assurance didn't make her feel any better. It wasn't even her fault that she had lost her job. Then Carl said, "Hey, at least I will see you more often now."

Elinore smiled when she saw the happiness in Carl's eyes as he said it. Now all she had to do was explain all of it to her father. She wasn't looking forward to that. She hated disappointing her father. They sat for a while longer and Elinore had to admit, it was nice to not be in such a hurry to leave. She did need to go home though and explain things to her parents. She promised to return tomorrow to spend more time with him and left.

When Elinore could see her house from the field, she stopped Lucky. She wanted a minute to collect her thoughts before she told her father what had happened at work that day. Elinore was saddened by losing her job. She had only completed her fifth week and didn't know how she would break this news. She hoped her father wouldn't be too disappointed in her because she hated to let him down. She sat still in that field atop her horse with her head hung low. She swatted hard at the bugs that flew around her face. They annoyed her and she was in no mood to be bothered by them. Elinore could feel the tears forming behind her eyes when she noticed a butterfly flying around her. It had landed on her arm and rested there for more than a moment before flying off to another flower. She hoped another job would come along, just as another flower had come along for that butterfly. When she finally reached home, she fed Lucky about as slowly as she ever had. Elinore was putting off going into the house for as long as she could but the inevitable was to come. Elinore reached for the door but hesitated to turn the knob. She would have done anything to not have to tell her father of her failure. She had been so proud of herself. The time had come, and she needed to open the door. Her shoulders were hunched over, and she was the epitome of the saddest individual on earth.

As she lifted her head to tell her tale she could see there was something wrong already. Porter and Rose were seated at the table and her mother was clearly upset. Elinore wondered if they already knew of what happened at the factory. But how? Porter called out Elinore's name in a very solemn voice. "Come darling, please sit down." Elinore made her way to the table and sat down. She didn't know what was about to happen, but she was very worried. Feeling like she would explode, she blurted out the words, "Father, I lost my job today." Elinore's eyes welled up and tears started to collect. Porter could see his daughter was devastated by what she had just told them and now he really felt horrible about what he was about to tell her. Porter stood up and pulled Elinore into his barrel chest for a hug. Rose joined in the hug and all three embraced each other. Porter placed his hand on Elinore's shoulder, easing her back down into the chair. Elinore prepared herself to now hear the scolding. She began to take her last wages out of her apron and placed them on the table. She pushed it toward her mother. Disheartened, Rose could not take Elinore's money and pushed the money back into Elinore's hand. "What's wrong mother?" Elinore asked. "I'll get another job in a week or two, I promise."

There was a long silent pause in their conversations. Elinore looked at her mother and could see her face was sadder than she could ever remember. It was swollen and red. Something else was bothering her. Something just wasn't right. Elinore then took notice of her father. He seemed sad too. Slowly, Porter began to speak. He needed to break some more upsetting news to her, and the timing couldn't have been worse. He started off with, "We want to tell you something and you are old enough now to understand. There has been a problem brewing at work for me concerning the orders and the money just isn't there anymore, Elinore. I've had to tell all my workers to go home. It's very bad right now. Your mother and I may even have to go back to farming to put food on the table."

Elinore thought for a minute. She had no idea things were so bad. But that surely explained why her father had been acting so grumpy lately. A look of concern came to her face, and she reached across the table for her father's hand. Her problems seemed so petty now to her. "How can I help?" she asked.

Porter bowed his head. He had no words. All he could say was, "I'm afraid darling, there isn't anything you can do to help." Porter knew Elinore could never make enough to pay for everything that was necessary by herself. He looked at

Rose and then back at Elinore. He felt dreadful. He had to tell his daughter the hardest thing he ever dreamed of but just couldn't find the words.

Rose couldn't take any more of the tension and decided to put it to rest. She sat up straight and cleared her throat. Rose took Elinore's hand and began to explain things to her oldest daughter. "Your father and I have decided that you are the one person in this family who is strong enough to do this. Elinore, we have decided you will go to stay with your Aunt Agnes, in the United States for a little while. When things get better, we will send for you to return home."

Elinore shouted, "NO! I don't want to go to another country! I don't even know Aunt Agnes! And what about Carl? I love him, and I don't want to leave him!"

Rose was shocked at Elinore's admission about Carl, and so was Porter, but at this point, it didn't make a difference. Porter simply did not have enough income to feed all the mouths in his family. Rose then said, "Elinore. it won't be forever, just for a little while until we can figure things out here. Carl will be here when you return, and it will be good for you to travel while you are still young." Rose knew that wasn't the entire truth of the matter and as she spoke, she had a sick feeling in her stomach. The truth of it was that they weren't sure if they would ever have enough money to bring her home again. They had no plan, but they were sure that Elinore was a strong girl, and she could make it on her own with a fresh start. Rose was confident her sister would take good care of Elinore.

Elinore's head spiraled with a sinking feeling. She slammed the palms of her hands down hard on the wooden table and shouted, "No, I don't want to go! I won't!" And with that, she picked herself up and ran to her room slamming the door behind her.

Margaret had heard the commotion and went to Elinore's door. She tried to open it, but it was locked. Margaret could hear Elinore sobbing and she didn't know what to do. She went looking for her parents, but they were in their room with the door locked too. What in the world was going on? she thought. Elinore's sobs could still be heard throughout the entire house.

She was inconsolable. She made sure of that when she locked her bedroom door. Elinore's world was crumbling around her. Going to another country; so far away from her parents. Never seeing Carl again, never seeing Margaret, Delilah, or Hans again. And Elsie or Emma, who had taught her so much. She had known Elsie and Emma for as long as she could remember. She hardly knew her Aunt Agnes. As a matter of fact, she couldn't even recall what she looked like. The only thing she could remember was her father making fun of how tight she wore her hair and that he wasn't particularly fond of her. Now, all she wanted to know was why her? No one else had to leave. She had even offered to get another job to help. Elinore felt betrayed by her parents. She questioned what she had done to deserve this. Elinore was very upset. Her pillow was wet from her tears, when she stood and looked out her window seemingly looking for an answer. She gazed across the field watching the cattle graze. She looked at the mountain range against the skyline. As the long yellow grass swayed in the breeze, a feeling of hopelessness sank into her soul. Elinore's eyes were bright red and swollen. Her nose whistled as she tried to breathe with each inhalation. Mucus ran down her upper lip. She wiped her nose with her sleeve. She needed to see Carl. Elinore brushed her hair and wiped her face in a flash. Elinore's mind was racing now. How could she get out of the house without anyone seeing her leave? She pressed her ear against her door, listening keenly. She could still hear Emma and Elsie talking. Leaving through her bedroom door was not an option. The only way she would be able to leave was from her window. Elinore piled the blankets on the bed to make it look like she had cried herself to sleep. Just in case her mother used a key to look in on her, she would see the pile of blankets and maybe she wouldn't go beyond the doorway. Outside, it was the darker end of twilight, and she knew she would be barely visible by anyone looking out. The only one that really concerned her was Hans. Elinore knew he was unpredictable. She quietly pushed the eyehook through the loop, releasing its grip on the window. Elinore had never done anything like this before, but now it just didn't matter. She just didn't care. If her parents truly loved her, as they had always told her, they wouldn't send her to live in another country with someone she didn't even know. Elinore hesitated briefly but in the next second, both her feet were on the ground outside her window. She pushed it closed and wedged a small stick in the corner so the window would stay closed. Elinore looked around to see if Hans was outside. Like a hunting lioness, she crept along, almost touching the ground, concealing herself with the tall grass until she reached the barn. Camouflaged by the darkness, Elinore and Lucky were swiftly on their way to Carl's house.

It wasn't long before Elinore was tapping on Carl's window, and he heard her. Looking out, he could see Elinore's horse just outside. Carl reached for his jacket and went to see why Elinore had come so late in the evening. Elinore stood in the shadows and with the moon's glow, Carl could see the reflection of tears running down Elinore's face. "What's wrong Elinore?" he asked as he put his arms around her. Carl believed this was all about Elinore losing her job, but she had much more to tell him. Elinore began to tell Carl the things her father had said, and Carl developed a heaviness in his heart. He didn't know what to say to her. He didn't know what he could say to make her feel better. He was sad himself, knowing he was about to lose the love of his life.

Elinore had a serious look on her face when she turned to Carl to speak. She asked, "Carl, did you mean it when you asked me to marry you?" "Why yes, Elinore," he said, "But when we get a little older." Elinore's eyes lowered and the disappointment on her face was clear. She questioned his disloyalty to her. Had he lied? "What, how old?" she asked angrily.

Carl struggled for something to say. "Elinore, I just don't think now is the right time. I still need to care for my mother and father. We are just starting over from our home burning down. Besides, I don't think your father would like it much either," he bravely said.

Elinore backed up and was clearly more upset than when she arrived, but now she was also disappointed. She shoved Carl, putting distance between them. "I thought you loved me,

Carl!" she growled. Carl lunged at Elinore, firmly grabbing hold of her arm and pulled her into himself. He knew she was desperate, but he didn't like being treated so unfairly. He held her face, looking deeply into her eyes and said, "Elinore, when I said I love you, that was forever. If you have to go to another country for a little while, I will still be here waiting when you return, I promise."

Carl had made her feel a little better about things, but she was still hurt that her parents had chosen her to be the one to be shipped off. No one could make that pain go away. She was also upset at the outcome of her foiled attempt to have Carl rescue her through marriage.

Carl decided to ride along with Elinore to make sure she got home safely, and in the moonlight, they traveled closely. Almost touching each other. When they were almost there, Carl kissed her once again. He did not want to leave her and wondered just how much more time he would have with her.

Elinore made her way through the darkness and snuck back in through her bedroom window. Once she got inside, she hastily put her night clothing back on and did a test yawn as if she had just gotten up from her bed. She opened her bedroom door with another fake yawn and made her way to the bathroom. Elinore played the part well, even remembering to mess up her hair. She had only come out of her room to see if anyone else was awake in the house, but there was no noise at all. It was still early, so Elinore returned to her room, anxious about what the morning would bring. She had no job to rush off to now. She lay on her bed, looking around her room. She stretched out her arms and her belly rose slightly. Another huge yawn came from her mouth, but this one was not pretend. She was tired from her long night out. She restlessly put her feet on the floor and noticed how cold it was. The mornings and nights were starting to grow colder now. It was Elinore's favorite time of year, but it didn't bring her the same joy as it always had. Over and over, her father and mother's words rang in her mind. She knew one thing for sure, she wasn't going to go willingly. Reality was beginning to set in again. Elinore needed a cup of coffee and went looking for it. But before she even reached the kitchen, she could smell a lovely aroma in the air.

Elsie had already poured her a cup and handed it to her as soon as she saw her. "Do you know where my mother is, Elsie?" Elinore asked. Elsie answered that she believed her mother was still in her bedroom. Elinore sucked her teeth just enough to make Elsie aware. "I guess you must know my parents are shipping me off to the United States?" Elinore stated with a snarky attitude. "NO!" Elsie cried. "Why? I don't understand!" Elinore could see that Elsie knew nothing about this. Elsie's jaw hung open. She shook her head, opposing the idea, when Rose entered the kitchen. Elsie looked like she had just swallowed a bug.

Elinore's eyes focused sharply on her mother. She was distressed and angry too. With her hand on her hip, Elinore asked, "So Mother, how much time do I have before you ship me off?"

Rose understood why Elinore wasn't happy, but she wasn't about to take any sass from her daughter either. "Watch your tone with me, Elinore," Rose sternly warned her. "Do you think it makes me happy to see you leave?" Elsie was feeling terribly uncomfortable. She offered to check on Delilah, excusing herself. Rose stood there in front of Elinore. Each facing each other, Elinore's broken heart was clear to see. Rose hugged Elinore and began to explain. "Darling, we are sending you for many reasons. You know Margaret wouldn't survive and Delilah is much too young. You are young and strong, and it is the best time for you to travel before you have children of your own." Then in a hushed voice, she told Elinore that they may even have to let Elsie and Emma go if their farming plan did not work out.

Elinore was taken by surprise, and that knowledge only made her feel worse, which she couldn't have imagined that that was even possible. "Mama, how long will I be there, please tell me the truth." Elinore desperately needed to know. But Rose could not tell her. Rose looked down at the floor. "Elinore, I won't lie to you, I'm really not sure. But I do know you will have many opportunities there to make a better life for yourself.

It is too late for your father and I, but you are at a turning point in your life, where you could make something of yourself. I do promise you, as soon as we can, we will send for you." Rose then tenderly kissed her daughter's forehead. Rose felt like the worst mother in the world and on the verge of breaking down herself. She couldn't leave the room fast enough, she really felt she would fall to pieces.

Elinore stood stunned. She set her cup in the sink and returned to her room to dress. Within minutes, she was on her way to the barn. Immediately, she noticed her father's automobile was gone. She wondered where it was and started to place her saddle on Lucky when Hans entered the barn behind her.

"Where are you going now, Elinore?" he asked. Elinore growled, "I'm going to Carl's." Hans cut her down. "Oh, last night wasn't enough?" Elinore froze and her blood ran cold. She thought she had gotten away with her plan undetected. She had underestimated Hans this time. Hans rarely missed anything happening on Porter's grounds. Elinore was thinking fast now. She wanted to change the subject quickly. The space where her father's auto had sat was empty. She asked Hans, "Where is my father's automobile?"

He told her that her father had decided to sell his auto to help with the expenses around the house. He continued to tell her that her father had confided in him and that he hadn't received an order in months at the factory. He had also told him that he would be laying off all his workers. Elinore was beyond words. It seemed her world was falling apart around her and furthermore, she had been outcasted from the entire situation. Did everyone know her family was struggling except her? She wondered if she was kept in the dark and pushed out of her family secretly until the last moment when it would be forced to be revealed. Her father had many employees and now she knew she wasn't the only one suffering, but that still didn't make her feel any better. Elinore couldn't help but wonder if Hans had to leave too. She had to ask, and Hans expected it. He was used to Elinore's candor. He did like the fact that she never minced words. He looked at her and simply said no, keeping his head down. He told her that her father would need help with the cattle and the farming. He'd be working for his food. Hans tried to look for something positive to say to make Elinore feel better about things. He reminded her that sometimes, absence makes the heart grow fonder. He knew that the part of leaving that bothered her most was likely to be Carl. Hans said, "Elinore, I never told you this, but I think Carl is a good man. He'll wait for you to return, I'm sure."

That did make Elinore smile, but she still did not want to go. "I don't know how much time I have left here, so I have to make my time count. I'm leaving to see Carl for now, tomorrow I will spend with Margaret. See you later Hans and thank you." Elinore tossed her hand in the air and gave Lucky a kick to gallop off.

Hans watched her until she was out of sight. He knew she would be fine in a big city, but Elinore just didn't seem right to him ever since she confronted the man who assaulted her mother inside their house. That traumatic day had somehow changed her, and she had never seemed quite right since then to him. He reasoned with himself that killing another person can do that.

Elinore was met by Carl who was tending to his farm when she arrived. Carl was sweaty and she found that appealing. As he always did, he helped her down off Lucky. He quickly tied her horse up and gave him a bucket of cold water. Elinore followed Carl. He leaned down to pick up some fresh hay that his horse had left behind to give to Lucky. Elinore took that opportunity to give him a good swat on his backside. She knew it was a bold move but looked forward to his reaction.

Carl was startled and he quickly stood up, turning to face her. He was grinning and retribution was coming her way! "Now you've done it!" he said loud and clear. Elinore knew she had seconds to make her getaway. She began to run toward the field of corn, all the while screeching and giggling with delight. She knew Carl was going to catch her. He was much faster than she was, and she could hear the beating of his boots on the ground quickly gaining on her. Then, all at once, she felt his hand reaching for her shoulder. Carl had a firm grip on her, and the two fell to the ground. Surrounded by the large stalks, they rested there in the brilliant sunshine. Elinore's mood was playful and that part of her was what made Carl fall in love with her in the first place. He turned his head to watch her laugh and he knew it might be a long time before he would see her laugh that way again.

Elinore had a plan hatching in her mind. Suddenly, she jumped on top of him and bit him gently on his neck. She could taste his salty sweat. "Ouch!" Carl yelled, recoiling from her bite, which only made her laugh louder. Elinore had straddled him and could feel his hardness below her. She reached down between her legs feeling around for the zipper on his trousers. Her hunger for him was growing and becoming hard to contain. She realized that this might be the last private time she would have with her love. She felt herself becoming uncontrollable in her fevered state. He was driving her mad.

Carl had never been able to find the right time or place for any real intimacy with Elinore, but it was about to happen, and Elinore surprised him by initiating it. His trousers were wide open, and Elinore's body rubbed against him driving him wild. They were in a passionate frenzy. Carl switched the tables on her suddenly, landing on top of her this time. Locking eyes, they kissed each other hard. His hands roamed her body fast and freely which made her breathing heavier. Her heart was pounding. His hands moved from her neck, over her bosom, downward to her inner thighs.

Elinore let a deep breath of air out. Carl lowered his head to kiss her neck and Elinore invited him by tilting her head to the side. She felt safe with him. He was her love and provided protection, security, patience and respect. She smiled at him as he ran his fingers through her hair. In that moment, Elinore wiggled her hips just enough to grab hold of her dress to expose her bare bottom. The tension led them to a physical union. The heat that lay within and between them sought to extract the elusive liquid lightning that ran through both of them. Elinore's legs trembled each time Carl thrust himself inside her. She moaned in pleasure. And then it came, like swimming in a warm pool of water. Panting with the passion to hold forever between them, they lay still caressing one another. Carl held her in his arms. He knew she was the one he wanted to spend the rest of his life with. He tried not to think about her leaving. Both fell silent, exhausted from their heightened pleasure. But in a raspy voice, Elinore tried to speak. She had to say it. "I will be lonely without you, Carl. I'm scared to leave here," she admitted.

Carl was feeling much the same way. He had developed a fondness for Elinore when he was only 7 years old. Now his heart had opened entirely for her. Carl thought for a minute and said, "Elinore, just promise me you won't find anyone else and come back to me as soon as you can." Elinore had a fast reply. "And as soon as I get back, we will marry, agreed?" "Yes, of course," he said happily. They took a few more minutes for themselves before fixing and brushing each other off.

Elinore wanted to say goodbye to Carl's parents before she would leave. As soon as they entered the house, Elinore could smell something buttery and delicious. Heidi had made some cake and it smelled heavenly to her. Heidi sliced off a piece for Elinore and on a white plate, with a cup of coffee, she slid it across the table to where Elinore was seated. "Oh, thank you!" she said taking a forkful of the warm buttery goodness. "What brings you here today, Elinore?" Heidi asked innocently. It made Elinore sad to tell her that she was going to live in the United States with her aunt in New York City for a while. Heidi didn't like that idea much at all. She had it fixed in her own mind that Elinore would become her son's wife. She couldn't understand why her parents would send their child off to a foreign land. Elinore did not want to spread her family's dirty laundry around so she tried to remain vague, but Heidi could see Elinore was wounded by her parent's decision. Heidi was sad as well. Her house was too small to take on a border and she simply couldn't afford to feed another mouth.

Otto was in the other room when he overheard the talking. He came out with one crutch under his arm to speak with Elinore. "I want to thank you for all you have done for me and my family, Elinore. Please continue to stay in touch with us, you know you are family to us." Otto was openly upset.

Unsteady on his own feet, he still managed to give her a hug. Otto had a small tear in his eye but quickly turned away, not wanting Elinore to see, but she did anyway.

She felt she would burst into tears herself if she didn't get out of there quick. The sun was low in the sky and Elinore had had a lovely day with Carl. Her memory of that day would need to last her a long time. On her way home, she passed the old gnarly apple tree that had died long ago, which Carl had given her the first of many apples from. She stopped to reflect for a moment on her relationship with Carl. She couldn't imagine life without him.

There was a small plate of food waiting for her in the kitchen as she passed through, and an already opened letter sat beside it. Elinore was hungry and only had eaten the piece of cake that Heidi had offered in the entire day thus far. She sat down at the table to eat. By her second mouthful, her curiosity was getting the better of her. Why would someone leave an open letter just lying on the table. Elinore peeked inside the envelope. She couldn't see the signature but when she turned it over, she could see it had come from the United States. Now, she had to read it! The house was quiet. She slowly took the single piece of paper quietly from the envelope so no one would hear it crinkle. She began to read it. The letter was from her aunt. It was addressed to her mother, and it told of the acceptance by her aunt to have Elinore stay there. Her aunt had already lined up a job for her and had bought some appropriate clothing for her to wear. Her aunt also stated she would pick her up at Ellis Island when she arrived. Elinore quickly shoved the letter back into the envelope and barely finished her food. She made sure to place the letter exactly the way she found it and went to Margaret's room. Margaret was sitting on the floor talking to her dolly. Elinore asked, "Are you having a good chat?" Elinore was amused by her sister. Margaret answered, "Not really, I'm bored to death." Elinore smiled at her. "Do you want to do something with me tomorrow?" Margaret jumped at the chance. "Sure, what do you want to do?" Elinore could see the excitement filling Margaret's mind. Elinore wanted it to be a special day. "You pick this time," she said with a smile. "Oh boy, we could go fishing, catching butterflies, or turtles, maybe pick some flowers like we used to, or gather some leaves and jump in the pile…or maybe…" Margaret was rambling off, barely taking time to breathe, but Elinore had a better idea. She asked, "Do you think you would like to go shopping? I have some extra money saved." Margaret exclaimed, "Would I! Will it be a long walk?" she asked. Elinore explained that she would put her on the back of Lucky and that she would have to hold onto her waist tightly. She told her that the plan she had was to ride over to where she used to work. "There are many stores there but first we will stop at the bakery," she said. Margaret began to lick her lips. She could almost taste the biscuits already. Then Elinore said, "There's a candy store and a hat store that I'd like you to see. Maybe you would like some pretty hair pins to wear for church. There's a pair of riding boots I saw there that I would really like to have, and I'd like to see if they're still available."

"Oh Elinore, that sounds like so much fun!" Margaret said. "I'll be ready as soon as the sun comes up." Margaret was vibrating with delight. Rubbing her hands together, she jumped onto her bed and began to sing. "I'm going shopping! I'm going shopping!"

Elinore knew she was going to miss Margaret as much as Carl. She was dying inside. Leaving her native country, but especially leaving Margaret and Carl, was more than she could handle. Margaret was her best friend aside from being her sister and anger began to replace her sadness about having to leave. All she had thought about over the past two days was how unfair it all was. There must be another solution, but her parents had already made the choice for her. It was almost like they didn't love her anymore. She fought hard to hold her tears back so no one would see her cry. Inside though, she felt as if she could rip someone to pieces. Elinore closed Margarets door and went to her room. She closed her door tightly and reached for the small wooden box under her bed. She opened the box and took out the ring Carl had given her. She placed it on her finger and swore never to take it off from that moment onward. Then she counted her money. She had saved 20 Goldmark. It would be enough to buy her boots and things for Margaret, plus some to take with her when she went to her aunt's.

The next morning, Margaret was ready, bright and early as she had promised. Elinore told Margaret to hold on tight as they rode straight to the bakery. Margaret had never been to the bakery. As they walked through the door, her eyes looked like giant saucers. They were open wide, and she bounced off each counter asking Elinore, "I'd like to have one of those, and one of those." She pointed to each biscuit gleefully. Elinore and the shopkeeper lady couldn't help but have some fun with it all. They laughed and the woman tried to keep up with Margaret's requests. Just as she had done with Elinore, on her first visit to the bakery, the nice lady put an extra of Margaret's favorite cookie in the bag.

Soon they were on their way again, to the many stores they would visit that day. At the end of the day, Margaret was tired. She clutched the filled bags they had purchased tightly. Elinore had bought Margaret a beautiful hat that was special. Margaret wanted badly to wear it home, but Elinore made her put it in the round hat box. She didn't want it to fall in the dirt as Lucky swiftly returned home carrying them. They had bought matching pins for their hair and Elinore treated herself to some additional cosmetics. Margaret enjoyed the bakery and candy store the most.

Elinore was disappointed that the boots she wanted were no longer available but was surely glad to return home with some money left over. It was very late when they finally got back, and Margaret's shoulders were hunched over. She dragged herself in and sat down on a chair in the kitchen. Barely able to hold her head up, Emma slid a plate of food under her nose. Elinore was happy to accept her plate from Emma. She hadn't eaten all day. A small snorting sound came from Margaret. Her head lay on the table, next to her untouched food. Elinore gently shook her shoulders, and she woke startled. "Come on, eat a little," Elinore said to Margaret. She tried but she was just too tired and asked to be excused. All she wanted to do was sleep. Elinore had to admit, she was tired too, but that wasn't going to stop her from devouring Emma's delicious food.

Elinore checked in on Margaret, on her way down the hallway to her room. Margaret was sound asleep, which made her smile. She took a minute to reflect on their childhood, remembering some of the times that made her the happiest in her life. She made her way to her room and sat down on the edge of her bed. Her life unfolded there like an open book. Memories flooded through Elinore's mind as far back as when she was a small child; even before she entered school. She remembered how her father would pick her up and spin her around while her feet flew through the air. She remembered the first apple that Carl gave her and the ring. She thought about Anna at school. She didn't like her so much. She thought about when Margaret fell in the creek. Many memories raced through her mind. They were becoming too much! Elinore looked around the room as she sat still in the same position. She ran her hand over her blanket, feeling each thread. Her eyes scanned each wooden board on the floor and the memories of her games with Margaret flashed in sequence, flooding her mind further. Elinore's tears were close to falling from her eyes. Breaking into her thoughts, there were two small taps on her door as it began to open with a creak. Elinore looked up when her father came in.

Porter could see that she was upset. He walked up to her and said, "Elinore, we need to talk." Her head dropped low, and her shoulders shrunk. Porter didn't want to upset her any more than she already was. He made it short. "We've heard from your aunt." "I know." Elinore interrupted. "You'll be beginning your journey there next week." He kissed her on top of her head and left the room as fast as he had come. Porter didn't see Elinore wipe the tears from her eyes as the door closed shut. Elinore never felt so unloved in all her life. Her parents had abandoned her and seemed to have lost any feeling of love they ever had for her. She fell back onto the bed with her arms above her head. She thought to herself, she had cried more this past week than she ever had in her whole life. She did not want to go, but now since her family didn't seem to care about her and Carl wouldn't marry her now, it didn't much matter anymore. She might as well go. She never planned on accepting this and was angry that she was being forced to. Elinore went to her closet and pulled out her tapestry bag that was covered over by many things. She hadn't used that bag often and it was dusty. She placed it on the chair and started to brush it off. All the dust made her sneeze. She decided once the bag was cleaned that she might as well pack it for the following day with the things she hardly used first. The very first thing she packed were her writing tablets. She had promised Carl that she would write to him every day. She knew it would probably be more realistically like once a month, but she would try to keep her word.

As the following week passed, Carl and Elinore spent as much time as they could together. Talking, laughing, crying and planning their future when she returned. She also made sure to spend time speaking with Hans and explaining things to Margaret. Margaret was the one she worried about most. She didn't quite understand the way things worked in life. Elinore often had to guide her through things, so trouble didn't come her way. Elinore knew that Margaret's mind didn't work quite right, but she loved her just the same. The news of her leaving had upset Margaret terribly.

Elinore continued to pack items into her bag a little at a time. A young woman at almost 18 years of age needed to pack very little. So, at the end of the week, her bag was full, and it sat on the floor waiting. She would need to wear her coat in the crisp, cold air over the ocean and that would be one bulky item that wouldn't need to be carried thankfully. That last week was filled with many tearful goodbyes, and it flew by. Elinore soon found herself sitting in the back of the wagon with her two bags, as Porter and Rose made their journey to the Northern part of the Elbe River downstream from Hamburg by sixty miles or so. It wasn't long before they could see the giant transatlantic ocean liner docked at Steubenhoft pier. There were many travelers waiting to board the giant vessel. On the side of the boat, Elinore could see the words, Hamburg-Amerika Linie. Many people also were gathered by a sign that read: Abschied nach Amerika. Rose pointed to the sign and told Elinore, "That is the pier you will go thru." Elinore felt sick. Porter helped his daughter down from the wagon and handed her the bags she had packed. From his pocket, he pulled a roll of money. He handed it to Elinore and told her to use it wisely. Porter, Elinore and Rose embraced one last time and Elinore couldn't stop the tears this time. They streamed down her face like a waterfall. Elinore didn't want to go and was petrified at getting on such a large boat on the ocean waters alone. The ocean was vast, and she had heard of many fishermen dying while at sea. Rose couldn't hold back the tears either and that made Porter want to cry too. Elinore just couldn't stay there for one more second. She quickly pecked a kiss to each of them and ran for the boat. She stood on the pier looking up at the boat. She asked herself what would happen if she didn't get on it. She would only have about a month or so before her parents found out she didn't get on board. Where would she go? The money her father gave her would only last so long. The large boat frightened her to her core. There was no place to go. Elinore stood, gawking at the enormous vessel.

Rose sat silent all the way home, occasionally wiping her eyes. Porter kept his handkerchief in his lap. He had used it so much that he had given up trying to put it back into his pocket. When they arrived home, they found Hans cradling a sobbing Margaret. Even Hans had some wetness on his cheeks. Porter had never seen Hans cry before. He wondered if he had done the right thing by sending Elinore away. He knew it was, but watching the fall out was almost too much for him to bear.

Elinore approached the gate and the man standing there asked, "Ticket please." Elinore didn't know what he meant. She thought her parents had already paid her fare. She replied, "I have no ticket, Sir." One of his eyebrows raised and he asked sternly, "NO TICKET? You need to buy a ticket to board!" He pushed her aside and pulled the man standing behind her forward. There was a man shouting, just a few steps from where she was amid the chaos. He was selling tickets and was sharply dressed in a uniform that was obviously provided for the ocean liners staff. Elinore asked him, "How much?" The man told her 30 Goldmark. That was almost as much money that she had made for the entire five weeks she had worked. She hid the roll of money her father had given her and handed the man 30 Goldmark. In exchange she received her ticket and returned to the line to board. She weaved her way through the crowd stopping at a clear space on the deck to look out over the water. There was a beautifully dressed woman standing alone that Elinore believed to be approachable. She sat her bags down next to her and began to speak to her. The woman told her she was going to America to visit family and had taken this trip many times. Elinore confided to the woman it was her first time and she was positively frightened out of her mind. They laughed together and the woman assured her it would be fine. Elinore asked her what her name was, and she told her. My name is Elinore. "That's my name too!" Elinore laughed again. She was comforted by this stranger and their special friendship began to form. Elinore had many questions. She asked how many days their journey would take. The woman told her if luck were with them, it would take a month and a half. "Oh my!" Elinore said surprised, as her mouth hung open. The woman gently lifted her chin to close her mouth. "You might not want to leave your mouth open Dear or you might eat a fly," she said with a smile. Elinore wondered how long this trip would take before she saw the aunt she barely remembered. She looked at her new friend quizzically and dared to ask, "What is the longest it took you to get to your destination?" The woman made a humf sound and said, "63 days!" Elinore's eyes bulged. She never thought it would take that long. Then the woman pulled Elinore close to her, wrapping her arm around her shoulder. She told her not to worry because she had said her prayers before she boarded. Elinore promised the smaller Elinore that she would guide her through Ellis Island, which she said would only be a few hours hopefully, and then bring her to where most people meet with their waiting families. Elinore was grateful and thanked the woman for her kindness.

They both made their way through the crowded decks to find a place to sleep for the night. There were long rows of large, shared bunks with straw mattresses that had no bed linens. Elinore thought it was rather disgusting and gently placed her bags under one of the bunks. The older Elinore carried a smaller bag, which she placed close to Elinore's. Over the next 45 days the two Elinore's had many conversations about their lives and shared plenty of laughs. They weathered only one storm, which made Elinore feel horrible. She witnessed many people vomiting over the side of the boat as the ocean sprayed the decks with water. Inside, there seemed to be a shortage of fresh air. Elinore tried to escape the stench, but it traveled throughout the entire boat and was terribly unpleasant. All through the entire trip she wondered if her parents knew how miserable this trip would be and became resentful about it. Their lack of compassion for her made her sick. Porter and Rose had sent her with good intentions, but Elinore did not see it that way. She knew there were other solutions to the financial problems that they were having that would have been a much better option than what she was going through now. But they didn't seem to give a damn. To her, she had been double-crossed in the worst way. After many days had passed, finally, Elinore could see a building as the ship entered the harbor. It was a long building with four turrets, pointing to the sky. Suddenly, the boat stopped, and Elinore was confused. Why would they stop here? What could be wrong; they were so close. The older woman began to explain; she told her not to worry. They had to stop the boat because it was the quarantine checkpoint, where doctors would board looking for contagious diseases among the passengers. It wasn't long before Elinore saw the men boarding the ship by rope ladders making their way through the crowd before it got to dock, just as she had been told. They finished quickly and seemed to rush the passengers into the immigration process. There were so many people, it reminded her of the laundry factory, but multiplied by a thousand times. Elinore felt herself becoming strangely dizzy and hoped the long lines would go quickly. Men began to bark orders at the passengers to form two lines. One was for women and children, and one was for men. The two women stood together as they approached the front of the line. Elinore handed her manifest tag to the inspector as he looked through her bags. Elinore was sweating now. She had hidden her pistol and billhook in her bloomers. She escaped without the inspectors noticing her awkwardness. Once the doctors left the boat, it docked, and they were allowed to get off. Elinore was so happy to finally be able to leave that dreadful boat. They made their way through the winding metal bars where some of the people were held for further inspection, but they were lucky and were released. She began to scan the crowd for the unfamiliar face that was supposed to be waiting on her. Elinore clutched the hand of her traveling companion tightly; afraid she would not find her aunt Agnes. It took a few minutes, but soon she heard a woman screaming her name. "Elinore Downing!" She heard it again and thanked her friend for her help. She followed the voice through the crowd until she saw a woman with braids wrapped tightly around her head. Elinore asked the woman if she were her Aunt Agnes. She did not recognize her.

Agnes latched onto her arm and said, "Of course I am, I'm not here for the excitement of this crowd, that's for sure. Now come along; let's get you home and wash that smell off you!" "You can't start working, smelling like that!" Elinore couldn't believe how rudely her aunt had welcomed her after such a long journey. Next, she found herself riding in a horse drawn carriage as her aunt hurried home. The house her aunt lived in looked nothing like hers, however it was quite nice. Mostly white brick and very tall. Her aunt showed her to her room and gave her fresh towels to take a bath. Agnes told her when she was finished with her bath, they needed to speak about what would be expected of her and about her job she was to start the following day.

Elinore was shocked! Work? My Lord, she said to herself. I just got here! Shaking her head and cursing under her breath she headed to the bathroom near what was to be her room, to get cleaned up. Soaking in the bathtub, she enjoyed every moment of her solitude. When the water turned cold, she stood and pulled the drain, watching the water swirl until it all had disappeared. Putting the towel to her face, she smelled it. It surely smelled better than anything else she had smelled in what seemed like forever. She dried herself slowly. She was careful not to get water on the floor and wrapped her hair in the other towel her aunt had given her. She made her way down the stairs to where her aunt sat waiting for her. She looked over the top of her glasses at Elinore and in that moment, she remembered some of the things her father and mother would say after she visited them back home, long ago.

Agnes began to speak. "Elinore, you will be expected to work and pay rent." "How much?" Elinore asked. Agnes replied, "Two dollars a week." Elinore was stunned! This was her aunt! Then Agnes told her to make sure she was ready to go by 8am to start her new job the following day and that she had better get to bed early. Agnes added, "Morning comes fast!" Elinore turned and rolled her eyes. But Agnes was still not finished. "Oh, two more things." Elinore stopped short in her tracks. Her head dropped as she listened for further instructions. "You will be expected to make supper on your days off, and you will find your new work clothes to start your new job in your closet." Elinore continued her way up the staircase and with each step, the thought of running from this house crossed her mind. She grumbled under her breath and had already begun to form an opinion about her miserable aunt. Elinore went to the closet to see the clothing her aunt had provided for her. She clutched the pretty glass doorknob that gleamed in her hand to open the door. It didn't creak like her closet door at home. Everything in the closet was white and black. She had never seen clothing like this before but didn't like it at all. It smelled funny too. There were 8 corsets, 7 black dresses, that went only to her ankles, and 7 white aprons. The aprons were lacey, and she didn't mind those as much as the ugly tight corsets that she would be expected to wear. The black dresses reminded her of the clothing people would wear to a burial but much too short. Elinore didn't want to seem ungrateful, but she much preferred her own clothing. She looked around the room. There was a desk, a bed, a wash table, and a chair. That was it! Elinore's thoughts returned to Carl. On the desk sat a writing tablet. Her heart was breaking. She already missed Carl more than she thought she would. She sat down on the poorly made chair at the desk, almost wanting to cry. It made noise and she hoped it wouldn't break from the stress of her weight. Elinore began to pen a letter to her love.

My dearest Darling, I have finally arrived here in New York City and already have formed a disdain for this country but furthermore, my aunt has not been the kindest. She is not the nicest person I have ever had the pleasure of meeting. However, I must be grateful to her for accommodating me since my parents no longer wanted me. I wish we could have continued to explore our lives together. In the split second that her pen ended that sentence, Elinore heard a voice that seemed to come from someone close to her age say, "Don't worry about him! He doesn't care about you, anyway!" Elinore looked around the room but saw no one. She shouted out, "Who's there?" But no one answered. She shook her head and thought, great! Now I'm hearing things! The sound of this unfamiliar voice seemed like it came from within her own mind, but she couldn't be sure. She tried to continue her letter but had trouble concentrating. Her mind wandered to the job her aunt had chosen for her and what that would be like. Elinore thought about what her aunt had told her about being ready at the crack of dawn. She couldn't believe she had only been in America less than 24 hours and her aunt was already preparing her for work. She decided to get ready for bed. She would need a good night's sleep. Elinore moved to the bed and picked up the pillow. When she held it to her face, she could smell the distinct odor of moth balls. Her nose scrunched up and the word 'Yuck' whispered from her mouth. She threw the pillow down on the bed but quickly picked it back up and began to fluff it roughly. She didn't like having to accept her current situation; knowing clearly that she didn't have much choice in the matter. A small feather floated around her nose, escaping from inside the pillow which was being pounded by her own hands. She blew the feather away from her face and set the pillow back down on the bed. Staring at the walls and feeling confused, Elinore wanted to return home again. She had just beaten the stuffing out of her pillow but wasn't exactly sure why. Her rage came on quickly and uncontrollably, but she didn't know why she had become so upset in the first place. She missed her life in Germany. If only she could go home, she thought. She admitted to herself that she was frustrated, but she wasn't angry anymore. Elinore had come to accept the fact that she couldn't change what had happened and needed to make the best of it. But out of nowhere, came a rage that was unfamiliar to her. She could not remember ever being so mad before in her life. Then she heard her aunt's heavy footsteps coming up the stairs. With each step, coming closer and closer. Elinore quickly tucked her letter away. There was a short stop in her aunt's climbing footsteps, and she knew that she had reached the top of the stairs. Dreading her entry to her private space, Elinore opened the door to see her aunt standing there.

She clung to the banister, breathing hard and looking annoyed. Agnes shoved a small plate of food into her hand. "Tomorrow, you will come to the kitchen to eat!" she said breathlessly. Through her strained voice, she still had enough air to continue. "When you are finished, bring your plate downstairs, wash it, and get to bed! The birds in the chimney will wake you at sunrise, so be ready for me to drop you off to meet with your new boss in time. It is not far, so you will be able to walk there after tomorrow." Agnes closed the door and Elinore stuck her tongue out. This whole new life was making her feel so insignificant. No one cared at all about her. Her sense of purpose had vanished. Her mind was becoming darker since she stepped onto the boat leaving her homeland. But she did as she was told, and headed for her bed when she finished putting her plate back in its proper place. Her last thought before she fell asleep was about her aunt's remark about the birds in the chimney. Elinore thought to herself how lucky they were to be able to just fly away whenever or wherever they liked.

Elinore slept lightly that night and she found her bed terribly uncomfortable. If she hadn't known better, she would've thought she slept on a rock. Her body ached that morning and she had no desire to start a new job. Elinore forced herself to go to the closet to pull out one of her dresses. Ugly! She thought as she put the dress on. The first thing she noticed was how short it was. It only came to just above her ankles. What will people think, she wondered. She could see it looked like a maid's dress and now she had a clue as to what type of job she would be doing. Next, she put the lacey apron on and tied it tight around her waist. Just as her aunt had warned her, she could hear the birds in the chimney chirping and fluttering around. A cap fell off the shelf when she was distracted by them, and she saw it just as she was about to close the closet door. Holding it her hands, she said, "Oh, you have got to be joking." She placed the small white cap on her head and imagined how stupid it must look. It came with two little clips which fastened into her braids, she knew that her excuse for losing it would be a lost cause. Just then, she heard Agnes shrieking up the stairs, "Come on Elinore! You don't want to be late on your first day, do you? It's time to leave!" Elinore hurried down the stairs.

Together the two women rode off down the street. Elinore listened to the clippety-clop of the horse's hooves against the street. Seated high in the carriage her aunt owned, it was only a few minutes and they had already arrived. Elinore sat looking at another brick building. In a flash, Agnes had her feet on the ground and was in a hurry. She came around to where Elinore sat. She glared at Elinore. "Are you waiting for Christmas? Come on, why does it take you so long?" Elinore snapped out of her transfixed state and hurried down from the carriage. Agnes reached for the heavy iron door knocker and hit it two times against the solid wood door. A man answered the door and ushered them in. He was a portly short man and introduced himself as Peter Quinn. As he spoke, Elinore could see splashes of saliva launching off his thick lips. She quickly ducked behind her aunt, seemingly shy. His lips were wet and as he spoke, she couldn't concentrate on anything he said. The only thing she could think about was how to avoid his projectiles. This is going to be disgusting, she thought to herself. Soon, her aunt was gone and the two stood alone looking at each other. Mr. Quinn began to tell Elinore what he wanted her to do. He looked her over hard and she felt uncomfortable as he pulled at his pants. They were cinched high around his middle tightly and she wondered how he was even able to breathe. He explained that he was a busy accountant and needed her to clean up around his office in addition to doing some small errands for him that he had no time to do himself. It didn't seem so bad she thought, and her pay was not bad either. Elinore wondered if her aunt had something to do with that.

She spent the first week shuffling around the office, mainly doing mundane things. Mr. Quinn rarely said much to her, and she wondered if he even liked her. He mostly kept his nose in his books, with one pencil in his hand and one tucked over his ear. She silently found humor in that because as he hoovered over his books, the one strand of hair that he still had and was wrapped around his head kept falling off over his glasses. Each time he moved it back into place, his pencil would consequently fall from his ear. It was a vicious cycle, one that seemed to irritate him. Over and over, the cycle continued but he still managed to keep that one hair in place. When Elinore reached her first month with Mr. Quinn, she noticed he had become very comfortable with having her around and her list of things to do for him was growing fast. He had even come in one day carrying a heavy metal bucket filled with water. He set it down in the front hallway, with some soap and a rag. Elinore knew what he was going to ask of her, and she was not pleased.

Peter briefly saw a glimpse of her outward expression of disgust before she could hide it. In his mind, he owned her. He paid her well and that should entitle him to ask whatever he wanted of her, or so he thought. He was a man who was used to getting his way. He decided to teach her a lesson, and with the side of his foot he kicked the bucket over. The water flowed across the floor and splashed against the wall. Mr. Quinn scolded her, "Now you have an even harder job! Clean that water up and get more fresh water from the pump out back." He turned to enter his office and Elinore could see the cheekbone on the side of his face sat higher. She knew he had a snide smile on his face and that angered her. His words and actions made her clench her teeth. Elinore lowered down to her hands and knees to clean up the water while she rubbed the soap into the wet rag. Before she was finished, her hands were a bright red and sore from the strong soap Mr. Quinn had given her.

When she finally finished, it was nearly the time she was supposed to leave. She knocked on Mr. Quinn's door to tell him she was leaving. Barely looking up, he lifted two fingers as if to say goodbye. Then he said, "One minute Elinore." She had had enough of Mr. Quinn for one day and didn't want to hear another peep from him. She tilted her head to one side waiting for his next demand. This time Elinore made sure to keep her face emotionless. He pointed to a huge stack of pencils that sat in the corner of the floor. He said, "Tomorrow, I need you to sharpen all of those." There is a sharpener on the wall in the back room." Elinore replied, "Yes sir." She stood waiting for just another second to see if he was finished with his requests. His head was still buried in his books. She watched him as he licked the tip of his pencil before he began to write. Suddenly, she found herself dreaming of slamming her hand to the back end of that pencil hard enough to push it through his throat, plunging it out to the backside of his neck. That thought only lasted a moment, but it even surprised Elinore. How could she have such violent thoughts? It was an awful thought surely, but Elinore kept the wicked smile on her face as she stared at the man she worked for. Mr. Quinn was surprised to see her still standing there when he finally looked up. Puzzled he said, "Good day now," and motioned for her to leave.

Elinore hurried home. She was hungry and thought about what kind of food Aunt Agnes would be making, but when she entered the house, she didn't smell anything. Not a scent of food at all. Elinore made her way to the kitchen to find her aunt sitting at the table with her legs wrapped around one of the legs of the chair she was sitting on. She was reading a newspaper. Elinore greeted her aunt with a simple hello and looked inside the icebox for something to eat. The icebox was cold, and in the corner sat one lone egg. There was nothing else! Elinore wanted to ask her aunt if she was going to make something to eat but decided against it. What would be the point? What could she possibly make with one egg? There was a loaf of bread in a pan on the table next to the sink and she asked if she could take a piece instead. Her aunt snapped back, "Yes, but why did you not stop at the market before you came home to buy some food?" Elinore's mouth hung open. She just couldn't believe her ears. How could her aunt be so mean?

Elinore snipped at Agnes. "Because I didn't know I had to!" Agnes raised her eyes and Elinore almost regretted saying that.

She decided to leave the room quickly and go to the market before they closed. There she purchased some meat, cheese and potatoes and when she returned, she found her aunt still seated in the same position. She took a pan out of the closet and began to make something to eat. Agnes was delighted by someone cooking other than herself. Elinore wasn't thrilled at all; she had just worked a long hard day. Not to mention that she had only been asked to cook on her days off. But the rules were already changing. She was tired and her hands were raw. She backed away from the stove to ask if there were any dried herbs in the house, but as she did so, she stepped right on top of Agnes's toe. She hadn't realized her aunt had been hoovering behind her. "Ouch!" Agnes yelled. Elinore apologized. She continued to make the evening meal and gave her aunt a portion of the food when she finished. It was then in her mind, she heard the words clearly, "Now you're even." Elinore placed her fingers on her temple and closed her eyes. She sat down quietly wondering about the words that she had just heard again. It sounded like the same voice she had heard before. She wasn't sure if they were her own thoughts or coming from somewhere else. Maybe outside? When they were done eating, she put the dishes in the sink and began to wash them. The water stung as it ran over her raw hands. She hurried to finish, and Agnes went back to her newspaper. In her room, Elinore finished her note to Carl and planned to stop by the postmaster on the way to work in the morning. It would take some time to reach him but better late than never, she reasoned. She closed the letter asking Carl to give her love to her family and tucked it into her apron for the next day.

Over the next several weeks, Elinore found many things about Mr. Quinn she did not like, but the one thing she found most deplorable was his insatiable love for coffee. One day she counted 22 cups that she brought him during an entire day. The coffee didn't bother her as much as the brown ring that formed around his already gross lips, and it disgusted her to the point of nausea. Then the last straw came when he asked her to go to his home to wash his laundry. He lived alone; never married. And she understood why. Mr. Quinn gave her the key to his door and told her there was a basket of laundry on the floor in the kitchen next to the washing machine. Elinore was astounded at his request. Laundry had nothing to do with what she was hired for. She was being taken advantage of and resented it. His house was a few doors away, just past the market. An evil thought crossed her mind as she passed the market and she decided to go inside. She asked the woman if she had any red pepper flakes. The woman replied that she did and put some in a small bag for her with a smile. Elinore left in a hurry. She went just a few more doors down the road until she reached a house with weeds that stood as high as she was tall. She entered the kitchen and could smell the dirty clothes from where she stood. She began to place the clothes in the washer and wring them tightly to put on the clothesline. There was a nice breeze in the air and Elinore knew the clothes would dry fast. Doing the laundry reminded her of Germany again, and she was reminded of just how much she missed it there.

The clothing dried very fast, and Elinore took the clothes off the line and brought them inside to fold. Everything was folded in no time. Except for his undergarments. She picked them up and took them to the bathroom. The tub was dry and clean to her surprise. She threw all his undergarments down into the tub forcefully and reached into her pocket for the red pepper flakes. Feeling wicked, she looked hard at the pepper flakes in her hand. She was very angry with Mr. Quinn. She had been galled and harassed long enough and now it was payback time. It would be one of the first times her alter personality Erika would show herself as her hand glided over the tub, sprinkling the flakes over the fresh garments, through her finger tips. She carefully shook off each piece of clothing, making sure there were no visible signs of the pepper on them; folding each piece as she had the others. She placed the rest of his clothing neatly in his bedroom and carefully wiped the tub clean of any residue. She locked the door behind her and returned to work. She smiled with anticipation as she said goodbye to Mr. Quinn at the end of the workday.

That night had brought her the best sleep that she had ever had since she came to America. The following day, Elinore could hardly wait to get back to work to watch the fun unfold. Mr. Quinn sat at his desk in his usual position. He was quiet and hadn't given Elinore a thing to do. She moved around the office, picking things up and emptying the trash. Elinore made some coffee in the small kitchen area that was in the back of the office. He barked to her to bring him some coffee as soon as it was ready. She had a good mind to tell him to get it himself, but she was not going to blow her chance to see the outcome of what she anticipated to come. The wait was killing her. She shouted back from the room loud enough for him to hear, "It'll be ready in a few minutes!" No good bastard, she whispered to herself.

Elinore poured the coffee and brought it to him. She was beginning to think her prank was useless. He had no reaction to the red pepper flakes at all, it seemed. She had almost resigned herself to giving up all hope of getting even for all the things he had made her do. But the coffee had done the trick. Elinore heard the bathroom door close! She continued doing her usual deeds, when suddenly, she heard a blood-curdling scream from behind the closed bathroom door. The piercing tone of his voice told her he was feeling some pain. Everything was fine for Mr. Quinn until his undergarment got a little wet from his urine. Her plan had worked, and she smiled at the success of her despicable underhandedness. Mr. Quinn came out of the bathroom in a fury. He glared at Elinore and demanded to know what she had done to his undergarments. His eyes bulged, making his pupils almost disappear. She wanted to burst out laughing but she held it back hard. He had got what he had coming, she thought. Elinore put the best shocking face on that she could muster up, and replied most innocently, "Who me? I didn't do a thing, only what you told me to." Elinore pressed one finger against her cheek, raising her eyebrows and tilting her head to one side. She was a picture of purity.

As soon as Mr. Quinn left the room, Elinore burst out laughing hard enough to pee herself. She was picturing inside her mind how Margaret would have loved this one. Margaret was a master at pranking. Her happy moment was short lived though. Mr. Quinn returned to the room and told Elinore that after careful thought, he no longer needed her services. She left that office with a smirk on her face. She hated the way Mr. Quinn had treated her and was glad she would no longer have to look at that disgusting brown ring around his mouth anymore. She had only been there for a few months and now she would have to look for another job.

She went back home that day knowing her aunt would be none too pleased with her, so she bought some things at the market on the way home to make a nice dinner to soften the blow. She had also figured out Aunt Agnes by now, which was making it easier for her to get along. Food made Aunt Agnes happy. She finally made her way to her room after dinner, dishes, and explaining to her aunt she would be looking for a new job the following day.

Elinore sat at her desk and propped her little mirror up to look at herself. Her hair was a mess. She took her brush out and began to pull it through her hair. She began to feel strange. She looked into the mirror as if she were looking through herself. Then she heard the voice she'd heard several times before. She slammed the mirror down on the desk, frightened. "Breaking the mirror will only give you seven years of bad luck, but it won't make me go away!" It seemed Elinore was observing this conversation instead of being part of it. Elinore had always felt there was something different about herself since she was young. There were times she couldn't remember, but others she could recall every detail of. Some of the extremely violent situations she had endured had triggered a cataclysmic psychological change within her. She was becoming aware of another identity inside her and the barrier between them was starting to crumble down. The different identities included herself, the more loving innocent person, and the older, stronger and angrier other identity. She dared to lift the mirror again. She stared at her reflection for a few minutes.

Soon, she felt the transfer of identity happen and she recognized it as something she had felt before but not as strongly. She felt a stern cold sensation and heard a voice ordering her to get back inside. She heard the commanding voice say, "I am Erika Heinreich. I protect you and handle all the things you are too weak for! You must do as I tell you!" Amid her confusion, the different voice of Erika became more conscious and with her came the explicitly detailed memory of the fisherman at the seaport, in her hometown years ago. Elinore remembered vaguely the details of what happened that day but couldn't specifically remember everything. She watched it happen from an observation point rather than being fully engaged. But Erika remembered everything as if it happened yesterday and she remembered cracking his skull open with the wine bottle gleefully. Elinore was abruptly aware that the different personalities were warring inside her, leaving her feeling overwhelmed. She wanted to hide, but where? How could she hide from herself? Erika was a frightening presence but protective of Elinore. Elinore had used this unconscious cognition to adapt in order to feel safe but was essentially unaware of Erika until now. It was the day in the seaport that Elinores mind had fragmented, and Erika took life.

Elinore was beginning to feel very unsure of herself. She had some memories but the emotions that went with each occasion vanished. Her sense of belonging in the world had seemed to vanish as well. Elinore was also becoming aware that her two parts were sharing her one life between them. Elinore co-existed with Erika, but they were not one. Erika provided the safety Elinore needed to continue life as she knew it. Still, her alters' fierceness frightened her but Erika clearly had defined areas of expertise. The moments Erika controlled seemed to not be a first-person memory to Elinore and were mostly the violent ones. Elinore was aware of things that had happened, but she wasn't part of them. As a matter of fact, the more she thought about things, she realized there were a lot of blank spots in her recollection where Erika had been in control. Still, she clung to the feelings of trust she had toward Margaret and Hans back home. She knew she could always trust them. But that didn't matter now. In fact, nothing seemed to matter now. She was in another land, far from where she grew up and she needed to survive.

The very next day, Elinore went looking for another job. She went to a few buildings that had "Help Wanted" signs hanging in their windows. She left her name everywhere she went. The search wasn't all bad for Elinore. She had saved some money while working for Mr. Quinn and now she was going into many businesses who often had things to sell too. Elinore found one particularly to her fancy. They had jewelry for sale. Fine crafted, gold and silver gems. Elinore found one ring that she just couldn't take her eyes off. It was silver with a black rose and embellished with 4 garnet stones. "How beautiful," she said holding it up to the stream of sunlight that came through the door. She asked the man who was seated at the counter, what the cost of the ring was. He replied, "Two dollars, Miss." She could easily afford that, so she purchased it on the spot. It was her treat to herself for all she had endured. The man took the ring and placed it in a blue velvet box. Then he remembered something. "Wait! I forgot to show you something!" He pulled the ring from the blue box and showed Elinore the secret compartment below the rose. Elinore asked, "What do you need a secret compartment in a ring for? It's such a small space." The man explained he had heard some women store medicine for a headache inside the ring and he snapped it shut returning it to the box again. As soon as Elinore stepped outside, she placed the ring on her right hand, ring finger. It fit that finger the best, she thought. It felt good to be able to buy something for herself on a whim. She took Carl's ring off, slipping it into her apron.

She continued her job search for a good part of the day. As it began to get colder Elinore clutched at her coat and her neck sunk deep into the collar. The last shop she saw on the way home did not have a sign in the window, but she could see a blazing fire in the fireplace from the street. Elinore stepped up to the door and gently knocked. A tall handsome man opened the door. At that moment, Elinore could no longer feel the cold anymore. Her eyes were wide as she stood almost gawking at him. He smiled and said, "Come in, you must be cold from this bitterness out here." He wrapped his arm around her and closed the door behind them. He asked if she would like some tea or coffee, but Elinore politely said, "No thank you." He then asked, "So, what can I do for you? Are you here to buy a newspaper?" She looked around, noticing a printing press on the other side of the room. Elinore was thinking fast. "Why yes, of course," she told him, handing the strapping man a penny for the paper. In no time she had scanned the room and noticed a lot of red very plush cushions on the seats and benches. She also noticed the leather apron he was wearing. It allowed her to view his very muscular physique, which made her feel a flutter deep within herself. He was rugged and she could immediately sense his strength and determination. She liked his roguish smile which gave her the impression he could also be playfully mischievous too. This excited her. He was dark and mysterious and the bristle on his face told her he hadn't had a shave in a day or two. She liked that too. It added to her excitement. Elinore decided to introduce herself. "I am Elinore Downing, pleased to meet you," she said extending her hand.

He tightly grabbed her hand and kissed the back of it. Now, she was feeling weak at the knees. He answered her back, "Pleased as well, my name is John Smith. My friend's father runs this newspaper and I've been here in this office for as long as I can remember." He laughed as he put the large machine in motion again.

Elinore found his laugh flirtatious and captivating. She was inclined to flirt back with an alluring smile and added an arousing interest in his work which she hoped would get her hired. To break the ice, she opened her coat, letting a portion of the top of her bosom out for show. She leaned toward him seductively to ask questions about what he was doing. She pretended to be very interested and impressed as he began to tell her about all he did and all his accolades. She reached for his arm and asked if he needed a helper, not forgetting to mention she was new to the area and didn't know many people. Elinore knew how to make her questions become a delicate dance. And if she executed them well enough, it could land her a job as well as an ultimate mental dance with him too. After all, she was intrigued by him. She was weaving her web, letting a waterfall loose filled with jokes and laughter. He loved being showered with her many compliments. John was falling right into her hands.

He answered her question, "Why yes, I was thinking of hiring someone to help me with all these papers." She batted her eyes at him and winked. Elinore told him, "Then I'm your girl! When do I start?" John smiled as his head whirled under Elinore's spell. "Monday?" he asked. Elinore was pleased with herself. Her charm was untouchable, and she seemed to smooth just about anything over by turning her flirt-o-meter up a smidge. "See you Monday morning sharp!" she said, giving him another wink as she rushed for the door. John's head was left spinning. He now had a possible apprentice and he never saw it coming. Elinore had developed a signature flirtation move that she deviously pulled from her coat pocket on the poor unsuspecting John, but he was tickled by it. Elinore walked home at a fast pace. She was happy and looked forward to giving her aunt the good news. On her way, she stopped to buy some chicken, green beans and potatoes. She opened the door but smelled nothing inside. Her aunt seemed to have forgotten how to cook, but it didn't bother her this day. She entered the kitchen clutching the brown paper sack that was piled to the top with things to eat. Elinore had not forgotten to buy some fresh herbs, butter and some bread as well. She set the bag down with a heavy thud. Agnes barely raised her eyes from the newspaper she was reading. She mumbled something to Elinore. Elinore couldn't make heads or tails of what she had just said. She turned to face her and found her seated on the same chair with her legs wrapped around the chair's leg exactly in the same fashion as in the days prior.

Elinore wanted to tell her aunt about the job she had just landed but her excitement was being dampened quickly. It was being replaced with annoyance. Elinore was beginning to think she was brought there to be her aunt's personal servant. This was no life. It certainly wasn't fair. She was not just expected to work. Now she was doing most of the cooking, cleaning and shopping while her aunt couldn't even be bothered to get dressed. Still in her bed clothes, she sat waiting for Elinore to drop food in front of her. All the tales Agnes had written about to her mother either happened before she had arrived or were a straight out lie, but her Aunt Agnes had not worked a day since she'd arrived. Now she understood why she wanted rent from her! And now even more, she felt like she had been set up. The house wasn't Elinore's; she barely had a furnished room and that was all!

She lost herself in the moments that passed as the chicken sizzled in the cast iron pan. The coal in the stove began to fill the kitchen with smoke. Elinore asked Agnes to open the window, but Agnes did not move. Elinore waited. Her body started to feel tense, and she could feel the temperature inside herself rising. Slowly, she became hypnotized by the beans rolling over the boiling water; suddenly she couldn't remember even putting them on the stove. Her alter, Erika, had taken control. It was now she who was looking at the chicken cooking in the pan and was beginning to choke from the smoke that filled the kitchen. In a fury, she went to the window and slammed it open with a crack. She delivered a fierce look to her aunt before returning to the stove. She stabbed the chicken with the fork and put it on a plate. "I hate chicken," she said to herself as she drained the beans from the boiling water. She put half of them in a bowl and the rest on the plate. She dropped the plate down hard in front of Agnes and took the bowl to her room. "Not much of a dinner," Erika said as she stomped up the staircase to her room. "One day I'm going to teach that woman a lesson!" she said under her breath.

Elinore remained hidden under Erika's safety until her bedroom door was closed and locked tight. She was allowed to come out then. The hostile atmosphere had been left in the kitchen and in the confinement of her room she found solace. Elinore missed the simple life she had back home. She rolled her bed down for the night. Climbing into it, she pulled the blankets up around herself. The warmth of the blankets comforted her. An image of Carl came to her mind. Elinore couldn't help but wonder what he was doing and if he'd forgotten her by now. Water began to fill her eyes. She wiped her nose with the edge of the blanket. Elinore's life was so unfulfilling, and she was lonely. She thought, even if she did find her way back to Germany, there wasn't much left for her to return to. She guessed she would need to find a job, a place to stay, and she suspected Carl had probably moved on to a new relationship by this time. She hadn't received a single letter from him since she left. Delilah probably wouldn't even remember her after a while. She was so young. She wondered if Hans and Margaret even noticed she was gone. She hadn't received a letter from them either. She hadn't made one friend since she'd come to New York City. Elinore's last thought before she fell asleep was maybe she would go for a walk in the morning and meet some local people while she still had the time. Once she started to work again, her time would be limited.

A chill was in the air that morning and the birds in the chimney were making quite a bit of a racket. Elinore got dressed in her own clothing which felt much more comfortable to her. Much better than the whorish dresses her aunt had bought for her. She despised those dresses. She left the house without a word and headed toward the market. She passed by the railroad tracks and stopped at a few stores along the way. Elinore didn't buy anything though. She had just bought her black rose ring, which she had worn every day since. The garnets sparkled beautifully, and she looked at them often throughout the day. The streets were filled with horse drawn carriages and Elinore enjoyed the hustle and bustle of it all. It was very much the opposite of what she was used to. As she passed the building she would be working in, she could see no one was inside. It was a Saturday and she started to think about how nice it would be to only have to work Monday through Friday. Compared to her job at the laundry factory, that would be as easy as pie. Elinore continued to walk being careful to stay close to the buildings. She did not want to be accidentally hit by a horse and carriage or worse yet, a train. As she approached 10th Avenue, she began to see men on horses waving red flags to warn pedestrians of oncoming trains. She had walked at least four miles before she thought about heading back. The dangerous conditions that these freight trains on the street level tracks caused frightened her and she wondered how many people had lost their lives to them. It seemed to her anything was available for purchase if one had the money.

On her way back, she passed many clothing stores, butchers, jewelry stores, street vendors, bakeries, and general stores. She was living in a big city now but after her long walk and taking it all in she wasn't sure she liked it all that much. There was a lot of noise which she minded terribly. Elinore couldn't wait to get home. And she was hungry now. On the way, she passed a small delicatessen. She entered the store and asked to buy a sandwich. The woman wrapped it in white paper and put it in a brown paper bag for her. Elinore decided to treat herself to a bottle of ginger ale with her sandwich and placed it on the counter. She liked the picture on the bottle of the lady with wings. The brand was White Rock and from her first sip she was sure that it was the only thing she would want to have daily. Before she knew it, Elinore had finished the food she had bought and turned the bottle upside down to let the last drops of sweet ginger ale fall into her mouth. Tonight, she swore she would not be cooking for anyone! She had spent the entire day out with no one to tell her what to do and it felt wonderful to her. The walk home seemed longer than it did when she was on her way.

She was only about a block away from her aunt's house when she noticed a young girl walking just slightly ahead of her. She looked a lot like her old friend Anna from Germany! She hurried to catch up and soon Elinore was close enough to put her hand on the girl's shoulder. The girl was quite startled and turned to face Elinore. She said, "I beg your pardon!" and quickly pushed Elinore's hand off herself. Elinore's eyes dropped to the ground. "I'm sorry, I thought you were someone I knew." The girl was not interested and walked off in a huff. Elinore's day went fine until that moment. Now she was sad again and she wondered if she would ever make friends with anyone in this big city. Feeling depressed, Elinore went straight to her room and locked the door. She was glad her Aunt Agnes did not come looking for her that evening. She just wanted to be left alone. Elinore sat on the bed and started to cry. She looked at the walls, the back of the door, and the fireplace that was attached to the chimney. She hated this place! It was hard to fit into these new surroundings. She started to write another letter to Carl but stopped at 'Dearest Darling.'

Elinore ripped the paper to shreds and threw the pieces into the desk drawer. She closed the drawer hard and the newspaper she had bought caught her eye. The first page told of an event to take place soon. It was a grand event. Many socialites and important people would be attending. She read the article thoroughly and was thrilled to see the man whom she was going to be working for was mentioned. A smile came across her face and she started drumming her fingers on the bed beside her. How could she get to attend such an elite event? Elinore wanted to go badly. She turned the page, looking at the many advertisements. One was of a local dressmaker. She would keep that in mind. The wheels inside Elinore's mind were turning fast now. She began to think of all types of scenarios that could play out involving her new boss. Elinore closed her eyes for a moment. She imagined herself dancing with her new handsome boss. She dreamed of herself living in high class style with more money than her father ever had. With her eyes still closed, she placed her hand on the waist of her imaginary dancing partner and began to dance. Elinore swirled around the room as the music played inside her mind. It all came to a screeching halt though when she stumbled over her own shoes. Landing on the cold floor next to her shoes, the corners of her mouth turned downward. She pressed her left cheek into the palm of her hand. Starring at her shoes, she picked one of them up and threw it across the room. "Dumb shoes!" she yelled.

The daylight began to fade, and Elinore climbed back into her bed again. She closed her eyes, tired from her long walk that day. Sleep came quickly that night. However, the next morning came with a fright. With only one eye open, Elinore believed the house was ablaze. But she smelled no smoke. Through the window, the room was illuminated with a fiery red color. Elinore leaped out of her bed and went to the window to have a look. The sun had risen, and the entire sky was a burning hot red. She remembered what her mother used to say. Rose always said, "Red sky in morning, sailor's warning, red sky at night sailors delight." Elinore's very next thought was that she needed a parasol! There was that lady's shop, and it wasn't far from the house! She washed up and brushed her long blonde hair. She put her shoes on, threw her coat over her shoulders and rushed for the shop. As soon as she stepped outside, she could taste the moisture in the air on her tongue. She hurried along the way hoping to get there before the rain started.

Elinore was not really paying attention to where she was going and walked smack square into a man's chest with a splat. "Oh, my goodness, I'm so sorry!" she exclaimed as she looked upwards at the man's face. It was John, her new boss! Her face turned red with embarrassment. Flustered, she began to explain she needed to buy a parasol before the rain came but stumbled over her words in her awkwardness. John could only laugh as her youthful innocence exuded and his laughter had lightened her uneasiness. Elinore smiled back at him. She liked making him laugh. He asked, "After you get your umbrella, would you like to have a cup of coffee with me?" Elinore didn't hesitate. "I would love to!" The rain had started to fall before she could even get out of the store, but John was still waiting for her. She quickly snapped open the parasol and the two walked arm and arm closely till they reached the building where she had first met him. John lit a fire and soon the water was hot enough to be poured over the coffee grounds. John placed his hands on Elinore's waist and guided her to a beautifully cushioned chair that sat behind a large oak desk. He pulled it out for her and tucked her into it. He poured two cups of coffee and handed one to her. The fire felt good to her, but her skin was still cold from the rain. The two sat for some time talking lightheartedly. John asked Elinore where she grew up. She could feel Erika not far, watching over her but for now, Elinore was left alone with John. She was mesmerized by his dark eyes. Elinore listened closely as each word rolled off his tongue.

He stood behind her and lowered his face, almost resting on her shoulder. He liked the way she smelled. A hint of violet talcum powder filled his nasal cavity. He liked it and it lingered in his thoughts. She had already begun to have a calming effect on his mood, increasing his focus enough to notice it. He told her the desk she was sitting at would be hers and where she would be working. His lips were so close to her ear she could feel his breath. It made her spine tingle and she sat silently. She wasn't sure where he was going with this, but she wasn't sure she would stop him either. John reached around her gently brushing her bosom to pull the top drawer open. In the drawer was a set of keys. John handed them to her and told her since she lived so close, she was likely to get there before him, so he wanted her to have her own set. Elinore took them from him and couldn't help but notice how well manicured his hands were. With such a rough job involving all that ink, letters, papers, and wheels, she thought his hands would be a little rougher.

The minutes turned into hours and Elinore was in no hurry to leave. But then John took the coffee cup from her and said he needed to be on his way. He put his hand on the small of her back and walked her to the door. They exited together and he fumbled looking for the key to lock the door behind them. He started to walk in the opposite direction of where Elinore needed to go. In three steps time, she heard him call her name. She looked back at him curiously. He shouted to her, "I think I will like having you around!" He waved to her and continued in the same direction. Elinore was thrilled! She had also noticed as he handed her the keys inside that he did not have a wedding ring on his finger. He had not spoken of any significant other in his life either. She thought to herself he could be a good catch. Before going home, she stopped to pick up some bits for her evening meal and didn't even mind the thought of having to cook. Today was a perfect day and it ended well for Elinore. She made herself and her aunt a delicious meal. Agnes even thanked her, which surprised her. Her Aunt had never said thank you for anything in the months that had passed since she had first arrived. But now, Elinore thought she might start doing things for herself and if it pleased her aunt too, it would be a plus.

Elinore's first day of work came on a beautiful morning. From out of her window, she saw not a cloud in the sky. She opened the window just about an inch and felt the crispness in the air. The season was changing and most of the leaves had fallen off the trees. Elinore looked through her small closet for something to wear. All her clothes were either ugly or too immature for her to continue to wear. She had held onto the money her father had given her. Elinore decided that this was the time to use some of it and buy herself some suitable clothing. Hurrying down the street she passed the dress shop she had read about in the newspaper. They had a stunning dress in the window that Elinore couldn't wait to try on. Elinore needed to go in and have a closer look at it. The woman inside had hardly noticed her even though the bell had rung at the top of the door when she opened it. She looked at the dress and thought it was the most beautiful dress she had ever seen. It was blue and had a petticoat to add to the fullness of it. The corset that came with it was beautifully made too. It had a lot of lacey details and frills which Elinore adored. This was the image she wanted to burn into any suitor's mind that would come her way from now on. She also saw many other lovely dresses with matching hats and gloves, in addition to some everyday dresses that were beautifully sewn too. In the smallest voice Elinore said, "Pardon me." But the woman did not look up. "Pardon." Elinore again said, raising her voice a little louder. The woman barely looked up to see who was calling her. It was almost as if she wasn't interested in making a sale, Elinore thought. She then asked the woman how much the dress was. She could feel the woman's impatience with her but couldn't understand why. Elinore knew her German accent was different from those who lived there but still she began to explain she had recently moved from Germany and needed to purchase some appropriate every day, working, and elegant clothing. The woman rolled her eyes and said, "Darling, these clothes are for women who have working husbands, they are much too expensive for a single girl such as yourself." "What do you mean, Mam, are you saying I can't buy a dress here?" Elinore was stunned. She was becoming angry with the woman and her attitude. Suddenly, Elinore became dizzy. The next thing she remembered was leaving the shop with a few very full bags of clothing in her hands. The woman inside the store flipped the sign on the door that read "closed" as she left. It was still early, and the beginning of a workday. Elinore had apparently caused the woman to close early for some reason. Elinore headed off once again toward the building where she would be working and looked over the sales slip on the way.

She noticed at the top of the list was the name Erika Heinreich and it appeared she had purchased many new dresses with all the necessary accessories including the elegant blue dress that was in the window. She looked in her pocket and there was still much of the money her father had given her left. Elinore shrugged her shoulders and continued onward. Her lips pressed tightly against one another, and she couldn't really remember what had occurred inside that store but was pleased she had come out with what she had wanted. She didn't bother to give it a second thought as she fumbled to find the keys John had given her. Not able to find them, she assumed she must have left them in the dress shop because she had them when she left her aunt's house. Elinore returned to the dress shop and tapped on the window.

The same woman came to the door but didn't open it. Elinore hollered through the closed glass door that she had left her keys. The woman had a terrified expression on her face and disappeared for a moment from behind the shade that covered the door. She came back quickly, and Elinore could see she held her keys in her hand. The woman only opened the door enough to toss the keys out onto the ground. She pushed the door closed and pulled the shade down fast. Elinore looked at the keys lying on the ground in front of her feet. According to the slip, Elinore had just spent quite a pretty sum inside this store and the woman couldn't even be bothered to put her keys in her hand. How rude, Elinore thought. Inside, the woman peered through the side of the shade to watch her leave. Shaken, she hoped she'd never return. The woman had just had her first encounter with Erika Heinreich and hoped it would be the last. She was demanding and much too scary for her liking.

Finally, Elinore reached her work with her keys in hand. She thought for sure she was late, but as soon as she opened the door, she found herself alone. Elinore quickly tucked her bags under her desk and started a fire to heat some water for coffee. She poured the water over the vessel John had for making it. The coffee smelled so good to her that she poured herself a cup. Just as she took her first sip, John came bursting through the door,

"I'm sorry I am so late!" He apologized as he rushed to his printer. She moved fast in his direction to help. He did not want the morning paper to come out at noon. She quickly handed him the fine paper as he pushed it through the machine. Soon, there was a pile of papers that Elinore took to her desk. She separated them and tied them into small bundles to be delivered. He had a list that hung on the wall noting all his regular customers. The postmaster, several general stores, and a few newspaper stands were at the top of his list. She tucked the piles neatly into the leather satchel that laid on the floor next to the fire. She lifted it carefully and placed it across her shoulders. Before she left, she poured a cup of coffee for John and placed it on his desk that sat across from hers. Elinore came back two more times and delivered the rest of the stacks before she was finished for the day.

Elinore had seemed to fit in quite perfectly and was right on time for all John needed. He found that her being there helped an enormous amount and that made him happy. Elinore sat in her chair exhausted after her final run. Now they had some time for some pleasant conversation, she thought. "Do you belong to any local churches?" John asked. That was an odd question that Elinore was not expecting from him. "No," Elinore replied. "I have not been to church since I first arrived here in America." John smiled and asked, "Would you be so kind as to attend services with me this Sunday?" Elinore was pleased and accepted his offer.

The week passed quickly, and Elinore found herself waiting that Sunday morning in their office for him to arrive. She had taken extreme care to apply her makeup, curling her hair, and picking an appropriate dress to attend the services on John's arm. Together they walked toward the church. They walked closely, but each time Elinore went to hold John's hand he seemed to avoid contact. His actions were peculiar, but she didn't think too hard about it. Elinore could hear the church bell as they got closer, and she became warmed by the reminiscent thoughts she had of her own country's church bells. There was happiness there that she shared with family and friends. Following that initial thought immediately, however, was a deep sadness because she knew it no longer existed. Elinore and John sat closely in a pew at the back of the church and Elinore struggled to hear the sermon. She leaned forward, listening hard, when for a moment, she felt John's hand resting on her leg. She dared not to move. She didn't want him to remove his hand, but he did anyway. Elinore turned to look at John and their eyes met. She gave her approval with a small smile and a twinkle in her eye.

Soon, they were at their usual places again. Both sat at their desks, with coffee in their hands. John was captivated by Elinore's beauty. He had never seen her in anything but her work clothes. He looked at her differently this day and Elinore noticed. She liked the fact that she had caught his eye. Being the temptress she was becoming, it seemed to flow more naturally for her than it ever had before. Elinore had stored Carl's love in a box in the attic of her mind and would be happy to unpack it if she ever had the opportunity to see him again. That seemed far away in a distant time to her and not likely to happen. It was a pure love that she was sure could endure anything that life could bring her way. In fact, that was the only subject that could honestly make her break down sobbing anymore, but on the occasion that she did, Elinore could sense the scolding from within. She could hear the familiar voice telling her to stop being foolish and that Carl didn't care about her anymore anyway. Elinore tried her best to just forget the hurt that still burned in her heart for Carl, only living in the moment and reacting to matters at hand presently. Elinore was adapting to her new life while still learning that Erika would take control when matters became too harsh for her to handle.

John could sense Elinore was deep in thought and very much distracted. Determined to get her attention, he asked the question Elinore wanted to hear most. He told her that there would be a ball that he needed to attend in a few weeks' time, and he wondered if she would grace him with her presence. "I would love to!" she exclaimed happily. John was happy too. He had her complete attention again. Time was escaping though, and the day was coming to an end. It would be hours until they would see each other again for work in the morning. At the end of that week, John placed her weekly pay in her hand. He handed her $20 for her work. Elinore was stunned. That was as much as a man could make! Quickly, she shoved it in her pocket, giving John a wink, and was on her way. Now, she could easily give her aunt the two dollars she wanted, and it wouldn't hurt at all.

John was already beginning to like his new apprentice, but his age bothered him. He wondered if he could keep someone so young for long. He judged his age must be at least twelve years her senior. He hoped the generous pay would help with that, and he didn't notice that she cared anyway. The thought of Elinore lingered on his mind as he put his coat on and went home for the evening. The pots were cold in his house and there was little food in the ice box. He lit a fire and the glow from it illuminated the room. He sat in his high-backed chair and began to eat the scraps of food he had on his plate. The flames that flickered within the fireplace, placed visions of Elinore being there with him. Being all alone in the darkness of his house, he was tempted to please himself. He was delighted with Elinore's interest in him. He was beginning to find it difficult to get through a single day without thinking of her. And it was even more difficult to hide his want for her. He had appeared quite innocent to Elinore, but John had his own motives for his interest in her. She was young and the skin she dared to show was plump and moist. John wanted her more with each day that passed. He was tantalized by the excitement that caused a burning desire within him, but also thought it might be unlikely that she would provide a way of satisfying that desire without attachment. Or maybe she would, he thought. After all, she was much younger than him. He reasoned that after a while she would surely find a younger man more suitable to her liking and he will have gotten what he wished from her. His attraction to her was undeniable and she was capable of exciting all his senses.

Elinore thought about John too. She was following the same path as she did with Carl. This time it was happening faster. A romantic whirlwind of her newest love interest. She hoped it would blossom into a lifelong partnership. She was completely infatuated with John and found it hard to think about little else. She doubted her parents would have approved, but they weren't there to stop her. She didn't know much about John in the short time she had worked for him but had every intention of finding out. The next time Elinore and John worked together; everything went perfectly. Elinore worked diligently as John pushed out the papers. After all the papers had been delivered, they both enjoyed some more personal time before the day finished out. They laughed together and talked about current events. They discussed the president, Theodore Roosevelt. They spoke about many things and John was surprised she knew so much. She had learned about the new subway system being built from city hall to the Bronx even though she had no idea where "the Bronx" was. He found it intriguing that she had knowledge of how it was being financed by the issue of rapid transit bonds. She knew about the Queensboro Bridge, and what Orville and his brother Wilbur Wright had accomplished, making the first flight in a small plane possible. Elinore read a lot in her spare time and kept it under her hat for occasions such as these. She made a habit of gobbling up any current news she came across eagerly. Her knowledge impressed him. Elinore's father had read a lot too. As a little girl she often saw him reading newspapers and he often read aloud to her. John found her intellectually stimulating. Elinore, for her age, was keen at reaching correct conclusions and determining truth or falseness of perceived relationships as well, it seemed. John knew from the start; she was a smart girl, and he would need to use caution. He had no idea how right he was about his own conclusion, but his day would come. The sky was becoming darker, and it was time for the two to say goodbye. John reached for her coat and gently helped her into it.

After he put his own coat on, he followed the same routine he had developed and walked Elinore to the door while casually placing his hand on the small of her back. She seemed to enjoy the attention, he thought. However, John had his own intention on this particular day. He planned something different and hoped he wouldn't get slugged. Just as Elinore reached for the door, John stopped her. Confused, Elinore thought she had forgotten something when John pulled her into himself and kissed her, lingering there for a few seconds longer than just a friendly goodbye gesture. Elinore's eyes rolled backward, and she looked as if she could use some smelling salt when his lips parted from hers. John smiled at her. Inside, he was laughing, and he thought to himself, I have her now!

Elinore was lightheaded and felt as if her knees would buckle. His kiss echoed of someone experienced. She had never been kissed like that before. Her heart fluttered. She smiled back at him but was speechless. His kiss had left her wanting more. But John left her with that and opened the door. He was playing a game of cat and mouse with her and quite enjoying himself. He liked her innocence, or so it seemed. He was unaware he had met his match with Elinore.

Her youth was no obstacle for her. She was smarter than he realized. Her father had taught her well about people's behaviors. Elinore still desired a permanent relationship with a man who would adore her but one that she was also attracted to. John was a magnet for her. He was appealing to her emotional and intellectual senses, but he was mostly visually pleasing to her. It was just a short walk when she found herself standing in front of her aunt's house. She hesitated before going in and dreaded having to now cook a meal. But when Elinore opened the door though, she was delightfully surprised! She could smell pork and sauerkraut cooking! That was one of her favorite dishes. She eagerly sat down and was ready to eat. Agnes made herself and Elinore a plate and the two women feasted on the delicious meal. It bothered Elinore slightly to listen to her aunt eat. Her manners weren't exceptional. She sucked the meat off the bones making a slurping noise. Elinore would have liked to savor the meal slowly, and she tried to ignore the sucking noise but hurried to finish it. She couldn't wash her plate fast enough to leave the room. She thanked her aunt and turned in for the night.

John's kiss was still on her mind. Her heart swelled with thoughts of his embrace. It had only been a few months since she had started to work for John, but she was beginning to think of him constantly. The grand event he had invited her to would arrive quickly. She decided to look over her clothes to make sure she had everything she wanted to wear to make her stunning entrance. It was most important to her to impress John. She needed to weave her web to draw him closer to her. She considered him to be the ideal image of a perfect man. The perfect material for a great father and husband. What a wonderful life she could have with him! He had a lot of money and was a great businessman. She saw him as classy, good-looking and having great notoriety in his circle of people. What more could she ask for? she wondered. Elinore decided the blue dress would be perfect for this occasion. She needed to be sure everything fit, and so she began to try her things on. The corset was tight, and it cinched her tighter as she hooked each eyehook. Her breathing became shallower, but she reasoned with herself that beauty would never come painlessly. She stood far enough away from her small mirror so she could get a full view of herself. The corset was even more pretty when she was wearing it. It was made with lovely ribbons and bows. Adorned with provocative lace, it thrusted her hips backward and forced her bosom forward, achieving that silhouette shape she loved so much. She checked the mirror and liked what she saw but had to admit that between the laces in the back and the hooks in the front, her beauty would suck the life from her. Elinore held her hair up and pushed a few pins in it. The pins she had bought with Margaret were perfect. She inventoried her makeup and began to put her dress on. Stuffing the petticoat under the dress was difficult for her but when she was finally finished, she knew John would not be able to take his eyes off her. The only thing that was missing was some jewelry for her long thin neck. She had the ring she had bought for herself and that would have to be enough. She sat on the bed feeling like she was sitting on a pillow. Elinore giggled with delight. All the frilly lace and bows made her feel pretty. Now, all she had to do was to figure out how she would bend over to lace up her leather shoes without breaking herself in half. In the end, she hoped it would all be worth it. She picked out the cosmetics she would wear and separated them inside her desk. The final touch would be to put her handkerchief in her small purse and wear the gloves that came with the dress. With them, she would be properly prepared if John asked her to dance. The gloves really added the finishing touch and made her look so elegant. Looking in the mirror one last time she held her two fingers to her lips holding an imaginary cigarette. Elinore pursed her lips and breathed outward deeply. She was happy with her stylish appearance. Now came the hard part. She needed to disrobe and hang the dress perfectly so that it would remain flawless.

That evening, John sat in his favorite chair again, picking at the scraps of food on the plate he had prepared. His thoughts returned to Elinore, and they filled his head again. He knew the event at the Knickerbocker would dazzle her and that was his intention. He had thought about this night a great deal too, but for different reasons. He had already made sure to reserve a room for that evening. He could no longer control his desire to have her. As they worked together each day, it was becoming more and more difficult for John to ignore his intense desire to explore her intimately. He certainly was aware that just her presence and grace made his body heat rise because he had never sweated so much in his entire life. His sexual gratification with her was becoming a primary focus and he was finding it harder to concentrate with each day that passed. It was so strong that it was affecting his sleep and he thought briefly that she could be the death of him if he bedded her more than once. His time would be limited with Elinore, but he doubted he could stop at just one encounter with her. His intense thoughts exhausted him and by the light of his lantern, he made his way to his bedroom. He was hoping to get a good night's sleep, but Elinore often invaded his dreams making that nearly impossible to attain. Sleep did not come for John that night and after a few hours of looking at the ceiling he was up again considering the next hook he would sink into Elinore. He just couldn't get the image of her face off his mind. He thought hard about things and decided the best thing he could do for the moment was to write her a note. Swirls of conjured scenarios ran rampant through his thoughts. The thought he settled on was to leave the note purposely on her desk, at the end of the following workday providing her the time to read it in her own solitude, the next morning. He had a plan to show up late to give her that time. In the darkness, lit only by his hand-held lantern, he pulled out his most elegant writing paper to pen his words. Resting his finger on one eyebrow, he thought carefully of how he would word his note. The words began to flow:

My dearest Elinore,

Ever since the propitious moment you entered my world, my heart has been riveted with your loveliness which I have fondly cherished. It is my hope Elinore, that you will relieve me from my inexpressible apprehension and secure me with the beautiful tranquility which is all of me that is yearning to touch the center of you. My body shall be yours and yours shall be mine, my love. Now, I only have the choice but to eagerly await your response to relieve me from this flustered anticipation of your heartened reply.

John paused for a moment, thinking about how to sign it. He tried a few choices out loud to himself, finally settling on one. He ended the note with *forever yours, John.*

John smiled a quite sickly smile as he folded the letter carefully, placing it into the folder. The outer edges of his mouth curled upward with his sinister overall expression. John thought to himself, if she misinterpreted his true intent after becoming aware of him, she would only have herself to blame and therefore he could deny any responsibility for his dastardly deed. He knew he could never fall in love with her as he wrote his words, and that was easy for him to ignore. Elinore was driving him quite mad and now he was focused on having her one way or another. He tucked the note inside his coat and muttered, "What a load of bolder dash!" He rubbed his eyes. They felt heavy now and he dragged himself back to his bed. His plan worked perfectly the next day and after a bit of conversation with Elinore, John slipped the note from under his coat, leaving it for Elinore to find in the morning when she returned.

Elinore enjoyed her walk to work that next day, as she noticed Christmas decorations slowly appearing. But it was early yet. Not even December 1st, but people were looking as if they were already ready for the upcoming festive cheer. The wind that blew through the city streets was cold and seemed to be there to stay. In fact, Elinore could no longer remember a warm day recently. She hurried on her way to John's building and the wind caught the door from her hand, slamming it into the wall behind it. Elinore quickly closed the door and shook from her neck to her legs. She was chilled to the bone. The office was cold and damp inside much to her dislike. She started a fire and thought about her first sip of coffee for the day. The stack of papers that had caught her eye on her desk reminded her of how much work she had to do that day. She began to look them over to remind herself of the order in which things needed to be done. That was when she noticed the folder that she didn't remember seeing the day before. She picked it up and opened the folder, curious as to how she could've missed it. She took the letter out and began to read. Soon, her eyes were wide and her mouth fell open. Her heart stopped and she became rooted to her chair. Elinore's stomach twisted as she rested her left hand on her chest. Her right hand trembled, making it more difficult to read each line but she couldn't put it down either. She now knew he wanted her as much as she wanted him. He expressed his passions to her, clarifying any doubt in her mind that they could become exclusive with one another. Elinore read every word more than once. She read between the lines too. She felt the weight of each sentence, even considering punctuation. Elinore returned the letter to the folder. She sat stunned in the empty room with only the crackling noise coming from the fire. She noticed John was late. She started the printer up and ran a few blank pieces of paper through it to get it warmed up. She didn't yet understand that John was a master at the game of come hither said the spider to the fly. He had her in his grip and he knew it. He was able to match her cunningness equally.

But there was something John had no knowledge of, and Elinore was only just becoming aware of herself, and that was the existence of Erika. Erika was moving through all of this with Elinore, but she did not feel the same way about John. She didn't care for him at all. But for now, she remained silent, keeping her hawk's eye on him. John finally arrived at work and crashed through the door. Elinore looked up at him and laughed. John's hair was twisted around his head like a bird's nest. She rose to her feet to take his coat from him. With it barely removed off his shoulders, the two met each other for a passionate kiss. Elinore felt as if she could melt into him but tried to compose herself. She turned around to place his coat on the hook and felt two small swats on her backside. She looked at John with one eyebrow raised. He ignored her not so pleased look and said, "Come on now, we need to get going here!" She didn't like being swatted like that, but Elinore let it slide and the two worked like a well-oiled machine till all the work was complete. He thanked her for her help and told her to go home early. He reminded her to meet him there for the event they were to attend at five o'clock sharp that evening.

That left her a few hours to prepare, and she wondered if she could make it out of the house without being interrogated by her aunt. She was glad she had already tried everything on ahead of time. She thought about many things on her fast-paced walk home. Elinore didn't see Agnes's carriage as she approached the house. She was happy she was alone in the house and assumed her aunt had gone out for the day. Elinore raced up the stairs and climbed into her dress. She moistened her hair and tied rags in it to curl her thick mane. She applied her cosmetics ever so lightly and painted her lips a cherry red. When her hair was finished drying, she decided to pin it up with the crystal pins she had brought from home, leaving her shoulders and thin youthful neck exposed. Strategically, she pulled a few pieces down to gently frame her face. She pulled the beautiful gloves on tightly adjusting each finger, grabbed her handbag, and hurried to the meeting place where John would be waiting. As she came upon the building, she could see a black carriage pulled by two horses. John was standing next to it dressed in an Edwardian lounge suit with a high hat. Black with stiff collars, he looked quite dashing. He had a dark frock coat draped over his shoulders and she could see it had a beautiful satin lining. It was finally going to happen, and Elinore was excited. John helped her up into the carriage and they were off. Elinore knew little about New York City.

John was spellbound by Elinore's beauty and was speechless. He gazed upon her and all he could muster up was to tell her she looked beautiful. It was the first time in his life he had no words. And his thoughts for the first time were truly honest. She returned his gesture and complimented him on his appearance too. The horses rolled over the Belgian blocked roads making a clip-pity-clop noise. Elinore felt like royalty as they glided along to their destination. They arrived after a short time. Elinore was awestruck by the high arches and banners hanging from the building which she counted fifteen stories high. The building was impressive to Elinore; she had never seen anything like it. The color was unusual to her. It was mostly red and made of brick and terracotta, making it stand out from the rest of the buildings that lined the streets. Above the doorway of the main entrance it read, "The Knickerbocker." She stepped down onto the pavement holding her head high. She was a debutante making her debut in society. She could hear music playing from inside and many women brushed past her and John on the arms of some very wealthy noblemen. All were dressed to kill. From the moment she entered the building, she knew she was in her own element. Elinore was so young, but way ahead of her time. There were many people already inside the building. They were dancing and talking loudly and seemed to be having the time of their life. Those who were seated sat in small groups so close that their elbows touched. She thought it was probably necessary for the amount of people in this lovely space. She moved slowly, noticing the beautiful crisp white linen tablecloths that people carelessly spilled their drinks upon. Many of them seemed to be drunk already and the party had only just begun.

Champagne and Martini glasses could be seen as far as one could see. It was an extravagant event taking place at the crossroads of 42nd street and Broadway. Elinore started to feel a bit lightheaded when she looked upward at the sky-high carved ceilings that had chandeliers hanging from everywhere. She lost her balance and held onto John's arm to steady herself. He sat her down in a lavishly upholstered chair. She felt the plush padding and noticed the imported rugs beneath her feet. John came to her holding a glass of champagne and handed it to her, sipping on his own drink. The music played continuously, and John now wanted to dance. Elinore had been anticipating this moment and was glad to oblige. They moved to the ballroom and on the marble tile, they looked into each other's fixed eyes. Elinore was falling in love hard with John. Her heart was beating fast. She felt it might pound its way right out of her chest! They danced light-footed and twirled with their arms intertwined with each turn. All the ladies' dresses became wide and swooshed across the floor, swaying to the music. Elinore laid her head on John's chest and could hear his heart racing too. John seized the moment and leaned down to kiss Elinore's long porcelain neck. She turned her head ever so slightly, enjoying the warmth of his lips against her skin which now tingled with delight. John moved his kiss from her neck and planted one directly on her mouth. Elinore felt weak in the knees again and John brought another glass of champagne to her.

Elinore was having a glorious time. After another dance, they took a short break to have a wonderful dinner with the most delicious food Elinore had ever tasted. John introduced her to a few people, but they mainly kept to themselves. She thought it was odd that he avoided conversations with much of the elite that were present, but she didn't dare ask why. She was enjoying John's attention. They returned to the dance floor, and Elinore was feeling the tightness of her corset beginning to pinch at her sides. It was becoming difficult for her to breathe. She was determined though not to let it ruin her night. John pulled her closer. Their bodies longed to taste each other and with each dance, it brought them to a higher frenzy. They danced the night away and the party continued long into the night. John could see Elinore was becoming tired. His moment had come. His patience had paid off. He whispered to Elinore. "I have a room upstairs for us, would you like to have a rest?" Elinore thought that would be lovely. She needed a rest badly. Her feet hurt and the corset was squeezing the life from her. They took a small elevator to his room. John mentioned to her on the way that he had ordered a bottle of champagne to be sent to the room in case they became thirsty. As John opened the door, Elinore was taken back by the elegance of the room. It was breathtaking! John sat in the chair in the corner of the room watching Elinore closely. Elinore sat on the bed and stretched her arms upward and slightly behind her, hoping to make breathing a little easier. There was a light knock at the door and John answered it. He accepted the bottle and signed for it. He closed the door and locked it. Right away, he opened the bottle, and the cork blew off, hitting the ceiling. Elinore laughed. The alcohol was impairing her, and John laughed noticing its effects. John poured the glasses full and handed one to Elinore. She knew she had drank enough and only finished half the glass.

John placed his glass on the small table next to him. He moved slowly toward her, biting his lower lip. Placing his hands on each side of her rib cage, he picked her up to a standing position. She was hot enough to start a fire. He began to kiss her again and she moaned with pleasure. John moved his hands up her sides to place her arms around his shoulders, leaving himself free to loosen her dress. Elinore, at the same time, began to open John's shirt, peeling it from him to expose his bare chest. Elinore's dress dropped to the floor, and she was left standing in only her corset and bare feet. John laid her down on the bed to crawl on top of her. John began his journey kissing her, starting just under her chin, working his way to nestling his head between her bust. He licked her skin, and she squirmed in ecstasy. John wanted her and he unhooked each hook of her corset exposing her entirely. His strong but gentle hands stroked her, and she felt her breasts rise to attention. John was breathing heavily and while hoovering over her, he whispered softly, "Relax, I won't hurt you." Slowly and rhythmically, he moved down her body. Suddenly, she felt him pierce her. It was only a brief pain that turned into a sweet spasm. Elinore arched her back and wanted more of John. She pressed hard against him and it pleased John intensely. John ran his hands over Elinore's thighs and lifted her legs over his shoulders so that Elinore was wide open for him. He slid himself inside her again and again. He was touching the center of her with himself as he had promised. He thrusted himself faster and harder and Elinore could feel herself vibrating. John felt as if he would explode. Not wanting it to end so soon, he withdrew himself, returning to her neck again. He let his fingers explore her every curve. Over her breasts, past her stomach, lightly passing over her hair and down her inner thighs to the insides of her knees. He leaned to kiss her stomach, opening her legs wider, almost flat to the bed. Elinore arched her back again in anticipation of where he would kiss next. It was the pink centered cleft of flesh he was after, and he licked it like a cat cleaning itself. Elinore had a tingling inside herself she had never felt before, and with her scream of delight, he plunged himself back inside her deeply. Finally, John couldn't hold out any longer, and with a jagged grunting breath, he himself felt ecstasy. Elinore lay beside John with her head on his chest. His heart pounded. Twisted together, they soon fell asleep under just the sheet.

Early that next morning, it was Erika who woke before John. Her eyes blurry from all the champagne she had drank. She rubbed the slight pain in her forehead with her fingers. She looked around the room, starting with the beautiful bed they were lying on. The light from the open windows off the balcony streamed through the room. The solid wood furniture was highly polished and had nip and tuck upholstery. All were covered in green velvet. Erika wasn't interested in such high-class stuff. She couldn't understand how people could get comfortable in furniture like that. She didn't think it was worth the money either. It's just furniture, she thought. The rugs that covered the floors were plush and vibrant with color. The long drapes caressed the walls and filtered the light from outside giving it a dreamy effect. But Erika felt sick, and even more so, disgusted. She needed to get them out of there fast. She was angered by Elinore's behavior. She looked at John's face as he lay sleeping beside her and cringed. She felt as if she would vomit. Dirty old man, she thought. Erika could see that Elinore was falling into John's clutches and she didn't like it one bit. She could see that he was up to no good. Erika was determined to get out of there as fast as she could. She was fueled by her anger with Elinore. She thought she was smarter than that. Erika slid out of the bed as quiet as a mouse. She looked for her clothes and found them scattered about in small, crumpled piles. She looked back at John to make sure he was still sleeping. Anger coursed through her veins. How dare he treat her like a common prostitute! She hurried to get dressed. In the bathroom she turned the faucet ever so slightly to let the smallest trickle of water out. She smoothed her hair quickly with it. Careful not to make any noise to wake the sleeping beast, she just wanted to forget any of this ever happened. She should not have trusted Elinore's judgement. She threw herself together and put the handkerchief from her purse over her head. She tip-toed toward the door but his pants lying across the chair caught her eye. If he was going to treat her like a whore, at least she would retrieve her pay for being so. Erika rifled through John's pockets and helped herself to most of his cash. "He should be glad I'm not taking all of it!" she mumbled. Slowly, she turned the knob on the door. Almost free, she thought! The breeze in the hallway hit her face. Erika made her getaway to the elevator and past the front desk, escaping to the street.

Outside the hotel, the streets were lined with horse and carriages with men standing by to take people to their destinations. She asked the first one she saw to take her to West 33rd street and hopped up inside the small carriage without any help from the driver. She just couldn't leave fast enough! With the crack of the whip, they were on their way and finally she could breathe again. Beside her in the seat someone had left a newspaper. It was one of John's papers from the day before.

She hadn't had time to read it yesterday, so she slipped it inside her purse. In a few minutes she arrived near her house, and she asked the driver to stop there. Erika paid her fare with the money she had taken from John. She walked the rest of the way and was finally at her aunt's house. She took a deep breath and opened the door. The first thing she smelled was bacon! Oh boy, she whispered and rolled her eyes. Elinore took a second to run her fingers through her hair and smooth her clothing over. She entered the kitchen to see her aunt cooking.

Agnes looked at her and asked where she had been. Elinore was feeling the throes of a panic attack setting in. She staggered at her aunt's question and now she was having trouble remembering the details of how she got home in the first place. The first thing that popped into her head blurted out from her mouth. With a wild look she said, "I went shopping and I bought this dress. Do you like it?" she asked. She stood paralyzed waiting for her aunt's response. Agnes looked up and down at her niece and then asked her to turn around. "I do like it, but you could have put it together a little neater." Elinore figured she would be critical in some sort of way, and she was right, but she imagined it would be much worse. Elinore told her aunt she wanted to wash the dress before she would wear it for a party. In her mind, this would be a good reason to discredit the dress's condition, hiding the fact that it had already been worn. To Elinore's surprise, Agnes agreed with her and offered her something to eat. With a sigh of relief, Elinore went to her room to hang the dress neatly in her closet. She returned to the kitchen in just a few minutes, looking forward to the meal Agnes had offered. She was more comfortable in her own clothing and sat down at the table accepting the coffee Agnes had put down for her. "Would you like a piece of toast with that?" she asked. Soon, Agnes was sitting across from her having the same. She took her usual position of burying her head in the newspaper and having her legs wrapped around the chair that held her. Both women sat quietly and the only noises that were heard by Elinore were the slurping sounds her aunt made as she sipped her hot coffee. Elinore began to think about her mother and father talking about Agnes's ill table manners.

As a child, she hadn't noticed but now it was hard to miss. Each sip made Elinore recoil in her seat.

John had arrived at work early, but Elinore was late that next day. Looking at the four walls, his toe tapped against the floor. He was impatient to confront her. When she entered the building, she immediately felt his eyes upon her. His gaze seemed to have an annoyed look, but she wasn't sure exactly why he would be angry with her. She wasn't late. She poured herself some coffee and sat down at her desk. John was still staring at her. Finally, Elinore shot out, "What? Why are you staring at me?" John shouted back, "Why did you leave without me?" Elinore really couldn't think of what to say. "Well…." she paused. "I needed to get home before my aunt noticed I was gone." That was all Elinore could honestly come up with. She walked slowly toward him from the opposite side of the room. She twirled her hair around her finger and tilted her head against her hair in the palm of her hand. When she reached the end of the strands she ran her index finger across her lips, moistening them with her tongue at the same time. She leaned into John who was seated at his desk and placed her knee hard against the inside of his thigh.

John began to babble. His words came from somewhere, but his tongue was disconnected from his brain. "What's wrong John?" Elinore enjoyed making him sweat. She wanted to burst out laughing as he stumbled over his words. Elinore's eyebrows raised and she looked down at him with an inquisitive look. John cleared his throat and asked Elinore if she would like to have a drink with him after work. Elinore wasn't sure she should. The champagne at the Knickerbocker had made her so uninhibited. She wasn't sure she could trust herself. "Oh, why not," she then reasoned with herself trying to convince herself nothing would happen. She agreed, despite her hesitation. As soon as the day was over, and the last of the papers were delivered, John pulled the horses around the building to the front. He sat patiently waiting for Elinore to lock the door. They headed in the direction of the flat iron district and Elinore asked where they were going. All he would tell her was that she would like it. They rode to 45 East 18th Street and stopped in front of a building named Old Town. Inside, they slipped into a booth quietly. The table between them was made of a high polished mahogany, with a brass rail that supported it from the tiled floor beneath their feet. All the traveling around the city excited Elinore. John went to the bar and asked the bartender for two glasses of Genesee. The bartender had a mustache that was very long. Elinore could see that he used wax to twirl and curl it upward toward his cheeks. She found it hilarious but held her laugh in so as not to embarrass John. It was funny to her because it looked like the handlebars of bicycles, she had seen people riding in the park. Her attention then was caught by a picture on the wall. It was a drawing of an old distillery vat that was used to make corn liquor and she had seen one like it before. It looked just like the one she and Margaret had found. She studied it closely until John returned with their refreshments.

They talked for a few hours and Elinore became hypnotized by John's dark eyes again. His stories fascinated her. He had traveled to many places and had even been to Germany, but only to Berlin, which was much further away from where she had lived. He bought a few more drinks and it was beginning to get late. It was when her hips began to ache from the hard benches, she asked John to take her back to the office. Elinore kissed him and thanked him for the outing. She passed the bakery on the way home and stopped to buy some bread to nibble on. The drinks had made her a little tipsy and she thought the bread might help with that. Elinore was unaware that she was swaying a bit as she walked, but the bread had done the trick. As she arrived home, she felt much better. All she could think of now was how comfortable she would be once she laid her head down for a good night of sleep. She was happy with the way her relationship with John was coming along. They were comfortable with each other. Every day their talks became more personal, as if they had already been married for a long time. Elinore thought John could very well become her husband.

Chapter 14

The season had changed, and it was becoming very cold outside. The snow was falling on a regular basis. Christmas was just days away now and Elinore didn't know if she should give John a gift. She had purchased a beautiful broach for her aunt, from the same store she had purchased her ring from. She thought about a walking stick that she had seen a street vendor selling. They were wonderfully carved with gems incrusted into the hand grip. Maybe John would like that, she thought. Elinore did eventually buy one and gave it to John the day before Christmas. John had a surprise for Elinore as well. From his pocket, he pulled a small box. He gave it to her after she had presented him with her gift. Elinore opened the box and found the daintiest golden locket. When she opened the locket, she found a small tuft of hair. The hair was the same color as John's. She asked him to help her put it on and he willingly did so. It was beautiful and she found it hard to believe he would buy something so exquisite for her. She thought it must have cost him a fortune. Christmas Day came, and she spent that day with her Aunt Agnes. Elinore gave her the broach she had bought, and it made her aunt cry. It was a circular one with vines of silver interweaved with no end. Agnes wiped the tears from her eyes and pinned it to her dress. It had made her so happy. Her niece had fine taste in jewelry. Agnes had a gift for Elinore too. She gave her a small box too. Elinore shook it trying to guess what was inside. Agnes smiled and said, "Go on now, open it!" Elinore opened the box to find 10 lovely new hairpins. She gleamed at their beauty. They were silver with Safire stones. "Oh, thank you," she cried out. Elinore felt lucky to have received such a special gift. That evening they shared a tasty meal of beef and potatoes with some bread pudding. Agnes had invited two of her friends over and Elinore blended with them. It was a glorious holiday for all of them. But at the end of the evening when everyone was tucked into their beds, Elinore could still not get John off her mind. She wondered where he was and if he was having a good time. She missed him and couldn't wait to get back to work.

Days and weeks passed fast as Elinore and John continued their relationship. The new year had come, and Elinore found it difficult to remember to change the year date as she wrote in John's ledgers. It was 1909 and that January was a cold one. In Germany it was even colder, as she remembered it, especially at night. Elinore had been in America five years now and had become accustomed to it. The day was January 15th when Elinore left her aunt's house to go to work. When she opened the door, a familiar smell entered her nostrils. It smelled like snow. She knew that smell well, since it snowed often in Germany. She pulled her coat tight around her body and was on her way. Before she closed the door, she shouted to her aunt that it smelled like snow and to get ready for it. "Goodbye," raising her voice before she closed the door tightly. She knew she would not be able to stop on the way home to shop, so she took a few extra minutes to pick up some bread, cheese, fruits and milk with a bit of smoked ham and coffee grounds before going to work. She could leave the things that needed to be kept cold on the back steps until she could leave. Small flakes of snow began to fall from the sky and Elinore caught some on her tongue. It was difficult to do while carrying the heavy bags, but it made her smile. As the morning became early afternoon, the snow began to fall heavier. A major snowstorm had come to the area with blizzard conditions at times. The winds howled. Elinore had seen many snowstorms, but this one was fierce. The roadways were starting to turn into thin trails as she looked out of the window of John's office. By late afternoon, she could barely see the buildings on the other side of the street. Even the people who dared to use a sleigh were becoming fewer. By the time Elinore and John had finished their work, the snow had piled halfway up the door and John pushed it hard to open it.

They both decided that it might be a good idea if they stayed right where they were till morning, but when morning came it was still snowing! Elinore looked out from the windows again. She became worried about her aunt and wondered when it would stop. It was hard to see anything now. The hardest falling of the snow seemed to be happening at that moment. There were small footpaths, but she could see no one. The familiar sounds of the trains had become silent. Some telegraph poles and wires had fallen and laid across the street. Elinore opened the window just enough to stick her hand outside and she could feel rain mixing with the snow. She told John that they were in for another bad night. Elinore knew the rain would freeze, making it very icy and possibly paralyze the city. Especially if it were like the snowstorms she had experienced! Elinore was glad she had stopped to get some food. That might be the only food they would have for a few days. She knew John and herself would be going nowhere for the time being. Elinore had experience when it came to snow. Being house bound with John made her happy. Elinore made a makeshift bed for the two of them in front of the fire and gathered all the cushions and blankets she could find. John had gone out to the back to check on the horses, and when he came in, he was carrying more coal and wood. His coat had snow stuck to it. His hat even had an inch of snow on top of it. He had only been outside for five minutes, Elinore guessed. John hung his coat on the pole by the fire and the snow dripped from it. Even his eyebrows had snow stuck on them. John stoked the fire and added another piece of wood to it. He held his hands out against the flames and the warmth felt good to him. The day had slipped by, and it was still snowing.

Elinore and John sipped some coffee and ate the sandwiches Elinore made. Eventually, they both laid in front of the fire and curled up against one another to let sleep take over their bodies. On Sunday night, the snow finally began to let up. Elinore knew by morning she would be able to return home. She didn't mind so much this time. She was looking forward to a hot bath and sleeping in her own bed. That Monday morning was a sight to behold. The largest and smallest of trees were coated with gleaming ice. Even the lampposts looked like they were made of glass. There were very few human or animal tracks to damage the visual beauty the storm had left in its wake. Elinore and John kissed, and each started out in the direction of their homes. John's kiss goodbye seemed short to her as she made her way carefully through the snow. Not anything she could put her finger on, but maybe he was just tired. The ice made it difficult to walk. With each step, she had to crack the ice first with her boot and let it sink through to the soft snow below it. The walk home was slow, and Elinore fell a few times before she got there. Her Aunt Agnes was happy to see her coming through the door and even hugged her. Agnes had made some nice biscuits and some chicken soup. She offered some to Elinore. That pleased her a great deal; it was the first hot food she'd had in days and her mouth watered when her aunt ladled some into a bowl for her. She sat down and took no time to put a spoonful into her mouth. The steam from the bowl rose and she gently blew on it. Her aunt asked her if she had stayed at work during the storm. Elinore replied, "Oh yes and it was most uncomfortable!" Agnes didn't ask any more questions and Elinore was glad.

Four days after the storm, the city workers had much of the ice and snow cleared away and Elinore made her way back to work. John had given some thought during his time away from Elinore as to how he would get out of the mess he had made with her. He had taken it a bit too far with her and he knew that, but he just couldn't control himself around her. He was running out of time, and he knew he should end it. Her help around the office was invaluable and he wondered if he could just keep her as an employee without the sexual tension. He also knew he was kidding himself for even thinking it.

In the morning the streets were still too rough to bring the horses, so he walked to work. He arrived first and started a fire. He hadn't finished making the coffee when Elinore came in. She hung up her coat and kissed John's cheek. She noticed he didn't lean into her as he usually did but she said nothing. She wondered if she'd done something wrong. She began to clean up the blankets and cushions that were still scattered about on the floor. The day went fast and there wasn't much news to print about. The city was still on its knees and many of John's customers weren't even open for business. John put his coat back on after a short time and told Elinore he would close early for the day. He told her, "I'll see you tomorrow." She didn't understand his casually cool manner with her. His lips barely touched hers as he headed for the door. Elinore hadn't even gotten the chance to tell him that she had brought him some of her aunt's chicken soup. She put her coat on and locked the door behind her, carrying the soup in her hand. She could still see John just a block away. In that moment, Elinore decided to follow him to see where he lived. Being careful not to follow too close so he wouldn't see her, Elinore moved slowly with him. It was only three blocks away and Elinore stood next to a building watching. She waited to watch John enter his home. It was a large house. Three times the size of her aunt's house. It was an enormous house for a single man, she thought. She was tempted to knock on the door to give him the chicken soup she had brought with her to give to him but decided not to. Elinore was satisfied with just knowing where he lived for the moment. She waited a little longer just watching. Nothing happened once he went inside; not even a light could be seen from within. She decided she should just go home.

Something seemed to bother John that day, but maybe he would tell her in the morning. Her thoughts circled around John for the rest of the day into that night. She couldn't help but wonder what would have happened if she had knocked on that door. Would he have greeted her lovingly, inviting her inside? Maybe he would have even invited her into his dudeoir for more intimacy. She was certainly becoming addicted to his attention. She thought about many things as she slowly made her way homeward. Her thoughts were interrupted by a little dog who joined her on her journey home. He seemed to be lost and she wanted to keep him, but she knew her aunt would not be happy about that. She put the soup down on the ground and the dog's tail wagged back and forth with excitement. He licked it up like he hadn't eaten in days. It was enough of a distraction for Elinore to get away without the dog following her. Elinore thought the dog was adorable and had a fleeting thought that maybe one day she would like to have a dog of her own. She continued at a slow pace, stopping to rest occasionally and watch birds. She felt very apathetic at this point. John was her reason to be excited lately. He brought a passion out in her that she hadn't felt in a while. Much too long for her liking. But he was at his home, and she would soon be at hers. That night Elinore sat soaking in the bathtub thinking about John. She was still concerned as to why he was being so distant with her, especially during the snowstorm when it was just the two of them with no chance of anyone coming in to pick up a paper. She had imagined as they sat in front of the fire that they would become passionate, but he hardly touched her. She was in love with him and needed to know why he was acting so strangely. Completely different from the way he treated her at the Knickerbocker. Unrecognizable really. Her appetite was becoming insatiable for him to touch her again the same way he had before. He had left his mark on her and now like a powerful drug, she had a voracious hunger to repeat their romantic entanglement. He had done things to her no man had ever done before and she wanted more at any cost. She was fully aware he was older than her and she assumed he was much more experienced because of that. She was determined to let their interludes progress with excitement but wasn't sure exactly how to adjust her flirt-o-meter. Too much and she could push him away, too little and he could think that she was disinterested. Elinore shook her head back and forth wildly. Bathwater flung off the ends of her hair. She exhaled hard and rolled her eyes. Frustrated, she stood up and took the towel from the small table beside the tub to dry herself. Elinore growled, "Enough thinking for now!"

John sat alone in his empty house too that night, in front of his fireplace. He stabbed the wood with the poker while his thoughts about Elinore consumed him. He watched the flames dance and visions of Elinore's body crept inside his head. He was used to being in control of his relationships, but this one was a loose cannon. Elinore was such an enchantress and he had lost his control like a schoolboy. He thought he had done well by avoiding her vampish ways while being held prisoner by the snowstorm but had to admit, it wasn't easy. He knew it would be likely that he would have to have one more tryst with her. Maybe two. He laughed to himself. He knew he had Elinore panting and heated for another encounter. She was so young and thirsty. At least he thought he had control as to when and where it would happen if at all. He was enjoying having her under his thumb drooling and was even developing a pompous attitude about it. Proud of his stealthy moves indeed. He was careful though to hide his true feelings. He dared not to let Elinore know that his appetite to taste her youthful porcelain skin again was still very hard for him to contain. It had been torturous to sleep next to his beauty and not touch her, but it was necessary to complete his plan on where he was going with their relationship. Pulling back, he knew would bring her on harder for their next romantic interlude.

Business was beginning to pick up again. All the walkways and entrances to most of the stores had been cleared. The sun had taken care of the rest of the snow and the roadways were clear enough that the horses could travel them again. John thought it might be nice to take the horses out for a sleigh ride through the park before it all melted soon. A lot of the holiday decorations were still up. Not many people had time to take them down before the storm left them encased in snowy ice. Elinore had already arrived at the office and was doing the most important thing first, making coffee. She waited patiently for John inside the chilly office. Her body was tense, and she had shivers run up her back from the coldness. Elinore put her coat back on and waited for the fire to warm the building. She paced the floor waiting for John. She had all but finished her first cup of coffee and was becoming impatient with John's lack of punctuality. She looked out of the window again and couldn't believe her eyes. John was riding in a sleigh and coming in her direction.

He saw her standing in the window and waved to her to come out. "What are you doing John?" she asked. "We have a paper to put out," she insisted. John smiled at her like the first time she had met him. "We are taking the day off! Come on!"

he said extending his hand downward to her. Elinore quickly pulled her coat around herself and locked the door. John helped her up into the sleigh and she sat nestled closely to him. They rode through Central Park which was mostly still untouched by human footprints. The snow and ice glistened in the sunshine, and they laughed together at the birds flopping around on the ice. John pulled back on the reins slowing the horse to a stop. "Elinore, would you be so kind as to go to a sporting event with me? I know women mostly don't care for sports, but…" Elinore was really a tomboy at heart so she was more than delighted at the invitation and John could see that from the expression on her face. "Sure!" she said with a grin. Elinore asked, "What type of sporting event will we be attending?" John told her about the indoor annual games of Columbia University, and that he had to cover it for the newspaper. He gave her the date. It was to take place on February 13th. "I know it's a workday, but I would really enjoy having your company," John told her. "Of course, I understand, and I'll be there with you," Elinore answered cheerfully. In a moment of stillness, John leaned into Elinore for a kiss. "Thank you," he whispered. With a crack of the whip, the horse continued their romantic outing.

But after an hour, Elinore asked John to take her home. She was chilled to the bone and needed warming. John had another idea on his mind though. He brought the sleigh back to their office and Elinore was confused. He had told her they were taking the day off, and now she would have to walk home through the ice that was still left on the ground. Didn't he hear her? She entered the office and John followed closely behind her. He could smell her violet perfumed body and he was losing control again. He looked at his desk piled with papers, but no longer cared about their importance. In one quick swipe of his long arm, the papers fell to the floor. Before Elinore knew it, John had rushed up behind her scooping her up and landed her on his massive wooden desk hard. He peeled her coat from her, and Elinore helped him. She became aroused by his spontaneity. Anyone from the street could have walked in on them, which added to the excitement. Both were breathing hard. He needed to feed his carnal appetite and Elinore complied willingly. She called his name softly, almost whispering between her deep breaths of satisfaction. Elinore loved the way her handsome man touched her. She felt her heart racing as his hands ran over her body. His forearms were thick, and he moved her with ease. She held his wrists tight and pulled herself into him inviting him to continue. John pushed Elinore's hair back as it spread wildly across her face. He kissed her hard. She just couldn't get enough of him. Her lips tasted sweet to him, and he kissed her again. Elinore gave a small wave of her head leading John to her neck area. He feasted there driving himself quite mad and she exhaled noticeably with excitement. Elinore trembled as she hooked one of her fingers onto his belt which still sat loosely around his waist. She arched her back and let out small moans encouraging John. She unbuttoned his shirt and reached to touch his exposed chest. Finally, both had pulled at each other's clothing enough to touch one another's skin. Their intense primal feeling could not be held back for another second. They enjoyed the waves of passion together until it had peaked, and the dam had burst.

John had physically exhausted himself and laid his body on top of Elinore, resting there comfortably. Their arms remained tangled around each other. John looked at Elinore's face with contention. "You are intoxicating!" he said with a satisfied smirk. She wiped the sweat from her brow and went to the bathroom to fix herself. She stood staring into the mirror. She examined herself and started to feel odd about herself, like she had just entered another world when she closed the bathroom door. Suddenly, she heard the word, "Tramp!" It was loud and clear! Elinore started to feel ashamed as her emotions swung, considering what she had just let happen. Erika was not happy with Elinore. Erika was about to make her presence known to John but as she opened the door, she saw John with his coat back on. Stunned, Elinore stood firm and asked, "Where are you going now?" John told her that he had forgotten that he was supposed to attend a meeting scheduled with his boss and he was late. He said, "I must go immediately, I'm sorry, but I will see you tomorrow." And with that, he closed the door. Erika was still mad, but Elinore was safe.

Saturday came quickly and Elinore took the arm of her lover into Madison Square Garden. She looked in awe of the noble establishment upon their arrival. All who attended were influential and she looked forward to meeting a few of these prominent people. Elinore had taken much care in the way she dressed for the event. John pranced around with his youthful arm candy feeling young himself again. He even held Elinore's hand on several occasions as they watched the athletes, but things still felt a little strange to Elinore. Something just wasn't right with him. Still, she reasoned with herself, she shouldn't complain. He took her there, maybe the stress of the job was affecting him. When the event was over, he rode with Elinore in his carriage to her house. She insisted though, she be let to leave him a few houses away from where she lived, insisting on not giving the neighbors anything to chew on. He helped her down to the street and kissed her goodbye. Elinore enjoyed the event and hoped many more would follow. Warmer temperatures had come in the weeks that followed, and the season was changing once again.

Erika's favorite season was on its way, the start of spring and new beginnings. Elinore was also looking forward to summer, but for different reasons. Every day, Elinore walked the same path to work, and it had been a while since anything exciting had happened. Elinore had noticed the first flowers starting to bloom on one of her walks. Pretty purple crocuses lined the well-worn cut through that many people walked over. One day, on her way to work, Elinore was not feeling particularly well and decided to stop by the apothecary. The lady inside asked if she could help her. Elinore told the nice lady that she had a bit of a headache and was looking for something to cure her ailment. Elinore kept looking around while the woman leafed through a very large book looking for a remedy behind the counter. The kind lady asked if anything else was bothering her to diagnose her more easily, but Elinore told her no. The woman placed a small bottle into a paper sack and Elinore thanked her for her help. As Elinore reached for the door, she saw a large sign posted on the wall in big red letters above it. It read:

WE DO NOT CARRY: Nightshade, Strychnine, arsenic, or Mandrake!

Elinore turned around and asked the lady why they did not carry the items listed on the sign, pointing to it. The woman was curious about her question. Most people knew. The lady simply said, "They are poisonous darling." She disappeared into the back of her store and Elinore didn't think about it anymore. Elinore stepped outside and reached into the bag. Inside she found a bottle she had seen before. It looked like the one her father had brought home for her mother a long time ago. She remembered he said it was a cure for a headache. Glad to have them, she popped two into her mouth when she got to work. She sat at her desk and sipped on a cup of coffee, waiting for them to take effect. The coffee seemed to make her feel better too. John noticed Elinore didn't look her usual self and asked her if she wanted to go home, but Elinore didn't want to leave. She liked being around John. She pushed herself through the day.

Over the next couple of weeks, the city seemed to come alive. The warmer weather brought people back outside again. The park seemed greener, and the animals became electrified by the warmth. The squirrels chased each other round and round the trees and the birds chirped beautiful songs happily. People were planning events and dances were being held. John often seemed too busy to even make small talk with Elinore and that made her upset with him. She missed their long conversations. Still, she kept at the same pace. At least she could be close to John at work and for now that would have to be enough. Elinore enjoyed the short walk to work every morning. As the temperatures had changed, she noticed all the wildflowers that were popping up to greet the sun. She was glad that she didn't need to wear her heavy coat anymore. The weight of it made her shoulders ache at times, but now she felt light as the spring breeze that caressed her face.

Agnes was happy, now that spring was in the air too, and thought about using the line outside for some freshly done laundry. The breeze in the air would dry the clothes quickly.

Agnes wanted to wash the curtains that were attached by rods at the top and bottom on each side of the front door too. She had been wanting to wash them for some time, but it was such a chore. It was simply a lot of bothersome work! The towels had stacked up too since Elinore needed two every time she bathed. It was a good day to do it. Agnes thought about the fact that Elinore had been so busy working that she didn't have much time for washing. That was when she decided to climb the staircase to Elinore's room to gather the dresses that she had come from Germany with. She held one of the dresses up, looking at it closely. She remembered when she and Rose wore very similar ones. The fabric was different than those in America. Much thicker and softer to the touch. She clutched at it and started to rub it against her cheek when she felt a deep stabbing pain in her hand. "OWW!" she shrieked in pain. Agnes held out the dress and blood dripped down her forearm. She examined herself and found a deep gash between her palm and ring finger on her right hand. Her life blood gushed from the wound. Quickly, she dug through the pockets of the dress to find what had cut her. Droplets of blood started to hit the floor where she stood. Astonished, she held in her opposite hand, Elinore's favorite choice of weapon. Her billhook, dripping with Agnes's blood. Agnes wondered why Elinore would need a billhook. There was no farming to be done where she lived. What on earth would she be doing with it, she wondered. She wrapped her bleeding hand tightly with one of the face towels she had given to Elinore and took the bloody dress with the billhook downstairs to the kitchen. She threw the dress in the sink and ran cold water over it. Agnes was feeling weak. The sight of the blood-soaked towel made her feel light-headed and sick to her stomach. She sat down at the table and waited for Elinore. Agnes expected her niece to be home from work shortly. It was getting late when she finally heard the front door open.

Elinore had stopped to pick up some food on her way home and was carrying two heavy paper sacks. She closed the door with her foot and stumbled to the kitchen. The paper bags crunched as she set them down, next to the sink. Immediately, the color of the water in the sink caught her eye. "What happened?" Elinore asked. Agnes remained silent and still had her hand wrapped in the towel. Concerned, Elinore asked again, "What happened?" Agnes pushed Elinore's precious billhook across the table. Elinore's eyes darted to the billhook that was still covered with blood. Elinore's face glazed over. "Why were you in my room?" she asked. Elinore felt heat rising throughout her body. Erika could feel the tension rising within Elinore and it was time for her to put an end to it. Elinore was losing control and Erika came out strong. She looked at Agnes and shouted, "You had no right to be snooping around my room!" Erika's eyes were dark and threatening. Erika didn't like Agnes to begin with, but the fact that she intruded into their private space made her break out in a rage. Almost feral.

Earlier that morning, Agnes had been chopping some ice for the ice box, and the ice pick she used was there sitting on the counter, next to the paper sacks. Erika was keenly aware of this convenient weapon that was within her reach. With precision, Erika firmly grasped the wooden handled tool and with a calculated intellectual quickness, she plunged the pointed end of the pick into the table, directly in front of Agnes. She bent over across the table, leaning on her elbows, looking straight into Agnes's eyes. Agnes was terrified of what her niece might do next. She felt the hairs on the back of her neck rise and a chill ran down her spine. Locked in place, she glared back at Erika, trying desperately not to show her fear. Erika growled at Agnes as if she were possessed. "You are never to go into my room again unless I say you can! I pay for that room! Do you hear me?" Erika began to leave the room but stopped for another lashing. She slowly turned her head, looking back at Agnes and spoke with gritted teeth, "You got what you deserved!" Agnes could feel the venom in her words but remained silent.

Agnes didn't like the way her niece spoke to her. She put the ice pick away quickly, hiding it under the doily in the drawer. She knew she would need to contact Rose if things got worse with Elinore and it had already gotten out of hand. It seemed that the situation between her and her niece was damn close to being just that. Elinore was unpredictable! Agnes realized she really didn't know her niece at all. She never knew what to expect. Elinore was moody. She could be pleasant and demonic all in the same day. Agnes had become dependent on Elinore's income, but it surely wasn't worth her life.

Erika finally left the kitchen and slammed the kitchen door. She stomped up the staircase. With each stomp of her foot, she was cementing in her words to Agnes. She slammed the door to her room to finalize her threats. Erika could feel Elinore's fear of what would happen now. She hadn't meant to cause her or the other identities more stress. Erika had come down hard on Agnes. For a few minutes within the confines of the safety of their room, Erika thought about the validity of what Elinore had transferred to her. What if they were evicted? Where would they live? Erika and Elinore blended their conversation inside Elinore's head. Erika could also feel the presence of other alters now coming forward with their input. They usually remained silent. But now there were younger ones making themselves known, and they were crying. Erika had not meant to make the other alters upset. Her job was to protect everyone inside though, and she took that seriously. Elinore was becoming more aware of the alters that lived within her now too. There was more than one voice she could hear now. It was all too much, and Elinore felt tired. She laid down and fell asleep, waking the following day feeling refreshed. She had slept soundly that night. Better than she ever had before. She went to her closet and noticed one of her dresses was missing. It didn't matter much, she didn't wear those dresses anymore, anyway. Then like a dream, she began to recall what had happened the day before in the kitchen. Elinore didn't want to be late for work. There was no time to think about that now. She focused on what she would wear. As she put the clothing on, her dress seemed tighter, especially around the waist. Another thought occurred to her. She knew her strawberry week would be arriving soon. Thinking about it for a moment, she couldn't remember the last time it had come. As she pulled her bodice up over her brazier, she noticed how tender her breasts felt. She planned to stop by the apothecary on her way home to find some relief. But for now, she needed to concentrate on getting to work. She ran down the stairs as fast as she could. She made a quick pass through the kitchen to grab a knuckle of bread and a sip of tea. Her Aunt Agnes was already seated at the table sipping on her own cup of tea.

Her hand was wrapped in gauze. Elinore stopped for a moment and spoke softly, "How is your hand today?" Elinore placed her hand on Agnes's shoulder and leaned into her face. Gently she kissed her cheek and whispered the words, "I'm sorry." Agnes was baffled. Was this the same person who had jammed the ice pick into her table? Elinore was in a rush and was gone in a flash. Agnes sat alone in the kitchen, shaking her head. She was thankful Elinore had left the house. Words escaped Agnes's mouth as she licked her thumb to turn the page of the newspaper she was reading. "That girl is nuts!"

Elinore ran toward John's office. She wanted to arrive before John. She enjoyed those first few minutes with John when they sipped on coffee and spoke privately before the rush of the days current events would be typed out. But when she came in, he was strictly business. Elinore tried to bring up lighter subjects, sensing his tension. John continued to move rigidly around the office. He limited his conversation with her to what he expected her to do that day. Elinore looked strangely at John and asked what was bothering him, but John insisted nothing was wrong. Yet he continued in an extremely business-like manner, incapable of any flexibility. Elinore's stomach was feeling queasy from John's coldness and her anxiety added to it. She told John she wanted to leave as soon as the first round of papers were delivered because she wasn't feeling well, and he seemed somewhat annoyed about it. His lack of concern angered Elinore. When she came back from her first deliveries, Elinore did exactly as she had planned, she left without so much as a kiss goodbye to John. John didn't care. He wasn't bothered by her leaving. He wanted some alone time and he had made Elinore miserable enough to leave on purpose. Elinore fell for his act.

On her way home, Elinore stopped by the apothecary to speak with the lady inside again. She told her she was feeling swollen and had another headache. The lady asked a random question. "Might you be with child, dear?" Elinore suddenly experienced a surge of strong emotions and her eyes started to well up with tears. Elinore felt weak in the knees in response to her question. She told the woman that she was expecting her strawberry week shortly, but her question left Elinore stressed and she wondered if it could possibly be true. The woman gave her some things for her headache and something to settle her stomach. Elinore was deep in thought when she found herself on her own doorstep. She didn't remember walking there, but she had come to a decision. She would wait another week or so and then tell John of her suspicions.

Another seven days had passed, and Elinore was out of her mind with worry. John was still cold toward her, and she wondered how he would react to what she was about to tell him. She worried about what her parents would do when they found out they would have a grandchild and that she was still unwed. She wondered if John would ask for her hand in marriage. She wondered what her Aunt Agnes would say. Elinore's head was spinning around faster than she could have thought. She found it difficult to concentrate on anything. Finally, she had had enough and couldn't carry this burden alone any longer. It would be Monday when she would tell him. Elinore planned to pop by his house after work since she knew where he lived. It surely wouldn't be proper to tell him such a thing while they were at work. Her thoughts were filled with only those thoughts that entire weekend and when Monday morning came with clear blue skies, she took that as a sign that things would turn out well.

On her way to work, she rehearsed in her head exactly how she would tell John the news. Beads of sweat dripped down her chest with the warm temperatures. She was more nervous than ever. The city had been quiet that weekend and there was only one page to print. John left work early that day and asked Elinore to lock up. She willingly agreed and he kissed her cheek as he left. Elinore waited until he was just out of sight to put her plan in motion. She walked a block behind him, being careful to stay well hidden. She wanted it to be a surprise when she showed up. She approached his house slowly, wanting to make sure he was alone. She didn't want any interruptions. Watching for just a few moments, she stood beside a building only a few doors away. He had no idea that Elinore had followed him home months ago. Her breathing was shallow, and she was frightened of how he would take the news.

Elinore took a big gulp of air and swallowed it hard. Finally, she gathered enough courage to step out from behind the building toward his home. But suddenly a black carriage being pulled by one horse rode past her almost hitting her. Sheer panic flowed through her veins and once again she took shelter behind the building again. The carriage stopped right in front of John's house. Aggravated and impatient, Elinore waited behind the streetlamp, standing on the cement path to watch. She bowed her head avoiding any contact with whomever was inside that carriage and waited for it to leave. A woman emerged with a small toddler from inside. The driver pulled a few carpet bags down off the back and set them down on the side of the road. Elinore saw her hand the driver some money and then watched as the carriage whisked away. In her clear view, she could see John exiting his house.

The small child broke free of the woman's hand and leaped into John's arms, who was already bent over to pick the child up. He had the biggest smile on his face that she had seen in months. The child screamed, "Daddy, I missed you!" Elinore watched every move John made. She wondered who was this woman? Elinore listened hard but could not hear what they spoke about. She continued watching as her heart ached. John obviously had hidden a few very important facts from her. The woman reached to take her bag from the curb, but John quickly took it from her. She put her arm around him as they entered his home with the child. It was clear to her now, John was married! Elinore could see that the woman was wearing a wedding ring. And the child had addressed John as daddy. It was all Elinore could take. Gutted, tears flowed from her eyes. He had been deceitful with her, and she felt sick to her stomach. The worst feeling was coming over her. She had never felt so bad. Not even comparable to when she had been made to come to this new land by her parents! Her heart was heavy, and it was even difficult for her to keep breathing. Her dreams were shattered. She looked back at the house they had entered in disgust. Elinore was aghast at what she had just witnessed and didn't know what to do now. She wandered home aimlessly not caring about where she walked. Staggering and feeling used, she wandered through the park that she and John had just ridden through only a short while ago. She was left feeling so insignificant to the world. Didn't anyone care about her, she wondered. No one seemed capable of loving her. Elinore sat on the first bench she saw, devastated by what had just happened. Why had he not told her that he was married? As the shock began to wear down, anger started to replace it. "Why would he do that to me?", she asked herself. How dare he! John had brought her to her knees in those few hours, but she would overcome her hopelessness. Elinore was not going to let him get away with it. She thought about the child inside her and decided she and her child deserved better. At the same time, Maniacal thoughts were filtering into her brain.

Erika wasn't happy observing Elinore's situation. But she knew it wouldn't be long before Elinore would be able to handle herself alone. Elinore's thoughts were becoming twisted, and it pleased Erika that they were now thinking in the same likeness. John was going to pay for his betrayal! If Elinore backed down, Erika would make sure his double-cross would be met with her vengeance. Elinore made her way home slowly. Her thoughts were overwhelming and filled with his backstabbing disloyalty. She moved around the house dazed by the events of the day and went to bed without eating a morsel of food. She cried herself to sleep and when she woke in the morning, she felt no better.

The next two weeks went by quickly, but John was still cold. He was all business and that fueled her anger. John had crossed that thin line between love and hate. Elinore considered occasionally over that time that maybe she could win him back, along with some other ideas, but in the end, she knew it would be of no use. She could never trust him again. She would have to raise their baby alone. At the end of the week, John gave Elinore her usual pay, but said nothing. Elinore leaned in to kiss him, just to see what his reaction would be. But John did something she never expected. He pulled away, pretending to cough, covering his mouth. That would be her last attempt. She decided that he was now out of chances with her to be honest and set things straight. Elinore would play his game now until she could make her final decision.

Erika was boiling over. She would have killed John herself, but Elinore was still too emotionally invested in this poor excuse of a man. She didn't want Elinore to suffer any more than she already had. She would give it a little more time but, in the end, Erika wanted John to pay for what he had done to the system! The calm before the storm was brewing. Elinore took the next two days to walk through the park again. It was comforting to her, and it took her mind off things. She cried as she watched the birds flutter in the pond. She found it difficult to sit long on the hard benches and mostly wandered around in a dazed state. She did notice the bees collecting their pollen from one flower to the next. It was then when she thought she recognized one plant that resembled another plant she knew from Germany. It was Hemlock! She looked closely at it, being careful not to touch it and was sure it was. She stopped to pick up some food to make a nice meal for herself and her aunt on the way home. Her life would be dull now, and Elinore was sad. She said nothing after their evening meal and Elinore went to her room after washing the dishes.

The birds were busy raising cane in the chimney that next day. She could hear the constant chirping of the baby birds calling for food, and it woke her from her blissful sleep. She took her time getting to work. She really didn't care if she saw John or not. As she passed the cut-through Erika was looking through Elinore's eyes. She remembered what Hans had told her about the Hemlock that grew in the pastures back home. The cows would never touch them because they knew they were poisonous. She planned to pick some on her way back home that day! It was so convenient for it to be growing right there along her way. Erika's psychotic thoughts were about to come to life. Elinore was drowning in self-pity and Erika couldn't tolerate it for another second. John was a bastard and

Erika found it incomprehensible that Elinore could go back and forth with her feelings for John. Erika hated the chaotic thought process Elinore was enduring. She needed to put an end to the torture. It was time to take care of it and be done with it all in just a few days.

When the day ended and she walked the same route as she had many times before, she felt the need to stop. Elinore stared at the ground, noticing the umbrella shaped cluster of the small white flowers. They were indeed Hemlock, she thought, and with a tissue, she carefully picked a handful. Elinore was operating mechanically. She was losing control against Erika. Erika knew all the parts of this plant. Its stems, leaves, and flowers were extremely poisonous, in fact deadly. She had remembered all the warnings that Elinore had heard from Hans as a child to stay away from this plant. A sinister grin came over her face while she processed a plan to attack John; step by step the plan took life. Erika had taken control, making the others hide in fear. She was becoming unstoppable. No one was stronger than her and she needed to make their world safe again at any cost. When she finally reached home, there was some food in a bowl sitting on the table. Erika was hungry and gobbled it down. She assumed it had been left there for her by Elinore's aunt, but she didn't care either way. She washed her hands, the bowl, and put everything away. She didn't do it in gratitude, she did it because that was where the dish was supposed to be. Erika proceeded to the room where they slept and hung the sprigs of plant matter inside the flue of the fireplace hoping they would dry quickly there. Her murderous plot was writing itself and she would joyously savor her vengeance; every step of it.

Elinore was aware of the plants hanging in the flue. She checked to see every day if the plants were dry enough to crunch but she really didn't understand why they had appeared out of nowhere. Still, she felt the need to check on them. Each day, she found herself checking for the sound that autumn leaves made when she stepped on them. She knew they were poisonous, so she used a branch from outside that she had picked up to continue her ritual of tapping on them. She knew how dangerous that plant was and continued to check with care. Finally, it was time to visit the apothecary to purchase a mortar and pestle. She had heard the crunching sound she had waited for! Erika watched as Elinore carefully handled the Hemlock. She put it in the mortar and began to grind it down into a fine powder. Elinore stopped for a moment. She couldn't remember if she had locked the door. She had but checked just the same. She didn't like surprises. She sat down at her desk and placed the fine powder on a creased piece of paper. Slowly, she poured the precious powder into the secret compartment beneath the black rose on her ring. Elinore was going through the motions and somehow knew that if she didn't, Erika would be very angry with her. She didn't want that; Erika was a force to be reckoned with. Elinore never believed Erika would hurt John. How could she hurt the father of her baby? Elinore looked at her swollen belly and started to rub it in a circular motion. She had figured that she was at least three weeks late for her strawberry week and was most certain a small life was growing inside her. Elinore remembered how well John had treated her and how she had fallen in love with him. Tears stained her cheeks when she thought about how their relationship had fallen to pieces and didn't understand why. She didn't know what she had done wrong. Then she thought about the woman kissing him at his doorstep and became enraged all over again. She never suspected, from the moment she had met him, that he was a liar. She was usually very good at spotting those type of people. He had tricked her, and she felt foolish. He was smooth and she deserved better. She wondered what she would do when she saw John the following day. Elinore wasn't about to tell him that she saw him with his wife and child. She'd keep that to herself for now. She wanted to splash him with some hot oatmeal!

Erika could feel the swaying back and forth of Elinore's emotions and it made her sick. She decided for all concerned, the torture needed to stop immediately. There had been so little peace since Elinore had been in America, and it needed to be restored. Erika was coming closer to a choice that would change everything. She had straightened out things with Agnes, so she felt that part of their lives was not part of the problem. It was peaceful at home and Agnes kept her course. Erika didn't really like Agnes, but she tolerated her and was glad she wasn't related to her. Now, she had to follow through with John. He was a stubborn man who didn't learn easily. He needed to learn a hard lesson and she was the perfect person to teach him that. Certainly, if Elinore had had Agnes and John in line, none of this would have needed to be done. Elinore was too naïve in Erika's eyes. She would worry about the possibility of a baby later. Her final decision had been made. No more suffering. No more confusion. Elinore was not strong enough to make the right choices for everyone. She was not responsible enough to have that control. Erika was going to make things good again. They just couldn't go on like this. It had to stop!

Erika woke and stretched her arms above her head. She was processing the day and what she had planned. She suddenly wanted to rush off. Throwing her feet on the floor, she hurried to get dressed and leave. She arrived at work before John and started the coffee. She fixed the paper to be run through the printer and straightened things up around the office. John still hadn't arrived yet. Erika was becoming annoyed with John for being late again. He was late often, much too unorderly for her liking. She had things to do. She was just about to sit down when John came through the door. "I'm sorry I'm late Elinore," he said as he placed his jacket on the coat hook. He poured a cup of coffee and went straight to the printer. Erika sat behind Elinore's eyes, watching the man she loved but who had betrayed her. Her eyes were piercing. Erika was ready, but she allowed Elinore one last look at John as he moved around the office. She was going to give him a chance to be honest with her as she continued to stare at him. John could feel the weight of her stare and moved toward her. She sat immobilized in the chair. John smiled and snidely looked into her face. He leaned forward and reached for the back of her neck. She could tell he was moving in for a kiss, but she resisted. John sensed her hesitation. He asked, "Elinore, are you angry with me?" His tone suggested that she had no right to be. Elinore shook her head, keeping her eyes focused on the floor. She couldn't look at him. She didn't want to. John placed his cup in her hand and asked, "Would you be a good pet and bring me another cup of coffee?"

That was it! Erika heard the starting gun! She presented herself with a crooked smile and replied, "Certainly Darling!" As she poured the coffee into the cup, her wicked grin grew wider. She checked over her shoulder to see if John was watching, but his back was turned to her, focusing his attention on his beloved machine. Slowly, Erika opened the secret compartment on her ring over his coffee and let the powder fall into it. It dissolved fast and disappeared into the brown liquid. She knew if she gave him the coffee it would be the end of everything. The Hemlock laced beverage would take only a short time to take effect. Erika hesitated a thin second and extended her hand holding the cup handle facing John. He took the cup from her and set it down on his desk. He hadn't even said thank you. But Erika didn't care. She was about to watch him take his last breath! Since Elinore had killed that wretched man back in Germany, they had not seen that type of violence, but Erika felt that Elinore had handled that properly. That man got what he asked for. Her eyes remained focused on the cup sitting on the very edge of his desk.

John finished his second set of papers and picked up the cup. The coffee had cooled, and he took a good taste of it. Erika smiled at him. His one eye closed and his lip turned up on one side. "That coffee doesn't taste right," he said. "Maybe you should get some fresh coffee. Can you pick some up for tomorrow?" he asked. Sarcastically she answered him, "Sure." John stood and moved toward his printer to start his third stack of papers. He had finished only half of it when the moment had come. She saw John wince in pain. He grabbed his stomach and folded over. His legs were becoming weak. The toxic Hemlock was beginning to course through his nervous system. She rushed to his side and snidely asked, "Is there something bothering you Darling? Awwe, let me help you." She placed her hand on his lower back. "Please help me, Elinore," desperately, he cried and reached for her hand. Erika answered him, "Would you like me to call your wife?" John's eyes opened wide, and his mouth fell open in shock. He wanted to ask her how she knew, but when he opened his mouth, vomit spewed out and hit the floor. John's heart was racing. He clutched at his chest and fell to the floor. His body was convulsing, and his face twisted. Saliva dripped from the side of his mouth and Erika watched with delight. She knelt beside him next to his ear and whispered softly to him, "Now you need to know, I know about your wife and your son. And by the way, I'm pregnant with your child, but soon none of that will matter because you will be dead darling." She kissed his cheek tenderly and rose to her feet. Erika stood over him watching as John's respiratory system began to fail. Periods of apnea interrupted his seizures and Erika knew the end was very near. She thought about it for a moment. Should she stay till the bitter end? She took her cardigan from her chair and wrapped it around her shoulders. She took one last look at John's crumpled body and opened the door.

Erika hated surprises. She left John lying on the floor as she closed the door, mixing in with the people on the street. She walked the same path as she always did with a wicked smile. She stopped to smell some wild roses that grew along the fence on her way. She picked one for Agnes and tugged at the stem to break one off. A thorn pricked her finger and a small drop of blood appeared. Erika licked the blood with her tongue and continued home. When she finally arrived and placed her hand on the doorknob; it suddenly opened. Startled, Erika stepped back. Agnes was just leaving and stepped out. Erika held the rose out. "This is for you," she said. Agnes took a sniff, and the pungent aroma made her close her eyes with delight. "Ah, that smells wonderful, thank you." She handed it back to Elinore and asked her to put it in water for her. Agnes mentioned that she had left some food on the table for her. She waved to her niece telling her that she was off to see a friend and jumped up into her horse drawn carriage. She was gone with the crack of the whip. Elinore entered the house and sat down at the table alone. She looked at the food her aunt had left. She looked at the rose Erika had picked. The faces of Elinore and Erika were now able to change in an instant, making life for the system much easier with each person they encountered. Elinore smiled as she put the food to her lips.

Chapter 15

Elinore did not really want to believe Erika had killed the father of her baby. She wanted to believe it was all just a bad dream when morning came. Her brain seemed foggy that morning. She couldn't put her thoughts together at all. She rushed toward the office in the rain that fell from the sky. It was a dreary day, and she didn't care if her boots got wet from the puddles she splashed through on her way. When she came within view, she could see that many carriages had surrounded the office. There was a real emergency going on. As she got closer, she could see the grim faces on all the people that were there. The watchmen were frantically running back and forth and many of them were writing things down. Droplets of rain dripped from the brims of their hats as they struggled to scribble things down onto their tablets. Two men were bringing a gurney into the office and Elinore knew that John was the only one who could be inside the building. Erika had done what she had already known.

A doctor came out with his black bag, and she could hear him tell one of the watchmen that it was too late to help him. The doctor just shook his head and left in his black horse drawn carriage. Sensing the tension within Elinore, Erika slowly walked toward the building, but a watchman stopped her. "You can't go in there right now Miss," he said, holding the palm of his hand up to face her. "Why not?" she asked. "I work here," she stated. "Oh dear," he said, "The man inside had died from a heart attack it seems." Erika dropped to her knees as the rain fell around her. "Oh no!" she howled, mustering up a shallow tear. The watchman helped her to her feet and saw her tears. He handed her a handkerchief from inside his jacket. "Have you been working here long?" he asked. Erika quickly said, "No, but he was an awfully nice man." "When did you last see him?" he asked gently. He didn't want to upset her any more than she already was. Erika responded in a traumatized voice, "I just saw him yesterday and he seemed fine. Do you need anything from me?" she asked, wiping the tear from her eye. The watchman told her that he didn't and thanked her for her help. He asked her for her address and let her go.

Erika sneered at the thought of John's final moments as she left the scene. She passed the apothecary on the way back home to buy one of John's last papers. She would need to look for another job now. She wandered home, trying her best to look as sad as she could. Her wolf in sheep's clothing act even convinced Agnes when she arrived home earlier than usual. Agnes looked confused as Elinore came through the door. "Is something wrong, Elinore?" Erika ignored her when she called her by that name, most times, but this time she said, "Yes, my boss dropped dead from a heart attack." She said it so bluntly, Agnes's mouth hung open. Her forehead wrinkled and her eyes squinted as she listened. "I'll need to look for another job tomorrow." Erika wiped another sad fake tear from her face, continuing her charade. "Don't worry though, it won't be long before I'm working again."

Agnes rushed to her and placed her arm around her shoulder. "I know, I wasn't worried. Would you like some tea?" Agnes asked. She was genuinely concerned about Elinore. What a terrible thing for her to go through. She could see her niece was upset but didn't know how to comfort her. Agnes was unaware that she really didn't know Elinore or her alter Erika the way she thought she did. In fact, she didn't know either at all. It was difficult for anyone to know who would present themselves at any given time; their personalities were becoming more individualized though. Each having their own likes and dislikes. Agnes only thought Elinore could be a bit fickle sometimes as young girls can often be.

The next day, it was Elinore who began to look for a new job. She carefully picked out the proper clothing and made her way to several locations she had read about in John's last paper.

She didn't feel particularly well this morning, but she pushed on anyway. As she walked up and down the city streets, she didn't have much luck, but one "help-wanted" sign caught her eye. It was a small sign at the bottom of a wooden staircase that went up the side of a very tall building. She opened the wrought iron gate and climbed her way to the top. Gently, she knocked on the door. Elinore was out of breath and her voice was raspy when she said hello to the man who answered the door. He was dressed in a white coat and had a stethoscope around his neck. Elinore cleared her throat and said, "I've come about the job you have posted on the sign at the bottom of your stairs. Is it still available?" she asked.

"It surely is!" he responded and grabbed at her hand to shake it. He had a firm grip and pulled her into his office. He introduced himself to her. "I'm Doctor Feelgood, but you can call me Ben." He was happy she had come, he told her because he desperately needed help. Elinore asked what the job required and how much did it pay. "I like a girl who gets straight to the point," he said, with a laugh. "I'll be glad to give you twenty dollars for the week, Monday through Friday, 9am to 5pm. That's if you want the job." Elinore was pleased. It was the same amount that John was paying her. Elinore then asked what she would be doing for that money.

Ben proceeded to tell her it was easy work, just a little tedious. He pointed to a bunch of small glass bottles. "These all need to be wrapped with labels." He told her, "With your tiny fingers, it should take no time at all." Elinore glanced at her hand and couldn't believe he noticed that about her in the five minutes that she was there. He was a kind of creepy man, she thought, but as long as he paid well, she wouldn't be looking for much else. Then she asked, "Is that all?" Ben replied with a smile, "Of course not. I will need you to make a few deliveries, but most people come here. I will need you to make appointments for customers while I work in my laboratory in the back room." He pointed to a door that was down the hallway behind him. That didn't sound too hard to Elinore, so she thought about it all for just a moment and said, "Well, I guess you have a new helper, Ben!" shaking his hand happily. Elinore started to walk toward the door to leave and Ben said, "Wait a minute! I don't even know your name!" "Oh yes," Elinore said, "Pardon me, my name is Elinore Downing, Sir."

Ben preferred to be called by his first name, except when his customers were around, and he had told her so. Again, he reminded her. But before he let her go, he wanted to show her one more thing. He held the inventory list in his hand, extending it out to her. "You will need to know this, memorize it and it will make your job so much easier," he said. She looked at the list and was amazed at all the cures he had listed. Curiously, she asked, "You make all of these here?" Ben smiled and said, "I most certainly do, and one more thing, please let me show you, my office." Ben was thrilled to have some help. His enthusiasm exuded in his smile. He opened a large sliding door that reminded her of the one on the cattle barn that they had at her home in Germany. Inside his office was a large solid wood desk, nice rugs and an examining table with a folding screen for privacy. In the corner, stood a glass medicine cabinet that held his medical equipment and a small bookshelf hung beside it. The room was well lit from the huge windows, opposite his desk. "This is where you will bring my patients when I ask you to." Elinore nodded her head in agreement. She smiled and said, "I think I've got everything now, when would you like me to start?" Ben said, "Monday, 9am sharp!" Elinore waved her hand in gesture, said goodbye, and closed the door behind her. She was happy she got a new job so quickly but was glad it didn't start until Monday. She needed some rest. Her body was aching.

She was excited to tell her Aunt Agnes when she got home, and Agnes was delighted at the good news. She even told Elinore to get changed into something more comfortable and she would make something for them both to celebrate with. Elinore climbed the stairs and with each step her legs and back throbbed. She undressed in the bathroom and sat down on the toilet. Surprised, when she wiped herself, she had found her strawberry week had finally arrived! For a moment, she thought of John. She felt a small sadness that he had forced that chapter of her life to close, but then quickly remembered watching him embracing that woman and child on the porch of his house. Those visions were too much for her. She closed her eyes tightly, wanting to cry again. They were burned into her memory and his betrayal hurt her heart again. She took the bottle she purchased from the apothecary off her desk and swallowed two tablets, flushing them down with a bit of water. She wiped her face and forehead with a fresh washcloth. Soon she began to smell something good cooking from the kitchen. Elinore was hungry and ready to eat.

There was not a scrap of food left when they were finished and both Elinore and Agnes leaned back in their chairs, finding it difficult to breathe. They laughed as they looked at each other, rubbing their bellies. The massive amount of food she had just devoured made her sleepy. Elinore was feeling better now and content with her new adventure that was about to begin. She knew there was no baby now and better yet, she would start this new chapter of her life on a full stomach. Elinore slept well that night, putting John, the baby and finding a new job, out of her mind. She had one more day before she would start working again. The door to the examination room at Doctor Feelgood's had brought back memories of home and Carl was on Elinore's mind as she lay awake but still cocooned under her blankets. The birds inside the chimney told her it was time to leave her bed. She had loved Carl very much; he was her first true love. It seemed so long ago since she had left that part of her life behind. She missed Carl. But she was so young then, she thought. She had learned and been through so much since then. She wondered how he was. She went to her desk, deciding to write him a note. It had been years since she had heard from anyone in her native home. She began to wonder how her parents and grandparents were. Hans and Margaret also crossed her mind, and she wondered if Delilah even remembered her now. Her head dropped in sadness. She remembered how simple her life used to be.

But no sense in crying over spilled milk, she thought, and finished her little note. She sealed it with a kiss and planned to send it off the next day on her way to her new job. She pushed the note into her apron so she wouldn't forget.

The day Elinore was to start her new job was a beautiful day. Warm sunny skies with a light breeze that gave her confidence. On her way, she had overheard people on the street talking about the newest president that had been elected. They were not sure if they liked him as much as Roosevelt. Then she heard three women talking about cherry trees being planted by the president's wife, Mrs. Taft, along the Potomac River. She didn't know where the Potomac River was, but assumed it ran through Washington DC, where the president lived somewhere. She stopped at the post office like she had planned and continued onward. It was a little longer of a walk than her last job, but Elinore didn't mind. She enjoyed it except during the times it would rain, but even then, it wasn't so bad. She immediately noticed that Ben had taken his "help wanted" sign down when she reached the bottom of the long wooden staircase.

At the top, Ben was waiting for her. He greeted her with a large smile. "Good morning, Elinore!" he shouted, opening the door for her. The minute she stepped inside, he handed her some tiny labels and a bottle of glue. There was a desk and a long counter just inside the door where Ben had already lined up hundreds of small bottles for her. Ben explained, "This is your desk," knocking twice on the desktop he had shown her before. "Please place the bottles after you've put the labels on them over there." He pointed to the table that was just outside his laboratory door toward the back part of the office. "Use this glass tray to transport them back and forth," he said and handed it to her. Soon there was a knock at the door and Elinore received the first of many patients to follow that day. As soon as Elinore started to label the bottles, another person came to the door. Elinore was starting to realize this was a very busy office and that she would be constantly interrupted as she tried to finish her job. Many people came by looking for cures for a multitude of ailments. Tuberculosis, which was also known as consumption, was on the rise. Many people were dying due to this horrible affliction. Elinore was careful and used a mask when she was around anyone who coughed. She wore it around her neck to make it convenient for herself. At any moment of the day, she could just pull it up, hoping that would keep her safe from contracting the dreaded disease. Some of the people who came to the door were very unusual, some were even scary. Elinore knew pain could make people act in the strangest manner and she tried her best to console all of them.

Ben hardly came out of his room and spent much of the day behind the door, down the hallway. Elinore thought it was odd that Ben hardly ever saw his patients but handed out medicine just on the patients' word. Sometimes it wasn't even the actual sick person, but the wife looking for help with a child or husband. All quite strange, she thought. Elinore studied the long list of remedies Ben had given her and before long, she was diagnosing some of the poorest of people in need. Ben seemed to like hibernating in his office, only briefly coming out to use the facilities occasionally. Elinore was keen to notice that he was always sure to lock the door of his laboratory each time he left it. It was always secure, no matter what.

Day after day, Elinore found each week the same in routine and rather boring. Ben was realistically more of the silent type it seemed to Elinore. Quite different from the first day she had met him. He spoke little throughout the day and the only conversation she had was with the patients. He was perky and upbeat when she first came to him but all that changed once she was hired. She would have even settled for some conversation with him on medical matters instead of sitting alone between clients. Listening to the customer's complaints about their afflictions could be depressing at times. When he did come out of his office, he would shuffle around making a sucking sound as if he was thinking hard about something. Elinore hated the way he didn't pick up his feet as he made his way around the small space. Her mother, Rose, would never have allowed that and she would have received a severe scolding if she had. Ben had nice leather shoes. Typical of a doctor, but he surely would wear them out quickly if he didn't learn to pick up his feet, she thought. By the end of each day, Elinore would need to count and hand over all the money she collected for each remedy to Ben. His eyes gleamed with joy when she deposited the fists full of money into his well-groomed hands.

Now that the warmer weather had arrived, working in a loft could be uncomfortable at times. She opened all the windows each day which created a nice cross draft inside the office. Elinore was also aware that it was healthier to have fresh air always flowing, from the articles she had read. On the rare occasion, she considered it a lucky day if she had the opportunity to make a delivery. It was then that she could meet all types of people. Patients would be grateful and sometimes offer her money for bringing them medicine. The conversations were sometimes sad then too, but most were pleasant, and many would tell a joke or two. Elinore always wore her mask during those times. Her visits were quite informal, but she protected herself just the same. One visit took her to a house with a long narrow cemented pathway. It was a tall three-story building. It was also the first time she had ever been there. She walked down the cemented alleyway next to the house which led to the back door and knocked. There was a beautiful rose bush that grew opposite the door, and she stopped to smell it. The door opened and a young lady appeared. "Pardon me," Elinore said, "This is the most beautiful rose bush I've ever seen!" "Yes," the lady said, "It has done well since I dumped Castor Oil on it!" Both women found humor in her wisecrack. Elinore had no idea why anyone would throw Castor Oil on anything, but it was the lady's tone of voice that struck her funny bone. Elinore handed the brown bag to the woman, and she thanked her for bringing her husband's medicine. "My name is Annie, and yours?" she asked. Elinore gave her name and told her it was nice to meet her. They spoke for a good while about many different things. Annie was enjoying talking with someone as much as Elinore, but Elinore needed to get back to work. Ben would surely be watching the time it took for her to make her deliveries. She didn't want to make him angry during her first week there.

She hurried back to the office but on her way a little black dog began to follow her. She had seen him before, but he was skinnier. She felt bad for him and stopped to buy a small bit of food for him. He gobbled down the food and wagged his tail happily. She decided to call him Blacky and continued quickly on her way. The dog followed and she wanted to keep him. She thought, if only she had a place to keep him. Maybe she could take him home and keep him in the small tool shed her aunt had in the backyard. All she would need would be a few towels to make a bed for him and two bowls for food and water. The little dog kept up with her quick pace and she enjoyed her new companion as she made her way back to Ben. The little dog seemed to enjoy her company too but then she heard a young boy calling out to him. "Dog! Get over here, dog!" Elinore looked at him shocked at the anger behind his calling. He was a disturbing young boy. Dirty too. Erika didn't care for the way he spoke to the dog either. He was hostile toward the dog she had developed a fondness for. The boy stood between two chairs, each having an elevated post where people could have their shoes shined by him for a modest fee. His hands were black with filth. His face and shirt were soiled with black shoe polish too. He looked at Elinore and shouted to her, "Give me back my dog!"

Before Elinore could get a word out, Erika took control and presented herself forcefully. "Who do you think you are talking to Buster? This is my dog! I found him!" The young boy reached down and grabbed the dog by the scruff of his neck. As he pulled the dog, Erika took a swipe at the boy knocking his hat to the ground. The boy said, "If you weren't a girl, I would give you what for!" holding his fist in the air. The boy gritted his teeth and his chin protruded. His face turned red, and she could see he was ready to fight. "He's my dog and you can't have him!" he demanded, taking the dog through the glass doors of the storefront behind him. Erika waited for a minute to see if the boy would return to his shoeshine stand, but he stayed inside the store. She was ready for the fight and wasn't going to back down.

Suddenly, Elinore appeared again, and she realized how much time had passed and was frantic to return to Ben's office. She had taken so long to make her delivery and if she were delayed any longer, she would never finish labeling all the bottles that needed to be done by the end of the day. Then, she would have to stay much later than she wanted to, so she hurried off and the dog vanished from her mind as quickly as he had come. Finally reaching the top of the stairs, there were five patients waiting to see the doctor. She tended to them all quickly, and three of the five asked for a remedy for a cough. Elinore again suspected Tuberculosis, so her mask became a constant necessity. Many times, by the end of the day, her face would have deep red marks from where the mask dug into her skin. It annoyed her because it made it hard for her to breathe in the warm temperatures. Elinore knew there were many knowledgeable scientists working on a vaccine, but Ben did not have it yet. She continued to label her bottles as fast as she could, and before long, she had finished. It was Ben who was behind now, and she could rest easy.

She sat down at her desk and waited for the next customer. Elinore noticed someone had left a newspaper on her desk in her absence. She picked it up and started to look it over. This one was a whole two pages! Elinore had lots of time until closing time. There was a big article advertising for help at a place just fifteen minutes from where she was. They paid even more than she was earning now, but Elinore wasn't sure she wanted to walk that far. She would keep it in her mind though. Just five dollars more a week could make such a difference and sway her thoughts about it. It was called The Triangle Shirtwaist Factory. Although it seemed much like the job she held in Germany, she wasn't sure she wanted to do that type of work again. She continued to read. There were so many interesting articles, but one had caught her eye. It was about a place called Coney Island. It looked like so much fun, Elinore felt she just had to go there. But how? She had no friends to ask, and she didn't even know how to get there. It seemed like it would take a miracle for her to get there. She would not ask her aunt. Elinore was sad that this place was just too far from her reach, but she was not about to give up either. She would need a little time to figure out a way to get herself there and she was determined. The first thing on her list was to find out where Brooklyn was. She assumed it couldn't be too far. Then a thought came to her. Maybe the girl she had just delivered the medicine to would want to go with her. She would ask Annie the next time she saw her.

On the last page there was a small article that made her nervous. There in bold print was a mention of the first fingerprint evidence used in a murder trial. She read the article closely. John entered her mind again although she knew she was not the responsible one. She had watched him die, but the blame sat squarely on Erika. She had not really wanted to see John die. Elinore truly loved John. But there was no controlling Erika once she had made her decision. Elinore had no choice but to hide inside. Erika was the only one within the system who would have been strong enough to carry out such a devious plot in order to keep things safe, and all the alters knew this. The article stated the Fingerprint Bureau was in Scotland Yard and Calcutta, India. She was sure after reading the entirety of it, she had nothing to worry about. Just as she put the paper down, Ben came out of his room. His lab coat was dotted with different colors, and he asked what took her so long to return from her delivery. Elinore thought for a moment and replied, "I lost my way. I don't know all the streets around here very well yet, I'm sorry."

Ben pressed his lips together and a small humph came out. Elinore knew Ben did not believe her, but there was nothing he could say. As soon as he turned around, Elinore stuck her tongue out at him. Ben was too busy fumbling for his keys as he shuffled back down the small hallway to lock his laboratory door. "I am closing early today; Elinore, I will see you tomorrow." He told her. She was happy to leave a little early. She wanted to stop at the market to buy some more food. Elinore flew down the stairs with a list of things in her mind to pick up. On her way this time though she saw the strangest thing. A man was pushing a cart that looked like a wheel barrel, only with larger wheels than normal. There was a bucket attached to the side that people who passed could drop change into. The man cranked the small musical organ that sat inside it. He had the cutest little monkey tethered to it for entertainment and he sure did his job. He was a smart monkey and had drawn a large crowd including Elinore. She watched the monkey while he danced and drew attention to himself. It was hilarious when suddenly that little monkey approached an older woman in the crowd and stole her purse. The older woman became enraged and chased the poor little creature, eventually getting her purse back, but Elinore along with others in the crowd couldn't help but laugh loudly. The monkey had made Elinore laugh hard enough to cry and it made her stomach hurt. She stopped at the market and then found herself at home in the kitchen making Agnes and herself their evening meal again. She told her aunt about the monkey and they both laughed together about it too.

It wasn't long before Elinore was sitting at her desk again, labeling more bottles. It was starting to get under her skin, having to do the same routine every day like clockwork. She was sorely in need of some fun. A bead of sweat dripped from her forehead and her thought returned to the sea breezes that she had read about at Coney Island. Ben came out of his laboratory. "Did you open all the windows?" Elinore wondered if Ben thought she was stupid. Her one eye closed and she looked at him. In a soft voice, she replied, "Yes, Sir." She remembered the bucket of water Mr. Quinn had kicked over and didn't want to have that happen again. Ben felt badly for her, being in the hottest part of the office and handed her a wet handkerchief. "Thank you," Elinore said as she took it from his hand. She wiped her forehead and then asked Ben if he had ever heard of Coney Island. "Why sure, I have, everybody knows about Coney Island. It's a wonderful place, plenty to do." He continued. "You should go there some time."

He shuffled off toward the bathroom and she rolled her eyes as he dragged his feet away. Elinore considered what he had told her for a moment though. Elinore heard the latch on the laboratory door turn and watched as Ben closed and locked himself inside his secret room. There were many customers that day for Elinore to take care of. Some were problems concerning arthritis, headaches, and stomach ailments. Ben seemed to have a cure for all the problems of these folks. It was the coughing ones that bothered her most. Ben had mentioned to her that a bad cold had been showing up a lot recently and he had a special remedy for that too. The charge for it was a little more money but it would do the trick to rid a person of the germ. She was hoping to see Annie that day, but she never came. Elinore interlaced her fingers behind her head and took a big stretch. Suddenly, her mouth opened wide with the biggest yawn from her boredom. Under her breath she said, "This is ridiculous, I need to get out of here!" She pulled the cash from the top desk drawer to count the earnings of the day. Ben had made much more than usual. She had barely knocked on his door to give him his profits when he opened the door.

Impatiently, he asked Elinore, "What is it, Elinore?" Sheepishly, Elinore said, "It has been very busy today, Ben and extremely warm. Is it ok if I go now?" Ben looked at the clock on the wall and returned a stern gaze to Elinore. She wasn't sure what he was thinking, and it was then that it occurred to her to hold the money out for him to see. She had now found what spoke to Ben. Cold hard cash. He eagerly took the money from her hand and began to count it. "Well done, Elinore. Do you want to go right now?" Ben asked. "Wow, yes, I would like that very much, if it's alright with you." Elinore jumped at the chance. She turned the sign on the door to read "closed" and hurried out before he changed his mind. "See you tomorrow!" she hollered as she slammed the door behind her.

Now that she was free, she thought, maybe she would stop by to speak with Annie for a minute. It wasn't long before she was walking down the familiar cemented walkway of her newly found friend. She hoped she wouldn't be disturbing her and was pleasantly surprised to find Annie sitting in a chair just outside her door. "Hello Annie!" she said gleefully. Annie looked confused. "I didn't send for any medicine today, what brings you here?" she asked. Elinore sat down on the chair next to her and asked if she wanted to go have some fun. Annie flatly told Elinore she wasn't sure she could because her husband was very sick, but that it had been a long time since she'd been anywhere. Elinore could see that Annie had an interest though in the thought. She began to tell her about the article that she had read about Coney Island. She told Annie how much she really wanted to go but hadn't the slightest idea about how to get there and doubted her aunt would let her use her horse and carriage.

"Horse and carriage?" Annie questioned and her forehead wrinkled. "Oh my!" Annie cried out and started to giggle. "Elinore, you really don't know your way around, do you?" Annie didn't mean to make fun of her and covered her mouth with her hand. "We could just take the 5th Avenue-West End Line from Sands Street to 36th Street and take the trolly pole the rest of the way." Annie was speaking a foreign language to Elinore and the expression on her face showed her confusion. "Do you have a bathing suit?" Annie asked. "If you don't, I have one you could borrow. It's too small for me now but it's so cute that I can't get rid of it." Annie giggled again and Elinore smiled. She felt their friendship starting and she also found it ironic that her name was Annie too. She had good luck with that name for sure. She missed her friend Anna in Germany. Elinore thanked Annie and told her how wonderful it would be if she could use her bathing suit because she did not have one. In a flash, Annie went inside to get it. She returned only moments later with a young girl's happiness. "Elinore, this is so adorable!" she busted out and began to peel away the tissue paper inside the small white box on her lap. She excitedly held it up to show Elinore and she had to admit, it was the cutest little thing she had ever seen. It was navy blue and tied at the waist. It had petite white lace around the neckline and on the edges of its capped sleeves. The bloomers came down, just below the knee. Elinore examined it as she held it up to herself. She loved the white lace accent and was happy it looked like it would fit. "Can you go Saturday?" Elinore eagerly asked. She waited patiently for her answer.

Annie hesitated for a minute. "Well, I guess my husband would be okay for a few hours." A big smile came over Annie's face and she slapped her thighs. "It's settled then! Meet me here 9am sharp and we'll go!" Elinore stood up and shouted, "That's wonderful, thank you so much!" Elinore was excited. She hadn't been anywhere since John took her to the Knickerbocker. This sounded like twice the fun to her, and she couldn't wait! Saturday took forever to arrive, but that morning she was up bright and early. She told Agnes where she was going and placed a few items in a bag to take with her. Ben had even given her an extra five dollars for all the hard work she had done, with her week's pay. That would come in handy today, she thought. Elinore arrived at Annie's house right on time, just as they had planned. Each of them changed into their bathing suits and wore their clothes over them. Before they left, Annie made sure Elinore had brought a towel with her. Sitting on sand without a towel was not very nice. Soon they were off on their girl's day outing. Elinore had grand hopes for the day and from what Annie had told her, she didn't think she would be disappointed. The public transportation made it easy and when they finally got there, they eagerly joined the line where many people were already standing to buy their tickets. Elinore could smell the water in the air, and she loved that smell. They each fastened their punch card by its string around the button on their dresses. Annie led Elinore straight to the entrance where there was a giant turning barrel that they had to walk through to get into the park. Elinore became anxious about it. She stood in front of the wooden barrel as it slowly turned looking for another way around it to enter the park. The last thing she wanted to do was fall and embarrass herself. Annie grabbed her hand and urged her to step forward as the crowd pushed them from behind. Together they made their way through to the other side. Elinore soon learned that each ride required a punch hole in their cards and promised much fun.

Elinore and Annie laughed loudly throughout the day enjoying every moment. There were so many things for them to do! Elinore shook with excitement when they came across a ride that allowed them to sit atop a mechanical horse. Annie thought it was peculiar the way her friend transformed into such a child-like manner about it. They weren't even real horses and she smiled at the expressions Elinore displayed. They rode side by side on a long track around a building to get off onto a stage where a crowd of onlookers cheered the riders on. There were two men waiting for them dressed as clowns at the end of the ride who led Elinore and Annie through a passage where air blew their dresses up. The crowd laughed when many of the women tried desperately to push their dresses back down.

Elinore was not amused and didn't like that part of the ride at all, but it was all meant for fun, Annie explained. Then, Annie decided to take Elinore on a ride called the Human Pool Table. Elinore loved that ride. Even though she skinned her elbow when she slid down the slide onto the circles that spun the people around on the floor, she laughed so hard that her stomach hurt, which quickly made her forget the pain to her elbow. As she lay on the floor spinning, Elinore silently wished the day would never end. There were many more things to come, and Annie led her to the best rides the park had to offer. They watched elephants slide into a pool of water to play joyfully. They also swung in seats that hung from metal chains high above the ground. They listened to men barking, trying to draw people's attention to enjoy a freak show. Elinore couldn't understand why people would find deformed people something to gawk at. Elinore was appalled by the woman who had no arms, but very talented feet. She felt sorry for the dog faced boy. It crossed Elinore's mind that he would have a hard time ever finding a wife. Then Elinore and Annie viewed a contortionist, a snake enchantress, and a man completely covered from head to toe with tattoos. They also saw women with stretched necks, dwarf people, amazingly obese people, and a man who could blow darts through reeds precisely hitting a target. Elinore knew she would never forget those people she viewed that day.

They had one more punch hole left on their ticket cards to use before they would need to purchase another, and so Elinore and Annie decided their last ride would be the merry-go-round. The attendee at the gate told them when they entered the circle of the beautifully decorated horses that if they could retrieve the brass ring from the outstretched mechanical arm as they passed it, they could win a free ride. Elinore knew she could and did! Excitedly, she handed the free-ride ticket to Annie as a gift of thanks. She really was having the best time! Annie was hungry when they got off their final ride and took Elinore to the boardwalk. The first smell Elinore detected again was the water. It was different from the North Sea that she would recognize anywhere, but she still appreciated that particular scent. That scent was followed by an even better one. It was a delicious smell. "Is that frankfurters I smell?" Elinore asked. Annie smiled back at her and asked, "Do you like frankfurters?" "You bet I do!" Elinore declared. Her stomach was grumbling. Her mouth watered as they got in another line for their tasty treat.

When she finally got to taste it, she couldn't help but think that it had to be the best frankfurter she had ever tasted! They both sat on the wooden benches watching the many people pass by as they ate. Elinore finished her second frankfurter in just a few minutes and only then did she dare to speak. She would never speak with her mouth full of food. Elinore had better manners than that. "I am having the time of my life; I can't thank you enough Annie!" Elinore felt the need to make sure Annie knew how grateful she was. "I'm having a good time too," she said with a smile and then asked, "Are you ready for a swim now?" Elinore's eyebrows rose. Her eyes opened wide, and she blurted out, "Sure!" They ran carrying their shoes onto the beach. Elinore loved the way the sand squished between her toes. Quickly, they spread their towels and neatly placed their clothing upon them. They both raced toward the water and splashed around. Elinore waded out into the water until she was waist high in it. Annie was a timid one, and only went in up to her knees, keeping a close eye on Elinore. Annie was afraid that Elinore was underestimating the strength of the waves that rushed in at times. Elinore was busy romping around like it was her own personal bathtub, when suddenly she fell silent. Her face had a bizarre look on it and Annie knew something was wrong. Elinore began violently shaking her leg. Annie could see that something was wrong. Elinore was kicking hard, and Annie raced toward her to help. Elinore reached down into the water and pulled up a crab! She held it up and shouted to Annie, "The bastard bit my toe!" Elinore fiercely threw the crab a good distance from where they were, back into the water. Annie was relieved that it was just a crab. Elinore's mood had changed, and she began to push her way through the water, back to the towels. Her toe was throbbing. She sat down looking at Annie, "Well, that didn't go very well!"

There was a long pause and then the two friends began to laugh at it all. The anger in Elinore's face had melted away. Elinore examined her toe, and a small spot of blood could be seen but otherwise, she would be fine. After a short time, Elinore decided to go for another dip in the water. Annie was thinking about her husband now and felt she should be getting back to him soon. Elinore swam out into the water, but not as far. She was enjoying the open water. Some people stood on the jetty's watching the swimmers. The waves crashed in against them. The sand under her feet felt good to her and so did the sun on her face. It was a great day, she thought until a large wave came toward her, turning her upside down. Being underwater, she didn't know which way was up. She could taste the saltwater and choked on the small amount she had inhaled. In an instant, she felt a large hand reaching down for her. A man that was watching his own children had seen what was happening and ran to help her. He was a large man and very strong. He scooped her up caringly and wrapped a towel around her waist. Elinore clung to him coughing. Unknowingly, her bloomers had come off in the wave exposing her bare bottom. They floated by as the man cradled her and he reached out to clutch them in the next incoming wave. The man carried her to her towel placing her down and promptly handed her bloomers back to her. Elinore was completely embarrassed but grateful for his kindness. She asked what his name was, and he told her his name was Ken. She was blushing nervously. Before he left, she made sure to thank him again. He had come to her rescue, and she didn't even know him. Annie asked if she was okay, as Elinore slipped her bloomers back on. All she could say was she supposed it could have been much worse if it weren't for Ken. Annie agreed and told Elinore that he was a nice man indeed.

The sun was beginning to set low in the sky and Annie needed to get home. They went back the same way they came, and Annie rushed down her walkway to check on her husband. Elinore waited outside and sat down in the chair just outside Annie's door. About ten minutes had gone by and Elinore wondered if she should just go home, but within one second more, Annie was back. "How is your husband?" Elinore asked.

Annie didn't answer her; only shaking her head slightly. Elinore waited for her response. Then Annie spoke in a whisper. She began to tell Elinore that she was sure he was dying from consumption. Elinore asked, "How do you know?" She knew that was serious. Annie continued, "Because he is having trouble breathing. It sounds like he is trying to breathe from under water. His glands are swollen, and he's been complaining that his joints hurt too. Sometimes, he says things that make no sense, like he's losing his mind," she said. Elinore asked Annie if she kept the windows open and explained that she had heard open-air practices with sunshine helped cull the effects of that disease. Then Elinore asked if he was coughing and Annie said, "That started a while ago." Elinore made sure to tell her friend that wearing a mask was important when caring for him. She reminded her that she could catch what he had from his cough. Elinore assured her that she would speak with Ben and get her the proper medicine. Annie began to cry. She covered her face with her hands and Elinore heard her say, "I love him so much, I don't want to lose him." Elinore hugged Annie. She really couldn't do much else, but her heart broke for her newest friend.

That Monday, Elinore approached Ben to see Annie's husband, but Ben refused. She couldn't understand why he wouldn't. He was a doctor, surely, he could help him. But Ben would not budge. His mind was set. "Don't bring that contagious man here and I will not go to see him either! Do you hear me?" Ben commanded. She sat at her desk, not saying much to Ben after that. She labeled all the bottles silently and placed them on the tray outside the door to the laboratory. She took care of the patients as they came in and she felt more like a doctor than Ben was. She was angry. How could Ben have so little compassion? As a doctor, he would be sworn to the responsibility of doing what he could to preserve anyone's life. Then a thought came to her. She was going to slip some of Ben's special medication for tuberculosis into her apron and bring it to Annie. If he wouldn't help her, she would. Surely, he would not miss a bottle or two.

Each morning Elinore came to work, there would be people lined up the stairs to Ben's office and the days were becoming busier with each passing day. Elinore was becoming overwhelmed by the number of people who were now extremely distressed. It seemed like an epidemic was on the rise. The patients just kept coming. When it came close to quitting time, Elinore closed the door five minutes early. Twice a week, she would stop by to see Annie and bring her a new bottle of Dr. Feelgood's extra strength cure to give to her husband, but only occasionally would he seem to feel better. Elinore would spend many days just sitting with Annie and that seemed to help her the most.

One day, Elinore noticed that her aunt was coughing too. She brought her some of Dr. Feelgood's remedies. She started to pay closer attention to her, making soup and putting her to bed. In a few days' time, Agnes was in a bad way too, making Elinore decide to stay home for a day. Elinore was worried about her Aunt Agnes. Erika was indifferent about the entire matter. She never liked Agnes anyway, but it was clear, Agnes provided shelter therefore allowing Elinore to continue to be a Florence Nightingale to Agnes and decided it wasn't something she would try to stop. If Elinore was busy, Erika could rest easily.

Life was calm but Erika still monitored everything. It was her responsibility, and she took that seriously. There were young ones that needed to be protected foremost. Elinore's personalities were fragmenting and more alters were beginning to show themselves. In fact, Charlotte, the youngest one, had shown herself briefly at Coney Island, twice. It was so subtle that Annie hadn't noticed the difference between Elinore and Charlotte. Charlotte had a fondness for horses. Even the mechanical ones on the Steeplechase ride and the horses on the merry-go-round made her happy too. It was the first time Erika had let her show herself and she had had a glorious time doing so.

On the way home that Friday from work, Elinore decided it would be nice to buy some flowers for Annie and her aunt. The pills had done the trick for Agnes, and she was feeling better, but Annie's husband wasn't doing well at all. She went to the store and picked out some lovely roses and beautiful yellow daisies to purchase. As she approached the counter, Elinore could hear what sounded like someone trying to get a machine to start from outside the store. It was a loud rough sound. She reached into her pocket for money, when she heard a loud bang, like gunfire. Elinore snapped to see what the noise was, and her eyes widened with fear. She dropped the flowers and ran to the door of the shop. Outside a man was trying to start his new Model T automobile. He lifted the side metal panel to expose the engine and rubbed his forehead in frustration. Elinore stood in the doorway watching as people gathered around him. One man in the crowd asked if he had run out of gas. There was a lot of chatter around the car that drew her interest.

A woman with a horse and carriage pulled up alongside of the car and asked Elinore if they still had fresh flowers inside and Elinore said that they did. The woman passed her to enter the store, but Elinore was interested more in this latest form of transportation and continued to watch, not paying any more attention to the woman's interruption. A flash of Hans's face appeared in her mind. She thought Hans would know what to do with this metal contraption. He could fix nearly anything. The man walked around the car many times and still didn't know what to do. A younger man stepped out from the crowd and asked the man if he could be of service to him. The older man explained to him everything he had done already, and the young man said, "Well, all you need then to do is turn the crank shaft in front." The man's eyes rolled inside his head, and he must have felt foolish for forgetting such a simple task. He thanked the fella and turned the crank a few times. He jumped up onto the seat to push the button next. The engine cranked a few times and made a puttering sound but then stopped. He tried it again. The engine sounded as if it would start, but then a loud bang echoed through the air. The horse that belonged to the woman who was still inside the store was frightened by the boom and raised up on its hind legs. All at once the horse began to break free of his constraints. Taking off wildly, he ran down the street as the carriage pitched from one side to the other.

The woman inside came running out screaming, watching in horror. "My baby is in that carriage! Help!" She pointed at the carriage and her face became contorted. Her body trembled uncontrollably, and she dropped to her knees from the sheer terror, crying. Elinore jumped on the horse next to where her carriage was and flew past everyone. Her riding skills were still alive, and she moved with the horse as she once had with Lucky. Elinore chased after the runaway horse and carriage, gaining on them quickly. She only hoped that no one would walk in their path. This wasn't like the fields in Germany. The horse did not slow down at all as Elinore gave chase. Determined to catch him, she kicked the belly of her horse. He was a magnificent beast and sure footed. Finally, the horse was slowed by a street vendor's cart that it had crashed into. The carriage had caught the edge of the man's cart and it dragged with them spilling all the vendor's produce to the ground. Elinore took that opportunity, reaching out for the reigns, bringing the horse to a stop. Both horses were breathing heavily and were drenched with sweat. A shop owner brought some water out to them. Elinore ran her hand over their thick necks to calm them. Speaking softly, she assured them that everything was okay now. She tied each to the hitching post in front of the store that the madness had ended near. Frantically, she scurried up inside the carriage that held the baby. She hoped the baby wasn't injured. The baby was wide awake and making cooing noises, like he may have even enjoyed the wild ride. Elinore smiled and patted the baby's head. She wondered how she would get the two horses plus the carriage back to the flower shop by herself. Deciding to walk it, she picked up the reigns of both horses and began her journey back.

A cheering crowd awaited her. In fact, not a soul had left the flower shop. Even more people had gathered there, including a reporter from the local newspaper. The mother of the child was still weeping and was the first to see her returning even through her bloodshot eyes. Elinore was proud of herself and glad her riding skills were still up to snuff. The baby's mother ran to Elinore who was holding the baby tightly to her chest. Elinore's first words were to her, assuring her that her baby was fine. She handed the small child over and the mother hugged Elinore hard enough to take her breath away. She said, "Thank you!" repeatedly, as she wiped the tears from her face. The reporter who was in the crowd, rushed to Elinore asking many questions. She heard the clicking of a camera. He asked her where she learned to ride like that and a few personal questions about herself. After the excitement, the crowd began to disperse and the woman who ran the flower shop called out to Elinore, capturing her attention. She still had the flowers in her hand that Elinore had initially intended to buy. She gave them to her, telling her that she deserved them. She placed them in her hand. Elinore never forgot her manners and told her thank you for them.

It was still early enough in the day for Elinore to visit Annie. When she reached the end of the alleyway, she found Annie sitting with a handkerchief in her hand. Elinore handed her half of the flowers she had brought with her and asked her how her husband was doing. Annie shook her head back and forth slowly. "Not good," she said. "He's slept most of the day today." She went into the house and returned, holding a pitcher of water. She placed the flowers in the pitcher and thanked Elinore for them. Elinore tried desperately to get Annie's mind off things by telling her what had happened before she got there. Annie's mouth hung open as she listened. "Well, at least the baby was okay," Annie said. "Well done, Elinore." Annie had not much else to say after that. She was worried about her husband and found it hard to think of little else.

After a long silence, Elinore asked Annie if she would like her to have a look at her husband. "My husband's name is Tom," Annie said and opened the door for her. Elinore quickly put her mask on and went inside. Tom was coughing and Annie led her to where Tom was. She opened the door and called out to him, but Tom did not respond. Elinore could see that he was having difficulty getting air into his lungs and his skin was a yellowish color. Elinore could hear his lungs whistle with each breath. She walked closer to his bedside and reached to touch his lymph glands just under his jaw. They were very swollen and hard. His eyes looked hollow to her and yellow too. Annie commented from the doorway, "He's lost a lot of weight." Elinore noticed Tom had a small rash developing on the bridge of his nose, forehead, and just above his upper lip. She could tell that Tom didn't have long, but she didn't want to tell Annie that. Just then, Tom erupted in a coughing fit that was the hardest she'd heard from any of the patients she had seen at Ben's office. Annie rushed to him, sitting him up, which seemed to help him breathe easier. She handed him a spittoon and he spit up a lot of phlegm. Annie put it down next to the bed and gave him some water in a glass. Elinore looked in the bucket when Annie left the room, and she could see that some blood was mixed in with his spit. She knew that wasn't a good sign.

The two women didn't stay long in the room, and only once they were outside, did they drop their masks. Elinore could see the strain on Annie's face and felt bad for her. She was so young to be a widow. Elinore promised to bring her more medicine tomorrow and she hurried home to give the rest of the flowers to her aunt. Agnes was pleased by the flowers. She had many in her garden, but these were especially fragrant. Elinore began to tell her about the day's events and started to dig out cooking pans from under the sink. She opened the icebox for the chicken she had bought the day before and began to brown it in the pan with some butter.

She was in the mood for some spaetzle and made some gravy to go along with it. Agnes had a tomato from the garden and sliced it up to have with their dinner. The two ladies sat talking and eating like old friends. Agnes was beginning to think her niece was becoming comfortable in New York and adjusting well now. She had to admit she was even beginning to appreciate having her around much more than at the start of her arrival. Elinore didn't even seem to notice Agnes's poor table manners anymore. It wasn't that often that they were home together at the same time and as long as Agnes didn't intrude in her personal space, things went well.

The next day, Ben sat in his laboratory reading the morning paper before beginning his work for the day. The first thing he saw was a picture of Elinore's face with a story of what had happened. Elinore was a hero, rescuing a small child from a runaway horse. He read the article and at the end it mentioned she had worked for another newspaper priorly, but that John Smith had died recently of a sudden heart attack. It also mentioned that he had left a wife and child at such a young age. Ben knew John and hadn't realized he had passed. He had seen him a few times and he had never mentioned he had heart problems. Ben thought that was odd. Why would he not have mentioned that? He wondered.

Elinore came in a few moments later and began to place labels on the empty bottles that were waiting for her. Ben heard the wooden door open and came out holding the paper. Carefully locking the laboratory door, he asked Elinore if she would like to see the morning paper. She sensed a little sarcasm in his tone of voice and looked inquisitively at him and now she knew why. Her eyes went directly to the article about herself and read its entire contents. Her mouth opened slightly, and her brow wrinkled. She liked the article until she got to the part about John. Ben knew John, but he kept that to himself. Ben watched her face closely as she read the paper. Elinore wanted to forget John ever existed. He was cruel to her in the end, and she wanted to put that all behind her. There was no mention of her working for Ben now and she thought that might be why he seemed a little annoyed with her. She put the paper down and continued with her work. Ben locked himself back in his laboratory and the two hardly spoke for the rest of the day. The patients that visited that day, were for minor problems and Elinore was happy about the break. Only one headache, a man with a bad tooth, and a young girl who had a sore ankle from falling while playing outside.

At the end of the day, she counted the money and gave it to Ben. Before she left, she made sure to put a bottle of medicine in her apron for Tom. She hurried to see Annie. Annie was waiting for her. She rushed her inside and Elinore could sense her urgency. Annie brought her to the room where Tom slept. The sheets that covered him were drenched with sweat. Annie stood in the doorway again, watching. Elinore was not a doctor, she wasn't even a nurse, but she was the only one who was willing to help Annie. Elinore felt Tom's head and he felt very warm to her. She could hear his lungs still struggling as he tried to breathe. Tom looked at her, but his far-off fixed look made her feel useless. He started to speak but Elinore could barely hear what he was saying. She did not want to get any closer. She didn't want to catch what he had. His whisper tried to get something important across to her. He asked her, "Please, take good care of my wife. Look after her for me." He reached for Elinore's hand and squeezed it. She placed her other hand on top of his and told him she would. She told him that he needn't worry about that. He smiled at her.

A few minutes passed and Elinore felt Tom's grip loosen. She looked at his chest and it had stopped moving. Elinore felt for a pulse, but there was none. She stood there knowing that the man she had tried to help had just passed before her eyes. She listened to his breathing to make sure, but she heard no sound at all. She placed a small mirror just under his nose, but no fog appeared on the mirror. She bowed her head and closed Tom's eyes with her trembling hand. Annie saw this and began to wail. "He's gone, isn't he?" Annie asked even though she knew the answer. Elinore hugged her friend. "Yes Annie, I'm sorry." Annie could barely stand. Her knees were buckling, and Elinore had to hold her up. Annie was gutted and Elinore cried with her. She and Tom had only been married a few years. Finally, Elinore could no longer hold her up and Annie slid down the wall to the floor. Her eyes were blank, and she kept asking Elinore what she was going to do now. Elinore asked Annie if she'd like to come home with her, but Annie didn't want to leave. She did ask Elinore if she would ask the pastor to come see her. She needed to make arrangements for her husband. "Will you be okay tonight?" Elinore asked. She would have stayed if Annie wanted her to, but she needed some time alone with her husband to say goodbye. Elinore told her she would be back the following day and started her walk home.

Elinore was dazed and crying herself. She walked slowly, trying to get Tom's last breath off her mind. Elinore was angry at Ben for refusing to treat Tom. She felt guilty for not being able to cure him for Annie with the medication she had given her. She had made a promise to Tom to look after Annie and she planned on keeping her word. Elinore felt numb as she made her way to the front door where she lived when she saw Blacky just outside the fence waiting for her. Elinore sat down with the dog and hugged him tightly. He was there at the perfect time when she needed him most. She didn't know how he found her but was glad he had. The dog licked her face and put his front paws on her shoulders. He seemed to know Elinore was upset. She sat with the dog for a few hours until it began to get dark. It was only then that the dog wandered off to wherever she assumed he lived. It was nice to see the dog she named Blacky again. She had missed him, and it was exactly what she needed. Elinore was glad he had come.

Elinore woke up with a horrible headache from the stress of watching poor Annie's husband die. She knew she needed to get to work and pushed herself to get up from her bed. There was no one waiting on the staircase, which allowed her to go into the office unnoticed. She was a little earlier than she normally arrived. Ben wasn't there yet so she took her time getting started. The first thing she did was wash her hands. The second thing she did was start to look for those little blessed white pills that promised to soothe her pounding head. Scanning the office, she knew they were there somewhere. They weren't inside her desk. Where could she have left them? As she made her way around, she immediately noticed that the forbidden door to Ben's laboratory was slightly open, and it caught her eye. She paused, placing her hand on the doorknob. She turned it slowly to see if Ben was inside. She called out Ben's name, but nobody answered. She couldn't help herself. Elinore couldn't resist the temptation. She had to find out what was so important inside, that he kept the door locked, always with the keys in his pocket. She entered the room sliding carefully through the doorway. Elinore didn't know what to expect but she didn't want to disturb anything. There on the counter sat a huge sack of powdered sugar with a small machine beside it. Elinore looked it over, paying close attention to every detail of it and could see it worked like a press. Elinore was putting two and two together. Ben was pressing out tablets of powdered sugar! Then she looked in the cabinets below

Ben's work area and saw many things to add color to the different tablets. He had berries, beets, saffron, green plant leaves, among other things stuffed under there, none of which she thought could cure any illness. They were not medicine at all, only colorants. As a matter of fact, there was nothing medical in the entire office space.

Ben was a charlatan! A fraud! He was practicing quackery to earn a living! Elinore wondered just how many people had died because of him. She stood, taking it all in for a moment. Elinore glanced at the clock on the wall and realized Ben would be there any minute. Her head was hot with anger for Ben's flagrant audacity that he had for the personal safety of his patients. The same people who supported his way of life. She hurried to close the cabinets but when she closed the last cabinet, she heard the front door open. She was trapped! She waited inside the laboratory silently, just behind the door, to see if he would use the bathroom first, as he always did. She could hear the shuffle of his shoes and hoped she'd be able to sneak out quietly. Elinore was motionless and made not a sound when Ben entered the room. Staring eye to eye with her, Ben was seething with anger. "What are you doing in here?" he said, his voice filled with rage. Elinore shook inside with fear. Her voice began with a stutter. "The door was open, I thought you were in here," she said. Ben quickly returned, "You have no business in here!" He growled like a rabid dog, scaring Elinore to her core. Ben pointed to the door and shrieked, "Get out now!"

Elinore's face felt hot, and her mouth dropped open. Elinore was not about to back down, even though she was afraid. How dare he speak to her in that manner, when he was the one who was entirely wrong! She thought for a minute about her words. "I have no business?" she asked. "I most certainly do!" Elinore turned and shot back. "You are an imposter; you are not a doctor! You proclaim to possess healing powers and have remedies to cure people, but it's all a sham! People are dying because of you and now you have involved me!"

Ben tried to justify his practice. He said, "If people think they're getting better than they will get better! It's a proven fact!" Elinore's jaw clenched and her eyes became dark. The image of Tom's dying face was burned into her memory. "Nonsense!" she hollered back. Then Ben shocked Elinore. His voice lowered and his face curled wide with a snide expression. "It's not like you've never killed someone before." One of his eyebrows raised and he gave her a sideward look. Ben had no proof at all, just suspicion. Only John and Elinore knew what happened between the two of them and John was dead. She had not told a soul about John. She knew he was bluffing. As a matter of fact, it was not Elinore at all anyway. Erika was responsible for John's death. But Ben's comment caught her by surprise, and she began to reflect over her past. A flashback of the bloody faced man that had worked for her father suddenly surfaced. Elinore winced and the image left as fast as it had come. Ben could never have known anything about that either. It had happened so long ago anyway.

Elinore's thoughts raced around her mind, but she knew she had him by his whiskers. Elinore continued to stand firm with her eyes still piercing Ben. She shrieked back at him with all her power, "I have never killed anyone, but you most certainly have! I should turn you into the watchmen!" Ben snapped around. His face displayed his anger and he snarled at her. "If you do, I will tell them this business was all your idea and I was only your mule." "They'll never believe you, Ben!" she shouted. "Really? Do you think they'll believe a young immigrant woman or a respected American doctor, who is well known?" he asked. Elinore looked at the floor. Her throat tightened and she found it hard to swallow. She knew he was probably right. But Elinore kept her poker face. Ben left the room and Elinore followed him out, leaving a good distance between them. Patients began to stop by, and she tended to them. Elinore was consumed by thoughts about what had happened that morning throughout the entire day. She wasn't sure what Ben was capable of now. Ben seemed to be nice, most times, but she knew there was a darker, more evil side to him. She had just seen an example of his rage. She no longer trusted Ben. She knew she needed to be always on guard with him from then on.

Ben closed himself in his office. He had given himself away and he was upset about it. Ben's mind was racing. What would he do now about Elinore? Ben sat with two fingers pressed against his forehead. What a problem Elinore had become. He was overwhelmed with worry and tried to think of a plan of what next to do about it. He had suspected she could have had something to do with John Smith's death. He would play that card if she tried to turn him in. Ben knew John was a ladies' man and would naturally have wanted to keep things quiet about an illicit affair with a woman so young. Ben also knew that John was married, but he rarely saw his wife. John had once mentioned to him that she had sickly parents and was gone often to help care for them. Either way, he had no proof, no concrete evidence to prove Elinore was involved in his death. If she went to the authorities, it could give them a reason to investigate him. He didn't want that. Even a small investigation could potentially harm his reputation, making people believe that he was guilty of running his own sham. Business would decline and he would be financially ruined. The schools listed on his accolades that hung in his office were all fake. It would only take days for people to realize everything was a lie. He pounded his fist on the counter. Bottles flew. Papers and broken glass littered the floor. He needed to do something. This would have never happened if he hadn't forgotten to lock that damn door! He knew she was too smart. He should never have hired her. He regretted underestimating her.

He decided to give it a few days to think about the conundrum he had put himself in and then decide what to do. Ben found it hard to concentrate that day. Elinore had gotten under his skin, and he wasn't going to stand for it. With the threat she had made, Elinore had unwittingly drawn the line in the sand. Exposing him would ruin him. Ben did not take kindly to that threat especially from a young woman, no less. Women had no rights, they weren't even allowed to vote, but this fallen woman had gained power against him and he had to stop her. Dead in her tracks at all costs, if necessary. Ben wouldn't stop at anything to save his reputation. How dare she think she could get away with this, he thought.

A picture on his office wall changed everything. For a moment, his eyes gazed at the map he had posted there a long time ago. It was a map of Manhattan, showing all the streets and waterways. A plan began to hatch in Ben's mind. He had overheard Elinore talking to one of his patients one day about the glorious days when she would go fishing with her sister and grandfather. He looked closer at the waterways on the map. His thoughts turned into an image of him throwing Elinore's lifeless body into the Hudson River. Bricks! The word whispered from his lips. He would need bricks to weigh her down! The currents were strong in that river, and they would drag her out into the Atlantic Ocean, never to be seen again. Without her around, there would be no more worries. And easy to explain, if anyone were to ask. He would say that she just stopped showing up to work. He started to think about every little detail thoroughly, including an excuse to get her out there in the first place. What an odd place for a doctor to ask his assistant to go, but he would make it work. The more he thought about his plan, the better it sounded to him. He just needed to smooth it out, so the plan would fall into place without a single hitch. He planned to feign his forgiveness and be sweet as pie over the next week so she wouldn't have an inkling as to what was coming. He could carry four bricks in his knapsack with some fishing tackle easily. One of the bricks he would use for the blow to the back of her head, hopefully knocking her unconscious. Then he would weigh down each of her limbs with the other bricks with some rope. He would need to work fast. He would need to do all of that before she came around if he didn't manage to kill her with the first blow. Ben had a small boat which he kept for fishing but hadn't used in years. He could bring it closer to the water beforehand and use it to bring her body out to the middle of the river, dropping her off the side. He estimated that she weighed no more than 110lbs., which presented no problem for him. He lifted 100 lb. bags of sugar every day.

He started his plan by asking Elinore if she would like to go home early that day, since it was slow, and he would pay her for the time she would have worked anyway. Elinore was happy to leave, because she wanted to check in on Annie, but she was no fool. She knew he was up to no good. Erika was standing guard, waiting and watching. She also saw that he was up to no good. Erika understood that Elinore could be naïve at times, and she considered that things could get out of hand. Either way, she would be the one to handle it. Erika was always suspicious of people. She was much stronger than Elinore in many ways. She was ready for the fight if Ben wanted to give one. Time would tell, but Erika didn't like Ben from the first day they met. She thought that Ben took advantage of Elinore. Erika didn't like many people and trusted no one. Ben had never met Erika in the time Elinore worked for him. He surely would have been surprised if he had.

Elinore walked the streets to Annie's house. She hadn't eaten or slept since Tom's passing. Annie looked pitiful. Her eyes were dark and had bags under them. She hadn't brushed her hair or washed her face. It was gut-wrenching for Elinore to see her friend grieving. She made a quick meal for her and sat with her. Elinore pushed the plate closer and closer, until she nibbled just a small amount. Elinore wanted to make sure she ate it. She made Annie a cup of tea and had one too. Still, Annie said nothing except to express her thanks. Annie was all but catatonic. It broke Elinore's heart, and she couldn't help feeling a little guilty with the knowledge she had of Ben. She hadn't known Ben was a charlatan before Tom had died, but that didn't seem to matter now. He was gone. If Tom had seen a real doctor, he may have lived, she silently thought. Elinore didn't tell Annie what she had discovered. It wouldn't bring Tom back. She decided to stay with Annie that night. She couldn't leave her friend. Tom's death was a grievous blow to Annie, and she was suffering. Ben was responsible for this, and she wished she would be able to see him pay for his grievous offense. Elinore was anguished by the thought that she was partially to blame. Her resentment toward Ben was growing into a heated ball of venom in the pit of her stomach.

Throughout that night, Annie didn't sleep much and neither did Elinore. Elinore put together breakfast and coffee for her friend before heading home in the morning. She was grateful that the weekend had come, and she would not see Ben for two entire days. Elinore visited often with Annie during that time, but Monday came fast. It seemed TB was on the rise, and there were many patients coughing and wheezing. Elinore was feeling unsafe about it all and began to wear her mask constantly. Her hands were red and hurt from washing them so often. Ben was still carrying on with his charade of being overly nice and it became sickening to Elinore. It was late in the day, when Ben told Elinore he intended to close early. Elinore was more than happy. She had had enough of handing out fake pills. She thought he would let her go home early again but was disappointed when he asked her to clean the windows in his examination room. He told her they disgusted him, and they needed to be ridden from germs. Elinore closed the front door and gathered her supplies. "Now I'm a window washer," she muttered under her breath. She dipped the corner of the rag into the vinegar solution and started to clean the dirt away. When the first window was finished, she unlatched the second one next to it and began to wipe it down. The windows were filthy, and Elinore thought they must not have been cleaned for a very long time.

The sun was starting to go down, which made it easier to see the dirt on the large farm windows. She pushed the window out, away from herself to reach the top. They were massive and her arms just weren't long enough. As she lifted them, it created a reflection of what was behind her. She could see the bookcase and Ben's desk. Then she saw Ben! He was watching her work from the opposite side of the room. She wasn't sure he knew she could see him. Her back was turned to him. She watched him closely, not taking her eye off him for a second. Ben continued watching her closely. Her white dress billowed out from the light breeze in the air. The silhouette of her body caught his attention. Pity, he would have to get rid of her, he thought. He followed the outline of her long thin legs up to her waist and they were clear to him as the sun streamed through her dress. He continued to watch and then he saw it! Ben had left his scalpel right there on top of his desk! It was time! This was the perfect moment! He could dispose of her body under the cover of nightfall and his problem would be solved. Slowly, he made his way into the room, positioning the room separator partially between them so Elinore would not catch even a glimpse of him as he prepared to take her down. But Elinore did see him and watched as he slowly approached her. The hair on the back of her neck stood up as he reached for his scalpel.

Erika knew it was time to take control. She was ready for battle and had been already watching. She was ready to deal with this low-life scum of the earth. Ben was unaware that he was about to meet his match. Suddenly, Ben lunged at her, but Erika was quick. She avoided his blow by turning to her side, setting Ben off balance. He tried in vain to grab hold of her, but he was no match for Erika's strength. Ben tried to regain his balance, but Erika pushed him hard, managing to tangle his feet with hers. His scalpel fell to the floor, and Erika barreled into him, making him fall against both unlatched windows. The windows gave way against the pressure of his weight, and he tried desperately not to fall. He teetered on the open sash, still trying to gain his balance and his eyes became wide with fear. Erika sneered at Ben, "You are such a fool!" There was an evil gleam in her eye. Another small push was all it took to make him lose his grip. In an instant, he disappeared from the window and Erika waited to hear something but heard nothing. The scalpel lay on the floor next to the bucket of vinegar with her rags. Quickly, she placed the scalpel back on the desk exactly the way it had been. Still, she heard no sound. From the loft, it was a long way to the ground, but she thought she would have at least heard him groaning in pain. Erika moved to look out of the windows slowly and stretched her neck out as far as possible. Erika could now see the ghastly view below. Ben's body was lying over the large spears of the wrought iron fence that surrounded the building. One of the spears had pierced through, impaling him. His blood drained from his lifeless body onto the earth below into large pools of deep crimson redness.

Erika needed to leave there at once! She gathered all evidence of her being there. She left the windows as they were, unlocked. The watchmen would discover the grizzly scene in the morning. She knew they would assume he fell while washing the windows. It was easy for Erika to make her escape into the twilight of the evening. Erika disappeared onto the street below, making her way home quickly.

Waking up the next morning, Elinore contemplated what she should do. She knew Erika had done something terrible, but she had closed her eyes to the outcome of it. There surely would be patients piled up waiting to be seen. But she was sure the authorities would have chased them away. She assumed Ben was likely dead now, and there was no point in going there, she argued with herself. She assumed Ben had already taken care of any evidence of her being there because she remembered that he had tried to kill her first. But something must have happened because she was still alive and breathing. She shrugged her shoulders and went to the kitchen to get something to eat. Ben had lost his gamble with Erika, and now Elinore would be looking for a new job yet again.

Chapter 16

Agnes was surprised to see that Elinore was still home and questioned why her niece had not left for work already. Agnes was afraid to ask but did anyway, "Why are you not at work dear, do you feel alright?" Elinore was not prepared to be questioned yet, but she always had a handful of excuses for occasions such as this. "I quit two days ago," she said. "There were too many people coming in with consumption right now, and I don't want to become one of them!" she said cementing her answer with a wink. "But don't worry, I'll have another job in no time." She wasn't really telling a lie, but it wasn't the exact truth of what happened either. Elinore's thoughts went straight to the factory she had read about a while back. She knew exactly where she would go. She always tried to aim for a higher status job than the one she had prior, but this time she would be going to the garment district. Any job would do at this point, but Elinore really liked being around elite people. She didn't plan to stay there for long, if she were hired, but it would at least pay for the things she needed right now.

She craved the power that John had shown her. He had wealth, privilege, political power, and swagger to boot. She enjoyed the prestige that came with his spotlight, and she was determined to be in that element again. She knew, one way or another, she would make sure that's where she would wind up. She had never lacked for anything as a child, and she wanted to improve on that lifestyle even further. She knew it would make her father proud if she ever got the chance to see him again. But since she had been in New York with her aunt, Elinore never felt at home. This new country was hard to adjust to. She simply had trouble adjusting to the different culture. At least that was until she found the street vendors, selling knishes and she bought one to eat on the way to the factory. The warm potato deliciousness she held in her hand of this tasty little treat gave her the little bit of home feeling she needed. Finally, she reached the building she was searching for. She stood on the sidewalk, looking up at the building. She followed it all the way to the top with her eyes, and she fell backwards from the height of it. With a giggle to herself, she entered the building and made her way up to the 8th floor. Elinore inquired about any available positions and was immediately hired. She would begin working the following day.

Elinore could smell the fibers in the air, as she walked through the tightly fitted rows of the machines that the women worked at. It made her cough. It was much like the laundry work she did in Germany, but on a much larger scale. The man that showed her where she would work told her that she would be expected to work 12-hour days, every day. That would be exhausting, Elinore thought. She could do it for a little while but wasn't sure how long she would be able to keep up with it. At least it could get her through Christmas, unless something came up in the meantime that was better. She also noticed many of the girls sitting at the bulky machines were very young. They were not speaking German or English, which Elinore was fluent in both by this time. She couldn't understand them. Some even looked as young as 10 years of age. Elinore was amazed they hired such young children. Considering all she had seen, and the harsh conditions, with not even enough room to stretch one's legs, Elinore decided to take the job anyway, and promised to return to work the following day.

Starting with Elinore's very first day, she excelled at all her tasks. She zipped shirts and dresses through her machine, like butter. Her boss, Howard noticed what an excellent worker she was and rewarded her with special privileges. He often overlooked her extra bathroom visits and extended minutes to her lunch time. It made the other ladies angry and even jealous, which made it harder for Elinore to make new friends. Elinore continued to work there through that summer. The heat inside the factory was stifling and, on several occasions, a few women had passed out from it. Howard had placed fans at both ends of the room, but it did little good. One day, a few of the women tried to open the exit doors, but they were locked. There was no way to get a cross breeze going except the small windows on each side of the room, which seemed to only let more heat in than anything else. Elinore had become unhappy with her job in the later end of that summer. She was only earning half of what she had previously made, and much of that went to rent and groceries. The article she had read that had brought her to where she was, was a complete lie. Her wages were not what she had expected, and the hours were extreme. She was doing nothing except working and sleeping, all week, every week.

Elinore's one friend, Annie, had never really recovered from the loss of her husband. She was sad much of the time, and cried often, still. It had seemed like forever, since Elinore had had any fun. Elinore was becoming depressed with her current situation. Her trip to Coney Island with Annie seemed like a lifetime ago to her. Elinore hadn't even been shopping. She hadn't treated herself to a new dress, since she had worked for John, which was also a very long time ago for her. She didn't have time to go shopping, even if she wanted to. Christmas would be coming soon again, and she would only be buying small gifts for Annie and her aunt. As Elinore's favorite season began to move in, the temperature outside became cooler. She looked forward to seeing the leaves change, but with the change of season, Elinore developed some more depression.

Iris, who was only 8 years old, loved fall and winter though. She was older than Charlotte, but the two alters liked one another. Iris took pride in collecting the most brilliant-colored leaves she could find, and kept them in a book, recording the date and where she found them meticulously, from year to year. Many times, Erika would let her show herself on their walks through the park; Iris would always have a handful of leaves and random flowers clenched in her fist, at the end of their journey. She was a very creative little girl. She often drew things and was a perfectionist when it came to blending her colors. She would often watch Elinore put her makeup on but thought she could do better with her application. Blending was certainly not her thing, as Iris saw it, and often became angry with her lack of patience for it. If she didn't hurry it along so much, Iris thought she could do a much nicer job. Elinore enjoyed walking through the park. The crisp air tantalized her senses with the feeling of a new beginning, but the winter only followed with frozen water and bare branches reaching into the sky. Food for the animals in the park became scarce, so Elinore would bring them the occasional stale pieces of bread slices her aunt had leftover. The town began to decorate as the holidays approached and Elinore enjoyed the beauty of it all, but still was not happy with her work and lack of money.

Agnes was busy planning her yearly holiday party that she always had just before Christmas Day. Elinore liked the dancing that came when her aunt would play tunes on her cylinder phonograph. She would only bring it out on special occasions, and the songs would only last three minutes or so, but it was fun. And of course, Elinore found the delicious treats her aunt would offer, yummy. The fruits and candies, the breads and meats, were all delicious. She looked forward to that each year. It was the only time her aunt would spare no expense. This year, Elinore intended to ask permission to invite Annie to join in the celebrations.

The new year followed, and 1911 was greeted with high hopes. Winter melted to spring without much fanfare and Elinore started to look around for a new job. Working so many endless hours had left her almost no social life. Even Annie was becoming impatient with Elinore's lack of time. Elinore hadn't courted anyone since John and was beginning to think she might die as an old spinster. She was feeling complacent and wanted more from life. She continued her search for a better job, and decided she would not quit until she found one. March 25th came, and the weather was so pleasant. Spring had sprung and Elinore simply just didn't feel like going to work that Saturday. Instead, she chose to go to the park. Flowers were popping up all over the place and Elinore sat on the bench to watch the birds flop around in the water. She enjoyed watching the children play and the many people who rode bicycles over the pathways. She had brought her sketching pad and pastels to earmark the new spring. Charlotte and Iris were having great fun too. Iris had picked a handful of flowers and looked forward to capturing the new tender grass with her pastels on paper. Charlotte was beside herself when she saw an open carriage being pulled by a beautiful brown and white horse that passed close enough for her to touch.

It was getting late when Elinore thought about going home. It was only then did she notice a great column of thick black smoke rising high in the sky. The smoke had an awful smell to it. She was surprised that she could smell it from where she was. It looked like it was quite a distance away. Her curiosity drove her to walk toward it to see where it was coming from. She walked in the same direction she would have walked if she had gone to work and worried that someone would catch her playing hooky. She was nearly at her job, and she could smell the strength of the awful smoke becoming worse. It made her choke, and she covered her face with the collar of her dress to breathe through. She watched in horror after realizing it was the factory that she worked at that was on fire. There were many firefighters with their wagons converged on the scene. It was all a mass of confusion, and many watched helplessly as dozens of workers screamed from the windows above. Elinore stood among the people in the crowd with her hands on her cheeks. She could not believe what she was seeing. Her eyes filled with tears at the realization that she would have been in there too, if she had not chosen to skip work that day. The fire seemed to have the strongest glow at the 8th floor but was working its way to the top of the building. Some firemen had put a net in place for people to jump but it tore when three girls jumped all at once. Those three women plunged to their deaths. Pressed by the heat as the fire grew, many more began to jump, crushing themselves into the sidewalk below. The sadness for her fellow workers grew, and the sheer terror reflected in her eyes that were now swollen from crying. Her face was red, and her cheeks were raw from witnessing the catastrophic loss of life. She became numb and all sound seemed to stop around her. Firefighters frantically scrambled around her to save the people inside, but their fire ladders were only able to reach up to the 7th

floor. Elinore overheard a man standing next to her say that they had no sprinklers in the building, and she knew that was true. She had not seen one inside anywhere.

Elinore made her way through the crowd of onlookers to begin her way home when she saw one of the firemen sitting on the curb of the building across the street. He was holding his head in his hands and his face was covered in black soot. He was clearly distraught from their inability to save the poor people dying inside the inferno. They had managed to put out the fire after about a half an hour, stretching their water hoses as far as they could reach, but now the hardest part was yet to come. Removing the bodies that awaited them. The water ran red through the gutters of the street. The wind carried pieces of burnt embers through the air. The dead and dying were everywhere. Some groaning in pain from their fall. Many workers were women. Elinore felt a deep sadness for the families they would leave behind. She made her way over to the fireman and placed her hand on his shoulder. She looked at him but said nothing. He looked back at her for a moment, and she could see that he had been crying. His eyes were red and his voice hoarse. Elinore was not used to seeing men cry and squatted down to his level to embrace him. Surprising her, he hugged her back, welcoming Elinore's comfort. She asked what his name was, and he told her it was Mark. Elinore told him her name and then told him that she worked there but had skipped work that day.

His forehead wrinkled and his eyebrows rose. He said, "That was the smartest decision you've ever made, I'm sure my dear lady!" He thought about all the lives lost inside that building, placing his hand on his forehead. When it was all over, and all the bodies were accounted for in total, 146 lives had been lost due to the fire. Some had gruesomely burned to death, and some had been suffocated by the thick smoke. Some lost their lives in the one elevator shaft that worked out of the four in the building. Some died from jumping to escape the flames, crushing themselves on the cement below, and some died in the stairwells when they reached the bottom only to find the doors locked from the outside. A measure that the owners of the factory used to prevent workers from stealing. Mark warned Elinore that they may need to talk with her again and asked for her address. She gladly gave it to him and told him it was nice to have met him but wished it was under better circumstances. He excused himself by saying he needed to get back and tell his men what was to be done next and left in a hurry.

When Elinore got home, she told Agnes about what had happened. Agnes was grateful that Elinore hadn't gone to work that day and gave her the biggest hug that she ever had. Elinore could feel the love in her hug. Up to that point, she had never really thought Agnes cared for her that much at all. That night as the moonlight filled her bedroom, Elinore's mind filled with thoughts of the fireman who felt so helpless that day. She wondered if he was okay. She thought about her own life. How close she had come to not being alive and breathing the air that she was. The sight of the women who jumped to their deaths, played over and over in her mind. The screams she heard echoed inside her head. It was a sight she would never forget. Elinore wasn't sure now if she wanted to go right back to work either. She felt she could really use a break and had managed to save some money over the past year to get through by not treating herself too much.

With the first rays of light, Elinore went to see Annie to tell her what happened and what she had decided about, not going back to work right away. Annie was happy about her choice and was glad to have her friend back. She felt that Elinore had been working too hard all along. Then Elinore started to tell Annie about the firefighter she had met and how badly she felt for him. Annie listened and they sat talking about what Elinore had witnessed. Each made the other feel a little better and they enjoyed each other's company. Annie cooked some food for supper, and they enjoyed their evening meal together. Before they knew it, it had gotten very late. Instead of going home, Elinore decided to stay at Annie's house for the night until morning, and when it came, they enjoyed a lovely breakfast, before Elinore went home. Agnes was not home when Elinore finally got there, so she thought it might be nice to have herself a nice, steamy, hot, bath. She drew herself a bath and treated herself to some fresh towels. She set them down on the side of the shiny porcelain clawfoot tub. She dipped her toe in and thought the tub was the loveliest piece of furniture in the entire house. She sat in the tub until the water turned cold and the skin on her fingers had pruned. That had always been her signal to get out since she was a little girl.

Elinore wrapped her long blonde hair in one towel and dried herself off with the other, before getting dressed. She stood in front of her tiny mirror, rubbing the water from her thick mane with the towel. The warm water had faded some of the stress from her body, but visions of the women who died on the sidewalk still lingered. Flashes of those faces paralyzed her, and Elinore tried with all she had to think of something else as best as she could. Unable, she returned to her bed for an afternoon nap, pulling the covers tightly up around her chin.

The warmth of her blanket made her eyes heavy, and Elinore felt she would finally be able to sleep when there was a knock at the door downstairs, Elinore went to the door and opened it. The fireman, she had just met, along with several watchmen stood in the doorway. They were demanding answers from her concerning the fire and insinuating that she could have been the one to have started it. Elinore tried to defend herself and told the group of men who were now surrounding her that she wasn't even at work that day, but it didn't convince them of her innocence. They pressed harder for answers that she did not have. Elinore started to cry. The watchmen demanded that she come with them, and two of them latched onto each of her arms. Elinore began to scream and kick as they pushed her into the patrol wagon that was parked just outside her house. She fought with them trying to escape their grip. Elinore landed on the floor next to her bed with a thud. Her heart was racing, and tears filled her eyes. She lay on the floor, realizing it was all just a bad dream. A very bad dream! She went downstairs to the kitchen to get a sip of water and wipe her forehead. Her hair was stuck to her face and the back of her neck was wet with sweat. Elinore returned to her room still bothered by her nightmare and it took some time before she was able to fall asleep again.

Elinore was exhausted and slept until almost noon, the next day. Agnes did not disturb her; she was busy looking at a catalogue a friend had given her for a department store called Sears and Roebuck. Agnes was amazed at all the things that were available to her through this publication. And it could all be shipped and picked up by train! Finally, Elinore got dressed, just after noon and wasn't sure what she wanted to do with the rest of the day. She sat down at the table, across from her aunt dazed. She thought about having a bite to eat but really wasn't hungry. Suddenly, there was a knock at the door. "Nuts, not again!" she whispered to herself rolling her eyes. She looked out of the window before opening the door. It was the fireman, but he was alone this time. She quickly ran her fingers through her hair and smoothed her dress, before opening the door with a smile. "Mark, how nice it is to see you and under much better circumstances." "Likewise," he said, nodding his head. There was an awkward moment of silence, when Elinore chose to step outside to speak with him. He had come to check on her, and she told him she had wondered how he was too. They talked about the fire. He asked her a few questions and told her that his fire chief had requested the fire inspector's assistance in the matter, for an investigation into the cause of the fire. He also mentioned to her that they had suspected that the fire had started on the lower level of the factory and that it was considered suspicious, but that was all he knew up to that point.

Elinore looked into his brown eyes, listening to his every word. He seemed to have a high position within the fire department, and she noticed how handsome he was without all that soot on his face immediately. And better yet, he was not wearing a wedding ring! But she was no fool, as she had discovered with John, that was not a sure sign as to whether he was married or not. Elinore had to ask. Boldy, the words came out. "Are you married?" Mark blushed and answered that he was not. He tilted his head to one side trying to hide his embarrassment at her question. Elinore's flirt-o-meter jumped to high alert. He told her the fire inspector was likely to come visit her to see if she could remember any details about how the fire may have started, which would be helpful in figuring it all out. But Elinore didn't know much more than she had already told him. Mark and Elinore sat talking on the small bench that Agnes had in front of the house for hours. They relaxed in their conversation, and Elinore guessed he was just a little older than she, but by no more than five years. He didn't leave until late that afternoon and Elinore was left intrigued by him. He was rugged, mysterious, but most of all, very professional. All the qualities that Elinore was attracted to. She was instantly smitten by his charm and when he left, he sealed the deal by kissing the back of her hand.

Elinore hoped she would see him again soon. Elinore couldn't wait to see Annie to tell her about Mark and that he had come to see her. When Elinore finally did get to see Annie, she was talking so fast that Annie had to ask her several times to slow down. Annie suggested to Elinore that she should take some time alone to get to know herself better, but Elinore wasn't hearing her. Elinore was doing as she had always done. She was falling for her newest love interest hard. Elinore really didn't even know Mark, but she wanted to, very much so. He was adorable and polite. Annie was becoming impatient with Elinore's school-girl antics and thought a distraction would do her good. She knew there was a dance being planned at the local dancehall and asked Elinore if she would like to go with her. Annie didn't care much for the way Elinore latched onto men she didn't know so quickly. Maybe Elinore might meet another man at the dance. Annie's heart was still hurting, and she missed Tom so much. She cried herself to sleep almost every night, but she knew she had to make something of the life she had left. She knew she would never get over the loss of him, but she needed to learn how to live with that. Her heart would be forever broken, but she also knew that Tom would not want her to stop living. Maybe she would meet someone that she could talk to at the dance too. She considered Elinore to be a good friend now, but the fact that she was so easily distracted by the next man that walked into her life bothered her. It made her feel insignificant in their friendship at times. Annie hesitated to tell Elinore everything because of it. She would have liked to have been able to confide in her the deepest and darkest secrets, but she wasn't convinced she always had Elinore's complete attention.

The night of the dance, Elinore and Annie had a wonderful time. They danced with each other and had a few dances separately with men who had asked, but neither found any of those men to stand out in the crowd. There were some delicious foods provided and refreshments for the participants, which Elinore ate her fair share of. Annie was particular about her choices and enjoyed a slice of cake with a hot cup of tea. There was a contest held that money could be won from, but they chose not to enter that. It was likely to last much past the time they wanted to be there. Later that night, both women were complaining about how much their feet hurt. Many people were beginning to leave, and Elinore wanted to leave too. The bright red exit sign led them down a long staircase, to the street. Annie laughed and grimaced simultaneously with the pain from each step that she took. "I feel like I am 100 years old tonight!" she said to Elinore as they got closer to the bottom. Elinore and Annie laughed a lot that night.

When they finally reached the sidewalk, Elinore thought she saw a glimpse of a man she was convinced was Mark. "Mark! Mark!" Elinore shouted, jumping up and down and waving her hands high in the air. Her face displayed her excitement. Annie became annoyed with her behavior and quickly clutched Elinore's hand, pulling it down. "Geese Louise!" Annie shouted at her. "Don't make a spectacle out of yourself! Stop acting so desperate! It's not likely that he'd be here, and could you please forget about Mark just for tonight?" Annie clutched Elinore's hand again, pulling her along as they walked in the direction of Annie's house. Elinore felt sort of bad from Annie's scolding. She agreed she wasn't being much of a friend to poor Annie. Annie still needed her support, and Elinore knew she could do that much for her. Elinore's mind was cooking now. She twisted her hair around her finger with each step and thought of an idea. Her eyes opened wide, and a smile came across her face. "Hey Annie? What do you think of going to the movie house next week?" she asked curiously. Annie was delighted with her suggestion. She thought finally maybe Elinore was thinking about something other than men!

Annie began to fumble for her keys to the door and found them after a few minutes of digging through her purse. It was becoming a habit for Elinore to stay at Annie's house since Tom passed and both changed into their night clothes. They both sat at the table in the kitchen and talked a little about the people they had encountered that evening. Both their faces were illuminated by the small lantern that Annie kept there. Elinore began to yawn and covered her mouth feeling embarrassed. Annie was feeling the same. She asked Elinore if she was ready for bed and turned the lamp down to go to sleep herself. Elinore made her way to the guest room that Annie had allowed her to sleep in and sat on the bed that had become hers there. Her thoughts returned to Mark, and she wondered if she had truly seen him earlier or if it was just her imagination. When she closed her eyes, she could feel his brown eyes looking back at her. She wondered just how long she would have to wait before she would see him again.

Mark sat comfortably in his own home, stoking the fire to make himself some coffee. He swore he couldn't do a thing until he had his first cup most days. He had lived alone most of his life. His father lived several houses down the block from where he lived and was a clockmaker. Mark enjoyed helping his father, Kyle, to make and repair clocks, but it was not his choice of livelihood. Mark was a very adrenaline-fueled man. Constantly on the move and always busy. Even with his fight or flight actions to the excitement under the stressful and dangerous constant circumstances he exposed himself to, he still found a few fleeting thoughts about the young woman who had embraced him on the curb that day. He kept that small piece of paper that he had written her address on in his pocket and looked at it occasionally, debating with himself if he should start another relationship with a female. Mark had had one other significant relationship, but under the constant obligations of being a firefighter and being called out at any given moment, it had put a lot of strain on them consequently killing the love they had for one another. Mark also had a short fuse at times.

Becoming impatient with people, he found difficult to control at times. Verbal shortness was not a great quality for gaining the affections of a woman. Still, he found her beauty alluring and couldn't get his mind off her. Her voice was seductive to him, but he could tell that she wasn't trying to come off that way. Her thick long hair and sparkling blue eyes dangled in front of him like a treasure, raising his interest in the deliciousness to be had. He considered what he had to offer in this new relationship should he choose to start one. He had a modest home, and his job paid well. He ranked second to his fire Chief which allowed him to live comfortably. And he had his faithful dog, Buster. A handsome German Shepard that was mostly black with brown highlights, but that was it. Mark liked a simple life.

Elinore was getting excited about the next outing she and Annie had planned. Movie houses were new on the scene. That following Friday, Annie and Elinore had a good time together preparing for their next night out of entertainment. They giggled and laughed as each tried on the choices of clothing that they had made. Elinore spent over a half of an hour applying her makeup. Iris was carefully watching. She took the opportunity to present herself for a few minutes, to make sure Elinore didn't make herself look like a clown. Erika was proud of Iris for taking that initiative. Iris had a creative hand, and as a result, Elinore's makeup was flawless. The system was happy within Elinore's mind, with no drama entering. Erika was comfortable lately and watching after Iris and Charlotte was her most favorite thing to do anyway. Erika had to admit though, Charlotte was her favorite. But ultimately, Elinore had to be her main concern for safety. Elinore had a way of getting herself and everyone else in trouble.

It was a nice evening that night. They walked to the movie house as the day faded to evening. It wasn't hot or cold, just comfortable, requiring no sweater. The banner on the outside of the theater displayed what they were about to see. It was a silent movie named, "Their First Misunderstanding." Mary Pickford was the lead actress, and the movie was only ten minutes long, but that didn't bother either of them. They were out and having a great time. After the movie, they stopped at the corner soda shop for an Egg Cream. Outside the soda shop, again, Elinore thought she saw Mark. This time, she tapped Annie on the shoulder and whispered, "Oh my goodness Annie, there he is again I think!" Annie slowly turned her head in the direction that Elinore was pointing, trying not to be obvious. This time, sure enough, it was Mark. Annie couldn't believe it. She thought this man must be following them! Before she knew it, Elinore had made her way over to him, boldly showing her fondness for him. Annie just shook her head. She didn't like seeing Elinore throwing herself at this man she barely knew. Annie thought maybe that it would be better if she just went home, without a word, when Elinore called out to Annie and motioned to her to come join them. Annie really didn't want to, but she did anyway. Elinore quickly introduced her to Mark, and they made some small talk before he was off again. "Isn't he dreamy?" she said to Annie.

Annie was not amused. She took a deep breath and blew it out hard. Her eyes rolled to the back of her head. Annie tossed her a stink eye, "How old are you?" Her tone of voice was stern. Elinore's eyes squinted and her bottom lip pushed up and out. "Don't you look at me like that!" Annie said with disgust. "You know what I'm talking about! You're acting like an 8-year-old!" Iris heard that and took offense to the statement. She was 8 and what was wrong with that? Iris didn't like Annie's insinuation at all. Elinore could feel a little rumbling inside herself. Annie's remark had caused a stirring which caught Erika's attention. Then Annie said, "Look Elinore, it's a little insulting when any half good looking guy walks by and I immediately lose your attention. It's just not right." Now Erika liked what Annie was saying. Finally, someone else was telling her to behave herself. "Could you just be a little more considerate and maybe discreet with your flirtatious moves on your next victim?" Elinore had a blank look on her face. "Next victim? What do you mean by that?" she asked. Annie started to laugh. "Oh, come on, I didn't mean that literally! But really El, could you put a cold rag between your legs?" For a few seconds they looked at each other expressionless. Annie wondered if Elinore understood what she meant when together, they both broke out laughing about the entire conversation. Each of them had laughed so hard that both had to hold their stomachs and wipe their eyes. Annie was always the first to break the ice, and they began to talk about where they would go on their next outing.

Elinore was excited to talk about it, but she needed to get home. She wanted to tell her Aunt Agnes all about the movie. The actors were so glamorous, and Elinore couldn't wait to tell her about it. Elinore really liked the way the lead actress dressed and wore her makeup. It was impeccable and she thought about buying herself some new makeup. Maybe she could try to copy it, although it was applied quite heavily. Maybe she would need a putty knife too, she joked with herself. She still found it funny when she entered her house. Agnes saw her laughing, but no one was with her. Agnes thought it was strange and hoped Elinore had not lost her mind altogether, like the last time with her billhook. That was scary! But she was laughing, and Agnes took that as a good sign. Elinore began talking about the movie and the glitz of it all, but Agnes didn't have much interest in it, as Elinore had hoped. As a matter of fact, she was a big fuddy duddy about it. Her kill joy attitude disappointed Elinore and it dampened her spirit. She hadn't even gotten to tell her about what the movie was about. Agnes seemed like she couldn't care less. Elinore made her story short and climbed the staircase to her room. What a wet blanket, she thought about her aunt. She pulled the wobbly old chair out from under the desk. It creaked the same way it always did when she sat on it. Elinore couldn't help but think about all the things Annie had told her regarding entertainment in New York City. Annie had mentioned tons of things, but Elinore really liked the idea of seeing a circus. Annie had also mentioned a wild, wild west show by a person named Buffalo Bill. Elinore thought that was a funny name for someone. Annie had also told her about live jazz music events and social clubs that had all sorts of lessons on a multitude of subjects, but the most interesting thing she mentioned was horseback riding. Horses made Elinore's heart sing. It also made little Charlotte happy too. She wondered if Annie would be upset if she invited Mark to come along with them at some point.

To Elinore's surprise, Annie had planned their next outing already. She had always wanted to take a cooking lesson but didn't want to go alone. Now, she could ask Elinore to go with her. Annie was excited about her plan, but Elinore was less than enthusiastic about it when she told her. Elinore already knew how to cook. She'd been cooking for years and learned from watching Elsie and Emma. Annie insisted it would be fun to try something different. She did her best to convince Elinore, but Elinore wasn't buying it. Still, she agreed to go. The dress was casual, which Elinore wasn't thrilled about either. She liked dressing to the nines. The class started out slowly and was held in a large kitchen. A man began to explain the use of a measuring cup and how to use measuring spoons correctly. Elinore was yawning. She never used those things. Real cooks didn't need them, she thought. She always cooked with a pinch of this and a handful of that. Annie asked questions and wrote everything down on a small notepad she had brought with her in her purse. The teacher began with a simple recipe of how to make oatmeal. He started with a thick batch and showed everyone there how to thin it out. Elinore didn't mean to be disrespectful but was yawning big now. Annie knew they wouldn't be coming back there, at least not together. She also was embarrassed by Elinore's behavior. She elbowed Elinore, "Would you cut that out!" adding an evil eye in her direction. Elinore responded by mouthing the word "Sorry.". Elinore ruined Annie's interest in learning that night and she placed her writing tablet back inside her purse. She put it on her lap in a huff and waited patiently for it all to end.

When the class was finished, Elinore couldn't wait to leave. As soon as they hit the air outside, Elinore turned to her friend and said, "If you want to learn how to cook, I can teach you better than that garbage. Everyone knows how to make oatmeal! That fruitcake is going to bore us to death!" Elinore begged, "Please, please, please, don't make me go back there again!" Elinore was smiling as she grabbed Annie's arm. She was cracking herself up making fun of the old teacher they had just left. "Let's go have some tea and talk about our next adventure, okay?" Elinore was still trying to control herself while clutching Annie's arm, but just couldn't. Annie agreed and the faintest smile came across her lips. She found Elinore's laughter contagious and had to admit, she was hilarious at times. Annie opened the door to her home and let Elinore in. She put on some water and they each sat in their familiar places. Annie began to talk about some dancing classes. She had heard about them and wondered what Elinore thought about it. It sounded much like what they had already done. Elinore wanted to do something else. She took that opportunity to ask about the horse-riding Annie had mentioned. "Do you like to horse ride?" Annie asked. Elinore's face lit up. "Oh yes!" Elinore began to spill out stories about Lucky and the fact that she missed him so much. Elinore went on to tell her about some of the most cherished times she had with her horse and how he loved the apples she would give him. Annie knew that would be where they would be going next but didn't know how to ride. She had never been on the back of a horse. When Annie told Elinore this, she couldn't believe her ears. "You never rode a horse?" The thought of someone not being able to ride a horse was unfathomable to her. Elinore's eyes reflected her mental confusion to Annie's admission. Elinore assured her that it would be fun, and she would show her how. Annie was feeling self-conscious and awkward. She didn't know how to cook, now she didn't know how to ride. She wondered what else Elinore would discover she didn't know how to do. Thankfully, Elinore was a good sport about it and followed through with her promise. Elinore began to teach Annie how to cook and they spent many evenings together.

The next week came, and Elinore was ready to ride. Elinore's pace picked up on their walk toward the park. She was over the top. Charlotte was giddy and waiting for Erika to give her permission to come out. Annie was nearly running, trying her best to keep up with Elinore. Charlotte could smell the stables. Horses had a distinct smell and she liked it. Elinore picked out a fine horse, brown with white spots, but not as high as Lucky. Then Elinore picked an older horse that was black and white for Annie. The man at the stable saddled them up and they were off. Elinore showed her how to hold the reigns and how to stop the horse. "Okay, let's go!" Elinore squealed. While Annie was fine, just sitting on the beast's back, letting it walk her around the park, Elinore took off like she did in the fields of her childhood home. A childish shrill came from Elinore's mouth and Annie called out to her but Charlotte paid her no mind. Charlotte was floating on air and delighted to be out on a horse. She was really enjoying herself.

Annie watched her friend from a distance and wondered why she was behaving so peculiarly. It was as if she was a child. Annie slowly clip-clopped around the park being careful of the children playing and Elinore ran circles around her. Annie really was not enjoying herself at all, but she stayed until Elinore had had enough. Finally, Elinore realized that riding in a crowded park was not like riding in the vast open fields of Germany, and she was disappointed. It annoyed her that she had to be careful not to run into anyone and couldn't gain the speed that exhilarated her. It wasn't the horse's fault. Just too many people there. Elinore asked Annie if she wanted to leave, and she jumped at the chance. She didn't like horse riding at all. Together they walked home and were tired from the day. Annie told Elinore on the way home, that she had found muscles that she didn't know she had and the two laughed about it. At the end of the day, Elinore decided to go back to her aunt's house to sleep in her own bed that night. And when she arrived, Agnes was waiting for her. She had become upset with Elinore for spending so much time away. Agnes had not started to cook their evening meal but had the chicken and potatoes out on the counter.

Elinore came through the front door, closing it softly behind her. "Is that you Elinore?" Agnes asked. "Yes, I'm home Aunt Agnes." Elinore shouted back. She made her way to the kitchen where her aunt was seated at the table. She was in her chair again, in her usual position. Elinore was not surprised, and she knew what that meant as soon as she went to the sink to wash her hands. She saw the chicken sitting there. To avoid a confrontation, she started dinner but was still annoyed that she had to cook. She was tired. Being out in the fresh air all day made her sleepy. Elinore had just put the butter in the pan when Agnes asked how her day was. Erika could hear the sarcasm in her voice, and she was paying close attention to it. She wondered what Agnes was trying to insinuate. Erika listened for the next clue. Elinore told her story about how she and Annie had gone to the park to ride horses. "You're spending a lot of time with your friend Annie." Agnes casually stated. "Will you be looking for a job soon?" The starting gun had sounded and now Agnes was getting under Erika's skin. It wouldn't take much more provocation from her to bring on her wrath. But Elinore answered perfectly. "Do you need to borrow money?" she asked. Agnes put her nose back into the newspaper and answered with a barely audible "No." Elinore boldly asked, "Then what is the problem? I paid you what you asked from me." Agnes thought about things for a minute. She had something on her mind. She put her glasses on top of her head and said, "To be honest dear, I miss your company at night here." Agnes was telling a fib, but realized Elinore was right. She really couldn't and shouldn't say much. Elinore was full grown. Elinore also knew that Agnes was just missing her being around to cook, clean, and do household chores while she went out and about. The two sat at the table and Elinore watched her aunt chomp over her plate. Bits of chicken fell off her greasy lips as she devoured her meal. Elinore was only half done, and Agnes had already finished. She got up to wash her plate and put it back in the cupboard; Elinore watched her closely. Agnes paused over the sink thinking. She thought that maybe it wasn't quite so much a fib. Elinore had grown on her, and she did miss her company at times. Elinore sat quietly in her chair and as Agnes passed her, she gave her a big hug from behind, squeezing her shoulders tightly. She whispered, "Thank you for the meal," adding, "That was delicious!" Elinore was in shock. Her aunt had never thanked her or shown her appreciation before.

Elinore finished her meal alone. She still felt she had been taken advantage of; Agnes's small gesture was not enough to convince her. She hurried to finish, wash her own plate, and make her way to her room. She mumbled to herself, "I should have stayed at Annie's!" She dressed for bed and pulled up the covers around herself. Her thoughts took her back to Mark. She wanted to see him again. Maybe she would go to the fire department and ask for him. Her eyes were heavy, and she was too sleepy to think up a plan to make that happen but thoughts of him still lingered on her mind as she fell into a blissfully sound sleep.

The morning sun came streaming in and Elinore awoke feeling much better. She stretched her arms up and a huge yawn escaped from her. Elinore felt adventurous. She went for a walk into town. She passed the building where she first worked after coming to this new land. She hoped she would see some "Help Wanted" signs but was sure she never wanted to work for Mr. Quinn again! Then something caught her eye. A new shop had opened, a gun shop. Guns always aroused Elinore's interest ever since Hans had shown her how to shoot one. Erika was stirred by them too, but not for the same reasons. She loved the fear in the eyes of those threatened by them. Thoughts of the gun Carl had bought for her many years ago crossed her mind. She couldn't remember what happened to that gun or where she had put it. She made a mental note to look for it and continued her journey. As she passed the flower shop, the woman who worked there waved to her from behind the large window. It made Elinore happy that people were becoming friendly to her, and she was being recognized as a local. She smiled and waved back to the woman. Then as she approached the butcher's shop, she saw they were looking for help too. Elinore couldn't picture herself working there. She cringed every time she had seen Emma cut the head off one of their chickens and take the feathers off. What an awful smell it had too.

At the end of her walk, she found herself knocking on Annie's door. Annie had not expected to see her but was glad she had come. They enjoyed some tea and began a conversation that lasted well into the night. It was warmer than usual that night, and a full moon lit the sky. They sat outside for a little while and enjoyed its glory. Elinore decided she would not make the same mistake by going back to her aunts this late and stayed at Annie's that night. Annie had bought some chicken and Elinore showed her how to cook it, making milk gravy and spaetzle to go with it. Annie had picked some tomatoes from her garden, and they paired well with the meal. Elinore thought twice about bringing the subject of Mark up again, but she really needed Annie's help with figuring out a good way to meet with him again. As soon as she mentioned his name, Annie shook her head laughing. "You're man crazy, Elinore! You know that?" Annie joked. The two began to hatch a plan. Annie started with something simple. "Maybe inviting him for dinner?" But Elinore thought that was kind of boring, but still a possibility. "What if we go to the movie house again?" Elinore asked. Annie admitted that was a good idea. "We could doll you up too!" Elinore was thrilled with her idea and so was Iris. It gave her a chance to paint Elinore's face again. It was a perfect plan, now all they had to do was get Mark to be there. Elinore was rapidly wiggling her fingers nervously.

Annie could see the excitement awakening in her friend. She even thought it could be more than just excitement. Elinore was fidgeting. To calm her down, Annie offered some tea again. But Elinore replied, "I don't like tea, I'd rather have some coffee, please." Annie was shocked! "But you drink tea with me all the time!" she said. Elinore answered, "I may but I don't really like it!" Annie looked at her dumbstruck. She realized she wasn't speaking to Elinore, but wondered who was behind those eyes. They had drunk tea a thousand times before. Now, she was sure, something was not quite right with Elinore. She had suspected something was a little off with her friend from the beginning but now, she was positive. Thankfully, Annie had never had any bad occasions with Elinore, but she wondered if she had a good reason to be alarmed. Elinore's personality seemed to change instantaneously throughout their friendship from day to day. Sometimes even minute to minute. She questioned whether she needed that complication in her life since Tom had passed, but she did enjoy Elinore's company. Erika rolled her eyes. She had finally had enough of all the tea she was being made to drink. Erika had to take a stand and didn't care how much Elinore liked tea. Erika just wanted a damn cup of coffee! That night, Annie thought about Elinore a lot. Her eyes were heavy, but her mind was troubled. Elinore's personality had changed in the blink of an eye. She found it odd. What could cause a person to change like that so abruptly. She had never met anyone quite like Elinore before. She was sure Elinore had something diagnosable but couldn't put her finger on it. The next time she saw a doctor, maybe she would ask about it.

Elinore felt as if she had just gone to bed when she heard Annie calling her name. Her eyes opened and she took a big stretch. "Oh, my goodness, I slept so good!" she said to Annie who was peeking in through the doorway. Annie was up and dressed already. "I'm going to the market; do you want to come with me? We need some things." Elinore really did not want to go but the food wasn't going to walk there on its own and she had been staying there quite a bit. She knew rightfully that she should go. And so, the two were off to do some shopping. They entered the shop where Annie liked to buy her dried goods. Annie noticed right away that the prices had gone up since the last time she'd been there. Coffee was 27 cents a pound now. Even though it was 5 cents higher than the time before, she thought she better get some since she didn't know what Elinore may want from time to time. A 5-pound bag of flour was now 18 cents and the bread had increased to 5 cents per pound! She added the things up in her mind as she moved along. She added some eggs, dried peas, bacon, butter and cornflakes to the counter next to the register. Annie watched anxiously with each pull of the registers handle. It added up quickly, and she hadn't noticed that Elinore was having a lively conversation with a gentleman in the corner at the back of the store. To her surprise, Elinore was talking with a man she hadn't seen when she first entered the store. Annie had asked her to come along because she knew she would need her help with the bags but apparently, Elinore had forgotten why they had come altogether.

As soon as she came close enough, she could hear Elinore carrying on like a young schoolgirl again. She was laughing in a very loud, unladylike manner that was noticeably forced. Annie was embarrassed, and she rolled her eyes back in her head with disgust. She really hated it when Elinore acted like that. Annie turned around in a huff and thought she'd be better off just doing it herself. She impatiently ruffled the tops of the bags closed. She was angry with Elinore. Elinore was watching her through a side view and saw she was just about finished with her shopping. She called out to her in a heightened voice. Annie's shoulders immediately shrunk, and her eyes lowered. She grumbled softly to herself. Once again, Elinore called out to her. Oh my God, she thought. Annie wished Elinore would just give up but with an even louder voice, she beckoned Annie to come join her for a third time. Annie was more than impatient and annoyed at this purposeless introduction. She just wanted to bring her things home. Elinore exclaimed, "Annie, this is Mark! The man I have been telling you about!" Annie minded her manners and shook Marks hand. "Very nice to meet you, Elinore has talked a lot about you," she said with a smile. Mark replied that he hoped that it was all good things that she had mentioned.

Annie made it as short as she possibly could and informed Elinore she had already paid for her items. Elinore asked for a minute and promised to hurry along. She took that moment to ask Mark if he would like to accompany her and Annie to the movie house that Friday. It was a bold move to ask him, but she was delighted when he said yes. Her daring attempt paid off! Elinore rushed off bursting to tell Annie what he had said. She could hardly contain herself; excited that their plan was working. She and Annie took the brown sacks off the counter and Elinore talked about Mark incessantly all the way home. It was the most unpleasant walk Annie could remember having in a long time. When Elinore finally left that night to go gather her makeup and things from her home, Annie was glad. She swore if she had heard Mark's name one more time, she was going to go insane!

Elinore walked as quickly as she could to her aunt's home through the twilight. On the way, Elinore passed the dress shop she had been to before. This time, they had a beautiful deep green dress on the mannequin in the window. It had a pretty white corset under it that peeped out at the edges of the neckline.

The mannequin was also adorned with gloves that went up to the elbows and a hat that matched, with a thin veil that hung over the edges. Elinore thought, how perfect! The store was still open, and she decided to go inside to ask about it. The shop owner came out when the bells on the back of the door rang. The woman tightened up immediately as soon as she saw Elinore, but Elinore didn't know why. It seemed to Elinore that she was uncomfortable with her presence and rushed her to make a purchase. Elinore wanted the dress and quickly bought it.

She left the store confused as to why the woman would treat her the way she did. That woman remained on Elinore's mind until she got home. She knew Erika didn't like her, but Erika didn't like anyone really, except for "precious" Charlotte. Elinore was still in a hurry and burst through the door once she made it home. She took the staircase, two steps at a time, to gather the rest of her things. She piled it all up on her chair and planned to bring it to Annie's in the morning. She had a small amount of green eye shade that she couldn't remember where it came from but thought it would go perfect with the dress. She needed to buy some red lipstick too, maybe it would give her pale face some color. But then again, on second thought, she didn't want to look like a harlot. She had always wanted a long-term relationship. She could have that if she kept her impression on Mark under a watchful eye. She was meticulously beginning to put together in her mind the image she wanted to portray to her newest interest in hopes it would land her among the elite again. She tried desperately not to make the same mistakes that she had made in the past. Her mind was becoming tired as it bounced from one subject to the next.

Movie night had finally arrived, and Elinore was vibrating with anticipation. This time they would see a movie named, "His Trust Fulfilled." Elinore loved the way she looked in her new dress. Annie had to admit, she looked flawless. Iris was proud of herself for putting her hand in it again too. Her makeup was blended perfectly. Her accessories polished her appearance considerably. Elinore was a vision of loveliness. Annie wore a dress that Tom had given her and had put a small wave in her hair with a metal clip she used, but Elinore outshined her. Elinore wanted to be the main attraction that night and dressed the part. Mark had arrived at the movie house first and saw them coming. Elinore immediately caught his eye. She was simply stunning, he thought. Elinore stood in front of him, and their eyes met. He complimented her on the way she looked and was careful to tell Annie the same. Mark was feeling his manliness by having a lovely lady on each arm. He smiled from ear to ear and Elinore took his facial expression as a personal reflection of what his thoughts were about her. Mark didn't know much about Elinore and was just out to have a good time, but he did find her very interesting. The movie lasted much longer than the one they had seen weeks ago. A full 17 minutes this time. Mark sat close to Elinore and after 5 minutes had passed; he placed his arm over Elinore's shoulder. She looked at his hand, dangling there. The light from the movie flickered through the darkened room and she felt the heaviness of his arm shift. His hand swayed with his movement and flowed like a feather over her breast. She was sure he knew but she remained completely still in her seat. Elinore was nervous and didn't know what to do. When the movie ended, Annie asked Mark if he'd like to come back to her house with them. Mark walked between Elinore and Annie and was very chatty. When they finally got to Annie's, she put on some coffee and asked Elinore what she would like to have. She handed Mark a cup filled with coffee when Elinore piped up, "I'd love a nice cup of tea if it's not too much trouble Annie." Elinore stood and asked her friend if she wanted help putting it all together. Annie had not been sure what Elinore's desire would be as to what beverage she would like but she wasn't surprised when she asked for tea. "No, I can get it," Annie answered. "You keep our guest company."

Mark couldn't take his eyes off Elinore and was smitten with her. She giggled at everything he said which made him smile. Their conversation went on for hours and Annie was beginning to feel like a third wheel. When she could take no more of it, she intentionally broke out a deck of cards to switch things up a little. This opened the conversations to the point that it made her feel more included in the night and could be okay with it. But Elinore didn't know much about playing cards and felt foolish. Mark and Annie were eager to teach her and the three enjoyed the games with much more conversation to follow. It was when Annie asked about what Mark did at his job that got to Elinore's core. Mark rambled on about his fire department history. The topic turned to his heroic deeds dotted with the dangers of firefighting. Annie was very intellectual and asked detailed questions which Mark enjoyed answering. Her interest in his work heightened his mood and Elinore keenly noticed. She became sullen, as she sipped on the last of her tea quietly. Annie noticed Elinore's change of mood but chalked it up to her being tired.

Mark didn't want to overstay his welcome and finished his coffee with a large gulp. He said goodbye to Annie and thanked her. He tipped his hat to Elinore as he left. The door closed behind him, and the silence was deafening that followed. Annie could now see that Elinore was upset about something. She waited for her to say something, but she said nothing. Elinore was upset because the evening had ended without her being the center of Mark's attention. Annie worried about the change in Elinore's attitude. She could feel the image of a bullseye of searing heat on her back from the imagined darkened glare that Elinore was sending. Annie wanted desperately to ask what was upsetting her but couldn't. She really didn't know what she had done to upset her in the first place. She hesitated, out of fear to what Elinore's response would be. The unanswered void was killing her. She stood at the sink and washed the last cup. Building up her nerve, Annie took a deep breath and turned around to face Elinore but discovered she had already left the room. She stared at the empty chair with a blank look on her face. Annie had not heard her get up. Where did she go? The water in the sink had covered the sound of Elinore's footsteps.

It was the very first time Annie felt anxious about being alone with her in her own home. Elinore's instability put her on edge. Slowly she made her way down the hall when she saw Elinore already in her nightclothes under her blanket with her eyes closed. Without another word, Annie soft footedly edged her way down the hallway to her room. She wondered about what had happened and hoped Elinore would want to talk about things in the morning. Darkness filled Annie's house that night with the new moon. She tried to be as quiet as she could. She was dreadfully tired, but what Annie had not noticed was that Elinore was not actually asleep and just after she had passed her bed, Elinore's eyes opened to watch her slowly walk down the hallway. There was a lot of chatter going on inside Elinore's head and she was tense. Even mild competition with Mark's affection upset her. She never expected Annie to be a competitor. And her plans with Mark didn't seem to be moving as quickly as she would have liked. She had first met Mark a few months ago and still did not have his undivided attention. She was aware of Erika's opinion that Annie was up to no good and Iris's comments validated her weakness. Even including that she had forgotten to freshen up after the movie. Iris thought she should have at least powdered her nose to cover up all that shine! There was no excuse for a woman to show the perspiration on her face at any time. Before Elinore closed her eyes, she made up her mind that she would march right down to Mark's house in the morning and thank him for teaching her how to play cards. He had told her where he lived during their conversations, and she was going to take advantage of that. That would ensure her another time to meet with him, but this time it would be by herself, and she would make sure she had his full attention, one way or another.

Annie didn't sleep well that night. She had even locked her bedroom door for good measure. Her intuition and gut were telling her something. She was up early that morning and started the stove. By the time Elinore awoke, she could smell sweetness in the air. Annie was making one of Tom's most favorite breakfast meals. Elinore could taste pancakes from where she was, and her stomach grumbled with delight. She had planned to go see Mark as soon as her feet hit the floor but maybe she could make time for this. She entered the kitchen and said, "Something smells delicious!" Annie had piled some on a plate with some berries already and handed it to Elinore. Elinore happily accepted the plate and Annie took the opportunity to speak. She blurted out, "I'm sorry if I upset you in any way last night. I didn't mean to." Elinore brushed it off and said, "It's fine, don't worry about it." Annie was surprised. She had seemed so very upset but now it was as if nothing had ever happened. She was baffled. Elinore was only interested in the pancakes in front of her and sat down to inhale them. Annie laughed, holding a small plate for herself. "Boy, you have a healthy appetite," and pulled the other chair out from under the table which made a small screeching sound as she dragged it over the floorboards to sit down. She told Elinore that it was Tom's favorite breakfast food. Elinore mumbled, "I can see why," but her words came out garbled. Her cheeks puffed out like a squirrel in autumn, packing away acorns with the sweet goodness of Annie's treat. Annie could see by the way Elinore was dressed that she had a plan. Her face was even made up. But Annie did not dare to ask a question. She didn't want a replay of the night before. Elinore quickly finished and washed her plate, placing it in the drainboard. She thanked Annie and rushed to the door. With her hand on the doorknob, she told Annie that she would see her later and, in a flash, she disappeared from Annie's view.

The warm sunlight brushed a rosy glow over Elinore's cheeks as she hurried down the street. She hoped her delay over silly pancakes wouldn't keep her from catching Mark at home. She could feel the skin around her upper body becoming moist. She remembered the small mirror she had in her handbag and checked herself when Mark's house was only a few doors away. Mark's house had a white wooden fence around it. Elinore stood in front of the house with her hand on the gate trying to gain her nerve to bang on his door. She knew he would be surprised. She was nervous and her fingers twitched slightly as she began to slowly open the gate. The next thing that she saw was the gnarling teeth of Mark's large German Shephard aggressively heading straight for her. Elinore slammed the gate closed just as the beast jumped to the top of the fence in attack mode. His nails were sharp, and one made a small tear into her finger. Her eyes widened as the massive, snarling dog barked at her with all his teeth showing angrily. Her presence created a threat to the large animal which made him instinctively defend his property. The animal was fierce. He wanted a piece of Elinore, but she backed away fast.

She was terrified by the dog but within seconds, Mark came out of his house. He commanded the dog to return to the house and ran to Elinore, who was still trembling outside the gate. A transition was taking place with her wide-eyed fear. "I didn't know you would be coming today, Elinore," he said. She looked at him and said, "Yes, I guess I should have told you!" Erika added the dog to the list of things she didn't like. Erika was now present, and Mark was too busy looking over Elinore to see if she was okay to notice the change in her. "You should put a chain on that dog, you know!" Erika reprimanded Mark. There was a sharpness to her voice that told Mark an apology was in order. "He could really hurt someone!" she scolded him. Mark brought Elinore inside his home and excused himself briefly to put his dog in his bathroom. With the dog quarantined, Erika allowed Elinore to come back out to be the focus. Mark could tell Elinore had calmed down and took the opportunity to apologize. The words had barely left his mouth when Elinore asked, "What are you apologizing for?" Mark was confused. He was speechless. Slowly, the words came to him, "The dog he..." Elinore responded as if she had already forgotten what had just happened, although clearly it had and was evident from her bloodied finger. Elinore looked down at her finger, raising her other hand, and said, "Oh that? It's nothing, really, the dog didn't mean it." Elinore then placed her finger against her lips licking the blood away. Mark's head was spinning. Through his mind ran a thought that he had not wanted to admit but couldn't ignore. This girl is beyond beautiful but she's half-baked! He decided to offer her some water and sat down beside her. The two sat like two bumps on a log, not saying much of anything. Mark couldn't think of a thing to say, and Elinore continued to sip on the cool water he had just given to her. Finally, Elinore began to speak. "I came here today to thank you for showing me how to play cards last night. I had a wonderful time." Mark thought back for a second about her, and how she had become so quiet the night before while he sat with her and her friend. Maybe she was just tired. After all, it was very late when he had left, reasoning with himself. "You're welcome, I enjoyed myself as well," he answered her. Something was still bothering him. It was just a gut feeling; she acted so strangely. Now that she had come to his house, he wondered what other reason could there possibly be for her visit except to thank him?

He tossed his thoughts aside and a few more awkward moments followed as Mark tried to think of something to say. He thought maybe he could tell her about the latest fire that he had been to just days before. It was a complicated one which was still under investigation. Mark figured that he couldn't go wrong by talking about himself. He began to tell her that the fire he had fought was an awful one. It was the home of a married couple of which the wife had been known to have some depression. The couple also had a beautiful two-year-old daughter. The wife seemed to have been doing better as was witnessed by neighbors, but in a wicked turn of events, she had shot her husband believing he was having an affair. She had shot the baby in the abdomen and started a fire in the child's bedroom. Then in her unbalanced mental state, shot herself. The fire department was made aware by neighbors when smoke could be seen coming from the house and sadly all of them perished.

As Mark told his story, Elinore sat on the edge of her seat listening intently. Within seconds, Elinore's facial expression had changed yet again. She was crying in a child-like manner. The terror Charlotte had once witnessed was being replayed in her mind. She remembered the man Elinore shot in her mother's bedroom. She remembered the look in the man's eyes. She remembered all the blood. She remembered the deafening sound of the gunfire that took the man's life and all the violence that came with it. She remembered clearly that day she stood behind Elinore, immobilized with fear, silently watching from between her legs. Mark noticed that Elinore's speech pattern also had changed. It was like she was a baby. He pulled Elinore closer to him to comfort her and handed her his handkerchief. Charlotte, the youngest alter, remembered all the details of that horrible day, but they had been buried deep. Mark felt badly for making her cry and in the split second of his effort to console her, Erika squinted her darkened eyes, piercing him. "Why did you have to tell us that story?. That man was evil, and he got what he had coming! I needed to make it safe for us again, some of us are too weak for all of this and I don't care for you to be telling us such awful things!" Erika was angry with Mark for upsetting the system.

Mark was baffled. Confused, he didn't know what to think. He was bewildered by the girl he knew as Elinore sitting next to him, but clearly something else was going on. His eyes lowered to the floor, and he wasn't sure what he should do next. What Elinore had just said made no sense to him. He wondered what his story had to do with what Elinore was talking about, but it seemed to be related in some way. He thought about the man who had been shot whom the firefighter's had tried to save and surely, he hadn't deserved to die. Mark tried hard to make sense of what she had just stated to him but couldn't. It was all so bizarre. He went to the kitchen for another drink of water. He needed that minute to collect his thoughts. He had heard of a type of condition once with a person who had severe mental disease, but it didn't quite fit the description of what he had just witnessed. Unknowingly, Mark had just met two of the personalities who resided within the original personality of Elinore Downing.

Quickly, Mark returned to Elinore holding two more glasses of water. "I thought you would like some more water," he said as he handed her a glassful. Elinore innocently looked up at him and accepted the water from him. "How did you know I was so thirsty?" she asked with a giggle. All traces of the emotional outburst Mark had just watched had vanished. Elinore had returned and she spoke as if nothing had ever occurred at all. It was evident to Mark though that he would need to tread lightly with Elinore from that moment forward. Now, Mark was back to thinking of what else they could talk about without another emotional train wreck. The most neutral thing he could come up with was the chickens he had in a coop behind his house. He had a rooster and three hens. Elinore had a wide grin on her face as he told her the story about how he wound up with the chickens. They were an unexpected gift from a friend whom he had lent some money to. Mark told Elinore that he liked having fresh eggs around and she agreed. She told him about the chickens that her mother kept when she lived in Germany. "They do taste a little different when they are fresh," she added. There was another long pause in their conversation and Elinore decided to seize the moment. She looked at Mark and said, "You know, I really think you're something special." Mark blushed. He was embarrassed and Elinore found his vulnerability charming. She began to twirl her hair around her finger, pulling it over her lip and gently tugging down on her lower lip displaying a pouty illusion. She reached with her other hand to gently knead his bicep. "Your arms are so strong," she whispered. Elinore had his attention just as she had planned. Then Elinore thought it was time for the kill and moved even closer. She soulfully looked into Mark's eyes and whispered again, "Kiss me." Mark was happy to oblige and leaned in for a taste of Elinore's soft wet lips. She closed her eyes and allowed him to linger. She could feel the bristle of the thick stubble on his face although he was mostly clean shaven. "Hummm…that was nice," she said.

Mark didn't want her to leave, even though he considered the preposterous conversation they had just had. Bravely, he said, "So tell me about yourself. Did you ever find a job after the fire at the factory? How old are you? I already know where you live, and it's a beautiful home." He was fishing for a lead into a pleasant conversation. He asked a few more questions, hoping to find out a little more about this beauty by his side. She captivated him, and even if the relationship would turn out to be strictly platonic, he still wished to keep her. He admitted to himself that he could tell she had some experience with men by the way she kissed him.

Elinore continued their conversation, telling Mark that she hadn't worked since the factory had burnt down but that she was going to start looking for a job soon. Elinore asked Mark if he knew of any place that might be looking for help. Mark didn't know of any offhand, but he would be on the lookout for her. That made Elinore happy. After some more small talk, each found difficulty in another subject. It was only the middle of the day, but Elinore made up an excuse that she needed to stop to pick up some things for the evening meal with her aunt. She knew that was a lie because she had planned to return to Annie's but her plan included leaving him with persistent thoughts of herself. Mark walked her to the door, but before she left, she made sure to sneak in another small peck to Mark's cheek. Conjuring up her most sultry voice, she whispered, "Goodbye, my love." And with the smallest feminine flutter of her hand, she bid him farewell. It was time to make her exit. It was her favorite time, the grand finale! She simply walked down his steps and out through the gate. Elinore could feel the weight of his stare on her lower extremities. She added an extra twitch to each step, knowing full well, this last look of her leaving would place her right where she wanted to be. In his ever-constant thoughts. She couldn't help but grin a wicked smile as she unlatched the gate. She knew she had him in her web and he'd be coming around to see her again soon.

Elinore was happy with herself as she made her way back to Annie's house. She was beginning to think fondly of Mark and wanted him for herself. He was so different from John. So much braver. And so much younger. His strength was a magnet to her. She found her pace picking up on the way, when she noticed the tiniest sign in the apothecary's window that drew her attention immediately. It was hardly noticeable, but to Elinore's surprise the lady inside who had been so nice to her in the past, needed help. Elinore was excited and wondered about the details. She remembered how she had lost a job once that she really wanted back in her homeland, making produce deliveries because she waited too long for an answer from the shopkeeper. This time she would not make that same mistake. She pounced on the opportunity and entered the store. A petite woman inside the store worked furiously, buzzing around with a feather duster in hand. The wooden floorboards made noise as she scampered over each of them. She smiled at Elinore, recognizing her immediately as she entered. "You know, I don't know how all this dust gets in here. It's so pesky!" she said with a laugh.

"How can I help you dear?" she asked. Elinore smiled back at the nice lady and said, "Maybe it is I who can help you this time." She laughed thinking about her clever answer. "I saw your sign in the window. Are you still looking for help?" she asked. "Why yes, I am!" the woman quickly responded. Placing her index finger on the corner of her mouth, "Funny, I only just put that sign up ten minutes ago. I'm in desperate need for some help with stocking my shelves, do you have any experience?" she asked. Elinore looked down, quickly thinking of what to say next. She had no prior experience working in a store but believed it couldn't be worse than taking orders from Elsie in the kitchen. Elinore really wanted this job. She looked up with a refreshed enthusiasm and replied, "No, but I learn fast and I'm sure you will be pleased with me!" Elinore stood proudly in front of the woman and sure enough, she had made a good impression. "Okay dear, you can start Monday. This store is open from 9am to 5pm, Monday through Friday, and you will do the stocking during that time." Then she added, "I can pay you 30 cents an hour, but sometimes, if it's slow, I close early." Elinore began adding it up in her mind. She would only be earning $15.00 for the week if she worked the full day, every day. Elinore wondered if the woman would still pay her if she decided to close early and as she began to ask, the woman interrupted. "By the way, my name is Gretchen, and yes I will still pay you if I send you home early." She said with a grin. Elinore thought it was like she was reading her mind and immediately knew this was going to be a nice place to work. It seemed to Elinore that Gretchen had an uncanny sense with her and that made her happy. Gretchen could see that Elinore was a smart young woman and that was just what she was looking for. Elinore shook her hand and paused. Gretchen looked inquisitively at her. "Is there something else dear?" Elinore smiled a wide grin again and said, "Gretchen is a German name. Are you German?" "Yes, I am," Gretchen returned. "Oh, I love that name!" Elinore told her. "I am German too!" Elinore added. Her eyes lit up and she felt a kinship develop inside herself. Elinore wondered if she spoke fluent German as well. She was sure to find out soon enough.

"See you Monday!" Gretchen shouted to Elinore. She breathed a sigh of relief with the knowledge that she would now have some help with her workload. It was getting busier every day and Gretchen was finding it hard to keep up. Elinore left the store excited and ran to Annie's house to tell her all about it. Annie was glad to hear Elinore had gotten a job. She thought it would be good for her. She had been watching Elinore closely as she continued to buy things on a whim but had no job. Annie knew Elinore was not good at managing a budget and this job came at a perfect time. The green dress Elinore had bought to wear to the movie house must have cost her a pretty penny and Annie took notice that Elinore didn't bat an eyelash about it. Annie was thrifty and didn't always agree with the way Elinore would spend her money so carelessly. But it wasn't her money, so there was nothing she could say. Elinore continued into that evening working Mark into every conversation that Annie and she had, wherever she could fit it in. Annie was starting to like the idea that Elinore would be going back to work. It would give her poor ears a break! Elinore also had a request for Annie. Unexpectedly, she asked if they could invite Mark over for dinner soon, before they turned in. She made sure to tell Annie what he had said about enjoying himself whilst they played their game of cards. It was not a big deal to Annie. Annie told her that she would enjoy having him and headed off to bed before Elinore could ask for another thing.

Elinore rose refreshed from her sleep. She was happy still with the knowledge that she was about to begin working again. She went to her Aunt Agnes's house to tell her the good news. Agnes was happy at the news too until Elinore informed her how much less she would be earning. Agnes looked over the top of her glasses and sternly said, "You are going to have to be more careful about your spending habits now, you know." Elinore had seen that look before and didn't like being told what to do. She shrugged her shoulders and assured her aunt it would all be okay and that she would still receive the money that she had always given her. Then Agnes asked, "So what about this young man who came here to see you a few weeks ago? My neighbor saw the two of you talking for hours outside." Elinore didn't realize she was being watched but was more than happy at the opportunity to talk about Mark again. "He's a firefighter and we've been trying to get to know each other but it's nothing serious," she said nonchalantly. She liked to keep things private about herself but found it hard when it came to the subject of Mark. Her answer was a far cry from her true feelings about Mark, but she was not ready to spill the beans altogether about him yet. It angered Elinore that her aunt's neighbors were so nosy, and she would need to be more careful in the future. Elinore hated people butting into her business! She liked being in control of what she wanted to tell people and to who. This time she would be apathetic about the subject though; not wanting to tip her hand. Elinore now wanted to lose her aunt's interest in the subject. She knew how to do that.

She changed the subject and asked the question that she knew would make her aunt forget all about things. "What would you like for our evening meal Aunt Agnes?" Agnes played right into Elinore's hand like a fiddle. She began to lick her plump lips, making them look wet and sticky. It disgusted Elinore, but she had become a master at manipulating people, and she had accomplished exactly that with the mere mention of food. "Soup with biscuits and cheese sounds excellent! What do you think, Aunt Agnes?" Elinore asked even though she knew what the answer would be. Elinore's eyebrows were raised with her question, and it was only seconds before her aunt responded. Again, she began to lick her lips. Elinore moved to the stove to avoid any further eye contact with her aunt. She was tired and just wanted to get the meal over with so that she could get some rest. She knew once the food was placed on the table, it would be devoured quickly, and she would be able to get comfortable in her own bed shortly after.

Soon, Elinore was hiking the mountain of stairs to her room as she had wanted to do from the moment she had walked through the door. Finally, she could get some rest. She wasted no time in turning her bed down and free-falling backwards into it. Elinore's eyes were fixed on a small imperfection in the ceiling. Her thoughts went back to a time when things were so much simpler. She wondered what her parents and sisters were doing at that moment. It seemed that they had forgotten her altogether. For that matter, in the entire time she had been in America she had only received two letters from them and only one from Carl. No one in Elinore's life thus far had been able to fill Carl's shoes completely. Her heart yearned to be near him again. Only John had come remotely close, but in the end, there was no comparison at all. Carl's love was honest and pure. Elinore wished she could have it back sorely but knew that wasn't likely to happen. She missed Carl. Her thoughts bounced back to Mark again. It was surely a different feeling with Mark for her. He was strong and handsome, but he didn't make her tingle inside, the way Carl did. Mark was just another conquest for Elinore, but a fine one for now. In time, maybe it could develop into more but only time would tell. For now, she would carry on a relationship with him and call him her own but also, at the same time, be in control of what she wanted to contribute to it. It certainly wasn't quite the same feeling. Elinore loved the idea of having a suitor tied around her little finger. She had mastered that even as a small child. There would never be a man in Elinore's life that could match her father, Hans or Carl. Elinore was convinced of that. She continued to think about Mark and her head ached as thoughts of him circled her mind. She rubbed her eyes with her thumb and index finger, squeezing them hard. There were disagreements going on inside Elinore's mind about exactly how to claim Mark and mold him into the exciting journey that Elinore craved.

Erika didn't much care for Mark but acknowledged that he was a much better choice than John. But Mark brought a lot of stress with him, and he had upset Charlotte too. Charlotte had the most powerful words of all the curse words in the world for him. She made it clear to everyone that she thought he was a poopy head. Charlotte had declared the next time he made her cry she would bite him! Iris disagreed with Charlotte. She liked Mark and the way he detailed his home. She especially liked a small plaque she noticed that hung on his bathroom door that said, "When I am called to duty, God, wherever flames rage, give me the strength to save a life, whatever be its age." Iris was smart though and realized she should be careful with her opinion. She dared not let it be known, especially to Erika, how she felt. Erika didn't like it when anyone disagreed with her. The repercussions could have grave consequences. Erika often said that she would kill any alter that would interfere with her judgement. Erika struck fear throughout the system in order to maintain the lifestyle they all wanted, simultaneously keeping the many other alters dormant. She didn't like being challenged at all and was in control most of the time even if another alter was out. In fact, there were alters that Erika had frightened in the past that had not been seen in years. Those had chosen to remain permanently dormant, letting time tell if they would ever appear again. Iris stayed soft spoken instead of having to deal with Erika's wrath.

Elinore woke bright and early that following Monday morning. She was to start her new job and was excited. She dressed in her regular work clothing and laced up her leather boots. Walking briskly, she noticed a different feeling and appearance on the people's faces who passed her in the street. Their faces all seemed to look weathered and grim. It was a glorious day and Elinore couldn't understand it. When she arrived at work, Gretchen was already there and placing the local paper in a pile near the door on a small metal crate. The paper had a picture of a huge vessel named the Titanic on the front page. It had sunk during the night! Operated by White Star Line, it was claimed to be unsinkable, but it had indeed sunk on its maiden voyage after hitting an iceberg. It took with it some 1500 people who perished in the frigid waters off the Atlantic Ocean. April 15th, 1912, had started out to be a lucky day for Elinore, but not so lucky for those poor people on that ship. Saddened by the news, Elinore and Gretchen looked over the long list of names of the people who were unaccounted for. Many of them were very wealthy, John Jacob Astor, and his wife. Benjamin Guggenheim, Macy's Department Store owner, former House of Representatives, Isidor Straus and his wife Ida, were among the people at the top of the list of missing. The price of a first-class ticket was $2,560 dollars, but Elinore thought even though it was a lot of money, it wasn't worth a person's life. The price of the second-class tickets was said to be $60, and the third-class tickets were between $15 and $40.

Elinore began to think about how cold and frightened the people must have been. In one moment of time, being so vibrantly alive switched to having unexpectedly be forced to confront death. Love, fear, hope, despair, bravery and cowardice, selfishness and brotherhood being felt all at once, by those aboard the doomed ship. The sheer madness must have been horrific. The paper reported the ocean temperature was a mere 28 degrees and it was said a person could succumb to those temperatures in as little as 15 minutes. Only one man escaped miraculously by swimming for hours. His name was listed as Charles Joughin. He was a baker who worked on board the massive vessel. Elinore could feel panic arising inside herself. That ice water must have felt like a thousand knives being plunged into the bodies of those that hit the water. Suddenly a flash of when she herself had fallen through the ice as a child. She remembered the pain as the ice scraped against her legs when Hans dragged her to safety with a rope. Gretchen took the paper from Elinore's trembling hand and placed it back on the pile. "Come on dear, we have work to do," she said. Gretchen could see that Elinore was a sensitive young lady and that she was deeply affected by the news.

Gretchen tried to make her think of something else by putting her to work. Elinore's first task was to work with the sections including liniments and salves. This section of the store often became quite messy, being the first that most of the patrons visited. Gretchen was overwhelmed by all the things that needed to be done and was happy that Elinore had come to help her. Next on the list Gretchen needed from her was to put away all the soaps that had just arrived, into the wooden drawers that each of the different fragrances belonged to. Each drawer had the name of the type of soap stored in it on a little slip of paper secured just under the handle. Elinore couldn't believe how many different scents of soap existed. Gretchen had task after task for Elinore, but she didn't seem to mind. She liked the work until Gretchen asked her to place the leeches into the great white tank that looked much like a gigantic tea pot, where they were stored. Elinore thought they were disgusting and didn't like that task one bit. She made an awful face as she picked up each one of them and Gretchen had to laugh. Elinore had not realized how busy she would be there and was tired after only the first two hours. She pushed herself to keep the pace, putting away the chalk for heartburn and the chinchona bark for fever. She placed the calamine inside small bottles and marked the price on each, just as Gretchen had asked her to. A few people had come in inquiring if surgical procedures were available there, but Gretchen did not do that, which Elinore was grateful for. Before she knew it the day was over, and it was closing time. Elinore was exhausted right down to her little toe.

Gretchen laughed and told her to get a good night's rest because there was a lot more to do the next day too. "Good Lord!" Elinore said faintly smiling and wiped her brow. "See you tomorrow," she said as she left before Gretchen could change her mind. Elinore made it to Annie's and collapsed in her chair in the kitchen. Annie had made some chicken soup and it smelled delicious to Elinore. Annie asked her if she wanted some and she gladly accepted the offer. Annie ladled out a bowl for Elinore and herself. She cut off two thick slices of bread that she had made that afternoon and put a thin layer of butter on each. Annie placed the meal in front of Elinore, and she inhaled the steam deeply into her lungs. "This soup smells delicious!" Elinore exclaimed. Immediately, she picked up the spoon beside her bowl and took a spoonful. Her mouth watered as she blew on it to cool it slightly. She dunked the bread into the soup and before she knew it, her bowl was empty. Annie suggested after looking at Elinore's appearance that it might be a good idea for her to get an early start on hitting the hay. Annie had never seen her looking so frumpy. Elinore agreed with her and at only 8 o'clock, she was sound asleep.

Annie took that opportunity to wash the dishes and read the paper that Elinore had brought home with her. She read the article about the Titanic and felt sad for the people involved. There were many children listed among the dead and Annie shook her head in disbelief. Soon after, Annie headed off to bed too, but she couldn't fall asleep that night. All the lives lost that she had read about turned her thoughts to her beloved Tom. Tears fell from her eyes and her heart still ached. She kept his nightrobe on the bed beside her and could smell him on it when she clutched it tightly against her face. His picture, she kept on her nightstand and kissed it each night before bed. Annie never had imagined that her life would end up like this. She flipped her pillow. It had become completely wet from her tears. Eventually, Annie did fall asleep but when the morning came, she still sorely missed Tom.

Elinore had a quick cup of tea and a small bowl of oatmeal before she flew out of the door. She was anxious about all the work that needed to be done at the store that Gretchen had warned her of. On this day Gretchen had Elinore work with the medicinal plants and botanicals. Elinore learned a lot about plants that day. She wondered how Gretchen had learned so much about the use of leaves, flowers and stems of certain plants. She questioned Gretchen as to how she knew so much about plants and Gretchen explained that she had studied with some Indigenous people for some time and spent much time in the forest learning. It was nearly lunchtime when Mark entered the store. Elinore was happy to see him. She introduced him to Gretchen as her boyfriend, which surprised Mark. Elinore and Mark left the store to get a bite to eat and Mark took the time to ask Elinore if she meant what she had said. "Of course, I meant it!" Elinore affirmed. "Don't you want to be my boyfriend?" she asked.

"Well… sure, okay," Mark answered. Elinore looked at him with the sweetest smile and reached for his hand. Clutching tightly, she announced, "Then it's official!" She kissed him on his cheek leaving a faint touch of lipstick there. Lunchtime ended in a short amount of time, and Elinore needed to return to the store. Mark stole another kiss from her before she left and as he made his way home, he realized he had forgotten to buy what he had gone there for in the first place. He was also concluding that Elinore was full of surprises. Just as he reached for the door to his house, he could hear the fire bell clanging loudly. Mark abruptly changed plans and rushed to the firehouse without entering his home for a second.

Elinore ended her second day at the store and was already looking forward to Friday. She didn't feel as tired as the day before and figured it was just something she would need to adjust to. Annie had kindly emptied out a dresser at her house weeks before so that Elinore could put some of her own clothing in it. Since her energy level was up, she decided to visit with her aunt and at the same time, gather some of her clothes to keep at Annie's. After all, she was spending a lot of time there. Surprisingly, Agnes was not there so Elinore gathered her clothing to make a quick getaway. She didn't want to be at the end of Agnes questioning about the mound of clothing in her hands. She hustled through the street carrying her large hemp bag. With all her extra energy now spent, she crashed through Annie's door and set the heavy bag on the floor with a thud. Annie barely looked up, so Elinore started to explain what she had in the bag.

Annie's mind was on other things. She was thinking about the final conversations she had with Tom and the fact that they had never had any children. She looked at her wedding ring that she had not taken off since he had passed, and Elinore knew Annie was becoming depressed about missing him so badly. She hated Ben for that, but he had gotten his deserved fate for what he had done. Elinore told Annie that she would put her clothing away shortly and she would be right back. Elinore had decided that she would make a nice meal for the two of them. She rushed to the market to buy some knockwurst and onions. She also bought some potatoes and vinegar to make a salad. What could be a better way to make someone feel better than to fill their belly with good food, she thought. She ran back to Annie's carrying the two paper sacks in her arms. Soon the delicious smells were reaching Annie's nostrils. Elinore's thoughts were undeniably correct. Annie was now thinking about the simmering onions in the pan and how nice it was going to taste on her tongue.

Annie did the dishes afterward while Elinore put her clothing away. It was then when Elinore noticed she had forgotten to bring her socks. She would have to borrow a pair for tomorrow from Annie but after work she would need to go back to her aunt's house for a few pairs. In the blink of an eye, it was closing time on Friday and Gretchen was giving Elinore her pay. She hustled back to her Aunt Agnes's home to give her the money she expected. And as she had already imagined, Agnes was indeed seated in the kitchen waiting for her. Elinore laughed as she thought about placing a whoopie cushion on her chair the next time she got up. It was of no surprise to Elinore that she was there. She was always there in that same chair. Elinore began to operate in a mindless way. She grabbed the pans and put them on the stove, tossed the meat from the icebox into the pan. The raw meat hit the cast iron with a thud. She peeled and sliced the potatoes and served up a meal. Then it was time to watch the show. Her ill-mannered aunt inhaled the food barely taking time to breathe. It wasn't long before Agnes had finished every morsel on her plate. Elinore reached to take her plate, but before she did, she handed her the weekly stipend she was expecting. Agnes smiled and snatched the money from Elinore's hand. "Thank you," Agnes said quietly as she left the room picking her teeth with her fingernail.

Elinore washed the dishes in the sink and went to her room. She sat on the bed looking down at her feet and the floorboards beneath her. It began to cross her mind that she really didn't like staying at her aunt's anymore, but she couldn't be sure she would like to be at Annie's all the time either. It was the first time Elinore had thought about finding a place to live by herself. That thought was fleeting when she came back to the memory that she still had not brought socks to Annie's for herself. She had a paper bag on the shelf in her closet and began to look through her socks to decide which ones she would take with her. The ones without holes would do quite nicely, she thought. She began to push them from side to side in the basket. Instantly, she could feel something that was certainly not a sock! Digging to the bottom of the basket, she found her pearl handled small pistol. Elinore remembered the day Carl had bought it for her but couldn't remember how it got into her sock basket. Or how did it get to her aunt's? She turned the basket over onto the floor and some of the bullets for the gun rolled across the floor. Quickly, Elinore got up and rushed to the door to make sure it was locked. She began to count the bullets in her hand. She held eight when she saw the small silver tin under the rest of the socks. Inside the tin, were sixteen more bullets. Elinore placed all the bullets back into the tin and secured it tightly. Elinore decided that it would be safer to take it with her to Annie's. It wasn't safe to leave them where they were. She wasn't there enough to keep her eye on them, and Annie would never snoop through her things. Elinore hid the gun and the tin, deep in the bag and covered them over with her socks. Then, she remembered her billhook. She took it from her apron in the closet where she had hidden it and placed it in the bag too. In the morning she would take them to Annie's to hide there. With all of that taken care of, Elinore rested more comfortably. Besides, she had better things to think about. Where would she and Annie go next was at the top of her list. Elinore was ready to have some more fun. Elinore was bored with having to work every day and was hoping either Annie or Mark could change that for her.

Mark especially could change her whole way of life under the right circumstances. Elinore realized just how much she loved John after he died. She knew Erika hated him. For a moment, she wished things could have been different but then Elinore's thoughts returned to Mark. She was obsessed with Mark and trying to figure out a way to make their relationship turn more serious. Elinore's thoughts flashed from one thing to the next exhausting herself into a deep slumber that night.

Night turned to daylight, and the birds in the chimney chirped joyously. Elinore woke early with the noise. She crawled out from under the blanket and saw that she hadn't even changed her clothes from the night before. She brushed her hair and was thankful it was Saturday because she didn't have to go to work. Not having to get dressed did save her some time getting to Annie's in time for breakfast too. That was a pleasing thought for Elinore. She enjoyed Tom's favorite pancakes very much. She grabbed the bag containing her socks and was off like the wind. But when she finally got to Annie's she was disappointed. She smelled nothing. The pans were cold with no sweetness in the air whatsoever. Elinore called out Annie's name. She could hear a faint reply from somewhere inside the house. Elinore followed the sound of Annie's voice, and it led her to the bedroom where she slept. Elinore looked inside the room not knowing what to expect. In the corner of the room there was a large grapevine basket, and it was overflowing with the sheets off both their beds. Today was wash day for Annie. "Won't it be nice to have some clean fresh sheets on your bed?" Annie asked but didn't really expect a reply. She picked up the heavy basket with a grunt. Elinore followed her to the kitchen where she began to place the sheets inside the tub of the washing machine that Tom had bought for her right before he had gotten sick. It was a wooden machine with a long metal handle to agitate the clothing in the wash pot. It had an adjustable wringer on the opposite side and Annie said she loved that machine every time she used it. In the small yard outside, there was a line where she hung the clothes to dry. Annie loved the smell of clean laundry once it was dry.

Elinore didn't like the scratchy sheets after they were hung out. Now it would take her a week to soften them up, but it was Annie's house. Elinore thought it was best to keep her comments to herself. She could hear Iris suggesting putting some talc on those sheets after Annie was done, but Elinore ignored her which made Iris mad. Elinore could hear Iris having a bit of a fit over being ignored but didn't care. She howled at Elinore, "You never listen to me!" Elinore had become aware that there were others living inside herself by now, but she liked being the one who everyone saw. After all, it was her body. But it was Erika who controlled most things. Elinore resented Erika at times however, she did what she needed to do to keep the peace and Erika was pretty good at what she did, she had to admit. It really was best for the system. Erika was a fierce warrior.

Annie was almost finished with the laundry and squeezed the water from the linens into the cedar basin. She began to tell Elinore about something she had overheard in town. There was a new movie out. It was called "The Keystone Cops." It was supposed to be a series of comical movies and it was soon to be released. Elinore was always up for a movie and was excited at the news. She had also heard about an invention called an electric blanket. Inventor Samuel Russell claimed it heated a bed better than the bed warmers people would pass over their sheets at night. Annie thought it would be nice to have electricity in the house but knew it could be very costly. A lively conversation between the two was taking place when there was a knock at the door. She wasn't expecting anyone and looked curiously at Elinore. Elinore held her hands up and shrugged her shoulders. Elinore left the room and Annie opened the door to find Mark standing there holding a box. "Is Elinore here?" he asked Annie. Annie held her finger to her lips, "One minute," she said. Annie let him in and closed the door behind him. She went looking for Elinore in the back room where they had just been. "Elinore, Mark is here to see you, and he's holding a box with a pretty gold ribbon on it."

Elinore's eyes gleamed with excitement. "Really? I wonder what he brought for me?" Elinore squealed with delight. She placed her hands on her cheeks and was barely able to hold her excitement in. She rushed to the kitchen to see Mark standing there. He was indeed holding a beautiful package with a sparkling golden bow! Elinore rushed to him and kissed him on the mouth. "Is that for me?" she asked. Her heart was beating fast, and she couldn't imagine what was inside the exquisite parcel he was holding out to her. Iris was thrilled and reached to receive the gift. The gold ribbon was shiny, and it glittered. Her eyes were wide, and she thought this must be something special. Iris pulled at the ribbon, being careful not to knot it and opened the box. Inside were luscious Belgium praline chocolates. She was speechless. She looked at Mark, knowing how expensive they must have been. Mark smiled and said, "Have one." Iris couldn't decide which one to eat first. She looked them over and chose the one with the nuts on it. Iris popped it right into her mouth and closed her eyes. "Oh, this is so good!" Soon, she had her hand in the box again, this time taking the one with caramel on it. Iris rubbed her stomach and smiled big. She thought quickly that this chocolate was much better than any of the other chocolate bars Elinore's father,

Porter, had ever brought home. "Would you like a piece?" Iris asked Mark. Mark just shook his head and told her that they were all for her.

Just then, Annie came into the kitchen and saw Elinore with her cheeks filled with sweet delicacies. Annie wanted to laugh, but she reminded Elinore it was very close to mealtime, and she better take it easy, or she'll ruin her appetite. Annie noticed the shift in Elinore's personality, and she was pretty sure it wasn't Elinore who was indulging herself. Iris put the lid on the box and presented a small pout. She placed the box on the sideboard in the kitchen and sat down at the table where Mark was seated now too. Iris was disappointed that she didn't get to have one more piece and looked down at the floor. A few minutes passed while Mark talked with Annie about how the prices of food were going up when Elinore interrupted. "I'm sorry Mark, I never said thank you for the chocolates you gave us." "Thank you for them!" she said. Mark smiled and asked if she had enjoyed them. "We did, oh yes!" she responded. Mark had not noticed how Elinore spoke in the third person at times. Annie, however, was noticing it more and more. Annie suspected that Elinore had as many as three different personalities and possibly more. She only knew of one positively that seemed typically angry, but each had specific traits that she could put her finger on. Most seemed gentle and kind, but there was that one that she was wary of. That one could seem dangerous, and Annie kept a watchful eye out for it.

Annie was just about to ask Mark if he would like to join them for dinner when the bell at the firehouse began to ring. Annie didn't live far from the firehouse and the bell was easy to hear. Mark stood up and excused himself in a hurry. He explained that he would try to stop by later if he could and in a flash, he was gone. Elinore didn't want Mark to leave. He had just gotten there. She started to think of ways she could capture him for a longer length of time when Annie asked what she would like to have for their evening meal. Elinore had a hankering for spaetzle and Wiener schnitzel and told her so. Annie let out a hardy laugh. "Veiner what?" she asked. "You're going to have to show me how to make that!" she said. Elinore laughed too. She told her it was as easy as pie and began to prepare the breadcrumbs. Annie paid close attention and once Elinore was done, she covered the meal in a flavorful mushroom sauce. Annie found the meal so enjoyable. Just the fragrance in the room made her stomach grumble. Annie had never had this dish but was more than willing to try it. She raised her fork to her lips and took a dainty first bite of the meal. It didn't take long before the meal had disappeared from their plates when Annie finally said, "My word, that was delightful!" Elinore was pleased that Annie had liked what she made and was proud of herself too for it.

Sleep came nicely for Elinore, but she woke in a pool of sweat. It was already warm, and she took extra care in washing up. She dressed herself nicely in her lightest cotton work dress. The walk to work was much shorter from Annie's than it was from her aunts. Gretchen was already working hard when Elinore arrived, and she put her to work right away. A woman had come in first thing as Gretchen opened the door looking for a cast iron pan. She tore through all the pots and pans that Gretchen had displayed throughout the store looking for the perfect one. When she finally found the one that suited her the store was a mess! Gretchen was in a bad mood for good reason. Elinore saw the mess and started placing the pans back on the hooks where they belonged. Gretchen was glad Elinore needed little direction. She seemed to know exactly what to do with a keen sense of priority. Gretchen was happy that she had hired Elinore and together they worked as a great team making the workload easier. It wasn't busy that day and they both had the store in ship-shape condition in a few hours.

Gretchen wanted to close early. It was Monday and typically slow most times. After lunchtime passed, she told Elinore what she wanted to do and complimented her on how much she appreciated having her as an employee. Gretchen also knew that nothing speaks louder than money and decided to give her a 5 cent raise too. Elinore was surprised and shook Gretchen's hand firmly in thanks. Elinore already made plans as to where she would go after leaving work.

She would go to Mark's and surprise him! This time though, she would stop at the market and purchase a bit of dried meat for Marks dog. Maybe she could make friends with the pooch even though she didn't like him much. On her way, she noticed that the sky had become very gray, so she hurried her way along picking up her pace. Getting caught in the rain in her white linen work dress was not what she had in mind. She hadn't brought a sweater with her, but wished she had when she felt the first drops of rain hit her face. There were only a few more blocks to go but a pending harsh storm was imminent and those few blocks seemed more like miles now. Clutching the bag for the dog closely, Elinore picked up her pace even more. She was all but running. She was only half the way there and now she was breathless. She wanted desperately to see Mark. She was looking forward to seeing him again. The rain that had started to fall soaked her dress which was now clinging to her skin. Elinore was becoming embarrassed as she raced toward Mark's home. She realized her dress was becoming transparent when she was only a few feet away. The weather had changed so fast, quite unexpectedly. The clouds had opened, and the rain was falling at a steady pace. Elinore's golden hair was drenched and dripping from every strand. She could taste the salt from her skin on the droplets that ran down her face, crossing her lips and landing on her tongue. She tried in vain to stop her thin dress from clinging to her, but with her every pull the dress attached itself to another part of her body, like a layer of new skin. Elinore was angry with herself for not at least wearing a hat that day. She looked dreadful.

She was just about there with only a few more steps to go when a crashing boom lit the sky. Her entire body stopped cold. She felt an excruciating pain and saw a great white light surrounding herself. Everything seemed to be in slow motion suddenly. The hair on the back of her neck stood up and so did the hair on her arms. Her ears were ringing, and she couldn't move. There was a tingling sensation throughout her body, especially in her arms and legs. She could smell something burnt. Elinore began to panic. She screamed for Mark, but no sound came from her mouth. The tree next to where she stood had split in half and partially lay across the ground almost touching her feet. Elinore felt very warm and deep dark roundish spots began to appear on her forearms and fingertips. Feeling confused, she tried again to call out to Mark but the words in her head were jumbled.

Mark had heard the crash from inside his home and opened the door to see what had happened. The tree in front of his neighbor's house was laying across the sidewalk. At the edges of the branches his eyes focused on someone lying on the ground. Mark's adrenaline pumped through his veins, and he sprang into action. Mark ran down his steps and flew out of the gate to the woman in distress. She was lying among the leaves of the fallen tree and injured. Buster, Mark's dog, was right behind him. He quickly kneeled down next to her, and his eyes opened wide. He found himself staring into familiar eyes he had already known. He was shocked when he realized it was Elinore. A burnt smell was noticeable to him. From her clothing, a small amount of smoke was visible. Buster licked her face and sensed the urgency of the moment. Buster circled Mark as he picked her up. He assured her that she would be okay but wasn't sure if that was the truth at all. Buster didn't miss the bag that Elinore had been carrying. He picked it up and followed Mark inside. He put Elinore down on his bed and began to look her over. Her clothing looked as if she had been blasted by a cannonball and it was burnt. He began to remove the pieces carefully from her body. Much of her clothing was already missing. Mark noticed a burn mark on her right arm that looked like leafy plant matter. But it was etched into her skin. At the crease of her elbow were a few blisters. Mark covered her with a blanket and sat quietly beside her. He stroked her hair and smiled at her. He knew it was important to reassure her that everything would be fine.

A few hours had passed when Elinore thought she would be able to sit up. She was confused as to what had happened. Mark listened to Elinore as she struggled to put her words together. Mark brushed her hair back from her face tenderly with his hand and spoke softly, "Elinore, I think you were struck by lightning." Elinore looked at his lips as he spoke, but she had trouble hearing him. Her ears were still ringing. Mark leaned in to kiss her forehead and she felt comforted by it, but also felt very vulnerable being only covered by the blanket she was under. Mark gave her some water and told her that he would go to Annie's to get some of her clothing. Buster had found the treats in the bag and was lying at the foot of the bed gnawing on them. Mark smiled at Elinore and said, "And by the way, Buster says thank you for the treats," pointing to the shredded bits of the bag that were scattered across the floor. Mark was only gone a few minutes and returned holding a couple of dresses and a few other things Annie had given him.

Annie was worried upon hearing the news about Elinore. She had asked Mark if there was anything she could do, but Mark declined her offer, telling her that he would take care of her himself. Annie thought maybe Elinore's aunt should be informed of what had happened and offered to be a messenger for her. Elinore was grateful for Mark's help and asked if he could stop by the store to tell Gretchen what had happened to her. Elinore hoped that Gretchen would understand. She had only been working there for just a few weeks and would need a few days off already. Mark assured her again that he would handle everything for her, and she could rest easily. He had only left her again briefly to return holding a cup of tea and a sliced apple to find Elinore fast asleep. He sat down on the small chair that he usually laid his clothes upon and was careful not to make any noise to wake her. He looked closely at Elinore. She looked so peaceful to him. He continued to watch her, and he fantasized about her. She was so beautiful. Elinore's chest gently lifted with each breath she took, and Mark started to feel a warm compassion for her within himself. Mark moved the chair closer to the bed. He studied Elinore's face. Her eyes moved rapidly under her closed lids. Her arms twitched occasionally.

Mark allowed her to continue to sleep and set the tea on the small table next to the bed. Elinore began to move back and forth, reacting to a dream. Mark leaned over her closer to look at the small creases around her eyes when one of her arms hurled into the air, violently hitting him on the side of his head.

The tea and apples crashed to the floor. Elinore woke at the impact and found a startled Mark looking back at her inches from her face. Elinore was alarmed. Her dream had continued the replay even further of what had just taken place. She latched onto Mark. Tears flowed from her eyes. She sobbed, soaking his shoulder. Mark held her body close to his and could feel her bare chest against his. He knew he shouldn't feel the way he was, but it had been a long time since he had been with a woman. Each time he tried to lay her back down on the bed to rest, she clung tighter to him resisting his efforts. Throughout the night he stood watch over her and when morning came, he decided that enough time had passed that he could draw Elinore a tepid bath. She still had much debris on her from the fallen tree. He was exhausted from staying up all night, watching her closely, but knew she would want to bathe before putting her fresh clothing on. He mixed a bath of water and soap to the perfect temperature. Mark knew a lot about burns from helping many people through fires.

The ringing had finally stopped in Elinore's ears, and she could hear his voice calling her out of her deep sleep. "How are you feeling this morning?" Mark asked. Elinore smiled and answered with one word, "Okay." Mark told her that he had drawn her a bath and gathered the blanket around her, draping it over her shoulders. Elinore put her feet on the floor and prepared herself to get up. She could feel her legs shaking and wobbled her way to the bathroom. She closed the door softly and dipped her hand into the warm water. Hanging on the back of the door was her dress with clean socks and knickers. Elinore balanced herself on the fresh towel Mark had left next to the tub and stepped into the water. The water swirled around her as she lowered herself into it. It felt good to her, and she sighed at the gentle relief. She smelled the small piece of soap in the dish at the tub's edge. It wasn't a typically feminine fragrance, but it was nice enough. She soaped up the washcloth and rubbed it over her body. Her burns had become very noticeable to her and were sensitive to the touch. In fact, one of her arms looked as if someone had stamped a picture of a fern leaf on it, but it was burnt into her skin. She tried to rub it off with the washcloth, but it remained. It was so peculiar, she thought. The round coin-shaped burns were the ones that hurt the most. They were the most sensitive. Elinore avoided touching them. When the water was cold, Elinore stood to remove herself from the tub. Watching the water drip off herself. A cold chill from the air made her tremble. She clutched at the towel that Mark had left for her and held it in a ball under her chin, against her chest. Elinore was still fragile, and she began to panic. All ordinary thoughts had left her. Elinore was frightened out of her mind, and she shrieked out to Mark. "Mark!" she cried. An intense wave of fear was taking over within her. It seemed to immobilize her to the point where she couldn't lift her leg over the side of the tub. Her heart raced and she found it difficult to breathe. She could hear Erika inside her inner self. This time, she seemed to be trying to reason with her. Erika wasn't in a rush to come out. This wasn't like Erika, which made Elinore's panic attack more severe. There was no clear trigger for her emotions and Elinore was in no danger.

Mark was making some toast and coffee when he heard Elinore's cries. Mark ran to the bathroom and opened the door. Elinore stood there in the empty tub trembling. She was overwhelmed with fear. She reached out to Mark and fell into his arms. Elinore was slippery and still wet, but Mark held onto her tightly and brought her back to the bed. She continued to lie just where Mark had placed her; not moving at all. He quickly went to the bathroom to pick up what covered the floor and when he returned Elinore still had not moved. He tried to cover her, but she pushed the blanket off herself. Mark wasn't sure what to do next. With a fresh towel he began to pat Elinore dry, beginning with her face. Her blue eyes looked desperately at him. She had a great sense of gratitude for him taking such care of her, which lead her to an intense attraction to him. She placed her hand on top of his and together they moved the towel downward toward her young breasts. Mark was now beginning to feel a little dizzy in his head. Her nipples were hard, but he tried to ignore what he was seeing. Elinore was still tired, but she didn't want to sleep now. She wanted Mark. She pulled at his hand, drawing him closer. She kissed his neck, and he could feel her breath. Her tongue felt soft to him, and he had an excitement growing within himself fast. Elinore was in a heated frenzy and pulled Mark even closer, knocking him down on the bed beside her. She pressed herself against him and he could smell the freshness of her newly cleansed skin. He was careful not to touch her burns, but he couldn't resist her temptations any longer. He pushed the blanket off the bed, sliding it into a pile on the floor. His manhood tingled unbearably; it was hot and swollen. Mark undressed himself, ripping at his clothing as he passionately pressed himself against her in return. The bed creaked with every move under the weight of both their bodies. Mark reached around her, and his hand flicked over Elinore's bottom. Elinore's face and neck lifted with pleasure, allowing her bare breasts to touch his face. He went mad; he bucked. Elinore's breath became short. Mark braced his hands on the wall as he hooked his knees inside of hers, splitting her in two. He lifted and heaved. Elinore pushed back, forcing more of him into herself. Elinore watched his face, and it told her he was feeling something beyond simple pleasure.

She wanted more and more, of him when suddenly, while he was still inside her, he lifted her entire body, seating her on his throbbing member, forcing the most of himself deeper into her. Elinore let out a primal scream which excited Mark even more. Elinore scratched Mark's back with her fingernails and felt that she would explode at any moment. She wrapped her legs around him tighter with each lift. He kissed her neck and breasts, adding to her delight. Elinore threw her head back inviting him to explore the rest of her. Mark gladly accepted her invitation and let her slip to his knees facing him but gently pushing back on her shoulders. Holding her face in his hands, he kissed her. He continued licking his way downward, stopping briefly at her navel. Elinore could feel the heat building below. No one had touched her there since John and she longed for that to happen again. Her lower abdomen ached for his touch. He let his tongue travel tasting the freshness of her skin, stopping just above her golden lovelock. With his massive arms he hoisted Elinore up and over, flipping her. Elinore trembled with anticipation of what Mark's next move would be. Quickly, he reached for his pillow and placed it directly under her hips, lifting her luscious bottom for his full view. Elinore's face became smushed into the sheets that covered his sleeping place. With each hand she bunched together a knot to take hold of in eager expectation of what was to come. She was in a vulnerable position but liked it. Mark had a lovely view of Elinore's curves. He placed his hands on her slender waist, moving slowly down the small of her back and around her bottom. He cupped each cheek in his strong hands and squeezed them firmly.

Elinore could feel the strength of his grip and it added to her excitement. Mark was firm but he was also gentle. She felt safe with Mark and was beginning to develop feelings for him. With Elinore's bottom lifted, Mark found places he wanted to explore. Out of the two places of entry, both pleased him as much as the other. Mark slid his finger back and forth making her hot and moist. Elinore moaned. He kneeled closer to her slapping his member against her bare bottom making it jiggle. Elinore smiled and Mark could see the edges of her cheekbones rise from behind her. He couldn't delay his delight any longer and placed his manhood along the small split between her two cheeks. Elinore groaned and lifted her hips higher. Finally, Mark plunged deep inside her. Mark was completely covered in Elinore's honey allowing him to do what excited him the most. He removed himself for a moment, confusing Elinore briefly but then she felt a gentle pressure against her anus. It was something Elinore had never experienced. Mark gently pushed against her bottom. Elinore felt pleasure and pain at the same time. Mark was driving her into an uncontrollable spasm of insanity. She moaned and moved her hips, riding him faster and faster. He lowered himself over her back to kiss her lips and in that motion, he found that he could sink himself entirely into her so that her bottom touched his stomach. Elinore gasped and squirmed with delight. Her appetite for him was insatiable, but it would be cut down in an instant as the fire bell began to ring.

"Damn it!" Mark cried out impatiently. He knew he had to go. Mark collapsed on top of Elinore in disappointment. Quickly, he ran to the bathroom, grabbing his clothes on the way. He apologized to Elinore and told her he would be back as soon as he could. Elinore laid flat on the bed. She was upset, covering herself with the blanket, she curled up into a ball. "I hate that bell!" she said to herself. Elinore still was thinking about Mark's rippled body. His strength was incredible. His muscular arms lifted her as if she were a feather. He also had very little body hair, something Elinore had come to like, and his broad shoulders and chest she loved most, when he laid them on top of her. His legs were so thick they reminded her of tree trunks. His waist was slim, attributing to his V-shape physique that she found irresistible. She looked at Buster trying to get him off her mind but found it impossible. She wondered how long she would have to wait before he came back. The morning turned into late afternoon, and she had heard that damn fire bell ring several more times that day. She knew she shouldn't be angry with Mark, but she was. She decided to write him a note and return to Annie's house.

Chapter 17

Annie could hear someone walking down the cemented pathway to her door. She looked out the window to see Elinore and rushed to greet her. She had many questions about what had happened to her. She'd never known a single soul who had been hit by lightning and survived. Elinore repeated to Annie what Mark had told her, but she honestly couldn't remember all the details. She could remember running through the rain to Mark's but didn't remember ever arriving. Elinore didn't tell Annie what had happened between herself and Mark. She wasn't ready to share that. Annie informed her that she had gone to her aunt's house to tell her what had happened before she heard about it in the street gossip. She hoped that she wouldn't mind. Elinore suggested that maybe the two of them could pay her aunt a visit and so they did. When they arrived, Agnes was making a large pot of Beef Barley soup. It smelled good to them. Agnes scooped up three bowls and they all sat together enjoying it at the kitchen table. Elinore showed Agnes the burn marks on her arms.

She was stunned at their appearance, but she was more concerned about the type of impact it would have on Elinore's mind. She knew her niece wasn't quite right. Agnes had sympathy for Elinore and even forgave her weekly stipend for the week. Elinore wanted to return to work, she liked her new job but still felt too weak. She told her aunt that her plan was to return to work on Monday, but she would have to see when it arrived. It was getting late when the two decided to return to Annie's home. Calling it a day, the two women settled into the fresh sheets in each of their own rooms. Elinore's eyes fixed on the ceiling and wondered what time Mark had eventually arrived home. She wondered how he reacted to her note. She knew he probably expected her to be there, but she didn't like being alone. Now, she was missing him already and found it difficult to relax enough to fall asleep.

It wasn't long before Elinore had returned to work and life was back to normal for her. The burns had faded and now Elinore was starting to give a lot of thought as to where her life was going again. Her fondness for Mark was growing every day and she thought their relationship might very well wind up being the love that would save her. She hadn't seen her parents for a very long time, and she wondered what her family would think of Mark. She also took time to think about Carl and wondered what had ever happened to him. She loved Mark in a different way now. It was becoming more of a love than she could have ever hoped for. One she had no idea could exist. It was a complete love. One that she could see herself spending the rest of her life in. She wondered if Carl would be mad that she had moved on without him? She had adored his parents and wondered about them too. Carl's father was not the healthiest. And then there was Hans. She hoped he would approve of Mark too. That was important to her. She would always compare the men she encountered to Hans and her father. Elinore felt that if they couldn't match up to either of them, then they were of no use to her. Elinore just couldn't help but to compare all the men she met to them. She always wanted a man with the same strengths, but knew they were large shoes to fill. Mark had a lot of integrity, and she was certain that both would like him without a doubt.

The person Elinore missed most though was her sister Margaret. There was no one else who enjoyed a good laugh more than Margaret. Elinore would have given just about anything to have another day with her. She thought about life in Germany with Mark by her side. She could only imagine how Margaret would get along with Mark. He could be a prankster when he wanted to be. She wondered if Mark could get on with life in her native country. It was so completely different than in America. Her best memories were when their grandfather would come, and the onslaught of a week's pranks would begin. They had so much fun! She remembered how they would laugh so hard that her stomach hurt. Surely, Mark would love that part of things. Elinore loved her grandfather's sense of humor; Mark had a great sense of humor too. She missed her grandparents so much. She convinced herself that Mark would get along brilliantly with her Oma and Opa. Elinore began to think of a plan. She decided to start putting some money aside to possibly one day return for a visit on her own to tell them all about the love she had found. Elinore liked planning ahead. Her mother had always taught her that it was better to be prepared. Since Elinore had come to America, she had gotten used to having things more accessible which led to spontaneous spending for her. In her homeland she had to wait for things. There was a big difference between living in her majestic countryside and the busy streets of New York City. Elinore had grown to like where she lived now, but the fond memories of her youngest days pulled at her heartstrings. She remembered her father picking her up as a young girl and twirling her in the air anchored to his large thick hands.

Elinore was enjoying a cup of tea in the kitchen when Annie came bursting through her door with more brown paper sacks in each arm. They needed some things. Elinore jumped up to help her, kicking the door closed behind her with her foot. Annie had gone shopping to buy some food and extra bits. The bags were heavy, and Annie shook her cramped arms as she set them down. She began putting things away when the subject of the movies crossed her mind. "The Keystone Kops are being shown at the movie house this Saturday, do you want to go?" Annie asked. "After working all week, I would love to!" Elinore jumped at the chance. She was excited about going to the movies again. "Do you mind if Mark comes along too?" Elinore asked. Annie didn't mind at all and said that it would be nice to see him again. And so, it was decided that they would go but Elinore needed to make time to ask Mark about it.

That week was very busy at the store and Gretchen was happy that Elinore had returned to work in the nick of time. Children had been dragging their mothers in droves to the store since the latest snack had come into town. Cracker Jacks had been putting toys inside their treats. Gretchen couldn't keep it on the shelves. Mothers, of course, would then pick up supplies while they were there. The store was crowded most of the time. Jell-O had become the latest craze in desserts and tootsie rolls were flying out of the door too. Zippers and studs were being used more often and so Gretchen began to carry these notions for the women who could sew their own clothing. The Farmer's Almanac was in great demand but there was a new book out that people had been requesting and so Gretchen had made a special effort to get her hands on a few published copies of *Tarzan of the Apes*. Gretchen enjoyed reading when the busy day at the shop was over and saved herself a copy. All these things kept the two very busy. Gretchen was finding it hard to keep up with it all without Elinore.

Mark had begun showing up at the store daily to see Elinore and Gretchen was getting used to seeing him often too. Gretchen liked the fact that he was so respectful and thought that he and Elinore made a nice couple. Mark always made small talk with her before leaving with Elinore for lunch. He had even helped Gretchen with some heavy boxes occasionally and she found that quite nice of him. At the first chance Elinore got, she asked Mark if he would accompany Annie and herself to the movie house on Saturday. Mark knew about the movie and had been wanting to see it himself. He had heard there would be many to follow and so he happily agreed. Elinore began her routine of putting together what she would wear in her mind for the remainder of that day. That was until Gretchen had a special delivery at the store. Six hat boxes showed up by a man in a black wagon being pulled by the most beautiful horse Elinore had seen in a long time. Elinore rushed to help Gretchen carry the boxes inside and was very curious to see what was inside of them. Gretchen opened the first one to check for any imperfections. As she raised it out of the box, Elinore was stunned by the beauty of it. It was a man's top hat. And it was made of beaver's skin. It had such a natural shine to it. It carried a hefty price tag of $8.67. Elinore was starting to think about Christmas already. She would need to save at least six weeks to buy one for Mark, but what a splendid idea of a gift to surprise him with. She promised herself that after buying that she would clamp down on her spending and absolutely make herself put some money aside.

When all was processed, unpacked and put away, Elinore asked Gretchen what she was going to make herself for supper. Elinore was out of ideas. She was tired of the same old thing and moaned about it. Gretchen laughed and pointed to the small section of Campbell soups. "Which one?" Elinore asked. There were so many choices. Gretchen had cleared a spot to hold a few cans each of the twenty-one different varieties. Elinore couldn't decide between the oxtail, tomato okra, or the mock turtle. For ten cents a can, it was entirely affordable. Finally, she took two cans of oxtail and a can of peas. She waved goodbye to Gretchen and was on her way. She hoped Annie had bought some fresh potatoes to go with it. That night, supper would be easy, Elinore thought. Her arms ached after the long day at the store. Elinore certainly didn't think Annie would mind a quick meal; five minutes and viola, supper would be on the table. She was pleased with herself to have come up with something so quickly. After all the things she'd seen that Annie considered dinner, this surely couldn't be that bad. Elinore hadn't had oxtail in a very long time and even looked forward to it herself.

After Elinore's feast, Annie had one thing left to do. She needed to trim the wicks on the kitchen lanterns and fill the oil lamps. She pushed herself to do it. She was tired and Elinore sympathized with her because she felt much the same. But Annie thought about how much she hated stumbling around in the dark so much more, and the thought of stubbing a toe made her complete her last task. Annie checked to make sure everything was secure, and began her nightly routine to get herself ready to turn in. She looked out the window and said a few words to Tom as she did every night. The stars sparkled bright that night like diamonds against the velvet black sky and she could feel Tom's presence. A candle illuminated the room softly and her body threw her shadow against the bedroom wall. The pain in her heart was still there. She wondered if it would ever leave.

Elinore crawled into her bed with her arms and feet aching. She was so tired and closed her eyes before her head hit the pillow. But Elinore was only asleep for a couple of hours when she woke from a nightmare. She dreamt that a huge bear was chasing her and wanted to eat her. She could see his razorblade teeth coming right for her when she awoke trembling with fear in the darkness with beads of sweat running down her neck. Now, Elinore could not go back to sleep. Again, Elinore began to think about Mark. Mark could surely handle a fire, but would he know what to do if a bear came after them? She thought about how big the bears were in her homeland. She thought, thought, thought about everything. Even her Aunt Agnes popped into her thoughts. She decided she should pay her a visit after she was through with work the following day. With all the thinking she was doing, Elinore finally fell back to sleep from the exhaustion of it.

It was early morning and Gretchen was getting ready to open the store. She began to unpack the freight that had arrived late the day before. She started to cut the boxes open to display what was inside. She had been expecting her order for some time, but it had been delayed and she was excited to see the latest invention. Inside the boxes were six Brownie Camera's; black small cubes to capture special moments in one's life. She was looking closely at one, when Elinore arrived at work. Elinore asked curiously what Gretchen was holding.

Gretchen extended the camera out to her and said, "They call this a brownie." Elinore began to inspect it. She had never seen such a small camera before! The only one's she had ever seen required two men; one with a flash and the other under a cape that held a large camera on a platform. Elinore held it with both her hands, being careful not to drop it. She looked down into it. It seemed easy enough to use. "How much is it, Gretchen?" Elinore inquired. "It cost one dollar and fifteen cents for the film," Gretchen told her. Elinore's eyebrow raised. "Hummmm, I'd like to buy one Friday, after you pay me if that's ok." Gretchen smiled and said, "Sure, but you better put one behind the counter because there'll be none left by Friday." Elinore thought about the lovely pictures she could take of her and Mark to send home to her parents. She smiled and placed one behind the counter as Gretchen had told her. Now, Elinore had to pay for the beaver skin hat and the camera, but by the end of the week she would only have enough to pay for the camera. She hoped that Gretchen would hold the hat for her and when she asked, Gretchen didn't mind at all. She liked Elinore and knew she had wide eyes about shopping. She was young, but Gretchen found Elinore funny and such a pleasure to work with. Her special requests were no problem. By the end of the day again, Elinore was tired. She took her time walking to her aunt's house. Dragging her feet, she seemed unable to control her gait. The uneven slabs on the sidewalk made it that much harder. She sighed when her aunt's house was in her sight. Elinore gently tapped on the door and opened it. She was greeted by the scent of what her aunt was cooking. It wasn't any special occasion, but her nose caught the aroma of turkey that filled the air. Her aunt usually only made turkey on holiday's. Elinore was hungry and she bit her lower lip, inhaling deeply. Her eyes closed, enjoying it. Elinore entered the kitchen and found her aunt hovering over the stove. Agnes was agitated. The turkey was golden brown and sitting in a pan full of its juices. Elinore asked, "What's wrong Aunt Agnes?" Agnes turned the bird around and back again. Poking it with a large fork, she said with a huff, "I can't tell if the damn things done!" Elinore laughed out loud. Agnes shot darts at Elinore with her eyes. "What's so funny?" she raised her voice asking sternly. Elinore quickly straightened out her crooked smile and asked, "Well, have you tried banging on it with a spoon?" "Banging on it, what's that going to do?" Agnes demanded and waited for her reply with her hands on her hips. Elinore giggled and told her that that was the only way she knew of to tell if the meat was thoroughly cooked. So, Agnes began banging on the turkey with a spoon. Elinore couldn't contain herself and had to leave the room. She laughed so hard. Hard enough to wet herself. She climbed the stairs to her room trying to compose herself. She wondered just how long her aunt would continue to hit the bird until she realized she'd been had. She was proud of herself and thought of Margaret. Margaret would have loved this one! Elinore sat on her bed, looking around the room. She felt uncomfortable there. Mostly awkward. Most of her things had been moved to Annie's already, but she purposely left a few insignificant things there just in case.

"Elinore, could you come down here please!" Agnes was shouting up the stairs. Her foot was tapping the floor where she stood with her hand still on her hip. Elinore gulped down the hard knot in her throat. Fearfully, she slowly approached the stairs and made her way down. Her aunt was still frustrated, and it was apparent to her. She wondered if she'd caught on to her practical joke. She asked innocently, "Is it done?" Agnes straightened her back. Her voice was strained but asked, "Could you help me please?" Elinore continued with her charade of innocence. "Sure," and went to the stove to see what she could do. By just looking at it, she could tell the bird was finished. The juice flowed clear from the bird; a sure indication that it was done and ready to be eaten. Agnes asked her niece if she would like to stay and have a bite to eat. Elinore thought she'd never ask. She happily carved the bird while her aunt finished with the potatoes, and it wasn't long before they were both leaning back finding it difficult to breathe. The turkey they had devoured, made Elinore sleepy. She had already been tired from the long day at the store. She rubbed her stomach in a circle. Her head nodded and she felt as if she could fall asleep where she sat. Deciding to stay there for the night, she found that her bed there was not quite as comfortable as the one she had gotten used to at Annie's home. She tried to get her mind off the hard horsehair mattress under her. Mark entered her thoughts once again. It would be another two long days until she would see him if he didn't stop in the store before that. That amount of time seemed unbearable to accept, but what could she do?

Mark was also thinking about Elinore. He was looking forward to seeing her lovely face again. He couldn't stop thinking about the way her hips twitched when she walked, and it just about drove him insane. He had thought about their first tryst a million times since it had happened and looked forward to another encounter. The thought of her made his heart race. He was counting the days until he would see her again at the movie house. It was hard to admit but he was also looking forward to the movie as well. He wanted her to believe she was the only reason he was there, but the firefighters he worked with had told him about the movie already. They told him it was hilarious.

It had seemed like forever, but Saturday finally arrived, and Elinore and Annie were excited. Elinore dressed for the occasion, but not as she usually did. She was tired from the week's work with Gretchen and wore a dress that didn't require a corset. She felt a little frumpy and didn't care much about it, but Iris was busy making her disapproval known. Iris didn't like it when Elinore didn't care about the way she presented herself. A girl should always look her best, she thought. But Elinore just couldn't be bothered. After all, it was her date, no one else's. She smoothed her dress and fixed her hair.

Annie came down the hall and asked Elinore if she was ready. Elinore looked at the way Annie had put herself together. No matter what Annie wore, Elinore always compared herself to her in her mind. She just always wanted to be the best looking. "Yes, I'm ready, and we should leave now, or we'll be late." Mark was waiting in front of the building as he had the time before. He moved toward them, centering himself between the two women. He moved so purposely, and Elinore wasn't sure how she felt about that. She thought at this point, he should have taken her arm before Annie, but she swallowed her pride and didn't want to spoil the evening. Once they were seated, Mark put his arm over Elinore's shoulder and that made her feel a little better. The lights dimmed and the movie began. Bright flashes of light filtered through the small theater and Elinore thought it was the funniest thing she had ever seen. The movie captured the comical police following the wrong person, displaying their crazy antics and eventually arresting the entirely wrong person. She was glad that the real watchmen didn't act as humorously incompetent as they had in the movie but believed the real one's weren't as smart as they thought they were either.

Soon, the movie was finished and a lot of the people who attended lingered about. Many talked and laughed among themselves. Annie asked Mark if he would like to come back to the house with her and Elinore for a slice of cake and some coffee. The invitation pleased him and again, he put his arms around both women as they began their walk toward Annie's place. Elinore was gritting her teeth now. Her little green horns were about to poke a hole through the top of her head. Mark and Annie were oblivious to Elinore's feigning of indifference to the way they enjoyed each other's company. Again, Elinore was feeling the competition of her good friend Annie and didn't like it. It turned late, and Mark was still sitting at the table with Annie and Elinore. He was enjoying himself and wanted to stay but decided against it. He thanked Annie for her hospitality and as he reached for the doorknob he stopped. Elinore watched him closely, waiting. She held her breath and wanted him to turn around. Mark needed to ask Elinore something but not in front of Annie. He thought for a moment about how he would work this. He decided on just asking Elinore to come outside with him for a minute. Elinore was delighted and smiled at his request. She was desperate to know what was going on in his mind. Mark wanted Elinore to come home with him. He was slow to speak once the two were outside. He wasn't sure if Elinore would come, and he didn't like the idea of being rejected.

But Elinore was reading his mind and winked at him. "Just give me a minute to tell Annie that I'm leaving with you," she said. Elinore sneered as she opened the door. She was becoming convinced that Annie might have some misguided feelings toward her newest interest. It made her happy to tell Annie that she was leaving with Mark. He was her boyfriend, not Annie's! The streets were dark that night and Elinore gripped Marks hand tightly. She was dying with anticipation of the excitement that awaited her. Mark put some wood in the fireplace and started a fire. They made themselves comfortable beside it. The night had brought a cool chill to the air. They whispered sweet things to each other and cuddled under a blanket on the small setae that was close enough to catch some of the fire's warmth. Elinore began to talk so much that she hadn't realized Mark had fallen asleep. When Elinore finally left an opening for Mark to speak, there was only silence. She looked at Mark sleeping like a baby, with his arms still wrapped around her. Her eyes rolled and she exhaled deeply. She began to think about how in the world she would get her man to his bed. This was not what she had in mind as to how she wanted the night to end. Elinore's hopes for the excitement she craved were dashed.

With the first rays of light, Elinore woke to find there was another disappointment waiting for her. The sun streamed through the window and warmed Elinore's face. She rubbed her eyes and arched her back to stretch. She rolled to her side and reached for Mark but only his pillow was there to take his place. Elinore was angry now. He hadn't even said goodbye. She wondered why he had asked her to come there in the first place. He hadn't even kissed her. A note on the table explained that another fire had occurred, and he would be back as soon as he could. But she hadn't heard a fire bell! It was so loud; she couldn't have slept through it. She took the note and crumbled it, throwing it to the floor. Elinore got dressed and left. She was disappointed, hurt and mad now.

Mark felt bad as he and the others tended to the small trash fire not far from his father's house. There was nothing suspicious and he was back home in a few hours. Mark opened his door only to find his dog and the crumpled note on the floor. He had planned to make it up to Elinore. He felt she would make a fine wife and he wanted to see if she felt the same. He even tossed the idea of asking her for her hand in marriage around his head. He had started to have serious feelings for her, and he needed someone who was as independent as she. He liked the fact that she did not get overly upset about being left alone and seemed to have a good head on her shoulders. Mark didn't really know Elinore at all, but he thought he did.

He hurried to Annie's expecting to find her there. He wanted to apologize, but when he got there, she was not to be found. Annie had not seen her since she had left with him the night before. He wondered where she could have gone and if she was alright. Mark took a minute to talk with Annie while Elinore was not present. He blurted out, "I want to buy a ring for Elinore." Annie was shocked. "Mark, you two haven't been courting long enough, are you sure?" "Yes," Mark said, "I'm sure." Annie tilted her head to one side. Her lips were pursed. An expression of disapproval was evident. Her eyebrows raised as she thought about the secrets she knew regarding her friend. Should she tell him, she wondered. Suddenly, Mark piped up. "Will you come with me to pick out a ring? You are her best friend," he said. "I guess I could do that, Mark," she agreed. Annie concluded that she wouldn't be able to change his mind. She took a sweater from the hook on the wall in the hallway and soon they walked along in the direction of the local jeweler. Mark just couldn't decide and looked at the many different rings. He asked Annie to try on a few to see how they looked on her hand, but Annie's hand was much more slender than Elinore's. Mark finally settled on a platinum setting with three diamonds; a smaller diamond on each side of the larger center diamond that sparkled as Annie moved her hand back and forth displaying it for him. Mark paid for the ring and the jeweler placed it in a box for him. Putting it in his pocket, he was satisfied with his purchase.

It didn't take long before Annie and Mark were back in her kitchen, waiting for Elinore to show up. Annie made some coffee, and they began to talk. "You made a beautiful choice, it is a lovely ring," Annie said. Memories of Tom flooded her mind. She started to think of the dreams they had had together. She went on to tell Mark some of them and then about the horrible death she watched him suffer. She cried and laughed with Mark. It was only then that she began to tell him something she hadn't told a single soul. Annie looked sadly at Mark, and he felt as if he could look through her. "What is it, Annie?" he asked. Annie placed her hand on top of his and whispered, "Please, this is not easy for me. Before Tom died, before he got sick, we lost our baby." Tears began to fall from her eyes. She clutched tighter to his hand. The pain made it hard for her to breathe. There was a silence that followed her admission.

Mark didn't know what to say, but he could see her suffering, bleeding from her soul. He felt badly for her and continued to listen closely as she struggled with her words. Annie tried to hide her face and wiped her tears with her handkerchief. "I'm sorry," she said. "Don't be silly," Mark said and reached out to comfort her. Annie sobbed on his shoulder making it wet. Between the tears from her eyes and the snot from her nose she pushed him away, ending the conversation with a final word. "We never did get to try again. All I have left now are my memories." Annie felt comfort in Mark's arms and had missed having a man hold her in that way.

Elinore was still upset about Mark falling asleep on her. Was she that boring? she thought. A familiar dizziness took hold of her. Iris had decided to come out with her playful self. She wanted to try to make Elinore's hurt go away. Soon Iris was walking through the park, which offered Elinore a much-needed break. Iris picked some pretty yellow buttercups and found some sweet-smelling honeysuckle. In her travels, she found some other beautiful wildflowers. They were lavender and white in color, and she needed to climb a small embankment to pick them. Iris's tiny hand was too small to hold the large bunch of flowers, but she was determined. She sat on a bench and arranged the bunch into an exquisite bouquet. She knew Elinore's aunt would love them. She carefully cascaded the honeysuckle down in the front and tied it all together with a long piece of cat tail leaves. Iris hurried back to Elinore's aunt's house hoping she would like them. Maybe they would even be able to enjoy another delicious meal and the bouquet would become a handsome gift of thanks. Iris was disappointed though when the offered supper meal was just some peas, potatoes, and pasta. It was one of the few times that Elinore, Iris, Erika, and Charlotte agreed. They all didn't like that and didn't eat one spoonful of it. They went to bed on an empty stomach.

Elinore didn't want to go to work the next day. She did not enjoy the weekend as she had expected to. She forced herself to get dressed and wash her face. She left without a word to her aunt. She only wanted to get through the day and get back to Annie's. She thought surely that Mark would've stopped by there looking for her. The hurt she had felt seemed to have left her memory quickly. The walk to work refreshed her. Elinore worked feverishly that entire day, but every time she looked at the clock it only seemed to move slightly. Elinore had hoped that Gretchen would let her leave early but as it turned out, she wound up staying a few minutes later than usual. A man had come to the store admiring the beaver skin top hats on the shelf. He fancied having one. He paced back and forth trying to make up his mind and asked Elinore's opinion more than once. Elinore just wanted to go home. It had been a long day. He sensed her impatience and offered her a ride home to make up for his indecision.

Gretchen told her to go and that she would lock up. Elinore thought that he was surely nice enough and she was really in a hurry to get back to Annie's. She thought about what she would make for supper. Supper, she thought, was an odd name for the evening meal but she had started to become used to the way people spoke in America. The man kindly opened the store's door for her and then the car door. Elinore admired the car. It had a small windshield and leather seats inside. The running board made it easy to hike herself up into the vehicle. The man asked where she lived, and Elinore gave him Annie's address. He cranked the engine to start it. It gave a small backfire and roared loudly. They rode down the street and Elinore enjoyed the ride. The man gripped the steering wheel with both hands and seemed to have something on his mind. Elinore sat silent and felt very regal sitting high in his vehicle as people walked slowly next to them on the sidewalk. The man looked at Elinore with his small eyes and asked, "Do you mind if I stop by my house for a minute before I drop you off? I've forgotten something." Elinore shrugged her shoulders and told him that it was fine with her. She waited in the vehicle, while the man ran inside his house. She noticed as he walked away how big he was. Not just tall but muscular too. Even his hands were big, like someone who did manual labor for a living. He quickly returned and they started off again.

Elinore was quick to notice railroad tracks as he drove, and she knew this was not the way they should be going. It was not the way to Annie's! Elinore began to feel nervous. She looked around for landmarks to figure out where she was and where he was taking her. She asked, "Why are you going this way? It is not where I told you I needed to go!" Elinore was beginning to panic. The man looked at her and his face seemed to have changed. It looked threatening to her now. Elinore knew something was wrong and wanted to jump from the car but knew that would not end well. She sat watching the street stones as they flashed by. Terror gripped her and Erika took her cue. Elinore surely couldn't handle this on her own. She was numb with fear. The black vehicle turned down a road that headed toward the river. There was not a single person in sight. Erika sat motionless waiting for the car to stop. She thought she could outrun him possibly but shouting out would be useless. No one would hear her screams. He was tall with long legs; difficult to escape. She began to prepare herself.

The man slowed the car down, pulling off to a place very well hidden by overgrowth. Erika's fists were clenched tightly. The man reached for her face and held it between his forefinger and thumb. She struggled to escape his tight grasp. "I just want one kiss!" he shouted at her. She hit him landing a hard shot against his ear. "No!" she screamed as he hit her face in return. A violent struggle began, and Erika tried desperately to free herself. They rolled back and forth inside the car, and it swayed as their heavy bodies tossed about. Erika screamed at the man, but he wouldn't stop. He gripped her leg, pulling her closer. Erika continued to pummel him as hard as she could, but it was of no use. He was big and very strong. Erika worked frantically to save "the system." She began to look over her surroundings. Desperately looking for anything she could use as a weapon. The man continued to try to position her in a compromised way. He locked her neck inside his elbow leaning against his shoulder. He leaned in toward her face with his, stopping only inches away. Erika spit at him. "You pig!" she shouted. His face became red and enraged. His small eyes grew darker and more evil.

Erika bit his arm but that only made him tighten his grip. Erika was finding it hard to get air into her lungs. Her life was being squeezed from her. Everything started to fade, but she was determined to break free from this brutal vermin. She tossed back and forth gasping. She felt as if she would pass out when she felt something sharp in her pocket. They continued to fight, and she followed the shape of the hardness, trying to hide her intention. Erika realized that she had Elinore's billhook! She must have left it in her apron! What luck! Erika began to smile; a smile that she intended to wound him with. The man saw her smile and loosened his grip momentarily, believing he may get the prize he had wanted from her. Her lips looked juicy to him, and he couldn't wait to taste them. "Alright," Erika said. "Just one kiss and then you'll take me home." Erika had a vicious plan. She told him to turn his back on her so that she could whisper in his ear what excited her most about him. Delighted with her words, he complied. Erika began kissing his neck, working her way to his ear. She worked slowly and carefully as the man enjoyed her tender kisses. Erika carefully reached inside the pocket of her apron holding the handle of her weapon tightly. She continued to work her magic on the man until the perfect moment. When it came, she stuck her tongue right into his ear. He tilted his head to give her more access. Perfect, she thought. Quickly, in a split second, she cut hard and deep across the men's neck. She cut his neck from ear to ear. His life's blood poured from his throat and Erika could hear a gurgle coming from him. It was a throaty bubbling noise that came as he must have known his life was about to end. The man slumped over the door. His blood splashed over the seat and door as his life ebbed away. More of his crimson blood pooled onto the floor near his feet.

Erika focused on his face that pressed against the door. She could see that she had sliced him within inches of his spine. She could view all the veins and muscles that barely kept his head from falling off. She whispered to him, "If you had just taken me home, none of this would have happened." Erika looked down at her hands. There was only a small amount of blood on them and some on the billhook. Her movements were quick and carefully executed. The door of the car was heavy. She pushed it open hard and started to run. Elinore did not look back. She was careful to stay well hidden by the overgrowth that lined the road. She tried not to transfer any of the blood on her hands to her clothing. She washed her hands and the billhook in a puddle along the way. She ran as fast as she could following the railroad tracks the same way he had driven. Her heart raced and she soon reached Annie's house exhausted. Out of breath and thirsty, she planned to enter Annie's house trying to appear as normal as possible.

Mark was already waiting at Annie's for Elinore to show up. He intended to give Elinore the ring. The same ring that had brought tears to Annie's eyes as she reminisced about the day that Tom had proposed to her. Their conversation led Mark to embrace Annie, telling her how sorry he was that she had to go through all that pain. He kissed her on the cheek and thanked her for helping him pick out the perfect ring, but just as his lips left her cheek,

Elinore walked in. "What is going on here?" she shouted. Elinore was angry. Mark tried to speak but only stuttered. He couldn't get a word out when Annie replied, "Don't be silly Elinore, nothing is going on here!" Elinore's face turned red. Her brows lowered and pulled closer together. Her eyes bulged as she became enraged. Her lips curled inward, and her face twisted. "I don't believe you Annie!" Elinore shrieked and now she was furious with both of them. She ran from the house, slamming the door behind herself.

Annie was afraid. She feared what Elinore might do in retaliation. Even though it was all very innocent, she knew how Elinore's mind worked and what she must have thought when she saw Mark kiss her. She worried and stayed tense for days. Annie was beginning to feel sick a lot after that. Her nerves were frayed from the constant drama. She also didn't feel safe anymore. Elinore was too unpredictable. It was days later when Annie thought about paying the doctor a visit. Her stomach had been bothering her. She had lots of headaches and was tense most always. She walked the short distance to Dr. Feel Good's office and climbed the long wooden staircase to the top. She was glad to see that there was no line. No one was waiting to see him. It was unusual she thought, but she was grateful. She got to the top only to find a note on the door. The note said, "Permanently closed" and had no other explanation. Annie's face scrunched up in disbelief. Why would he close, she thought. Annie scratched her head and began her descent back down the long staircase. Two ladies had seen her and waited for her at the bottom. The older of the two women called out to her. "Haven't you heard?" Annie walked closer to the ladies. "Heard what?" she asked. "Dr. Feel Good had a nasty fall while he was cleaning his windows." "He died right there," as her long finger pointed to the spot where Ben's body had landed. "The poor thing bought the farm right there," she said.

Annie had seen these two women before and knew they had all the gossip of the town. Then Annie asked if they knew of another doctor that she could go to, but their answer was vague. The ladies had told her of a doctor that they had tried near 42nd street but weren't exactly pleased with. Annie decided that it would be better to just go home and take her time to ask others that were more reliable for a recommendation. On the way Annie's mind started to wander. John died, and now she knew Ben died. She was beginning to think that Elinore may have had something to do with their deaths.

Her mind took her back to when she had first met Elinore and why she had never mentioned the doctor's death to her. The sickness in her stomach also had returned. Annie had no proof of what she was thinking. Only her intuition and the gossip from the two busy bodies of the town. She chose to ask Elinore if she knew what happened to the doctor she worked for. Simply and not accusatory would be her approach. Annie just wanted to see what Elinore's reaction would be to her question. It wasn't long before Elinore came by for a cup of tea and some chitchat. She seemed to have forgiven her and there was no mention of Mark at all. Annie had noticed something about Elinore lately too. Her personality would change from one minute to the next much faster than when they had first started to become friends. She never could be sure what form of Elinore would be visiting.

Elinore had Annie on her mind that entire day too and wanted to see her. She left Gretchen early with the intention of visiting with her right after work. She entered in her usual way but kept a noticeable distance between herself and Annie. Annie poured the tea and began to tell Elinore that she had gone to see the doctor. Annie was setting up the conversation that she already had planned in her mind. Slowly, she injected her question into the broadly common conversation they were having, and Annie immediately noticed Elinore's interest perk up. "Have you been feeling ill?" Elinore asked. Annie told her that she had but then asked the catching portion of her question. "I went to see the doctor, but you'd never believe that when I got there, I found out that the good doctor has died! Did you know about this?" Elinore didn't take her bait. Annie was surprised by her return. "Yes, I know," Elinore said slyly. "I heard that he died right after I quit working for him." Elinore didn't like where Annie's conversation was leading. She did not want to talk about Ben. Her answer though was enough for Annie. Elinore had answered so blasé, that she was almost certain now that Elinore did indeed have something to do with the doctor's death. She tried to hide her face by pouring another cup of tea, but Elinore was watching her every move.

It all made sense to Annie why she had never mentioned his death. Her gut told her that Elinore was involved in some way, and it frightened her. Annie decided to try to change the subject but struggled to find common ground. She didn't dare ask about Mark. She turned the conversation to ask about the latest things to be available at Gretchen's store. She explained that she was tired of the same old things and would be going shopping soon. Erika had been listening carefully the whole time and had been coming out more and more often lately. Annie had moved to the top of Erika's most suspicious list. Elinore was beginning to mistrust people too and knew Annie all too well. She knew Annie did things methodically. Everything had a purpose for the way she did things. There was a reason for even moving one hair on her head. Elinore was starting to have doubts about the friendship she had made with Annie and Erika was keenly aware of that. Erika was pleased that Elinore's thoughts were aligning with hers more often and that her innocence was fading quickly. Erika and Elinore were finally intertwining their framework on the clever ways of interacting with people. Erika felt that she could almost trust Elinore's judgement a little more, but she would remain the most powerful within the system. She would not let her guard down for a minute. It was vital to keep "the system" safe.

Elinore was still very angry with Annie and Mark. She hadn't forgotten catching them red handed. There was even a moment that she thought of killing them both for what they had done. Her trust in both had been destroyed. She never thought that Annie would betray her like that. She could never, and wouldn't ever, forgive her for that. There was a long uncomfortable silence between the two as they sat when Elinore decided that it was time to go. She had hoped to see Mark there, but he didn't show. Elinore picked herself up and quickly went inside to the room she had been given by Annie without explanation. All the clothes could be replaced but she wanted her pistol. She took the pistol and shoved it deep into her pocket with the billhook.

Annie remained on the edge of her seat in the kitchen wondering what on earth she could be doing. To take her mind off Elinore being out of sight yet still in her house, she moved to wash the dishes in the sink, still trying to remain calm. Annie didn't like having Elinore there anymore. She had become afraid of her. She was unpredictable. And now with what her mind was conjuring up, she wasn't sure what she was capable of. She was sure Elinore was a murderer. Elinore waved goodbye to Annie as she rushed by her, and she was glad to see her leaving. She didn't like walking on pins and needles in her own home. Elinore remained fixed on seeing Mark. She wanted to see what he had to say for himself.

Mark had been thinking about Elinore too. He was second guessing his original thought about marrying her. He had also decided to hold off on giving her the ring he had bought. Maybe he had rushed things too quickly. If he slowed things down, it couldn't hurt. If it was meant to be it would still happen. He felt bad about what Elinore had thought she had seen. He felt bad about having hurt her like that. He was deep in thought when there was a knock at the door. Mark's dog had become accustomed to seeing Elinore and wasn't alarmed. He started to jump up on her and his tail wagged fast when he saw her at the door. It made Elinore smile to see him so happy. Animals are so loyal, she thought. She sat down next to Mark, and he slowly started to speak. "I'm sorry about what happened at Annie's," he said. And he was truly sorry. "Elinore, nothing was going on between me and Annie, I swear!" he continued. He wanted her to understand that he loved only her. Mark had never seen the jealous side of Elinore before but now that he had, he didn't like it at all. He tried to explain to her that he wasn't that type of person, and she had nothing to worry about.

She kissed him and smiled at him. She told him that she forgave him but that she needed to get back to her aunt's house. She left him with another kiss, and an easy smile. She thought it was important that she be trusted by the people she lied to in case she needed to plan for retribution. That would ensure a surprise retaliation for the dirty deed. He watched her walk out of sight. Elinore didn't really need to get to her Aunt Agnes's. She wasn't even home. And she most certainly did not forgive him! She lied. She didn't believe a word he had said either. She did believe Mark and Annie had betrayed her! How dare he think she would share him with Annie, Elinore thought. Her mind was twisting, and Erika was guiding the way. Elinore's thoughts were becoming as malicious as Erika's, and both were equally capable of spewing their venom on someone. Elinore passed the burnt building where she had worked and exactly where she had first met Mark on her way home. She remembered the fire and the thick smoke. She spit on the ground with disgust as she walked by. She remembered that the smoke had such a foul smell. Then it came to her in a flash. The fire! The next time Mark tried to bring her to his bed, she might just set it on fire. With him in it!

Her anger was becoming uncontrollable, and Elinore's reality was warping. Her twisted views of the people in her life were becoming unrealistic. Elinore's life had been filled with much pain. After her parents' abandonment of her and Carl had ended his correspondence with her, then John's deceitful ways, and now Mark's cheating ways, Elinore's pain and hurt were too much for her to bear. Crying nightly into her pillow, Elinore began to think she would never find her perfect hero. And Erika would always take that opportunity to reinforce that thought every chance she could. Elinore, as hard as she could, would try to ignore that reinforcement, clinging to the hope that maybe some day things could turn out well for her, but Erika was becoming hard to ignore. Her own self-esteem was suffering. She could hear Erika loud and clear. Elinore shouted at her to go away but Erika was much stronger than she, and Erika was not going anywhere. She was there to stay. Elinore was almost home when she passed the local saloon. She looked in the window and saw a lively crowd. There was an old piano being played by someone and she could hear the music from outside the establishment. She could see a large brass clock on the wall that had a pendulum which swung back and forth, keeping time. She hadn't been to a saloon since John had taken her. She was in no rush to be anywhere. There was a table toward the back of the long room where five men sat around a table and there were at least that many crowded around them watching what they were doing. It was a happy crowd and all of them seemed to be having a grand time.

Elinore wanted to go in but hesitated. She wasn't sure if she should. Suddenly she reached for the door and threw caution to the wind. One drink won't hurt, she thought to herself. As soon as she stepped inside, she saw a large wheel with a spindle sticking straight up in the center. There were black and red squares on it with numbers all the way around it. There was a young man leaning against the bar with one foot on the gold rail at the base of it. He had his eyes on Elinore as soon as she walked in. Elinore could feel the heaviness of his stare. Her legs seemed to tighten, and her feet tangled up with each other. She grabbed a seat and sat down next to the odd wheel. The man was still staring at her, but she avoided making eye contact with him. Finally, she dared to look over her shoulder. And he was still looking! He tipped his hat and winked at Elinore. Slowly, he swaggered over to where Elinore was seated, carrying his glass of spirits. "They don't play roulette here tonight, Miss, tonight is poker night," he said pointing to the table at the rear of the saloon. "Can I get you something to drink?" he asked. He stood tall in front of her, and she had to look up at him to speak. Elinore was thinking fast and came up with something to say.

"Why yes please, I thought you'd never ask." Elinore wanted a free drink and she had heard that phrase in one of the last of the movies that she and Annie had seen. It worked for the woman in the plot. The man smiled and quickly returned with some bourbon. He handed it to her, and she immediately took a sip. It burned her throat and nostrils at first, but then an overall warm sensation came that was pleasing. The man asked many questions that Elinore felt he had no right to ask. He continued by asking her name but thinking fast Elinore told him that Annie was her name. "What's yours?" she shot back. "Fred's the name, pleasure to meet you my fine lady," he said reaching for her hand and kissing the back of it. "It's not that often that we get such a lovely lady in here. Do you live around here?" he asked. Elinore had had enough. All these questions. And she wasn't in the mood for random chit-chat. She just wanted a drink and to watch the people. This man was starting to get on her last nerve. Then she had an idea. She blurted out, "I'm new to the area and I just needed to take a minute before I go home to cook supper for my eight children. They're a handful, you know." The man coughed and nearly spit his drink onto the floor. His eyes bulged. "But you look so young," he exclaimed. "Thank you, kind sir," she replied as she gathered her things to leave. Walking straight for the door she shook her head thinking to herself, what a dumb cluck he was. Glad to be going while the getting was good, Elinore continued her way to her aunt's.

Chapter 18

Annie stood in front of the massive brick building watching the watchmen go up and down the small staircase. They seemed much more organized than the watchmen of earlier years. On each side of the staircase were two posts which every officer that came down the stairs seemed to swing from. Panes of red glass enclosed the lights that glowed at the highest peak of the posts. Those lights were grand with purpose. Everyone that passed there knew that the police were inside that building. She stood there wondering if she had made the right decision to go there. She had nothing, no proof of what she was about to tell them. But she was sure right down to her toes that Elinore was a killer. The more she thought about it the more certain she became. Annie made her way up into the rounded stone doorway. Cautiously, she stepped inside. There was a high wooden desk to the left, with three uniformed men standing behind it who were ruffling through some paperwork. They hardly noticed her standing there. Annie waited a minute before clearing her throat. One of the men finally noticed her and approached her. "Can I help you?" he asked.

Annie looked down at her shoes. "Yes," she whispered. "I want to tell you about something." Pausing a minute to scan the room, she asked, "Is there a place a little more private that I can speak freely?" The man motioned for her to move to a small desk that sat at the back of the room in the corner. Annie sat down; still not sure she was doing the right thing. The watchman looked deeply concerned about what she had to say. "Now what can I do for you, is there a problem I can help you with?" Annie nervously bit her lower lip. "Well, I have no proof of what I'm about to tell you, but I have some serious suspicions and my intuition tells me I'm right." Intrigued by her statement, his one brow lifted. Annie was starting to think that he wasn't going to believe her. She asked the man if he knew John Smith. The men replied that he did and that almost everyone did. Then she asked about Dr. Feelgood. The man asked impatiently, "Now what's this about? Both those men are dead; John died of natural causes and the doctor died of a nasty accident. Why do you ask if I know them?" he asked. Annie held up a forefinger and asked, "Do you think you could be wrong about the cause of their deaths?" Annie now had his attention. "Explain please," he said as he picked up a pencil and some paper. He took her name first and then listened to what she had to say. Annie told the man that she had a friend whom she suspected had some mental sickness and could have been responsible for both their deaths. But when Annie mentioned Elinore's full name, they had no record of her. It had not been noted anywhere that she was involved or even near the scene when the watchmen arrived. She was not a suspect.

Without warning, there was a great commotion just inside the doorway of the office. A young boy, no more than ten years of age, came running in screaming at the top of his lungs. "Help, help!" he cried. He had caught the attention of everyone that was inside the room. The boy's face was dirty, and his pants were tattered. He shrieked, "There's a dead man inside a car down by the waterway! He's all bloody!" The other two officers in the room gathered around him. "Are you sure, boy? How do you know he's dead?" The boy's eyes opened wide, and he gulped hard. He had ran all the way there from finding the gruesome sight. He screeched, "His throat is cut; his head is hanging and there's a lot of blood all over him, that's how I know! I poked him, but he's stiff. I think he's dead, really I do!" the boy shouted as he continued to gasp for air. The boy beckoned the two men to come with him, tugging one of them by the hand. "I'll show you where he is!" he said. The boy's face reflected the terror he had just witnessed, and his voice remained urgent.

The precinct emptied out and only Annie remained with the officer she had first approached. Annie could see that the officer's interest had faded. She just wanted to leave, feeling somewhat silly. "Maybe it was wrong for me to have come here Sir." Annie said. The officer told her that it wasn't and that they were interested in all leads. He went on further to say that the leads people provided were a necessary part of putting all the pieces of a crime together. He thanked her for coming and told her to come back if she had anything else that she wanted to tell him. In a split second, the officer stopped short and said, "By the way, just what makes you think your friend might be involved?" Annie looked at him. He had his pencil still resting on his ear. Annie wondered how she could explain things to him in a way that he would understand. She was only a few steps from the door and looked back at him over her right shoulder. "It's my intuition Sir, and the way she responded when I asked her about it, that's all." The officer nodded his head and told her that he understood. Annie continued out of the doorway and down the stone staircase. She still was uncertain she had done the right thing at the end of their conversation.

Elinore was feeling still a bit tipsy from the bourbon when she entered her aunt's home. She was also hungry. She went to the kitchen to have a look to see what the ice box had to offer. There was some bratwurst and onions in there but not much else. She had just started up the fire inside the stove and had the meat and onions in a pan with some butter when she heard the front door open. Agnes was home. She had shopping bags in her hands. Agnes was quick to show Elinore the new shoes, dress and handbag she had bought. Elinore heard Iris's comments in her mind. "What a dreadful color!" Elinore minded her manners and told her that they were pretty. She remembered her mother's words; if you can't say something nice, say nothing at all. Iris was laughing because Charlotte was laughing. Charlotte's laugh was contagious. Charlotte looked up to Iris and always thought Iris was funny. Elinore and Agnes both sat down to eat, and Agnes was truly happy to see her niece. She had to admit to herself that she got lonesome at times living alone. It was nice to have someone to eat with occasionally and Elinore had grown on her.

Elinore did the dishes when they were finished and excused herself. She thought about her beautiful clothing still at Annie's. All her nice dresses were there. She thought after work the following day that she should bring some back to her aunt's house. Just a few things. Annie hadn't told her that she couldn't stay there but Elinore didn't feel welcome there either. She was still upset with Annie too and thought it would be best to put some distance between them. It was for the best, she thought. Elinore lit the small candle lantern that was on her desk and sat on her bed. All alone in her room she gazed at the candle as it flickered in the darkened room. The flame hypnotized her. She focused on the flame and nothing else. Everything in the room faded away from her awareness. Erika joined in on the view of the flame as well. She loved the way it danced and licked the air. Erika always did like fire. Invasive thoughts began to swirl around Elinore's mind. Annie and Mark's faces appeared in her thoughts behind her closed eyelids again. She pictured them laughing together and smiling at one another. Her view was becoming more distorted every day. Her reality was warped. Elinore knew it wouldn't be long before Annie tried to steal Mark from her. Mark was the one person she was sure could save her from the wretched poor life she had been made to live. Why couldn't Annie get her own man? Why did she need to take Mark? Elinore asked herself over and over.

Elinore knew that Mark was smart enough to climb the ladder to the top of the firehouse echelon. She had found out that firemen at the highest levels could make a handsome $1200.00 a year. With money like that she wouldn't ever have to worry. Another thing that Elinore had considered was something she had heard about. There was going to be an upcoming event; a fireman's parade was in the works with a grand ball to take place afterward. Mark had not mentioned it to her and she speculated as to why. Maybe he was going to take Annie. Her mind was spiraling out of control. Elinore became enraged again and kicked her chair. It wobbled and her toe hurt from it, but she ignored it. "Stupid chair!" she growled. She thought about killing Mark and Annie again. It was Elinore this time thinking the murderous thoughts and Erika's eyes gleamed feverishly with delight. She was following each of Elinore's thoughts one after another rapidly with extraordinary clarity. Elinore fidgeted on her bed. She whispered to herself that she should never have trusted Mark or Annie. Elinore lifted herself and blew the candle out. A small swirl of smoke rose through the air, and she could smell the burnt wick. Crawling into her bed, she pulled the blanket tightly up to her neck.

Elinore slept soundly that night and didn't stir once. It was late in the morning before Elinore's eyes opened. The birds in the flue of the chimney had not made much noise like they usually had done before. Elinore could tell it was late and rushed to get ready for work. She stumbled across the floor trying to put on her boots. She put on the first dress that her hands touched in her closet, washed up and ran down the stairs. She closed the door and struggled with the key to lock it, when out of the corner of her eye, she saw Mark sitting on the bench waiting. "What are you doing here, I'm late for work!" she said impatiently. Mark stood and reached for her hand. "I know, but I wanted to walk you to work," he answered persistently. He held her hand tightly and they talked on the way. He asked if she had forgiven him again and Elinore said that she had. He asked her to come to his house after she was done working that day and she agreed reluctantly. Mark kissed her on the cheek and left her on the porch of Gretchen's store.

As soon as he was out of sight, Elinore wiped her cheek with her sleeve. She had a disgusted look on her face when she entered the store. "Good morning!" Gretchen said upon seeing Elinore. "We have a lot of work today, El. We got more leeches, I know how you love them," she said jokingly. "They need to be put in the tank and we received some more candy. Can you believe they are making candy cigarettes now! What will they think of next?" Gretchen babbled on. But Elinore wasn't really paying her much mind. She was thinking a lot about other things. Then Gretchen asked, "What's wrong Elinore?" Elinore shook her head and left the trance she seemed to be under. "Oh nothing," she said. "I think I ate a bug on the way to work this morning." Her face scrunched and Gretchen laughed. "Ewwe!" she said, returning the same face. That made Elinore laugh.

Elinore could hear little Charlotte's wild laughter which made her laugh too. Gretchen knew that she had made a funny face, but it wasn't that funny. Secretly rolling her eyes, she returned to working again and Elinore helped.

At noon, Mark returned. Gretchen waved and smiled at him. "Nice to see you, Mark!" she happily greeted him. Elinore could see that he had a brown paper bag as he walked toward her. Handing it to her, he said, "I hope you're hungry, I made you a sandwich." Elinore had to admit that she was. Mark sat close to her while she ate. It was a warm day, and the sun was bright. It wouldn't be long before the seasons would change again and the leaves on the trees would begin to fall, Elinore thought. Lunchtime went by fast, and it was time for Elinore to return to work. This time Mark kissed her on the lips, and she briefly remembered the excitement she first felt with him. Mark could see a faint smile appear on Elinore's face and thought he'd try his luck. "I'll see you tonight?" he asked and left before she could answer.

When Elinore entered the store again, Gretchen was still working hard. She knew it was going to be a long day and didn't take a break. She stacked off all the candy in all the places it needed to be and neatly placed all the sewing notions where they belonged. Gretchen had received a new candy and pointed it out to Elinore. They were pep-o-mint lifesavers and some goo-goo clusters which looked very interesting to Elinore. Gretchen joked about the hole in the middle of the peppermints and that some poor unsuspecting child would probably get their tongue caught inside it. Elinore loved working with the candy and had to try each one as they came in. In a motherly way, Gretchen was quick to remind her that all that sugar wasn't good for her lady-like figure, but Elinore didn't care. She just had to try them all. There were so many new candies that came in everyday that Elinore's sweet tooth began to control her, especially when it came to the chocolate Necco wafers and the butterscotch Reed's rolls. They were her favorites. But then again, if you asked her, there was nothing better than a box of good-n-plenty or a bag of Richardson's Pastel Mints. There were just so many choices that Elinore found all of them hard to resist. Gretchen had one last thing to ask of Elinore before they closed the shop for the day. This time Gretchen wanted Elinore to count the days cash drawer out. Surprised, Elinore looked at the big brass register and pulled the side handle down hard. The bottom drawer kicked out, hitting her in the stomach. Elinore looked at all the money inside. She hadn't realized that they had made so much in one day and her eyes were wide. Elinore was a wiz at counting money. Her father had taught her well. The cool coins fell quickly through Elinore's slender fingers quickly. It had been a good day for Gretchen.

By the clock on the store wall, Elinore knew quitting time was near. She also knew Mark was expecting her. Gretchen had thanked her for her help and all her hard work; she told her that she would lock up behind them. Elinore waved as she left the store. She walked her way down the familiar route that she had taken many times before to Mark's, but this time she didn't want to arrive so timely. She purposely wanted to keep him waiting. She decided to sit on the bench where people waited to catch the trolley. Elinore took that time to think about her relationship with Mark. She didn't know if she could ever trust him. Her entire view of him had changed when she caught him embracing Annie. She didn't believe either one of them when they protested their innocence. Without trust, she would never be able to truly love him, she thought. She had considered, before the day that she had walked into Annie's kitchen, that she might have already been in love with him, but now she would never allow either of them to know how much they had hurt her. She would keep her steady path and continue her pretense of calm detachment. She would not allow herself to display any emotional involvement if she still considered serving up her cool dish of revenge. Elinore could not throw that off the table yet. She couldn't believe that they could think that she was that stupid. She vowed if it came their way, they would never see it coming. Elinore was going back and forth with it all in her heart. She missed the friendship that she had grown to count on with Annie.

Elinore wavered on her second thoughts and felt maybe it would be best to just give things more time. If she did that, each of them would decide their own fate. The thread of distrust that had been spun in Elinore's mind though was constant. She had little control over it, and when she closed her eyes, Mark with Annie was all she could see. Nearly an hour had passed before Elinore had realized it and she was still seated on the bench. She was very late, and she rushed toward Mark's house. Buster greeted her at the fence, wagging his tail as he usually did. He was always so happy to see her. Elinore liked Buster now and she gently patted him on his head. After a little scratch behind his ears, she walked up to the door and opened it without knocking. "Sorry I'm late," she said. She could smell something good cooking. Mark greeted her at the door and pulled her in for a kiss. He guided her into the kitchen where a lovely setting of fresh flowers and lit candles awaited her. She smiled and joined him next to the stove. "Where did you learn to cook so well?" she asked. Mark touched Elinore's nose and told her that his mother had taught him. She was surprised, he had never spoken about his mother before. She wanted to know more about this woman but didn't think it was the right time to ask. She knew his father lived alone and didn't want to be nosey.

Mark had made a lovely meal of pork chops and potatoes. Her stomach started to growl when he handed a spoonful of the gravy from the pan to her. Mark's kitchen was his domain. He was used to living alone and asked her to sit down at the table. Elinore smiled and laid the napkin neatly in her lap that he had provided. She found it so unusual for a man to think ahead like that. She had only known women to be in control of the kitchen. Mark served up the dish and the milk gravy to go with the potatoes was delicious. Elinore thought she could not have done better herself. As Mark sat down across from her, she noticed that he never once put his elbows on the table. He wiped his mouth after every bite too. The placement of the fork and knife were perfect. He had impeccable manners. Rose had always felt a person's manners were most important and she instilled that in her girls. Elinore was impressed. It was the first time that they both sat down together for a formal evening meal. After the meal, Mark put the dishes in the sink but did not want to wash them. Elinore offered but he would have no part of it and asked her to go inside. He had a small table in front of his sofa with a deck of cards on it. It was clear to her that Mark had playing cards in mind. Mark thought again about giving her the ring but poured two glasses of lemonade to bring inside with him, leaving the ring in its hidden place. They talked for hours. Elinore even believed that Mark may have yielded some of the games to her that she had won. It had gotten very late, and Mark asked if he could walk her home. She accepted his offer but told him she would be staying at her aunt's house instead of Annie's that night. Mark placed his arm around her shoulder, holding her tightly as they walked together through the streets. The moon was full and bright, and Elinore thought it was so romantic. She felt safe with Mark and that made her happy. Elinore thought to herself that it was such a glorious night and wished it could stay like that forever frozen in time. As they reached Agnes's door, Mark turned to Elinore and said, "I had a wonderful night, thank you for joining me." Elinore declined to kiss him again, merely smiling, and melted behind the closed door. Oh, how she truly wanted to kiss him once more. Elinore went straight to her room and off to bed. She did not want to be late for work for a second day in the morning. She did not want to make Gretchen angry with her. She really liked Gretchen.

The night had passed so quickly, and Elinore had felt as if she hadn't slept a wink. Already, she was on her way to work again. Yawning with every third step she took. Elinore thought she would have given almost anything if she could have stayed home. Elinore pushed the store door open to find Gretchen stacking the coffee tins on the shelf in the corner. Beside the door, Gretchen had already put the newspaper out for buyers. A picture of the man she had taken a ride from was on the front page. Elinore recognized his face as soon as she saw it. She wanted to read the article desperately and had trouble taking her eyes away from it. Gretchen asked her to come help her, but Elinore couldn't detach from the gruesome picture of the man with his head lying against the door of his car, covered in his own blood. Gretchen was standing on a small stool struggling to reach the highest shelf and had dropped a tin.

She called out to Elinore again to come help her. "Sorry, sorry," Elinore said as she rushed to help Gretchen. "It's ok," Gretchen replied, adding, "It is a ghastly picture, isn't it? Isn't that the man you took a ride home with?"

Elinore was stunned. She didn't know what to say. Her mind was racing for an explanation. And it finally came to her. "I don't know, but he was fine when he dropped me off at my house." Gretchen thought it was odd the way she answered her. She had only asked if that was the man because that day had been so busy, she frankly couldn't remember his face. "It says in the article that they think the killer must have been a man because the poor chap had literally almost been decapitated. Only a man could have that kind of strength." Elinore didn't want to draw attention to herself. She paused a moment with the most pensive expression on her face. "Yes, it's a shame, poor thing," was all she could push out of her mouth. She had watched Erika put that man in his place, shutting down his illicit desires for good. Elinore worked all day trying to ignore the picture on the front page of that paper, but it was like the man's ghost had come back to haunt her. She couldn't wait to leave.

Elinore had wanted to go to Annie's to pick up some of her dresses, but now all she wanted to do was go back to bed. And at the end of the workday, that was exactly what she did. She felt fresh and clear in her mind when the morning came with a golden silence. Her precious dresses were still on her mind though and she still wanted to retrieve them from Annie's house. After she finished working with Gretchen, that was exactly what she would do. She received her weekly pay when the store closed and hurried off to Annie's. Slowly, she walked down the long cement driveway to the back of Annie's house. Elinore looked in the window to see if Annie was home. She didn't see her, and the house was dark. The door was locked. What luck, Elinore thought. She let herself in quietly and stuffed all her things in the large hemp bag she had taken from Gretchen. Elinore worked with lightning speed and left, locking the door behind herself. She had made it out of the house without having to explain a thing to Annie. Glad about that, she dragged the large bag back to her aunt's house and as luck would have it, Agnes was not home either. Elinore put her things away and raced down the stairs to start supper. By the time Agnes had come home, Elinore had made a big pot of chicken soup with dumplings. Agnes was happy as soon as she stepped into her home. The smell of the soup enticed her, and she went to the kitchen straight away. Agnes was hungry and the two women sat together to eat. Elinore gave her the weekly stipend she owed her and that made her happy.

What Elinore would do the next day was the only thing that was on her mind. She just needed to clean up all the dishes first. She wished she didn't have to, but at least tomorrow was Saturday and she had the day to herself. Everyone was happy to have a free day except Erika. Erika was always a bit grumpy, whether she was busy or not. Everyone in the system knew that, but each had their own agenda to be concerned about. Erika could be harsh but since she kept everyone safe, she deserved the respect of all. Charlotte would try extra hard to make Erika smile. It was surprising that she was so responsible; being the youngest of all the alters.

Elinore woke to a beautiful day with blue skies and abundant sunshine. It had already been decided overnight that they would go to the park today. Elinore wandered about, watching birds and picking flowers as she usually did. It was still her favorite thing to do after all the years that had passed. The squirrels chased each other, and she could even see a few turtles pop their heads out of the water. There were a lot of people in the park. There were many children running and shouting. Charlotte wished she could come out to play but Erika wouldn't allow it. It was not the right time. There were many people walking together holding hands. There was a man taking photographs too.

Suddenly, Elinore spotted a man further up from where she was sitting that looked very familiar. Elinore wanted to be sure and looked hard at him. Sure enough, it was Mark! But he was sitting with another woman, and not Annie either. She had never seen this woman before. Quickly, Elinore tried to blend into her surroundings so he would not see her. She wanted to watch him. Her focus was fixed on his every move. They talked and laughed as if they had known each other for awhile. Elinore couldn't hear what they were saying, but she did notice how close they sat to one another. The young girl's eyes sparkled with delight, and they talked for a lengthy time there on the bench that they sat upon. Elinore watched the whole time, gritting her teeth.

Mark was happy to see his sister. He hadn't seen her in a very long time. She had come to visit with their father but needed to return to Boston where she worked at Boston City Hospital as a nurse. It was a busy hospital and she told Mark she could only stay a short time. Mark hugged his sister Sarah tightly and kissed both her cheeks. She smiled largely at him as they parted ways, but she promised to return as soon as she was able. He hugged her again and she waved goodbye as she turned to leave him.

Elinore could feel the fury inside herself. She had reached her boiling point. She was seething at his betrayal once again! She angrily dodged amongst the others in the park. She stomped along vowing to make him pay. This was the last straw, and she would challenge anyone who tried to stop her, including Erika! Elinore had never been this angry before. Emotionally charged, Elinore's undercurrents of frustration and disgust were bubbling to the surface. She threw the flowers in her hand to the ground and vanished from sight. Iris cried over her flowers that had been thrown with such disregard.

Mark had never told Elinore that he had a sister. Mark was so delighted to see Sarah that he had not noticed Elinore in the distance. No explanation would do now though. Elinore was convinced that Mark had crossed the line with her. There would be no return. When Elinore finally reached home, she went straight to her room, locking the door. Enraged with herself, she wondered how it could have ever crossed her mind to give him a second chance to make things right between them. Trusting him now would be impossible! She regretted making that mistake and beat herself up over it throughout the night. The tears flowed down her face turning it to a brightly inflamed red color. Her eyes were swollen into small slits that she could barely see from. She found it difficult to breathe. Elinore didn't wish to see anyone in the shape she was, choosing to become a recluse. Work would be the only reason to leave the comfort of her room, but that wouldn't be until the morning came. She couldn't process another blow. She wondered how Mark could do this to her again! She had been convinced the worst was over but now she was certain that it had just begun, but not for her. It was becoming clearer to her that Mark would be meeting his fate for hurting her so badly once again.

Monday morning Mark was seated on the bench outside Agnes's home again. He waited patiently for Elinore to come out. Elinore opened the door to see him sitting waiting for her. They walked together to Gretchen's store when Elinore asked, "So, how was your weekend, Mark?" She intentionally asked him with deceptive casualness. She would hide her anger at all costs. She wanted to see if he would lie to her about where he had been. However, Mark simply stated that it was nice. Elinore remained silent for the rest of the way. Mark sensed Elinore's coolness, but it was early morning. He had seen her in the morning before and knew she wasn't much of a morning person. He returned to the store at lunch as he had done many times before, yet Elinore still displayed little affection and was short on conversation. Still, Mark persisted onward. He wanted to try to make her smile again and asked her if she would join him for supper again. Elinore accepted and asked what he would cook. Elinore's mind was plotting on her unsuspecting so-called boyfriend. Mark hadn't thought about what he would make, he didn't think that far ahead often. He told her it would be a surprise and kissed her goodbye.

Gretchen could tell by Elinore's demeanor that something was bothering her. She didn't want to pry in Elinore's personal affairs, but she did feel that maybe she needed a break. Gretchen thought she could do that by asking Elinore to work in the candy section, which she knew she enjoyed. At last, the day finally ended on a quiet note and Elinore couldn't wait to leave. Elinore felt very apathetic as to what to do with the rest of her day. Her days were becoming constant treadmills of the same routine. She knew Mark was expecting her and she wasn't even excited about it. She longed for some excitement in a good way to happen. Life was becoming depressing and complicated to her. All the lies being told to her, lack of money, no purpose to anything. She followed the same path to Mark's and only uttered a few words to herself on the way. "Same food, same work, same dung, day in, day out." But when Elinore opened Mark's gate, Buster came running to greet her. Buster jumped on her, excited to see her, knocking her to the ground. He wagged his tail and licked her face. For a short minute, she had forgotten she had been so upset at all. She rolled with Buster on the ground getting her apron dirty but enjoying every second of it.

Elinore didn't care about her stupid apron. She really had grown to like Buster. Inside, Mark had supper waiting. Elinore hadn't eaten much all day except for the sandwich Mark had brought her earlier. They sat and ate but Elinore still couldn't get the woman she had seen Mark with off her mind. It bothered her. She continued to wait to see if he would tell her about the woman, but not a word came. Mark started a fire, and they sat together to play cards again. This time though, Elinore only won two games. The dirty dishes in the sink were on her mind and she insisted on washing them. Her mother would have never allowed her to leave them just sitting. She just couldn't leave them! As soon as she turned the water on in the sink, she felt Mark's hands around her waist. He nibbled on her neck, and she squirmed hoping to discourage him long enough to take care of the dishes. His lack of integrity was getting to her. She had initially thought he had much of it but due to her latest findings she knew it was untrue. He disappointed her and she couldn't put up with the lies.

She had felt a strong passion for him when they first had met. Now her negative emotions were leading her to want to physically harm him. Oh, how she tried to forget her feelings for him after finding him with Annie. And that image was seared into her mind. Now, the little quirks that once endeared him to her started to make her eye twitch. Her quiet disgust and resentment caused an intense dislike which she promised herself to hide; it was exhausting for her. The girl in the park only made the situation worse. It was nearly impossible to keep from spewing her venom on Mark. Elinore was constantly reminding herself to stay focused. She finished the dishes and dried her hands on the towel hanging on the hook next to the sink. Mark had not left the room and was patiently waiting for her to finish. He watched her sway back and forth. Her delicate silhouette excited him. There was heat building inside of him and he was unaware of Elinore's wrath that was hiding just below the surface. Mark couldn't help himself. He came up from behind her fast. He twirled her around and planted a kiss on her soft lips. Mark lingered there momentarily before moving to her neck for another taste. Elinore loved the excitement he gave her, and she craved it from him, ignoring her anger toward him. His actions were so spontaneous and her passion for him was getting the best of her momentarily. Mark was doing his best to make her smile. But it wasn't going to be that easy for him, Elinore thought.

Mark could sense her resistance. Mark looked curiously at her. "What? Did I do something wrong?" Her eyes narrowed and her lips pursed. She placed her hand on her hip. "I bet you say that to all the ladies!" Mark was baffled. "What are you talking about, Elinore?" he asked. "I saw you in the park with that girl!" she bemoaned. "Who is she?" she demanded. Elinore had blurted it out and blew her plan. She was so angry at him that she couldn't contain herself, but Mark only laughed. "That was my sister, Sarah, dear God, Elinore, are you talking about my sister?"

Elinore suddenly felt ashamed of herself. She covered her mouth and lowered her eyes to the floor. Elinore didn't know what to say. She looked at Mark and was speechless. In the smallest voice she whispered, "I'm sorry." Mark was still laughing. "Oh, forget it!" he said and picked her up, carrying her to his bed where he dropped her playfully hard. He wanted to feast on her and Elinore's feelings for Mark were returning fast. They rolled in each other's arms and tasted the salt from one another's skin. Their passion together came hurried and heated. Clothing fell to the floor at their feet. The tension between them exploded. Elinore's legs trembled as they wrapped around Mark. Her hips moved in rhythm to his slow but steady thrusts. Their heightened pleasure made each of their breathing shallower. Elinore had surrendered herself to him, heightening his pleasure. Finally, Mark rolled over the edge and his body opened, overflowing from a highly energized state to a fully emptied one. He collapsed beside her, and they remained wrapped around each other for some time; drained of strength, they blissfully fell asleep.

It always seemed that Elinore never slept for long, and she awoke, still lying in Mark's arms. She studied his face, so close to hers. She took note of the curve of his face. Her heart couldn't hide her feelings inside now. She was falling in love with Mark all over again. Untangling herself from his arms, she slithered from his bed. Closing the bathroom door gently, she could let herself go. Erika was close. Elinore could hear her words. "Kill Him! Kill Him Now! He can't be trusted!" Elinore felt the familiar dizziness, but she fought back this time. "No! I don't want to," she said as quietly as she could, trying not to wake Mark.

Elinore had never fought with Erika on this level before. But this time was different. She stood her ground, and Erika was fierce. "You are too weak, and he will never be what you want him to be!" Elinore could hear Erika and she continued to try to gain dominance. She closed her eyes and held her fists against her forehead. "Go away!" Elinore cried desperately. Quickly, she left the bathroom, hoping to leave Erika behind. She walked to the bed and stared at Mark who was still sleeping peacefully. Elinore stood for a minute just looking at him. In a small cabinet close to the bed, Mark kept a kraft of brandy. She opened the cabinet and poured herself a shot, drinking half in one gulp. Still standing there, next to his bedside, she spilled the remaining brandy onto the blanket. Erika was gaining on her, and it looked like Elinore was losing the fight. Erika was beginning her plan; she had set things up so carefully. Elinore had fiery eyes like never before and was still trying to gain her strength against Erika. She wasn't willing to give up yet and surely wasn't ready to let go of her beloved Mark. An internal war was raging inside Elinore's body. Elinore struggled to maintain her power as Erika moved to the fireplace. Using the small shovel that Mark used to remove the ashes, she picked up some of the red-hot embers. Her eyes glistened as she held them. She imagined how the bed would ignite when she spilled them onto the alcohol from the brandy.

Finally, Elinore had grown strong enough inside to dare to do something that she had never done before. She took back control, forcing Erika to return to the inside. Elinore hadn't realized it until that moment, but she had already forgiven Mark in her heart. She tossed the embers back into the fireplace and returned the shovel to its stand. Elinore again looked lovingly at Mark. She kissed his forehead and ran her fingers lightly around the curve of his chin. She couldn't take her eyes off him; her heart grew for him with every breath she took. She took notice of his long eyelashes before creeping back into the bed, pulling the blanket up over them. Elinore was the happiest she'd ever been.

The break of day came too soon, but Elinore needed to get to work. Mark made some toast and coffee and told her that he would meet her for lunch in a few hours as she ran to the door. Elinore's mind overflowed with thoughts from the night before, and about Mark along the way. She took stock in everything that had happened and was glad that the damn fire bell hadn't rung once. Grateful for that, she entered Gretchen's store. As usual, there was so much work to be done but business was slow that day and Elinore wound up looking for things to do to keep herself busy. Gretchen handed Elinore a large feather duster and so she started to move about with it. Getting to the soaps, she took great care of dusting the ribbons tied around each one of them. Gretchen called out to Elinore from the back room and as she turned to face her, something crashed to the floor. Startled, Elinore turned around to see what she had accidentally knocked over. White powder and shattered glass were scattered all about the wooden floor. She had knocked over the carbolic acid jar. Elinore quickly reached for the broom and began to sweep it up when Gretchen appeared in the doorway to see what had broken. "Be careful with that," she said, "And wash your hands when you are through, that disinfectant is pretty harsh." Elinore thought about what she had said. Keeping that in mind, she took a flyer from the counter, creased it down the middle and neatly enclosed some of the chemical inside it. Before Gretchen had time to return, Elinore had placed the folded paper inside her apron pocket. Elinore continued to casually finish cleaning up her mess. "I'm sorry Gretchen," Elinore said, washing her hands as Gretchen has told her. "No sense in crying over spilt milk," Gretchen commented.

Elinore continued to work until lunchtime when Mark came in. Gretchen was always happy to see Mark. She waved hello to him and smiled widely. A few hours had passed when Gretchen had a thought. "Elinore," she said, "Why don't you take the rest of the day off. I think I will close early today." Elinore was happy to go. It had been boring to her at the store, and she just wanted to be with Mark anyway. Elinore walked down the street as fast as her legs would carry her. Adrenaline raced through her veins with anticipation of seeing Mark again sooner than she had expected. But running was Charlotte's favorite thing to do. Her young thin legs gave her incredible speed and as Elinore's pace picked up, Charlotte sprang forward to take the lead. Her feet hit the pavement beneath them with great swiftness and she couldn't help but giggle with delight. She adored the way her speed made her pretty hair fly out following behind her; carried by the wind. She even imagined that she had superhuman strength that could increase by her running faster than the speed of light. And with her invisible cape, no one could match her. Charlotte did reach Mark's house, but she didn't want to stop. She wanted to keep running but Mark was outside of his house with Buster. The dog started to bark and wag his tail. He had seen Elinore coming and became excited. Jumping and scratching at the fence, Charlotte patted the dog's head. "Silly puppy," she said in her childish voice. She opened the gate and said hello to Mark. Charlotte stood in front of Mark twisting about. Her fingers twirled her hair around them. Mark looked strangely at her. "Why are you looking at me like that? It's not nice to stare," Charlotte said. Mark couldn't understand why she was talking baby-talk.

He found it so odd. He had to ask, "Why are you talking baby talk, Elinore?" Mark was confused. He asked most innocently and, in a flash, within that moment, Elinore returned. "Are you trying to make fun of me? I just like playing with Buster! I thought you'd be happy to see us getting along so well!" she said sternly. Mark did not feel like arguing another round with Elinore. He picked Elinore up and tossed her over his shoulder holding onto her legs tightly. He marched up the pathway to his door whilst Elinore let out a shriek of laughter. She couldn't help herself. She began to kick and pound him on his back with her fists, but Mark wasn't about to let her get away by provoking another argument again. He would handle things his own way this time. He brought her inside and sat her down hard on the setae. "Now you listen," pointing his finger at her. "I'm not going to argue with you every time I see you!" She started to laugh, and it was so contagious that Mark had to laugh himself.

Hours went by when Elinore remembered the paper in her pocket containing the powdery substance she had spilled at Gretchen's. She reached nervously into her pocket, checking to see if it was still there. And it was. Relieved, she told Mark that she needed to go to Annie's to get a few things, but she would only be gone for a short time. Mark told her that he would start supper and that it should be ready by the time she returned. Elinore gathered herself, kissed Mark goodbye and left for Annie's. She was on a mission now. Clearing her head with each step, Elinore thought about what she would say to Annie when she got there. It had been several weeks since she had seen her but some of her things were still there, and she wanted them back. She gave consideration to the friendship that she missed, but she still could not forgive Annie for trying to steal Mark from her. That was not going to happen. Elinore walked down the pathway to Annie's door. She paused for a moment looking at the beautiful roses in Annie's small yard. Then, she knocked at the door. Annie was surprised to see her. "I came because I want to talk with you." "I'm not sorry for the way I acted, but I am sorry that our friendship has been hurt by it," she stated. "Can I come in?" Elinore asked.

Annie was uncomfortable but she opened the door, allowing her to enter. The two women sat at the table and looked at each other. No words came from either of them. Then, Annie asked if she would like a cup of tea. "Yes, I would love that," Elinore said. The ice was broken finally. Annie started the conversation. "I didn't mean to make you angry, and I wasn't trying to make a pass at Mark," she continued. "I had just become emotional thinking about Tom." Annie had never shared with her the secret fact of the baby they had lost, and it became clear to her that Mark had never given her the ring. Elinore's hand was void of any jewelry. Annie decided to keep mum about those two things. Elinore had no emotion on her face as she took another sip of her tea. "I'm sorry that Tom passed away, and I am sorry for you, but Mark cannot replace him," Elinore said.

Annie was becoming impatient by the nonsense. She could see that Elinore still had it in her mind that she was trying to take Mark from her. Annie also knew that Elinore was a loose cannon and unpredictable. Now she was certain that she needed to end what was left of their friendship. Annie straightened out her shoulders and mustered up her courage. "Elinore, I've become pleased with living in this house by myself now, however, I will always be grateful to you for being such a good friend in my time of need." Annie went on to say, "I don't think you can be here anymore to stay, with the way our friendship has turned." Annie was shaking inside but wanted to make herself clear. She feared what would happen next.

Elinore bit her lip in vexation. Then a vengeful, evil, felonious thought began to take hold of her. Sweetly sickening, she told Annie not to give it any more thought. "No hard feelings," she added when she asked Annie for another cup of tea. But Elinore's mind was thinking fast. How dare she kick me out of here when she was the one who was wrong. She had feigned friendship with an ulterior motive. She used me, Elinore thought. She felt that she had mistaken Annie's warmness for a true friendship, but now she could see Annie had a cold heart. Annie needed to heat some more water and it took her a few minutes to cover her hand with a towel to bring the hot kettle to the sink to refill it. Annie foolishly turned her back to Elinore and in those quick minutes, she mixed the carbolic acid from her pocket into Annie's sugar bowl. Every household carried this deadly product for disinfecting, but it also blended well and became virtually undetectable with sugar. Elinore knew it would eventually make Annie sick. Maybe even kill her. Annie shouldn't have overstepped her bounds with her, Elinore reasoned. She quickly finished her cup of tea with Annie and asked if it would be okay if she took her things. Annie was happy to oblige. She just wanted Elinore out. Elinore checked the drawers and closets twice to make sure that nothing was left behind. She had no intention of returning. Annie moved her hand across her forehead as soon as Elinore left the house. Thankful, Annie dead bolted the door. She was happy to see the last of Elinore. The thought crossed Annie's mind that she couldn't have left fast enough. Annie was completely unaware that on her table sat a waiting deathtrap.

Carrying the heavy load of remaining clothing from Annie's, Elinore headed straight for her aunt's house. She hadn't realized how many things she had left at Annie's. Her arms ached trying not to drop anything on the way. Almost there, she rounded the corner, barely able to see around the pile of clothing in her arms. But she could see just enough to notice that there were three watchmen's cars parked just in front of her aunt's house. Her aunt stood in the doorway talking to them. Quickly, Elinore ducked behind the corner of the neighbor's house. She was close enough to hear pieces of what they were talking about. Elinore heard her aunt say that she hadn't seen her in days. The watchmen pushed on, wanting to know where Elinore could be found but her aunt gave them no information. She couldn't have because Elinore had not told her much since the neighbor had ratted her out. She changed direction and decided to head off to Mark's in a hurry. She knew she could be safe there. Mark was respected by many, and he was known throughout the community as an important figure. Still, with her clothing in hand, she finally arrived at Mark's feeling much like she would faint. Mark had been waiting for her and dinner was beginning to dry out. He took the heavy load from Elinore and set it down. "What took you so long El?" he asked.

Elinore stumbled over her words. "Well…I had a lot more stuff than I thought." Elinore's mind was still on the watchmen that were at her aunt's. She wondered if she should have waited to go to see Annie. She wondered why the watchmen were at her aunts at all. Elinore was going back and forth between the two subjects that bothered her the most in her mind. If only she could be rid of those two things, she thought. Then maybe she could get on with her life with Mark. She reasoned with herself; Annie should never have crossed me like that! And those pesky watchmen! All the while, she could also hear Erika inside her mind since she had left Annie's, reminding her continually of her betrayal and how she tried to take away her only means of survival. Over and over, Erika pounded the words that Annie could not be trusted into Elinore's mind. Those kinds of people get what they deserve, she would reiterate. Elinore squeezed her eyes closed tightly. Erika was giving her a headache and she wished for her to go away.

Mark was anxious to eat and set the table. He was hungry. He filled the plates and brought them to the table. Elinore was in the bathroom when she heard Mark call out to her. "Coming," she answered him back. He had made another wonderful meal and Elinore raised her fork to her lips. It smelled wonderful to her, but it was a dish she had never tasted or heard of before. They spoke over their meals for a short time but before they were through, there was a knock at the door. Mark answered it. The three watchmen that had been standing at her aunt's door hours before, were now there! Elinore felt a cold chill run up her spine. She found it hard to breathe and was terrified as to why they were there. They wanted to speak with Elinore! Her dream was coming true! She knew if they had their way, they would haul her off to jail. Why couldn't they just leave her alone! Deep down, she knew they had no proof of anything. Because if truth be told, she hadn't even done anything wrong. Erika had done most of the violent things that had occurred. Elinore was only an observer. She wasn't capable, that was until Annie started her nonsense. And Annie wasn't dead yet! She was sure of that.

Mark called Elinore to the door and the watchmen showed her a picture of the man she had taken a ride home with that fateful day after work. She was aware Erika had killed him, but she wasn't going to tell the watchmen that. Instead, she denied even knowing him. Again, Elinore was justifying things to herself. I really didn't know him at all, she thought to herself. The watchmen were slowly putting things together though. Because of Annie, they knew Elinore had dated John and worked for Ben. They had no way to connect her to the dead man by the waterway, but they were not about to give up that easily.

Mark defended Elinore to the watchmen. He told them that he was with her almost always and that she was living there with him. She would not be entertaining another man because they were engaged. Elinore couldn't believe her ears. She was shocked by what he had said. And when they left, she had to ask what he meant by that. She looked at him curiously. "Why did you tell them that we are engaged, Mark?" she asked inquisitively. Mark held his finger up to Elinore's lip. "One minute," he said and left the room. Elinore waited in anticipation for him to return. Mark thought to himself, he may as well do it now. It seemed like the right time. But first he needed to know something. He returned but kept the ring in his pocket. Mark sat down beside her and asked very seriously, "Elinore, I need to know, did you have anything to do with the death of that man they showed you the picture of, down by the water's edge?"

Elinore considered telling him about what Erika had done. But how could she explain things to him in a way that he could understand correctly and not ruin her life with him? Was it possible? Now she was wishing she had waited to make Annie pay for her deceit. But she had already set the trap, putting her plan in motion. "No," she answered firmly. It just blurted from her mouth. Mark kissed her and smiled. "I didn't think so, but I had to ask," he said, still smiling. Mark slipped off the setae onto one knee. He looked lovingly into her eyes and pulled the ring from his pocket. Holding it out to her, he stated, "This ring is a symbol of my love and my plans to marry you. It is also a symbol of my commitment to you and our relationship until the day that we are joined in marriage. I vow to honor that bond forever with you, Elinore," he said.

Elinore was speechless. Mark placed the ring on her finger and saw a tear of joy in her eye. Elinore looked closely at the dazzling ring on her finger and her only thought was that out of all her fingers, that one was now her favorite. She began to kiss Mark, wrapping her arms around his shoulders. She whispered in his ear, "You have just stolen my heart." She held her hand out to have another look at her beautiful ring. "I will never take it off," Elinore declared.

That night the two slept blissfully and their breathing mingled softly together. It had been a long time since Elinore, the original personality, had felt so safe. Wrapped in each other's arms, both were unaware of what was happening outside the home. The watchmen had a man posted outside Mark's house, right near the call box. They were there to watch Elinore's every move. They wanted to see if she would give them something to chew on.

The sun was just beginning to show itself and Elinore had already been awake. While Mark lay sleeping beside her, she held her hand out to have another look at her new ring. It is simply beautiful, she thought. The way it sparkled almost hurt her eyes. She tried not to move too much so as not to wake her love. Elinore tried out her new name in her mind. Mrs. Elinore Bailey, she said quietly. A smile came across her face. She looked back at Mark. She couldn't believe how soundly he could sleep, unless of course that damn fire bell went off. Then, he would be out the door in a flash with his pants half done! Instantly, an image of Annie's face appeared in her mind. She needed to get that sugar bowl back! In a panic, Elinore slipped out of their bed and put her clothes on in the bathroom. She thought to herself, I must get that bowl back now! I have everything I've ever wanted now, and I'll be damned if I'll allow that tramp to take it from me! Elinore penciled a quick note to Mark and escaped to the street. Her feet carried her quickly. Elinore hoped to catch Annie before she had her morning tea. Trying to think of what she could say, she made her way to the back of Annie's house. She paused before she knocked on the door. Her ring! Yes, that's it! How perfect, she thought. She would tell Annie that Mark had proposed. Elinore would tell her she needed to borrow some sugar because she planned to make a special meal to celebrate their engagement. Approving her own thought, she agreed; Yes, that is what I will say! In those few seconds, she had planned out the entire scenario and knocked upon Annie's door. Annie answered the door and was quite startled to see Elinore again.

It was a mental blow to Annie, why wouldn't she just leave her alone? She never expected to see Elinore again, furthermore, what could she possibly want? she wondered. Annie's one eyebrow raised and was about to ask Elinore what she wanted when she pushed her way through the door excitedly. "Annie, Annie, come here and look!" She shrieked with enthusiasm. Elinore proudly held out the ring on her finger. It was the same ring she had picked out with Mark weeks ago. "Oh, yes, it is beautiful," Annie said. Elinore coyly looked around as she went on with her charade. She didn't want to look obvious. Elinore could see an empty cup on the table, but no sugar bowl. Elinore asked, "Don't you think it's the most beautiful ring you've ever seen?" Annie had had enough of Elinore and her grandstanding but in order not to make waves, Annie asked her if she would like a cup of tea again. She hoped she would refuse, but Elinore responded agreeably, "Oh yes, I would love a cup." Cunningly, Elinore thought, "Perfect!"

Annie went to the cupboard and pulled out a cup. She prayed Elinore would end this all quickly and placed the cup on the table. "I was just about to have a cup myself," she said. Annie poured the water, and the tea began to steep. She placed two spoons on the table and sat down. Elinore picked up her spoon and placed it into the boiling water. She pushed the water back and forth. With the disguise of a most genuine face, she looked into Annie's eyes and said, "I just wanted you to be the first to know. We've been friends for so long." Annie didn't know what to say. She had a blank expression. All she really wanted was for Elinore to leave. She wondered what was really behind all this façade of bonding.

The wheels in Elinore's mind were turning. She remained focused on undoing the trap she had set for Annie's demise. "Oh, I'm sorry," Annie said, "You like sugar in your tea, right?" She was trying to hurry her along and stood to get it. Elinore was willing to do anything she needed to do to retrieve her fatal mistake. Annie placed the bowl on the table. Elinore stared at it and then lifted the lid. Her thoughts were racing faster than ever. She could feel a familiar dizziness setting in, but Elinore was determined to take care of this herself immediately. She lifted the burning hot spoon from the cup and pretended to burn herself with it. Quickly, she used that action to knock her scalding tea water over and into the sugar bowl, spilling both across the table. "Oh dear, I'm so sorry!" Elinore said, keeping up with her masquerade. She rushed to the sink, grabbing a towel as fast as she could to mop up the substance. "It seems I've ruined your towel too," she said as she tried to rinse the tea stains from the towel. "I will replace your towel tomorrow," Elinore told Annie, but Annie didn't care. She said, "It's an old towel, don't bother, it's fine." Elinore made sure that she rinsed the acid clean from the towel before placing it in the bin for garbage. "I can't believe I did that, Annie. I'm so sorry," she repeated. Elinore had one last thing to do before her plan was undone. She needed to wash out the sugar bowl. She reached for it, but Annie put her hand on top of Elinore's and said, "It's okay, you've done enough." Elinore had to wash that sugar bowl! She was frightened now! She needed to complete her plan! She pushed Annie's hand aside and said, "Don't' be silly, I made the mess, and I will clean it up!" Elinore wasn't taking no for an answer. "I'm just glad I didn't break your sugar bowl!" she added. Elinore scurried to the sink and ran the water as fast as she could. She didn't want Annie to try to stop her. She placed the bowl in the drainboard and sat back down.

Annie asked, "Are you happy with the idea of marrying Mark? Do you think you will be able to tolerate him leaving every time there is a fire?" Elinore didn't like her questions. But she did accomplish what she had set out to do. Elinore didn't answer her. She said, "Annie, I just wanted to tell you that Mark proposed and show you the ring. I must be going now. I've got to get supper on, I want to be ready when Mark comes home." Elinore was annoyed by Annie's questions and was finished with her. She abruptly opened the door to let herself out. She parted her way with, "Have a lovely day, Annie!" A sinister grin came over Elinore's face as she made her way back to Mark's. She could hear Erika in the background taunting her. "I would have let her die," she said with an evil whisper. Elinore shook her head. "Shut up," she uttered. A woman walking along the street saw Elinore talking to herself. Heeding caution, she moved to the other side of the street. Elinore had a crazy look about her and the woman tried her best not to make eye contact with her as they passed each other.

Buster greeted Elinore at the door as usual when she came into the house and Mark was already up. He had a cup of coffee in his hand. Mark had something else to tell Elinore. He asked her to come and sit with him. Once she was settled, he told her that his initial plan was to wait to give her the ring that he had the night before. He felt he should explain. Elinore was curious. "Why?" she asked. "Well, there's going to be a fireman's ball after the parade that is planned for the fall, and I was going to announce it there. I thought you would like that with all the important people who will be there and all the fanfare."

"Oh no Mark," Elinore assured him. "The way you gave me the ring was perfect!" It was one of the few times Elinore was honestly, truly, happy. "I wouldn't have liked it any other way," she insisted. Now, Elinore realized why Mark hadn't asked her to the ball! She wondered how long he had had the ring before he gave it to her but decided not to ask. She would let this one be.

The watchmen had followed Elinore to Annie's. They discovered nothing unusual about her being there though. They knew that the two were acquainted. That fact had already been established by Annie herself. But they were still determined to bring her in for questioning and trying to gather necessary additional evidence to do so. They continued to watch Elinore for that purpose. They were preparing to question the shop keep where Elinore worked and speak with Annie again too. They needed to catch the brutal murderer who had the city on edge. People on the street had started to talk about the rash of deaths. Especially the two busy-bodies, Mrs. Clatchey and Mrs. Humner. These two women loved to keep tabs on all the neighbors, invading privacy whenever possible. They were always up for a good stirring of the pot, sending gossip out to all who would lend an ear. Even though it had been some time since the good doctor had died and even more time since John Smith fell ill, it took the brutal slaying of Mr. Sharp, who was a strong and brawny brick layer to get the neighborhood worrying that a monster may be among them. Calls to the watchmen were ringing constantly with concern. The newspaper's article with the gruesome picture showing Mr. Sharp, made officials demand the capture of the individual who was responsible.

Elinore had her aunt on her mind in the following days after Mark had given her the ring. She was the only one who hadn't seen her beautiful ring. Elinore had shown it off to almost everyone. She knew and thought that she ought to now show it to her aunt. At the start of the following day, Elinore informed Mark that she had made plans to go have a visit with her Aunt Agnes to announce the good news to her and let her see the brilliant piece of jewelry on her hand. Mark was preoccupied with cleaning his fire gear but asked if she'd like him to come along with her. Elinore declined, saying it wasn't necessary and Mark happily accepted her response. There was a warm breeze that touched her face when she opened the door that late summer day. Elinore decided that maybe on the way home she would pick up some delightful strawberries and surprise Mark with a delicious strawberry pie for dessert after supper. Elinore even had time to sniff the flowers on the way. Elinore was feeling good and couldn't remember the last time that she had been so happy. Her spirit was high and felt as if maybe she might be able to stop worrying for a moment. Throughout Elinore's internal being, things seemed peaceful, but it never seemed to stay that way too long for her.

When Elinore finally reached Agnes's house, she was glad. Even too much of a good thing is no good, she thought, as the sunshine began to draw sweat to her forehead. Her cheeks were a rosy color, and she was quite parched. She entered the house looking for a cool glass of lemonade. Luckily a fresh block of ice had just been delivered and Agnes's icebox was very cold. There, sitting on the first shelf was a pitcher of lemonade, as luck would have it. Elinore drank her first glass in seconds and then poured another half glass right after. Agnes came into the kitchen to see what the noise was all about. She saw Elinore and said, "Oh it's you dear." In an instant the sparkle from Elinore's hand caught Agnes's eye. "Ah…what have you got there," taking Elinore's hand. "Come here and let me have a look," Agnes said. Elinore proudly held her hand out. "Mark gave me this ring, Auntie. Do you like it?" she asked. "Yes, it's a stunner," Agnes complimented.

Suddenly there was a hard knock at the door. "Who could be knocking at my door with such an ill manner?" Agnes asked aloud. It was completely unexpected by her to find the watchmen standing there again. They had followed Elinore there, and the first officer asked if they could speak with Elinore. Elinore's blood ran cold. Why were they showing up all the time, she asked herself and began to become bothered by their intrusiveness. "Listen to me," she shouted, "I have told you everything I know." She rushed toward the door but stood behind Agnes. "I don't have anything further to tell you! Please, leave me alone," she cried. But the watchmen were determined and one of them grasped at her arm. Elinore swatted his hand as if it were a fly. "You take your hand off me at once Sir! You have no right!" The watchmen were trying to strong arm her into coming down to the station to answer more of their questions, but Elinore stood her ground. She fiercely replied, "I don't have anything to add to what I've already told you! Kindly leave here at once!"

Agnes slammed the door and peeked through the curtain to watch them leave. Agnes turned to Elinore and asked softly, "What have you gotten yourself into dear?" Elinore's lips pressed tightly against one another, and she shrugged her shoulders. "I have no idea what they are talking about." Trying her best to remain calm, she rolled her eyes. She didn't want to leave her aunt's just yet for fear that the watchmen were still lurking about outside, but she just wanted to get back to Mark's. At least she had some protection there. She waited a couple hours before leaving to return to Mark, completely forgetting about the strawberries she had planned to pick up. Along the way, she wondered how long it would take her aunt to tell her mother and father about her engagement. When she opened the door to Mark's everything was as it always was. Buster greeted her, Mark called out to her from the kitchen, the house had a delicious smell from whatever was cooking on the stove and a fire was softly burning in the fireplace. The air smelled like bread and Elinore was amazed that Mark could cook so well. But Elinore didn't feel so well. And the supper Mark had made didn't help with that. She had lost her appetite when the watchmen had come around again. Mark plated the food and the two sat at the table in the kitchen to eat. Mark had even lit the candles and made the water cold for Elinore. She forced herself to eat, not wanting to insult her beloved. She pushed the food around the plate with her fork. But it did not sit well and soon Elinore found herself running for the toilet.

Mark was concerned. He didn't feel ill himself, so he knew it wasn't the food. Elinore looked kind of green to Mark as she crouched in front of the toilet. He picked her up and placed her down softly in his bed. Mark didn't struggle under Elinore's weight, and she loved being pampered by him. Mark placed a cool rag on Elinore's forehead, and she smiled at him. Elinore was tired, more so than ever. She just wanted to stay in bed where she was. She blamed the watchmen for getting her so upset for it. Elinore fell asleep until the sun came through the window waking her again. She rubbed the sand from her eyes. Mark was beside her making terrible noises. Snoring like he was his own sawmill; she was surprised the neighbors had not banged on the door to see what the commotion was all about. She swore he could wake the dead. She ruffled the sheets, moving them to see if she could gently wake him but he didn't budge. Mark was sound asleep, and Elinore was hungry now. She had gone to bed with no supper and now it felt like she hadn't eaten in days. Elinore got up to wash her face and brush her teeth. She still didn't feel so good once she got out of bed.

The toothbrush in her mouth made her gag. Maybe some toast and tea would make her feel better, she thought.

Her movement across the floorboards woke Mark. He liked overseeing things in his own kitchen and asked Elinore what she was doing. When she told him that she wanted some tea and toast, he jumped up to fix it for her. He made some for himself too and joined her. Over the table, they spoke about mundane things. Suddenly, Elinore felt a little gas bubble roll across her stomach, and she clutched at it. Mark had noticed. "Sick again?" he asked, but Elinore nodded her head back and forth. "It'll pass, I think the watchmen were trying to frighten me into confessing something I didn't do. It literally made me sick, but this too shall pass," she said. Mark stirred his tea and blinked his eyes in agreement.

It was just a few seconds and the fire bell sounded loudly. Elinore hated that bell. Mark picked up his gear, kissed Elinore and ran for the door. Elinore didn't know when he would be back, so she returned to bed wanting to sleep an hour or so more. She felt as if she had just fallen asleep when she heard Mark coming back through the door again. Two hours had passed since he had left but it didn't feel like it to Elinore. Mark took the opportunity to crawl back into bed with Elinore. He was tired too now and the fire that he had just come from was a small one, so the smoke had not clung to the fibers of his clothing. He stood next to the bed adoring his lovely lady sprawled across it, wearing his short white night shirt. The sheets surrounded her like billowing clouds caressing her softly. He stroked her hair and tenderly kissed her. She fondly looked at her gallant hero. He had saved her from the wretched life that inevitably seemed to be her destiny. He was becoming more dashing to her every day. Her life was becoming what she had wanted it to be for so long. But now the watchmen were hoovering closely, and she didn't know how she could get rid of them. Maybe if she could kill off Erika, they would leave her alone and she would be better off without her anyway.

What Elinore could not seem to understand was that her alters were part of her and none of them could die if she was alive. The best possibility she could ever hope for would be that she could become integrated with Erika, but that would be something she would come to learn. Erika was a strong one and she had tried in the past to take over the entire system, shutting everyone down, including Elinore, but Elinore had gained much strength over the past years. Erika had begun to realize that she could still torment Elinore and took great pleasure in dropping hints of self-doubt in her mind.

Mark dropped his clothing to the floor and snuggled up behind Elinore under the linen sheet. He pulled her thick mane back to look at the side of her face. She was smiling and Mark pulled her closer to him. Reaching around her waist, his hands roamed freely across her thin frame. He asked, "How are you feeling now?" She hesitated a moment, not wanting to complain and said, "I'm okay." Mark liked having a woman in his home. He had fallen in love with Elinore and thought about her at least a million times a day. Her body felt warm to him. He had a firm grasp on her. Her bare bottom was squarely pushed against his hips. He gently pushed the nightshirt up exploring her. Elinore did not push him away. They wrapped themselves together enjoying the waves of pleasure that started from the base of their spines and moved throughout their bodies. Mark's breathing was heavy, and moans escaped from Elinore's lips. Both enjoyed the overwhelming heat that was building. Mark was becoming consumed with a sense of animalistic focus in his biological hardwiring that was taking over. It flooded his body into a frenzy. Mark's force became faster and sweat began to build around his neck. His nerves were tingling, and a euphoric pleasure released all his tension. Elinore rolled onto her back revealing her two sensual bare tips standing erect as sweet peas. Stretching both her arms up over her head, she continued to breathe heavily too. Turning her head, she looked lovingly at Mark. Mark snuggled into her in response. He was sleepy now and Elinore was happy to join him in his slumber.

Chapter 19

Gretchen was almost ready to open the door for business that day. She had just finished sweeping the floor. Orders were expected to come in and there would be plenty of work to do for the day. Elinore was running a little late and Gretchen hoped she wouldn't take long to show. Gretchen turned the paper sign on the front door to read "open" and she started to sweep the pile of dirt that she had collected into the metal dustpan. People had tracked in a lot of dirt from outside the day before, and she didn't like it. It hadn't rained in some time, and everything was dry to the bone. She looked at all the shelves and everything had a fine coating of dust on it. Under her breath she uttered, "It's drier than a popcorn fart in a whirlwind around here lately!" Gretchen was meticulously clean, and the dust drove her crazy. She needed to be that way for the business she ran. Fresh flowers were the first to arrive and she placed them into the sleeves that were filled with water outside. Then the papers came. She cut the strings and placed them by the door as usual. Still Elinore had not shown up.

Gretchen was starting to to worry when Elinore frantically turned up. "Sorry I'm so late," she explained to Gretchen. "I simply haven't felt well these past few days." Gretchen was just glad she was okay. It was busy as the afternoon came, so busy that Elinore didn't sit with Mark for lunch. She did take the brown paper sack from him and thanked him for it, but Elinore didn't feel very hungry at lunchtime. A lot of soaps had come in that afternoon and Elinore struggled with the weight of them. It was unusual. She didn't ever remember struggling before with them, but she was getting older. After all, she would be turning twenty-four soon. Elinore stacked the soaps neatly into the wooden drawers according to size and scent but when she got to the bottom shelf, she became a little light-headed. Elinore excused herself and went out the back door for a breath of fresh air. She sat down on the small bench near Gretchen's herbal garden. Gretchen kept that bench for such occasions. She watched the bees float from flower to flower. She remembered how she would watch the bees in the fields with Lucky in Germany. She wondered how Lucky was and thought about how much she missed him.

While Elinore enjoyed her moment of solitude, three watchmen had entered Gretchen's store. They wanted to speak with Gretchen about Mr. Sharp. They asked if she had ever seen Elinore with him. They asked if Elinore was there. Gretchen liked Elinore and didn't want to lose her. She was a remarkable employee. The day Mr. Sharp had come to her store was a mental blur to her. It had been extremely busy that day. She didn't want to give false information. She honestly couldn't remember if it was Mr. Sharp who had given Elinore a ride that day or not. He wasn't a regular at her store. And when they asked if she was there, Gretchen's answer sided in favor of Elinore. She told them, "Not at the moment," and thought that was quite the truth. Her only hope was that Elinore would stay put. The watchmen were very intimidating, and Gretchen believed that they may just be looking for a scapegoat to not tarnish themselves. Maybe they were truly interested in finding the real killer, but she couldn't be sure. They were under a lot of pressure to find the murderer, but Gretchen truly believed Elinore couldn't have done what they claimed. She thought it over with herself. Elinore would even cup up the spiders on the floor at times and throw them outside rather than kill them, but Gretchen had never met any of Elinore's alters.

The watchmen pressed on with their questions when Elinore was about to return inside. She could hear them talking as she entered the back door and stood listening closely to their conversation. Carefully staying out of sight, she soon realized it was the watchmen again! Fear gripped her and her eyes widened. She turned tail quickly and returned outside. She hid behind the two large rain barrels and the side of the building, but they did not come looking for her. She waited there until she heard their car start up before she came back into the store. It was then that

Gretchen had told her that they had just been there. "Oh, really?" Elinore asked innocently. "I don't know what they want from me. I don't know anything about that man," she concluded. Gretchen figured the less she knew the better and asked no questions except only to know if Elinore was feeling any better, to which Elinore nodded her head in response.

Elinore worked until closing that day and rang up many customers as they filed through. Gretchen had made a lot of money that day. The cash drawer was so full that Elinore had a hard time fitting the money into the slots. At the end of the day, Gretchen gave her an extra two dollars for all her hard work. As she left the store, Gretchen made sure to tell Elinore to get some rest. Elinore was glad to be going to what she called home now and she walked fast. The watchmen were still on her mind. They were closing in on her. She was anxious and worried. Erika's anger had landed her in a real pickle. It was the first time that she felt comfortable in her life and now it could all be taken away.

A little boy riding his tricycle was coming toward Elinore, but she was so deep in thought, worrying about what she would do, that the two collided. Elinore tried to catch herself but fell to the ground, landing hard on the sidewalk. Her wrist stung. Her skin was shredded from the impact. The boy's mother came running to help Elinore up. She limped to her feet, thanking the woman for her hand. The woman was concerned for Elinore and asked over and over if she were okay, apologizing many times. Elinore also apologized for not seeing the young child. After the impact, she couldn't help but think about the fact that Mark may want a child someday. She didn't know how she honestly felt about that, but her thoughts were quick to return to the jam Erika had gotten her into as she made her way through the fence and up the small staircase into Mark's house. The sun was just going down and an orange glow reflected from it through the front windows. Mark wasn't home yet. Elinore was getting used to him not being there all the time. She began to appreciate being alone occasionally, but this time was not one of those.

She reached to close the drapes. It was difficult to pick him out of the shadows, but there he was. Watching her. The watchmen were beginning to become so familiar to her that she thought of giving them each their own pet names. She closed the drapes with a swish. Buster lifted his head and his ears stood up. She looked at him and patted the top of his head. "You'll protect me, won't you boy? You're a good dog." Elinore went to the kitchen next. She knew Mark liked to cook meals, but she thought it might be nice to surprise him with something. She started to prepare the potatoes that he had set out that morning before he left. Elinore wondered when he would be home and when she should start preparing the meal when she abruptly heard him enter the front room. She dropped what she was doing to greet him. He was a sight. His face was covered in soot. He smelled heavily from burnt wood. Elinore went straight for the bathroom to draw her pet a bath. She brought him fresh towels as he had done for her. She sat on the toilet, next to the tub to wash his back for him.

Mark told her about the fire he had been to and that it was a bad one. "It had been started by a lit cigarette that wasn't extinguished properly and the people inside had lost everything they owned. They had escaped with only minor burns but there was nothing salvageable from the charred remains. It was a hot fire," and Mark showed her the hair on his face that had been burned by it. Elinore gently wiped his face with the wet cloth. He winced as the water ran down his cheek. "It's a little sensitive," he said, laying his hand over hers. Elinore couldn't help but notice the way the water made Mark's skin shimmer. It defined his brawny masculinity. She was fond of his physique, and especially attracted to his broad shoulders. She loved a man who was beefy with a large heavy body and a strong muscular build.

Elinore left him to soak alone and changed her plans about making supper. Instead, she made a quick bite to eat for the two of them. When she returned, Mark was out of the tub and dressed. Surprised, she told Mark that she had made something already for them to eat and this time Mark was grateful. He was tired and hungry. Cooking was the last thing that he wanted to do. They both sat down after Elinore placed the food on the table. "I have to tell you something," Mark said. Elinore prepared herself. He looked serious to her. "What is it?" she asked. "My father and sister wanted to come over tonight for a visit to meet you. Sarah is in town again and I'd really like you to meet her too," he said.

"Tonight?" Elinore asked in a heightened voice. "Are they coming tonight?" she asked again. Mark smiled, "Yes," he answered. Elinore was stunned. She looked around the house. It was an utter pigsty! Scurryfunge! Her panic level rose through the top of her head! "Oh Mark, how could you not warn me?" Elinore began ripping through the house; picking up clothing, towels, shoes and everything else that was out of place. She threw it all on the bed that they slept in. Panic mode had set in firmly. Mark couldn't help but laugh. She looked like a bird to him trying to escape. She was here and there and then everywhere. She looked at him with beady eyes. Mark saw the hostility that she was conveying but that only made him laugh harder. "They won't be here for at least an hour," he explained. With her hand on her hip, Elinore replied, "Good, then you'll have time to do the dishes!" She returned to her fluffing frenzy until she was satisfied.

A half hour had passed, and for a moment, Elinore stood still. She looked around. It was clean enough for her liking. She had swept the floor and prettified the home. Buster sat in his bed with his tail curled under him, making sure to stay out of the way, when her eyes took hold of the mound of stuff on the bed that she had accumulated. Panic returned, making her heart race again. Her eyes bulged at the sight. What to do, what to do, she thought! Elinore focused on the bed, giving it some thought. "What an eyesore," she muttered under her breath. Then, she did the only thing she could think of, she began to shove everything as fast as she could beneath the bed, pulling the dust ruffle over it to hide it. Mark had finished his part and stood in the doorway smiling big. "What's so amusing?" she demanded. Mark looked around and returned with, "It looks pretty good." Elinore's eyes rolled back a little and she sucked her teeth just a bit.

Soon enough, there was a knock at the door. Mark's father and Sarah stood in the doorway as Elinore opened it. Suddenly, she felt a sharp pinch on her backside which startled her, pushing her into a very friendly greeting for his father. Mark always thought and tried to be a real barrel of laughs, but Elinore wasn't finding it funny at all. She was already uncomfortable enough. Her father had always emphasized how important first impressions were and Mark wasn't making it easy for her. The "system" inside Elinore's head was quiet. The only comment being made came from Iris, who kept reminding her that she should check her appearance in the mirror. The shine from the sweat she gave herself from running around the house was not becoming, and she was thankful for Iris's thoughts. Elinore found Mark's father enjoyable, but she would have much preferred less conversation about clocks. He was a charming man with thin wire glasses and a large white beard. Mark had many of his father's features and Elinore wondered what his mother looked like. Again, there was absolutely no mention of her, and Elinore did not want to ask. Maybe someday she would ask but now was not the moment. Sarah was a beautiful woman and she mostly talked about her work at the hospital. Her hair was neatly pinned back, and Elinore had remembered she wore it in the same fashion the day she saw her in the park with Mark. What she had initially assumed was her competition would now likely become family. The thought made her a little ashamed of herself again, but she wasn't planning on telling on herself. Elinore found she had little in common with Sarah but still found her pleasant to be around. The two only stayed a short while before calling it a night. Sarah had plans to catch a train back to Boston that evening, and his father was tired. Elinore kissed both goodbye, as did Mark.

The old man paused for a moment, heavy in thought upon exiting. He turned around, holding one finger up. "By the way Mark, have you heard the watchmen are getting closer to capturing the killer of Mr. Sharp?" Mark's ears perked up and his forehead wrinkled. "Is that a fact?" he asked. "Father, you know you can't believe everything you hear." Mark's father confirmed his thought with a nod of his head, but continued, "Mrs. Humner told me that they found a small piece of fabric, caught in the door of Mr. Sharp's car and some blonde hairs wrapped around his fingers." "Have the guys at the fire station heard anything?" he asked. Mark shook his head, "No, nothing." He watched his father and Sarah go down the steps and through the gate to the street. Closing the door, Mark said, "I'm so tired, let's go to bed, El." He hadn't given his father's words a second thought, but Elinore silently was. She lay there next to Mark with her eyes fixed on the ceiling. She wondered if there was any truth to what his father had said. Elinore couldn't get comfortable, and her fidgeting would not let Mark fall off to sleep like he wanted. "What's wrong El, why are you fussing so?" Elinore blamed it on the lumpy mattress. "I'll need to fix that first thing in the morning," she told him, but she lied. That wasn't what was bothering her at all. If they did have her hair and a piece of her apron that she had on that day, maybe they could connect her to the man's death. She blamed Erika for her predicament and now she was nervous. Why couldn't Erika just run away instead of killing him, she thought. Elinore started to make a mental check list of things to do as she still laid beside Mark. She needed to cover herself. She needed to check all her aprons to see if any had tears. She couldn't remember which apron or dress she had worn that day. It was all such a blur to her. Erika had been in control during that vicious attack. It was all her fault! Elinore solely laid the blame squarely on her. She didn't sleep well that night. She was worried. The thought of going to jail and losing Mark frightened her.

Mark seemed to linger over his cup of coffee that morning for an eternity. She secretly hoped that the stupid fire bell would ring. She sat across the table from him quietly. Watching and waiting for him to finish. Mark asked if she had any plans for the day. They made some small talk and Mark commented that it might be nice to have lunch in the park. It was a glorious summer day that Sunday morning. But Elinore didn't feel much like going out nor being tailed by the watchmen. Mark was oblivious to their constant presence. When Elinore had asked once if it bothered him, he only stated that they were just doing their job. He knew most of them. They were often at the scene of a fire. Elinore knew better than that though. She knew they were only there because of her. Her feelings of anxiety were becoming overwhelming, and it was beginning to impact her overall being. She was having trouble concentrating on what Mark was saying to her. Even when he had asked her about her plans that morning, she just couldn't answer immediately. The only thing she was sure about was that she needed to get those aprons looked over. Elinore busied herself and went back to the bedroom to make the bed up. She cleared the wrinkles and tucked the edges under in the European style she had been taught as a young girl. She mounted the bed sitting straight up with her legs crossed in an Indian fashion. She looked out of the window, staring into space. She did not see anyone sharply eyeing her movements within the house. She thought about the fact that she was so close to having it all. It depressed her knowing she could be on the verge of losing everything. She needed to find a safe place.

Mark poked his head into the doorway and Elinore looked like she was about to cry to him. She held her head in her hands. He couldn't understand what she was upset about. Things had gone well with his father and Sarah the night before. "You, okay?" he asked Elinore. Elinore remembered another thing her father had always said. "Never cry in front of your boss or a man," he would tell her. "It shows your weakness." He had told her that for as long as she could remember. In hindsight, she thought that her father could be harsh, but he was teaching her survival skills that would come in handy. "Yes, I'll be fine, I think I'm getting ready for my strawberry week," she returned. Mark didn't want to be any part of that conversation. With her last statement, he decided to scram. He told Elinore that he was going to the butcher to pick up a few things.

She waited to hear the door close. She parted the thin shear that covered the window to watch him leave. Quickly, Elinore went to the closet and emptied all her aprons onto the bed. She inspected each one. All seemed fine until she got to the last one.

As she checked all the edges, pockets and ties, her eyes opened wide. Her mouth hung open. She couldn't believe that she had not noticed, but there it was. A piece no bigger than the size of her thumb was missing from the bottom corner. "Oh no," she whispered. She looked around herself from side to side. Elinore wanted to hide the apron somewhere, but where? Where could she put it to be sure that no one would find it? She crumpled it up and squeezed it tight. She snarled in frustration and then it came to her. The barrel outback that Mark burned the garbage in! Yes! In a fury she pushed the curtain open just enough to look for the man who was always posted somewhere around the front of the house. But he wasn't there. Quickly, she raced through the kitchen, flew open the door, grabbing hold of the big stick Mark used to push the garbage down with inside the can and threw the apron into the barrel. He had started a fire up early that morning with all the garbage and some newspapers too. It was still smoldering, and her apron caught fire quickly. She watched the tiny fire heighten as the white apron turned brown. Elinore pushed it down in the barrel hard with the stick, then placed it back leaning against the house where she had taken it from. Hastily, she returned to the kitchen to wash her hands, returning to the bedroom. The pile under the bed needed to be taken care of. Elinore was feeling better. She thought she had finished tying up all the loose ends. Maybe now she could rest. But as she reached for the pile, dipping her head under the bed, she felt a dizziness return. She held onto the edge of the bed tightly, waiting for the strange feeling to leave. But each time she bent her head over, the dizziness also returned. Elinore had to lie down. She rested her head on the cool pillow, and it felt good to her.

Outside and unseen, Elinore had not been alone. A new watchman had been lurking about. He had changed the position from the usual man who took the afternoon shift. Instead, he had chosen to watch from the back of the house. As luck would have it, he was able to retrieve the burnt apron from the barrel. At full tilt he ran with it, closing the gate that surrounded Mark's house. The gate's latch alerted Buster inside the house, and he began to bark. Elinore got up and looked outside for a moment but saw nothing. She went back to bed, scolding Buster to hush. The officer ran down the street shaking the hot embers from the burning apron. He needed to get it to the station where it could be analyzed. He was proud of himself; he had their first piece of hard evidence in his hands!

The mornings news headlines read: "New Evidence Surfaced- Police Closing In On Killer!" It captured Elinore's eye as soon as she stepped through the door to Gretchen's store. A cold chill ran through her blood right down to her toes. Gretchen was too busy with a customer to notice the immediate look on Elinore's face. Desperately trying not to raise suspicion, Elinore turned away hoping to erase what she had seen from her mind, but it was impossible. She could not unsee it. She tried hard to hide her fear and picked up a broom to begin to sweep. The lady at the counter started a conversation with Gretchen whilst she tallied up her bill. "Oh dear, I forgot a newspaper. Could you please add that to my bill, Gretchen?" she asked. "I want to read about this killer." She went on to say, "I heard Mrs. Clatchey talking in church after the service and she said they had the apron of the killer! Have you heard anything?" she asked boldly. Gretchen just shook her head. She didn't like taking part in town gossip. "No, but I don't read the paper much, I'm so busy," she said softly. If they made an arrest, everyone in town would find out about it soon enough, she thought. After all, it was a big city.

Elinore thought back to the moment when she heard Buster bark, after she had thrown her apron into the barrel. She had not checked the backside of the house for any of the watchmen. If it was true about what the customer had said that they had the apron, that would have been a big mistake for her to have made. They could have all the evidence they needed now! As the conversation continued, Elinore's strokes of the broom became harder and faster. The woman was really getting on Elinore's last nerve, and she just wanted her to leave. She opened the door and swept the dust out with a swish, slamming the door closed so it couldn't blow back in. Elinore had slammed the door with such force that it stopped the ladies' chatter long enough for her to lose track of what she was saying. Startled by Elinore's action, she promptly paid her tab and left.

Elinore was glad to see her leave. She and Gretchen had a lot to do as usual, but it helped little to keep her mind off what she should do next. Elinore knew it was only a matter of time now until she would have to do some real explaining. It made her want to cry. She knew she was going to have to change her plans. She knew she was going to have to say goodbye to everything she had finally found. Elinore's heart was breaking. The choice of fight or flight seemed to be being made not in her favor. Her fate did not look good. She had liked working for Gretchen but knew that would come to an end too once she found out about what Erika had done. Elinore had not spoken to Annie in a very long time, but she wondered how she would feel once everything came to light. A little whisper inside her head told her, "To hell with that girl, she never was a true friend anyway!" Elinore was taking stock of all the people in her life. She hated the idea of losing it all. And Agnes. Well, overall, she hadn't been that bad to her, but Elinore believed that the only thing she would really miss would be her weekly money that she gave her. It was leaving Mark that hurt Elinore to her core the most. She honestly loved him at this point. Everyone inside Elinore loved him too. But like all the men she had known, she wasn't going to be able to keep him. Her hero was not going to be able to get her out of this mess.

She clutched at her stomach which was giving her the colly-wobbles and she felt as if she would faint again. Elinore pushed herself to finish the day. She did as much as she could for Gretchen as a plan started to hatch in her mind. She was going to have to run. She just had to figure out where and when. It got close to closing time and Gretchen asked Elinore if she wouldn't mind closing the store for her. She had some errands to run, and it would help her to get a head start. Elinore was fine with that and told Gretchen to go. Gretchen hugged Elinore and left. As the door closed, Elinore flipped the paper sign to read "closed." The last copy of the paper sat on the crate by the door. She looked at it and kicked it hard. She stood inside the store she had spent so much time in, alone. Looking at all the things that surrounded her, she began to weep. She didn't want to leave. She was finally happy. But Elinore was spiraling down a deep rabbit hole. Her fate had been sealed and she was paranoid. She looked outside the storefront. She didn't see anyone, but she still felt they were there, hiding. Elinore went to the register and shoveled the day's money into the small bag they filled nightly for Gretchen to bring to the bank in the morning. It was an awful lot of money, she thought. It had been very busy. Elinore was not a thief and Gretchen had been good to her. She looked at the register and paused for a moment. Without another hesitation, she emptied the register into the small bag, cinching it tightly, and stuffed it into her apron. Elinore imagined how Gretchen would feel when she returned the next day to discover what she had done, and she felt bad about it. She was disappointed in herself. She promised herself out loud that she would pay every penny back to her and with a pencil, next to the register, she wrote a quick note. "I'm sorry Gretchen, I will pay you back as soon as I can. Thank you for all you have done for me," it read. Elinore doublechecked the front door to make sure it was locked. She left through the back door, closing herself out. Elinore looked at the key in her trembling hand and slowly placed it under the mat. She wouldn't be returning to this place again and would miss it very much. She took a minute to look at the small building and yard that surrounded her. Elinore wiped the tears from her eyes and walked through the alleyway to the street. She was sad to leave Gretchen; she had been so kind to her.

Elinore made her way to Mark's knowing what she needed to do next. That would be the hardest yet. The sunset was beautiful that evening, but it left Elinore with a sadness in her heart. Holding back the tears that were so close to her eyes she feasted on her last glimpses of her beloved. Sitting across the table from each other, they enjoyed what would be their last meal together. Mark had a ferocious appetite and ate every morsel on his plate, while Elinore only tried. Hunger had eluded her, but she would not have given up the chance to sit next to the man who she had grown to love so deeply, one last time. With their stomachs full, they sat snuggled to watch the fire softly burn to talk about the day's events. Daylight had faded to darkness and the two took joy in disrobing one another. Mark's breath was taken from him in anticipation of his nightly views of Elinore's nakedness. They rolled in unabashed passion. They fell together with fiery eyes. Real and raw, Elinore did her best to hold back her tears that were becoming nearly impossible to control. Leaving would be the hardest thing she ever had to do.

Mark was soon fast asleep, but Elinore was restless. She looked closely at Mark's face; silently lying next to him. She had painted a picture in her mind what life would have been like with him. She had worked so hard to have everything taken from her. What a mess Erika had made, she thought. She wondered where his dreams took him and she continued to take her last looks, studying his face closely. She had come so close to becoming Mrs. Bailey. Finally, she had taken her fill and could take no more, slipping out of the bed carefully. Elinore took Mark's carpet bag from the closet and stuffed it quickly with some clothes, her billhook, and pistol. She looked at her ring. For an instant, she thought about leaving it on the table, but it was the only thing she had to remember him by except for her memories. All the love he had given her was wrapped inside those memories and she would take them with her. Her stomach felt nauseous, and she tried hard to ignore it. Elinore placed the bag by the front door. She looked at it and put her hand on the knob. Elinore thought about Mark again. How could she leave him like this? He would wake to her absence. She couldn't hurt him like that. Elinore quickly went to the kitchen and by the smallest flicker of a candle, she penned him her final thoughts. She could no longer hold back the tears as she began to write. Elinore held her closed fist against her mouth. She cried for him on the kitchen floor. Her breath was labored, and it was difficult for her to stay quiet. Slowly, the words began to form.

Dearest Mark:

Though you still lie sleeping, my thoughts are with you, my love. Sadly, I never thought our story would end like this, but it has. The pain in my heart makes me wish I need not say farewell. I had hoped we would last forever and grow together until death parted us. You have brought me so much happiness, I will always love thee. However, the time has come that I must tear myself from this bliss, my love, never again will I kiss thy sweet lips. Our bodies, never again, in the moonlight, will roam freely in love. I never wished to deceive thee, but for reasons which I cannot explain, I must leave. In my heart and head, you will always remain my hero throughout eternity.

All my love,
Elinore

Elinore broke down. Signing her name to the letter shattered her heart. Her tears hit the paper under her hand leaving water marks. Her sorrow was uncontrollable. Short of breath, she choked back her gasps. She needed to go and didn't want Mark to wake. Frantically, she pushed herself out through the door. Down the street in the darkness, she ran. She looked side to side for the watchmen through her blurry vision but found it hard to care now if they caught her or not. She had followed her heart, but darkness covered it now. The distance she had been willing to go wasn't enough in the end and getting over Mark would be slow. She'd lost everything and felt hopeless. She asked herself repeatedly why did love always have to be such a losing game for her. The physical exertion of running made her stomach even more nauseous. She took every opportunity along the way to catch her breath and still remain out of sight. She needed to stop at her aunt's. She would need her coat for her journey.

In the darkness, there was unseen danger. The watchman was following Elinore. Inside the apron that they had retrieved from the burning trash, they found two small initials. E.D. was carefully embroidered near the hem. They were untouched by the flames and perfectly preserved. They had the evidence that they needed to prove Elinore's responsibility for at least Mr. Sharp's death and possibly others. That small piece that they had found inside Mr. Sharp's car, fit perfectly into the small section missing from the apron in their possession that Elinore had tried to get rid of. The watchman stopped at the call box along the way to notify his superiors. He continued tracking her as she slithered through the streets. Elinore had reached her aunt's house and entered quietly. Careful not to creak the wooden stairs up to her room, she slowly opened the door. She knew her way around and needed no light. Inside her closet she wrapped her coat over her arm that tightly held Mark's carpet bag. She would not have time to leave her aunt a note and felt badly about that, but Elinore did leave her weekly stipend and her key on the kitchen table. She closed the door behind herself, turning her head over her shoulder to have one last look at the house she had spent so much time in. Elinore left hastily. She had no time to spare. It would take her three more hours to walk to the port where she had first arrived in this new land.

She moved her bag from hand to hand to keep her strength. It wasn't very warm that late August night and she was glad. Wearing a coat in the warm air would have made the trip unbearable. She ran by the moonlight through the streets, hiding when she could, and keeping watch of her surroundings. She hadn't noticed anyone following her but that didn't mean they weren't there. The watchman was still there and in close pursuit. He was waiting to make his arrest. They wanted to try to catch her red-handed if she were on her way to claim another victim. It would seal the case firmly if they could do that. A piece of an apron was not very hard evidence, but they were convinced they had their killer. His superior had ordered him to observe her every move for the moment. He had no idea where she was headed. After two and a half hours, Elinore was close. Her feet were sore, but she pushed on. The air had become humid, and she could feel the droplets of mist on her face from the open water. A fog had set in and there was a crowd of people standing near the dock. Elinore pulled a dark shawl up over her head from under her coat and wrapped it tightly around her face. She had taken her aunt's shawl from the back of the kitchen chair and knew Agnes would probably be angry. It was her favorite one.

Elinore could see the enormous ship docked amid the fog. In big letters on the side it read, Hamburgh Amerikas Linie. It was not the same boat that she had initially come on, but she knew it was the right one. She had read about it recently and had all the information she needed. Elinore moved to the ticket booth to purchase her way with the money she had taken from Gretchen. She was quick to mingle with the crowd that was waiting to board. The watchman had taken the chance to use the call box at the edge of the pier for more orders. Looking at the many people who now surrounded him, his vision was blurred by the murky gloom that enveloped the ship and its passengers. He had lost sight of Elinore! It was only seconds when the loud clanging of the boarding bell rang through the foggy darkness. The passengers hurried to board. Elinore hid between as many women and children as she could stand between.

Keeping her head down and covered, Charlotte was excited. She loved a good game of hide and seek. Charlotte pushed her way through the crowd, blending with her imaginary invisible coat. She was delighted that the coolness of the water had developed the fog that added to the mystery of the evening. Charlotte gave her ticket to the man. He punched a small hole in it and waved his hand for her to pass. Playfully, she ran across the wooden plank and entered the vessel. Many people were already on board. She looked around. Her eyes were shifty and small, scanning for a great hiding place. She held the carpet bag close to her that Elinore had packed. It was far too heavy for a person her age to carry. She blamed Elinore for that as she struggled to drag it along. She knew Elinore would be angry if she left it behind though, so she did her best. There were many people who were very well dressed on board. Charlotte was momentarily distracted by how pretty every lady she saw looked. This ship was much bigger and nicer than the one she had been on years ago with Elinore. She was tickled by the many places it provided for a person to hide. The people were all speaking so loudly, and they shuffled past Charlotte to get settled.

The chatter was beginning to hurt Charlotte's ears when she saw it! A stairwell, with a small area behind it. There was a small enough space to pass through for her to get behind it. It would be a grand place to hide! Using all the might of the four-year old she had become; she hurled the carpet bag through the passageway. She was proud of herself and well-hidden there. She pulled an empty hemp bag that lay in the corner over herself. With her invisible coat and the hemp bag she knew no one would see her. But through the darkness she could hear whistles being blown. Watchmen had entered the boat. The bad men were chasing her! They were searching for Elinore. The watchman who had lost her at the pier, headed the group through the search. He had not seen her board the vessel, but the watchman's superior had sent every available officer to help in the search. In large groups, they searched each deck with lanterns blazing. Charlotte could hear the footsteps of their boots passing by her. Their whistles pierced the air as they shouted back and forth to one another. She could hear them travel up the metal staircase just above her head to the next level of the boat. Charlotte held her breath and stayed as quiet as a church mouse. She feared they would find her in her secret hiding space, but at the same time, she enjoyed the thrill of it all.

With such an enormous crowd, it was impossible for them to see the faces of everyone on board. After an hour though, the captain of the ship was becoming impatient. He needed to push off for the long journey ahead of him. The watchmen exited the ship, disappointed that their search ended fruitless. They had lost their most wanted criminal! Soon, the ship's foghorn began to blow. Charlotte could hear the engines of the boat start to run. They made a vibration against the floor that she sat on. Slowly, she crawled out from beneath the hemp bag and peeked out from behind the staircase. Everyone had seemed to find their places by now and the deck had mostly cleared from what she could see. Charlotte was tired from all the excitement and crawled back behind the staircase for a nap. The ship was on its way.

People on board hoped for good weather and their voyage of forty to ninety days depended on it. An older gentleman with a large gray beard was trying to speak over the crowd to a younger man standing beside him. He was talking about a handbook that one of the deckhands had given him. He laughed in jest about the advice it offered on what a person could expect while on board the ship. He joked with his friend about how they had forgotten to mention the mice and lice that had also come along for the ride. "Just give me my cap, some warm clothing and my stout boots and I'll be fine," he said loudly. The conversation interrupted Elinore's sleep. She woke groggy. Dazed, weak and feeling unsteady, she stood slowly. Her head touched the back side of the stairs above her. Her stomach was ill again, and the swell of the ship made her feel worse. Elinore needed some fresh air. She carefully left the safety of her small space to the outer deck area. Many people were still standing and talking. Some had small bites to eat that they had brought with them. The only thing Elinore had was the apple she had taken from her Aunt Agnes's kitchen seconds before she left. She would save that for later.

There was a beautifully dressed young woman standing looking over the side of the boat. Wearing a dark velvet green dress with a white linen bonnet, Elinore admired her. She came up beside her and said hello. "Guten Morgen, Liebchen." The woman spoke German to her and that made her feel good. But Elinore had not spoken in her native tongue in a long time and was a little unsure. The woman could see immediately that Elinore was of German descent but then spoke English to her. "You are German, correct?" she asked. Elinore nodded in affirmation. "Yes, and I am on my way home," she said with a laugh. "You will have to pardon me as I am not feeling well today." "You poor thing," the woman said. "It will be a long journey till you reach home; I hope you feel better shortly," looking concerned at Elinore. They both looked over the side of the deck to watch the water splash against the hull of the ship. The woman turned to Elinore and said, "I must be getting back to my space, my children are waiting." Elinore forced a smile and watched her disappear into the crowd.

The weather was calm and bright, but Elinore just wanted some water and to close her eyes for some more sleep. She was exhausted. She had never felt so tired in all her life. Suddenly, she felt a rumble in her belly. She clutched at her stomach instinctively. Elinore felt something move inside herself. She extended her neck out over the edge of the boat and the little bit that she had in her stomach splashed out into the water. Elinore coughed and felt even worse than she had earlier. Again, she felt something. It bubbled straight across her stomach and stopped. She thought about the last strawberry week she had had but couldn't remember it. Could she be carrying Mark's baby? she wondered. If she were, she wouldn't be able to return to her mother and father's until after the baby was born. Now, she was worried her parents would be disappointed in her.

How she wished she could have asked Mark to come with her, but after having to tell him about what Erika had done, she was convinced he would never have understood. Elinore looked vacantly over the endless ocean, thinking about her time in America. Her Aunt, John, Ben, Mr. Quinn, Gretchen, Sarah, Mark's father and even Annie crossed her mind. She thought about her own mother, father, Margaret, Delilah, Carl, Hans, and Lucky too. She wondered how time had changed them. She wondered where she would go, once she got home. Minutes turned into hours and Elinore still stood in the same place. She missed Mark already. She wished she could just touch him one more time. She caught a small tear in her hand that dripped from her chin. Mark had had a light in his eye that she had found irresistible. That light had made her fall in love with him. Her shoulders shrunk and her head hung low at the thought that she would never see him again. She wondered why love had to be so cruel. Why did everything have to be so hard for her? Her memories of her life with Mark began to leak from her eyes and roll down her cheek once again.

She began to daydream about the next chapter of her life and where it would take her. Leaving the spot where she stood, for only minutes to search for sustenance, Elinore watched the sun set into a brilliant purple and deep blue sky. It was just a short time after that when Elinore witnessed the first of many moons she was to see and stars that lit up the sky over the vast ocean. Mark entered her thoughts each night as she gazed out across the endless sea. She had not planned to leave America so hastily or to bring a baby inside her, with her. Leaving Mark destroyed her, and her future was now questionable. The moon highlighted each wave, hypnotizing Elinore. She knew she had at least forty days to ponder over it all. For now, though, she would be satisfied with a comfortable place to sleep and something to eat.

She turned with a sadness in her heart to find just that. Elinore crept back into her tiny space and laid her head on her carpet bag. She cried hard. She longed for Mark. Her life would be miserable without him. She wondered if she would ever be able to allow all the sentiments and emotional stirrings to come forth without crumbling with each passing day and yet still try to embrace the transition that she had been forced to accept. She felt another movement inside herself and was certain now that she was carrying Mark's baby. She remembered her childhood love with Carl and wondered what he would think about that. But Mark was her true love now and Carl mattered little. She continued to weep, unsure where life was going to take her. How would she raise this baby on her own, alone? Would she ever be able to tell Mark of the life they had created together? She also wondered if by the time she was able to reconnect with her beloved would he still remember her in the same way. She knew she could never return to America. But trying to forget Mark would just be a waste of time. She hoped the journey would end quickly on the ship. Exhausted, her head throbbed. She closed her eyes and sleep overtook her.

Elinore's new chapter in life was about to begin. Pieces of her shattered life in America would now need to form a new one for Elinore Downing to be discovered. Her native country awaited her return with many obstacles and uncertainty. And the hardest thing to do would be that she would have to do it all without Mark.

THE END

If you enjoyed *When Birds Fly*, I would really appreciate a short review, your help in spreading the word is highly valued and reviews make it much easier for readers to find the book.

Amazon Link:

https://www.amazon.com/dp/B0CXLVYDGY